T0086684

Pierre

Pierre

or

The Ambiguities

HERMAN MELVILLE

EDITED BY
Harrison Hayford
Hershel Parker
G. Thomas Tanselle

HISTORICAL NOTE BY
Leon Howard and Hershel Parker

Northwestern University Press
Evanston, Illinois

Northwestern University Press
www.nupress.northwestern.edu

First published in 1971 as volume 7 of the Northwestern–Newberry Edition of *The Writings of Herman Melville.* Historical Note copyright © 1971 by Leon Howard and Hershel Parker. Northwestern University Press edition published 1995.

10 9 8 7 6 5 4

Printed in the United States of America

ISBN-13: 978-0-8101-1412-8
ISBN-10: 0-8101-1412-7

TO

Greylock's Most Excellent Majesty

IN OLD TIMES authors were proud of the privilege of dedicating their works to Majesty. A right noble custom, which we of Berkshire must revive. For whether we will or no, Majesty is all around us here in Berkshire, sitting as in a grand Congress of Vienna of majestical hill-tops, and eternally challenging our homage.

But since the majestic mountain, Greylock—my own more immediate sovereign lord and king—hath now, for innumerable ages, been the one grand dedicatee of the earliest rays of all the Berkshire mornings, I know not how his Imperial Purple Majesty (royal-born: Porphyrogenitus) will receive the dedication of my own poor solitary ray.

Nevertheless, forasmuch as I, dwelling with my loyal neighbors, the Maples and the Beeches, in the amphitheater over which his central majesty presides, have received his most bounteous and unstinted fertilizations, it is but meet, that I here devoutly kneel, and render up my gratitude, whether, thereto, The Most Excellent Purple Majesty of Greylock benignantly incline his hoary crown or no.

Pittsfield, Mass.

Contents

EDITORIAL APPENDIX

Pierre

Book I

Pierre Just Emerging from His Teens

THERE ARE some strange summer mornings in the country, when he who is but a sojourner from the city shall early walk forth into the fields, and be wonder-smitten with the trance-like aspect of the green and golden world. Not a flower stirs; the trees forget to wave; the grass itself seems to have ceased to grow; and all Nature, as if suddenly become conscious of her own profound mystery, and feeling no refuge from it but silence, sinks into this wonderful and indescribable repose.

Such was the morning in June, when, issuing from the embowered and high-gabled old home of his fathers, Pierre, dewily refreshed and spiritualized by sleep, gayly entered the long, wide, elm-arched street of the village, and half unconsciously bent his steps toward a cottage, which peeped into view near the end of the vista.

The verdant trance lay far and wide; and through it nothing came but the brindled kine, dreamily wandering to their pastures, followed, not driven, by ruddy-cheeked, white-footed boys.

As touched and bewitched by the loveliness of this silence, Pierre neared the cottage, and lifted his eyes, he swiftly paused, fixing his glance upon one upper, open casement there. Why now this impassioned, youthful pause? Why this enkindled cheek and eye? Upon the sill of the casement, a snow-white glossy pillow reposes, and a trailing shrub has softly rested a rich, crimson flower against it.

Well mayst thou seek that pillow, thou odoriferous flower, thought Pierre; not an hour ago, her own cheek must have rested there. "Lucy!"

"Pierre!"

As heart rings to heart those voices rang, and for a moment, in the bright hush of the morning, the two stood silently but ardently eying each other, beholding mutual reflections of a boundless admiration and love.

"Nothing but Pierre," laughed the youth, at last; "thou hast forgotten to bid me good-morning."

"That would be little. Good-mornings, good-evenings, good days, weeks, months, and years to thee, Pierre;—bright Pierre!—Pierre!"

Truly, thought the youth, with a still gaze of inexpressible fondness; truly the skies do ope, and this invoking angel looks down.—"I would return thee thy manifold good-mornings, Lucy, did not that presume thou had'st lived through a night; and by Heaven, thou belong'st to the regions of an infinite day!"

"Fie, now, Pierre; why should ye youths always swear when ye love?"

"Because in us love is profane, since it mortally reaches toward the heaven in ye!"

"There thou fly'st again, Pierre; thou art always circumventing me so. Tell me, why should ye youths ever show so sweet an expertness in turning all trifles of ours into trophies of yours?"

"I know not how that is, but ever was it our fashion to do." And shaking the casement shrub, he dislodged the flower, and conspicuously fastened it in his bosom.—"I must away now, Lucy; see! under these colors I march."

"Bravissimo! oh, my only recruit!"

ii

Pierre was the only son of an affluent, and haughty widow; a lady who externally furnished a singular example of the preservative and beautifying influences of unfluctuating rank, health, and wealth, when joined to a fine mind of medium culture, uncankered by any inconsolable grief, and never worn by sordid cares. In mature age, the rose still miraculously clung to her cheek; litheness had not yet completely uncoiled itself from her waist, nor smoothness unscrolled itself from her brow, nor diamondness departed from her eyes. So that when lit up and bediademed by ball-room lights, Mrs. Glendinning still eclipsed far younger charms, and had she chosen to encourage them, would have been followed by a train of infatuated suitors, little less young than her own son Pierre.

But a reverential and devoted son seemed lover enough for this widow Bloom; and besides all this, Pierre when namelessly annoyed, and sometimes even jealously transported by the too ardent admiration of the handsome youths, who now and then, caught in unintended snares, seemed to entertain some insane hopes of wedding this unattainable being; Pierre had more than once, with a playful malice, openly sworn, that the man—gray-beard, or beardless—who should dare to propose marriage to his mother, that man would by some peremptory unrevealed agency immediately disappear from the earth.

This romantic filial love of Pierre seemed fully returned by the triumphant maternal pride of the widow, who in the clear-cut lineaments and noble air of the son, saw her own graces strangely translated into the opposite sex. There was a striking personal resemblance between them; and as the mother seemed to have long stood still in her beauty, heedless of the passing years; so Pierre seemed to meet her half-way, and by a splendid precocity of form and feature, almost advanced himself to that mature stand-point in Time, where his pedestaled mother so long had stood. In the playfulness of their unclouded love, and with that strange license which a perfect confidence and mutual understanding at all points, had long bred between them, they were wont to call each other brother and sister. Both in public and private this was their usage; nor when thrown among strangers, was this mode of address ever suspected for a sportful assumption; since the amaranthineness of Mrs. Glendinning fully sustained this youthful pretension.—Thus freely and lightsomely for mother and son flowed on the pure joined current of life. But as yet the fair river had not borne its waves to those sideways repelling rocks, where it was thenceforth destined to be forever divided into two unmixing streams.

An excellent English author of these times enumerating the prime advantages of his natal lot, cites foremost, that he first saw the rural light. So with Pierre. It had been his choice fate to have been born and nurtured in the country, surrounded by scenery whose uncommon loveliness was the perfect mould of a delicate and poetic mind; while the popular names of its finest features appealed to the proudest patriotic and family associations of the historic line of Glendinning. On the meadows which sloped away from the shaded rear of the manorial mansion, far to the winding river, an Indian battle had been fought, in the earlier days of the colony, and in that battle the paternal great-grandfather of Pierre, mortally wounded, had sat unhorsed on his saddle in the grass, with his dying voice, still cheering his men in the fray. This was Saddle-Meadows, a name likewise extended to the mansion and the village. Far beyond these plains, a day's walk for Pierre, rose the storied heights, where in the Revolutionary War his grandfather had for several months defended a rude but all-important stockaded fort, against the repeated combined assaults of Indians, Tories, and Regulars. From before that fort, the gentlemanly, but murderous half-breed, Brandt, had fled, but had survived to dine with General Glendinning, in the amicable times which followed that vindictive war. All the associations of Saddle-Meadows were full of pride to Pierre. The Glendinning deeds by which their estate had so long been held, bore the cyphers of three Indian kings, the aboriginal and only conveyancers of those noble woods and plains. Thus loftily, in the days of his circumscribed youth, did Pierre glance along the background of his race; little recking of that maturer and larger interior development, which should forever deprive these things of their full power of pride in his soul.

But the breeding of Pierre would have been unwisely contracted, had his youth been unintermittingly passed in these rural scenes. At a very early period he had begun to accompany his father and mother—and afterwards his mother alone—in their annual visits to the city; where naturally mingling in a large and polished society, Pierre had insensibly formed himself in the airier graces of life, without enfeebling the vigor derived from a martial race, and fostered in the country's clarion air.

Nor while thus liberally developed in person and manners, was Pierre deficient in a still better and finer culture. Not in vain had he spent long summer afternoons in the deep recesses of his father's fastidiously picked and decorous library; where the Spenserian nymphs had early led him into many a maze of all-bewildering beauty. Thus, with a graceful glow on his limbs, and soft, imaginative flames in his heart, did this Pierre glide toward maturity, thoughtless of that period of remorseless insight, when all these delicate warmths should seem frigid to him, and he should madly demand more ardent fires.

Nor had that pride and love which had so bountifully provided for the youthful nurture of Pierre, neglected his culture in the deepest element of all. It had been a maxim with the father of Pierre, that all gentlemanhood was vain; all claims to it preposterous and absurd, unless the primeval gentleness and golden humanities of religion had been so thoroughly wrought into the complete texture of the character, that he who pronounced himself gentleman, could also rightfully assume the meek, but kingly style of Christian.

At the age of sixteen, Pierre partook with his mother of the Holy Sacraments.

It were needless, and more difficult, perhaps, to trace out precisely the absolute motives which prompted these youthful vows. Enough, that as to Pierre had descended the numerous other noble qualities of his ancestors; and as he now stood heir to their forests and farms; so by the same insensible sliding process, he seemed to have inherited their docile homage to a venerable Faith, which the first Glendinning had brought over sea, from beneath the shadow of an English minister. Thus in Pierre was the complete polished steel of the gentleman, girded with Religion's silken sash; and his great-grandfather's soldierly fate had taught him that the generous sash should, in the last bitter trial, furnish its wearer with Glory's shroud; so that what through life had been worn for Grace's sake, in death might safely hold the man. But while thus all alive to the beauty and poesy of his father's faith, Pierre little foresaw that this world hath a secret deeper than beauty, and Life some burdens heavier than death.

So perfect to Pierre had long seemed the illuminated scroll of his life thus far, that only one hiatus was discoverable by him in that sweetly-writ manuscript. A sister had been omitted from the text. He mourned that so delicious a feeling as fraternal love had been denied him. Nor could the fictitious title, which he so often lavished upon his mother, at all supply the absent reality. This emotion was most natural; and the full cause and reason of it even Pierre did not at that time entirely appreciate. For surely a gentle sister is the second best gift to a man; and it is first in point of occurrence; for the wife comes after. He who is sisterless, is as a bachelor before his time. For much that goes to make up the deliciousness of a wife, already lies in the sister.

"Oh, had my father but had a daughter!" cried Pierre; "some one whom I might love, and protect, and fight for, if need be. It must be a glorious thing to engage in a mortal quarrel on a sweet sister's behalf! Now, of all things, would to heaven, I had a sister!"

Thus, ere entranced in the gentler bonds of a lover; thus often would Pierre invoke heaven for a sister; but Pierre did not then know, that if there be any thing a man might well pray against, that thing is the responsive gratification of some of the devoutest prayers of his youth.

It may have been that this strange yearning of Pierre for a sister, had part of its origin in that still stranger feeling of loneliness he sometimes experienced, as not only the solitary head of his family, but the only surnamed male Glendinning extant. A powerful and populous family had by degrees run off into the female branches; so that Pierre found himself surrounded by numerous kinsmen and kinswomen, yet companioned by no surnamed male Glendinning, but the duplicate one reflected to him in the mirror. But in his more wonted natural mood, this thought was not wholly sad to him. Nay, sometimes it mounted into an exultant swell. For in the ruddiness, and flushfulness, and vaingloriousness of his youthful soul, he fondly hoped to have a monopoly of glory in capping the fame-column, whose tall shaft had been erected by his noble sires.

In all this, how unadmonished was our Pierre by that foreboding and prophetic lesson taught, not less by Palmyra's quarries, than by Palmyra's ruins. Among those ruins is a crumbling, uncompleted shaft, and some leagues off, ages ago left in the quarry, is the crumbling corresponding capital, also incomplete. These Time seized and spoiled; these Time crushed in the egg; and the proud stone that should have stood among the clouds, Time left abased beneath the soil. Oh, what quenchless feud is this, that Time hath with the sons of Men!

iii

It has been said that the beautiful country round about Pierre appealed to very proud memories. But not only through the mere chances of things, had that fine country become ennobled by the deeds of his sires, but in Pierre's eyes, all its hills and swales seemed as sanctified through their very long uninterrupted possession by his race.

That fond ideality which, in the eyes of affection, hallows the least trinket once familiar to the person of a departed love; with Pierre that talisman touched the whole earthly landscape about him; for remembering that on those hills his own fine fathers had gazed; through those woods, over these lawns, by that stream, along these tangled paths, many a grand-dame of his had merrily strolled when a girl; vividly recalling these things, Pierre deemed all that part of the earth a love-token; so that his very horizon was to him as a memorial ring.

The monarchical world very generally imagines, that in demagoguical America the sacred Past hath no fixed statues erected to it, but all things irreverently seethe and boil in the vulgar caldron of an everlasting uncrystalizing Present. This conceit would seem peculiarly applicable to the social condition. With no chartered aristocracy, and no law of entail, how can any family in America imposingly perpetuate itself? Certainly that common saying among us, which declares, that be a family conspicuous as it may, a single half-century shall see it abased; that maxim undoubtedly holds true with the commonalty. In our cities families rise and burst like bubbles in a vat. For indeed the democratic element operates as a subtile acid among us; forever producing new things by corroding the old; as in the south of France verdigris, the primitive material of one kind of green paint, is produced by grape-vinegar poured upon copper plates. Now in general nothing can be more significant of decay than the idea of corrosion; yet on the other hand, nothing can more vividly suggest luxuriance of life, than the idea of green as a color; for green is the peculiar signet of all-fertile Nature herself. Herein by apt analogy we behold the marked anomalousness of America; whose character abroad, we need not be surprised, is misconceived, when we consider how strangely she contradicts all prior notions of human things; and how wonderfully to her, Death itself becomes transmuted into Life. So that political institutions, which in other lands seem above all things intensely artificial, with America seem to possess the divine virtue of a natural law; for the most mighty of nature's laws is this, that out of Death she brings Life.

Still, are there things in the visible world, over which ever-shifting Nature hath not so unbounded a sway. The grass is annually changed; but the limbs of the oak, for a long term of years, defy that annual decree. And if in America the vast mass of families be as the blades of grass, yet some few there are that stand as the oak; which, instead of decaying, annually puts forth new branches; whereby Time, instead of subtracting, is made to capitulate into a multiple virtue.

In this matter we will—not superciliously, but in fair spirit—compare pedigrees with England, and strange as it may seem at the first blush, not without some claim to equality. I dare say, that in this thing the Peerage Book is a good statistical standard whereby to judge her; since the compilers of that work can not be entirely insensible on whose patronage they most rely; and the common intelligence of our own people shall suffice to judge us. But the magnificence of names must not mislead us as to the humility of things. For as the breath in all our lungs is hereditary, and my present breath at this moment, is further descended than the body of the present High Priest of the Jews, so far as he can assuredly trace it; so mere names, which are also but air, do likewise revel in this endless descendedness. But if Richmond, and St. Albans, and Grafton, and Portland, and Buccleugh, be names almost old as England herself, the present Dukes of those names stop in their own genuine pedigrees at Charles II., and there find no very fine fountain; since what we would deem the least glorious parentage under the sun, is precisely the parentage of a Buccleugh, for example; whose ancestress could not well avoid being a mother, it is true, but had accidentally omitted the preliminary rite. Yet a king was the sire. Then only so much the worse; for if it be small insult to be struck by a pauper, but mortal offense to receive a blow from a gentleman, then of all things the bye-blows of kings must be signally unflattering. In England the Peerage is kept alive by incessant restorations and creations. One man, George III., manufactured five hundred and twenty-two peers. An earldom, in abeyance for five centuries, has suddenly been assumed by some commoner, to whom it had not so much descended, as through the art of the lawyers been made flexibly to bend in that direction. For not Thames is so sinuous in his natural course, not the Bridgewater Canal more artificially conducted, than blood in the veins of that winding or manufactured nobility. Perishable as stubble, and fungous as the fungi, those grafted families successively live and die on the eternal soil of a name. In England this day, twenty-five hundred peerages are extinct; but the names survive. So that the empty air of a name is more endurable than a man, or than dynasties of men; the air fills man's lungs and puts life into a man, but man fills not the air, nor puts life into that.

All honor to the names then, and all courtesy to the men; but if St. Albans tell me he is all-honorable and all-eternal, I must still politely refer him to Nell Gwynne.

Beyond Charles II. very few indeed—hardly worthy of note—are the present titled English families which can trace any thing like a direct unvitiated blood-descent from the thief knights of the Norman. Beyond Charles II. their direct genealogies seem vain as though some Jew clothesman, with a tea-canister on his head, turned over the first chapter of St. Matthew to make out his unmingled participation in the blood of King Saul, who had long died ere the career of the Cæsar began.

Now, not preliminarily to enlarge upon the fact that, while in England an immense mass of state-masonry is brought to bear as a buttress in upholding the hereditary existence of certain houses, while with us nothing of that kind can possibly be admitted; and to omit all mention of the hundreds of unobtrusive families in New England who, nevertheless, might easily trace their uninterrupted English lineage to a time before Charles the Blade: not to speak of the old and oriental-like English planter families of Virginia and the South; the Randolphs for example, one of whose ancestors, in King James' time, married Pocahontas the Indian Princess, and in whose blood therefore an underived aboriginal royalty was flowing over two hundred years ago; consider those most ancient and magnificent Dutch Manors at the

North, whose perches are miles—whose meadows overspread adjacent counties—and whose haughty rent-deeds are held by their thousand farmer tenants, so long as grass grows and water runs; which hints of a surprising eternity for a deed, and seems to make lawyer's ink unobliterable as the sea. Some of those manors are two centuries old; and their present patroons or lords will show you stakes and stones on their estates put there—the stones at least—before Nell Gwynne the Duke-mother was born, and genealogies which, like their own river, Hudson, flow somewhat farther and straighter than the Serpentine brooklet in Hyde Park.

These far-descended Dutch meadows lie steeped in a Hindooish haze; an eastern patriarchalness sways its mild crook over pastures, whose tenant flocks shall there feed, long as their own grass grows, long as their own water shall run. Such estates seem to defy Time's tooth, and by conditions which take hold of the indestructible earth seem to cotemporize their fee-simples with eternity. Unimaginable audacity of a worm that but crawls through the soil he so imperially claims!

In midland counties of England they boast of old oaken dining-halls where three hundred men-at-arms could exercise of a rainy afternoon, in the reign of the Plantagenets. But our lords, the Patroons, appeal not to the past, but they point to the present. One will show you that the public census of a county, is but part of the roll of his tenants. Ranges of mountains, high as Ben Nevis or Snowdon, are their walls; and regular armies, with staffs of officers, crossing rivers with artillery, and marching through primeval woods, and threading vast rocky defiles, have been sent out to distrain upon three thousand farmer-tenants of one landlord, at a blow. A fact most suggestive two ways; both whereof shall be nameless here.

But whatever one may think of the existence of such mighty lordships in the heart of a republic, and however we may wonder at their thus surviving, like Indian mounds, the Revolutionary flood; yet survive and exist they do, and are now owned by their present proprietors, by as good nominal title as any peasant owns his father's old hat, or any duke his great-uncle's old coronet.

For all this, then, we shall not err very widely if we humbly conceive, that—should she choose to glorify herself in that inconsiderable way—our America will make out a good general case with England in this short little matter of large estates, and long pedigrees—pedigrees I mean, wherein is no flaw.

iv

In general terms we have been thus decided in asserting the great genealogical and real-estate dignity of some families in America, because in so doing we poetically establish the richly aristocratic condition of Master Pierre Glendinning, for whom we have before claimed some special family distinction. And to the observant reader the sequel will not fail to show, how important is this circumstance, considered with reference to the singularly developed character and most singular life-career of our hero. Nor will any man dream that the last chapter was merely intended for a foolish bravado, and not with a solid purpose in view.

Now Pierre stands on this noble pedestal; we shall see if he keeps that fine footing; we shall see if Fate hath not just a little bit of a small word or two to say in this world. But it is not laid down here that the Glendinnings dated back beyond Pharaoh, or the deeds of Saddle-Meadows to the Three Magi in the Gospels. Nevertheless, those deeds, as before hinted, did indeed date back to three kings—Indian kings—only so much the finer for that.

But if Pierre did not date back to the Pharaohs, and if the English farmer Hampdens were somewhat the seniors of even the oldest Glendinning; and if some American manors boasted a few additional years and square miles over his, yet think you that it is at all possible, that a youth of nineteen should —merely by way of trial of the thing—strew his ancestral kitchen hearthstone with wheat in the stalk, and there standing in the chimney thresh out that grain with a flail, whose aerial evolutions had free play among all that masonry; were it not impossible for such a flailer so to thresh wheat in his own ancestral kitchen chimney without feeling just a little twinge or two of what one might call family pride? I should say not.

Or how think you it would be with this youthful Pierre, if every day descending to breakfast, he caught sight of an old tattered British banner or two, hanging over an arched window in his hall; and those banners captured by his grandfather, the general, in fair fight? Or how think you it would be if every time he heard the band of the military company of the village, he should distinctly recognize the peculiar tap of a British kettle-drum also captured by his grandfather in fair fight, and afterwards suitably inscribed on the brass and bestowed upon the Saddle-Meadows Artillery Corps? Or how think you it would be, if sometimes of a mild meditative Fourth of July morning in the country, he carried out with him into the garden by way of ceremonial cane, a long, majestic, silver-tipped staff, a Major-General's baton, once wielded on the plume-nodding and musket-flashing review by the same grandfather several times herein-before mentioned? I should say that considering Pierre was quite young and very unphilosophical as yet, and withal rather high-blooded; and sometimes read the History of the Revolutionary War, and possessed a mother who very frequently made remote social allusions to the epaulettes of the Major-General his grandfather;—I should say that upon all of these occasions, the way it must have been with him, was a very proud, elated sort of way. And if this seem but too fond and foolish in Pierre; and if you tell me that this sort of thing in him showed him no sterling Democrat, and that a truly noble man should never brag of any arm but his own; then I beg you to consider again that this Pierre was but a youngster as yet. And believe me you will pronounce Pierre a thorough-going Democrat in time; perhaps a little too Radical altogether to your fancy.

In conclusion, do not blame me if I here make repetition, and do verbally quote my own words in saying that *it had been the choice fate of Pierre to have been born and bred in the country*. For to a noble American youth this indeed—more than in any other land—this indeed is a most rare and choice lot. For it is to be observed, that while in other countries, the finest families boast of the country as their home; the more prominent among us, proudly cite the city as their seat. Too often the American that himself makes his fortune, builds him a great metropolitan house, in the most metropolitan street of the most metropolitan town. Whereas a European of the same sort would thereupon migrate into the country. That herein the European hath the better of it, no poet, no philosopher, and no aristocrat will deny. For the country is not only the most poetical and philosophical, but it is the most aristocratic part of this earth, for it is the most venerable, and numerous bards have ennobled it by many fine titles. Whereas the town is the more plebeian portion: which, besides many other things, is plainly evinced by the dirty unwashed face perpetually worn by the town; but the country, like any Queen, is ever attended by scrupulous lady's maids in the guise of the seasons, and the town hath but one dress of brick turned up with stone; but the country hath a brave dress for every week in the year; sometimes she changes her dress twenty-four times in the twenty-four hours; and the country weareth her sun by day as a diamond on a Queen's brow; and the stars by night as necklaces of gold beads; whereas the town's sun is smoky paste, and no diamond, and the town's stars are pinchbeck and not gold.

In the country then Nature planted our Pierre; because Nature intended a rare and original development in Pierre. Never mind if hereby she proved ambiguous to him in the end; nevertheless, in the beginning she did bravely.

She blew her wind-clarion from the blue hills, and Pierre neighed out lyrical thoughts, as at the trumpet-blast, a war-horse paws himself into a lyric of foam. She whispered through her deep groves at eve, and gentle whispers of humanness, and sweet whispers of love, ran through Pierre's thought-veins, musical as water over pebbles. She lifted her spangled crest of a thickly-starred night, and forth at that glimpse of their divine Captain and Lord, ten thousand mailed thoughts of heroicness started up in Pierre's soul, and glared round for some insulted good cause to defend.

So the country was a glorious benediction to young Pierre; we shall see if that blessing pass from him as did the divine blessing from the Hebrews; we shall yet see again, I say, whether Fate hath not just a little bit of a word or two to say in this world; we shall see whether this wee scrap of latinity be very far out of the way—*Nemo contra Deum nisi Deus ipse.*

V

"Sister Mary," said Pierre, returned from his sunrise stroll, and tapping at his mother's chamber door:—"do you know, sister Mary, that the trees which have been up all night, are all abroad again this morning before you? —Do you not smell something like coffee, my sister?"

A light step moved from within toward the door; which opened, showing Mrs. Glendinning, in a resplendently cheerful morning robe, and holding a gay wide ribbon in her hand.

"Good morning, madam," said Pierre, slowly, and with a bow, whose genuine and spontaneous reverence amusingly contrasted with the sportive manner that had preceded it. For thus sweetly and religiously was the familiarity of his affections bottomed on the profoundest filial respect.

"Good afternoon to you, Pierre, for I suppose it is afternoon. But come, you shall finish my toilette;—here, brother—" reaching the ribbon—"now acquit yourself bravely—" and seating herself away from the glass, she awaited the good offices of Pierre.

"First Lady in waiting to the Dowager Duchess Glendinning," laughed Pierre, as bowing over before his mother, he gracefully passed the ribbon round her neck, simply crossing the ends in front.

"Well, what is to hold it there, Pierre?"

"I am going to try and tack it with a kiss, sister,—there!—oh, what a pity that sort of fastening won't always hold!—where's the cameo with the fawns, I gave you last night?—Ah! on the slab—you were going to wear it then?—Thank you, my considerate and most politic sister—there!—but stop—here's a ringlet gone romping—so now, dear sister, give that Assyrian toss to your head."

The haughtily happy mother rose to her feet, and as she stood before the mirror to criticize her son's adornings, Pierre, noticing the straggling tie of her slipper, knelt down and secured it. "And now for the urn," he cried, "madam!" and with a humorous gallantry, offering his arm to his mother, the pair descended to breakfast.

With Mrs. Glendinning it was one of those spontaneous maxims, which women sometimes act upon without ever thinking of, never to appear in the presence of her son in any dishabille that was not eminently becoming. Her own independent observation of things, had revealed to her many very common maxims, which often become operatively lifeless from a vicarious reception of them. She was vividly aware how immense was that influence, which, even in the closest ties of the heart, the merest appearances make upon the mind. And as in the admiring love and graceful devotion of Pierre lay now her highest joy in life; so she omitted no slightest trifle which could possibly contribute to the preservation of so sweet and flattering a thing.

Besides all this, Mary Glendinning was a woman, and with more than the ordinary vanity of women—if vanity it can be called—which in a life of nearly fifty years had never betrayed her into a single published impropriety, or caused her one known pang at the heart. Moreover, she had never yearned for admiration; because that was her birthright by the eternal privilege of beauty; she had always possessed it; she had not to turn her head for it, since spontaneously it always encompassed her. Vanity, which in so many women approaches to a spiritual vice, and therefore to a visible blemish; in her peculiar case—and though possessed in a transcendent degree —was still the token of the highest health; inasmuch as never knowing what it was to yearn for its gratification, she was almost entirely unconscious of possessing it at all. Many women carry this light of their lives flaming on their foreheads; but Mary Glendinning unknowingly bore hers within. Through all the infinite traceries of feminine art, she evenly glowed like a vase which, internally illuminated, gives no outward sign of the lighting flame, but seems to shine by the very virtue of the exquisite marble itself. But that bluff corporeal admiration, with which some ball-room women are content, was no admiration to the mother of Pierre. Not the general homage of men, but the selected homage of the noblest men, was what she felt to be her appropriate right. And as her own maternal partialities were added to, and glorified the rare and absolute merits of Pierre; she considered the voluntary allegiance of his affectionate soul, the representative fealty of the choicest guild of his race. Thus, though replenished through all her veins with the subtlest vanity, with the homage of Pierre alone she was content.

But as to a woman of sense and spirit, the admiration of even the noblest and most gifted man, is esteemed as nothing, so long as she remains conscious of possessing no directly influencing and practical sorcery over his soul; and as notwithstanding all his intellectual superiority to his mother, Pierre, through the unavoidable weakness of inexperienced and unexpanded youth, was strangely docile to the maternal tuitions in nearly all the things which thus far had any ways interested or affected him; therefore it was, that to Mary Glendinning this reverence of Pierre was invested with all the proudest delights and witcheries of self-complacency, which it is possible for the most conquering virgin to feel. Still more. That nameless and infinitely delicate aroma of inexpressible tenderness and attentiveness which, in every refined and honorable attachment, is cotemporary with the courtship, and precedes the final banns and the rite; but which, like the *bouquet* of the costliest German wines, too often evaporates upon pouring love out to drink, in the disenchanting glasses of the matrimonial days and nights; this highest and airiest thing in the whole compass of the experience of our mortal life; this heavenly evanescence—still further etherealized in the filial breast—was for Mary Glendinning, now not very far from her grand climacteric, miraculously revived in the courteous lover-like adoration of Pierre.

Altogether having its origin in a wonderful but purely fortuitous combination of the happiest and rarest accidents of earth; and not to be limited in duration by that climax which is so fatal to ordinary love; this softened spell which still wheeled the mother and son in one orbit of joy, seemed a glimpse of the glorious possibility, that the divinest of those emotions, which are incident to the sweetest season of love, is capable of an indefinite translation into many of the less signal relations of our many chequered life. In a detached and individual way, it seemed almost to realize here below the sweet dreams of those religious enthusiasts, who paint to us a Paradise to come, when etherealized from all drosses and stains, the holiest passion of man shall unite all kindreds and climes in one circle of pure and unimpairable delight.

vi

There was one little uncelestial trait, which, in the opinion of some, may mar the romantic merits of the gentlemanly Pierre Glendinning. He always had an excellent appetite, and especially for his breakfast. But when we consider that though Pierre's hands were small, and his ruffles white, yet his arm was by no means dainty, and his complexion inclined to brown; and that he generally rose with the sun, and could not sleep without riding his twenty, or walking his twelve miles a day, or felling a fair-sized hemlock in the forest, or boxing, or fencing, or boating, or performing some other gymnastical feat; when we consider these athletic habitudes of Pierre, and the great fullness of brawn and muscle they built round about him; all of which manly brawn and muscle, three times a day loudly clamored for attention; we shall very soon perceive that to have a bountiful appetite, was not only no vulgar reproach, but a right royal grace and honor to Pierre; attesting him a man and a gentleman; for a thoroughly developed gentleman is always robust and healthy; and Robustness and Health are great trenchermen.

So when Pierre and his mother descended to breakfast, and Pierre had scrupulously seen her supplied with whatever little things were convenient to her; and had twice or thrice ordered the respectable and immemorial Dates, the servitor, to adjust and re-adjust the window-sashes, so that no unkind current of air should take undue liberties with his mother's neck; after seeing to all this, but in a very quiet and inconspicuous way; and also after directing the unruffled Dates, to swing out, horizontally into a particular light, a fine joyous painting, in the good-fellow, Flemish style (which painting was so attached to the wall as to be capable of that mode of adjusting), and furthermore after darting from where he sat a few invigorating glances over the river-meadows to the blue mountains beyond; Pierre made a masonic sort of mysterious motion to the excellent Dates, who in automaton obedience thereto, brought from a certain agreeable little side-stand, a very prominent-looking cold pasty; which, on careful inspection with the knife, proved to be the embossed savory nest of a few uncommonly tender pigeons of Pierre's own shooting.

"Sister Mary," said he, lifting on his silver trident one of the choicest of the many fine pigeon morsels; "Sister Mary," said he, "in shooting these pigeons, I was very careful to bring down one in such a manner that the breast is entirely unmarred. It was intended for you! and here it is. Now Sergeant Dates, help hither your mistress' plate. No?—nothing but the crumbs of French rolls, and a few peeps into a coffee-cup—is that a breakfast for the daughter of yonder bold General?"—pointing to a full-length of his gold-laced grandfather on the opposite wall. "Well, pitiable is my case when I have to breakfast for two. Dates!"

"Sir."

"Remove that toast-rack, Dates; and this plate of tongue, and bring the rolls nearer, and wheel the stand farther off, good Dates."

Having thus made generous room for himself, Pierre commenced operations, interrupting his mouthfuls by many sallies of mirthfulness.

"You seem to be in prodigious fine spirits this morning, brother Pierre," said his mother.

"Yes, very tolerable; at least I can't say, that I am low-spirited exactly, sister Mary;—Dates, my fine fellow, bring me three bowls of milk."

"One bowl, sir, you mean," said Dates, gravely and imperturbably.

As the servitor left the room, Mrs. Glendinning spoke. "My dear Pierre, how often have I begged you never to permit your hilariousness to betray you into overstepping the exact line of propriety in your intercourse with servants. Dates' look was a respectful reproof to you just now. You must not call Dates, *My fine fellow*. He *is* a fine fellow, a very fine fellow, indeed; but there is no need of telling him so at my table. It is very easy to be entirely kind and pleasant to servants, without the least touch of any shade of transient good-fellowship with them."

"Well, sister, no doubt you are altogether right; after this I shall drop the *fine*, and call Dates nothing but *fellow*;—Fellow, come here!—how will that answer?"

"Not at all, Pierre—but you are a Romeo, you know, and so for the present I pass over your nonsense."

"Romeo! oh, no. I am far from being Romeo—" sighed Pierre. "I laugh, but he cried; poor Romeo! alas Romeo! woe is me, Romeo! he came to a very deplorable end, did Romeo, sister Mary."

"It was his own fault though."

"Poor Romeo!"

"He was disobedient to his parents."

"Alas Romeo!"

"He married against their particular wishes."

"Woe is me, Romeo!"

"But you, Pierre, are going to be married before long, I trust, not to a Capulet, but to one of our own Montagues; and so Romeo's evil fortune will hardly be yours. You will be happy."

"The more miserable Romeo!"

"Don't be so ridiculous, brother Pierre; so you are going to take Lucy that long ride among the hills this morning? She is a sweet girl; a most lovely girl."

"Yes, that is rather my opinion, sister Mary.—By heavens, mother, the five zones hold not such another! She is—yes—though I say it—Dates!—he's a precious long time getting that milk!"

"Let him stay.—Don't be a milk-sop, Pierre!"

"Ha! my sister is a little satirical this morning. I comprehend."

"Never rave, Pierre; and never rant. Your father never did either; nor is it written of Socrates; and both were very wise men. Your father was profoundly in love—that I know to my certain knowledge—but I never heard him rant about it. He was always exceedingly gentlemanly: and gentlemen never rant. Milk-sops and Muggletonians rant, but gentlemen never."

"Thank you, sister.—There, put it down, Dates; are the horses ready?"

"Just driving round, sir, I believe."

"Why, Pierre," said his mother, glancing out at the window, "are you going to Santa Fe De Bogota with that enormous old phaeton;—what do you take that Juggernaut out for?"

"Humor, sister, humor; I like it because it's old-fashioned, and because the seat is such a wide sofa of a seat, and finally because a young lady by the name of Lucy Tartan cherishes a high regard for it. She vows she would like to be married in it."

"Well, Pierre, all I have to say, is, be sure that Christopher puts the coach-hammer and nails, and plenty of cords and screws into the box. And you had better let him follow you in one of the farm wagons, with a spare axle and some boards."

"No fear, sister; no fear;—I shall take the best of care of the old phaeton. The quaint old arms on the panel, always remind me who it was that first rode in it."

"I am glad you have that memory, brother Pierre."

"And who it was that *next* rode in it."

"Bless you!—God bless you, my dear son!—always think of him and you can never err; yes, always think of your dear perfect father, Pierre."

"Well, kiss me now, dear sister, for I must go."

"There; this is my cheek, and the other is Lucy's; though now that I look at them both, I think that hers is getting to be the most blooming; sweeter dews fall on that one, I suppose."

Pierre laughed, and ran out of the room, for old Christopher was getting impatient. His mother went to the window and stood there.

"A noble boy, and docile"—she murmured—"he has all the frolicsomeness of youth, with little of its giddiness. And he does not grow vain-glorious in sophomorean wisdom. I thank heaven I sent him not to college. A noble boy, and docile. A fine, proud, loving, docile, vigorous boy. Pray God, he never becomes otherwise to me. His little wife, that is to be, will not estrange him from me; for she too is docile,—beautiful, and reverential, and most docile. Seldom yet have I known such blue eyes as hers, that were not docile, and would not follow a bold black one, as two meek blue-ribboned ewes, follow their martial leader. How glad am I that Pierre loves her so, and not some dark-eyed haughtiness, with whom I could never live in peace; but who would be ever setting her young married state before my elderly widowed one, and claiming all the homage of my dear boy—the fine, proud, loving, docile, vigorous boy!—the lofty-minded, well-born, noble boy; and with such sweet docilities! See his hair! He does in truth illustrate that fine saying of his father's, that as the noblest colts, in three points—abundant hair, swelling chest, and sweet docility—should resemble a fine woman, so should a noble youth. Well, good-bye, Pierre, and a merry morning to ye!"

So saying she crossed the room, and—resting in a corner—her glad proud eye met the old General's baton, which the day before in one of his frolic moods Pierre had taken from its accustomed place in the pictured-bannered hall. She lifted it, and musingly swayed it to and fro; then paused, and staff-wise rested with it in her hand. Her stately beauty had ever somewhat martial in it; and now she looked the daughter of a General, as she was; for Pierre's was a double revolutionary descent. On both sides he sprung from heroes.

"This is his inheritance—this symbol of command! and I swell out to think it. Yet but just now I fondled the conceit that Pierre was so sweetly docile! Here sure is a most strange inconsistency! For is sweet docility a general's badge? and is this baton but a distaff then?—Here's something widely wrong. Now I almost wish him otherwise than sweet and docile to me, seeing that it must be hard for man to be an uncompromising hero and a commander among his race, and yet never ruffle any domestic brow. Pray heaven he show his heroicness in some smooth way of favoring fortune, not be called out to be a hero of some dark hope forlorn;—of some dark hope forlorn, whose cruelness makes a savage of a man. Give him, O God, regardful gales! Fan him with unwavering prosperities! So shall he remain all docility to me, and yet prove a haughty hero to the world!"

Book II

Love, Delight, and Alarm

ON THE PREVIOUS EVENING, Pierre had arranged with Lucy the plan of a long winding ride, among the hills which stretched around to the southward from the wide plains of Saddle-Meadows.

Though the vehicle was a sexagenarian, the animals that drew it, were but six-year colts. The old phaeton had outlasted several generations of its drawers.

Pierre rolled beneath the village elms in billowy style, and soon drew up before the white cottage door. Flinging his reins upon the ground he entered the house.

The two colts were his particular and confidential friends; born on the same land with him, and fed with the same corn, which, in the form of Indian-cakes, Pierre himself was often wont to eat for breakfast. The same fountain that by one branch supplied the stables with water, by another supplied Pierre's pitcher. They were a sort of family cousins to Pierre, those horses; and they were splendid young cousins; very showy in their redundant manes and mighty paces, but not at all vain or arrogant. They acknowledged Pierre as the undoubted head of the house of Glendinning. They well knew that they were but an inferior and subordinate branch of the Glendinnings, bound in perpetual feudal fealty to its headmost representative. Therefore, these young cousins never permitted themselves to run from

Pierre; they were impatient in their paces, but very patient in the halt. They were full of good-humor too, and kind as kittens.

"Bless me, how can you let them stand all alone that way, Pierre," cried Lucy, as she and Pierre stepped forth from the cottage door, Pierre laden with shawls, parasol, reticule, and a small hamper.

"Wait a bit," cried Pierre, dropping his load; "I will show you what my colts are."

So saying, he spoke to them mildly, and went close up to them, and patted them. The colts neighed; the nigh colt neighing a little jealously, as if Pierre had not patted impartially. Then, with a low, long, almost inaudible whistle, Pierre got between the colts, among the harness. Whereat Lucy started, and uttered a faint cry, but Pierre told her to keep perfectly quiet, for there was not the least danger in the world. And Lucy did keep quiet; for somehow, though she always started when Pierre seemed in the slightest jeopardy, yet at bottom she rather cherished a notion that Pierre bore a charmed life, and by no earthly possibility could die from her, or experience any harm, when she was within a thousand leagues.

Pierre, still between the horses, now stepped upon the pole of the phaeton; then stepping down, indefinitely disappeared, or became partially obscured among the living colonnade of the horses' eight slender and glossy legs. He entered the colonnade one way, and after a variety of meanderings, came out another way; during all of which equestrian performance, the two colts kept gayly neighing, and good-humoredly moving their heads perpendicularly up and down; and sometimes turning them sideways toward Lucy; as much as to say—We understand young master; we understand him, Miss; never fear, pretty lady: why, bless your delicious little heart, we played with Pierre before you ever did.

"Are you afraid of their running away now, Lucy?" said Pierre, returning to her.

"Not much, Pierre; the superb fellows! Why, Pierre, they have made an officer of you—look!" and she pointed to two foam-flakes epauletting his shoulders. "Bravissimo again! I called you my recruit, when you left my window this morning, and here you are promoted."

"Very prettily conceited, Lucy. But see, you don't admire their coats; they wear nothing but the finest Genoa velvet, Lucy. See! did you ever see such well-groomed horses?"

"Never!"

"Then what say you to have them for my groomsmen, Lucy? Glorious groomsmen they would make, I declare. They should have a hundred ells of white favors all over their manes and tails; and when they drew us to church, they would be still all the time scattering white favors from their mouths, just as they did here on me. Upon my soul, they shall be my groomsmen, Lucy. Stately stags! playful dogs! heroes, Lucy. We shall have no marriage bells; they shall neigh for us, Lucy; we shall be wedded to the martial sound of Job's trumpeters, Lucy. Hark! they are neighing now to think of it."

"Neighing at your lyrics, Pierre. Come, let us be off. Here, the shawl, the parasol, the basket: what are you looking at them so for?"

"I was thinking, Lucy, of the sad state I am in. Not six months ago, I saw a poor affianced fellow, an old comrade of mine, trudging along with his Lucy Tartan, a hillock of bundles under either arm; and I said to myself—There goes a sumpter, now; poor devil, he's a lover. And now look at me! Well, life's a burden, they say; why not be burdened cheerily? But look ye, Lucy, I am going to enter a formal declaration and protest before matters go further with us. When we are married, I am not to carry any bundles, unless in cases of real need; and what is more, when there are any of your young lady acquaintances in sight, I am not to be unnecessarily called upon to back up, and load for their particular edification."

"Now I am really vexed with you, Pierre; that is the first ill-natured innuendo I ever heard from you. Are there any of my young lady acquaintances in sight now, I should like to know?"

"Six of them, right over the way," said Pierre; "but they keep behind the curtains. I never trust your solitary village streets, Lucy. Sharp-shooters behind every clap-board, Lucy."

"Pray, then, dear Pierre, do let us be off!"

ii

While Pierre and Lucy are now rolling along under the elms, let it be said who Lucy Tartan was. It is needless to say that she was a beauty; because chestnut-haired, bright-cheeked youths like Pierre Glendinning, seldom fall in love with any but a beauty. And in the times to come, there must be—as in the present times, and in the times gone by—some splendid men, and some transcendent women; and how can they ever be, unless always, throughout all time, here and there, a handsome youth weds with a handsome maid?

But though owing to the above-named provisions of dame Nature, there always will be beautiful women in the world; yet the world will never see another Lucy Tartan. Her cheeks were tinted with the most delicate white and red, the white predominating. Her eyes some god brought down from heaven; her hair was Danae's, spangled with Jove's shower; her teeth were dived for in the Persian Sea.

If long wont to fix his glance on those who, trudging through the humbler walks of life, and whom unequal toil and poverty deform; if that man shall haply view some fair and gracious daughter of the gods, who, from unknown climes of loveliness and affluence, comes floating into sight, all symmetry and radiance; how shall he be transported, that in a world so full of vice and misery as ours, there should yet shine forth this visible semblance of the heavens. For a lovely woman is not entirely of this earth. Her own sex regard her not as such. A crowd of women eye a transcendent beauty entering a room, much as though a bird from Arabia had lighted on the window sill. Say what you will, their jealousy—if any—is but an after-birth to their open admiration. Do men envy the gods? And shall women envy the goddesses? A beautiful woman is born Queen of men and women both, as Mary Stuart was born Queen of Scots, whether men or women. All mankind are her Scots; her leal clans are numbered by the nations. A true gentleman in Kentucky would cheerfully die for a beautiful woman in Hindostan, though he never saw her. Yea, count down his heart in death-drops for her; and go to Pluto, that she might go to Paradise. He would turn Turk before he would disown an allegiance hereditary to all gentlemen, from the hour their Grand Master, Adam, first knelt to Eve.

A plain-faced Queen of Spain dwells not in half the glory a beautiful milliner does. Her soldiers can break heads, but her Highness can not crack a heart; and the beautiful milliner might string hearts for necklaces. Undoubtedly, Beauty made the first Queen. If ever again the succession to the German Empire should be contested, and one poor lame lawyer should present the claims of the first excellingly beautiful woman he chanced to see —she would thereupon be unanimously elected Empress of the Holy Roman German Empire;—that is to say, if all the Germans were true, free-hearted and magnanimous gentlemen, at all capable of appreciating so immense an honor.

It is nonsense to talk of France as the seat of all civility. Did not those French heathen have a Salique law? Three of the most bewitching creatures, —immortal flowers of the line of Valois—were excluded from the French throne by that infamous provision. France, indeed! whose Catholic millions still worship Mary Queen of Heaven; and for ten generations refused cap and knee to many angel Maries, rightful Queens of France. Here is cause for universal war. See how vilely nations, as well as men, assume and wear unchallenged the choicest titles, however without merit. The Americans, and not the French, are the world's models of chivalry. Our Salique Law provides that universal homage shall be paid all beautiful women. No man's most solid rights shall weigh against her airiest whims. If you buy the best seat in the coach, to go and consult a doctor on a matter of life and death, you shall cheerfully abdicate that best seat, and limp away on foot, if a pretty woman, traveling, shake one feather from the stage-house door.

Now, since we began by talking of a certain young lady that went out riding with a certain youth; and yet find ourselves, after leading such a merry dance, fast by a stage-house window;—this may seem rather irregular sort of writing. But whither indeed should Lucy Tartan conduct us, but among mighty Queens, and all other creatures of high degree; and finally set us roaming, to see whether the wide world can match so fine a wonder. By immemorial usage, am I not bound to celebrate this Lucy Tartan? Who shall stay me? Is she not my hero's own affianced? What can be gainsaid? Where underneath the tester of the night sleeps such another?

Yet, how would Lucy Tartan shrink from all this noise and clatter! She is bragged of, but not brags. Thus far she hath floated as stilly through this life, as thistle-down floats over meadows. Noiseless, she, except with Pierre; and even with him she lives through many a panting hush. Oh, those love-pauses that they know—how ominous of their future; for pauses precede the earthquake, and every other terrible commotion! But blue be their sky awhile, and lightsome all their chat, and frolicsome their humors.

Never shall I get down the vile inventory! How, if with paper and with pencil I went out into the starry night to inventorize the heavens? Who shall tell stars as teaspoons? Who shall put down the charms of Lucy Tartan upon paper?

And for the rest; her parentage, what fortune she would possess, how many dresses in her wardrobe, and how many rings upon her fingers; cheerfully would I let the genealogists, tax-gatherers, and upholsterers attend to that. My proper province is with the angelical part of Lucy. But as in some quarters, there prevails a sort of prejudice against angels, who are merely angels and nothing more; therefore I shall martyrize myself, by letting such gentlemen and ladies into some details of Lucy Tartan's history.

She was the daughter of an early and most cherished friend of Pierre's father. But that father was now dead, and she resided an only daughter with her mother, in a very fine house in the city. But though her home was in the city, her heart was twice a year in the country. She did not at all love the city and its empty, heartless, ceremonial ways. It was very strange, but most eloquently significant of her own natural angelhood that, though born among brick and mortar in a sea-port, she still pined for unbaked earth and inland grass. So the sweet linnet, though born inside of wires in a lady's chamber on the ocean coast, and ignorant all its life of any other spot; yet, when spring-time comes, it is seized with flutterings and vague impatiences; it can not eat or drink for these wild longings. Though unlearned by any experience, still the inspired linnet divinely knows that the inland migrating time has come. And just so with Lucy in her first longings for the verdure. Every spring those wild flutterings shook her; every spring, this sweet linnet girl did migrate inland. Oh God grant that those other and long after nameless flutterings of her inmost soul, when all life was become weary to her—God grant, that those deeper flutterings in her were equally significant of her final heavenly migration from this heavy earth.

It was fortunate for Lucy that her Aunt Llanyllyn—a pensive, childless, white-turbaned widow—possessed and occupied a pretty cottage in the village of Saddle-Meadows; and still more fortunate, that this excellent old aunt was very partial to her, and always felt a quiet delight in having Lucy near her. So Aunt Llanyllyn's cottage, in effect, was Lucy's. And now, for some years past, she had annually spent several months at Saddle Meadows; and it was among the pure and soft incitements of the country that Pierre first had felt toward Lucy the dear passion which now made him wholly hers.

Lucy had two brothers; one her senior, by three years, and the other her junior by two. But these young men were officers in the navy; and so they did not permanently live with Lucy and her mother.

Mrs. Tartan was mistress of an ample fortune. She was, moreover, perfectly aware that such was the fact, and was somewhat inclined to force it upon the notice of other people, nowise interested in the matter. In other words, Mrs. Tartan, instead of being daughter-proud, for which she had infinite reason, was a little inclined to being purse-proud, for which she had not the slightest reason; seeing that the Great Mogul probably possessed a larger fortune than she, not to speak of the Shah of Persia and Baron Rothschild, and a thousand other millionaires; whereas, the Grand Turk, and all their other majesties of Europe, Asia, and Africa to boot, could not, in all their joint dominions, boast so sweet a girl as Lucy. Nevertheless, Mrs. Tartan was an excellent sort of lady, as this lady-like world goes. She subscribed to charities, and owned five pews in as many churches, and went about trying to promote the general felicity of the world, by making all the handsome young people of her acquaintance marry one another. In other words, she was a match-maker—not a Lucifer match-maker—though, to tell the truth, she may have kindled the matrimonial blues in certain dissatisfied gentlemen's breasts, who had been wedded under her particular auspices, and by her particular advice. Rumor said—but rumor is always fibbing—that there was a secret society of dissatisfied young husbands, who were at the pains of privately circulating handbills among all unmarried young strangers, warning them against the insidious approaches of Mrs. Tartan; and, for reference, named themselves in cipher. But this could not have been true; for, flushed with a thousand matches—burning blue or bright, it made little matter—Mrs. Tartan sailed the seas of fashion, causing all topsails to lower to her; and towing flotillas of young ladies, for all of whom she was bound to find the finest husband harbors in the world.

But does not match-making, like charity, begin at home? Why is her own daughter Lucy without a mate? But not so fast; Mrs. Tartan years ago laid out that sweet programme concerning Pierre and Lucy; but in this case, her programme happened to coincide, in some degree, with a previous one in heaven, and only for that cause did it come to pass, that Pierre Glendinning was the proud elect of Lucy Tartan. Besides, this being a thing so nearly affecting herself, Mrs. Tartan had, for the most part, been rather circumspect and cautious in all her manœuvrings with Pierre and Lucy. Moreover, the thing demanded no manœuvring at all. The two Platonic particles, after roaming in quest of each other, from the time of Saturn and Ops till now; they came together before Mrs. Tartan's own eyes; and what more could Mrs. Tartan do toward making them forever one and indivisible? Once, and only once, had a dim suspicion passed through Pierre's mind, that Mrs. Tartan was a lady thimble-rigger, and slyly rolled the pea.

In their less mature acquaintance, he was breakfasting with Lucy and her mother in the city, and the first cup of coffee had been poured out by Mrs. Tartan, when she declared she smelt matches burning somewhere in the house, and she must see them extinguished. So banning all pursuit, she rose to seek for the burning matches, leaving the pair alone to interchange the civilities of the coffee; and finally sent word to them, from above stairs, that the matches, or something else, had given her a headache, and begged Lucy to send her up some toast and tea, for she would breakfast in her own chamber that morning.

Upon this, Pierre looked from Lucy to his boots, and as he lifted his eyes again, saw Anacreon on the sofa on one side of him, and Moore's Melodies on the other, and some honey on the table, and a bit of white satin on the floor, and a sort of bride's veil on the chandelier.

Never mind though—thought Pierre, fixing his gaze on Lucy—I'm entirely willing to be caught, when the bait is set in Paradise, and the bait is such an angel. Again he glanced at Lucy, and saw a look of infinite subdued vexation, and some unwonted pallor on her cheek. Then willingly he would have kissed the delicious bait, that so gently hated to be tasted in the trap. But glancing round again, and seeing that the music, which Mrs. Tartan, under the pretense of putting in order, had been adjusting upon the piano; seeing that this music was now in a vertical pile against the wall, with—"*Love was once a little boy*," for the outermost and only visible sheet; and thinking this to be a remarkable coincidence under the circumstances; Pierre could not refrain from a humorous smile, though it was a very gentle one, and immediately repented of, especially as Lucy seeing and interpreting it, immediately arose, with an unaccountable, indignant, angelical, adorable, and all-persuasive "Mr. Glendinning?" utterly confounded in him the slightest germ of suspicion as to Lucy's collusion in her mother's imagined artifices.

Indeed, Mrs. Tartan's having any thing whatever to do, or hint, or finesse in this matter of the loves of Pierre and Lucy, was nothing less than immensely gratuitous and sacrilegious. Would Mrs. Tartan doctor lilies when they blow? Would Mrs. Tartan set about match-making between the steel and magnet? Preposterous Mrs. Tartan! But this whole world is a preposterous one, with many preposterous people in it; chief among whom was Mrs. Tartan, match-maker to the nation.

This conduct of Mrs. Tartan, was the more absurd, seeing that she could not but know that Mrs. Glendinning desired the thing. And was not Lucy wealthy?—going to be, that is, very wealthy when her mother died;—(sad thought that for Mrs. Tartan)—and was not her husband's family of the best; and had not Lucy's father been a bosom friend of Pierre's father? And though Lucy might be matched to some one man, where among women was the match for Lucy? Exceedingly preposterous Mrs. Tartan! But when a lady like Mrs. Tartan has nothing positive and useful to do, then she will do just such preposterous things as Mrs. Tartan did.

Well, time went on; and Pierre loved Lucy, and Lucy, Pierre; till at last the two young naval gentlemen, her brothers, happened to arrive in Mrs. Tartan's drawing-room, from their first cruise—a three years' one up the Mediterranean. They rather stared at Pierre, finding him on the sofa, and Lucy not very remote.

"Pray, be seated, gentlemen," said Pierre. "Plenty of room."

"My darling brothers!" cried Lucy, embracing them.

"My darling brothers and sister!" cried Pierre, folding them together.

"Pray, hold off, sir," said the elder brother, who had served as a passed midshipman for the last two weeks. The younger brother retreated a little, and clapped his hand upon his dirk, saying, "Sir, we are from the Mediterranean. Sir, permit me to say, this is decidedly improper! Who may you be, sir?"

"I can't explain for joy," cried Pierre, hilariously embracing them all again.

"Most extraordinary!" cried the elder brother, extricating his shirt-collar from the embrace, and pulling it up vehemently.

"Draw!" cried the younger, intrepidly.

"Peace, foolish fellows," cried Lucy—"this is your old playfellow, Pierre Glendinning."

"Pierre? why, Pierre?" cried the lads—"a hug all round again! You've grown a fathom!—who would have known you? But, then—Lucy? I say, Lucy?—what business have you here in this—eh? eh?—hugging-match, I should call it?"

"Oh! Lucy don't mean any thing," cried Pierre—"come, one more all round."

So they all embraced again; and that evening it was publicly known that Pierre was to wed with Lucy.

Whereupon, the young officers took it upon themselves to think—though they by no means presumed to breathe it—that they had authoritatively, though indirectly, accelerated a before ambiguous and highly incommendable state of affairs between the now affianced lovers.

iii

In the fine old robust times of Pierre's grandfather, an American gentleman of substantial person and fortune spent his time in a somewhat different style from the green-house gentlemen of the present day. The grandfather of Pierre measured six feet four inches in height; during a fire in the old manorial mansion, with one dash of his foot, he had smitten down an oaken door, to admit the buckets of his negro slaves; Pierre had often tried on his military vest, which still remained an heirloom at Saddle Meadows, and found the pockets below his knees, and plenty additional room for a fair-sized quarter-cask within its buttoned girth; in a night-scuffle in the wilderness before the Revolutionary War, he had annihilated two Indian savages by making reciprocal bludgeons of their heads. And all this was done by the mildest hearted, and most blue-eyed gentleman in the world, who, according to the patriarchal fashion of those days, was a gentle, white-haired worshiper of all the household gods; the gentlest husband, and the gentlest father; the kindest of masters to his slaves; of the most wonderful unruffledness of temper; a serene smoker of his after-dinner pipe; a forgiver of many injuries; a sweet-hearted, charitable Christian; in fine, a pure, cheerful, childlike, blue-eyed, divine old man; in whose meek, majestic soul, the lion and the lamb embraced—fit image of his God.

Never could Pierre look upon his fine military portrait without an infinite and mournful longing to meet his living aspect in actual life. The majestic sweetness of this portrait was truly wonderful in its effects upon any sensitive and generous-minded young observer. For such, that portrait possessed the heavenly persuasiveness of angelic speech; a glorious gospel framed and hung upon the wall, and declaring to all people, as from the Mount, that man is a noble, god-like being, full of choicest juices; made up of strength and beauty.

Now, this grand old Pierre Glendinning was a great lover of horses; but not in the modern sense, for he was no jockey;—one of his most intimate friends of the masculine gender was a huge, proud, gray horse, of a surprising reserve of manner, his saddle-beast; he had his horses' mangers carved like old trenchers, out of solid maple logs; the key of the corn-bin hung in his library; and no one grained his steeds, but himself; unless his absence from home promoted Moyar, an incorruptible and most punctual old black, to that honorable office. He said that no man loved his horses, unless his own hands grained them. Every Christmas he gave them brimming measures. "I keep Christmas with my horses," said grand old Pierre. This grand old Pierre always rose at sunrise; washed his face and chest in the open air; and then, returning to his closet, and being completely arrayed at last, stepped forth to make a ceremonious call at his stables, to bid his very honorable friends there a very good and joyful morning. Woe to Cranz, Kit, Douw, or any other of his stable slaves, if grand old Pierre found one horse unblanketed, or one weed among the hay that filled their rack. Not that he ever had Cranz, Kit, Douw, or any of them flogged—a thing unknown in that patriarchal time and country—but he would refuse to say his wonted pleasant word to them; and that was very bitter to them, for Cranz, Kit, Douw, and all of them, loved grand old Pierre, as his shepherds loved old Abraham.

What decorous, lordly, gray-haired steed is this? What old Chaldean rides abroad?—'Tis grand old Pierre; who, every morning before he eats, goes out promenading with his saddle-beast; nor mounts him, without first asking leave. But time glides on, and grand old Pierre grows old: his life's glorious grape now swells with fatness; he has not the conscience to saddle his majestic beast with such a mighty load of manliness. Besides, the noble beast himself is growing old, and has a touching look of meditativeness in his large, attentive eyes. Leg of man, swears grand old Pierre, shall never more bestride my steed; no more shall harness touch him! Then every spring he sowed a field with clover for his steed; and at mid-summer sorted all his meadow grasses, for the choicest hay to winter him; and had his destined grain thrashed out with a flail, whose handle had once borne a flag in a brisk battle, into which this same old steed had pranced with grand old Pierre; one waving mane, one waving sword!

Now needs must grand old Pierre take a morning drive; he rides no more with the old gray steed. He has a phaeton built, fit for a vast General, in whose sash three common men might hide. Doubled, trebled are the huge S shaped leather springs; the wheels seem stolen from some mill; the canopied seat is like a testered bed. From beneath the old archway, not one horse, but two, every morning now draw forth old Pierre, as the Chinese draw their fat god Josh, once every year from out his fane.

But time glides on, and a morning comes, when the phaeton emerges not; but all the yards and courts are full; helmets line the ways; sword-points strike the stone steps of the porch; muskets ring upon the stairs; and mournful martial melodies are heard in all the halls. Grand old Pierre is dead; and like a hero of old battles, he dies on the eve of another war; ere wheeling to fire on the foe, his platoons fire over their old commander's grave; in A.D. 1812, died grand old Pierre. The drum that beat in brass his funeral march, was a British kettle-drum, that had once helped beat the vain-glorious march, for the thirty thousand predestined prisoners, led into sure captivity by that bragging boy, Burgoyne.

Next day the old gray steed turned from his grain; turned round, and vainly whinnied in his stall. By gracious Moyar's hand, he refuses to be patted now; plain as horse can speak, the old gray steed says—"I smell not the wonted hand; where is grand old Pierre? Grain me not, and groom me not;—Where is grand old Pierre?"

He sleeps not far from his master now; beneath the field he cropt, he has softly lain him down; and long ere this, grand old Pierre and steed have passed through that grass to glory.

But his phaeton—like his plumed hearse, outlives the noble load it bore. And the dark bay steeds that drew grand old Pierre alive, and by his testament drew him dead, and followed the lordly lead of the led gray horse; those dark bay steeds are still extant; not in themselves or in their issue; but in the two descendants of stallions of their own breed. For on the lands of Saddle Meadows, man and horse are both hereditary; and this bright morning Pierre Glendinning, grandson of grand old Pierre, now drives forth with Lucy Tartan, seated where his own ancestor had sat, and reining steeds, whose great-great-great-grandfathers grand old Pierre had reined before.

How proud felt Pierre: In fancy's eye, he saw the horse-ghosts a-tandem in the van; "These are but wheelers"—cried young Pierre—"the leaders are the generations."

iv

But Love has more to do with his own possible and probable posterities, than with the once living but now impossible ancestries in the past. So Pierre's glow of family pride quickly gave place to a deeper hue, when Lucy bade love's banner blush out from his cheek.

That morning was the choicest drop that Time had in his vase. Ineffable distillations of a soft delight were wafted from the fields and hills. Fatal morning that, to all lovers unbetrothed; "Come to your confessional," it cried. "Behold our airy loves," the birds chirped from the trees; far out at sea, no more the sailors tied their bowline-knots; their hands had lost their cunning; will they, nill they, Love tied love-knots on every spangled spar.

Oh, praised be the beauty of this earth, the beauty, and the bloom, and the mirthfulness thereof! The first worlds made were winter worlds; the second made, were vernal worlds; the third, and last, and perfectest, was this summer world of ours. In the cold and nether spheres, preachers preach of earth, as we of Paradise above. Oh, there, my friends, they say, they have a season, in their language known as summer. Then their fields spin themselves green carpets; snow and ice are not in all the land; then a million strange, bright, fragrant things powder that sward with perfumes; and high, majestic beings, dumb and grand, stand up with outstretched arms, and hold their green canopies over merry angels—men and women—who love and wed, and sleep and dream, beneath the approving glances of their visible god and goddess, glad-hearted sun, and pensive moon!

Oh, praised be the beauty of this earth; the beauty, and the bloom, and the mirthfulness thereof. We lived before, and shall live again; and as we hope for a fairer world than this to come; so we came from one less fine. From each successive world, the demon Principle is more and more dislodged; he is the accursed clog from chaos, and thither, by every new translation, we drive him further and further back again. Hosannahs to this world! so beautiful itself, and the vestibule to more. Out of some past Egypt, we have come to this new Canaan; and from this new Canaan, we press on to some Circassia. Though still the villains, Want and Woe, followed us out of Egypt, and now beg in Canaan's streets: yet Circassia's gates shall not admit them; they, with their sire, the demon Principle, must back to chaos, whence they came.

Love was first begot by Mirth and Peace, in Eden, when the world was young. The man oppressed with cares, he can not love; the man of gloom finds not the god. So, as youth, for the most part, has no cares, and knows no gloom, therefore, ever since time did begin, youth belongs to love. Love may end in grief and age, and pain and need, and all other modes of human mournfulness; but love begins in joy. Love's first sigh is never breathed, till after love hath laughed. Love laughs first, and then sighs after. Love has not hands, but cymbals; Love's mouth is chambered like a bugle, and the instinctive breathings of his life breathe jubilee notes of joy!

That morning, two bay horses drew two Laughs along the road that led to the hills from Saddle Meadows. Apt time they kept; Pierre Glendinning's young, manly tenor, to Lucy Tartan's girlish treble.

Wondrous fair of face, blue-eyed, and golden-haired, the bright blonde, Lucy, was arrayed in colors harmonious with the heavens. Light blue be thy perpetual color, Lucy; light blue becomes thee best—such the repeated azure counsel of Lucy Tartan's mother. On both sides, from the hedges, came to Pierre the clover bloom of Saddle Meadows, and from Lucy's mouth and cheek came the fresh fragrance of her violet young being.

"Smell I the flowers, or thee?" cried Pierre.

"See I lakes, or eyes?" cried Lucy, her own gazing down into his soul, as two stars gaze down into a tarn.

No Cornwall miner ever sunk so deep a shaft beneath the sea, as Love will sink beneath the floatings of the eyes. Love sees ten million fathoms down, till dazzled by the floor of pearls. The eye is Love's own magic glass, where all things that are not of earth, glide in supernatural light. There are not so many fishes in the sea, as there are sweet images in lovers' eyes. In those miraculous translucencies swim the strange eye-fish with wings, that sometimes leap out, instinct with joy; moist fish-wings wet the lover's cheek. Love's eyes are holy things; therein the mysteries of life are lodged; looking in each other's eyes, lovers see the ultimate secret of the worlds; and with thrills eternally untranslatable, feel that Love is god of all. Man or woman who has never loved, nor once looked deep down into their own lover's eyes, they know not the sweetest and the loftiest religion of this earth. Love is both Creator's and Saviour's gospel to mankind; a volume bound in rose-leaves, clasped with violets, and by the beaks of humming-birds printed with peach-juice on the leaves of lilies.

Endless is the account of Love. Time and space can not contain Love's story. All things that are sweet to see, or taste, or feel, or hear, all these things were made by Love; and none other things were made by Love. Love made not the Arctic zones, but Love is ever reclaiming them. Say, are not the fierce things of this earth daily, hourly going out? Where now are your wolves of Britain? Where in Virginia now, find you the panther and the pard? Oh, Love is busy everywhere. Everywhere Love hath Moravian missionaries. No Propagandist like to Love. The south wind wooes the barbarous north; on many a distant shore the gentler west wind persuades the arid east.

All this Earth is Love's affianced; vainly the demon Principle howls to stay the banns. Why round her middle wears this world so rich a zone of torrid verdure, if she be not dressing for the final rites? And why provides she orange blossoms and lilies of the valley, if she would not that all men and maids should love and marry? For every wedding where true lovers wed, helps on the march of universal Love. Who are brides here shall be Love's bridemaids in the marriage world to come. So on all sides Love allures; can contain himself what youth who views the wonders of the beauteous woman-world? Where a beautiful woman is, there is all Asia and her Bazars. Italy hath not a sight before the beauty of a Yankee girl; nor heaven a blessing beyond her earthly love. Did not the angelical Lotharios come down to earth, that they might taste of mortal woman's Love and Beauty? even while her own silly brothers were pining after the self-same Paradise they left? Yes, those envying angels did come down; did emigrate; and who emigrates except to be better off?

Love is this world's great redeemer and reformer; and as all beautiful women are her selectest emissaries, so hath Love gifted them with a magnetical persuasiveness, that no youth can possibly repel. The own heart's choice of every youth, seems ever as an inscrutable witch to him; and by ten thousand concentric spells and circling incantations, glides round and round him, as he turns: murmuring meanings of unearthly import; and summoning up to him all the subterranean sprites and gnomes; and unpeopling all the sea for naiads to swim round him; so that mysteries are evoked as in exhalations by this Love;—what wonder then that Love was aye a mystic?

V

And this self-same morning Pierre was very mystical; not continually, though; but most mystical one moment, and overflowing with mad, unbridled merriment, the next. He seemed a youthful Magian, and almost a mountebank together. Chaldaic improvisations burst from him, in quick Golden Verses, on the heel of humorous retort and repartee. More especially, the bright glance of Lucy was transporting to him. Now, reckless of his horses, with both arms holding Lucy in his embrace, like a Sicilian diver he dives deep down in the Adriatic of her eyes, and brings up some king's-cup of joy. All the waves in Lucy's eyes seemed waves of infinite glee to him. And as if, like veritable seas, they did indeed catch the reflected irradiations of that pellucid azure morning; in Lucy's eyes, there seemed to shine all the blue glory of the general day, and all the sweet inscrutableness of the sky. And certainly, the blue eye of woman, like the sea, is not uninfluenced by the atmosphere. Only in the open air of some divinest, summer day, will you see its ultramarine,—its fluid lapis lazuli. Then would Pierre burst forth in some screaming shout of joy; and the striped tigers of his chestnut eyes leaped in their lashed cages with a fierce delight. Lucy shrank from him in extreme love; for the extremest top of love, is Fear and Wonder.

Soon the swift horses drew this fair god and goddess nigh the wooded hills, whose distant blue, now changed into a variously-shaded green, stood before them like old Babylonian walls, overgrown with verdure; while here and there, at regular intervals, the scattered peaks seemed mural towers; and the clumped pines surmounting them, as lofty archers, and vast, out-looking watchers of the glorious Babylonian City of the Day. Catching that hilly air, the prancing horses neighed; laughed on the ground with gleeful feet. Felt they the gay delightsome spurrings of the day; for the day was mad with excessive joy; and high in heaven you heard the neighing of the horses of the sun; and down dropt their nostrils' froth in many a fleecy vapor from the hills.

From the plains, the mists rose slowly; reluctant yet to quit so fair a mead. At those green slopings, Pierre reined in his steeds, and soon the twain were seated on the bank, gazing far, and far away; over many a grove and lake; corn-crested uplands, and Herd's-grass lowlands; and long-stretching swales of vividest green, betokening where the greenest bounty of this earth seeks its winding channels; as ever, the most heavenly bounteousness most seeks the lowly places; making green and glad many a humble mortal's breast, and leaving to his own lonely aridness, many a hill-top prince's state.

But Grief, not Joy, is a moralizer; and small moralizing wisdom caught Pierre from that scene. With Lucy's hand in his, and feeling, softly feeling of its soft tinglingness; he seemed as one placed in linked correspondence with the summer lightnings; and by sweet shock on shock, receiving intimating foretastes of the etherealest delights of earth.

Now, prone on the grass he falls, with his attentive upward glance fixed on Lucy's eyes. "Thou art my heaven, Lucy; and here I lie thy shepherd-king, watching for new eye-stars to rise in thee. Ha! I see Venus' transit now;—lo! a new planet there;—and behind all, an infinite starry nebulousness, as if thy being were backgrounded by some spangled vail of mystery."

Is Lucy deaf to all these ravings of his lyric love? Why looks she down, and vibrates so; and why now from her over-charged lids, drops such warm drops as these? No joy now in Lucy's eyes, and seeming tremor on her lips.

"Ah! thou too ardent and impetuous Pierre!"

"Nay, thou too moist and changeful April! know'st thou not, that the moist and changeful April is followed by the glad, assured, and showerless joy of June? And this, Lucy, this day should be thy June, even as it is the earth's!"

"Ah Pierre! not June to me. But say, are not the sweets of June made sweet by the April tears?"

"Ay, love! but here fall more drops,—more and more;—these showers are longer than beseem the April, and pertain not to the June."

"June! June!—thou bride's month of the summer,—following the spring's sweet courtship of the earth,—my June, my June is yet to come!"

"Oh! yet to come, but fixedly decreed;—good as come, and better."

"Then no flower that, in the bud, the April showers have nurtured; no such flower may untimely perish, ere the June unfolds it? Ye will not swear that, Pierre?"

"The audacious immortalities of divinest love are in me; and I now swear to thee all the immutable eternities of joyfulness, that ever woman dreamed of, in this dream-house of the earth. A god decrees to thee unchangeable felicity; and to me, the unchallenged possession of thee and them, for my inalienable fief.—Do I rave? Look on me, Lucy; think on me, girl."

"Thou art young, and beautiful, and strong; and a joyful manliness invests thee, Pierre; and thy intrepid heart never yet felt the touch of fear;—But—"

"But what?"

"Ah, my best Pierre!"

"With kisses I will suck thy secret from thy cheek!—but what?"

"Let us hie homeward, Pierre. Some nameless sadness, faintness, strangely comes to me. Foretaste I feel of endless dreariness. Tell me once more the story of that face, Pierre,—that mysterious, haunting face, which thou once told'st me, thou didst thrice vainly try to shun. Blue is the sky, oh, bland the air, Pierre;—but—tell me the story of the face,—the dark-eyed, lustrous, imploring, mournful face, that so mystically paled, and shrunk at thine. Ah, Pierre, sometimes I have thought,—never will I wed with my best Pierre, until the riddle of that face be known. Tell me, tell me, Pierre;—as a fixed basilisk, with eyes of steady, flaming mournfulness, that face this instant fastens me."

"Bewitched! bewitched!—Cursed be the hour I acted on the thought, that Love hath no reserves. Never should I have told thee the story of that face, Lucy. I have bared myself too much to thee. Oh, never should Love know all!"

"Knows not all, then loves not all, Pierre. Never shalt thou so say again; —and Pierre, listen to me. Now,—now, in this inexplicable trepidation that I feel, I do conjure thee, that thou wilt ever continue to do as thou hast done; so that I may ever continue to know all that agitateth thee, the airiest and most transient thought, that ever shall sweep into thee from the wide atmosphere of all things that hem mortality. Did I doubt thee here;—could I ever think, that thy heart hath yet one private nook or corner from me;—fatal disenchanting day for me, my Pierre, would that be. I tell thee, Pierre—and 'tis Love's own self that now speaks through me—only in unbounded confidence and interchangings of all subtlest secrets, can Love possibly endure. Love's self is a secret, and so feeds on secrets, Pierre. Did I only know of thee, what the whole common world may know—what then were Pierre to me?—Thou must be wholly a disclosed secret to me; Love is vain and proud; and when I walk the streets, and meet thy friends, I must still be laughing and hugging to myself the thought,—They know him not;—I only know my Pierre;—none else beneath the circuit of yon sun. Then, swear to me, dear Pierre, that thou wilt never keep a secret from me—no, never, never;—swear!"

"Something seizes me. Thy inexplicable tears, falling, falling on my heart, have now turned it to a stone. I feel icy cold and hard; I will not swear!"

"Pierre! Pierre!"

"God help thee, and God help me, Lucy. I can not think, that in this most mild and dulcet air, the invisible agencies are plotting treasons against our loves. Oh! if ye be now nigh us, ye things I have no name for; then by a name that should be efficacious—by Christ's holy name, I warn ye back from her and me. Touch her not, ye airy devils; hence to your appointed hell! why come ye prowling in these heavenly purlieus? Can not the chains of Love omnipotent bind ye, fiends?"

"Is this Pierre? His eyes glare fearfully; now I see layer on layer deeper in him; he turns round and menaces the air and talks to it, as if defied by the air. Woe is me, that fairy love should raise this evil spell!—Pierre?"

"But now I was infinite distances from thee, oh my Lucy, wandering baffled in the choking night; but thy voice might find me, though I had wandered to the Boreal realm, Lucy. Here I sit down by thee; I catch a soothing from thee."

"My own, own Pierre! Pierre, into ten trillion pieces I could now be torn for thee; in my bosom would yet hide thee, and there keep thee warm, though I sat down on Arctic ice-floes, frozen to a corpse. My own, best, blessed Pierre! Now, could I plant some poniard in me, that my silly ailings should have power to move thee thus, and pain thee thus. Forgive me, Pierre; thy changed face hath chased the other from me; the fright of thee exceeds all other frights. It does not so haunt me now. Press hard my hand; look hard on me, my love, that its last trace may pass away. Now I feel almost whole again; now, 'tis gone. Up, my Pierre; let us up, and fly these hills, whence, I fear, too wide a prospect meets us. Fly we to the plain. See, thy steeds neigh for thee—they call thee—see, the clouds fly down toward the plain—lo, these hills now seem all desolate to me, and the vale all verdure. Thank thee, Pierre.—See, now, I quit the hills, dry-cheeked; and leave all tears behind to be sucked in by these evergreens, meet emblems of the unchanging love, my own sadness nourishes in me. Hard fate, that Love's best verdure should feed so on tears!"

Now they rolled swiftly down the slopes; nor tempted the upper hills; but sped fast for the plain. Now the cloud hath passed from Lucy's eye; no more the lurid slanting light forks upward from her lover's brow. In the plain they find peace, and love, and joy again.

"It was the merest, idling, wanton vapor, Lucy!"

"An empty echo, Pierre, of a sad sound, long past. Bless thee, my Pierre!"

"The great God wrap thee ever, Lucy. So, now, we are home."

vi

After seeing Lucy into her aunt's most cheerful parlor, and seating her by the honeysuckle that half clambered into the window there; and near to which was her easel for crayon-sketching, upon part of whose frame Lucy had cunningly trained two slender vines, into whose earth-filled pots two of the three legs of the easel were inserted; and sitting down himself by her, and by his pleasant, lightsome chat, striving to chase the last trace of sadness from her; and not till his object seemed fully gained; Pierre rose to call her good aunt to her, and so take his leave till evening, when Lucy called him back, begging him first to bring her the blue portfolio from her chamber, for she wished to kill her last lingering melancholy—if any indeed did linger now—by diverting her thoughts, in a little pencil sketch, to scenes widely different from those of Saddle Meadows and its hills.

So Pierre went up stairs, but paused on the threshold of the open door. He never had entered that chamber but with feelings of a wonderful reverentialness. The carpet seemed as holy ground. Every chair seemed sanctified by some departed saint, there once seated long ago. Here his book of Love was all a rubric, and said—Bow now, Pierre, bow. But this extreme loyalty to the piety of love, called from him by such glimpses of its most secret inner shrine, was not unrelieved betimes by such quickenings of all his pulses, that in fantasy he pressed the wide beauty of the world in his embracing arms; for all his world resolved itself into his heart's best love for Lucy.

Now, crossing the magic silence of the empty chamber, he caught the snow-white bed reflected in the toilet-glass. This rooted him. For one swift instant, he seemed to see in that one glance the two separate beds—the real one and the reflected one—and an unbidden, most miserable presentiment thereupon stole into him. But in one breath it came and went. So he advanced, and with a fond and gentle joyfulness, his eye now fell upon the spotless bed itself, and fastened on a snow-white roll that lay beside the pillow. Now he started; Lucy seemed coming in upon him; but no—'tis only the foot of one of her little slippers, just peeping into view from under the narrow nether curtains of the bed. Then again his glance fixed itself upon the slender, snow-white, ruffled roll; and he stood as one enchanted. Never precious parchment of the Greek was half so precious in his eyes. Never trembling scholar longed more to unroll the mystic vellum, than Pierre longed to unroll the sacred secrets of that snow-white, ruffled thing. But his hands touched not any object in that chamber, except the one he had gone thither for.

"Here is the blue portfolio, Lucy. See, the key hangs to its silver lock; —were you not fearful I would open it?—'twas tempting, I must confess."

"Open it!" said Lucy—"why, yes, Pierre, yes; what secret thing keep I from thee? Read me through and through. I am entirely thine. See!" and tossing open the portfolio, all manner of rosy things came floating from it, and a most delicate perfume of some invisible essence.

"Ah! thou holy angel, Lucy!"

"Why, Pierre, thou art transfigured; thou now lookest as one who—why, Pierre?"

"As one who had just peeped in at paradise, Lucy; and——"

"Again wandering in thy mind, Pierre; no more—Come, you must leave me, now. I am quite rested again. Quick, call my aunt, and leave me. Stay, this evening we are to look over the book of plates from the city, you know. Be early;—go now, Pierre."

"Well, good-bye, till evening, thou height of all delight."

vii

As Pierre drove through the silent village, beneath the vertical shadows of the noon-day trees, the sweet chamber scene abandoned him, and the mystical face recurred to him, and kept with him. At last, arrived at home, he found his mother absent; so passing straight through the wide middle hall of the mansion, he descended the piazza on the other side, and wandered away in reveries down to the river bank.

Here one primeval pine-tree had been luckily left standing by the otherwise unsparing woodmen, who long ago had cleared that meadow. It was once crossing to this noble pine, from a clump of hemlocks far across the river, that Pierre had first noticed the significant fact, that while the hemlock and the pine are trees of equal growth and stature, and are so similar in their general aspect, that people unused to woods sometimes confound them; and while both trees are proverbially trees of sadness, yet the dark hemlock hath no music in its thoughtful boughs; but the gentle pine-tree drops melodious mournfulness.

At its half-bared roots of sadness, Pierre sat down, and marked the mighty bulk and far out-reaching length of one particular root, which, straying down the bank, the storms and rains had years ago exposed.

"How wide, how strong these roots must spread! Sure, this pine-tree takes powerful hold of this fair earth! Yon bright flower hath not so deep a root. This tree hath outlived a century of that gay flower's generations, and will outlive a century of them yet to come. This is most sad. Hark, now I hear the pyramidical and numberless, flame-like complainings of this Eolean pine;—the wind breathes now upon it:—the wind,—that is God's breath! Is He so sad? Oh, tree! so mighty thou, so lofty, yet so mournful! This is most strange! Hark! as I look up into thy high secrecies, oh, tree, the face, the face, peeps down on me!—'Art thou Pierre? Come to me'—oh, thou mysterious girl,—what an ill-matched pendant thou, to that other countenance of sweet Lucy, which also hangs, and first did hang within my heart! Is grief a pendant then to pleasantness? Is grief a self-willed guest that *will* come in? Yet I have never known thee, Grief;—thou art a legend to me. I have known some fiery broils of glorious frenzy; I have oft tasted of revery; whence comes pensiveness; whence comes sadness; whence all delicious poetic presentiments;—but thou, Grief! art still a ghost-story to me. I know thee not,—do half disbelieve in thee. Not that I would be without my too little cherished fits of sadness now and then; but God keep me from thee, thou other shape of far profounder gloom! I shudder at thee! The face!—the face!—forth again from thy high secrecies, oh, tree! the face steals down upon me. Mysterious girl! who art thou? by what right snatchest thou thus my deepest thoughts? Take thy thin fingers from me;—I am affianced, and not to thee. Leave me!—what share hast thou in me? Surely, thou lovest not me?—that were most miserable for thee, and me, and Lucy. It can not be. What, *who* art thou? Oh! wretched vagueness—too familiar to me, yet inexplicable,—unknown, utterly unknown! I seem to founder in this perplexity. Thou seemest to know somewhat of me, that I know not of myself,—what is it then? If thou hast a secret in thy eyes of mournful mystery, out with it; Pierre demands it; what is that thou has veiled in thee so imperfectly, that I seem to see its motion, but not its form? It visibly rustles behind the concealing screen. Now, never into the soul of Pierre, stole there before, a muffledness like this! If aught really lurks in it, ye sovereign powers that claim all my leal worshipings, I conjure ye to lift the veil; I must see it face to face. Tread I on a mine, warn me; advance I on a precipice, hold me back; but abandon me to an unknown misery, that it shall suddenly seize me, and possess me, wholly,—that ye will never do; else, Pierre's fond faith in ye—now clean, untouched—may clean depart; and give me up to be a railing atheist! Ah, now the face departs. Pray heaven it hath not only stolen back, and hidden again in thy high secrecies, oh tree! But 'tis gone—gone—entirely gone; and I thank God, and I feel joy again; joy, which I also feel to be my right as man; deprived of joy, I feel I should find cause for deadly feuds with things invisible. Ha! a coat of iron-mail seems to grow round, and husk me now; and I have heard, that the bitterest winters are foretold by a thicker husk upon the Indian corn; so our old farmers say. But 'tis a dark similitude. Quit thy analogies; sweet in the orator's mouth, bitter in the thinker's belly. Now, then, I'll up with my own joyful will; and with my joy's face scare away all phantoms:—so, they go; and Pierre is Joy's, and Life's again. Thou pine-tree!—henceforth I will resist thy too treacherous persuasiveness. Thou'lt not so often woo me to thy airy tent, to ponder on the gloomy rooted stakes that bind it. Hence now I go; and peace be with thee, pine! That blessed sereneness which lurks ever at the heart of sadness—mere sadness—and remains when all the rest has gone;—that sweet feeling is now mine, and cheaply mine. I am not sorry I was sad, I feel so blessed now. Dearest Lucy!—well, well;—'twill be a pretty time we'll have this evening; there's the book of Flemish prints—that first we must look over; then, second, is Flaxman's Homer—clear-cut outlines, yet full of unadorned barbaric nobleness. Then Flaxman's Dante;—Dante! Night's and Hell's poet he. No, we will not open Dante. Methinks now the face—the face—minds me a little of pensive, sweet Francesca's face—or, rather, as it had been Francesca's daughter's face—wafted on the sad dark wind, toward observant Virgil and the blistered Florentine. No, we will not open Flaxman's Dante. Francesca's mournful face is now ideal to me. Flaxman might evoke it wholly,—make it present in lines of misery—bewitching power. No! I will not open Flaxman's Dante! Damned be the hour I read in Dante! more damned than that wherein Paolo and Francesca read in fatal Launcelot!"

Book III

The Presentiment and the Verification

THE FACE, of which Pierre and Lucy so strangely and fearfully hinted, was not of enchanted air; but its mortal lineaments of mournfulness had been visibly beheld by Pierre. Nor had it accosted him in any privacy; or in any lonely byeway; or beneath the white light of the crescent moon; but in a joyous chamber, bright with candles, and ringing with two score women's gayest voices. Out of the heart of mirthfulness, this shadow had come forth to him. Encircled by bandelets of light, it had still beamed upon him; vaguely historic and prophetic; backward, hinting of some irrevocable sin; forward, pointing to some inevitable ill. One of those faces, which now and then appear to man, and without one word of speech, still reveal glimpses of some fearful gospel. In natural guise, but lit by supernatural light; palpable to the senses, but inscrutable to the soul; in their perfectest impression on us, ever hovering between Tartarean misery and Paradisaic beauty; such faces, compounded so of hell and heaven, overthrow in us all foregone persuasions, and make us wondering children in this world again.

The face had accosted Pierre some weeks previous to his ride with Lucy to the hills beyond Saddle Meadows; and before her arrival for the summer at the village; moreover it had accosted him in a very common and homely scene; but this enhanced the wonder.

On some distant business, with a farmer-tenant, he had been absent from the mansion during the best part of the day, and had but just come home, early of a pleasant moonlight evening, when Dates delivered a message to him from his mother, begging him to come for her about half-past seven that night to Miss Llanyllyn's cottage, in order to accompany her thence to that of the two Miss Pennies. At the mention of that last name, Pierre well knew what he must anticipate. Those elderly and truly pious spinsters, gifted with the most benevolent hearts in the world, and at mid-age deprived by envious nature of their hearing, seemed to have made it a maxim of their charitable lives, that since God had not given them any more the power to hear Christ's gospel preached, they would therefore thenceforth do what they could toward practicing it. Wherefore, as a matter of no possible interest to them now, they abstained from church; and while with prayer-books in their hands the Rev. Mr. Falsgrave's congregation were engaged in worshiping their God, according to the divine behest; the two Miss Pennies, with thread and needle, were hard at work in serving him; making up shirts and gowns for the poor people of the parish. Pierre had heard that they had recently been at the trouble of organizing a regular society, among the neighboring farmers' wives and daughters, to meet twice a month at their own house (the Miss Pennies) for the purpose of sewing in concert for the benefit of various settlements of necessitous emigrants, who had lately pitched their populous shanties further up the river. But though this enterprise had not been started without previously acquainting Mrs. Glendinning of it,—for indeed she was much loved and honored by the pious spinsters,—and their promise of solid assistance from that gracious manorial lady; yet Pierre had not heard that his mother had been officially invited to preside, or be at all present at the semi-monthly meetings; though he supposed, that far from having any scruples against so doing, she would be very glad to associate that way, with the good people of the village.

"Now, brother Pierre"—said Mrs. Glendinning, rising from Miss Llanyllyn's huge cushioned chair—"throw my shawl around me; and good-evening to Lucy's aunt.—There, we shall be late."

As they walked along, she added—"Now, Pierre, I know you are apt to be a little impatient sometimes, of these sewing scenes; but courage; I merely want to peep in on them; so as to get some inkling of what they would indeed be at; and then my promised benefactions can be better selected by me. Besides, Pierre, I could have had Dates escort me, but I preferred you; because I want you to know who they are you live among; how many really pretty, and naturally-refined dames and girls you shall one day be lord of the manor of. I anticipate a rare display of rural red and white."

Cheered by such pleasant promises, Pierre soon found himself leading his mother into a room full of faces. The instant they appeared, a gratuitous old body, seated with her knitting near the door, squeaked out shrilly— "Ah! dames, dames,—Madam Glendinning!—Master Pierre Glendinning!"

Almost immediately following this sound, there came a sudden, long-drawn, unearthly, girlish shriek, from the further corner of the long, double room. Never had human voice so affected Pierre before. Though he saw not the person from whom it came, and though the voice was wholly strange to him, yet the sudden shriek seemed to split its way clean through his heart, and leave a yawning gap there. For an instant, he stood bewildered; but started at his mother's voice; her arm being still in his. "Why do you clutch my arm so, Pierre? You pain me. Pshaw! some one has fainted,—nothing more."

Instantly Pierre recovered himself, and affecting to mock at his own trepidation, hurried across the room to offer his services, if such were needed. But dames and maidens had been all beforehand with him; the lights were wildly flickering in the air-current made by the flinging open of the casement, near to where the shriek had come. But the climax of the tumult was soon past; and presently, upon closing the casement, it subsided almost wholly. The elder of the spinster Pennies, advancing to Mrs. Glendinning, now gave her to understand, that one of the further crowd of industrious girls present, had been attacked by a sudden, but fleeting fit, vaguely imputable to some constitutional disorder or other. She was now quite well again. And so the company, one and all, seemingly acting upon their natural good-breeding, which in any one at bottom, is but delicacy and charity, refrained from all further curiosity; reminded not the girl of what had passed; noted her scarce at all; and all needles stitched away as before.

Leaving his mother to speak with whom she pleased, and attend alone to her own affairs with the society; Pierre, oblivious now in such a lively crowd, of any past unpleasantness, after some courtly words to the Miss Pennies,—insinuated into their understandings through a long coiled trumpet, which, when not in use, the spinsters wore, hanging like a powder-horn from their girdles:—and likewise, after manifesting the profoundest and most intelligent interest in the mystic mechanism of a huge woolen sock, in course of completion by a spectacled old lady of his more particular acquaintance; after all this had been gone through, and something more too tedious to detail, but which occupied him for nearly half an hour, Pierre, with a slightly blushing, and imperfectly balanced assurance, advanced toward the further crowd of maidens; where, by the light of many a well-snuffed candle, they clubbed all their bright contrasting cheeks, like a dense bed of garden tulips. There were the shy and pretty Maries, Marthas, Susans, Betties, Jennies, Nellies; and forty more fair nymphs, who skimmed the cream, and made the butter of the fat farms of Saddle Meadows.

Assurance is in presence of the assured. Where embarrassments prevail, they affect the most disembarrassed. What wonder, then, that gazing on such a thick array of wreathing, roguish, half-averted, blushing faces—still audacious in their very embarrassment—Pierre, too, should flush a bit, and stammer in his attitudes a little? Youthful love and graciousness were in his heart; kindest words upon his tongue; but there he stood, target for the transfixing glances of those ambushed archers of the eye.

But his abashments last too long; his cheek hath changed from blush to pallor; what strange thing does Pierre Glendinning see? Behind the first close, busy breast-work of young girls, are several very little stands, or circular tables, where sit small groups of twos and threes, sewing in small comparative solitudes, as it were. They would seem to be the less notable of the rural company; or else, for some cause, they have voluntarily retired into their humble banishment. Upon one of these persons engaged at the furthermost and least conspicuous of these little stands, and close by a casement, Pierre's glance is palely fixed.

The girl sits steadily sewing; neither she nor her two companions speak. Her eyes are mostly upon her work; but now and then a very close observer would notice that she furtively lifts them, and moves them sideways and timidly toward Pierre; and then, still more furtively and timidly toward his lady mother, further off. All the while, her preternatural calmness sometimes seems only made to cover the intensest struggle in her bosom. Her unadorned and modest dress is black; fitting close up to her neck, and clasping it with a plain, velvet border. To a nice perception, that velvet shows elastically; contracting and expanding, as though some choked, violent thing were risen up there within from the teeming region of her heart. But her dark, olive cheek is without a blush, or sign of any disquietude. So far as this girl lies upon the common surface, ineffable composure steeps her. But still, she sideways steals the furtive, timid glance. Anon, as yielding to the irresistible climax of her concealed emotion, whatever that may be, she lifts her whole marvelous countenance into the radiant candlelight, and for one swift instant, that face of supernaturalness unreservedly meets Pierre's. Now, wonderful loveliness, and a still more wonderful loneliness, have with inexplicable implorings, looked up to him from that henceforth immemorial face. There, too, he seemed to see the fair ground where Anguish had contended with Beauty, and neither being conqueror, both had laid down on the field.

Recovering at length from his all too obvious emotion, Pierre turned away still farther, to regain the conscious possession of himself. A wild, bewildering, and incomprehensible curiosity had seized him, to know something definite of that face. To this curiosity, at the moment, he entirely surrendered himself; unable as he was to combat it, or reason with it in the slightest way. So soon as he felt his outward composure returned to him, he purposed to chat his way behind the breastwork of bright eyes and cheeks, and on some parlor pretense or other, hear, if possible, an audible syllable from one whose mere silent aspect had so potentially moved him. But at length, as with this object in mind, he was crossing the room again, he heard his mother's voice, gayly calling him away; and turning, saw her shawled and bonneted. He could now make no plausible stay, and smothering the agitation in him, he bowed a general and hurried adieu to the company, and went forth with his mother.

They had gone some way homeward, in perfect silence, when his mother spoke.

"Well, Pierre, what can it possibly be?"

"My God, mother, did you see her then?"

"My son!" cried Mrs. Glendinning, instantly stopping in terror, and withdrawing her arm from Pierre, "what—what under heaven ails you? This is most strange! I but playfully asked, what you were so steadfastly thinking of; and here you answer me by the strangest question, in a voice that seems to come from under your great-grandfather's tomb! What, in heaven's name, does this mean, Pierre? Why were you so silent, and why now are you so ill-timed in speaking? Answer me;—explain all this;—*she*—*she*—what *she* should you be thinking of but Lucy Tartan?—Pierre, beware, beware! I had thought you firmer in your lady's faith, than such strange behavior as this would seem to hint. Answer me, Pierre, what may this mean? Come, I hate a mystery; speak, my son."

Fortunately, this prolonged verbalized wonder in his mother afforded Pierre time to rally from his double and aggravated astonishment, brought about by first suspecting that his mother also had been struck by the strange aspect of the face, and then, having that suspicion so violently beaten back upon him, by her apparently unaffected alarm at finding him in some region of thought wholly unshared by herself at the time.

"It is nothing—nothing, sister Mary; just nothing at all in the world. I believe I was dreaming—sleep-walking, or something of that sort. They were vastly pretty girls there this evening, sister Mary, were they not? Come, let us walk on—do, sister mine."

"Pierre, Pierre!—but I will take your arm again;—and have you really nothing more to say? were you really wandering, Pierre?"

"I swear to you, my dearest mother, that never before in my whole existence, have I so completely gone wandering in my soul, as at that very moment. But it is all over now." Then in a less earnest and somewhat playful tone, he added: "And sister mine, if you know aught of the physical and sanitary authors, you must be aware, that the only treatment for such a case of harmless temporary aberration, is for all persons to ignore it in the subject. So no more of this foolishness. Talking about it only makes me feel very unpleasantly silly, and there is no knowing that it may not bring it back upon me."

"Then by all means, my dear boy, not another word about it. But it's passing strange—very, very strange indeed. Well, about that morning business; how fared you? Tell me about it."

ii

So Pierre, gladly plunging into this welcome current of talk, was enabled to attend his mother home without furnishing further cause for her concern or wonderment. But not by any means so readily could he allay his own concern and wonderment. Too really true in itself, however evasive in its effect at the time, was that earnest answer to his mother, declaring that never in his whole existence had he been so profoundly stirred. The face haunted him as some imploring, and beauteous, impassioned, ideal Madonna's haunts the morbidly longing and enthusiastic, but ever-baffled artist. And ever, as the mystic face thus rose before his fancy's sight, another sense was touched in him; the long-drawn, unearthly, girlish shriek pealed through and through his soul; for now he knew the shriek came from the face—such Delphic shriek could only come from such a source. And wherefore that shriek? thought Pierre. Bodes it ill to the face, or me, or both? How am I changed, that my appearance on any scene should have power to work such woe? But it was mostly the face—the face, that wrought upon him. The shriek seemed as incidentally embodied there.

The emotions he experienced seemed to have taken hold of the deepest roots and subtlest fibres of his being. And so much the more that it was so subterranean in him, so much the more did he feel its weird inscrutableness. What was one unknown, sad-eyed, shrieking girl to him? There must be sad-eyed girls somewhere in the world, and this was only one of them. And what was the most beautiful sad-eyed girl to him? Sadness might be beautiful, as well as mirth—he lost himself trying to follow out this tangle. "I will no more of this infatuation," he would cry; but forth from regions of irradiated air, the divine beauty and imploring sufferings of the face, stole into his view.

Hitherto I have ever held but lightly, thought Pierre, all stories of ghostly mysticalness in man; my creed of this world leads me to believe in visible, beautiful flesh, and audible breath, however sweet and scented; but only in visible flesh, and audible breath, have I hitherto believed. But now! —now!—and again he would lose himself in the most surprising and preternatural ponderings, which baffled all the introspective cunning of his mind. Himself was too much for himself. He felt that what he had always before considered the solid land of veritable reality, was now being audaciously encroached upon by bannered armies of hooded phantoms, disembarking in his soul, as from flotillas of specter-boats.

The terrors of the face were not those of Gorgon; not by repelling hideousness did it smite him so; but bewilderingly allured him, by its nameless beauty, and its long-suffering, hopeless anguish.

But he was sensible that this general effect upon him, was also special; the face somehow mystically appealing to his own private and individual affections; and by a silent and tyrannic call, challenging him in his deepest moral being, and summoning Truth, Love, Pity, Conscience, to the stand. Apex of all wonders! thought Pierre; this indeed almost unmans me with its wonderfulness. Escape the face he could not. Muffling his own in his bedclothes—that did not hide it. Flying from it by sunlight down the meadows, was as vain.

Most miraculous of all to Pierre was the vague impression, that somewhere he had seen traits of the likeness of that face before. But where, he could not say; nor could he, in the remotest degree, imagine. He was not unaware—for in one or two instances, he had experienced the fact—that sometimes a man may see a passing countenance in the street, which shall irresistibly and magnetically affect him, for a moment, as wholly unknown to him, and yet strangely reminiscent of some vague face he has previously encountered, in some fancied time, too, of extreme interest to his life. But not so was it now with Pierre. The face had not perplexed him for a few speculative minutes, and then glided from him, to return no more. It stayed close by him; only—and not invariably—could he repel it, by the exertion of all his resolution and self-will. Besides, what of general enchantment lurked in his strange sensations, seemed concentringly condensed, and pointed to a spear-head, that pierced his heart with an inexplicable pang, whenever the specializing emotion—to call it so—seized the possession of his thoughts, and waved into his visions, a thousand forms of by-gone times, and many an old legendary family scene, which he had heard related by his elderly relations, some of them now dead.

Disguising his wild reveries as best he might from the notice of his mother, and all other persons of her household, for two days Pierre wrestled with his own haunted spirit; and at last, so effectually purged it of all weirdnesses, and so effectually regained the general mastery of himself, that for a time, life went with him, as though he had never been stirred so strangely. Once more, the sweet unconditional thought of Lucy slid wholly into his soul, dislodging thence all such phantom occupants. Once more he rode, he walked, he swam, he vaulted; and with new zest threw himself into the glowing practice of all those manly exercises, he so dearly loved. It almost seemed in him, that ere promising forever to protect, as well as eternally to love, his Lucy, he must first completely invigorate and embrawn himself into the possession of such a noble muscular manliness, that he might champion Lucy against the whole physical world.

Still—even before the occasional reappearance of the face to him—Pierre, for all his willful ardor in his gymnasticals and other diversions, whether in-doors or out, or whether by book or foil; still, Pierre could not but be secretly annoyed, and not a little perplexed, as to the motive, which, for the first time in his recollection, had impelled him, not merely to conceal from his mother a singular circumstance in his life (for that, he felt would have been but venial; and besides, as will eventually be seen, he could find one particular precedent for it, in his past experience) but likewise, and superaddedly, to parry, nay, to evade, and, in effect, to return something alarmingly like a fib, to an explicit question put to him by his mother;—such being the guise, in which part of the conversation they had had that eventful night, now appeared to his fastidious sense. He considered also, that his evasive answer had not pantheistically burst from him in a momentary interregnum of self-command. No; his mother had made quite a lengthy speech to him; during which he well remembered, he had been carefully, though with trepidation, turning over in his mind, how best he might recall her from her unwished-for and untimely scent. Why had this been so? Was this his wont? What inscrutable thing was it, that so suddenly had seized him, and made him a falsifyer—ay, a falsifyer and nothing less—to his own dearly-beloved, and confiding mother? Here, indeed, was something strange for him; here was stuff for his utmost ethical meditations. But, nevertheless, on strict introspection, he felt, that he would not willingly have it otherwise; not willingly would he now undissemble himself in this matter to his mother. Why was this, too? Was this his wont? Here, again, was food for mysticism. Here, in imperfect inklings, tinglings, presentiments, Pierre began to feel—what all mature men, who are Magians, sooner or later know, and more or less assuredly—that not always in our actions, are we our own factors. But this conceit was very dim in Pierre; and dimness is ever suspicious and repugnant to us; and so, Pierre shrank abhorringly from the infernal catacombs of thought, down into which, this fœtal fancy beckoned him. Only this, though in secret, did he cherish; only this, he felt persuaded of; namely, that not for both worlds would he have his mother made a partner to his sometime mystic mood.

But with this nameless fascination of the face upon him, during those two days that it had first and fully possessed him for its own, did perplexed Pierre refrain from that apparently most natural of all resources,—boldly seeking out, and returning to the palpable cause, and questioning her, by look or voice, or both together—the mysterious girl herself? No; not entirely did Pierre here refrain. But his profound curiosity and interest in the matter—strange as it may seem—did not so much appear to be embodied in the mournful person of the olive girl, as by some radiations from her, embodied in the vague conceits which agitated his own soul. *There*, lurked the subtler secret: *that*, Pierre had striven to tear away. From without, no wonderful effect is wrought within ourselves, unless some interior, responding wonder meets it. That the starry vault shall surcharge the heart with all rapturous marvelings, is only because we ourselves are greater miracles, and superber trophies than all the stars in universal space. Wonder interlocks with wonder; and then the confounding feeling comes. No cause have we to fancy, that a horse, a dog, a fowl, ever stand transfixed beneath yon skyey load of majesty. But our soul's arches underfit into its; and so, prevent the upper arch from falling on us with unsustainable inscrutableness. "Explain ye my deeper mystery," said the shepherd Chaldean king, smiting his breast, lying on his back upon the plain; "and then, I will bestow all my wonderings upon ye, ye stately stars!" So, in some sort, with Pierre. Explain thou this strange integral feeling in me myself, he thought—turning upon the fancied face—and I will then renounce all other wonders, to gaze wonderingly at thee. But thou hast evoked in me profounder spells than the evoking one, thou face! For me, thou hast uncovered one infinite, dumb, beseeching countenance of mystery, underlying all the surfaces of visible time and space.

But during those two days of his first wild vassalage to his original sensations, Pierre had not been unvisited by less mysterious impulses. Two or three very plain and practical plannings of desirable procedures in reference to some possible homely explication of all this nonsense—so he would momentarily denominate it—now and then flittingly intermitted his pervading mood of semi-madness. Once he had seized his hat, careless of his accustomed gloves and cane, and found himself in the street, walking very rapidly in the direction of the Miss Pennies'. But whither now? he disenchantingly interrogated himself. Where would you go? A million to one, those deaf old spinsters can tell you nothing you burn to know. Deaf old spinsters are not used to be the depositaries of such mystical secrecies. But then, they may reveal her name—where she dwells, and something, however fragmentary and unsatisfactory, of who she is, and whence. Ay; but then, in ten minutes after your leaving them, all the houses in Saddle Meadows would be humming with the gossip of Pierre Glendinning engaged to marry Lucy Tartan, and yet running about the country, in ambiguous pursuit of strange young women. That will never do. You remember, do you not, often seeing the Miss Pennies, hatless and without a shawl, hurrying through the village, like two postmen intent on dropping some tit-bit of precious gossip? What a morsel for them, Pierre, have you, if you now call upon them. Verily, their trumpets are both for use and for significance. Though very deaf, the Miss Pennies are by no means dumb. They blazon very wide.

"Now be sure, and say that it was the Miss Pennies, who left the news—be sure—we—the Miss Pennies—remember—say to Mrs. Glendinning it was we." Such was the message that now half-humorously occurred to Pierre, as having been once confided to him by the sister spinsters, one evening when they called with a choice present of some very *recherche* chit-chat for his mother; but found the manorial lady out; and so charged her son with it; hurrying away to all the inferior houses, so as not to be anywhere forestalled in their disclosure.

Now, I wish it had been any other house than the Miss Pennies; any other house but theirs, and on my soul I believe I should have gone. But not to them—no, that I can not do. It would be sure to reach my mother, and then she would put this and that together—stir a little—let it simmer—and farewell forever to all her majestic notions of my immaculate integrity.

Patience, Pierre, the population of this region is not so immense. No dense mobs of Nineveh confound all personal identities in Saddle Meadows. Patience; thou shalt see it soon again; catch it passing thee in some green lane, sacred to thy evening reveries. She that bears it can not dwell remote. Patience, Pierre. Ever are such mysteries best and soonest unraveled by the eventual unraveling of themselves. Or, if you will, go back and get your gloves, and more especially your cane, and begin your own secret voyage of discovery after it. Your cane, I say; because it will probably be a very long and weary walk. True, just now I hinted, that she that bears it can not dwell very remote; but then her nearness may not be at all conspicuous. So, homeward, and put off thy hat, and let thy cane stay still, good Pierre. Seek not to mystify the mystery so.

Thus, intermittingly, ever and anon during those sad two days of deepest sufferance, Pierre would stand reasoning and expostulating with himself; and by such meditative treatment, reassure his own spontaneous impulses. Doubtless, it was wise and right that so he did; doubtless: but in a world so full of all dubieties as this, one can never be entirely certain whether another person, however carefully and cautiously conscientious, has acted in all respects conceivable for the very best.

But when the two days were gone by, and Pierre began to recognize his former self, as restored to him from its mystic exile, then the thoughts of personally and pointedly seeking out the unknown, either preliminarily by a call upon the sister spinsters, or generally by performing the observant lynx-eyed circuit of the country on foot, and as a crafty inquisitor, dissembling his cause of inquisition; these and all similar intentions completely abandoned Pierre.

He was now diligently striving, with all his mental might, forever to drive the phantom from him. He seemed to feel that it begat in him a certain condition of his being, which was most painful, and every way uncongenial to his natural, wonted self. It had a touch of he knew not what sort of unhealthiness in it, so to speak; for, in his then ignorance, he could find no better term; it seemed to have in it a germ of somewhat which, if not quickly extirpated, might insidiously poison and embitter his whole life—that choice, delicious life which he had vowed to Lucy for his one pure and comprehensive offering—at once a sacrifice and a delight.

Nor in these endeavorings did he entirely fail. For the most part, he felt now that he had a power over the comings and the goings of the face; but not on all occasions. Sometimes the old, original mystic tyranny would steal upon him; the long, dark, locks of mournful hair would fall upon his soul, and trail their wonderful melancholy along with them; the two full, steady, over-brimming eyes of loveliness and anguish would converge their magic rays, till he felt them kindling he could not tell what mysterious fires in the heart at which they aimed.

When once this feeling had him fully, then was the perilous time for Pierre. For supernatural as the feeling was, and appealing to all things ultramontane to his soul; yet was it a delicious sadness to him. Some hazy fairy swam above him in the heavenly ether, and showered down upon him the sweetest pearls of pensiveness. Then he would be seized with a singular impulse to reveal the secret to some one other individual in the world. Only one, not more; he could not hold all this strange fullness in himself. It must be shared. In such an hour it was, that chancing to encounter Lucy (her, whom above all others, he did confidingly adore), she heard the story of the face; nor slept at all that night; nor for a long time freed her pillow completely from wild, Beethoven sounds of distant, waltzing melodies, as of ambiguous fairies dancing on the heath.

iii

This history goes forward and goes backward, as occasion calls. Nimble center, circumference elastic you must have. Now we return to Pierre, wending homeward from his reveries beneath the pine-tree.

His burst of impatience against the sublime Italian, Dante, arising from that poet being the one who, in a former time, had first opened to his shuddering eyes the infinite cliffs and gulfs of human mystery and misery;—though still more in the way of experimental vision, than of sensational presentiment or experience (for as yet he had not seen so far and deep as Dante, and therefore was entirely incompetent to meet the grim bard fairly on his peculiar ground), this ignorant burst of his young impatience,—also arising from that half contemptuous dislike, and sometimes selfish loathing, with which, either naturally feeble or undeveloped minds, regard those dark ravings of the loftier poets, which are in eternal opposition to their own fine-spun, shallow dreams of rapturous or prudential Youth;—this rash, untutored burst of Pierre's young impatience, seemed to have carried off with it, all the other forms of his melancholy—if melancholy it had been—and left him now serene again, and ready for any tranquil pleasantness the gods might have in store. For his, indeed, was true Youth's temperament,—summary with sadness, swift to joyfulness, and long protracting, and detaining with that joyfulness, when once it came fully nigh to him.

As he entered the dining-hall, he saw Dates retiring from another door with his tray. Alone and meditative, by the bared half of the polished table, sat his mother at her dessert; fruit-baskets and a decanter were before her. On the other leaf of the same table, still lay the cloth, folded back upon itself, and set out with one plate and its usual accompaniments.

"Sit down, Pierre; when I came home, I was surprised to hear that the phaeton had returned so early, and here I waited dinner for you, until I could wait no more. But go to the green pantry now, and get what Dates has but just put away for you there. Heigh-ho! too plainly I foresee it—no more regular dinner-hours, or tea-hours, or supper-hours, in Saddle Meadows, till its young lord is wedded. And that puts me in mind of something, Pierre; but I'll defer it till you have eaten a little. Do you know, Pierre, that if you continue these irregular meals of yours, and deprive me so entirely almost of your company, that I shall run fearful risk of getting to be a terrible wine-bibber;—yes, could you unalarmed see me sitting all alone here with this decanter, like any old nurse, Pierre; some solitary, forlorn old nurse, Pierre, deserted by her last friend, and therefore forced to embrace her flask?"

"No, I did not feel any great alarm, sister," said Pierre, smiling, "since I could not but perceive that the decanter was still full to the stopple."

"Possibly it may be only a fresh decanter, Pierre;" then changing her voice suddenly—"but mark me, Mr. Pierre Glendinning!"

"Well, Mrs. Mary Glendinning!"

"Do you know, sir, that you are very shortly to be married,—that indeed the day is all but fixed?"

"How!" cried Pierre, in real joyful astonishment, both at the nature of the tidings, and the earnest tones in which they were conveyed—"dear, dear mother, you have strangely changed your mind then, my dear mother."

"It is even so, dear brother;—before this day month I hope to have a little sister Tartan."

"You talk very strangely, mother," rejoined Pierre, quickly. "I suppose, then, I have next to nothing to say in the matter?"

"Next to nothing, Pierre! What indeed could you say to the purpose? what at all have you to do with it, I should like to know? Do you so much as dream, you silly boy, that men ever have the marrying of themselves? Juxtaposition marries men. There is but one match-maker in the world, Pierre, and that is Mrs. Juxtaposition, a most notorious lady!"

"Very peculiar, disenchanting sort of talk, this, under the circumstances, sister Mary," laying down his fork. "Mrs. Juxtaposition, ah! And in your opinion, mother, does this fine glorious passion only amount to that?"

"Only to that, Pierre; but mark you: according to my creed—though this part of it is a little hazy—Mrs. Juxtaposition moves her pawns only as she herself is moved to so doing by the spirit."

"Ah! that sets it all right again," said Pierre, resuming his fork—"my appetite returns. But what was that about my being married so soon?" he added, vainly striving to assume an air of incredulity and unconcern; "you were joking, I suppose; it seems to me, sister, either you or I was but just now wandering in the mind a little, on that subject. Are you really thinking of any such thing? and have you really vanquished your sagacious scruples by yourself, after I had so long and ineffectually sought to do it for you? Well, I am a million times delighted; tell me quick!"

"I will, Pierre. You very well know, that from the first hour you apprised me—or rather, from a period prior to that—from the moment that I, by my own insight, became aware of your love for Lucy, I have always approved it. Lucy is a delicious girl; of honorable descent, a fortune, well-bred, and the very pattern of all that I think amiable and attractive in a girl of seventeen."

"Well, well, well," cried Pierre rapidly and impetuously; "we both knew that before."

"Well, well, well, Pierre," retorted his mother, mockingly.

"It is not well, well, well; but ill, ill, ill, to torture me so, mother; go on, do!"

"But notwithstanding my admiring approval of your choice, Pierre; yet, as you know, I have resisted your entreaties for my consent to your speedy marriage, because I thought that a girl of scarcely seventeen, and a boy scarcely twenty, should not be in such a hurry;—there was plenty of time, I thought, which could be profitably employed by both."

"Permit me here to interrupt you, mother. Whatever you may have seen in me; she,—I mean Lucy,—has never been in the slightest hurry to be married;—that's all. But I shall regard it as a *lapsus-linguae* in you."

"Undoubtedly, a *lapsus*. But listen to me. I have been carefully observing both you and Lucy of late; and that has made me think further of the matter. Now, Pierre, if you were in any profession, or in any business at all; nay, if I were a farmer's wife, and you my child, working in my fields; why, then, you and Lucy should still wait awhile. But as you have nothing to do but to think of Lucy by day, and dream of her by night, and as she is in the same predicament, I suppose, with respect to you; and as the consequence of all this begins to be discernible in a certain, just perceptible, and quite harmless thinness, so to speak, of the cheek; but a very conspicuous and dangerous febrileness of the eye; therefore, I choose the lesser of two evils; and now you have my permission to be married, as soon as the thing can be done with propriety. I dare say you have no objection to have the wedding take place before Christmas, the present month being the first of summer."

Pierre said nothing; but leaping to his feet, threw his two arms around his mother, and kissed her repeatedly.

"A most sweet and eloquent answer, Pierre; but sit down again. I desire now to say a little concerning less attractive, but quite necessary things connected with this affair. You know, that by your father's will, these lands and—"

"Miss Lucy, my mistress;" said Dates, throwing open the door.

Pierre sprang to his feet; but as if suddenly mindful of his mother's presence, composed himself again, though he still approached the door.

Lucy entered, carrying a little basket of strawberries.

"Why, how do you do, my dear," said Mrs. Glendinning affectionately. "This is an unexpected pleasure."

"Yes; and I suppose that Pierre here is a little surprised too; seeing that he was to call upon me this evening, and not I upon him before sundown. But I took a sudden fancy for a solitary stroll,—the afternoon was such a delicious one; and chancing—it was only chancing—to pass through the Locust Lane leading hither, I met the strangest little fellow, with this basket in his hand.—'Yes, buy them, miss'—said he. 'And how do you know I want to buy them,' returned I, 'I don't want to buy them.'—'Yes you do, miss; they ought to be twenty-six cents, but I'll take thirteen cents, that being my shilling. I always want the odd half cent, I do. Come, I can't wait, I have been expecting you long enough.'"

"A very sagacious little imp," laughed Mrs. Glendinning.

"Impertinent little rascal," cried Pierre.

"And am I not now the silliest of all silly girls, to be telling you my adventures so very frankly," smiled Lucy.

"No; but the most celestial of all innocents," cried Pierre, in a rhapsody of delight. "Frankly open is the flower, that hath nothing but purity to show."

"Now, my dear little Lucy," said Mrs. Glendinning, "let Pierre take off your shawl, and come now and stay to tea with us. Pierre has put back the dinner so, the tea-hour will come now very soon."

"Thank you; but I can not stay this time. Look, I have forgotten my own errand; I brought these strawberries for you, Mrs. Glendinning, and for Pierre;—Pierre is so wonderfully fond of them."

"I was audacious enough to think as much," cried Pierre, "for you *and* me, you see, mother; for you *and* me, you understand that, I hope."

"Perfectly, my dear brother."

Lucy blushed.

"How warm it is, Mrs. Glendinning."

"Very warm, Lucy. So you won't stay to tea?"

"No, I must go now; just a little stroll, that's all; good-bye! Now don't be following me, Pierre. Mrs. Glendinning, will you keep Pierre back? I know you want him; you were talking over some private affair when I entered; you both looked so very confidential."

"And you were not very far from right, Lucy," said Mrs. Glendinning, making no sign to stay her departure.

"Yes, business of the highest importance," said Pierre, fixing his eyes upon Lucy significantly.

At this moment, Lucy just upon the point of her departure, was hovering near the door; the setting sun, streaming through the window, bathed her whole form in golden loveliness and light; that wonderful, and most vivid transparency of her clear Welsh complexion, now fairly glowed like rosy snow. Her flowing, white, blue-ribboned dress, fleecily invested her. Pierre almost thought that she could only depart the house by floating out of the open window, instead of actually stepping from the door. All her aspect to him, was that moment touched with an indescribable gayety, buoyancy, fragility, and an unearthly evanescence.

Youth is no philosopher. Not into young Pierre's heart did there then come the thought, that as the glory of the rose endures but for a day, so the full bloom of girlish airiness and bewitchingness, passes from the earth almost as soon; as jealously absorbed by those frugal elements, which again incorporate that translated girlish bloom, into the first expanding flower-bud. Not into young Pierre, did there then steal that thought of utmost sadness; pondering on the inevitable evanescence of all earthly loveliness; which makes the sweetest things of life only food for ever-devouring and omnivorous melancholy. Pierre's thought was different from this, and yet somehow akin to it.

This to be my wife? I that but the other day weighed an hundred and fifty pounds of solid avoirdupois;—*I* to wed this heavenly fleece? Methinks one husbandly embrace would break her airy zone, and she exhale upward to that heaven whence she hath hither come, condensed to mortal sight. It can not be; I am of heavy earth, and she of airy light. By heaven, but marriage is an impious thing!

Meanwhile, as these things ran through his soul, Mrs. Glendinning also had thinkings of her own.

"A very beautiful tableau," she cried, at last, artistically turning her gay head a little sideways—"very beautiful, indeed; this, I suppose is all premeditated for my entertainment. Orpheus finding his Eurydice; or Pluto stealing Proserpine. Admirable! It might almost stand for either."

"No," said Pierre, gravely; "it is the last. Now, first I see a meaning there." Yes, he added to himself inwardly, I am Pluto stealing Proserpine; and every accepted lover is.

"And you would be very stupid, brother Pierre, if you did not see something there," said his mother, still that way pursuing her own different train of thought. "The meaning thereof is this: Lucy has commanded me to stay you; but in reality she wants you to go along with her. Well, you may go as far as the porch; but then, you must return, for we have not concluded our little affair, you know. Adieu, little lady!"

There was ever a slight degree of affectionate patronizing in the manner of the resplendent, full-blown Mrs. Glendinning, toward the delicate and shrinking girlhood of young Lucy. She treated her very much as she might have treated some surpassingly beautiful and precocious child; and this was precisely what Lucy was. Looking beyond the present period, Mrs. Glendinning could not but perceive, that even in Lucy's womanly maturity, Lucy would still be a child to her; because, she, elated, felt, that in a certain intellectual vigor, so to speak, she was the essential opposite of Lucy, whose sympathetic mind and person had both been cast in one mould of wondrous delicacy. But here Mrs. Glendinning was both right and wrong. So far as she here saw a difference between herself and Lucy Tartan, she did not err; but so far—and that was very far—as she thought she saw her innate superiority to her in the absolute scale of being, here she very widely and immeasurably erred. For what may be artistically styled angelicalness, this is the highest essence compatible with created being; and angelicalness hath no vulgar vigor in it. And that thing which very often prompts to the display of any vigor—which thing, in man or woman, is at bottom nothing but ambition—this quality is purely earthly, and not angelical. It is false, that any angels fell by reason of ambition. Angels never fall; and never feel ambition. Therefore, benevolently, and affectionately, and all-sincerely, as thy heart, oh, Mrs. Glendinning! now standeth affected toward the fleecy Lucy; still, lady, thou dost very sadly mistake it, when the proud, double-arches of the bright breastplate of thy bosom, expand with secret triumph over one, whom thou so sweetly, but still so patronizingly stylest, The Little Lucy.

But ignorant of these further insights, that very superb-looking lady, now waiting Pierre's return from the portico door, sat in a very matronly revery; her eyes fixed upon the decanter of amber-hued wine before her. Whether it was that she somehow saw some lurking analogical similitude between that remarkably slender, and gracefully cut little pint-decanter, brimfull of light, golden wine, or not, there is no absolute telling now. But really, the peculiarly, and reminiscently, and forecastingly complacent expression of her beaming and benevolent countenance, seemed a tell-tale of some conceit very much like the following:—Yes, she's a very pretty little pint-decanter of a girl: a very pretty little Pale Sherry pint-decanter of a girl; and I—I'm a quart decanter of—of—Port—potent Port! Now, Sherry for boys, and Port for men—so I've heard men say; and Pierre is but a boy; but when his father wedded me,—why, his father was turned of five-and-thirty years.

After a little further waiting for him, Mrs. Glendinning heard Pierre's voice—"Yes, before eight o'clock at least, Lucy—no fear;" and then the hall door banged, and Pierre returned to her.

But now she found that this unforeseen visit of Lucy had completely routed all business capacity in her mercurial son; fairly capsizing him again into, there was no telling what sea of pleasant pensiveness.

"Dear me! some other time, sister Mary."

"Not this time; that is very certain, Pierre. Upon my word I shall have to get Lucy kidnapped, and temporarily taken out of the country, and you handcuffed to the table, else there will be no having a preliminary understanding with you, previous to calling in the lawyers. Well, I shall yet manage you, one way or other. Good-bye, Pierre; I see you don't want me now. I suppose I shan't see you till to-morrow morning. Luckily, I have a very interesting book to read. Adieu!"

But Pierre remained in his chair; his gaze fixed upon the stilly sunset beyond the meadows, and far away to the now golden hills. A glorious, softly glorious, and most gracious evening, which seemed plainly a tongue to all humanity, saying: I go down in beauty to rise in joy; Love reigns throughout all worlds that sunsets visit; it is a foolish ghost story; there is no such thing as misery. Would Love, which is omnipotent, have misery in his domain? Would the god of sunlight decree gloom? It is a flawless, speckless, fleckless, beautiful world throughout; joy now, and joy forever!

Then the face, which before had seemed mournfully and reproachfully looking out upon him from the effulgent sunset's heart; the face slid from him; and left alone there with his soul's joy, thinking that that very night he would utter the magic word of marriage to his Lucy; not a happier youth than Pierre Glendinning sat watching that day's sun go down.

iv

After this morning of gayety, this noon of tragedy, and this evening so full of chequered pensiveness; Pierre now possessed his soul in joyful mildness and steadfastness; feeling none of that wild anguish of anticipative rapture, which, in weaker minds, too often dislodges Love's sweet bird from her nest.

The early night was warm, but dark—for the moon was not risen yet—and as Pierre passed on beneath the pendulous canopies of the long arms of the weeping elms of the village, an almost impenetrable blackness surrounded him, but entered not the gently illuminated halls of his heart. He had not gone very far, when in the distance beyond, he noticed a light moving along the opposite side of the road, and slowly approaching. As it was the custom for some of the more elderly, and perhaps timid inhabitants of the village, to carry a lantern when going abroad of so dark a night, this object conveyed no impression of novelty to Pierre; still, as it silently drew nearer and nearer, the one only distinguishable thing before him, he somehow felt a nameless presentiment that the light must be seeking him. He had nearly gained the cottage door, when the lantern crossed over toward him; and as his nimble hand was laid at last upon the little wicket-gate, which he thought was now to admit him to so much delight; a heavy hand was laid upon himself, and at the same moment, the lantern was lifted toward his face, by a hooded and obscure-looking figure, whose half-averted countenance he could but indistinctly discern. But Pierre's own open aspect, seemed to have been quickly scrutinized by the other.

"I have a letter for Pierre Glendinning," said the stranger, "and I believe this is he." At the same moment, a letter was drawn forth, and sought his hand.

"For me!" exclaimed Pierre, faintly, starting at the strangeness of the encounter;—"methinks this is an odd time and place to deliver your mail; —who are you?—Stay!"

But without waiting an answer, the messenger had already turned about, and was re-crossing the road. In the first impulse of the moment, Pierre stept forward, and would have pursued him; but smiling at his own causeless curiosity and trepidation, paused again; and softly turned over the letter in his hand. What mysterious correspondent is this, thought he, circularly moving his thumb upon the seal; no one writes me but from abroad; and their letters come through the office; and as for Lucy—pooh!—when she herself is within, she would hardly have her notes delivered at her own gate. Strange! but I'll in, and read it;—no, not that;—I come to read again in her own sweet heart—that dear missive to me from heaven,—and this impertinent letter would pre-occupy me. I'll wait till I go home.

He entered the gate, and laid his hand upon the cottage knocker. Its sudden coolness caused a slight, and, at any other time, an unaccountable sympathetic sensation in his hand. To his unwonted mood, the knocker seemed to say—"Enter not!—Begone, and first read thy note."

Yielding now, half alarmed, and half bantering with himself, to these shadowy interior monitions, he half-unconsciously quitted the door; repassed the gate; and soon found himself retracing his homeward path.

He equivocated with himself no more; the gloom of the air had now burst into his heart, and extinguished its light; then, first in all his life, Pierre felt the irresistible admonitions and intuitions of Fate.

He entered the hall unnoticed, passed up to his chamber, and hurriedly locking the door in the dark, lit his lamp. As the summoned flame illuminated the room, Pierre, standing before the round center-table, where the lamp was placed, with his hand yet on the brass circle which regulated the wick, started at a figure in the opposite mirror. It bore the outline of Pierre, but now strangely filled with features transformed, and unfamiliar to him; feverish eagerness, fear, and nameless forebodings of ill! He threw himself into a chair, and for a time vainly struggled with the incomprehensible power that possessed him. Then, as he avertedly drew the letter from his bosom, he whispered to himself—Out on thee, Pierre! how sheepish now will ye feel when this tremendous note will turn out to be an invitation to a supper to-morrow night; quick, fool, and write the stereotyped reply: Mr. Pierre Glendinning will be very happy to accept Miss so and so's polite invitation.

Still for the moment he held the letter averted. The messenger had so hurriedly accosted him, and delivered his duty, that Pierre had not yet so much as gained one glance at the superscription of the note. And now the wild thought passed through his mind of what would be the result, should he deliberately destroy the note, without so much as looking at the hand that had addressed it. Hardly had this half-crazy conceit fully made itself legible in his soul, when he was conscious of his two hands meeting in the middle of the sundered note! He leapt from his chair—By heaven! he murmured, unspeakably shocked at the intensity of that mood which had caused him unwittingly as it were, to do for the first time in his whole life, an act of which he was privately ashamed. Though the mood that was on him was none of his own willful seeking; yet now he swiftly felt conscious that he had perhaps a little encouraged it, through that certain strange infatuation of fondness, which the human mind, however vigorous, sometimes feels for any emotion at once novel and mystical. Not willingly, at such times—never mind how fearful we may be—do we try to dissolve the spell which seems, for the time, to admit us, all astonished, into the vague vestibule of the spiritual worlds.

Pierre now seemed distinctly to feel two antagonistic agencies within him; one of which was just struggling into his consciousness, and each of which was striving for the mastery; and between whose respective final ascendencies, he thought he could perceive, though but shadowly, that he himself was to be the only umpire. One bade him finish the selfish destruction of the note; for in some dark way the reading of it would irretrievably entangle his fate. The other bade him dismiss all misgivings; not because there was no possible ground for them, but because to dismiss them was the manlier part, never mind what might betide. This good angel seemed mildly to say—Read, Pierre, though by reading thou may'st entangle thyself, yet may'st thou thereby disentangle others. Read, and feel that best blessedness which, with the sense of all duties discharged, holds happiness indifferent. The bad angel insinuatingly breathed—Read it not, dearest Pierre; but destroy it, and be happy. Then, at the blast of his noble heart, the bad angel shrunk up into nothingness; and the good one defined itself clearer and more clear, and came nigher and more nigh to him, smiling sadly but benignantly; while forth from the infinite distances wonderful harmonies stole into his heart; so that every vein in him pulsed to some heavenly swell.

V

"The name at the end of this letter will be wholly strange to thee. Hitherto my existence has been utterly unknown to thee. This letter will touch thee and pain thee. Willingly would I spare thee, but I can not. My heart bears me witness, that did I think that the suffering these lines would give thee, would, in the faintest degree, compare with what mine has been, I would forever withhold them.

Pierre Glendinning, thou art not the only child of thy father; in the eye of the sun, the hand that traces this is thy sister's; yes, Pierre, Isabel calls thee her brother—her brother! oh, sweetest of words, which so often I have thought to myself, and almost deemed it profanity for an outcast like me to speak or think. Dearest Pierre, my brother, my own father's child! art thou an angel, that thou canst overleap all the heartless usages and fashions of a banded world, that will call thee fool, fool, fool! and curse thee, if thou yieldest to that heavenly impulse which alone can lead thee to respond to the long tyrannizing, and now at last unquenchable yearnings of my bursting heart? Oh, my brother!

But, Pierre Glendinning, I will be proud with thee. Let not my hapless condition extinguish in me, the nobleness which I equally inherit with thee. Thou shalt not be cozened, by my tears and my anguish, into any thing which thy most sober hour will repent. Read no further. If it suit thee, burn this letter; so shalt thou escape the certainty of that knowledge, which, if thou art now cold and selfish, may hereafter, in some maturer, remorseful, and helpless hour, cause thee a poignant upbraiding. No, I shall not, I will not implore thee.—Oh, my brother, my dear, dear Pierre,—help me, fly to me; see, I perish without thee;—pity, pity,—here I freeze in the wide, wide world;—no father, no mother, no sister, no brother, no living thing in the fair form of humanity, that holds me dear. No more, oh no more, dear Pierre, can I endure to be an outcast in the world, for which the dear Savior died. Fly to me, Pierre;—nay, I could tear what I now write,—as I have torn so many other sheets, all written for thy eye, but which never reached thee, because in my distraction, I knew not how to write to thee, nor what to say to thee; and so, behold again how I rave.

Nothing more; I will write no more;—silence becomes this grave;—the heart-sickness steals over me, Pierre, my brother.

Scarce know I what I have written. Yet will I write thee the fatal line, and leave all the rest to thee, Pierre, my brother.—She that is called Isabel Banford dwells in the little red farm-house, three miles from the village, on the slope toward the lake. To-morrow night-fall—not before—not by day, not by day, Pierre.

THY SISTER, ISABEL."

vi

This letter, inscribed in a feminine, but irregular hand, and in some places almost illegible, plainly attesting the state of the mind which had dictated it; —stained, too, here and there, with spots of tears, which chemically acted upon by the ink, assumed a strange and reddish hue—as if blood and not tears had dropped upon the sheet;—and so completely torn in two by Pierre's own hand, that it indeed seemed the fit scroll of a torn, as well as bleeding heart;—this amazing letter, deprived Pierre for the time of all lucid and definite thought or feeling. He hung half-lifeless in his chair; his hand, clutching the letter, was pressed against his heart, as if some assassin had stabbed him and fled; and Pierre was now holding the dagger in the wound, to stanch the outgushing of the blood.

Ay, Pierre, now indeed art thou hurt with a wound, never to be completely healed but in heaven; for thee, the before undistrusted moral beauty of the world is forever fled; for thee, thy sacred father is no more a saint; all brightness hath gone from thy hills, and all peace from thy plains; and now, now, for the first time, Pierre, Truth rolls a black billow through thy soul! Ah, miserable thou, to whom Truth, in her first tides, bears nothing but wrecks!

The perceptible forms of things; the shapes of thoughts; the pulses of life, but slowly came back to Pierre. And as the mariner, shipwrecked and cast on the beach, has much ado to escape the recoil of the wave that hurled him there; so Pierre long struggled, and struggled, to escape the recoil of that anguish, which had dashed him out of itself, upon the beach of his swoon.

But man was not made to succumb to the villain Woe. Youth is not young and a wrestler in vain. Pierre staggeringly rose to his feet; his wide eyes fixed, and his whole form in a tremble.

"Myself am left, at least," he slowly and half-chokingly murmured. "With myself I front thee! Unhand me all fears, and unlock me all spells! Henceforth I will know nothing but Truth; glad Truth, or sad Truth; I will know what *is*, and do what my deepest angel dictates.—The letter!—Isabel,—sister,—brother,—me, *me*—my sacred father!—This is some accursed dream!—nay, but this paper thing is forged,—a base and malicious forgery, I swear;—Well didst thou hide thy face from me, thou vile lanterned messenger, that didst accost me on the threshold of Joy, with this lying warrant of Woe! Doth Truth come in the dark, and steal on us, and rob us so, and then depart, deaf to all pursuing invocations? If this night, which now wraps my soul, be genuine as that which now wraps this half of the world; then Fate, I have a choice quarrel with thee. Thou art a palterer and a cheat; thou hast lured me on through gay gardens to a gulf. Oh! falsely guided in the days of my Joy, am I now truly led in this night of my grief?—I will be a raver, and none shall stay me! I will lift my hand in fury, for am I not struck? I will be bitter in my breath, for is not this cup of gall? Thou Black Knight, that with visor down, thus confrontest me, and mockest at me; Lo! I strike through thy helm, and will see thy face, be it Gorgon!—Let me go, ye fond affections; all piety leave me;—I will be impious, for piety hath juggled me, and taught me to revere, where I should spurn. From all idols, I tear all veils; henceforth I will see the hidden things; and live right out in my own hidden life!—Now I feel that nothing but Truth can move me so. This letter is not a forgery. Oh! Isabel, thou art my sister; and I will love thee, and protect thee, ay, and own thee through all. Ah! forgive me, ye heavens, for my ignorant ravings, and accept this my vow.—Here I swear myself Isabel's. Oh! thou poor castaway girl, that in loneliness and anguish must have long breathed that same air, which I have only inhaled for delight; thou who must even now be weeping, and weeping, cast into an ocean of uncertainty as to thy fate, which heaven hath placed in my hands; sweet Isabel! would I not be baser than brass, and harder, and colder than ice, if I could be insensible to such claims as thine? Thou movest before me, in rainbows spun of thy tears! I see thee long weeping, and God demands me for thy comforter; and comfort thee, stand by thee, and fight for thee, will thy leapingly-acknowledging brother, whom thy own father named Pierre!"

He could not stay in his chamber: the house contracted to a nut-shell around him; the walls smote his forehead; bare-headed he rushed from the place, and only in the infinite air, found scope for that boundless expansion of his life.

Book IV

Retrospective

IN THEIR PRECISE TRACINGS-OUT and subtile causations, the strongest and fieriest emotions of life defy all analytical insight. We see the cloud, and feel its bolt; but meteorology only idly essays a critical scrutiny as to how that cloud became charged, and how this bolt so stuns. The metaphysical writers confess, that the most impressive, sudden, and overwhelming event, as well as the minutest, is but the product of an infinite series of infinitely involved and untraceable foregoing occurrences. Just so with every motion of the heart. Why this cheek kindles with a noble enthusiasm; why that lip curls in scorn; these are things not wholly imputable to the immediate apparent cause, which is only one link in the chain; but to a long line of dependencies whose further part is lost in the mid-regions of the impalpable air.

Idle then would it be to attempt by any winding way so to penetrate into the heart, and memory, and inmost life, and nature of Pierre, as to show why it was that a piece of intelligence which, in the natural course of things, many amiable gentlemen, both young and old, have been known to receive with a momentary feeling of surprise, and then a little curiosity to know more, and at last an entire unconcern; idle would it be, to attempt to show how to Pierre it rolled down on his soul like melted lava, and left so deep a deposit of desolation, that all his subsequent endeavors never restored the original temples to the soil, nor all his culture completely revived its buried bloom.

But some random hints may suffice to deprive a little of its strangeness, that tumultuous mood, into which so small a note had thrown him.

There had long stood a shrine in the fresh-foliaged heart of Pierre, up to which he ascended by many tableted steps of remembrance; and around which annually he had hung fresh wreaths of a sweet and holy affection. Made one green bower of at last, by such successive votive offerings of his being; this shrine seemed, and was indeed, a place for the celebration of a chastened joy, rather than for any melancholy rites. But though thus mantled, and tangled with garlands, this shrine was of marble—a niched pillar, deemed solid and eternal, and from whose top radiated all those innumerable sculptured scrolls and branches, which supported the entire one-pillared temple of his moral life; as in some beautiful gothic oratories, one central pillar, trunk-like, upholds the roof. In this shrine, in this niche of this pillar, stood the perfect marble form of his departed father; without blemish, unclouded, snow-white, and serene; Pierre's fond personification of perfect human goodness and virtue. Before this shrine, Pierre poured out the fullness of all young life's most reverential thoughts and beliefs. Not to God had Pierre ever gone in his heart, unless by ascending the steps of that shrine, and so making it the vestibule of his abstractest religion.

Blessed and glorified in his tomb beyond Prince Mausolus is that mortal sire, who, after an honorable, pure course of life, dies, and is buried, as in a choice fountain, in the filial breast of a tender-hearted and intellectually appreciative child. For at that period, the Solomonic insights have not poured their turbid tributaries into the pure-flowing well of the childish life. Rare preservative virtue, too, have those heavenly waters. Thrown into that fountain, all sweet recollections become marbleized; so that things which in themselves were evanescent, thus became unchangeable and eternal. So, some rare waters in Derbyshire will petrify birds'-nests. But if fate preserves the father to a later time, too often the filial obsequies are less profound; the canonization less ethereal. The eye-expanded boy perceives, or vaguely thinks he perceives, slight specks and flaws in the character he once so wholly reverenced.

When Pierre was twelve years old, his father had died, leaving behind him, in the general voice of the world, a marked reputation as a gentleman and a Christian; in the heart of his wife, a green memory of many healthy days of unclouded and joyful wedded life, and in the inmost soul of Pierre, the impression of a bodily form of rare manly beauty and benignity, only rivaled by the supposed perfect mould in which his virtuous heart had been cast. Of pensive evenings, by the wide winter fire, or in summer, in the southern piazza, when that mystical night-silence so peculiar to the country would summon up in the minds of Pierre and his mother, long trains of the images of the past; leading all that spiritual procession, majestically and holily walked the venerated form of the departed husband and father. Then their talk would be reminiscent and serious, but sweet; and again, and again, still deep and deeper, was stamped in Pierre's soul the cherished conceit, that his virtuous father, so beautiful on earth, was now uncorruptibly sainted in heaven. So choicely, and in some degree, secludedly nurtured, Pierre, though now arrived at the age of nineteen, had never yet become so thoroughly initiated into that darker, though truer aspect of things, which an entire residence in the city from the earliest period of life, almost inevitably engraves upon the mind of any keenly observant and reflective youth of Pierre's present years. So that up to this period, in his breast, all remained as it had been; and to Pierre, his father's shrine seemed spotless, and still new as the marble of the tomb of him of Arimathea.

Judge, then, how all-desolating and withering the blast, that for Pierre, in one night, stripped his holiest shrine of all overlaid bloom, and buried the mild statue of the saint beneath the prostrated ruins of the soul's temple itself.

ii

As the vine flourishes, and the grape empurples close up to the very walls and muzzles of cannoned Ehrenbreitstein; so do the sweetest joys of life grow in the very jaws of its perils.

But is life, indeed, a thing for all infidel levities, and we, its misdeemed beneficiaries, so utterly fools and infatuate, that what we take to be our strongest tower of delight, only stands at the caprice of the minutest event—the falling of a leaf, the hearing of a voice, or the receipt of one little bit of paper scratched over with a few small characters by a sharpened feather? Are we so entirely insecure, that that casket, wherein we have placed our holiest and most final joy, and which we have secured by a lock of infinite deftness; can that casket be picked and desecrated at the merest stranger's touch, when we think that we alone hold the only and chosen key?

Pierre! thou art foolish; rebuild—no, not that, for thy shrine still stands; it stands, Pierre, firmly stands; smellest thou not its yet undeparted, embowering bloom? Such a note as thine can be easily enough written, Pierre; impostors are not unknown in this curious world; or the brisk novelist,

Pierre, will write thee fifty such notes, and so steal gushing tears from his reader's eyes; even as *thy* note so strangely made thine own manly eyes so arid; so glazed, and so arid, Pierre—foolish Pierre!

Oh! mock not the poniarded heart. The stabbed man knows the steel; prate not to him that it is only a tickling feather. Feels he not the interior gash? What does this blood on my vesture? and what does this pang in my soul?

And here again, not unreasonably, might invocations go up to those Three Weird Ones, that tend Life's loom. Again we might ask them, What threads were those, oh, ye Weird Ones, that ye wove in the years foregone; that now to Pierre, they so unerringly conduct electric presentiments, that his woe is woe, his father no more a saint, and Isabel a sister indeed?

Ah, fathers and mothers! all the world round, be heedful,—give heed! Thy little one may not now comprehend the meaning of those words and those signs, by which, in its innocent presence, thou thinkest to disguise the sinister thing ye would hint. Not now he knows; not very much even of the externals he consciously remarks; but if, in after-life, Fate puts the chemic key of the cipher into his hands; then how swiftly and how wonderfully, he reads all the obscurest and most obliterate inscriptions he finds in his memory; yea, and rummages himself all over, for still hidden writings to read. Oh, darkest lessons of Life have thus been read; all faith in Virtue been murdered, and youth gives itself up to an infidel scorn.

But not thus, altogether, was it now with Pierre; yet so like, in some points, that the above true warning may not misplacedly stand.

His father had died of a fever; and, as is not uncommon in such maladies, toward his end, he at intervals lowly wandered in his mind. At such times, by unobserved, but subtle arts, the devoted family attendants, had restrained his wife from being present at his side. But little Pierre, whose fond, filial love drew him ever to that bed; they heeded not innocent little Pierre, when his father was delirious; and so, one evening, when the shadows intermingled with the curtains; and all the chamber was hushed; and Pierre but dimly saw his father's face; and the fire on the hearth lay in a broken temple of wonderful coals; then a strange, plaintive, infinitely pitiable, low voice, stole forth from the testered bed; and Pierre heard,—"My daughter! my daughter!"

"He wanders again," said the nurse.

"Dear, dear father!" sobbed the child—"thou hast not a daughter, but here is thy own little Pierre."

But again the unregardful voice in the bed was heard; and now in a sudden, pealing wail,—"My daughter!—God! God!—my daughter!"

The child snatched the dying man's hand; it faintly grew to his grasp;

but on the other side of the bed, the other hand now also emptily lifted itself, and emptily caught, as if at some other childish fingers. Then both hands dropped on the sheet; and in the twinkling shadows of the evening little Pierre seemed to see, that while the hand which he held wore a faint, feverish flush, the other empty one was ashy white as a leper's.

"It is past," whispered the nurse, "he will wander so no more now till midnight,—that is his wont." And then, in her heart, she wondered how it was, that so excellent a gentleman, and so thoroughly good a man, should wander so ambiguously in his mind; and trembled to think of that mysterious thing in the soul, which seems to acknowledge no human jurisdiction, but in spite of the individual's own innocent self, will still dream horrid dreams, and mutter unmentionable thoughts; and into Pierre's awe-stricken, childish soul, there entered a kindred, though still more nebulous conceit. But it belonged to the spheres of the impalpable ether; and the child soon threw other and sweeter remembrances over it, and covered it up; and at last, it was blended with all other dim things, and imaginings of dimness; and so, seemed to survive to no real life in Pierre. But though through many long years the henbane showed no leaves in his soul; yet the sunken seed was there: and the first glimpse of Isabel's letter caused it to spring forth, as by magic. Then, again, the long-hushed, plaintive and infinitely pitiable voice was heard,—"My daughter! my daughter!" followed by the compunctious "God! God!" And to Pierre, once again the empty hand lifted itself, and once again the ashy hand fell.

iii

In the cold courts of justice the dull head demands oaths, and holy writ proofs; but in the warm halls of the heart one single, untestified memory's spark shall suffice to enkindle such a blaze of evidence, that all the corners of conviction are as suddenly lighted up as a midnight city by a burning building, which on every side whirls its reddened brands.

In a locked, round-windowed closet connecting with the chamber of Pierre, and whither he had always been wont to go, in those sweetly awful hours, when the spirit crieth to the spirit, Come into solitude with me, twin-brother; come away: a secret have I; let me whisper it to thee aside; in this closet, sacred to the Tadmor privacies and repose of the sometimes solitary Pierre, there hung, by long cords from the cornice, a small portrait in oil, before which Pierre had many a time trancedly stood. Had this painting hung in any annual public exhibition, and in its turn been described in print by the casual glancing critics, they would probably have described it thus, and truthfully: "An impromptu portrait of a fine-looking, gay-hearted, youthful gentleman. He is lightly, and, as it were, airily and but grazingly seated in, or rather flittingly tenanting an old-fashioned chair of Malacca. One arm confining his hat and cane is loungingly thrown over the back of the chair, while the fingers of the other hand play with his gold watch-seal and key. The free-templed head is sideways turned, with a peculiarly bright, and care-free, morning expression. He seems as if just dropped in for a visit upon some familiar acquaintance. Altogether, the painting is exceedingly clever and cheerful; with a fine, off-handed expression about it. Undoubtedly a portrait, and no fancy-piece; and, to hazard a vague conjecture, by an amateur."

So bright, and so cheerful then; so trim, and so young; so singularly healthful, and handsome; what subtile element could so steep this whole portrait, that, to the wife of the original, it was namelessly unpleasant and repelling? The mother of Pierre could never abide this picture which she had always asserted did signally belie her husband. Her fond memories of the departed refused to hang one single wreath around it. It is not he, she would emphatically and almost indignantly exclaim, when more urgently besought to reveal the cause for so unreasonable a dissent from the opinion of nearly all the other connections and relatives of the deceased. But the portrait which she held to do justice to her husband, correctly to convey his features in detail, and more especially their truest, and finest, and noblest combined expression; this portrait was a much larger one, and in the great drawing-room below occupied the most conspicuous and honorable place on the wall.

Even to Pierre these two paintings had always seemed strangely dissimilar. And as the larger one had been painted many years after the other, and therefore brought the original pretty nearly within his own childish recollections; therefore, he himself could not but deem it by far the more truthful and life-like presentation of his father. So that the mere preference of his mother, however strong, was not at all surprising to him, but rather coincided with his own conceit. Yet not for this, must the other portrait be so decidedly rejected. Because, in the first place, there was a difference in time, and some difference of costume to be considered, and the wide difference of the styles of the respective artists, and the wide difference of those respective, semi-reflected, ideal faces, which, even in the presence of the original, a spiritual artist will rather choose to draw from than from the fleshy face, however brilliant and fine. Moreover, while the larger portrait was that of a middle-aged, married man, and seemed to possess all the nameless and slightly portly tranquillities, incident to that condition when a felicitous one; the smaller portrait painted a brisk, unentangled, young bachelor, gayly ranging up and down in the world; light-hearted, and a very little bladish perhaps; and charged to the lips with the first uncloying morning fullness and freshness of life. Here, certainly, large allowance was to be made in any careful, candid estimation of these portraits. To Pierre this conclusion had become well-nigh irresistible, when he placed side by side two portraits of himself; one taken in his early childhood, a frocked and belted boy of four years old; and the other, a grown youth of sixteen. Except an indestructible, all-surviving something in the eyes and on the temples, Pierre could hardly recognize the loud-laughing boy in the tall, and pensively smiling youth. If a few years, then, can have in *me* made all this difference, why not in my father? thought Pierre.

Besides all this, Pierre considered the history, and, so to speak, the family legend of the smaller painting. In his fifteenth year, it was made a present to him by an old maiden aunt, who resided in the city, and who cherished the memory of Pierre's father, with all that wonderful amaranthine devotion which an advanced maiden sister ever feels for the idea of a beloved younger brother, now dead and irrevocably gone. As the only child of that brother, Pierre was an object of the warmest and most extravagant attachment on the part of this lonely aunt, who seemed to see, transformed into youth once again, the likeness, and very soul of her brother, in the fair, inheriting brow of Pierre. Though the portrait we speak of was inordinately prized by her, yet at length the strict canon of her romantic and imaginative love asserted the portrait to be Pierre's—for Pierre was not only his father's only child, but his namesake—so soon as Pierre should be old enough to value aright so holy and inestimable a treasure. She had accordingly sent it to him, trebly boxed, and finally covered with a water-proof cloth; and it was delivered at Saddle Meadows, by an express, confidential messenger, an old gentleman of leisure, once her forlorn, because rejected gallant, but now her contented, and chatty neighbor. Henceforth, before a gold-framed and gold-lidded ivory miniature,—a fraternal gift—aunt Dorothea now offered up her morning and her evening rites, to the memory of the noblest and handsomest of brothers. Yet an annual visit to the far closet of Pierre—no slight undertaking now for one so stricken in years, and every way infirm—attested the earnestness of that strong sense of duty, that painful renunciation of self, which had induced her voluntarily to part with the precious memorial.

iv

"Tell me, aunt," the child Pierre had early said to her, long before the portrait became his—"tell me, aunt, how this chair-portrait, as you call it, was painted;—who painted it?—whose chair was this?—have you the chair now?—I don't see it in your room here;—what is papa looking at so strangely?—I should like to know now, what papa was thinking of, then. Do, now, dear aunt, tell me all about this picture, so that when it is mine, as you promise me, I shall know its whole history."

"Sit down, then, and be very still and attentive, my dear child," said aunt Dorothea; while she a little averted her head, and tremulously and inaccurately sought her pocket, till little Pierre cried—"Why, aunt, the story of the picture is not in any little book, is it, that you are going to take out and read to me?"

"My handkerchief, my child."

"Why, aunt, here it is, at your elbow; here, on the table; here, aunt; take it, do; Oh, don't tell me any thing about the picture, now; I won't hear it."

"Be still, my darling Pierre," said his aunt, taking the handkerchief, "draw the curtain a little, dearest; the light hurts my eyes. Now, go into the closet, and bring me my dark shawl;—take your time.—There; thank you, Pierre; now sit down again, and I will begin.—The picture was painted long ago, my child; you were not born then."

"Not born?" cried little Pierre.

"Not born," said his aunt.

"Well, go on, aunt; but don't tell me again that once upon a time I was not little Pierre at all, and yet my father was alive. Go on, aunt,—do, do!"

"Why, how nervous you are getting, my child;—Be patient; I am very old, Pierre; and old people never like to be hurried."

"Now, my own dear Aunt Dorothea, do forgive me this once, and go on with your story."

"When your poor father was quite a young man, my child, and was on one of his long autumnal visits to his friends in this city, he was rather intimate at times with a cousin of his, Ralph Winwood, who was about his own age,—a fine youth he was, too, Pierre."

"I never saw him, aunt; pray, where is he now?" interrupted Pierre;—"does he live in the country, now, as mother and I do?"

"Yes, my child; but a far-away, beautiful country, I hope;—he's in heaven, I trust."

"Dead," sighed little Pierre—"go on, aunt."

"Now, cousin Ralph had a great love for painting, my child; and he spent many hours in a room, hung all round with pictures and portraits; and there he had his easel and brushes; and much liked to paint his friends, and hang their faces on his walls; so that when all alone by himself, he yet had plenty of company, who always wore their best expressions to him, and never once ruffled him, by ever getting cross or ill-natured, little Pierre. Often, he had besought your father to sit to him; saying, that his silent circle of friends would never be complete, till your father consented to join them. But in those days, my child, your father was always in motion. It was hard for me to get him to stand still, while I tied his cravat; for he never came to any one but me for that. So he was always putting off, and putting off cousin Ralph. 'Some other time, cousin; not to-day;—to-morrow, perhaps;—or next week;'—and so, at last cousin Ralph began to despair. But I'll catch him yet, cried sly cousin Ralph. So now he said nothing more to your father about the matter of painting him; but every pleasant morning kept his easel and brushes and every thing in readiness; so as to be ready the first moment your father should chance to drop in upon him from his long strolls; for it was now and then your father's wont to pay flying little visits to cousin Ralph in his painting-room.—But, my child, you may draw back the curtain now—it's getting very dim here, seems to me."

"Well, I thought so all along, aunt," said little Pierre, obeying; "but didn't you say the light hurt your eyes."

"But it does not now, little Pierre."

"Well, well; go on, go on, aunt; you can't think how interested I am," said little Pierre, drawing his stool close up to the quilted satin hem of his good Aunt Dorothea's dress.

"I will, my child. But first let me tell you, that about this time there arrived in the port, a cabin-full of French emigrants of quality;—poor people, Pierre, who were forced to fly from their native land, because of the cruel, blood-shedding times there. But you have read all that in the little history I gave you, a good while ago."

"I know all about it;—the French Revolution," said little Pierre.

"What a famous little scholar you are, my dear child,"—said Aunt Dorothea, faintly smiling—"Among those poor, but noble emigrants, there was a beautiful young girl, whose sad fate afterward made a great noise in the city, and made many eyes to weep, but in vain, for she never was heard of any more."

"How? how? aunt;—I don't understand;—did she disappear then, aunt?"

"I was a little before my story, child. Yes, she did disappear, and never was heard of again; but that was afterward, some time afterward, my child. I am very sure it was; I could take my oath of that, Pierre."

"Why, dear aunt," said little Pierre, "how earnestly you talk—after what? your voice is getting very strange; do now;—don't talk that way; you frighten me so, aunt."

"Perhaps it is this bad cold I have to-day; it makes my voice a little hoarse, I fear, Pierre. But I will try and not talk so hoarsely again. Well, my child, some time before this beautiful young lady disappeared, indeed it was only shortly after the poor emigrants landed, your father made her acquaintance; and with many other humane gentlemen of the city, provided for the wants of the strangers, for they were very poor indeed, having been stripped of every thing, save a little trifling jewelry, which could not go very far. At last, the friends of your father endeavored to dissuade him from visiting these people so much; they were fearful that as the young lady was so very beautiful, and a little inclined to be intriguing—so some said—your father might be tempted to marry her; which would not have been a wise thing in him; for though the young lady might have been very beautiful, and good-hearted, yet no one on this side of the water certainly knew her history; and she was a foreigner; and would not have made so suitable and excellent a match for your father as your dear mother afterward did, my child. But, for myself, I—who always knew your father very well in all his intentions, and he was very confidential with me, too—I, for my part, never credited that he would do so unwise a thing as marry the strange young lady. At any rate, he at last discontinued his visits to the emigrants; and it was after this that the young lady disappeared. Some said that she must have voluntarily but secretly returned into her own country; and others declared that she must have been kidnapped by French emissaries; for, after her disappearance, rumor began to hint that she was of the noblest birth, and some ways allied to the royal family; and then, again, there were some who shook their heads darkly, and muttered of drownings, and other dark things; which one always hears hinted when people disappear, and no one can find them. But though your father and many other gentlemen moved heaven and earth to find trace of her, yet, as I said before, my child, she never re-appeared."

"The poor French lady!" sighed little Pierre. "Aunt, I'm afraid she was murdered."

"Poor lady, there is no telling," said his aunt. "But listen, for I am coming to the picture again. Now, at the time your father was so often visiting the emigrants, my child, cousin Ralph was one of those who a little fancied that your father was courting her; but cousin Ralph being a quiet young man, and a scholar, not well acquainted with what is wise, or what is foolish in the great world; cousin Ralph would not have been at all mortified had your father really wedded with the refugee young lady. So vainly thinking, as I told you, that your father was courting her, he fancied it would be a very fine thing if he could paint your father as her wooer; that is, paint him just after his coming from his daily visits to the emigrants. So he watched his chance; every thing being ready in his painting-room, as I told you before; and one morning, sure enough, in dropt your father from his walk. But before he came into the room, cousin Ralph had spied him from the window; and when your father entered, cousin Ralph had the sitting-chair ready drawn out, back of his easel, but still fronting toward him, and pretended to be very busy painting. He said to your father—'Glad to see you, cousin Pierre; I am just about something here; sit right down there now, and tell me the news; and I'll sally out with you presently. And tell us something of the emigrants, cousin Pierre,' he slyly added—wishing, you see, to get your father's thoughts running that supposed wooing way, so that he might catch some sort of corresponding expression you see, little Pierre."

"I don't know that I precisely understand, aunt; but go on, I am so interested; do go on, dear aunt."

"Well, by many little cunning shifts and contrivances, cousin Ralph kept your father there sitting, and sitting in the chair, rattling and rattling away, and so self-forgetful too, that he never heeded that all the while sly cousin Ralph was painting and painting just as fast as ever he could; and only making believe laugh at your father's wit; in short, cousin Ralph was stealing his portrait, my child."

"Not *stealing* it, I hope," said Pierre, "that would be very wicked."

"Well, then, we won't call it stealing, since I am sure that cousin Ralph kept your father all the time off from him, and so, could not have possibly picked his pocket, though indeed, he slyly picked his portrait, so to speak. And if indeed it was stealing, or any thing of that sort; yet seeing how much comfort that portrait has been to me, Pierre, and how much it will yet be to you, I hope; I think we must very heartily forgive cousin Ralph, for what he then did."

"Yes, I think we must indeed," chimed in little Pierre, now eagerly eying the very portrait in question, which hung over the mantle.

"Well, by catching your father two or three times more in that way, cousin Ralph at last finished the painting; and when it was all framed, and every way completed, he would have surprised your father by hanging it boldly up in his room among his other portraits, had not your father one morning suddenly come to him—while, indeed, the very picture itself was placed face down on a table and cousin Ralph fixing the cord to it—came to him, and frightened cousin Ralph by quietly saying, that now that he thought of it, it seemed to him that cousin Ralph had been playing tricks with him; but he hoped it was not so. 'What do you mean?' said cousin Ralph, a little flurried. 'You have not been hanging my portrait up here, have you, cousin Ralph?' said your father, glancing along the walls. 'I'm glad I don't see it. It is my whim, cousin Ralph,—and perhaps it is a very silly one,—but if you have been lately painting my portrait, I want you to destroy it; at any rate, don't show it to any one, keep it out of sight. What's that you have there, cousin Ralph?'

"Cousin Ralph was now more and more fluttered; not knowing what to make—as indeed, to this day, I don't completely myself—of your father's strange manner. But he rallied, and said—'This, cousin Pierre, is a secret portrait I have here; you must be aware that we portrait-painters are sometimes called upon to paint such. I, therefore, can not show it to you, or tell you any thing about it.'

"'Have you been painting my portrait or not, cousin Ralph?' said your father, very suddenly and pointedly.

"'I have painted nothing that looks as you there look,' said cousin Ralph, evasively, observing in your father's face a fierce-like expression, which he had never seen there before. And more than that, your father could not get from him."

"And what then?" said little Pierre.

"Why not much, my child; only your father never so much as caught one glimpse of that picture; indeed, never knew for certain, whether there was such a painting in the world. Cousin Ralph secretly gave it to me, knowing how tenderly I loved your father; making me solemnly promise never to expose it anywhere where your father could ever see it, or any way hear of it. This promise I faithfully kept; and it was only after your dear father's death, that I hung it in my chamber. There, Pierre, you now have the story of the chair-portrait."

"And a very strange one it is," said Pierre—"and so interesting, I shall never forget it, aunt."

"I hope you never will, my child. Now ring the bell, and we will have a little fruit-cake, and I will take a glass of wine, Pierre;—do you hear, my child?—the bell—ring it. Why, what do you do standing there, Pierre?"

"*Why* did'nt papa want to have cousin Ralph paint his picture, aunt?"

"How these children's minds do run!" exclaimed old aunt Dorothea staring at little Pierre in amazement—"That indeed is more than I can tell you, little Pierre. But cousin Ralph had a foolish fancy about it. He used to tell me, that being in your father's room some few days after the last scene I described, he noticed there a very wonderful work on Physiognomy, as they call it, in which the strangest and shadowiest rules were laid down for detecting people's innermost secrets by studying their faces. And so, foolish cousin Ralph always flattered himself, that the reason your father did not want his portrait taken was, because he was secretly in love with the French young lady, and did not want his secret published in a portrait; since the wonderful work on Physiognomy had, as it were, indirectly warned him against running that risk. But cousin Ralph being such a retired and solitary sort of a youth, he always had such curious whimsies about things. For my part, I don't believe your father ever had any such ridiculous ideas on the subject. To be sure, I myself can not tell you *why* he did not want his picture taken; but when you get to be as old as I am, little Pierre, you will find that every one, even the best of us, at times, is apt to act very queerly and unaccountably; indeed some things we do, we can not entirely explain the reason of, even to ourselves, little Pierre. But you will know all about these strange matters by and by."

"I hope I shall, aunt," said little Pierre—"But, dear aunt, I thought Marten was to bring in some fruit-cake?"

"Ring the bell for him, then, my child."

"Oh! I forgot," said little Pierre, doing her bidding.

By-and-by, while the aunt was sipping her wine; and the boy eating his cake, and both their eyes were fixed on the portrait in question; little Pierre, pushing his stool nearer the picture exclaimed—"Now, aunt, did papa really look exactly like that? Did you ever see him in that same buff vest, and huge-figured neckcloth? I remember the seal and key, pretty well; and it was only a week ago that I saw mamma take them out of a little locked drawer in her wardrobe—but I don't remember the queer whiskers; nor the buff vest; nor the huge white-figured neckcloth; did you ever see papa in that very neckcloth, aunt?"

"My child, it was I that chose the stuff for that neckcloth; yes, and hemmed it for him, and worked P.G. in one corner; but that aint in the picture. It is an excellent likeness, my child, neckcloth and all; as he looked at that time. Why, little Pierre, sometimes I sit here all alone by myself, gazing, and gazing, and gazing at that face, till I begin to think your father is looking at me, and smiling at me, and nodding at me, and saying—Dorothea! Dorothea!"

"How strange," said little Pierre, "I think it begins to look at me now, aunt. Hark! aunt, it's so silent all round in this old-fashioned room, that I think I hear a little jingling in the picture, as if the watch-seal was striking against the key—Hark! aunt."

"Bless me, don't talk so strangely, my child."

"I heard mamma say once—but she did not say so to me—that, for her part, she did not like aunt Dorothea's picture; it was not a good likeness, so she said. Why don't mamma like the picture, aunt?"

"My child, you ask very queer questions. If your mamma don't like the picture, it is for a very plain reason. She has a much larger and finer one at home, which she had painted for herself; yes, and paid I don't know how many hundred dollars for it; and that, too, is an excellent likeness, *that* must be the reason, little Pierre."

And thus the old aunt and the little child ran on; each thinking the other very strange; and both thinking the picture still stranger; and the face in the picture still looked at them frankly, and cheerfully, as if there was nothing kept concealed; and yet again, a little ambiguously and mockingly, as if slyly winking to some other picture, to mark what a very foolish old sister, and what a very silly little son, were growing so monstrously grave and speculative about a huge white-figured neckcloth, a buff vest, and a very gentleman-like and amiable countenance.

And so, after this scene, as usual, one by one, the fleet years ran on; till the little child Pierre had grown up to be the tall Master Pierre, and could call the picture his own; and now, in the privacy of his own little closet, could stand, or lean, or sit before it all day long, if he pleased, and keep thinking, and thinking, and thinking, and thinking, till by-and-by all thoughts were blurred, and at last there were no thoughts at all.

Before the picture was sent to him, in his fifteenth year, it had been only through the inadvertence of his mother, or rather through a casual passing into a parlor by Pierre, that he had any way learned that his mother did not approve of the picture. Because, as then Pierre was still young, and the picture was the picture of his father, and the cherished property of a most excellent, and dearly-beloved, affectionate aunt; therefore the mother, with an intuitive delicacy, had refrained from knowingly expressing her peculiar opinion in the presence of little Pierre. And this judicious, though half-unconscious delicacy in the mother, had been perhaps somewhat singularly answered by a like nicety of sentiment in the child; for children of a naturally refined organization, and a gentle nurture, sometimes possess a wonderful, and often undreamed of, daintiness of propriety, and thoughtfulness, and forbearance, in matters esteemed a little subtile even by their elders, and self-elected betters. The little Pierre never disclosed to his mother that he had, through another person, become aware of her thoughts concerning Aunt Dorothea's portrait; he seemed to possess an intuitive knowledge of the circumstance, that from the difference of their relationship to his father, and for other minute reasons, he could in some things, with the greater propriety, be more inquisitive concerning him, with his aunt, than with his mother, especially touching the matter of the chair-portrait. And Aunt Dorothea's reasons accounting for his mother's distaste, long continued satisfactory, or at least not unsufficiently explanatory.

And when the portrait arrived at the Meadows, it so chanced that his mother was abroad; and so Pierre silently hung it up in his closet; and when after a day or two his mother returned, he said nothing to her about its arrival, being still strangely alive to that certain mild mystery which invested it, and whose sacredness now he was fearful of violating, by provoking any discussion with his mother about Aunt Dorothea's gift, or by permitting himself to be improperly curious concerning the reasons of his mother's private and self-reserved opinions of it. But the first time—and it was not long after the arrival of the portrait—that he knew of his mother's having entered his closet; then, when he next saw her, he was prepared to hear what she should voluntarily say about the late addition to its embellishments; but as she omitted all mention of any thing of that sort, he unobtrusively scanned her countenance, to mark whether any little clouding emotion might be discoverable there. But he could discern none. And as all genuine delicacies are by their nature accumulative; therefore this reverential, mutual, but only tacit forbearance of the mother and son, ever after continued uninvaded. And it was another sweet, and sanctified, and sanctifying bond between them. For, whatever some lovers may sometimes say, love does not always abhor a secret, as nature is said to abhor a vacuum. Love is built upon secrets, as lovely Venice upon invisible and incorruptible piles in the sea. Love's secrets, being mysteries, ever pertain to the transcendent and the infinite; and so they are as airy bridges, by which our further shadows pass over into the regions of the golden mists and exhalations; whence all poetical, lovely thoughts are engendered, and drop into us, as though pearls should drop from rainbows.

As time went on, the chasteness and pure virginity of this mutual reservation, only served to dress the portrait in sweeter, because still more mysterious attractions; and to fling, as it were, fresh fennel and rosemary around the revered memory of the father. Though, indeed, as previously recounted, Pierre now and then loved to present to himself for some fanciful solution the penultimate secret of the portrait, in so far, as that involved his mother's distaste; yet the cunning analysis in which such a mental procedure would involve him, never voluntarily transgressed that sacred limit, where his mother's peculiar repugnance began to shade off into ambiguous considerations, touching any unknown possibilities in the character and early life of the original. Not, that he had altogether forbidden his fancy to range in such fields of speculation; but all such imaginings must be contributory to that pure, exalted idea of his father, which, in his soul, was based upon the known acknowledged facts of his father's life.

V

If, when the mind roams up and down in the ever-elastic regions of evanescent invention, any definite form or feature can be assigned to the multitudinous shapes it creates out of the incessant dissolvings of its own prior creations; then might we here attempt to hold and define the least shadowy of those reasons, which about the period of adolescence we now treat of, more frequently occurred to Pierre, whenever he essayed to account for his mother's remarkable distaste for the portrait. Yet will we venture one sketch.

Yes—sometimes dimly thought Pierre—who knows but cousin Ralph, after all, may have been not so very far from the truth, when he surmised that at one time my father did indeed cherish some passing emotion for the beautiful young Frenchwoman. And this portrait being painted at that precise time, and indeed with the precise purpose of perpetuating some shadowy testification of the fact in the countenance of the original: therefore, its expression is not congenial, is not familiar, is not altogether agreeable to my mother: because, not only did my father's features never look so to her (since it was afterward that she first became acquainted with him), but also, that certain womanliness of women; that thing I should perhaps call a tender jealousy, a fastidious vanity, in any other lady, enables her to perceive that the glance of the face in the portrait, is not, in some nameless way, dedicated to herself, but to some other and unknown object; and therefore, is she impatient of it, and it is repelling to her; for she must naturally be intolerant of any imputed reminiscence in my father, which is not in some way connected with her own recollections of him.

Whereas, the larger and more expansive portrait in the great drawing-room, taken in the prime of life; during the best and rosiest days of their wedded union; at the particular desire of my mother; and by a celebrated artist of her own election, and costumed after her own taste; and on all hands considered to be, by those who know, a singularly happy likeness at the period; a belief spiritually reinforced by my own dim infantile remembrances; for all these reasons, this drawing-room portrait possesses an inestimable charm to her; there, she indeed beholds her husband as he had really appeared to her; she does not vacantly gaze upon an unfamiliar phantom called up from the distant, and, to her, well-nigh fabulous days of my father's bachelor life. But in that other portrait, she sees rehearsed to her fond eyes, the latter tales and legends of his devoted wedded love. Yes, I think now that I plainly see it must be so. And yet, ever new conceits come vaporing up in me, as I look on the strange chair-portrait: which, though so very much more unfamiliar to me, than it can possibly be to my mother, still sometimes seems to say—Pierre, believe not the drawing-room painting; that is not thy father; or, at least, is not *all* of thy father. Consider in thy mind, Pierre, whether we two paintings may not make only one. Faithful wives are ever over-fond to a certain imaginary image of their husbands; and faithful widows are ever over-reverential to a certain imagined ghost of that same imagined image, Pierre. Look again, I am thy father as he more truly was. In mature life, the world overlays and varnishes us, Pierre; the thousand proprieties and polished finenesses and grimaces intervene, Pierre; then, we, as it were, abdicate ourselves, and take unto us another self, Pierre; in youth we *are*, Pierre, but in age we *seem*. Look again. I am thy real father, so much the more truly, as thou thinkest thou recognizest me not, Pierre. To their young children, fathers are not wont to unfold themselves entirely, Pierre. There are a thousand and one odd little youthful peccadilloes, that we think we may as well not divulge to them, Pierre. Consider this strange, ambiguous smile, Pierre; more narrowly regard this mouth. Behold, what is this too ardent and, as it were, unchastened light in these eyes, Pierre? I am thy father, boy. There was once a certain, oh, but too lovely young Frenchwoman, Pierre. Youth is hot, and temptation strong, Pierre; and in the minutest moment momentous things are irrevocably done, Pierre; and Time sweeps on, and the thing is not always carried down by its stream, but may be left stranded on its bank; away beyond, in the young, green countries, Pierre. Look again. Doth thy mother dislike me for naught? Consider. Do not all her spontaneous, loving impressions, ever strive to magnify, and spiritualize, and deify, her husband's memory, Pierre? Then why doth she cast despite upon me; and never speak to thee of me; and why dost thou thyself keep silence before her, Pierre? Consider. Is there no little mystery here? Probe a little, Pierre. Never fear, never fear. No matter for thy father now. Look, do I not smile?—yes, and with an unchangeable smile; and thus have I unchangeably smiled for many long years gone by, Pierre. Oh, it is a permanent smile! Thus I smiled to cousin Ralph; and thus in thy dear old Aunt Dorothea's parlor, Pierre; and just so, I smile here to thee, and even thus in thy father's later life, when his body may have been in grief, still—hidden away in Aunt Dorothea's secretary—I thus smiled as before; and just so I'd smile were I now hung up in the deepest dungeon of the Spanish Inquisition, Pierre; though suspended in outer darkness, still would I smile with this smile, though then not a soul should be near. Consider; for a smile is the chosen vehicle for all ambiguities, Pierre. When we would deceive, we smile; when we are hatching any nice little artifice, Pierre; only just a little gratifying our own sweet little appetites, Pierre; then watch us, and out comes the odd little smile. Once upon a time, there was a lovely young Frenchwoman, Pierre. Have you carefully, and analytically, and psychologically, and metaphysically, considered her belongings and surroundings, and all her incidentals, Pierre? Oh, a strange sort of story, that, thy dear old Aunt Dorothea once told thee, Pierre. I once knew a credulous old soul, Pierre. Probe, probe a little—see—there seems one little crack there, Pierre—a wedge, a wedge. Something ever comes of all persistent inquiry; we are not so continually curious for nothing, Pierre; not for nothing, do we so intrigue and become wily diplomatists, and glozers with our own minds, Pierre; and afraid of following the Indian trail from the open plain into the dark thickets, Pierre; but enough; a word to the wise.

Thus sometimes in the mystical, outer quietude of the long country nights; either when the hushed mansion was banked round by the thick-fallen December snows, or banked round by the immovable white August moonlight; in the haunted repose of a wide story, tenanted only by himself; and sentineling his own little closet; and standing guard, as it were, before the mystical tent of the picture; and ever watching the strangely concealed lights of the meanings that so mysteriously moved to and fro within; thus sometimes stood Pierre before the portrait of his father, unconsciously throwing himself open to all those ineffable hints and ambiguities, and undefined half-suggestions, which now and then people the soul's atmosphere, as thickly as in a soft, steady snow-storm, the snow-flakes people the air. Yet as often starting from these reveries and trances, Pierre would regain the assured element of consciously bidden and self-propelled thought; and then in a moment the air all cleared, not a snow-flake descended, and Pierre, upbraiding himself for his self-indulgent infatuation, would promise never again to fall into a midnight revery before the chair-portrait of his father. Nor did the streams of these reveries seem to leave any conscious sediment in his mind; they were so light and so rapid, that they rolled their own alluvial along; and seemed to leave all Pierre's thought-channels as clean and dry as though never any alluvial stream had rolled there at all.

And so still in his sober, cherishing memories, his father's beatification remained untouched; and all the strangeness of the portrait only served to invest his idea with a fine, legendary romance; the essence whereof was that very mystery, which at other times was so subtly and evilly significant.

But now, *now!*—Isabel's letter read: swift as the first light that slides from the sun, Pierre saw all preceding ambiguities, all mysteries ripped open as if with a keen sword, and forth trooped thickening phantoms of an infinite gloom. Now his remotest infantile reminiscences—the wandering mind of his father—the empty hand, and the ashen—the strange story of Aunt Dorothea—the mystical midnight suggestions of the portrait itself; and, above all, his mother's intuitive aversion, all, all overwhelmed him with reciprocal testimonies.

And now, by irresistible intuitions, all that had been inexplicably mysterious to him in the portrait, and all that had been inexplicably familiar in the face, most magically these now coincided; the merriness of the one not inharmonious with the mournfulness of the other, but by some ineffable correlativeness, they reciprocally identified each other, and, as it were, melted into each other, and thus interpenetratingly uniting, presented lineaments of an added supernaturalness.

On all sides, the physical world of solid objects now slidingly displaced itself from around him, and he floated into an ether of visions; and, starting to his feet with clenched hands and outstaring eyes at the transfixed face in the air, he ejaculated that wonderful verse from Dante, descriptive of the two mutually absorbing shapes in the Inferno:

> "Ah! how dost thou change,
> Agnello! See! thou art nor double now,
> Nor only one!"

Book V

Misgivings and Preparations

IT WAS LONG AFTER MIDNIGHT when Pierre returned to the house. He had rushed forth in that complete abandonment of soul, which, in so ardent a temperament, attends the first stages of any sudden and tremendous affliction; but now he returned in pallid composure, for the calm spirit of the night, and the then risen moon, and the late revealed stars, had all at last become as a strange subduing melody to him, which, though at first trampled and scorned, yet by degrees had stolen into the windings of his heart, and so shed abroad its own quietude in him. Now, from his height of composure, he firmly gazed abroad upon the charred landscape within him; as the timber man of Canada, forced to fly from the conflagration of his forests, comes back again when the fires have waned, and unblinkingly eyes the immeasurable fields of fire-brands that here and there glow beneath the wide canopy of smoke.

It has been said, that always when Pierre would seek solitude in its material shelter and walled isolation, then the closet communicating with his chamber was his elected haunt. So, going to his room, he took up the now dim-burning lamp he had left there, and instinctively entered that retreat, seating himself, with folded arms and bowed head, in the accustomed dragon-footed old chair. With leaden feet, and heart now changing from iciness to a strange sort of indifference, and a numbing sensation stealing over him, he sat there awhile, till, like the resting traveler in snows, he began to struggle against this inertness as the most treacherous and deadliest of symptoms. He looked up, and found himself fronted by the no longer wholly enigmatical, but still ambiguously smiling picture of his father. Instantly all his consciousness and his anguish returned, but still without power to shake the grim tranquillity which possessed him. Yet endure the smiling portrait he could not; and obeying an irresistible nameless impulse, he rose, and without unhanging it, reversed the picture on the wall.

This brought to sight the defaced and dusty back, with some wrinkled, tattered paper over the joints, which had become loosened from the paste. "Oh, symbol of thy reversed idea in my soul," groaned Pierre; "thou shalt not hang thus. Rather cast thee utterly out, than conspicuously insult thee so. I will no more have a father." He removed the picture wholly from the wall, and the closet; and concealed it in a large chest, covered with blue chintz, and locked it up there. But still, in a square space of slightly discolored wall, the picture still left its shadowy, but vacant and desolate trace. He now strove to banish the least trace of his altered father, as fearful that at present all thoughts concerning him were not only entirely vain, but would prove fatally distracting and incapacitating to a mind, which was now loudly called upon, not only to endure a signal grief, but immediately to act upon it. Wild and cruel case, youth ever thinks; but mistakenly; for Experience well knows, that action, though it seems an aggravation of woe, is really an alleviative; though permanently to alleviate pain, we must first dart some added pangs.

Nor now, though profoundly sensible that his whole previous moral being was overturned, and that for him the fair structure of the world must, in some then unknown way, be entirely rebuilded again, from the lowermost corner stone up; nor now did Pierre torment himself with the thought of that last desolation; and how the desolate place was to be made flourishing again. He seemed to feel that in his deepest soul, lurked an indefinite but potential faith, which could rule in the interregnum of all hereditary beliefs, and circumstantial persuasions; not wholly, he felt, was his soul in anarchy. The indefinite regent had assumed the scepter as its right; and Pierre was not entirely given up to his grief's utter pillage and sack.

To a less enthusiastic heart than Pierre's the foremost question in respect to Isabel which would have presented itself, would have been, *What* must I do? But such a question never presented itself to Pierre; the spontaneous responsiveness of his being left no shadow of dubiousness as to the direct point he must aim at. But if the object was plain, not so the path to it. *How* must I do it? was a problem for which at first there seemed no chance of solution. But without being entirely aware of it himself, Pierre was one of those spirits, which not in a determinate and sordid scrutiny of small pros and cons—but in an impulsive subservience to the god-like dictation of events themselves, find at length the surest solution of perplexities, and the brightest prerogative of command. And as for him, *What* must I do? was a question already answered by the inspiration of the difficulty itself; so now he, as it were, unconsciously discharged his mind, for the present, of all distracting considerations concerning *How* he should do it; assured that the coming interview with Isabel could not but unerringly inspire him there. Still, the inspiration which had thus far directed him had not been entirely mute and undivulging as to many very bitter things which Pierre foresaw in the wide sea of trouble into which he was plunged.

If it be the sacred province and—by the wisest, deemed—the inestimable compensation of the heavier woes, that they both purge the soul of gay-hearted errors and replenish it with a saddened truth; that holy office is not so much accomplished by any covertly inductive reasoning process, whose original motive is received from the particular affliction; as it is the magical effect of the admission into man's inmost spirit of a before unexperienced and wholly inexplicable element, which like electricity suddenly received into any sultry atmosphere of the dark, in all directions splits itself into nimble lances of purifying light; which at one and the same instant discharge all the air of sluggishness and inform it with an illuminating property; so that objects which before, in the uncertainty of the dark, assumed shadowy and romantic outlines, now are lighted up in their substantial realities; so that in these flashing revelations of grief's wonderful fire, we see all things as they are; and though, when the electric element is gone, the shadows once more descend, and the false outlines of objects again return; yet not with their former power to deceive; for now, even in the presence of the falsest aspects, we still retain the impressions of their immovable true ones, though, indeed, once more concealed.

Thus with Pierre. In the joyous young times, ere his great grief came upon him, all the objects which surrounded him were concealingly deceptive. Not only was the long-cherished image of his father now transfigured before him from a green foliaged tree into a blasted trunk, but every other image in his mind attested the universality of that electral light which had darted into his soul. Not even his lovely, immaculate mother, remained entirely untouched, unaltered by the shock. At her changed aspect, when first revealed to him, Pierre had gazed in a panic; and now, when the electrical storm had gone by, he retained in his mind, that so suddenly revealed image, with an infinite mournfulness. She, who in her less splendid but finer and more spiritual part, had ever seemed to Pierre not only as a beautiful saint before whom to offer up his daily orisons, but also as a gentle lady-counsellor and confessor, and her revered chamber as a soft satin-hung cabinet and confessional;—his mother was no longer this all-alluring thing; no more, he too keenly felt, could he go to his mother, as to one who entirely sympathized with him; as to one before whom he could almost unreservedly unbosom himself; as to one capable of pointing out to him the true path where he seemed most beset. Wonderful, indeed, was that electric insight which Fate had now given him into the vital character of his mother. She well might have stood all ordinary tests; but when Pierre thought of the touchstone of his immense strait applied to her spirit; he felt profoundly assured that she would crumble into nothing before it.

She was a noble creature, but formed chiefly for the gilded prosperities of life, and hitherto mostly used to its unruffled serenities; bred and expanded, in all developments, under the sole influence of hereditary forms and world-usages. Not his refined, courtly, loving, equable mother, Pierre felt, could unreservedly, and like a heaven's heroine, meet the shock of his extraordinary emergency, and applaud, to his heart's echo, a sublime resolve, whose execution should call down the astonishment and the jeers of the world.

My mother!—dearest mother!—God hath given me a sister, and unto thee a daughter, and covered her with the world's extremest infamy and scorn, that so I and thou—*thou*, my mother, mightest gloriously own her, and acknowledge her, and,——Nay, nay, groaned Pierre, never, never, could such syllables be one instant tolerated by her. Then, high-up, and towering, and all-forbidding before Pierre grew the before unthought of wonderful edifice of his mother's immense pride;—her pride of birth, her pride of affluence, her pride of purity, and all the pride of high-born, refined, and wealthy Life, and all the Semiramian pride of woman. Then he staggered back upon himself, and only found support in himself. Then Pierre felt that deep in him lurked a divine unidentifiableness, that owned no earthly kith or kin. Yet was this feeling entirely lonesome, and orphan-like. Fain, then, for one moment, would he have recalled the thousand sweet illusions of Life; tho' purchased at the price of Life's Truth; so that once more he might not feel himself driven out an infant Ishmael into the desert, with no maternal Hagar to accompany and comfort him.

Still, were these emotions without prejudice to his own love for his mother, and without the slightest bitterness respecting her; and, least of all, there was no shallow disdain toward her of superior virtue. He too plainly saw, that not his mother had made his mother; but the Infinite Haughtiness had first fashioned her; and then the haughty world had further molded her; nor had a haughty Ritual omitted to finish her.

Wonderful, indeed, we repeat it, was the electrical insight which Pierre now had into the character of his mother, for not even the vivid recalling of her lavish love for him could suffice to gainsay his sudden persuasion. Love me she doth, thought Pierre, but how? Loveth she me with the love past all understanding? that love, which in the loved one's behalf, would still calmly confront all hate? whose most triumphing hymn, triumphs only by swelling above all opposing taunts and despite?—Loving mother, here have I a loved, but world-infamous sister to own;—and if thou lovest me, mother, thy love will love her, too, and in the proudest drawing-room take her so much the more proudly by the hand.—And as Pierre thus in fancy led Isabel before his mother; and in fancy led her away, and felt his tongue cleave to the roof of his mouth, with her transfixing look of incredulous, scornful horror; then Pierre's enthusiastic heart sunk in and in, and caved clean away in him, as he so poignantly felt his first feeling of the dreary heart-vacancies of the conventional life. Oh heartless, proud, ice-gilded world, how I hate thee, he thought, that thy tyrannous, insatiate grasp, thus now in my bitterest need—thus doth rob me even of my mother; thus doth make me now doubly an orphan, without a green grave to bedew. My tears,—could I weep them,—must now be wept in the desolate places; now to me is it, as though both father and mother had gone on distant voyages, and, returning, died in unknown seas.

She loveth me, ay;—but why? Had I been cast in a cripple's mold, how then? Now, do I remember that in her most caressing love, there ever gleamed some scaly, glittering folds of pride. Me she loveth with pride's love; in me she thinks she seeth her own curled and haughty beauty; before my glass she stands,—pride's priestess—and to her mirrored image, not to me, she offers up her offerings of kisses. Oh, small thanks I owe thee, Favorable Goddess, that didst clothe this form with all the beauty of a man, that so thou mightest hide from me all the truth of a man. Now I see that in his beauty a man is snared, and made stone-blind, as the worm within its silk. Welcome then be Ugliness and Poverty and Infamy, and all ye other crafty ministers of Truth, that beneath the hoods and rags of beggars hide yet the belts and crowns of kings. And dimmed be all beauty that must own the clay; and dimmed be all wealth, and all delight, and all the annual prosperities of earth, that but gild the links, and stud with diamonds the base rivets and the chains of Lies. Oh, now methinks I a little see why of old the men of Truth went barefoot, girded with a rope, and ever moving under mournfulness as underneath a canopy. I remember now those first wise words, wherewith our Savior Christ first spoke in his first speech to men:—'Blessed are the poor in spirit, and blessed they that mourn.' Oh, hitherto I have but piled up words; bought books, and bought some small experiences, and builded me in libraries; now I sit down and read. Oh, now I know the night, and comprehend the sorceries of the moon, and all the dark persuadings that have their birth in storms and winds. Oh, not long will Joy abide, when Truth doth come; nor Grief her laggard be. Well may this head hang on my breast,—it holds too much; well may my heart knock at my ribs,—prisoner impatient of his iron bars. Oh, men are jailers all; jailers of themselves; and in Opinion's world ignorantly hold their noblest part a captive to their vilest; as disguised royal Charles when caught by peasants. The heart! the heart! 'tis God's anointed; let me pursue the heart!

ii

But if the presentiment in Pierre of his mother's pride, as bigotedly hostile to the noble design he cherished; if this feeling was so wretched to him; far more so was the thought of another and a deeper hostility, arising from her more spiritual part. For her pride would not be so scornful, as her wedded memories reject with horror, the unmentionable imputation involved in the mere fact of Isabel's existence. In what galleries of conjecture, among what horrible haunting toads and scorpions, would such a revelation lead her? When Pierre thought of this, the idea of at all divulging his secret to his mother, not only was made repelling by its hopelessness, as an infirm attack upon her citadel of pride, but was made in the last degree inhuman, as torturing her in her tenderest recollections, and desecrating the whitest altar in her sanctuary.

Though the conviction that he must never disclose his secret to his mother was originally an unmeditated, and as it were, an inspired one; yet now he was almost pains-taking in scrutinizing the entire circumstances of the matter, in order that nothing might be overlooked. For already he vaguely felt, that upon the concealment, or the disclosure of this thing, with reference to his mother, hinged his whole future course of conduct, his whole earthly weal, and Isabel's. But the more and the more that he pondered upon it, the more and the more fixed became his original conviction. He considered that in the case of a disclosure, all human probability pointed to his mother's scornful rejection of his suit as a pleader for Isabel's honorable admission into the honorable mansion of the Glendinnings. Then in that case, unconsciously thought Pierre, I shall have given the deep poison of a miserable truth to my mother, without benefit to any, and positive harm to all. And through Pierre's mind there then darted a baleful thought; how that the truth should not always be paraded; how that sometimes a lie is heavenly, and truth infernal. Filially infernal, truly, thought Pierre, if I should by one vile breath of truth, blast my father's blessed memory in the bosom of my mother, and plant the sharpest dagger of grief in her soul. I will not do it!

But as this resolution in him opened up so dark and wretched a background to his view, he strove to think no more of it now, but postpone it until the interview with Isabel should have in some way more definitely shaped his purposes. For, when suddenly encountering the shock of new and unanswerable revelations, which he feels must revolutionize all the circumstances of his life, man, at first, ever seeks to shun all conscious definitiveness in his thoughts and purposes; as assured, that the lines that shall precisely define his present misery, and thereby lay out his future path; these can only be defined by sharp stakes that cut into his heart.

iii

Most melancholy of all the hours of earth, is that one long, gray hour, which to the watcher by the lamp intervenes between the night and day; when both lamp and watcher, over-tasked, grow sickly in the pallid light; and the watcher, seeking for no gladness in the dawn, sees naught but garish vapors there; and almost invokes a curse upon the public day, that shall invade his lonely night of sufferance.

The one small window of his closet looked forth upon the meadow, and across the river, and far away to the distant heights, storied with the great deeds of the Glendinnings. Many a time had Pierre sought this window before sunrise, to behold the blood-red, out-flinging dawn, that would wrap those purple hills as with a banner. But now the morning dawned in mist and rain, and came drizzlingly upon his heart. Yet as the day advanced, and once more showed to him the accustomed features of his room by that natural light, which, till this very moment, had never lighted him but to his joy; now that the day, and not the night, was witness to his woe; now first the dread reality came appallingly upon him. A sense of horrible forlornness, feebleness, impotence, and infinite, eternal desolation possessed him. It was not merely mental, but corporeal also. He could not stand; and when he tried to sit, his arms fell floorwards as tied to leaden weights. Dragging his ball and chain, he fell upon his bed; for when the mind is cast down, only in sympathetic proneness can the body rest; whence the bed is often Grief's first refuge. Half stupefied, as with opium, he fell into the profoundest sleep.

In an hour he awoke, instantly recalling all the previous night; and now finding himself a little strengthened, and lying so quietly and silently there, almost without bodily consciousness, but his soul unobtrusively alert; careful not to break the spell by the least movement of a limb, or the least turning of his head, Pierre steadfastly faced his grief, and looked deep down into its eyes; and thoroughly, and calmly, and summarily comprehended it now—so at least he thought—and what it demanded from him; and what he must quickly do in its more immediate sequences; and what that course of conduct was, which he must pursue in the coming unevadable breakfast interview with his mother; and what, for the present must be his plan with Lucy. His time of thought was brief. Rising from his bed, he steadied himself upright a moment; and then going to his writing-desk, in a few at first faltering, but at length unlagging lines, traced the following note:

"I must ask pardon of you, Lucy, for so strangely absenting myself last night. But you know me well enough to be very sure that I would not have done so without important cause. I was in the street approaching your cottage, when a message reached me, imperatively calling me away. It is a matter which will take up all my time and attention for, possibly, two or three days. I tell you this, now, that you may be prepared for it. And I know that however unwelcome this may be to you, you will yet bear with it for my sake; for, indeed, and indeed, Lucy dear, I would not dream of staying from you so long, unless irresistibly coerced to it. Do not come to the mansion until I come to you; and do not manifest any curiosity or anxiety about me, should you chance in the interval to see my mother in any other place. Keep just as cheerful as if I were by you all the time. Do this, now, I conjure you; and so farewell!"

He folded the note, and was about sealing it, when he hesitated a moment, and instantly unfolding it, read it to himself. But he could not adequately comprehend his own writing, for a sudden cloud came over him. This passed; and taking his pen hurriedly again, he added the following postscript:

"Lucy, this note may seem mysterious; but if it shall, I did not mean to make it so; nor do I know that I could have helped it. But the only reason is this, Lucy: the matter which I have alluded to, is of such a nature, that, for the present I stand virtually pledged not to disclose it to any person but those more directly involved in it. But where one can not reveal the thing itself, it only makes it the more mysterious to write round it this way. So merely know me entirely unmenaced in person, and eternally faithful to you; and so be at rest till I see you."

Then sealing the note, and ringing the bell, he gave it in strict charge to a servant, with directions to deliver it at the earliest practicable moment, and not wait for any answer. But as the messenger was departing the chamber, he called him back, and taking the sealed note again, and hollowing it in his hand, scrawled inside of it in pencil the following words: "Don't write me; don't inquire for me;" and then returned it to the man, who quitted him, leaving Pierre rooted in thought in the middle of the room.

But he soon roused himself, and left the mansion; and seeking the cool, refreshing meadow stream, where it formed a deep and shady pool, he bathed; and returning invigorated to his chamber, changed his entire dress; in the little trifling concernments of his toilette, striving utterly to banish all thought of that weight upon his soul. Never did he array himself with more solicitude for effect. It was one of his fond mother's whims to perfume the lighter contents of his wardrobe; and it was one of his own little femininenesses—of the sort sometimes curiously observable in very robust-bodied and big-souled men, as Mohammed, for example—to be very partial to all pleasant essences. So that when once more he left the mansion in order to freshen his cheek anew to meet the keen glance of his mother—to whom the secret of his possible pallor could not be divulged; Pierre went forth all redolent; but alas! his body only the embalming cerements of his buried dead within.

iv

His stroll was longer than he meant; and when he returned up the Linden walk leading to the breakfast-room, and ascended the piazza steps, and glanced into the wide window there, he saw his mother seated not far from the table; her face turned toward his own; and heard her gay voice, and peculiarly light and buoyant laugh, accusing him, and not her, of being the morning's laggard now. Dates was busy among some spoons and napkins at a side-stand.

Summoning all possible cheerfulness to his face, Pierre entered the room.

Remembering his carefulness in bathing and dressing; and knowing that there is no air so calculated to give bloom to the cheek as that of a damply fresh, cool, and misty morning, Pierre persuaded himself that small trace would now be found on him of his long night of watching.

"Good morning sister;—Such a famous stroll! I have been all the way to"—

"Where? good heavens! where? for such a look as that!—why, Pierre, Pierre? what ails thee? Dates, I will touch the bell presently."

As the good servitor fumbled for a moment among the napkins, as if unwilling to stir so summarily from his accustomed duty, and not without some of a well and long-tried old domestic's vague, intermitted murmuring, at being wholly excluded from a matter of family interest; Mrs. Glendinning kept her fixed eye on Pierre, who, unmindful that the breakfast was not yet entirely ready, seating himself at the table, began helping himself—though but nervously enough—to the cream and sugar. The moment the door closed on Dates, the mother sprang to her feet, and threw her arms around her son; but in that embrace, Pierre miserably felt that their two hearts beat not together in such unison as before.

"What haggard thing possesses thee, my son? Speak, this is incomprehensible! Lucy;—fie!—not she?—no love-quarrel there;—speak, speak, my darling boy!"

"My dear sister," began Pierre.

"Sister me not, now, Pierre;—I am thy mother."

"Well, then, dear mother, thou art quite as incomprehensible to me as I to"—

"Talk faster, Pierre—this calmness freezes me. Tell me; for, by my soul, something most wonderful must have happened to thee. Thou art my son, and I command thee. It is not Lucy; it is something else. Tell me."

"My dear mother," said Pierre, impulsively moving his chair backward from the table, "if thou wouldst only believe me when I say it, I have really nothing to tell thee. Thou knowest that sometimes, when I happen to feel very foolishly studious and philosophical, I sit up late in my chamber; and then, regardless of the hour, foolishly run out into the air, for a long stroll across the meadows. I took such a stroll last night; and had but little time left for napping afterward; and what nap I had I was none the better for. But I won't be so silly again, soon; so do, dearest mother, stop looking at me, and let us to breakfast.—Dates! Touch the bell there, sister."

"Stay, Pierre!—There is a heaviness in this hour. I feel, I know, that thou art deceiving me;—perhaps I erred in seeking to wrest thy secret from thee;

but believe me, my son, I never thought thou hadst any secret thing from me, except thy first love for Lucy—and that, my own womanhood tells me, was most pardonable and right. But now, what can it be? Pierre, Pierre! consider well before thou determinest upon withholding confidence from me. I am thy mother. It may prove a fatal thing. Can that be good and virtuous, Pierre, which shrinks from a mother's knowledge? Let us not loose hands so, Pierre; thy confidence from me, mine goes from thee. Now, shall I touch the bell?"

Pierre, who had thus far been vainly seeking to occupy his hands with his cup and spoon; he now paused, and unconsciously fastened a speechless glance of mournfulness upon his mother. Again he felt presentiments of his mother's newly-revealed character. He foresaw the supposed indignation of her wounded pride; her gradually estranged affections thereupon; he knew her firmness, and her exaggerated ideas of the inalienable allegiance of a son. He trembled to think, that now indeed was come the first initial moment of his heavy trial. But though he knew all the significance of his mother's attitude, as she stood before him, intently eying him, with one hand upon the bell-cord; and though he felt that the same opening of the door that should now admit Dates, could not but give eternal exit to all confidence between him and his mother; and though he felt, too, that this was his mother's latent thought; nevertheless, he was girded up in his well-considered resolution.

"Pierre, Pierre! shall I touch the bell?"

"Mother, stay!—yes do, sister."

The bell was rung; and at the summons Dates entered; and looking with some significance at Mrs. Glendinning, said,—"His Reverence has come, my mistress, and is now in the west parlor."

"Show Mr. Falsgrave in here immediately; and bring up the coffee; did I not tell you I expected him to breakfast this morning?"

"Yes, my mistress; but I thought that—that—just then"—glancing alarmedly from mother to son.

"Oh, my good Dates, nothing has happened," cried Mrs. Glendinning, lightly, and with a bitter smile, looking toward her son,—"show Mr. Falsgrave in. Pierre, I did not see thee, to tell thee, last night; but Mr. Falsgrave breakfasts with us by invitation. I was at the parsonage yesterday, to see him about that wretched affair of Delly, and we are finally to settle upon what is to be done this morning. But my mind is made up concerning Ned; no such profligate shall pollute this place; nor shall the disgraceful Delly."

Fortunately, the abrupt entrance of the clergyman, here turned away attention from the sudden pallor of Pierre's countenance, and afforded him time to rally.

"Good morning, madam; good morning, sir;" said Mr. Falsgrave, in a singularly mild, flute-like voice, turning to Mrs. Glendinning and her son; the lady receiving him with answering cordiality, but Pierre too embarrassed just then to be equally polite. As for one brief moment Mr. Falsgrave stood before the pair, ere taking the offered chair from Dates, his aspect was eminently attractive.

There are certain ever-to-be-cherished moments in the life of almost any man, when a variety of little foregoing circumstances all unite to make him temporarily oblivious of whatever may be hard and bitter in his life, and also to make him most amiably and ruddily disposed; when the scene and company immediately before him are highly agreeable; and if at such a time he chance involuntarily to put himself into a scenically favorable bodily posture; then, in that posture, however transient, thou shalt catch the noble stature of his Better Angel; catch a heavenly glimpse of the latent heavenliness of man. It was so with Mr. Falsgrave now. Not a house within a circuit of fifty miles that he preferred entering before the mansion-house of Saddle Meadows; and though the business upon which he had that morning come, was any thing but relishable to him, yet that subject was not in his memory then. Before him stood united in one person, the most exalted lady and the most storied beauty of all the country round; and the finest, most intellectual, and most congenial youth he knew. Before him also, stood the generous foundress and the untiring patroness of the beautiful little marble church, consecrated by the good Bishop, not four years gone by. Before him also, stood—though in polite disguise—the same untiring benefactress, from whose purse, he could not help suspecting, came a great part of his salary, nominally supplied by the rental of the pews. He had been invited to breakfast; a meal, which, in a well-appointed country family, is the most cheerful circumstance of daily life; he smelt all Java's spices in the aroma from the silver coffee-urn; and well he knew, what liquid deliciousness would soon come from it. Besides all this, and many more minutenesses of the kind, he was conscious that Mrs. Glendinning entertained a particular partiality for him (though not enough to marry him, as he ten times knew by very bitter experience), and that Pierre was not behindhand in his esteem.

And the clergyman was well worthy of it. Nature had been royally bountiful to him in his person. In his happier moments, as the present, his face was radiant with a courtly, but mild benevolence; his person was nobly robust and dignified; while the remarkable smallness of his feet, and the almost infantile delicacy, and vivid whiteness and purity of his hands, strikingly contrasted with his fine girth and stature. For in countries like America, where there is no distinct hereditary caste of gentlemen, whose order is factitiously perpetuated as race-horses and lords are in kingly lands; and especially, in those agricultural districts, where, of a hundred hands, that drop a ballot for the Presidency, ninety-nine shall be of the brownest and the brawniest; in such districts, this daintiness of the fingers, when united with a generally manly aspect, assumes a remarkableness unknown in European nations.

This most prepossessing form of the clergyman lost nothing by the character of his manners, which were polished and unobtrusive, but peculiarly insinuating, without the least appearance of craftiness or affectation. Heaven had given him his fine, silver-keyed person for a flute to play on in this world; and he was nearly the perfect master of it. His graceful motions had the undulatoriness of melodious sounds. You almost thought you heard, not saw him. So much the wonderful, yet natural gentleman he seemed, that more than once Mrs. Glendinning had held him up to Pierre as a splendid example of the polishing and gentlemanizing influences of Christianity upon the mind and manners; declaring, that extravagant as it might seem, she had always been of his father's fancy,—that no man could be a complete gentleman, and preside with dignity at his own table, unless he partook of the church's sacraments. Nor in Mr. Falsgrave's case was this maxim entirely absurd. The child of a poor northern farmer who had wedded a pretty sempstress, the clergyman had no heraldic line of ancestry to show, as warrant and explanation of his handsome person and gentle manners; the first, being the willful partiality of nature; and the second, the consequence of a scholastic life, attempered by a taste for the choicest female society, however small, which he had always regarded as the best relish of existence. If now his manners thus responded to his person, his mind answered to them both, and was their finest illustration. Besides his eloquent persuasiveness in the pulpit, various fugitive papers upon subjects of nature, art, and literature, attested not only his refined affinity to all beautiful things, visible or invisible; but likewise that he possessed a genius for celebrating such things, which in a less indolent and more ambitious nature, would have been sure to have gained a fair poet's name ere now. For this Mr. Falsgrave was just hovering upon his prime of years; a period which, in such a man, is the sweetest, and, to a mature woman, by far the most attractive of manly life. Youth has not yet completely gone with its beauty, grace, and strength;

nor has age at all come with its decrepitudes; though the finest undrossed parts of it—its mildness and its wisdom—have gone on before, as decorous chamberlains precede the sedan of some crutched king.

Such was this Mr. Falsgrave, who now sat at Mrs. Glendinning's breakfast table, a corner of one of that lady's generous napkins so inserted into his snowy bosom, that its folds almost invested him as far down as the table's edge; and he seemed a sacred priest, indeed, breakfasting in his surplice.

"Pray, Mr. Falsgrave," said Mrs. Glendinning, "break me off a bit of that roll."

Whether or not his sacerdotal experiences had strangely refined and spiritualized so simple a process as breaking bread; or whether it was from the spotless aspect of his hands: certain it is that Mr. Falsgrave acquitted himself on this little occasion, in a manner that beheld of old by Leonardo, might have given that artist no despicable hint touching his celestial painting. As Pierre regarded him, sitting there so mild and meek; such an image of white-browed and white-handed, and napkined immaculateness; and as he felt the gentle humane radiations which came from the clergyman's manly and rounded beautifulness; and as he remembered all the good that he knew of this man, and all the good that he had heard of him, and could recall no blemish in his character; and as in his own concealed misery and forlornness, he contemplated the open benevolence, and beaming excellent-heartedness of Mr. Falsgrave, the thought darted through his mind, that if any living being was capable of giving him worthy counsel in his strait; and if to any one he could go with Christian propriety and some small hopefulness, that person was the one before him.

"Pray, Mr. Glendinning," said the clergyman, pleasantly, as Pierre was silently offering to help him to some tongue—"don't let me rob you of it—pardon me, but you seem to have very little yourself this morning, I think. An execrable pun, I know: but"—turning toward Mrs. Glendinning—"when one is made to feel very happy, one is somehow apt to say very silly things. Happiness and silliness—ah, it's a suspicious coincidence."

"Mr. Falsgrave," said the hostess—"Your cup is empty. Dates!—We were talking yesterday, Mr. Falsgrave, concerning that vile fellow, Ned."

"Well, Madam," responded the gentleman, a very little uneasily.

"He shall not stay on any ground of mine; my mind is made up, sir. Infamous man!—did he not have a wife as virtuous and beautiful now, as when I first gave her away at your altar?—It was the sheerest and most gratuitous profligacy."

The clergyman mournfully and assentingly moved his head.

"Such men," continued the lady, flushing with the sincerest indignation —"are to my way of thinking more detestable than murderers."

"That is being a little hard upon them, my dear Madam," said Mr. Falsgrave, mildly.

"Do you not think so, Pierre—now," said the lady, turning earnestly upon her son—"is not the man, who has sinned like that Ned, worse than a murderer? Has he not sacrificed one woman completely, and given infamy to another—to both of them—for their portion. If his own legitimate boy should now hate him, I could hardly blame him."

"My dear Madam," said the clergyman, whose eyes having followed Mrs. Glendinning's to her son's countenance, and marking a strange trepidation there, had thus far been earnestly scrutinizing Pierre's not wholly repressible emotion;—"My dear Madam," he said, slightly bending over his stately episcopal-looking person—"Virtue has, perhaps, an over-ardent champion in you; you grow too warm; but Mr. Glendinning, here, he seems to grow too cold. Pray, favor us with your views, Mr. Glendinning?"

"I will not think now of the man," said Pierre, slowly, and looking away from both his auditors—"let us speak of Delly and her infant—she has, or had one, I have loosely heard;—their case is miserable indeed."

"The mother deserves it," said the lady, inflexibly—"and the child—Reverend sir, what are the words of the Bible?"

"'The sins of the father shall be visited upon the children to the third generation,'" said Mr. Falsgrave, with some slight reluctance in his tones. "But Madam, that does not mean, that the community is in any way to take the infamy of the children into their own voluntary hands, as the conscious delegated stewards of God's inscrutable dispensations. Because it is declared that the infamous consequences of sin shall be hereditary, it does not follow that our personal and active loathing of sin, should descend from the sinful sinner to his sinless child."

"I understand you, sir," said Mrs. Glendinning, coloring slightly, "you think me too censorious. But if we entirely forget the parentage of the child, and every way receive the child as we would any other, feel for it in all respects the same, and attach no sign of ignominy to it—how then is the Bible dispensation to be fulfilled? Do we not then put ourselves in the way of its fulfilment, and is that wholly free from impiety?"

Here it was the clergyman's turn to color a little, and there was a just perceptible tremor of the under lip.

"Pardon me," continued the lady, courteously, "but if there is any one blemish in the character of the Reverend Mr. Falsgrave, it is that the benevolence of his heart, too much warps in him the holy rigor of our Church's doctrines. For my part, as I loathe the man, I loathe the woman, and never desire to behold the child."

A pause ensued, during which it was fortunate for Pierre, that by the social sorcery of such occasions as the present, the eyes of all three were intent upon the cloth; all three for the moment, giving loose to their own distressful meditations upon the subject in debate, and Mr. Falsgrave vexedly thinking that the scene was becoming a little embarrassing.

Pierre was the first who spoke; as before, he steadfastly kept his eyes away from both his auditors; but though he did not designate his mother, something in the tone of his voice showed that what he said was addressed more particularly to her.

"Since we seem to have been strangely drawn into the ethical aspect of this melancholy matter," said he, "suppose we go further in it; and let me ask, how it should be between the legitimate and the illegitimate child—children of one father—when they shall have passed their childhood?"

Here the clergyman quickly raising his eyes, looked as surprised and searchingly at Pierre, as his politeness would permit.

"Upon my word"—said Mrs. Glendinning, hardly less surprised, and making no attempt at disguising it—"this is an odd question you put; you have been more attentive to the subject than I had fancied. But what do you mean, Pierre? I did not entirely understand you."

"Should the legitimate child shun the illegitimate, when one father is father to both?" rejoined Pierre, bending his head still further over his plate.

The clergyman looked a little down again, and was silent; but still turned his head slightly sideways toward his hostess, as if awaiting some reply to Pierre from her.

"Ask the world, Pierre"—said Mrs. Glendinning warmly—"and ask your own heart."

"My own heart? I will, Madam"—said Pierre, now looking up steadfastly; "but what do *you* think, Mr. Falsgrave?" letting his glance drop again—"should the one shun the other? should the one refuse his highest sympathy and perfect love for the other, especially if that other be deserted by all the rest of the world? What think you would have been our blessed Savior's thoughts on such a matter? And what was that he so mildly said to the adulteress?"

A swift color passed over the clergyman's countenance, suffusing even his expanded brow; he slightly moved in his chair, and looked uncertainly from Pierre to his mother. He seemed as a shrewd, benevolent-minded man, placed between opposite opinions—merely opinions—who, with a full, and doubly-differing persuasion in himself, still refrains from uttering it, because of an irresistible dislike to manifesting an absolute dissent from the honest convictions of any person, whom he both socially and morally esteems.

"Well, what do you reply to my son?"—said Mrs. Glendinning at last.

"Madam and sir"—said the clergyman, now regaining his entire self-possession. "It is one of the social disadvantages which we of the pulpit labor under, that we are supposed to know more of the moral obligations of humanity than other people. And it is a still more serious disadvantage to the world, that our unconsidered, conversational opinions on the most complex problems of ethics, are too apt to be considered authoritative, as indirectly proceeding from the church itself. Now, nothing can be more erroneous than such notions; and nothing so embarrasses me, and deprives me of that entire serenity, which is indispensable to the delivery of a careful opinion on moral subjects, than when sudden questions of this sort are put to me in company. Pardon this long preamble, for I have little more to say. It is not every question, however direct, Mr. Glendinning, which can be conscientiously answered with a yes or no. Millions of circumstances modify all moral questions; so that though conscience may possibly dictate freely in any known special case; yet, by one universal maxim, to embrace all moral contingencies,—this is not only impossible, but the attempt, to me, seems foolish."

At this instant, the surplice-like napkin dropped from the clergyman's bosom, showing a minute but exquisitely cut cameo brooch, representing the allegorical union of the serpent and dove. It had been the gift of an appreciative friend, and was sometimes worn on secular occasions like the present.

"I agree with you, sir"—said Pierre, bowing. "I fully agree with you. And now, madam, let us talk of something else."

"You madam me very punctiliously this morning, Mr. Glendinning"—said his mother, half-bitterly smiling, and half-openly offended, but still more surprised at Pierre's frigid demeanor.

"'Honor thy father and mother;'" said Pierre—"*both* father and mother," he unconsciously added. "And now that it strikes me, Mr. Falsgrave, and now that we have become so strangely polemical this morning, let me say, that as that command is justly said to be the only one with a promise, so it seems to be without any contingency in the application. It would seem—would it not, sir?—that the most deceitful and hypocritical of fathers should be equally honored by the son, as the purest."

"So it would certainly seem, according to the strict letter of the Decalogue—certainly."

"And do you think, sir, that it should be so held, and so applied in actual life? For instance, should I honor my father, if I knew him to be a seducer?"

"Pierre! Pierre!" said his mother, profoundly coloring, and half rising; "there is no need of these argumentative assumptions. You very immensely forget yourself this morning."

"It is merely the interest of the general question, Madam," returned Pierre, coldly. "I am sorry. If your former objection does not apply here, Mr. Falsgrave, will you favor me with an answer to my question?"

"There you are again, Mr. Glendinning," said the clergyman, thankful for Pierre's hint; "that is another question in morals absolutely incapable of a definite answer, which shall be universally applicable." Again the surplice-like napkin chanced to drop.

"I am tacitly rebuked again then, sir," said Pierre, slowly; "but I admit that perhaps you are again in the right. And now, Madam, since Mr. Falsgrave and yourself have a little business together, to which my presence is not necessary, and may possibly prove quite dispensable, permit me to leave you. I am going off on a long ramble, so you need not wait dinner for me. Good morning, Mr. Falsgrave; good morning, Madam," looking toward his mother.

As the door closed upon him, Mr. Falsgrave spoke—"Mr. Glendinning looks a little pale to-day: has he been ill?"

"Not that I know of," answered the lady, indifferently, "but did you ever see young gentleman so stately as he was? Extraordinary!" she murmured; "what can this mean—Madam—Madam? But your cup is empty again, sir"—reaching forth her hand.

"No more, no more, Madam," said the clergyman.

"Madam? pray don't Madam me any more, Mr. Falsgrave; I have taken a sudden hatred to that title."

"Shall it be Your Majesty, then?" said the clergyman, gallantly; "the May Queens are so styled, and so should be the Queens of October."

Here the lady laughed. "Come," said she, "let us go into another room, and settle the affair of that infamous Ned and that miserable Delly."

V

The swiftness and unrepellableness of the billow which, with its first shock, had so profoundly whelmed Pierre, had not only poured into his soul a tumult of entirely new images and emotions, but, for the time, it almost entirely drove out of him all previous ones. The things that any way bore directly upon the pregnant fact of Isabel, these things were all animate and vividly present to him; but the things which bore more upon himself, and his own personal condition, as now forever involved with his sister's, these things were not so animate and present to him. The conjectured past of Isabel took mysterious hold of his father; therefore, the idea of his father tyrannized over his imagination; and the possible future of Isabel, as so essentially though indirectly compromisable by whatever course of conduct his mother might hereafter ignorantly pursue with regard to himself, as henceforth, through Isabel, forever altered to her; these considerations brought his mother with blazing prominence before him.

Heaven, after all, hath been a little merciful to the miserable man; not entirely untempered to human nature are the most direful blasts of Fate. When on all sides assailed by prospects of disaster, whose final ends are in terror hidden from it, the soul of man—either, as instinctively convinced that it can not battle with the whole host at once; or else, benevolently blinded to the larger arc of the circle which menacingly hems it in;—whichever be the truth, the soul of man, thus surrounded, can not, and does never intelligently confront the totality of its wretchedness. The bitter drug is divided into separate draughts for him: to-day he takes one part of his woe; to-morrow he takes more; and so on, till the last drop is drunk.

Not that in the despotism of other things, the thought of Lucy, and the unconjecturable suffering into which she might so soon be plunged, owing to the threatening uncertainty of the state of his own future, as now in great part and at all hazards dedicated to Isabel; not that this thought had thus far been alien to him. Icy-cold, and serpent-like, it had overlayingly crawled in upon his other shuddering imaginings; but those other thoughts would as often upheave again, and absorb it into themselves, so that it would in that way soon disappear from his cotemporary apprehension. The prevailing thoughts connected with Isabel he now could front with prepared and open eyes; but the occasional thought of Lucy, when *that* started up before him, he could only cover his bewildered eyes with his bewildered hands. Nor was this the cowardice of selfishness, but the infinite sensitiveness of his soul. He could bear the agonizing thought of Isabel, because he was immediately resolved to help her, and to assuage a fellow-being's grief; but, as yet, he could not bear the thought of Lucy, because the very resolution that promised balm to Isabel obscurely involved the everlasting peace of Lucy, and therefore aggravatingly threatened a far more than fellow-being's happiness.

Well for Pierre it was, that the penciling presentiments of his mind concerning Lucy as quickly erased as painted their tormenting images. Standing half-befogged upon the mountain of his Fate, all that part of the wide panorama was wrapped in clouds to him; but anon those concealings slid aside, or rather, a quick rent was made in them; disclosing far below, half-vailed in the lower mist, the winding tranquil vale and stream of Lucy's previous happy life; through the swift cloud-rent he caught one glimpse of her expectant and angelic face peeping from the honey-suckled window of her cottage; and the next instant the stormy pinions of the clouds locked themselves over it again; and all was hidden as before; and all went confused in whirling rack and vapor as before. Only by unconscious inspiration, caught from the agencies invisible to man, had he been enabled to write that first obscurely announcing note to Lucy; wherein the collectedness, and the mildness, and the calmness, were but the natural though insidious precursors of the stunning bolts on bolts to follow.

But, while thus, for the most part wrapped from his consciousness and vision, still, the condition of his Lucy, as so deeply affected now, was still more and more disentangling and defining itself from out its nether mist, and even beneath the general upper fog. For when unfathomably stirred, the subtler elements of man do not always reveal themselves in the concocting act; but, as with all other potencies, show themselves chiefly in their ultimate resolvings and results. Strange wild work, and awfully symmetrical and reciprocal, was that now going on within the self-apparently chaotic breast of Pierre. As in his own conscious determinations, the mournful Isabel was being snatched from her captivity of world-wide abandonment; so, deeper down in the more secret chambers of his unsuspecting soul, the smiling Lucy, now as dead and ashy pale, was being bound a ransom for Isabel's salvation. Eye for eye, and tooth for tooth. Eternally inexorable and unconcerned is Fate, a mere heartless trader in men's joys and woes.

Nor was this general and spontaneous self-concealment of all the most momentous interests of his love, as irretrievably involved with Isabel and his resolution respecting her; nor was this unbidden thing in him unseconded by the prompting of his own conscious judgment, when in the tyranny of the master-event itself, that judgment was permitted some infrequent play. He could not but be aware, that all meditation on Lucy now was worse than useless. How could he now map out his and her young life-chart, when all was yet misty-white with creamy breakers! Still more: divinely dedicated as he felt himself to be; with divine commands upon him to befriend and champion Isabel, through all conceivable contingencies of Time and Chance; how could he insure himself against the insidious inroads of self-interest, and hold intact all his unselfish magnanimities, if once he should permit the distracting thought of Lucy to dispute with Isabel's the pervading possession of his soul?

And if—though but unconsciously as yet—he was almost superhumanly prepared to make a sacrifice of all objects dearest to him, and cut himself away from his last hopes of common happiness, should they cross his grand enthusiast resolution;—if this was so with him; then, how light as gossamer, and thinner and more impalpable than airiest threads of gauze, did he hold all common conventional regardings;—his hereditary duty to his mother, his pledged worldly faith and honor to the hand and seal of his affiancement?

Not that at present all these things did thus present themselves to Pierre; but these things were fœtally forming in him. Impregnations from high enthusiasms he had received; and the now incipient offspring which so stirred, with such painful, vague vibrations in his soul; this, in its mature development, when it should at last come forth in living deeds, would scorn all personal relationship with Pierre, and hold his heart's dearest interests for naught.

Thus, in the Enthusiast to Duty, the heaven-begotten Christ is born; and will not own a mortal parent, and spurns and rends all mortal bonds.

vi

One night, one day, and a small part of the one ensuing evening had been given to Pierre to prepare for the momentous interview with Isabel.

Now, thank God, thought Pierre, the night is past,—the night of Chaos and of Doom; the day only, and the skirt of evening now remain. May heaven new-string my soul, and confirm me in the Christ-like feeling I first felt. May I, in all my least shapeful thoughts still square myself by the inflexible rule of holy right. Let no unmanly, mean temptation cross my path this day; let no base stone lie in it. This day I will forsake the censuses of men, and seek the suffrages of the god-like population of the trees, which now seem to me a nobler race than man. Their high foliage shall drop heavenliness upon me; my feet in contact with their mighty roots, immortal vigor shall so steal into me. Guide me, gird me, guard me, this day, ye sovereign powers! Bind me in bonds I can not break; remove all sinister allurings from me; eternally this day deface in me the detested and distorted images of all the convenient lies and duty-subterfuges of the diving and ducking moralities of this earth. Fill me with consuming fire for them; to my life's muzzle, cram me with your own intent. Let no world-syren come to sing to me this day, and wheedle from me my undauntedness. I cast my eternal die this day, ye powers. On my strong faith in ye Invisibles, I stake three whole felicities, and three whole lives this day. If ye forsake me now,—farewell to Faith, farewell to Truth, farewell to God; exiled for aye from God and man, I shall declare myself an equal power with both; free to make war on Night and Day, and all thoughts and things of mind and matter, which the upper and the nether firmaments do clasp!

vii

But Pierre, though charged with the fire of all divineness, his containing thing was made of clay. Ah, muskets the gods have made to carry infinite combustions, and yet made them of clay!

Save me from being bound to Truth, liege lord, as I am now. How shall I steal yet further into Pierre, and show how this heavenly fire was helped to be contained in him, by mere contingent things, and things that he knew not. But I shall follow the endless, winding way,—the flowing river in the cave of man; careless whither I be led, reckless where I land.

Was not the face—though mutely mournful—beautiful, bewitchingly? How unfathomable those most wondrous eyes of supernatural light! In those charmed depths, Grief and Beauty plunged and dived together. So beautiful, so mystical, so bewilderingly alluring; speaking of a mournfulness infinitely sweeter and more attractive than all mirthfulness; that face of glorious suffering; that face of touching loveliness; that face was Pierre's own sister's; that face was Isabel's; that face Pierre had visibly seen; into those same supernatural eyes our Pierre had looked. Thus, already, and ere the proposed encounter, he was assured that, in a transcendent degree, womanly beauty, and not womanly ugliness, invited him to champion the right. Be naught concealed in this book of sacred truth. How, if accosted in some squalid lane, a humped, and crippled, hideous girl should have snatched his garment's hem, with—"Save me, Pierre—love me, own me, brother; I am thy sister!"—Ah, if man were wholly made in heaven, why catch we hell-glimpses? Why in the noblest marble pillar that stands beneath the all-comprising vault, ever should we descry the sinister vein? We lie in nature very close to God; and though, further on, the stream may be corrupted by the banks it flows through; yet at the fountain's rim, where mankind stand, there the stream infallibly bespeaks the fountain.

So let no censorious word be here hinted of mortal Pierre. Easy for me to slyly hide these things, and always put him before the eye as immaculate; unsusceptible to the inevitable nature and the lot of common men. I am more frank with Pierre than the best men are with themselves. I am all unguarded and magnanimous with Pierre; therefore you see his weakness, and therefore only. In reserves men build imposing characters; not in revelations. He who shall be wholly honest, though nobler than Ethan Allen; that man shall stand in danger of the meanest mortal's scorn.

Book VI

Isabel, and the First Part of the Story of Isabel

HALF WISHFUL that the hour would come; half shuddering that every moment it still came nearer and more near to him; dry-eyed, but wet with that dark day's rain; at fall of eve, Pierre emerged from long wanderings in the primeval woods of Saddle Meadows, and for one instant stood motionless upon their sloping skirt.

Where he stood was in the rude wood road, only used by sledges in the time of snow; just where the out-posted trees formed a narrow arch, and fancied gateway leading upon the far, wide pastures sweeping down toward the lake. In that wet and misty eve the scattered, shivering pasture elms seemed standing in a world inhospitable, yet rooted by inscrutable sense of duty to their place. Beyond, the lake lay in one sheet of blankness and of dumbness, unstirred by breeze or breath; fast bound there it lay, with not life enough to reflect the smallest shrub or twig. Yet in that lake was seen the duplicate, stirless sky above. Only in sunshine did that lake catch gay, green images; and these but displaced the imaged muteness of the unfeatured heavens.

On both sides, in the remoter distance, and also far beyond the mild lake's further shore, rose the long, mysterious mountain masses; shaggy with pines and hemlocks, mystical with nameless, vapory exhalations, and in that dim air black with dread and gloom. At their base, profoundest forests lay entranced, and from their far owl-haunted depths of caves and rotted leaves, and unused and unregarded inland overgrowth of decaying wood—for smallest sticks of which, in other climes many a pauper was that moment perishing; from out the infinite inhumanities of those profoundest forests, came a moaning, muttering, roaring, intermitted, changeful sound: rain-shakings of the palsied trees, slidings of rocks undermined, final crashings of long-riven boughs, and devilish gibberish of the forest-ghosts.

But more near, on the mild lake's hither shore, where it formed a long semi-circular and scooped acclivity of corn-fields, there the small and low red farm-house lay; its ancient roof a bed of brightest mosses; its north front (from the north the moss-wind blows), also moss-incrusted, like the north side of any vast-trunked maple in the groves. At one gabled end, a tangled arbor claimed support, and paid for it by generous gratuities of broad-flung verdure, one viny shaft of which pointed itself upright against the chimney-bricks, as if a waving lightning-rod. Against the other gable, you saw the lowly dairy-shed; its sides close netted with traced Madeira vines; and had you been close enough, peeping through that imprisoning tracery, and through the light slats barring the little embrasure of a window, you might have seen the gentle and contented captives—the pans of milk, and the snow-white Dutch cheeses in a row, and the molds of golden butter, and the jars of lily cream. In front, three straight gigantic lindens stood guardians of this verdant spot. A long way up, almost to the ridge-pole of the house, they showed little foliage; but then, suddenly, as three huge green balloons, they poised their three vast, inverted, rounded cones of verdure in the air.

Soon as Pierre's eye rested on the place, a tremor shook him. Not alone because of Isabel, as there a harborer now, but because of two dependent and most strange coincidences which that day's experience had brought to him. He had gone to breakfast with his mother, his heart charged to overflowing with presentiments of what would probably be her haughty disposition concerning such a being as Isabel, claiming her maternal love: and lo! the Reverend Mr. Falsgrave enters, and Ned and Delly are discussed, and that whole sympathetic matter, which Pierre had despaired of bringing before his mother in all its ethic bearings, so as absolutely to learn her thoughts upon it, and thereby test his own conjectures; all that matter had been fully talked about; so that, through that strange coincidence, he now perfectly knew his mother's mind, and had received forewarnings, as if from heaven, not to make any present disclosure to her. That was in the morning; and now, at eve catching a glimpse of the house where Isabel was harboring, at once he recognized it as the rented farm-house of old Walter Ulver, father to the self-same Delly, forever ruined through the cruel arts of Ned.

Strangest feelings, almost supernatural, now stole into Pierre. With little power to touch with awe the souls of less susceptible, reflective, and poetic beings, such coincidences, however frequently they may recur, ever fill the finer organization with sensations which transcend all verbal renderings. They take hold of life's subtlest problem. With the lightning's flash, the query is spontaneously propounded—chance, or God? If too, the mind thus influenced be likewise a prey to any settled grief, then on all sides the query magnifies, and at last takes in the all-comprehending round of things. For ever is it seen, that sincere souls in suffering, then most ponder upon final causes. The heart, stirred to its depths, finds correlative sympathy in the head, which likewise is profoundly moved. Before miserable men, when intellectual, all the ages of the world pass as in a manacled procession, and all their myriad links rattle in the mournful mystery.

Pacing beneath the long-skirting shadows of the elevated wood, waiting for the appointed hour to come, Pierre strangely strove to imagine to himself the scene which was destined to ensue. But imagination utterly failed him here; the reality was too real for him; only the face, the face alone now visited him; and so accustomed had he been of late to confound it with the shapes of air, that he almost trembled when he thought that face to face, that face must shortly meet his own.

And now the thicker shadows begin to fall; the place is lost to him; only the three dim, tall lindens pilot him as he descends the hill, hovering upon the house. He knows it not, but his meditative route is sinuous; as if that moment his thought's stream was likewise serpentining: laterally obstructed by insinuated misgivings as to the ultimate utilitarian advisability of the enthusiast resolution that was his. His steps decrease in quickness as he comes more nigh, and sees one feeble light struggling in the rustic double-casement. Infallibly he knows that his own voluntary steps are taking him forever from the brilliant chandeliers of the mansion of Saddle Meadows, to join company with the wretched rush-lights of poverty and woe. But his sublime intuitiveness also paints to him the sun-like glories of god-like truth and virtue; which though ever obscured by the dense fogs of earth, still shall shine eventually in unclouded radiance, casting illustrative light upon the sapphire throne of God.

ii

He stands before the door; the house is steeped in silence; he knocks; the casement light flickers for a moment, and then moves away; within, he hears a door creak on its hinges; then his whole heart beats wildly as the outer latch is lifted; and holding the light above her supernatural head, Isabel stands before him. It is herself. No word is spoken; no other soul is seen. They enter the room of the double casement; and Pierre sits down, overpowered with bodily faintness and spiritual awe. He lifts his eyes to Isabel's gaze of loveliness and loneliness; and then a low, sweet, half-sobbing voice of more than natural musicalness is heard:—

"And so, thou art my brother;—shall I call thee Pierre?"

Steadfastly, with his one first and last fraternal inquisition of the person of the mystic girl, Pierre now for an instant eyes her; and in that one instant sees in the imploring face, not only the nameless touchingness of that of the sewing-girl, but also the subtler expression of the portrait of his then youthful father, strangely translated, and intermarryingly blended with some before unknown, foreign feminineness. In one breath, Memory and Prophecy, and Intuition tell him—"Pierre, have no reserves; no minutest possible doubt;—this being is thy sister; thou gazest on thy father's flesh."

"And so thou art my brother?—shall I call thee Pierre?"

He sprang to his feet, and caught her in his undoubting arms.

"Thou art! thou art!"

He felt a faint struggling within his clasp; her head drooped against him; his whole form was bathed in the flowing glossiness of her long and unimprisoned hair. Brushing the locks aside, he now gazed upon the deathlike beauty of the face, and caught immortal sadness from it. She seemed as dead; as suffocated,—the death that leaves most unimpaired the latent tranquillities and sweetnesses of the human countenance.

He would have called aloud for succor; but the slow eyes opened upon him; and slowly he felt the girl's supineness leaving her; and now she recovers herself a little,—and again he feels her faintly struggling in his arms, as if somehow abashed, and incredulous of mortal right to hold her so. Now Pierre repents his overardent and incautious warmth, and feels himself all reverence for her. Tenderly he leads her to a bench within the double casement; and sits beside her; and waits in silence, till the first shock of this encounter shall have left her more composed and more prepared to hold communion with him.

"How feel'st thou now, my sister?"

"Bless thee! bless thee!"

Again the sweet, wild power of the musicalness of the voice, and some soft, strange touch of foreignness in the accent,—so it fancifully seemed to Pierre, thrills through and through his soul. He bent and kissed her brow; and then feels her hand seeking his, and then clasping it without one uttered word.

All his being is now condensed in that one sensation of the clasping hand. He feels it as very small and smooth, but strangely hard. Then he knew that by the lonely labor of her hands, his own father's daughter had earned her living in the same world, where he himself, her own brother, had so idly dwelled. Once more he reverently kissed her brow, and his warm breath against it murmured with a prayer to heaven.

"I have no tongue to speak to thee, Pierre, my brother. My whole being, all my life's thoughts and longings are in endless arrears to thee; then how can I speak to thee? Were it God's will, Pierre, my utmost blessing now, were to lie down and die. Then should I be at peace. Bear with me, Pierre."

"Eternally will I do that, my beloved Isabel! Speak not to me yet awhile, if that seemeth best to thee, if that only is possible to thee. This thy clasping hand, my sister, *this* is now thy tongue to me."

"I know not where to begin to speak to thee, Pierre; and yet my soul o'erbrims in me."

"From my heart's depths, I love and reverence thee; and feel for thee, backward and forward, through all eternity!"

"Oh, Pierre, can'st thou not cure in me this dreaminess, this bewilderingness I feel? My poor head swims and swims, and will not pause. My life can not last long thus; I am too full without discharge. Conjure tears for me, Pierre; that my heart may not break with the present feeling,—more deathlike to me than all my grief gone by!"

"Ye thirst-slaking evening skies, ye hilly dews and mists, distil your moisture here! The bolt hath passed; why comes not the following shower? —Make her to weep!"

Then her head sought his support; and big drops fell on him; and anon, Isabel gently slid her head from him, and sat a little composedly beside him.

"If thou feelest in endless arrears of thought to me, my sister; so do I feel toward thee. I too, scarce know what I should speak to thee. But when thou lookest on me, my sister, thou beholdest one, who in his soul hath taken vows immutable, to be to thee, in all respects, and to the uttermost bounds and possibilities of Fate, thy protecting and all-acknowledging brother!"

"Not mere sounds of common words, but inmost tones of my heart's deepest melodies should now be audible to thee. Thou speakest to a human thing, but something heavenly should answer thee;—some flute heard in the air should answer thee; for sure thy most undreamed-of accents, Pierre, sure they have not been unheard on high. Blessings that are imageless to all mortal fancyings, these shall be thine for this."

"Blessing like to thine, doth but recoil and bless homeward to the heart that uttered it. I can not bless thee, my sister, as thou dost bless thyself in blessing my unworthiness. But, Isabel, by still keeping present the first wonder of our meeting, we shall make our hearts all feebleness. Let me then rehearse to thee what Pierre is; what life hitherto he hath been leading; and what hereafter he shall lead;—so thou wilt be prepared."

"Nay, Pierre, that is my office; thou art first entitled to my tale, then, if it suit thee, thou shalt make me the unentitled gift of thine. Listen to me, now. The invisible things will give me strength;—it is not much, Pierre;—nor aught very marvelous. Listen then;—I feel soothed down to utterance now."

During some brief, interluding, silent pauses in their interview thus far, Pierre had heard a soft, slow, sad, to-and-fro, meditative stepping on the floor above; and in the frequent pauses that intermitted the strange story in the following chapter, that same soft, slow, sad, to-and-fro, meditative, and most melancholy stepping, was again and again audible in the silent room.

iii

"I never knew a mortal mother. The farthest stretch of my life's memory can not recall one single feature of such a face. If, indeed, mother of mine hath lived, she is long gone, and cast no shadow on the ground she trod. Pierre, the lips that do now speak to thee, never touched a woman's breast; I seem not of woman born. My first dim life-thoughts cluster round an old, half-ruinous house in some region, for which I now have no chart to seek it out. If such a spot did ever really exist, that too seems to have been withdrawn from all the remainder of the earth. It was a wild, dark house, planted in the midst of a round, cleared, deeply-sloping space, scooped out of the middle of deep stunted pine woods. Ever I shrunk at evening from peeping out of my window, lest the ghostly pines should steal near to me, and reach out their grim arms to snatch me into their horrid shadows. In summer the forest unceasingly hummed with unconjecturable voices of unknown birds and beasts. In winter its deep snows were traced like any paper map, with dotting night-tracks of four-footed creatures, that, even to the sun, were never visible, and never were seen by man at all. In the round open space the dark house stood, without one single green twig or leaf to shelter it; shadeless and shelterless in the heart of shade and shelter. Some of the windows were rudely boarded up, with boards nailed straight up and down; and those rooms were utterly empty, and never were entered, though they were doorless. But often, from the echoing corridor, I gazed into them with fear; for the great fire-places were all in ruins; the lower tier of back-stones were burnt into one white, common crumbling; and the black bricks above had fallen upon the hearths, heaped here and there with the still falling soot of long-extinguished fires. Every hearth-stone in that house had one long crack through it; every floor drooped at the corners; and outside, the whole base of the house, where it rested on the low foundation of greenish stones, was strewn with dull, yellow molderings of the rotting sills. No name; no scrawled or written thing; no book, was in the house; no one memorial speaking of its former occupants. It was dumb as death. No grave-stone, or mound, or any little hillock around the house, betrayed any past burials of man or child. And thus, with no trace then to me of its past history, thus it hath now entirely departed and perished from my slightest knowledge as to where that house so stood, or in what region it so stood. None other house like it have I ever seen. But once I saw plates of the outside of French chateaux which powerfully recalled its dim image to me, especially the two rows of small dormer windows projecting from the inverted hopper-roof. But that house was of wood, and these of stone. Still, sometimes I think that house was not in this country, but somewhere in Europe; perhaps in France; but it is all bewildering to me; and so you must not start at me, for I can not but talk wildly upon so wild a theme.

"In this house I never saw any living human soul, but an old man and woman. The old man's face was almost black with age, and was one purse of wrinkles, his hoary beard always tangled, streaked with dust and earthy crumbs. I think in summer he toiled a little in the garden, or some spot like that, which lay on one side of the house. All my ideas are in uncertainty and confusion here. But the old man and the old woman seem to have fastened themselves indelibly upon my memory. I suppose their being the only human things around me then, *that* caused the hold they took upon me. They seldom spoke to me; but would sometimes, of dark, gusty nights, sit by the fire and stare at me, and then mumble to each other, and then stare at me again. They were not entirely unkind to me; but, I repeat, they seldom or never spoke to me. What words or language they used to each other, this it is impossible for me to recall. I have often wished to; for then I might at least have some additional idea whether the house was in this country or somewhere beyond the sea. And here I ought to say, that sometimes I have, I know not what sort of vague remembrances of at one time—shortly after the period I now speak of—chattering in two different childish languages; one of which waned in me as the other and latter grew. But more of this anon. It was the woman that gave me my meals; for I did not eat with them. Once they sat by the fire with a loaf between them, and a bottle of some thin sort of reddish wine; and I went up to them, and asked to eat with them, and touched the loaf. But instantly the old man made a motion as if to strike me, but did not, and the woman, glaring at me, snatched the loaf and threw it into the fire before them. I ran frightened from the room; and sought a cat, which I had often tried to coax into some intimacy, but, for some strange cause, without success. But in my frightened loneliness, then, I sought the cat again, and found her up-stairs, softly scratching for some hidden thing among the litter of the abandoned fire-places. I called to her, for I dared not go into the haunted chamber; but she only gazed sideways and unintelligently toward me; and continued her noiseless searchings. I called again, and then she turned round and hissed at me; and I ran down stairs, still stung with the thought of having been driven away there, too. I now knew not where to go to rid myself of my loneliness. At last I went outside of the house, and sat down on a stone, but its coldness went up to my heart, and I rose and stood on my feet. But my head was dizzy; I could not stand; I fell, and knew no more. But next morning I found myself in bed in my uncheerable room, and some dark bread and a cup of water by me.

"It has only been by chance that I have told thee this one particular reminiscence of my early life in that house. I could tell many more like it, but this is enough to show what manner of life I led at that time. Every day that I then lived, I felt all visible sights and all audible sounds growing stranger and stranger, and fearful and more fearful to me. To me the man and the woman were just like the cat; none of them would speak to me; none of them were comprehensible to me. And the man, and the woman, and the cat, were just like the green foundation stones of the house to me; I knew not whence they came, or what cause they had for being there. I say again, no living human soul came to the house but the man and the woman; but sometimes the old man early trudged away to a road that led through the woods, and would not come back till late in the evening; he brought the dark bread, and the thin, reddish wine with him. Though the entrance to the wood was not so very far from the door, yet he came so slowly and infirmly trudging with his little load, that it seemed weary hours on hours between my first descrying him among the trees, and his crossing the splintered threshold.

"Now the wide and vacant blurrings of my early life thicken in my mind. All goes wholly memoryless to me now. It may have been that about that time I grew sick with some fever, in which for a long interval I lost myself. Or it may be true, which I have heard, that after the period of our very earliest recollections, then a space intervenes of entire unknowingness, followed again by the first dim glimpses of the succeeding memory, more or less distinctly embracing all our past up to that one early gap in it.

"However this may be, nothing more can I recall of the house in the wide open space; nothing of how at last I came to leave it; but I must have been still extremely young then. But some uncertain, tossing memory have I of being at last in another round, open space, but immensely larger than the first one, and with no encircling belt of woods. Yet often it seems to me that there were three tall, straight things like pine-trees somewhere there nigh to me at times; and that they fearfully shook and snapt as the old trees used to in the mountain storms. And the floors seemed sometimes to droop at the corners still more steeply than the old floors did; and changefully drooped too, so that I would even seem to feel them drooping under me.

"Now, too, it was that, as it sometimes seems to me, I first and last chattered in the two childish languages I spoke of a little time ago. There seemed people about me, some of whom talked one, and some the other; but I talked both; yet one not so readily as the other; and but beginningly as it were; still this other was the one which was gradually displacing the former. The men who—as it sometimes dreamily seems to me at times—often climbed the three strange tree-like things, they talked—I needs must think—if indeed I have any real thought about so bodiless a phantom as this is—they talked the language which I speak of as at this time gradually waning in me. It was a bonny tongue; oh, seems to me so sparkling-gay and lightsome; just the tongue for a child like me, if the child had not been so sad always. It was pure children's language, Pierre; so twittering—such a chirp.

"In thy own mind, thou must now perceive, that most of these dim remembrances in me, hint vaguely of a ship at sea. But all is dim and vague to me. Scarce know I at any time whether I tell you real things, or the unrealest dreams. Always in me, the solidest things melt into dreams, and dreams into solidities. Never have I wholly recovered from the effects of my strange early life. This it is, that even now—this moment—surrounds thy visible form, my brother, with a mysterious mistiness; so that a second face, and a third face, and a fourth face peep at me from within thy own. Now dim, and more dim, grows in me all the memory of how thou and I did come to meet. I go groping again amid all sorts of shapes, which part to me; so that I seem to advance through the shapes; and yet the shapes have eyes that look at me. I turn round, and they look at me; I step forward, and they look at me.—Let me be silent now; do not speak to me."

iv

Filled with nameless wonderings at this strange being, Pierre sat mute, intensely regarding her half-averted aspect. Her immense soft tresses of the jettiest hair had slantingly fallen over her as though a curtain were half drawn from before some saint enshrined. To Pierre, she seemed half unearthly; but this unearthliness was only her mysteriousness, not any thing that was repelling or menacing to him. And still, the low melodies of her far interior voice hovered in sweet echoes in the room; and were trodden upon, and pressed like gushing grapes, by the steady invisible pacing on the floor above.

She moved a little now, and after some strange wanderings more coherently continued.

"My next memory which I think I can in some degree rely upon, was yet another house, also situated away from human haunts, in the heart of a not entirely silent country. Through this country, and by the house, wound a green and lagging river. That house must have been in some lowland; for the first house I spoke of seems to me to have been somewhere among mountains, or near to mountains;—the sounds of the far waterfalls,—I seem to hear them now; the steady up-pointed cloud-shapes behind the house in the sunset sky—I seem to see them now. But this other house, this second one, or third one, I know not which, I say again it was in some lowland. There were no pines around it; few trees of any sort; the ground did not slope so steeply as around the first house. There were cultivated fields about it, and in the distance farm-houses and out-houses, and cattle, and fowls, and many objects of that familiar sort. This house I am persuaded was in this country; on this side of the sea. It was a very large house, and full of people; but for the most part they lived separately. There were some old people in it, and there were young men, and young women in it,—some very handsome; and there were children in it. It seemed a happy place to some of these people; many of them were always laughing; but it was not a happy place for me.

"But here I may err, because of my own consciousness I can not identify in myself—I mean in the memory of my whole foregoing life,—I say, I can not identify that thing which is called happiness; that thing whose token is a laugh, or a smile, or a silent serenity on the lip. I may have been happy, but it is not in my conscious memory now. Nor do I feel a longing for it, as though I had never had it; my spirit seeks different food from happiness; for I think I have a suspicion of what it is. I have suffered wretchedness, but not because of the absence of happiness, and without praying for happiness. I pray for peace—for motionlessness—for the feeling of myself, as of some plant, absorbing life without seeking it, and existing without individual sensation. I feel that there can be no perfect peace in individualness. Therefore I hope one day to feel myself drank up into the pervading spirit animating all things. I feel I am an exile here. I still go straying.—Yes; in thy speech, thou smilest.—But let me be silent again. Do not answer me. When I resume, I will not wander so, but make short end."

Reverently resolved not to offer the slightest let or hinting hindrance to the singular tale rehearsing to him, but to sit passively and receive its marvelous droppings into his soul, however long the pauses; and as touching less mystical considerations, persuaded that by so doing he should ultimately derive the least nebulous and imperfect account of Isabel's history; Pierre still sat waiting her resuming, his eyes fixed upon the girl's wonderfully beautiful ear, which chancing to peep forth from among her abundant tresses, nestled in that blackness like a transparent sea-shell of pearl.

She moved a little now; and after some strange wanderings more coherently continued; while the sound of the stepping on the floor above—it seemed to cease.

"I have spoken of the second or rather the third spot in my memory of the past, as it first appeared to me; I mean, I have spoken of the people in the house, according to my very earliest recallable impression of them. But I stayed in that house for several years—five, six, perhaps, seven years—and during that interval of my stay, all things changed to me, because I learned more, though always dimly. Some of its occupants departed; some changed from smiles to tears; some went moping all the day; some grew as savages and outrageous, and were dragged below by dumb-like men into deep places, that I knew nothing of, but dismal sounds came through the lower floor, groans and clanking fallings, as of iron in straw. Now and then, I saw coffins silently at noon-day carried into the house, and in five minutes' time emerge again, seemingly heavier than they entered; but I saw not who was in them. Once, I saw an immense-sized coffin, endwise pushed through a lower window by three men who did not speak; and watching, I saw it pushed out again, and they drove off with it. But the numbers of those invisible persons who thus departed from the house, were made good by other invisible persons arriving in close carriages. Some in rags and tatters came on foot, or rather were driven on foot. Once I heard horrible outcries, and peeping from my window, saw a robust but squalid and distorted man, seemingly a peasant, tied by cords with four long ends to them, held behind by as many ignorant-looking men who with a lash drove the wild squalid being that way toward the house. Then I heard answering hand-clappings, shrieks, howls, laughter, blessings, prayers, oaths, hymns, and all audible confusions issuing from all the chambers of the house.

"Sometimes there entered the house—though only transiently, departing within the hour they came—people of a then remarkable aspect to me. They were very composed of countenance; did not laugh; did not groan; did not weep; did not make strange faces; did not look endlessly fatigued; were not strangely and fantastically dressed; in short, did not at all resemble any people I had ever seen before, except a little like some few of the persons of the house, who seemed to have authority over the rest. These people of a remarkable aspect to me, I thought they were strangely demented people; —composed of countenance, but wandering of mind; soul-composed and bodily-wandering, and strangely demented people.

"By-and-by, the house seemed to change again, or else my mind took in more, and modified its first impressions. I was lodged up-stairs in a little room; there was hardly any furniture in the room; sometimes I wished to go out of it; but the door was locked. Sometimes the people came and took me out of the room, into a much larger and very long room, and here I would collectively see many of the other people of the house, who seemed likewise brought from distant and separate chambers. In this long room they would vacantly roam about, and talk vacant talk to each other. Some would stand in the middle of the room gazing steadily on the floor for hours together, and never stirred, but only breathed and gazed upon the floor. Some would sit crouching in the corner, and sit crouching there, and only breathe and crouch in the corners. Some kept their hands tight on their hearts, and went slowly promenading up and down, moaning and moaning to themselves. One would say to another—'Feel of it—here, put thy hand in the break.' Another would mutter—'Broken, broken, broken'—and would mutter nothing but that one word *broken*. But most of them were dumb, and could not, or would not speak, or had forgotten how to speak. They were nearly all pale people. Some had hair white as snow, and yet were quite young people. Some were always talking about Hell, Eternity, and God; and some of all things as fixedly decreed; others would say nay to this, and then they would argue, but without much conviction either way. But once nearly all the people present—even the dumb moping people, and the sluggish persons crouching in the corners—nearly all of them laughed once, when after a whole day's loud babbling, two of these predestinarian opponents, said each to the other—'Thou hast convinced me, friend; but we are quits; for so also, have I convinced thee, the other way; now then, let's argue it all over again; for still, though mutually converted, we are still at odds.' Some harangued the wall; some apostrophized the air; some hissed at the air; some lolled their tongues out at the air; some struck the air; some made motions, as if wrestling with the air, and fell out of the arms of the air, panting from the invisible hug.

"Now, as in the former thing, thou must, ere this, have suspected what manner of place this second or third house was, that I then lived in. But do not speak the word to me. That word has never passed my lips; even now, when I hear the word, I run from it; when I see it printed in a book, I run from the book. The word is wholly unendurable to me. Who brought me to the house; how I came there, I do not know. I lived a long time in the house; that alone I know; I say I know, but still I am uncertain; still Pierre, still the—oh the dreaminess, the bewilderingness—it never entirely leaves me. Let me be still again."

She leaned away from him; she put her small hard hand to her forehead; then moved it down, very slowly, but still hardly over her eyes, and kept it there, making no other sign, and still as death. Then she moved and continued her vague tale of terribleness.

"I must be shorter; I did not mean to turn off into the mere offshootings of my story, here and there; but the dreaminess I speak of leads me sometimes; and I, as impotent then, obey the dreamy prompting. Bear with me; now I will be briefer.

"It came to pass, at last, that there was a contention about me in the house; some contention which I heard in the after rumor only, not at the actual time. Some strangers had arrived; or had come in haste, being sent for to the house. Next day they dressed me in new and pretty, but still plain clothes, and they took me down stairs, and out into the air, and into a carriage with a pleasant-looking woman, a stranger to me; and I was driven off a good way, two days nearly we drove away, stopping somewhere overnight; and on the evening of the second day we came to another house, and went into it, and stayed there.

"This house was a much smaller one than the other, and seemed sweetly quiet to me after that. There was a beautiful infant in it; and this beautiful infant always archly and innocently smiling on me, and strangely beckoning me to come and play with it, and be glad with it; and be thoughtless, and be glad and gleeful with it; this beautiful infant first brought me to my own mind, as it were; first made me sensible that I was something different from stones, trees, cats; first undid in me the fancy that all people were as stones, trees, cats; first filled me with the sweet idea of humanness; first made me aware of the infinite mercifulness, and tenderness, and beautifulness of humanness; and this beautiful infant first filled me with the dim thought of Beauty; and equally, and at the same time, with the feeling of the Sadness; of the immortalness and universalness of the Sadness. I now feel that I should soon have gone,———stop me now; do not let me go that way. I owe all things to that beautiful infant. Oh, how I envied it, lying in its happy mother's breast, and drawing life and gladness, and all its perpetual smilingness from that white and smiling breast. That infant saved me; but still gave me vague desirings. Now I first began to reflect in my mind; to endeavor after the recalling past things; but try as I would, little could I recall, but the bewilderingness;—and the stupor, and the torpor, and the blankness, and the dimness, and the vacant whirlingness of the bewilderingness. Let me be still again."

And the stepping on the floor above,—it then resumed.

V

"I must have been nine, or ten, or eleven years old, when the pleasant-looking woman carried me away from the large house. She was a farmer's wife; and now that was my residence, the farm-house. They taught me to sew, and work with wool, and spin the wool; I was nearly always busy now. This being busy, too, this it must have been, which partly brought to me the power of being sensible of myself as something human. Now I began to feel strange differences. When I saw a snake trailing through the grass, and darting out the fire-fork from its mouth, I said to myself, That thing is not human, but I am human. When the lightning flashed, and split some beautiful tree, and left it to rot from all its greenness, I said, That lightning is not human, but I am human. And so with all other things. I can not speak coherently here; but somehow I felt that all good, harmless men and women were human things, placed at cross-purposes, in a world of snakes and lightnings, in a world of horrible and inscrutable inhumanities. I have had no training of any sort. All my thoughts well up in me; I know not whether they pertain to the old bewilderings or not; but as they are, they are, and I can not alter them, for I had nothing to do with putting them in my mind, and I never affect any thoughts, and I never adulterate any thoughts; but when I speak, think forth from the tongue, speech being sometimes before the thought; so, often, my own tongue teaches me new things.

"Now as yet I never had questioned the woman, or her husband, or the young girls, their children, why I had been brought to the house, or how long I was to stay in the house. There I was; just as I found myself in the world; there I was; for what cause I had been brought into the world, would have been no stranger question to me, than for what cause I had been brought to the house. I knew nothing of myself, or any thing pertaining to myself; I felt my pulse, my thought; but other things I was ignorant of, except the general feeling of my humanness among the inhumanities. But as I grew older, I expanded in my mind. I began to learn things out of me; to see still stranger, and minuter differences. I called the woman mother, and so did the other girls; yet the woman often kissed them, but seldom me. She always helped them first at table. The farmer scarcely ever spoke to me. Now months, years rolled on, and the young girls began to stare at me. Then the bewilderingness of the old starings of the solitary old man and old woman, by the cracked hearth-stone of the desolate old house, in the desolate, round, open space; the bewilderingness of those old starings now returned to me; and the green starings, and the serpent hissings of the uncompanionable cat, recurred to me, and the feeling of the infinite forlornness of my life rolled over me. But the woman was very kind to me; she taught the girls not to be cruel to me; she would call me to her, and speak cheerfully to me, and I thanked—not God, for I had been taught no God—I thanked the bright human summer, and the joyful human sun in the sky; I thanked the human summer and the sun, that they had given me the woman; and I would sometimes steal away into the beautiful grass, and worship the kind summer and the sun; and often say over to myself the soft words, summer and the sun.

"Still, weeks and years ran on, and my hair began to vail me with its fullness and its length; and now often I heard the word beautiful, spoken of my hair, and beautiful, spoken of myself. They would not say the word openly to me, but I would by chance overhear them whispering it. The word joyed me with the human feeling of it. They were wrong not to say it openly to me; my joy would have been so much the more assured for the openness of their saying beautiful, to me; and I know it would have filled me with all conceivable kindness toward every one. Now I had heard the word beautiful, whispered, now and then, for some months, when a new being came to the house; they called him gentleman. His face was wonderful to me. Something strangely like it, and yet again unlike it, I had seen before, but where, I could not tell. But one day, looking into the smooth water behind the house, there I saw the likeness—something strangely like, and yet unlike, the likeness of his face. This filled me with puzzlings. The new being, the gentleman, he was very gracious to me; he seemed astonished, confounded at me; he looked at me, then at a very little, round picture—so it seemed—which he took from his pocket, and yet concealed from me. Then he kissed me, and looked with tenderness and grief upon me; and I felt a tear fall on me from him. Then he whispered a word into my ear. 'Father,' was the word he whispered; the same word by which the young girls called the farmer. Then I knew it was the word of kindness and of kisses. I kissed the gentleman.

"When he left the house I wept for him to come again. And he did come again. All called him my father now. He came to see me once every month or two; till at last he came not at all; and when I wept and asked for him, they said the word *Dead* to me. Then the bewilderings of the comings and the goings of the coffins at the large and populous house; these bewilderings came over me. What was it to be dead? What is it to be living? Wherein is the difference between the words Death and Life? Had I been ever dead? Was I living? Let me be still again. Do not speak to me."

And the stepping on the floor above; again it did resume.

"Months ran on; and now I somehow learned that my father had every now and then sent money to the woman to keep me with her in the house; and that no more money had come to her after he was dead; the last penny of the former money was now gone. Now the farmer's wife looked troubledly and painfully at me; and the farmer looked unpleasantly and impatiently at me. I felt that something was miserably wrong; I said to myself, I am one too many; I must go away from the pleasant house. Then the bewilderings of all the loneliness and forlornness of all my forlorn and lonely life; all these bewilderings and the whelmings of the bewilderings rolled over me; and I sat down without the house, but could not weep.

"But I was strong, and I was a grown girl now. I said to the woman—Keep me hard at work; let me work all the time, but let me stay with thee. But the other girls were sufficient to do the work; me they wanted not. The farmer looked out of his eyes at me, and the out-lookings of his eyes said plainly to me—Thee we do not want; go from us; thou art one too many; and thou art more than one too many. Then I said to the woman—Hire me out to some one; let me work for some one.—But I spread too wide my little story. I must make an end.

"The woman listened to me, and through her means I went to live at another house, and earned wages there. My work was milking the cows, and making butter, and spinning wool, and weaving carpets of thin strips of cloth. One day there came to this house a pedler. In his wagon he had a guitar, an old guitar, yet a very pretty one, but with broken strings. He had got it slyly in part exchange from the servants of a grand house some distance off. Spite of the broken strings, the thing looked very graceful and beautiful to me; and I knew there was melodiousness lurking in the thing, though I had never seen a guitar before, nor heard of one; but there was a strange humming in my heart that seemed to prophesy of the hummings of the guitar. Intuitively, I knew that the strings were not as they should be. I said to the man—I will buy of thee the thing thou callest a guitar. But thou must put new strings to it. So he went to search for them; and brought the strings, and restringing the guitar, tuned it for me. So with part of my earnings I bought the guitar. Straightway I took it to my little chamber in the gable, and softly laid it on my bed. Then I murmured; sung and murmured to it; very lowly, very softly; I could hardly hear myself. And I changed the modulations of my singings and my murmurings; and still sung, and murmured, lowly, softly,—more and more; and presently I heard a sudden sound: sweet and low beyond all telling was the sweet and sudden sound. I clapt my hands; the guitar was speaking to me; the dear guitar was singing to me; murmuring and singing to me, the guitar. Then I sung and murmured to it with a still different modulation; and once more it answered me from a different string; and once more it murmured to me, and it answered to me with a different string. The guitar was human; the guitar taught me the secret of the guitar; the guitar learned me to play on the guitar. No music-master have I ever had but the guitar. I made a loving friend of it; a heart friend of it. It sings to me as I to it. Love is not all on one side with my guitar. All the wonders that are unimaginable and unspeakable; all these wonders are translated in the mysterious melodiousness of the guitar. It knows all my past history. Sometimes it plays to me the mystic visions of the confused large house I never name. Sometimes it brings to me the bird-twitterings in the air; and sometimes it strikes up in me rapturous pulsations of legendary delights eternally unexperienced and unknown to me. Bring me the guitar."

VI

Entranced, lost, as one wandering bedazzled and amazed among innumerable dancing lights, Pierre had motionlessly listened to this abundant-haired, and large-eyed girl of mystery.

"Bring me the guitar!"

Starting from his enchantment, Pierre gazed round the room, and saw the instrument leaning against a corner. Silently he brought it to the girl, and silently sat down again.

"Now listen to the guitar; and the guitar shall sing to thee the sequel of my story; for not in words can it be spoken. So listen to the guitar."

Instantly the room was populous with sounds of melodiousness, and mournfulness, and wonderfulness; the room swarmed with the unintelligible but delicious sounds. The sounds seemed waltzing in the room; the sounds hung pendulous like glittering icicles from the corners of the room; and fell upon him with a ringing silveryness; and were drawn up again to the ceiling, and hung pendulous again, and dropt down upon him again with the ringing silveryness. Fire-flies seemed buzzing in the sounds; summer-lightnings seemed vividly yet softly audible in the sounds.

And still the wild girl played on the guitar; and her long dark shower of curls fell over it, and vailed it; and still, out from the vail came the swarming sweetness, and the utter unintelligibleness, but the infinite significancies of the sounds of the guitar.

"Girl of all-bewildering mystery!" cried Pierre—"Speak to me;—sister, if thou indeed canst be a thing that's mortal—speak to me, if thou be Isabel!"

"Mystery! Mystery!
Mystery of Isabel!
Mystery! Mystery!
Isabel and Mystery!"

Among the waltzings, and the droppings, and the swarmings of the sounds, Pierre now heard the tones above deftly stealing and winding among the myriad serpentinings of the other melody:—deftly stealing and winding as respected the instrumental sounds, but in themselves wonderfully and abandonedly free and bold—bounding and rebounding as from multitudinous reciprocal walls; while with every syllable the hair-shrouded form of Isabel swayed to and fro with a like abandonment, and suddenness, and wantonness:—then it seemed not like any song; seemed not issuing from any mouth; but it came forth from beneath the same vail concealing the guitar.

Now a strange wild heat burned upon his brow; he put his hand to it. Instantly the music changed; and drooped and changed; and changed and changed; and lingeringly retreated as it changed; and at last was wholly gone.

Pierre was the first to break the silence.

"Isabel, thou hast filled me with such wonderings; I am so distraught with thee, that the particular things I had to tell to thee, when I hither came; these things I can not now recall, to speak them to thee:—I feel that something is still unsaid by thee, which at some other time thou wilt reveal. But now I can stay no longer with thee. Know me eternally as thy loving, revering, and most marveling brother, who will never desert thee, Isabel. Now let me kiss thee and depart, till to-morrow night; when I shall open to thee all my mind, and all my plans concerning me and thee. Let me kiss thee, and adieu!"

As full of unquestioning and unfaltering faith in him, the girl sat motionless and heard him out. Then silently rose, and turned her boundlessly confiding brow to him. He kissed it thrice, and without another syllable left the place.

Book VII

Intermediate between Pierre's Two Interviews with Isabel at the Farm-house

NOT IMMEDIATELY, not for a long time, could Pierre fully, or by any approximation, realize the scene which he had just departed. But the vague revelation was now in him, that the visible world, some of which before had seemed but too common and prosaic to him; and but too intelligible; he now vaguely felt, that all the world, and every misconceivedly common and prosaic thing in it, was steeped a million fathoms in a mysteriousness wholly hopeless of solution. First, the enigmatical story of the girl, and the profound sincerity of it, and yet the ever accompanying haziness, obscurity, and almost miraculousness of it;—first, this wonderful story of the girl had displaced all commonness and prosaicness from his soul; and then, the inexplicable spell of the guitar, and the subtleness of the melodious appealings of the few brief words from Isabel sung in the conclusion of the melody—all this had bewitched him, and enchanted him, till he had sat motionless and bending over, as a tree-transformed and mystery-laden visitant, caught and fast bound in some necromancer's garden.

But as now burst from these sorceries, he hurried along the open road, he strove for the time to dispel the mystic feeling, or at least postpone it for a while, until he should have time to rally both body and soul from the more immediate consequences of that day's long fastings and wanderings, and that night's never-to-be-forgotten scene. He now endeavored to beat away all thoughts from him, but of present bodily needs.

Passing through the silent village, he heard the clock tell the mid hour of night. Hurrying on, he entered the mansion by a private door, the key of which hung in a secret outer place. Without undressing, he flung himself upon the bed. But remembering himself again, he rose and adjusted his alarm-clock, so that it would emphatically repeat the hour of five. Then to bed again, and driving off all intrudings of thoughtfulness, and resolutely bending himself to slumber, he by-and-by fell into its at first reluctant, but at last welcoming and hospitable arms. At five he rose; and in the east saw the first spears of the advanced-guard of the day.

It had been his purpose to go forth at that early hour, and so avoid all casual contact with any inmate of the mansion, and spend the entire day in a second wandering in the woods, as the only fit prelude to the society of so wild a being as his new-found sister Isabel. But the familiar home-sights of his chamber strangely worked upon him. For an instant, he almost could have prayed Isabel back into the wonder-world from which she had so slidingly emerged. For an instant, the fond, all-understood blue eyes of Lucy displaced the as tender, but mournful and inscrutable dark glance of Isabel. He seemed placed between them, to choose one or the other; then both seemed his; but into Lucy's eyes there stole half of the mournfulness of Isabel's, without diminishing hers.

Again the faintness, and the long life-weariness benumbed him. He left the mansion, and put his bare forehead against the restoring wind. He re-entered the mansion, and adjusted the clock to repeat emphatically the call of seven; and then lay upon his bed. But now he could not sleep. At seven he changed his dress; and at half-past eight went below to meet his mother at the breakfast table, having a little before overheard her step upon the stair.

ii

He saluted her; but she looked gravely and yet alarmedly, and then in a sudden, illy-repressed panic, upon him. Then he knew he must be wonderfully changed. But his mother spoke not to him, only to return his good-morning. He saw that she was deeply offended with him, on many accounts; moreover, that she was vaguely frightened about him, and finally that notwithstanding all this, her stung pride conquered all apprehensiveness in her; and he knew his mother well enough to be very certain that, though he should unroll a magician's parchment before her now, she would verbally express no interest, and seek no explanation from him. Nevertheless, he could not entirely abstain from testing the power of her reservedness.

"I have been quite an absentee, sister Mary," said he, with ill-affected pleasantness.

"Yes, Pierre. How does the coffee suit you this morning? It is some new coffee."

"It is very nice; very rich and odorous, sister Mary."

"I am glad you find it so, Pierre."

"Why don't you call me brother Pierre?"

"Have I not called you so? Well, then, brother Pierre,—is that better?"

"Why do you look so indifferently and icily upon me, sister Mary?"

"Do I look indifferently and icily? Then I will endeavor to look otherwise. Give me the toast there, Pierre."

"You are very deeply offended at me, my dear mother."

"Not in the slightest degree, Pierre. Have you seen Lucy lately?"

"I have not, my mother."

"Ah! A bit of salmon, Pierre."

"You are too proud to show toward me what you are this moment feeling, my mother."

Mrs. Glendinning slowly rose to her feet, and her full stature of womanly beauty and majesty stood imposingly over him.

"Tempt me no more, Pierre. I will ask no secret from thee; all shall be voluntary between us, as it ever has been, until very lately, or all shall be nothing between us. Beware of me, Pierre. There lives not that being in the world of whom thou hast more reason to beware, so you continue but a little longer to act thus with me."

She reseated herself, and spoke no more. Pierre kept silence; and after snatching a few mouthfuls of he knew not what, silently quitted the table, and the room, and the mansion.

iii

As the door of the breakfast-room closed upon Pierre, Mrs. Glendinning rose, her fork unconsciously retained in her hand. Presently, as she paced the room in deep, rapid thought, she became conscious of something strange in her grasp, and without looking at it, to mark what it was, impulsively flung it from her. A dashing noise was heard, and then a quivering. She turned; and hanging by the side of Pierre's portrait, she saw her own smiling picture pierced through, and the fork, whose silver tines had caught in the painted bosom, vibratingly rankled in the wound.

She advanced swiftly to the picture, and stood intrepidly before it.

"Yes, thou art stabbed! but the wrong hand stabbed thee; this should have been *thy* silver blow," turning to Pierre's portrait face. "Pierre, Pierre, thou hast stabbed me with a poisoned point. I feel my blood chemically changing in me. I, the mother of the only surnamed Glendinning, I feel now as though I had borne the last of a swiftly to be extinguished race. For swiftly to be extinguished is that race, whose only heir but so much as impends upon a deed of shame. And some deed of shame, or something most dubious and most dark, is in thy soul, or else some belying specter, with a cloudy, shame-faced front, sat at yon seat but now! What can it be? Pierre, unbosom. Smile not so lightly upon my heavy grief. Answer; what is it, boy? Can it? can it? no—yes—surely—can it? it can not be! But he was not at Lucy's yesterday; nor was she here; and she would not see me when I called. What can this bode? But not a mere broken match—broken as lovers sometimes break, to mend the break with joyful tears, so soon again—not a mere broken match can break my proud heart so. If that indeed be part, it is not all. But no, no, no; it can not, can not be. He would not, could not, do so mad, so impious a thing. It was a most surprising face, though I confessed it not to him, nor even hinted that I saw it. But no, no, no, it can not be. Such young peerlessness in such humbleness, can not have an honest origin. Lilies are not stalked on weeds, though polluted, they sometimes may stand among them. She must be both poor and vile—some chance-blow of a splendid, worthless rake, doomed to inherit both parts of her infecting portion—vileness and beauty. No, I will not think it of him. But what then? Sometimes I have feared that my pride would work me some woe incurable, by closing both my lips, and varnishing all my front, where I perhaps ought to be wholly in the melted and invoking mood. But who can get at one's own heart, to mend it? Right one's self against another, that, one may sometimes do; but when that other is one's own self, these ribs forbid. Then I will live my nature out. I will stand on pride. I will not budge. Let come what will, I shall not half-way run to meet it, to beat it off. Shall a mother abase herself before her stripling boy? Let him tell me of himself, or let him slide adown!"

iv

Pierre plunged deep into the woods, and paused not for several miles; paused not till he came to a remarkable stone, or rather, smoothed mass of rock, huge as a barn, which, wholly isolated horizontally, was yet sweepingly overarched by beech-trees and chestnuts.

It was shaped something like a lengthened egg, but flattened more; and, at the ends, pointed more; and yet not pointed, but irregularly wedge-shaped. Somewhere near the middle of its under side, there was a lateral ridge; and an obscure point of this ridge rested on a second lengthwise-sharpened rock, slightly protruding from the ground. Beside that one obscure and minute point of contact, the whole enormous and most ponderous mass touched not another object in the wide terraqueous world. It was a breathless thing to see. One broad haunched end hovered within an inch of the soil, all along to the point of teetering contact; but yet touched not the soil. Many feet from that—beneath one part of the opposite end, which was all seamed and half-riven—the vacancy was considerably larger, so as to make it not only possible, but convenient to admit a crawling man; yet no mortal being had ever been known to have the intrepid heart to crawl there.

It might well have been the wonder of all the country round. But strange to tell, though hundreds of cottage hearthstones—where, of long winter-evenings, both old men smoked their pipes and young men shelled their corn—surrounded it, at no very remote distance, yet had the youthful Pierre been the first known publishing discoverer of this stone, which he had thereupon fancifully christened the Memnon Stone. Possibly, the reason why this singular object had so long remained unblazoned to the world, was not so much because it had never before been lighted on—though indeed, both belted and topped by the dense deep luxuriance of the aboriginal forest, it lay like Captain Kidd's sunken hull in the gorge of the river Hudson's Highlands,—its crown being full eight fathoms under high-foliage mark during the great spring-tide of foliage;—and besides this, the cottagers had no special motive for visiting its more immediate vicinity at all; their timber and fuel being obtained from more accessible woodlands—as because, even, if any of the simple people should have chanced to have beheld it, they, in their hoodwinked unappreciativeness, would not have accounted it any very marvelous sight, and therefore, would never have thought it worth their while to publish it abroad. So that in real truth, they might have seen it, and yet afterward have forgotten so inconsiderable a circumstance. In short, this wondrous Memnon Stone could be no Memnon Stone to them; nothing but a huge stumbling-block, deeply to be regretted as a vast prospective obstacle in the way of running a handy little cross-road through that wild part of the Manor.

Now one day while reclining near its flank, and intently eying it, and thinking how surprising it was, that in so long-settled a country he should have been the first discerning and appreciative person to light upon such a great natural curiosity, Pierre happened to brush aside several successive layers of old, gray-haired, close cropped, nappy moss, and beneath, to his no small amazement, he saw rudely hammered in the rock some half-obliterate initials—"S. ye W." Then he knew, that ignorant of the stone, as all the simple country round might immemorially have been, yet was not himself the only human being who had discovered that marvelous impending spectacle: but long and long ago, in quite another age, the stone had been beheld, and its wonderfulness fully appreciated—as the painstaking initials seemed to testify—by some departed man, who, were he now alive, might possibly wag a beard old as the most venerable oak of centuries' growth. But who,—who in Methuselah's name,—who might have been this "S. ye W.?" Pierre pondered long, but could not possibly imagine; for the initials, in their antiqueness, seemed to point to some period before the era of Columbus' discovery of the hemisphere. Happening in the end to mention the strange matter of these initials to a white-haired old gentleman, his city kinsman, who, after a long and richly varied, but unfortunate life, had at last found great solace in the Old Testament, which he was continually studying with ever-increasing admiration; this white-haired old kinsman, after having learnt all the particulars about the stone—its bulk, its height, the precise angle of its critical impendings, and all that,—and then, after much prolonged cogitation upon it, and several long-drawn sighs, and aged looks of hoar significance, and reading certain verses in Ecclesiastes; after all these tedious preliminaries, this not-at-all-to-be-hurried white-haired old kinsman, had laid his tremulous hand upon Pierre's firm young shoulder, and slowly whispered—"Boy; 'tis Solomon the Wise." Pierre could not repress a merry laugh at this; wonderfully diverted by what seemed to him so queer and crotchety a conceit; which he imputed to the alledged dotage of his venerable kinsman, who he well knew had once maintained, that the old Scriptural Ophir was somewhere on our northern sea-coast; so no wonder the old gentleman should fancy that King Solomon might have taken a trip—as a sort of amateur supercargo—of some Tyre or Sidon gold-ship across the water, and happened to light on the Memnon Stone, while rambling about with bow and quiver shooting partridges.

But merriment was by no means Pierre's usual mood when thinking of this stone; much less when seated in the woods, he, in the profound significance of that deep forest silence, viewed its marvelous impendings. A flitting conceit had often crossed him, that he would like nothing better for a head-stone than this same imposing pile; in which, at times, during the soft swayings of the surrounding foliage, there seemed to lurk some mournful and lamenting plaint, as for some sweet boy long since departed in the antediluvian time.

Not only might this stone well have been the wonder of the simple country round, but it might well have been its terror. Sometimes, wrought to a mystic mood by contemplating its ponderous inscrutableness, Pierre had called it the Terror Stone. Few could be bribed to climb its giddy height, and crawl out upon its more hovering end. It seemed as if the dropping of one seed from the beak of the smallest flying bird would topple the immense mass over, crashing against the trees.

It was a very familiar thing to Pierre; he had often climbed it, by placing long poles against it, and so creeping up to where it sloped in little crumbling stepping-places; or by climbing high up the neighboring beeches, and then lowering himself down upon the forehead-like summit by the elastic branches. But never had he been fearless enough—or rather fool-hardy enough, it may be, to crawl on the ground beneath the vacancy of the higher end; that spot first menaced by the Terror Stone should it ever really topple.

V

Yet now advancing steadily, and as if by some interior predetermination, and eying the mass unfalteringly; he then threw himself prone upon the wood's last year's leaves, and slid himself straight into the horrible interspace, and lay there as dead. He spoke not, for speechless thoughts were in him. These gave place at last to things less and less unspeakable; till at last, from beneath the very brow of the beetlings and the menacings of the Terror Stone came the audible words of Pierre:—

"If the miseries of the undisclosable things in me, shall ever unhorse me from my manhood's seat; if to vow myself all Virtue's and all Truth's, be but to make a trembling, distrusted slave of me; if Life is to prove a burden I can not bear without ignominious cringings; if indeed our actions are all foreordained, and we are Russian serfs to Fate; if invisible devils do titter at us when we most nobly strive; if Life be a cheating dream, and Virtue as unmeaning and unsequeled with any blessing as the midnight mirth of wine; if by sacrificing myself for Duty's sake, my own mother re-sacrifices me; if Duty's self be but a bugbear, and all things are allowable and unpunishable to man;—then do thou, Mute Massiveness, fall on me! Ages thou hast waited; and if these things be thus, then wait no more; for whom better canst thou crush than him who now lies here invoking thee?"

A down-darting bird, all song, swiftly lighted on the unmoved and eternally immovable balancings of the Terror Stone, and cheerfully chirped to Pierre. The tree-boughs bent and waved to the rushes of a sudden, balmy wind; and slowly Pierre crawled forth, and stood haughtily upon his feet, as he owed thanks to none, and went his moody way.

VI

When in his imaginative ruminating moods of early youth, Pierre had christened the wonderful stone by the old resounding name of Memnon, he had done so merely from certain associative remembrances of that Egyptian marvel, of which all Eastern travelers speak. And when the fugitive thought had long ago entered him of desiring that same stone for his head-stone, when he should be no more; then he had only yielded to one of those innumerable fanciful notions, tinged with dreamy painless melancholy, which are frequently suggested to the mind of a poetic boy. But in aftertimes, when placed in far different circumstances from those surrounding him at the Meadows, Pierre pondered on the stone, and his young thoughts concerning it, and, later, his desperate act in crawling under it; then an immense significance came to him, and the long-passed unconscious movements of his then youthful heart, seemed now prophetic to him, and allegorically verified by the subsequent events.

For, not to speak of the other and subtler meanings which lie crouching behind the colossal haunches of this stone, regarded as the menacingly impending Terror Stone—hidden to all the simple cottagers, but revealed to Pierre—consider its aspects as the Memnon Stone. For Memnon was that dewey, royal boy, son of Aurora, and born King of Egypt, who, with enthusiastic rashness flinging himself on another's account into a rightful quarrel, fought hand to hand with his overmatch, and met his boyish and most dolorous death beneath the walls of Troy. His wailing subjects built a monument in Egypt to commemorate his untimely fate. Touched by the breath of the bereaved Aurora, every sunrise that statue gave forth a mournful broken sound, as of a harp-string suddenly sundered, being too harshly wound.

Herein lies an unsummed world of grief. For in this plaintive fable we find embodied the Hamletism of the antique world; the Hamletism of three thousand years ago: "The flower of virtue cropped by a too rare mischance." And the English Tragedy is but Egyptian Memnon, Montaignized and modernized; for being but a mortal man Shakspeare had his fathers too.

Now as the Memnon Statue survives down to this present day, so does that nobly-striving but ever-shipwrecked character in some royal youths (for both Memnon and Hamlet were the sons of kings), of which that statue is the melancholy type. But Memnon's sculptured woes did once melodiously resound; now all is mute. Fit emblem that of old, poetry was a consecration and an obsequy to all hapless modes of human life; but in a bantering, barren, and prosaic, heartless age, Aurora's music-moan is lost among our drifting sands, which whelm alike the monument and the dirge.

vii

As Pierre went on through the woods, all thoughts now left him but those investing Isabel. He strove to condense her mysterious haze into some definite and comprehensible shape. He could not but infer that the feeling of bewilderment, which she had so often hinted of during their interview, had caused her continually to go aside from the straight line of her narration; and finally to end it in an abrupt and enigmatical obscurity. But he also felt assured, that as this was entirely unintended, and now, doubtless, regretted by herself, so their coming second interview would help to clear up much of this mysteriousness; considering that the elapsing interval would do much to tranquilize her, and rally her into less of wonderfulness to him; he did not therefore so much accuse his unthinkingness in naming the postponing hour he had. For, indeed, looking from the morning down the vista of the day, it seemed as indefinite and interminable to him. He could not bring himself to confront any face or house; a plowed field, any sign of tillage, the rotted stump of a long-felled pine, the slightest passing trace of man was uncongenial and repelling to him. Likewise in his own mind all remembrances and imaginings that had to do with the common and general humanity had become, for the time, in the most singular manner distasteful to him. Still, while thus loathing all that was common in the two different worlds—that without, and that within—nevertheless, even in the most withdrawn and subtlest region of his own essential spirit, Pierre could not now find one single agreeable twig of thought whereon to perch his weary soul.

Men in general seldom suffer from this utter pauperism of the spirit. If God hath not blessed them with incurable frivolity, men in general have still some secret thing of self-conceit or virtuous gratulation; men in general have always done some small self-sacrificing deed for some other man; and so, in those now and then recurring hours of despondent lassitude, which must at various and differing intervals overtake almost every civilized human being; such persons straightway bethink them of their one, or two, or three small self-sacrificing things, and suck respite, consolation, and more or less compensating deliciousness from it. But with men of self-disdainful spirits; in whose chosen souls heaven itself hath by a primitive persuasion unindoctrinally fixed that most true Christian doctrine of the utter nothingness of good works; the casual remembrance of their benevolent well-doings, does never distill one drop of comfort for them, even as (in harmony with the correlative Scripture doctrine) the recalling of their outlived errors and misdeeds, conveys to them no slightest pang or shadow of reproach.

Though the clew-defying mysteriousness of Isabel's narration, did now for the time, in this particular mood of his, put on a repelling aspect to our Pierre; yet something must occupy the soul of man; and Isabel was nearest to him then; and Isabel he thought of; at first, with great discomfort and with pain, but anon (for heaven eventually rewards the resolute and duteous thinker) with lessening repugnance, and at last with still-increasing willingness and congenialness. Now he recalled his first impressions, here and there, while she was rehearsing to him her wild tale; he recalled those swift but mystical corroborations in his own mind and memory, which by shedding another twinkling light upon her history, had but increased its mystery, while at the same time remarkably substantiating it.

Her first recallable recollection was of an old deserted chateau-like house in a strange, French-like country, which she dimly imagined to be somewhere beyond the sea. Did not this surprisingly correspond with certain natural inferences to be drawn from his Aunt Dorothea's account of the disappearance of the French young lady? Yes; the French young lady's disappearance on this side the water was only contingent upon her reappearance on the other; then he shuddered as he darkly pictured the possible sequel of her life, and the wresting from her of her infant, and its immurement in the savage mountain wilderness.

But Isabel had also vague impressions of herself crossing the sea;—*re*-crossing, emphatically thought Pierre, as he pondered on the unbidden conceit, that she had probably first unconsciously and smuggledly crossed it hidden beneath her sorrowing mother's heart. But in attempting to draw any inferences, from what he himself had ever heard, for a coinciding proof or elucidation of this assumption of Isabel's actual crossing the sea at so tender an age; here Pierre felt all the inadequateness of both his own and Isabel's united knowledge, to clear up the profound mysteriousness of her early life. To the certainty of this irremovable obscurity he bowed himself, and strove to dismiss it from his mind, as worse than hopeless. So, also, in a good degree, did he endeavor to drive out of him, Isabel's reminiscence of the, to her, unnameable large house, from which she had been finally removed by the pleasant woman in the coach. This episode in her life, above all other things, was most cruelly suggestive to him, as possibly involving his father in the privity to a thing, at which Pierre's inmost soul fainted with amazement and abhorrence. Here the helplessness of all further light, and the eternal impossibility of logically exonerating his dead father, in his own mind, from the liability to this, and many other of the blackest self-insinuated suppositions; all this came over Pierre with a power so infernal and intense, that it could only have proceeded from the unretarded malice of the Evil One himself. But subtilly and wantonly as these conceits stole into him, Pierre as subtilly opposed them; and with the hue-and-cry of his whole indignant soul, pursued them forth again into the wide Tartarean realm from which they had emerged.

The more and the more that Pierre now revolved the story of Isabel in his mind, so much the more he amended his original idea, that much of its obscurity would depart upon a second interview. He saw, or seemed to see, that it was not so much Isabel who had by her wild idiosyncrasies mystified the narration of her history, as it was the essential and unavoidable mystery of her history itself, which had invested Isabel with such wonderful enigmas to him.

viii

The issue of these reconsiderings was the conviction, that all he could now reasonably anticipate from Isabel, in further disclosure on the subject of her life, were some few additional particulars bringing it down to the present moment; and, also, possibly filling out the latter portion of what she had already revealed to him. Nor here, could he persuade himself, that she would have much to say. Isabel had not been so digressive and withholding as he had thought. What more, indeed, could she now have to impart, except by what strange means she had at last come to find her brother out; and the dreary recital of how she had pecuniarily wrestled with her destitute condition; how she had come to leave one place of toiling refuge for another, till now he found her in humble servitude at farmer Ulver's? Is it possible then, thought Pierre, that there lives a human creature in this common world of every-days, whose whole history may be told in little less than two-score words, and yet embody in that smallness a fathomless fountain of ever-welling mystery? Is it possible, after all, that spite of bricks and shaven faces, this world we live in is brimmed with wonders, and I and all mankind, beneath our garbs of common-placeness, conceal enigmas that the stars themselves, and perhaps the highest seraphim can not resolve?

The intuitively certain, however literally unproven fact of Isabel's sisterhood to him, was a link that he now felt binding him to a before unimagined and endless chain of wondering. His very blood seemed to flow through all his arteries with unwonted subtileness, when he thought that the same tide flowed through the mystic veins of Isabel. All his occasional pangs of dubiousness as to the grand governing thing of all—the reality of the physical relationship—only recoiled back upon him with added tribute of both certainty and insolubleness.

She is my sister—my own father's daughter. Well; why do I believe it? The other day I had not so much as heard the remotest rumor of her existence; and what has since occurred to change me? What so new and incontestable vouchers have I handled? None at all. But I have seen her. Well; grant it; I might have seen a thousand other girls, whom I had never seen before; but for that, I would not own any one among them for my sister. But the portrait, the chair-portrait, Pierre? Think of that. But that was painted before Isabel was born; what can that portrait have to do with Isabel? It is not the portrait of Isabel, it is my father's portrait; and yet my mother swears it is not he.

Now alive as he was to all these searching argumentative itemizings of the minutest known facts any way bearing upon the subject; and yet, at the same time, persuaded, strong as death, that in spite of them, Isabel was indeed his sister; how could Pierre, naturally poetic, and therefore piercing as he was; how could he fail to acknowledge the existence of that all-controlling and all-permeating wonderfulness, which, when imperfectly and isolatedly recognized by the generality, is so significantly denominated The Finger of God? But it is not merely the Finger, it is the whole outspread Hand of God; for doth not Scripture intimate, that He holdeth all of us in the hollow of His hand?—a Hollow, truly!

Still wandering through the forest, his eye pursuing its ever-shifting shadowy vistas; remote from all visible haunts and traces of that strangely wilful race, who, in the sordid traffickings of clay and mud, are ever seeking to denationalize the natural heavenliness of their souls; there came into the mind of Pierre, thoughts and fancies never imbibed within the gates of towns; but only given forth by the atmosphere of primeval forests, which, with the eternal ocean, are the only unchanged general objects remaining to this day, from those that originally met the gaze of Adam. For so it is, that the apparently most inflammable or evaporable of all earthly things, wood and water, are, in this view, immensely the most endurable.

Now all his ponderings, however excursive, wheeled round Isabel as their center; and back to her they came again from every excursion; and again derived some new, small germs for wonderment.

The question of Time occurred to Pierre. How old was Isabel? According to all reasonable inferences from the presumed circumstances of her life, she was his elder, certainly, though by uncertain years; yet her whole aspect was that of more than childlikeness; nevertheless, not only did he feel his muscular superiority to her, so to speak, which made him spontaneously alive to a feeling of elderly protectingness over her; not only did he experience the thoughts of superior world-acquaintance, and general cultured knowledge; but spite of reason's self, and irrespective of all mere computings, he was conscious of a feeling which independently pronounced him her senior in point of Time, and Isabel a child of everlasting youngness. This strange, though strong conceit of his mysterious persuasion, doubtless, had its untraced, and but little-suspected origin in his mind, from ideas born of his devout meditations upon the artless infantileness of her face; which, though profoundly mournful in the general expression, yet did not, by any means, for that cause, lose one whit in its singular infantileness; as the faces of real infants, in their earliest visibleness, do oft-times wear a look of deep and endless sadness. But it was not the sadness, nor indeed, strictly speaking, the infantileness of the face of Isabel which so singularly impressed him with the idea of her original and changeless youthfulness. It was something else; yet something which entirely eluded him.

Imaginatively exalted by the willing suffrages of all mankind into higher and purer realms than men themselves inhabit; beautiful women—those of them at least who are beautiful in soul as well as body—do, notwithstanding the relentless law of earthly fleetingness, still seem, for a long interval, mysteriously exempt from the incantations of decay; for as the outward loveliness touch by touch departs, the interior beauty touch by touch replaces that departing bloom, with charms, which, underivable from earth, possess the ineffaceableness of stars. Else, why at the age of sixty, have some women held in the strongest bonds of love and fealty, men young enough to be their grandsons? And why did all-seducing Ninon unintendingly break scores of hearts at seventy? It is because of the perennialness of womanly sweetness.

Out from the infantile, yet eternal mournfulness of the face of Isabel, there looked on Pierre that angelic childlikeness, which our Savior hints is the one only investiture of translated souls; for of such—even of little children—is the other world.

Now, unending as the wonderful rivers, which once bathed the feet of the primeval generations, and still remain to flow fast by the graves of all succeeding men, and by the beds of all now living; unending, ever-flowing, ran through the soul of Pierre, fresh and fresher, further and still further, thoughts of Isabel. But the more his thoughtful river ran, the more mysteriousness it floated to him; and yet the more certainty that the mysteriousness was unchangeable. In her life there was an unraveled plot; and he felt that unraveled it would eternally remain to him. No slightest hope or dream had he, that what was dark and mournful in her would ever be cleared up into some coming atmosphere of light and mirth. Like all youths, Pierre had conned his novel-lessons; had read more novels than most persons of his years; but their false, inverted attempts at systematizing eternally unsystemizable elements; their audacious, intermeddling impotency, in trying to unravel, and spread out, and classify, the more thin than gossamer threads which make up the complex web of life; these things over Pierre had no power now. Straight through their helpless miserableness he pierced; the one sensational truth in him, transfixed like beetles all the speculative lies in them. He saw that human life doth truly come from that, which all men are agreed to call by the name of *God;* and that it partakes of the unravelable inscrutableness of God. By infallible presentiment he saw, that not always doth life's beginning gloom conclude in gladness; that wedding-bells peal not ever in the last scene of life's fifth act; that while the countless tribes of common novels laboriously spin vails of mystery, only to complacently clear them up at last; and while the countless tribe of common dramas do but repeat the same; yet the profounder emanations of the human mind, intended to illustrate all that can be humanly known of human life; these never unravel their own intricacies, and have no proper endings; but in imperfect, unanticipated, and disappointing sequels (as mutilated stumps), hurry to abrupt intermergings with the eternal tides of time and fate.

So Pierre renounced all thought of ever having Isabel's dark-lantern illuminated to him. Her light was lidded, and the lid was locked. Nor did he feel a pang at this. By posting hither and thither among the reminiscences of his family, and craftily interrogating his remaining relatives on his father's side, he might possibly rake forth some few small grains of dubious and most unsatisfying things, which, were he that way strongly bent, would only serve the more hopelessly to cripple him in his practical resolves. He determined to pry not at all into this sacred problem. For him now the mystery of Isabel possessed all the bewitchingness of the mysterious vault of night, whose very darkness evokes the witchery.

The thoughtful river still ran on in him, and now it floated still another thing to him.

Though the letter of Isabel gushed with all a sister's sacred longings to embrace her brother, and in the most abandoned terms painted the anguish of her life-long estrangement from him; and though, in effect, it took vows to this,—that without his continual love and sympathy, further life for her was only fit to be thrown into the nearest unfathomed pool, or rushing stream; yet when the brother and the sister had encountered, according to the set appointment, none of these impassionedments had been repeated. She had more than thrice thanked God, and most earnestly blessed himself, that now he had come near to her in her loneliness; but no gesture of common and customary sisterly affection. Nay, from his embrace had she not struggled? nor kissed him once; nor had he kissed her, except when the salute was solely sought by him.

Now Pierre began to see mysteries interpierced with mysteries, and mysteries eluding mysteries; and began to seem to see the mere imaginariness of the so supposed solidest principle of human association. Fate had done this thing for them. Fate had separated the brother and the sister, till to each other they somehow seemed so not at all. Sisters shrink not from their brother's kisses. And Pierre felt that never, never would he be able to embrace Isabel with the mere brotherly embrace; while the thought of any other caress, which took hold of any domesticness, was entirely vacant from his uncontaminated soul, for it had never consciously intruded there.

Therefore, forever unsistered for him by the stroke of Fate, and apparently forever, and twice removed from the remotest possibility of that love which had drawn him to his Lucy; yet still the object of the ardentest and deepest emotions of his soul; therefore, to him, Isabel wholly soared out of the realms of mortalness, and for him became transfigured in the highest heaven of uncorrupted Love.

Book VIII

The Second Interview at the Farm-House, and the Second Part of the Story of Isabel • Their Immediate Impulsive Effect upon Pierre

HIS SECOND INTERVIEW with Isabel was more satisfying, but none the less affecting and mystical than the first, though in the beginning, to his no small surprise, it was far more strange and embarrassing.

As before, Isabel herself admitted him into the farm-house, and spoke no word to him till they were both seated in the room of the double casement, and himself had first addressed her. If Pierre had any way predetermined how to deport himself at the moment, it was to manifest by some outward token the utmost affection for his sister; but her rapt silence and that atmosphere of unearthliness which invested her, now froze him to his seat; his arms refused to open, his lips refused to meet in the fraternal kiss; while all the while his heart was overflowing with the deepest love, and he knew full well, that his presence was inexpressibly grateful to the girl. Never did love and reverence so intimately react and blend; never did pity so join with wonder in casting a spell upon the movements of his body, and impeding him in its command.

After a few embarrassed words from Pierre, and a brief reply, a pause ensued, during which not only was the slow, soft stepping overhead quite audible, as at intervals on the night before, but also some slight domestic sounds were heard from the adjoining room; and noticing the unconsciously interrogating expression of Pierre's face, Isabel thus spoke to him:

"I feel, my brother, that thou dost appreciate the peculiarity and the mystery of my life, and of myself, and therefore I am at rest concerning the possibility of thy misconstruing any of my actions. It is only when people refuse to admit the uncommonness of some persons and the circumstances surrounding them, that erroneous conceits are nourished, and their feelings pained. My brother, if ever I shall seem reserved and unembracing to thee, still thou must ever trust the heart of Isabel, and permit no doubt to cross thee there. My brother, the sounds thou hast just overheard in yonder room, have suggested to thee interesting questions connected with myself. Do not speak; I fervently understand thee. I will tell thee upon what terms I have been living here; and how it is that I, a hired person, am enabled to receive thee in this seemly privacy; for as thou mayest very readily imagine, this room is not my own. And this reminds me also that I have yet some few further trifling things to tell thee respecting the circumstances which have ended in bestowing upon me so angelical a brother."

"I can not retain that word"—said Pierre, with earnest lowness, and drawing a little nearer to her—"of right, it only pertains to thee."

"My brother, I will now go on, and tell thee all that I think thou couldst wish to know, in addition to what was so dimly rehearsed last night. Some three months ago, the people of the distant farm-house, where I was then staying, broke up their household and departed for some Western country. No place immediately presented itself where my services were wanted, but I was hospitably received at an old neighbor's hearth, and most kindly invited to tarry there, till some employ should offer. But I did not wait for chance to help me; my inquiries resulted in ascertaining the sad story of Delly Ulver, and that through the fate which had overtaken her, her aged parents were not only plunged into the most poignant grief, but were deprived of the domestic help of an only daughter, a circumstance whose deep discomfort can not be easily realized by persons who have always been ministered to by servants. Though indeed my natural mood—if I may call it so, for want of a better term—was strangely touched by thinking that the misery of Delly should be the source of benefit to me; yet this had no practically operative effect upon me,—my most inmost and truest thoughts seldom have;—and so I came hither, and my hands will testify that I did not come entirely for naught. Now, my brother, since thou didst leave me yesterday, I have felt no small surprise, that thou didst not then seek from me, how and when I came to learn the name of Glendinning as so closely associated with myself;

and how I came to know Saddle Meadows to be the family seat, and how I at last resolved upon addressing thee, Pierre, and none other; and to what may be attributed that very memorable scene in the sewing-circle at the Miss Pennies."

"I have myself been wondering at myself that these things should hitherto have so entirely absented themselves from my mind," responded Pierre;—"but truly, Isabel, thy all-abounding hair falls upon me with some spell which dismisses all ordinary considerations from me, and leaves me only sensible to the Nubian power in thine eyes. But go on, and tell me every thing and any thing. I desire to know all, Isabel, and yet, nothing which thou wilt not voluntarily disclose. I feel that already I know the pith of all; that already I feel toward thee to the very limit of all; and that, whatever remains for thee to tell me, can but corroborate and confirm. So go on, my dearest,—ay, my only sister."

Isabel fixed her wonderful eyes upon him with a gaze of long impassionment; then rose suddenly to her feet, and advanced swiftly toward him; but more suddenly paused, and reseated herself in silence, and continued so for a time, with her head averted from him, and mutely resting on her hand, gazing out of the open casement upon the soft heat-lightning, occasionally revealed there.

She resumed anon.

ii

"My brother, thou wilt remember that certain part of my story which in reference to my more childish years spent remote from here, introduced the gentleman—my—yes, *our* father, Pierre. I can not describe to thee, for indeed, I do not myself comprehend how it was, that though at the time I sometimes called him my father, and the people of the house also called him so, sometimes when speaking of him to me; yet—partly, I suppose, because of the extraordinary secludedness of my previous life—I did not then join in my mind with the word father, all those peculiar associations which the term ordinarily inspires in children. The word father only seemed a word of general love and endearment to me—little or nothing more; it did not seem to involve any claims of any sort, one way or the other. I did not ask the name of my father; for I could have had no motive to hear him named, except to individualize the person who was so peculiarly kind to me; and individualized in that way he already was, since he was generally called by us *the gentleman*, and sometimes *my father*. As I have no reason to suppose that had I then or afterward, questioned the people of the house as to what more particular name my father went by in the world, they would have at all disclosed it to me; and, indeed, since, for certain singular reasons, I now feel convinced that on that point they were pledged to secrecy; I do not know that I ever would have come to learn my father's name,—and by consequence, ever have learned the least shade or shadow of knowledge as to you, Pierre, or any of your kin—had it not been for the merest little accident, which early revealed it to me, though at the moment I did not know the value of that knowledge. The last time my father visited the house, he chanced to leave his handkerchief behind him. It was the farmer's wife who first discovered it. She picked it up, and fumbling at it a moment, as if rapidly examining the corners, tossed it to me, saying, 'Here, Isabel, here is the good gentleman's handkerchief; keep it for him now, till he comes to see little Bell again.' Gladly I caught the handkerchief, and put it into my bosom. It was a white one; and upon closely scanning it, I found a small line of fine faded yellowish writing in the middle of it. At that time I could not read either print or writing, so I was none the wiser then; but still, some secret instinct told me, that the woman would not so freely have given me the handkerchief, had she known there was any writing on it. I forbore questioning her on the subject; I waited till my father should return, to secretly question him. The handkerchief had become dusty by lying on the uncarpeted floor. I took it to the brook and washed it, and laid it out on the grass where none would chance to pass; and I ironed it under my little apron, so that none would be attracted to it, to look at it again. But my father never returned; so, in my grief, the handkerchief became the more and the more endeared to me; it absorbed many of the secret tears I wept in memory of my dear departed friend, whom, in my child-like ignorance, I then equally called *my father* and *the gentleman*. But when the impression of his death became a fixed thing to me, then again I washed and dried and ironed the precious memorial of him, and put it away where none should find it but myself, and resolved never more to soil it with my tears; and I folded it in such a manner, that the name was invisibly buried in the heart of it, and it was like opening a book and turning over many blank leaves before I came to the mysterious writing, which I knew should be one day read by me, without direct help from any one. Now I resolved to learn my letters, and learn to read, in order that of myself I might learn the meaning of those faded characters. No other purpose but that only one, did I have in learning then to read. I easily induced the woman to give me my little teachings, and being uncommonly quick, and moreover, most eager to learn, I soon mastered the alphabet, and went on to spelling, and by-and-by to reading, and at last to the complete deciphering of the talismanic word—Glendinning. I was yet very ignorant. *Glendinning*, thought I, what is that? It sounds something like *gentleman*;—Glen-din-ning;—just as many syllables as *gentleman;* and—G—it begins with the same letter; yes, it must mean *my father*. I will think of him by that word now;—I will not think of the *gentleman*, but of *Glendinning*. When at last I removed from that house and went to another, and still another, and as I still grew up and thought more to myself, that word was ever humming in my head, I saw it would only prove the key to more. But I repressed all undue curiosity, if any such has ever filled my breast. I would not ask of any one, who it was that had been Glendinning; where he had lived; whether, ever any other girl or boy had called him father as I had done. I resolved to hold myself in perfect patience, as somehow mystically certain, that Fate would at last disclose to me, of itself, and at the suitable time, whatever Fate thought it best for me to know. But now, my brother, I must go aside a little for a moment.—Hand me the guitar."

Surprised and rejoiced thus far at the unanticipated newness, and the sweet lucidness and simplicity of Isabel's narrating, as compared with the obscure and marvelous revelations of the night before, and all eager for her to continue her story in the same limpid manner, but remembering into what a wholly tumultuous and unearthly frame of mind the melodies of her guitar had formerly thrown him; Pierre now, in handing the instrument to Isabel, could not entirely restrain something like a look of half-regret, accompanied rather strangely with a half-smile of gentle humor. It did not pass unnoticed by his sister, who receiving the guitar, looked up into his face with an expression which would almost have been arch and playful, were it not for the ever-abiding shadows cast from her infinite hair into her unfathomed eyes, and redoubledly shot back again from them.

"Do not be alarmed, my brother; and do not smile at me; I am not going to play the Mystery of Isabel to thee to-night. Draw nearer to me now. Hold the light near to me."

So saying she loosened some ivory screws of the guitar, so as to open a peep lengthwise through its interior.

"Now hold it thus, my brother; thus; and see what thou wilt see; but wait one instant till I hold the lamp." So saying, as Pierre held the instrument before him as directed, Isabel held the lamp so as to cast its light through the round sounding-hole into the heart of the guitar.

"Now, Pierre, now."

Eagerly Pierre did as he was bid; but somehow felt disappointed, and yet surprised at what he saw. He saw the word *Isabel*, quite legibly but still fadedly gilded upon a part of one side of the interior, where it made a projecting curve.

"A very curious place thou hast chosen, Isabel, wherein to have the ownership of the guitar engraved. How did ever any person get in there to do it, I should like to know?"

The girl looked surprisedly at him a moment; then took the instrument from him, and looked into it herself. She put it down, and continued.

"I see, my brother, thou dost not comprehend. When one knows every thing about any object, one is too apt to suppose that the slightest hint will suffice to throw it quite as open to any other person. *I* did not have the name gilded there, my brother."

"How?" cried Pierre.

"The name was gilded there when I first got the guitar, though then I did not know it. The guitar must have been expressly made for some one by the name of Isabel; because the lettering could only have been put there before the guitar was put together."

"Go on—hurry," said Pierre.

"Yes, one day, after I had owned it a long time, a strange whim came into me. Thou know'st that it is not at all uncommon for children to break their dearest playthings in order to gratify a half-crazy curiosity to find out what is in the hidden heart of them. So it is with children, sometimes. And, Pierre, I have always been, and feel that I must always continue to be a child, though I should grow to three score years and ten. Seized with this sudden whim, I unscrewed the part I showed thee, and peeped in, and saw 'Isabel.' Now I have not yet told thee, that from as early a time as I can remember, I have nearly always gone by the name of Bell. And at the particular time I now speak of, my knowledge of general and trivial matters was sufficiently advanced to make it quite a familiar thing to me, that Bell was often a diminutive for Isabella, or Isabel. It was therefore no very strange affair, that considering my age, and other connected circumstances at the time, I should have instinctively associated the word Isabel, found in the guitar, with my own abbreviated name, and so be led into all sorts of fancyings. They return upon me now. Do not speak to me."

She leaned away from him, toward the occasionally illuminated casement, in the same manner as on the previous night, and for a few moments seemed struggling with some wild bewilderment. But now she suddenly turned, and fully confronted Pierre with all the wonderfulness of her most surprising face.

"I am called woman, and thou, man, Pierre; but there is neither man nor woman about it. Why should I not speak out to thee? There is no sex in our immaculateness. Pierre, the secret name in the guitar even now thrills me through and through. Pierre, think! think! Oh, canst thou not comprehend? see it?—what I mean, Pierre? The secret name in the guitar thrills me, thrills me, whirls me, whirls me; so secret, wholly hidden, yet constantly carried about in it; unseen, unsuspected, always vibrating to the hidden heart-strings—broken heart-strings; oh, my mother, my mother, my mother!"

As the wild plaints of Isabel pierced into his bosom's core, they carried with them the first inkling of the extraordinary conceit, so vaguely and shrinkingly hinted at in her till now entirely unintelligible words.

She lifted her dry burning eyes of long-fringed fire to him.

"Pierre—I have no slightest proof—but the guitar was *hers*, I know, I feel it was. Say, did I not last night tell thee, how it first sung to me upon the bed, and answered me, without my once touching it? and how it always sung to me and answered me, and soothed and loved me,—Hark now; thou shalt hear my mother's spirit."

She carefully scanned the strings, and tuned them carefully; then placed the guitar in the casement-bench, and knelt before it; and in low, sweet, and changefully modulated notes, so barely audible, that Pierre bent over to catch them; breathed the word *mother, mother, mother!* There was profound silence for a time; when suddenly, to the lowest and least audible note of all, the magical untouched guitar responded with a quick spark of melody, which in the following hush, long vibrated and subsidingly tingled through the room; while to his augmented wonder, he now espied, quivering along the metallic strings of the guitar, some minute scintillations, seemingly caught from the instrument's close proximity to the occasionally irradiated window.

The girl still kept kneeling; but an altogether unwonted expression suddenly overcast her whole countenance. She darted one swift glance at Pierre; and then with a single toss of her hand tumbled her unrestrained locks all over her, so that they tent-wise invested her whole kneeling form close to the floor, and yet swept the floor with their wild redundancy. Never Saya of Limeean girl, at dim mass in St. Dominic's cathedral, so completely muffled the human figure. To Pierre, the deep oaken recess of the double-casement, before which Isabel was kneeling, seemed now the immediate vestibule of some awful shrine, mystically revealed through the obscurely open window, which ever and anon was still softly illumined by the mild heat-lightnings and ground-lightnings, that wove their wonderfulness without, in the unsearchable air of that ebonly warm and most noiseless summer night.

Some unsubduable word was on Pierre's lip, but a sudden voice from out the vail bade him be silent.

"Mother—mother—mother!"

Again, after a preluding silence, the guitar as magically responded as before; the sparks quivered along its strings; and again Pierre felt as in the immediate presence of the spirit.

"Shall I, mother?—Art thou ready? Wilt thou tell me?—Now? Now?"

These words were lowly and sweetly murmured in the same way with the word *mother*, being changefully varied in their modulations, till at the last *now*, the magical guitar again responded; and the girl swiftly drew it to her beneath her dark tent of hair. In this act, as the long curls swept over the strings of the guitar, the strange sparks—still quivering there—caught at those attractive curls; the entire casement was suddenly and wovenly illumined; then waned again; while now, in the succeeding dimness, every downward undulating wave and billow of Isabel's tossed tresses gleamed here and there like a tract of phosphorescent midnight sea; and, simultaneously, all the four winds of the world of melody broke loose; and again as on the previous night, only in a still more subtile, and wholly inexplicable way, Pierre felt himself surrounded by ten thousand sprites and gnomes, and his whole soul was swayed and tossed by supernatural tides; and again he heard the wondrous, rebounding, chanted words:

"Mystery! Mystery!
Mystery of Isabel!
Mystery! Mystery!
Isabel and Mystery!
Mystery!"

iii

Almost deprived of consciousness by the spell flung over him by the marvelous girl, Pierre unknowingly gazed away from her, as on vacancy; and when at last stillness had once more fallen upon the room—all except the stepping—and he recovered his self-possession, and turned to look where he might now be, he was surprised to see Isabel composedly, though avertedly, seated on the bench; the longer and fuller tresses of her now ungleaming hair flung back, and the guitar quietly leaning in the corner.

He was about to put some unconsidered question to her, but she half-anticipated it by bidding him, in a low, but nevertheless almost authoritative tone, not to make any allusion to the scene he had just beheld.

He paused, profoundly thinking to himself, and now felt certain that the entire scene, from the first musical invocation of the guitar, must have unpremeditatedly proceeded from a sudden impulse in the girl, inspired by the peculiar mood into which the preceding conversation, and especially the handling of the guitar under such circumstances, had irresistibly thrown her.

But that certain something of the preternatural in the scene, of which he could not rid his mind:—the, so to speak, voluntary and all but intelligent responsiveness of the guitar—its strangely scintillating strings—the so suddenly glorified head of Isabel; altogether, these things seemed not at the time entirely produced by customary or natural causes. To Pierre's dilated senses Isabel seemed to swim in an electric fluid; the vivid buckler of her brow seemed as a magnetic plate. Now first this night was Pierre made aware of what, in the superstitiousness of his rapt enthusiasm, he could not help believing was an extraordinary physical magnetism in Isabel. And—as it were derived from this marvelous quality thus imputed to her—he now first became vaguely sensible of a certain still more marvelous power in the girl over himself and his most interior thoughts and motions;—a power so hovering upon the confines of the invisible world, that it seemed more inclined that way than this;—a power which not only seemed irresistibly to draw him toward Isabel, but to draw him away from another quarter—wantonly as it were, and yet quite ignorantly and unintendingly; and, besides, without respect apparently to any thing ulterior, and yet again, only under cover of drawing him to her. For over all these things, and interfusing itself with the sparkling electricity in which she seemed to swim, was an ever-creeping and condensing haze of ambiguities. Often, in after-times with her, did he recall this first magnetic night, and would seem to see that she then had bound him to her by an extraordinary atmospheric spell—both physical and spiritual—which henceforth it had become impossible for him to break, but whose full potency he never recognized till long after he had become habituated to its sway. This spell seemed one with that Pantheistic master-spell, which eternally locks in mystery and in muteness the universal subject world, and the physical electricalness of Isabel seemed reciprocal with the heat-lightnings and the ground-lightnings nigh to which it had first become revealed to Pierre. She seemed molded from fire and air, and vivified at some Voltaic pile of August thunder-clouds heaped against the sunset.

The occasional sweet simplicity, and innocence, and humbleness of her story; her often serene and open aspect; her deep-seated, but mostly quiet, unobtrusive sadness, and that touchingness of her less unwonted tone and air; —these only the more signalized and contrastingly emphasized the profounder, subtler, and more mystic part of her. Especially did Pierre feel this, when after another silent interval, she now proceeded with her story in a manner so gently confiding, so entirely artless, so almost peasant-like in its simplicity, and dealing in some details so little sublimated in themselves, that it seemed well nigh impossible that this unassuming maid should be the same dark, regal being who had but just now bade Pierre be silent in so imperious a tone, and around whose wondrous temples the strange electric glory had been playing. Yet not very long did she now thus innocently proceed, ere, at times, some fainter flashes of her electricalness came from her, but only to be followed by such melting, human, and most feminine traits as brought all his soft, enthusiast tears into the sympathetic but still unshedding eyes of Pierre.

iv

"Thou rememberest, my brother, my telling thee last night, how the—the—thou knowest what I mean—*that, there*"—avertedly pointing to the guitar; "thou rememberest how it came into my possession. But perhaps I did not tell thee, that the pedler said he had got it in barter from the servants of a great house some distance from the place where I was then residing."

Pierre signed his acquiescence, and Isabel proceeded:

"Now, at long though stated intervals, that man passed the farm-house in his trading route between the small towns and villages. When I discovered the gilding in the guitar, I kept watch for him; for though I truly felt persuaded that Fate had the dispensing of her own secrets in her own good time; yet I also felt persuaded that in some cases Fate drops us one little hint, leaving our own minds to follow it up, so that we of ourselves may come to the grand secret in reserve. So I kept diligent watch for him; and the next time he stopped, without permitting him at all to guess my motives, I contrived to steal out of him what great house it was from which the guitar had come. And, my brother, it was the mansion of Saddle Meadows."

Pierre started, and the girl went on:

"Yes, my brother, Saddle Meadows; 'old General Glendinning's place,' he said; 'but the old hero's long dead and gone now; and—the more's the pity—so is the young General, his son, dead and gone; but then there is a still younger grandson General left; that family always keep the title and the name a-going; yes, even to the christian name,—Pierre. Pierre Glendinning was the white-haired old General's name, who fought in the old French and Indian wars; and Pierre Glendinning is his young great-grandson's name.' Thou may'st well look at me so, my brother;—yes, he meant thee, *thee*, my brother."

"But the guitar—the guitar!"—cried Pierre—"how came the guitar openly at Saddle Meadows, and how came it to be bartered away by servants? Tell me that, Isabel!"

"Do not put such impetuous questions to me, Pierre; else thou mayst recall the old—may be, it is the evil spell upon me. I can not precisely and knowingly answer thee. I could surmise; but what are surmises worth? Oh, Pierre, better, a million times, and far sweeter are mysteries than surmises: though the mystery be unfathomable, it is still the unfathomableness of fullness; but the surmise, that is but shallow and unmeaning emptiness."

"But this is the most inexplicable point of all. Tell me, Isabel; surely thou must have thought something about this thing."

"Much, Pierre, very much; but only about the mystery of it—nothing more. Could I, I would not now be fully told, how the guitar came to be at Saddle Meadows, and came to be bartered away by the servants of Saddle Meadows. Enough, that it found me out, and came to me, and spoke and sung to me, and soothed me, and has been every thing to me."

She paused a moment; while vaguely to his secret self Pierre revolved these strange revealings; but now he was all attention again as Isabel resumed.

"I now held in my mind's hand the clew, my brother. But I did not immediately follow it further up. Sufficient to me in my loneliness was the knowledge, that I now knew where my father's family was to be found. As yet not the slightest intention of ever disclosing myself to them, had entered my mind. And assured as I was, that for obvious reasons, none of his surviving relatives could possibly know me, even if they saw me, for what I really was, I felt entire security in the event of encountering any of them by chance. But my unavoidable displacements and migrations from one house to another, at last brought me within twelve miles of Saddle Meadows. I began to feel an increasing longing in me; but side by side with it, a newborn and competing pride,—yes, pride, Pierre. Do my eyes flash? They belie me, if they do not. But it is no common pride, Pierre; for what has

Isabel to be proud of in this world? It is the pride of—of—a too, too longing, loving heart, Pierre—the pride of lasting suffering and grief, my brother! Yes, I conquered the great longing with the still more powerful pride, Pierre; and so I would not now be here, in this room,—nor wouldst thou ever have received any line from me; nor, in all worldly probability, ever so much as heard of her who is called Isabel Banford, had it not been for my hearing that at Walter Ulver's, only three miles from the mansion of Saddle Meadows, poor Bell would find people kind enough to give her wages for her work. Feel my hand, my brother."

"Dear divine girl, my own exalted Isabel!" cried Pierre, catching the offered hand with ungovernable emotion, "how most unbeseeming, that this strange hardness, and this still stranger littleness should be united in any human hand. But hard and small, it by an opposite analogy hints of the soft capacious heart that made the hand so hard with heavenly submission to thy most undeserved and martyred lot. Would, Isabel, that these my kisses on the hand, were on the heart itself, and dropt the seeds of eternal joy and comfort there."

He leaped to his feet, and stood before her with such warm, god-like majesty of love and tenderness, that the girl gazed up at him as though he were the one benignant star in all her general night.

"Isabel," cried Pierre, "I stand the sweet penance in my father's stead, thou, in thy mother's. By our earthly acts we shall redeemingly bless both their eternal lots; we will love with the pure and perfect love of angel to an angel. If ever I fall from thee, dear Isabel, may Pierre fall from himself; fall back forever into vacant nothingness and night!"

"My brother, my brother, speak not so to me; it is too much; unused to any love ere now, thine, so heavenly and immense, falls crushing on me! Such love is almost hard to bear as hate. Be still; do not speak to me."

They were both silent for a time; when she went on.

"Yes, my brother, Fate had now brought me within three miles of thee; and—but shall I go straight on, and tell thee all, Pierre? all? every thing? art thou of such divineness, that I may speak straight on, in all my thoughts, heedless whither they may flow, or what things they may float to me?"

"Straight on, and fearlessly," said Pierre.

"By chance I saw thy mother, Pierre, and under such circumstances that I *knew* her to be thy mother; and—but shall I go on?"

"Straight on, my Isabel; thou didst see my mother—well?"

"And when I saw her, though I spake not to her, nor she to me, yet straightway my heart knew that she would love me not."

"Thy heart spake true," muttered Pierre to himself; "go on."

"I re-swore an oath never to reveal myself to thy mother."

"Oath well sworn," again he muttered; "go on."

"But I saw *thee*, Pierre; and, more than ever filled my mother toward thy father, Pierre, then upheaved in me. Straightway I knew that if ever I should come to be made known to thee, then thy own generous love would open itself to me."

"Again thy heart spake true," he murmured; "go on—and didst thou re-swear again?"

"No, Pierre; but yes, I did. I swore that thou wert my brother; with love and pride I swore, that young and noble Pierre Glendinning was my brother!"

"And only that?"

"Nothing more, Pierre; not to thee even, did I ever think to reveal myself."

"How then? thou *art* revealed to me."

"Yes; but the great God did it, Pierre—not poor Bell. Listen.

"I felt very dreary here; poor, dear Delly—thou must have heard something of her story—a most sorrowful house, Pierre. Hark! that is her seldom-pausing pacing thou hearest from the floor above. So she keeps ever pacing, pacing, pacing; in her track, all thread-bare, Pierre, is her chamber-rug. Her father will not look upon her; her mother, she hath cursed her to her face. Out of yon chamber, Pierre, Delly hath not stept, for now four weeks and more; nor ever hath she once laid upon her bed; it was last made up five weeks ago; but paces, paces, paces, all through the night, till after twelve; and then sits vacant in her chair. Often I would go to her to comfort her; but she says, 'Nay, nay, nay,' to me through the door; says 'Nay, nay, nay,' and only nay to me, through the bolted door; bolted three weeks ago—when I by cunning arts stole her dead baby from her, and with these fingers, alone, by night, scooped out a hollow, and, seconding heaven's own charitable stroke, buried that sweet, wee symbol of her not unpardonable shame far from the ruthless foot of man—yes, bolted three weeks ago, not once unbolted since; her food I must thrust through the little window in her closet. Pierre, hardly these two handfuls has she eaten in a week."

"Curses, wasp-like, cohere on that villain, Ned, and sting him to his death!" cried Pierre, smit by this most piteous tale. "What can be done for her, sweet Isabel; can Pierre do aught?"

"If thou or I do not, then the ever-hospitable grave will prove her quick refuge, Pierre. Father and mother both, are worse than dead and gone to her. They would have turned her forth, I think, but for my own poor petitionings, unceasing in her behalf."

Pierre's deep concern now gave place to a momentary look of benevolent intelligence.

"Isabel, a thought of benefit to Delly has just entered me; but I am still uncertain how best it may be acted on. Resolved I am though to succor her. Do thou still hold her here yet awhile, by thy sweet petitionings, till my further plans are more matured. Now run on with thy story, and so divert me from the pacing;—her every step steps in my soul."

"Thy noble heart hath many chambers, Pierre; the records of thy wealth, I see, are not bound up in the one poor book of Isabel, my brother. Thou art a visible token, Pierre, of the invisible angel-hoods, which in our darker hours we do sometimes distrust. The gospel of thy acts goes very far, my brother. Were all men like to thee, then were there no men at all,—mankind extinct in seraphim!"

"Praises are for the base, my sister, cunningly to entice them to fair Virtue by our ignorings of the ill in them, and our imputings of the good not theirs. So make not my head to hang, sweet Isabel. Praise me not. Go on now with thy tale."

"I have said to thee, my brother, how most dreary I found it here, and from the first. Wonted all my life to sadness—if it be such—still, this house hath such acuteness in its general grief, such hopelessness and despair of any slightest remedy—that even poor Bell could scarce abide it always, without some little going forth into contrasting scenes. So I went forth into the places of delight, only that I might return more braced to minister in the haunts of woe. For continual unchanging residence therein, doth but bring on woe's stupor, and make us as dead. So I went forth betimes; visiting the neighboring cottages; where there were chattering children, and no one place vacant at the cheerful board. Thus at last I chanced to hear of the Sewing Circle to be held at the Miss Pennies'; and how that they were anxious to press into their kind charity all the maidens of the country round. In various cottages, I was besought to join; and they at length persuaded me; not that I was naturally loth to it, and needed such entreaties; but at first I felt great fear, lest at such a scene I might closely encounter some of the Glendinnings; and that thought was then namelessly repulsive to me. But by stealthy inquiries I learned, that the lady of the manorial-house would not be present;—it proved deceptive information;—but I went; and all the rest thou knowest."

"I do, sweet Isabel, but thou must tell it over to me; and all thy emotions there."

V

"Though but one day hath passed, my brother, since we first met in life, yet thou hast that heavenly magnet in thee, which draws all my soul's interior to thee. I will go on.—Having to wait for a neighbor's wagon, I arrived but late at the Sewing Circle. When I entered, the two joined rooms were very full. With the farmer's girls, our neighbors, I passed along to the further corner, where thou didst see me; and as I went, some heads were turned, and some whisperings I heard, of—'She's the new help at poor Walter Ulver's—the strange girl they've got—she thinks herself 'mazing pretty, I'll be bound;—but nobody knows her—Oh, how demure!—but not over-good, I guess;—I wouldn't be her, not I—mayhap she's some other ruined Delly, run away;—minx!' It was the first time poor Bell had ever mixed in such a general crowded company; and knowing little or nothing of such things, I had thought, that the meeting being for charity's sweet sake, uncharity could find no harbor there; but no doubt it was mere thoughtlessness, not malice in them. Still, it made my heart ache in me sadly; for then I very keenly felt the dread suspiciousness, in which a strange and lonely grief invests itself to common eyes; as if grief itself were not enough, nor innocence any armor to us, but despite must also come, and icy infamy! Miserable returnings then I had—even in the midst of bright-budding girls and full-blown women—miserable returnings then I had of the feeling, the bewildering feeling of the inhumanities I spoke of in my earlier story. But Pierre, blessed Pierre, do not look so sadly and half-reproachfully upon me. Lone and lost though I have been, I love my kind; and charitably and intelligently pity them, who uncharitably and unintelligently do me despite. And thou, *thou*, blessed brother, hast glorified many somber places in my soul, and taught me once for all to know, that my kind are capable of things which would be glorious in angels. So look away from me, dear Pierre, till thou hast taught thine eyes more wonted glances."

"They are vile falsifying telegraphs of me, then, sweet Isabel. What my look was I can not tell, but my heart was only dark with ill-restrained upbraidings against heaven that could unrelentingly see such innocence as thine so suffer. Go on with thy too-touching tale."

"Quietly I sat there sewing, not brave enough to look up at all, and thanking my good star, that had led me to so concealed a nook behind the rest: quietly I sat there, sewing on a flannel shirt, and with each stitch praying God, that whatever heart it might be folded over, the flannel might hold it truly warm; and keep out the wide-world-coldness which I felt myself; and which no flannel, or thickest fur, or any fire then could keep off from me; quietly I sat there sewing, when I heard the announcing words—oh, how deep and ineffaceably engraved they are!—'Ah, dames, dames, Madame Glendinning,—Master Pierre Glendinning.' Instantly, my sharp needle went through my side and stitched my heart; the flannel dropt from my hand; thou heard'st my shriek. But the good people bore me still nearer to the casement close at hand, and threw it open wide; and God's own breath breathed on me; and I rallied; and said it was some merest passing fit—'twas quite over now—I was used to it—they had my heart's best thanks—but would they now only leave me to myself, it were best for me;—I would go on and sew. And thus it came and passed away; and again I sat sewing on the flannel, hoping either that the unanticipated persons would soon depart, or else that some spirit would catch me away from there; I sat sewing on—till, Pierre! Pierre!—without looking up—for that I dared not do at any time that evening—only once—without looking up, or knowing aught but the flannel on my knee, and the needle in my heart, I felt,—Pierre, *felt*—a glance of magnetic meaning on me. Long, I, shrinking, sideways turned to meet it, but could not; till some helping spirit seized me, and all my soul looked up at thee in my full-fronting face. It was enough. Fate was in that moment. All the loneliness of my life, all the choked longings of my soul, now poured over me. I could not away from them. Then first I felt the complete deplorableness of my state; that while thou, my brother, had a mother, and troops of aunts and cousins, and plentiful friends in city and in country—I, I, Isabel, thy own father's daughter, was thrust out of all hearts' gates, and shivered in the winter way. But this was but the least. Not poor Bell can tell thee all the feelings of poor Bell, or what feelings she felt first. It was all one whirl of old and new bewilderings, mixed and slanted with a driving madness. But it was most the sweet, inquisitive, kindly interested aspect of thy face,—so strangely like thy father's, too—the one only being that I first did love—it was that which most stirred the distracting storm in me; most charged me with the immense longings for some one of my blood to know me, and to own me, though but once, and then away. Oh, my dear brother —Pierre! Pierre!—could'st thou take out my heart, and look at it in thy hand, then thou would'st find it all over written, this way and that, and crossed again, and yet again, with continual lines of longings, that found no end but in suddenly calling thee. Call him! Call him! He will come!—so cried my heart to me; so cried the leaves and stars to me, as I that night went home. But pride rose up—the very pride in my own longings,—and as one arm pulled, the other held. So I stood still, and called thee not. But Fate will be Fate, and it was fated. Once having met thy fixed regardful glance; once having seen the full angelicalness in thee, my whole soul was undone by thee; my whole pride was cut off at the root, and soon showed a blighting in the bud; which spread deep into my whole being, till I knew, that utterly decay and die away I must, unless pride let me go, and I, with the one little trumpet of a pen, blew my heart's shrillest blast, and called dear Pierre to me. My soul was full; and as my beseeching ink went tracing o'er the page, my tears contributed their mite, and made a strange alloy. How blest I felt that my so bitterly tear-mingled ink—that last depth of my anguish—would never be visibly known to thee, but the tears would dry upon the page, and all be fair again, ere the so submerged-freighted letter should meet thine eye."

"Ah, there thou wast deceived, poor Isabel," cried Pierre impulsively; "thy tears dried not fair, but dried red, almost like blood; and nothing so much moved my inmost soul as that tragic sight."

"How? how? Pierre, my brother? Dried they red? Oh, horrible! enchantment! most undreamed of!"

"Nay, the ink—the ink! something chemic in it changed thy real tears to seeming blood;—only that, my sister."

"Oh Pierre! thus wonderfully is it—seems to me—that our own hearts do not ever know the extremity of their own sufferings; sometimes we bleed blood, when we think it only water. Of our sufferings, as of our talents, others sometimes are the better judges. But stop me! force me backward to my story! Yet methinks that now thou knowest all;—no, not entirely all. Thou dost not know what planned and winnowed motive I did have in writing thee; nor does poor Bell know that; for poor Bell was too delirious to have planned and winnowed motives then. The impulse in me called thee, not poor Bell. God called thee, Pierre, not poor Bell. Even now, when I have passed one night after seeing thee, and hearkening to all thy full love and graciousness; even now, I stand as one amazed, and feel not what may be coming to me, or what will now befall me, from having so rashly claimed thee for mine. Pierre, now, *now*, this instant a vague anguish fills me. Tell me, by loving me, by owning me, publicly or secretly,—tell me, doth it involve any vital hurt to thee? Speak without reserve; speak honestly; as I do to thee! Speak now, Pierre, and tell me all!"

"Is Love a harm? Can Truth betray to pain? Sweet Isabel, how can hurt come in the path to God? Now, when I know thee all, now did I forget thee, fail to acknowledge thee, and love thee before the wide world's whole brazen width—could I do that; then might'st thou ask thy question reasonably and say—Tell me, Pierre, does not the suffocating in thee of poor Bell's holy claims, does not that involve for thee unending misery? And my truthful soul would echo—Unending misery! Nay, nay, nay. Thou art my sister and I am thy brother; and that part of the world which knows me, shall acknowledge thee; or by heaven I will crush the disdainful world down on its knees to thee, my sweet Isabel!"

"The menacings in thy eyes are dear delights to me; I grow up with thy own glorious stature; and in thee, my brother, I see God's indignant embassador to me, saying—Up, up, Isabel, and take no terms from the common world, but do thou make terms to it, and grind thy fierce rights out of it! Thy catching nobleness unsexes me, my brother; and now I know that in her most exalted moment, then woman no more feels the twin-born softness of her breasts, but feels chain-armor palpitating there!"

Her changed attitude of beautiful audacity; her long scornful hair, that trailed out a disheveled banner; her wonderful transfigured eyes, in which some meteors seemed playing up; all this now seemed to Pierre the work of an invisible enchanter. Transformed she stood before him; and Pierre, bowing low over to her, owned that irrespective, darting majesty of humanity, which can be majestical and menacing in woman as in man.

But her gentler sex returned to Isabel at last; and she sat silent in the casement's niche, looking out upon the soft ground-lightnings of the electric summer night.

vi

Sadly smiling, Pierre broke the pause.

"My sister, thou art so rich, that thou must do me alms; I am very hungry; I have forgotten to eat since breakfast;—and now thou shalt bring me bread and a cup of water, Isabel, ere I go forth from thee. Last night I went rummaging in a pantry, like a bake-house burglar; but to-night thou and I must sup together, Isabel; for as we may henceforth live together, let us begin forthwith to eat in company."

Isabel looked up at him, with sudden and deep emotion, then all acquiescing sweetness, and silently left the room.

As she returned, Pierre, casting his eyes toward the ceiling, said—"She is quiet now, the pacing hath entirely ceased."

"Not the beating, tho'; her foot hath paused, not her unceasing heart. My brother, she is not quiet now; quiet for her hath gone; so that the pivoted stillness of this night is yet a noisy madness to her."

"Give me pen or pencil, and some paper, Isabel."

She laid down her loaf, and plate, and knife, and brought him pen, and ink, and paper.

Pierre took the pen.

"Was this the one, dear Isabel?"

"It is the one, my brother; none other is in this poor cot."

He gazed at it intensely. Then turning to the table, steadily wrote the following note:

"For Delly Ulver: with the deep and true regard and sympathy of Pierre Glendinning.

"Thy sad story—partly known before—hath now more fully come to me, from one who sincerely feels for thee, and who hath imparted her own sincerity to me. Thou desirest to quit this neighborhood, and be somewhere at peace, and find some secluded employ fitted to thy sex and age. With this, I now willingly charge myself, and insure it to thee, so far as my utmost ability can go. Therefore—if consolation be not wholly spurned by thy great grief, which too often happens, though it be but grief's great folly so to feel—therefore, two true friends of thine do here beseech thee to take some little heart to thee, and bethink thee, that all thy life is not yet lived; that Time hath surest healing in his continuous balm. Be patient yet a little while, till thy future lot be disposed for thee, through our best help; and so, know me and Isabel thy earnest friends and true-hearted lovers."

He handed the note to Isabel. She read it silently, and put it down, and spread her two hands over him, and with one motion lifted her eyes toward Delly and toward God.

"Thou think'st it will not pain her to receive the note, Isabel? Thou know'st best. I thought, that ere our help do really reach her, some promise of it now might prove slight comfort. But keep it, and do as thou think'st best."

"Then straightway will I give it her, my brother," said Isabel quitting him.

An infixing stillness, now thrust a long rivet through the night, and fast nailed it to that side of the world. And alone again in such an hour, Pierre could not but listen. He heard Isabel's step on the stair; then it approached him from above; then he heard a gentle knock, and thought he heard a rustling, as of paper slid over a threshold underneath a door. Then another advancing and opposite step tremblingly met Isabel's; and then both steps stepped from each other, and soon Isabel came back to him.

"Thou did'st knock, and slide it underneath the door?"

"Yes, and she hath it now. Hark! a sobbing! Thank God, long arid grief hath found a tear at last. Pity, sympathy hath done this.—Pierre, for thy dear deed thou art already sainted, ere thou be dead."

"Do saints hunger, Isabel?" said Pierre, striving to call her away from this. "Come, give me the loaf; but no, thou shalt help me, my sister.—Thank thee;—this is twice over the bread of sweetness.—Is this of thine own making, Isabel?"

"My own making, my brother."

"Give me the cup; hand it me with thine own hand. So:—Isabel, my heart and soul are now full of deepest reverence; yet I do dare to call this the real sacrament of the supper.—Eat with me."

They eat together without a single word; and without a single word, Pierre rose, and kissed her pure and spotless brow, and without a single word departed from the place.

vii

We know not Pierre Glendinning's thoughts as he gained the village and passed on beneath its often shrouding trees, and saw no light from man, and heard no sound from man, but only, by intervals, saw at his feet the soft ground-lightnings, snake-like, playing in and out among the blades of grass; and between the trees, caught the far dim light from heaven, and heard the far wide general hum of the sleeping but still breathing earth.

He paused before a detached and pleasant house, with much shrubbery about it. He mounted the portico and knocked distinctly there, just as the village clock struck one. He knocked, but no answer came. He knocked again, and soon he heard a sash thrown up in the second story, and an astonished voice inquired who was there?

"It is Pierre Glendinning, and he desires an instant interview with the Reverend Mr. Falsgrave."

"Do I hear right?—in heaven's name, what is the matter, young gentleman?"

"Every thing is the matter; the whole world is the matter. Will you admit me, sir?"

"Certainly—but I beseech thee—nay, stay, I will admit thee."

In quicker time than could have been anticipated, the door was opened to Pierre by Mr. Falsgrave in person, holding a candle, and invested in his very becoming student's wrapper of Scotch plaid.

"For heaven's sake, what is the matter, Mr. Glendinning?"

"Heaven and earth is the matter, sir! shall we go up to the study?"

"Certainly, but—but—"

"Well, let us proceed, then."

They went up-stairs, and soon found themselves in the clergyman's retreat, and both sat down; the amazed host still holding the candle in his hand, and intently eying Pierre, with an apprehensive aspect.

"Thou art a man of God, sir, I believe."

"I? I? I? upon my word, Mr. Glendinning!"

"Yes, sir, the world calls thee a man of God. Now, what hast thou, the man of God, decided, with my mother, concerning Delly Ulver?"

"Delly Ulver! why, why—what can this madness mean?"

"It means, sir, what have thou and my mother decided concerning Delly Ulver."

"She?—Delly Ulver? She is to depart the neighborhood; why, her own parents want her not."

"*How* is she to depart? *Who* is to take her? Art *thou* to take her? *Where* is she to go? *Who* has food for her? *What* is to keep her from the pollution to which such as she are every day driven to contribute, by the detestable uncharitableness and heartlessness of the world?"

"Mr. Glendinning," said the clergyman, now somewhat calmly putting down the candle, and folding himself with dignity in his gown; "Mr. Glendinning, I will not now make any mention of my natural astonishment at this most unusual call, and the most extraordinary time of it. Thou hast sought information upon a certain point, and I have given it to thee, to the best of my knowledge. All thy after and incidental questions, I choose to have no answer for. I will be most happy to see thee at any other time, but for the present thou must excuse my presence. Good-night, sir."

But Pierre sat entirely still, and the clergyman could not but remain standing still.

"I perfectly comprehend the whole, sir. Delly Ulver, then, is to be driven out to starve or rot; and this, too, by the acquiescence of a man of God. Mr. Falsgrave, the subject of Delly, deeply interesting as it is to me, is only the preface to another, still more interesting to me, and concerning which I once cherished some slight hope that thou wouldst have been able, in thy Christian character, to sincerely and honestly counsel me. But a hint from heaven assures me now, that thou hast no earnest and world-disdaining counsel for me. I must seek it direct from God himself, who, I now know, never delegates his holiest admonishings. But I do not blame thee; I think I begin to see how thy profession is unavoidably entangled by all fleshly alliances, and can not move with godly freedom in a world of benefices. I am more sorry than indignant. Pardon me for my most uncivil call, and know me as not thy enemy. Good-night, sir."

Book IX

More Light, and the Gloom of That Light • More Gloom, and the Light of That Gloom

IN THOSE HYPERBOREAN REGIONS, to which enthusiastic Truth, and Earnestness, and Independence, will invariably lead a mind fitted by nature for profound and fearless thought, all objects are seen in a dubious, uncertain, and refracting light. Viewed through that rarefied atmosphere the most immemorially admitted maxims of men begin to slide and fluctuate, and finally become wholly inverted; the very heavens themselves being not innocent of producing this confounding effect, since it is mostly in the heavens themselves that these wonderful mirages are exhibited.

But the example of many minds forever lost, like undiscoverable Arctic explorers, amid those treacherous regions, warns us entirely away from them; and we learn that it is not for man to follow the trail of truth too far, since by so doing he entirely loses the directing compass of his mind; for arrived at the Pole, to whose barrenness only it points, there, the needle indifferently respects all points of the horizon alike.

But even the less distant regions of thought are not without their singular introversions. Hardly any sincere man of ordinary reflective powers, and accustomed to exercise them at all, but must have been independently struck by the thought, that, after all, what is so enthusiastically applauded as the march of mind,—meaning the inroads of Truth into Error—which has ever been regarded by hopeful persons as the one fundamental thing most earnestly to be prayed for as the greatest possible Catholic blessing to the world;—almost every thinking man must have been some time or other struck with the idea, that, in certain respects, a tremendous mistake may be lurking here, since all the world does never gregariously advance to Truth, but only here and there some of its individuals do; and by advancing, leave the rest behind; cutting themselves forever adrift from their sympathy, and making themselves always liable to be regarded with distrust, dislike, and often, downright—though, ofttimes, concealed—fear and hate. What wonder, then, that those advanced minds, which in spite of advance, happen still to remain, for the time, ill-regulated, should now and then be goaded into turning round in acts of wanton aggression upon sentiments and opinions now forever left in their rear. Certain it is, that in their earlier stages of advance, especially in youthful minds, as yet untranquilized by long habituation to the world as it inevitably and eternally is; this aggressiveness is almost invariably manifested, and as invariably afterward deplored by themselves.

That amazing shock of practical truth, which in the compass of a very few days and hours had not so much advanced, as magically transplanted the youthful mind of Pierre far beyond all common discernments; it had not been entirely unattended by the lamentable rearward aggressiveness we have endeavored to portray above. Yielding to that unwarrantable mood, he had invaded the profound midnight slumbers of the Reverend Mr. Falsgrave, and most discourteously made war upon that really amiable and estimable person. But as through the strange force of circumstances his advance in insight had been so surprisingly rapid, so also was now his advance in some sort of wisdom, in charitableness; and his concluding words to Mr. Falsgrave, sufficiently evinced that already, ere quitting that gentleman's study, he had begun to repent his ever entering it on such a mission.

And as he now walked on in the profound meditations induced by the hour; and as all that was in him stirred to and fro, intensely agitated by the ever-creative fire of enthusiastic earnestness, he became fully alive to many palliating considerations, which had they previously occurred to him would have peremptorily forbidden his impulsive intrusion upon the respectable clergyman.

But it is through the malice of this earthly air, that only by being guilty of Folly does mortal man in many cases arrive at the perception of Sense. A thought which should forever free us from hasty imprecations upon our ever-recurring intervals of Folly; since though Folly be our teacher, Sense is the lesson she teaches; since if Folly wholly depart from us, Further Sense will be her companion in the flight, and we will be left standing midway in wisdom. For it is only the miraculous vanity of man which ever persuades him, that even for the most richly gifted mind, there ever arrives an earthly period, where it can truly say to itself, I have come to the Ultimate of Human Speculative Knowledge; hereafter, at this present point I will abide. Sudden onsets of new truth will assail him, and overturn him as the Tartars did China; for there is no China Wall that man can build in his soul, which shall permanently stay the irruptions of those barbarous hordes which Truth ever nourishes in the loins of her frozen, yet teeming North; so that the Empire of Human Knowledge can never be lasting in any one dynasty, since Truth still gives new Emperors to the earth.

But the thoughts we here indite as Pierre's are to be very carefully discriminated from those we indite concerning him. Ignorant at this time of the ideas concerning the reciprocity and partnership of Folly and Sense, in contributing to the mental and moral growth of the mind; Pierre keenly upbraided his thoughtlessness, and began to stagger in his soul; as distrustful of that radical change in his general sentiments, which had thus hurried him into a glaring impropriety and folly; as distrustful of himself, the most wretched distrust of all. But this last distrust was not of the heart; for heaven itself, so he felt, had sanctified that with its blessing; but it was the distrust of his intellect, which in undisciplinedly espousing the manly enthusiast cause of his heart, seemed to cast a reproach upon that cause itself.

But though evermore hath the earnest heart an eventual balm for the most deplorable error of the head; yet in the interval small alleviation is to be had, and the whole man droops into nameless melancholy. Then it seems as though the most magnanimous and virtuous resolutions were only intended for fine spiritual emotions, not as mere preludes to their bodily translation into acts; since in essaying their embodiment, we have but proved ourselves miserable bunglers, and thereupon taken ignominious shame to ourselves. Then, too, the never-entirely repulsed hosts of Commonness, and Conventionalness, and Worldly Prudent-mindedness return to the charge; press hard on the faltering soul; and with inhuman hootings deride all its nobleness as mere eccentricity, which further wisdom and experience shall assuredly cure. The man is as seized by arms and legs, and convulsively pulled either way by his own indecisions and doubts. Blackness advances her banner over this cruel altercation, and he droops and swoons beneath its folds.

It was precisely in this mood of mind that, at about two in the morning, Pierre, with a hanging head, now crossed the private threshold of the Mansion of Saddle Meadows.

ii

In the profoundly silent heart of a house full of sleeping serving-men and maids, Pierre now sat in his chamber before his accustomed round table, still tossed with the books and the papers which, three days before, he had abruptly left, for a sudden and more absorbing object. Uppermost and most conspicuous among the books were the Inferno of Dante, and the Hamlet of Shakspeare.

His mind was wandering and vague; his arm wandered and was vague. Soon he found the open Inferno in his hand, and his eye met the following lines, allegorically overscribed within the arch of the outgoings of the womb of human life:

> "Through me you pass into the city of Woe;
> Through me you pass into eternal pain;
> Through me, among the people lost for aye.
> *   *   *   *   *   *
> All hope abandon, ye who enter here."

He dropped the fatal volume from his hand; he dropped his fated head upon his chest.

His mind was wandering and vague; his arm wandered and was vague. Some moments passed, and he found the open Hamlet in his hand, and his eyes met the following lines:

> "The time is out of joint;—Oh cursed spite,
> That ever I was born to set it right!"

He dropped the too true volume from his hand; his petrifying heart dropped hollowly within him, as a pebble down Carrisbrook well.

iii

The man Dante Alighieri received unforgivable affronts and insults from the world; and the poet Dante Alighieri bequeathed his immortal curse to it, in the sublime malediction of the Inferno. The fiery tongue whose political forkings lost him the solacements of this world, found its malicious counterpart in that muse of fire, which would forever bar the vast bulk of mankind from all solacement in the worlds to come. Fortunately for the felicity of the Dilletante in Literature, the horrible allegorical meanings of the Inferno, lie not on the surface; but unfortunately for the earnest and youthful piercers into truth and reality, those horrible meanings, when first discovered, infuse their poison into a spot previously unprovided with that sovereign antidote of a sense of uncapitulatable security, which is only the possession of the furthest advanced and profoundest souls.

Judge ye, then, ye Judicious, the mood of Pierre, so far as the passage in Dante touched him.

If among the deeper significances of its pervading indefiniteness, which significances are wisely hidden from all but the rarest adepts, the pregnant tragedy of Hamlet convey any one particular moral at all fitted to the ordinary uses of man, it is this:—that all meditation is worthless, unless it prompt to action; that it is not for man to stand shillyshallying amid the conflicting invasions of surrounding impulses; that in the earliest instant of conviction, the roused man must strike, and, if possible, with the precision and the force of the lightning-bolt.

Pierre had always been an admiring reader of Hamlet; but neither his age nor his mental experience thus far, had qualified him either to catch initiating glimpses into the hopeless gloom of its interior meaning, or to draw from the general story those superficial and purely incidental lessons, wherein the painstaking moralist so complacently expatiates.

The intensest light of reason and revelation combined, can not shed such blazonings upon the deeper truths in man, as will sometimes proceed from his own profoundest gloom. Utter darkness is then his light, and cat-like he distinctly sees all objects through a medium which is mere blindness to common vision. Wherefore have Gloom and Grief been celebrated of old as the selectest chamberlains to knowledge? Wherefore is it, that not to know Gloom and Grief is not to know aught that an heroic man should learn?

By the light of that gloom, Pierre now turned over the soul of Hamlet in his hand. He knew not—at least, felt not—then, that Hamlet, though a thing of life, was, after all, but a thing of breath, evoked by the wanton magic of a creative hand, and as wantonly dismissed at last into endless halls of hell and night.

It is the not impartially bestowed privilege of the more final insights, that at the same moment they reveal the depths, they do, sometimes, also reveal—though by no means so distinctly—some answering heights. But when only midway down the gulf, its crags wholly conceal the upper vaults, and the wanderer thinks it all one gulf of downward dark.

Judge ye, then, ye Judicious, the mood of Pierre, so far as the passage in Hamlet touched him.

iv

Torn into a hundred shreds the printed pages of Hell and Hamlet lay at his feet, which trampled them, while their vacant covers mocked him with their idle titles. Dante had made him fierce, and Hamlet had insinuated that there was none to strike. Dante had taught him that he had bitter cause of quarrel; Hamlet taunted him with faltering in the fight. Now he began to curse anew his fate, for now he began to see that after all he had been finely juggling with himself, and postponing with himself, and in meditative sentimentalities wasting the moments consecrated to instant action.

Eight-and-forty hours and more had passed. Was Isabel acknowledged? Had she yet hung on his public arm? Who knew yet of Isabel but Pierre? Like a skulking coward he had gone prowling in the woods by day, and like a skulking coward he had stolen to her haunt by night! Like a thief he had sat and stammered and turned pale before his mother, and in the cause of Holy Right, permitted a woman to grow tall and hector over him! Ah! Easy for man to think like a hero; but hard for man to act like one. All imaginable audacities readily enter into the soul; few come boldly forth from it.

Did he, or did he not vitally mean to do this thing? Was the immense stuff to do it his, or was it not his? Why defer? Why put off? What was there to be gained by deferring and putting off? His resolution had been taken, why was it not executed? What more was there to learn? What more which was essential to the public acknowledgment of Isabel, had remained to be learned, after his first glance at her first letter? Had doubts of her identity come over him to stay him?—None at all. Against the wall of the thick darkness of the mystery of Isabel, recorded as by some phosphoric finger was the burning fact, that Isabel was his sister. Why then? How then? Whence then this utter nothing of his acts? Did he stagger at the thought, that at the first announcement to his mother concerning Isabel, and his resolution to own her boldly and lovingly, his proud mother, spurning the reflection on his father, would likewise spurn Pierre and Isabel, and denounce both him and her, and hate them both alike, as unnatural accomplices against the good name of the purest of husbands and parents? Not at all.

Such a thought was not in him. For had he not already resolved, that his mother should know nothing of the fact of Isabel?—But how now? What then? How was Isabel to be acknowledged to the world, if his mother was to know nothing of that acknowledgment?—Short-sighted, miserable palterer and huckster, thou hast been playing a most fond and foolish game with thyself! Fool and coward! Coward and fool! Tear thyself open, and read there the confounding story of thy blind dotishness! Thy two grand resolutions—the public acknowledgment of Isabel, and the charitable withholding of her existence from thy own mother,—these are impossible adjuncts.—Likewise, thy so magnanimous purpose to screen thy father's honorable memory from reproach, and thy other intention, the open vindication of thy fraternalness to Isabel,—these also are impossible adjuncts. And the having individually entertained four such resolves, without perceiving that once brought together, they all mutually expire; this, this ineffable folly, Pierre, brands thee in the forehead for an unaccountable infatuate!

Well may'st thou distrust thyself, and curse thyself, and tear thy Hamlet and thy Hell! Oh! fool, blind fool, and a million times an ass! Go, go, thou poor and feeble one! High deeds are not for such blind grubs as thou! Quit Isabel, and go to Lucy! Beg humble pardon of thy mother, and hereafter be a more obedient and good boy to her, Pierre—Pierre, Pierre,—infatuate!

Impossible would it be now to tell all the confusion and confoundings in the soul of Pierre, so soon as the above absurdities in his mind presented themselves first to his combining consciousness. He would fain have disowned the very memory and the mind which produced to him such an immense scandal upon his common sanity. Now indeed did all the fiery floods in the Inferno, and all the rolling gloom in Hamlet suffocate him at once in flame and smoke. The cheeks of his soul collapsed in him: he dashed himself in blind fury and swift madness against the wall, and fell dabbling in the vomit of his loathed identity.

Book X

The Unprecedented Final Resolution of Pierre

GLORIFIED BE HIS GRACIOUS MEMORY who first said, The deepest gloom precedes the day. We care not whether the saying will prove true to the utmost bounds of things; sufficient that it sometimes does hold true within the bounds of earthly finitude.

Next morning Pierre rose from the floor of his chamber, haggard and tattered in body from his past night's utter misery, but stoically serene and symmetrical in soul, with the foretaste of what then seemed to him a planned and perfect Future. Now he thinks he knows that the wholly unanticipated storm which had so terribly burst upon him, had yet burst upon him for his good; for the place, which in its undetected incipiency, the storm had obscurely occupied in his soul, seemed now clear sky to him; and all his horizon seemed distinctly commanded by him.

His resolution was a strange and extraordinary one; but therefore it only the better met a strange and extraordinary emergency. But it was not only strange and extraordinary in its novelty of mere aspect, but it was wonderful in its unequaled renunciation of himself.

From the first, determined at all hazards to hold his father's fair fame inviolate from any thing he should do in reference to protecting Isabel, and extending to her a brother's utmost devotedness and love; and equally determined not to shake his mother's lasting peace by any useless exposure of unwelcome facts; and yet vowed in his deepest soul some way to embrace Isabel before the world, and yield to her his constant consolation and companionship; and finding no possible mode of unitedly compassing all these ends, without a most singular act of pious imposture, which he thought all heaven would justify in him, since he himself was to be the grand self-renouncing victim; therefore, this was his settled and immovable purpose now; namely: to assume before the world, that by secret rites, Pierre Glendinning was already become the husband of Isabel Banford—an assumption which would entirely warrant his dwelling in her continual company, and upon equal terms, taking her wherever the world admitted him; and at the same time foreclose all sinister inquisitions bearing upon his deceased parent's memory, or any way affecting his mother's lasting peace, as indissolubly linked with that. True, he in embryo, foreknew, that the extraordinary thing he had resolved, would, in another way, indirectly though inevitably, dart a most keen pang into his mother's heart; but this then seemed to him part of the unavoidable vast price of his enthusiastic virtue; and, thus minded, rather would he privately pain his living mother with a wound that might be curable, than cast world-wide and irremediable dishonor—so it seemed to him—upon his departed father.

Probably no other being than Isabel could have produced upon Pierre impressions powerful enough to eventuate in a final resolution so unparalleled as the above. But the wonderful melodiousness of her grief had touched the secret monochord within his breast, by an apparent magic, precisely similar to that which had moved the stringed tongue of her guitar to respond to the heart-strings of her own melancholy plaints. The deep voice of the being of Isabel called to him from out the immense distances of sky and air, and there seemed no veto of the earth that could forbid her heavenly claim.

During the three days that he had personally known her, and so been brought into magnetic contact with her, other persuasions and potencies than those direct ones, involved in her bewildering eyes and marvelous story, had unconsciously left their ineffaceable impressions on him, and perhaps without his privity, had mainly contributed to his resolve. She had impressed him as the glorious child of Pride and Grief, in whose countenance were traceable the divinest lineaments of both her parents. Pride gave to her her nameless nobleness; Grief touched that nobleness with an angelical softness; and again that softness was steeped in a most charitable humility, which was the foundation of her loftiest excellence of all.

Neither by word or letter had Isabel betrayed any spark of those more common emotions and desires which might not unreasonably be ascribed to an ordinary person placed in circumstances like hers. Though almost penniless, she had not invoked the pecuniary bounty of Pierre; and though she was altogether silent on that subject, yet Pierre could not but be strangely sensible of something in her which disdained to voluntarily hang upon the mere bounty even of a brother. Nor, though she by various nameless ways, manifested her consciousness of being surrounded by uncongenial and inferior beings, while yet descended from a generous stock, and personally meriting the most refined companionships which the wide world could yield; nevertheless, she had not demanded of Pierre that he should array her in brocade, and lead her forth among the rare and opulent ladies of the land. But while thus evincing her intuitive, true lady-likeness and nobleness by this entire freedom from all sordid motives, neither had she merged all her feelings in any sickly sentimentalities of sisterly affection toward her so suddenly discovered brother; which, in the case of a naturally unattractive woman in her circumstances, would not have been altogether alluring to Pierre. No. That intense and indescribable longing, which her letter by its very incoherencies had best embodied, proceeded from no base, vain, or ordinary motive whatever; but was the unsuppressible and unmistakable cry of the godhead through her soul, commanding Pierre to fly to her, and do his highest and most glorious duty in the world.

Nor now, as it changedly seemed to Pierre, did that duty consist in stubbornly flying in the marble face of the Past, and striving to reverse the decree which had pronounced that Isabel could never perfectly inherit all the privileges of a legitimate child of her father. And thoroughly now he felt, that even as this would in the present case be both preposterous in itself and cruel in effect to both the living and the dead, so was it entirely undesired by Isabel, who though once yielding to a momentary burst of aggressive enthusiasm, yet in her more wonted mood of mournfulness and sweetness, evinced no such lawless wandering. Thoroughly, now he felt, that Isabel was content to live obscure in her paternal identity, so long as she could any way appease her deep longings for the constant love and sympathy and close domestic contact of some one of her blood. So that Pierre had no slightest misgiving that upon learning the character of his scheme, she would deem it to come short of her natural expectations; while so far as its apparent strangeness was concerned,—a strangeness, perhaps invincible to squeamish and humdrum women—here Pierre anticipated no obstacle in Isabel; for her whole past was strange, and strangeness seemed best befitting to her future.

But had Pierre now reread the opening paragraph of her letter to him, he might have very quickly derived a powerful anticipative objection from his sister, which his own complete disinterestedness concealed from him. Though Pierre had every reason to believe that—owing to her secluded and humble life—Isabel was in entire ignorance of the fact of his precise relation to Lucy Tartan:—an ignorance, whose first indirect and unconscious manifestation in Isabel, had been unspeakably welcome to him;—and though, of course, he had both wisely and benevolently abstained from enlightening her on that point; still, notwithstanding this, was it possible that any true-hearted, noble girl like Isabel, would, to benefit herself, willingly become a participator in an act, which would prospectively and forever bar the blessed boon of marriageable love from one so young and generous as Pierre, and eternally entangle him in a fictitious alliance, which, though in reality but a web of air, yet in effect would prove a wall of iron; for the same powerful motive which induced the thought of forming such an alliance, would always thereafter forbid that tacit exposure of its fictitiousness, which would be consequent upon its public discontinuance, and the real nuptials of Pierre with any other being during the lifetime of Isabel.

But according to what view you take of it, it is either the gracious or the malicious gift of the great gods to man, that on the threshold of any wholly new and momentous devoted enterprise, the thousand ulterior intricacies and emperilings to which it must conduct; these, at the outset, are mostly withheld from sight; and so, through her ever-primeval wilderness Fortune's Knight rides on, alike ignorant of the palaces or the pitfalls in its heart. Surprising, and past all ordinary belief, are those strange oversights and inconsistencies, which the enthusiastic meditation upon unique or extreme resolves will sometimes beget in young and over-ardent souls. That all-comprehending oneness, that calm representativeness, by which a steady philosophic mind reaches forth and draws to itself, in their collective entirety, the objects of its contemplations; that pertains not to the young enthusiast. By his eagerness, all objects are deceptively foreshortened; by his intensity each object is viewed as detached; so that essentially and relatively every thing is misseen by him. Already have we exposed that passing preposterousness in Pierre, which by reason of the above-named cause which we have endeavored to portray, induced him to cherish for a time four unitedly impossible designs. And now we behold this hapless youth all eager to involve himself in such an inextricable twist of Fate, that the three dextrous maids themselves could hardly disentangle him, if once he tie the complicating knots about him and Isabel.

Ah, thou rash boy! are there no couriers in the air to warn thee away from these emperilings, and point thee to those Cretan labyrinths, to which thy life's cord is leading thee? Where now are the high beneficences? Whither fled the sweet angels that are alledged guardians to man?

Not that the impulsive Pierre wholly overlooked all that was menacing to him in his future, if now he acted out his most rare resolve; but eagerly foreshortened by him, they assumed not their full magnitude of menacing; nor, indeed,—so riveted now his purpose—were they pushed up to his face, would he for that renounce his self-renunciation; while concerning all things more immediately contingent upon his central resolution; these were, doubtless, in a measure, foreseen and understood by him. Perfectly, at least, he seemed to foresee and understand, that the present hope of Lucy Tartan must be banished from his being; that this would carry a terrible pang to her, which in the natural recoil would but redouble his own; that to the world all his heroicness, standing equally unexplained and unsuspected, therefore the world would denounce him as infamously false to his betrothed; reckless of the most binding human vows; a secret wooer and wedder of an unknown and enigmatic girl; a spurner of all a loving mother's wisest counselings; a bringer down of lasting reproach upon an honorable name; a besotted self-exile from a most prosperous house and bounteous fortune; and lastly, that now his whole life would, in the eyes of the wide humanity, be covered with an all-pervading haze of incurable sinisterness, possibly not to be removed even in the concluding hour of death.

Such, oh thou son of man! are the perils and the miseries thou callest down on thee, when, even in a virtuous cause, thou steppest aside from those arbitrary lines of conduct, by which the common world, however base and dastardly, surrounds thee for thy worldly good.

Ofttimes it is very wonderful to trace the rarest and profoundest things, and find their probable origin in something extremely trite or trivial. Yet so strange and complicate is the human soul; so much is confusedly evolved from out itself, and such vast and varied accessions come to it from abroad, and so impossible is it always to distinguish between these two, that the wisest man were rash, positively to assign the precise and incipient origination of his final thoughts and acts. Far as we blind moles can see, man's life seems but an acting upon mysterious hints; it is somehow hinted to us, to do thus or thus. For surely no mere mortal who has at all gone down into himself will ever pretend that his slightest thought or act solely originates in his own defined identity. This preamble seems not entirely unnecessary as usher of the strange conceit, that possibly the latent germ of Pierre's proposed extraordinary mode of executing his proposed extraordinary resolve—namely, the nominal conversion of a sister into a wife—might have been found in the previous conversational conversion of a mother into a sister; for hereby he had habituated his voice and manner to a certain fictitiousness in one of the closest domestic relations of life; and since man's moral texture is very porous, and things assumed upon the surface, at last strike in—hence, this outward habituation to the above-named fictitiousness had insensibly disposed his mind to it as it were; but only innocently and pleasantly as yet. If, by any possibility, this general conceit be so, then to Pierre the times of sportfulness were as pregnant with the hours of earnestness; and in sport he learnt the terms of woe.

ii

If next to that resolve concerning his lasting fraternal succor to Isabel, there was at this present time any determination in Pierre absolutely inflexible, and partaking at once of the sacredness and the indissolubleness of the most solemn oath, it was the enthusiastic, and apparently wholly supererogatory resolution to hold his father's memory untouched; nor to one single being in the world reveal the paternity of Isabel. Unrecallably dead and gone from out the living world, again returned to utter helplessness, so far as this world went; his perished father seemed to appeal to the dutifulness and mercifulness of Pierre, in terms far more moving than though the accents proceeded from his mortal mouth. And what though not through the sin of Pierre, but through his father's sin, that father's fair fame now lay at the mercy of the son, and could only be kept inviolate by the son's free sacrifice of all earthly felicity;—what if this were so? It but struck a still loftier chord in the bosom of the son, and filled him with infinite magnanimities. Never had the generous Pierre cherished the heathenish conceit, that even in the general world, Sin is a fair object to be stretched on the cruelest racks by self-complacent Virtue, that self-complacent Virtue may feed her lily-liveredness on the pallor of Sin's anguish. For perfect Virtue does not more loudly claim our approbation, than repented Sin in its concludedness does demand our utmost tenderness and concern. And as the more immense the Virtue, so should be the more immense our approbation; likewise the more immense the Sin, the more infinite our pity. In some sort, Sin hath its sacredness, not less than holiness. And great Sin calls forth more magnanimity than small Virtue. What man, who is a man, does not feel livelier and more generous emotions toward the great god of Sin—Satan,—

than toward yonder haberdasher, who only is a sinner in the small and entirely honorable way of trade?

Though Pierre profoundly shuddered at that impenetrable yet blackly significant nebulousness, which the wild story of Isabel threw around the early life of his father; yet as he recalled the dumb anguish of the invocation of the empty and the ashy hand uplifted from his father's death-bed, he most keenly felt that of whatsoever unknown shade his father's guilt might be, yet in the final hour of death it had been most dismally repented of; by a repentance only the more full of utter wretchedness, that it was a consuming secret in him. Mince the matter how his family would, had not his father died a raver? Whence that raving, following so prosperous a life? Whence, but from the cruelest compunctions?

Touched thus, and strung in all his sinews and his nerves to the holding of his father's memory intact,—Pierre turned his confronting and unfrightened face toward Lucy Tartan, and stilly vowed that not even she should know the whole; no, not know the least.

There is an inevitable keen cruelty in the loftier heroism. It is not heroism only to stand unflinched ourselves in the hour of suffering; but it is heroism to stand unflinched both at our own and at some loved one's united suffering; a united suffering, which we could put an instant period to, if we would but renounce the glorious cause for which ourselves do bleed, and see our most loved one bleed. If he would not reveal his father's shame to the common world, whose favorable opinion for himself, Pierre now despised; how then reveal it to the woman he adored? To her, above all others, would he now uncover his father's tomb, and bid her behold from what vile attaintings he himself had sprung? So Pierre turned round and tied Lucy to the same stake which must hold himself, for he too plainly saw, that it could not be, but that both their hearts must burn.

Yes, his resolve concerning his father's memory involved the necessity of assuming even to Lucy his marriage with Isabel. Here he could not explain himself, even to her. This would aggravate the sharp pang of parting, by self-suggested, though wholly groundless surmising in Lucy's mind, in the most miserable degree contaminating to her idea of him. But on this point, he still fondly trusted that without at all marring his filial bond, he would be enabled by some significant intimations to arrest in Lucy's mind those darker imaginings which might find entrance there; and if he could not set her wholly right, yet prevent her from going wildly wrong.

For his mother Pierre was more prepared. He considered that by an inscrutable decree, which it was but foolishness to try to evade, or shun, or deny existence to, since he felt it so profoundly pressing on his inmost soul; the family of the Glendinnings was imperiously called upon to offer up a victim to the gods of woe; one grand victim at the least; and that grand victim must be his mother, or himself. If he disclosed his secret to the world, then his mother was made the victim; if at all hazards he kept it to himself, then himself would be the victim. A victim as respecting his mother, because under the peculiar circumstances of the case, the non-disclosure of the secret involved her entire and infamy-engendering misconception of himself. But to this he bowed submissive.

One other thing—and the last to be here named, because the very least in the conscious thoughts of Pierre; one other thing remained to menace him with assured disastrousness. This thing it was, which though but dimly hinted of as yet, still in the apprehension must have exerted a powerful influence upon Pierre, in preparing him for the worst.

His father's last and fatal sickness had seized him suddenly. Both the probable concealed distraction of his mind with reference to his early life as recalled to him in an evil hour, and his consequent mental wanderings; these, with other reasons, had prevented him from framing a new will to supersede one made shortly after his marriage, and ere Pierre was born. By that will which as yet had never been dragged into the courts of law; and which, in the fancied security of her own and her son's congenial and loving future, Mrs. Glendinning had never but once, and then inconclusively, offered to discuss, with a view to a better and more appropriate ordering of things to meet circumstances non-existent at the period the testament was framed; by that will, all the Glendinning property was declared his mother's.

Acutely sensible to those prophetic intimations in him, which painted in advance the haughty temper of his offended mother, as all bitterness and scorn toward a son, once the object of her proudest joy, but now become a deep reproach, as not only rebellious to her, but glaringly dishonorable before the world; Pierre distinctly foresaw, that as she never would have permitted Isabel Banford in her true character to cross her threshold; neither would she now permit Isabel Banford to cross her threshold in any other, and disguised character; least of all, as that unknown and insidious girl, who by some pernicious arts had lured her only son from honor into infamy. But not to admit Isabel, was now to exclude Pierre, if indeed on independent grounds of exasperation against himself, his mother would not cast him out.

Nor did the same interior intimations in him which forepainted the above bearing of his mother, abstain to trace her whole haughty heart as so unrelentingly set against him, that while she would close her doors against both him and his fictitious wife, so also she would not willingly contribute one copper to support them in a supposed union so entirely abhorrent to her. And though Pierre was not so familiar with the science of the law, as to be quite certain what the law, if appealed to concerning the provisions of his father's will, would decree concerning any possible claims of the son to share with the mother in the property of the sire; yet he prospectively felt an invincible repugnance to dragging his dead father's hand and seal into open Court, and fighting over them with a base mercenary motive, and with his own mother for the antagonist. For so thoroughly did his infallible presentiments paint his mother's character to him, as operated upon and disclosed in all those fiercer traits,—hitherto held in abeyance by the mere chance and felicity of circumstances,—that he felt assured that her exasperation against him would even meet the test of a public legal contention concerning the Glendinning property. For indeed there was a reserved strength and masculineness in the character of his mother, from which on all these points Pierre had every thing to dread. Besides, will the matter how he would, Pierre for nearly two whole years to come, would still remain a minor, an infant in the eye of the law, incapable of personally asserting any legal claim; and though he might sue by his next friend, yet who would be his voluntary next friend, when the execution of his great resolve would, for him, depopulate all the world of friends?

Now to all these things, and many more, seemed the soul of this infatuated young enthusiast braced.

iii

There is a dark, mad mystery in some human hearts, which, sometimes, during the tyranny of a usurper mood, leads them to be all eagerness to cast off the most intense beloved bond, as a hindrance to the attainment of whatever transcendental object that usurper mood so tyrannically suggests. Then the beloved bond seems to hold us to no essential good; lifted to exalted mounts, we can dispense with all the vale; endearments we spurn; kisses are blisters to us; and forsaking the palpitating forms of mortal love, we emptily embrace the boundless and the unbodied air. We think we are not human; we become as immortal bachelors and gods; but again, like the Greek gods themselves, prone we descend to earth; glad to be uxorious once more; glad to hide these god-like heads within the bosoms made of too-seducing clay.

Weary with the invariable earth, the restless sailor breaks from every enfolding arm, and puts to sea in height of tempest that blows off shore. But in long night-watches at the antipodes, how heavily that ocean gloom lies in vast bales upon the deck; thinking that that very moment in his deserted hamlet-home the household sun is high, and many a sun-eyed maiden meridian as the sun. He curses Fate; himself he curses; his senseless madness, which is himself. For whoso once has known this sweet knowledge, and then fled it; in absence, to him the avenging dream will come.

Pierre was now this vulnerable god; this self-upbraiding sailor; this dreamer of the avenging dream. Though in some things he had unjuggled himself, and forced himself to eye the prospect as it was; yet, so far as Lucy was concerned, he was at bottom still a juggler. True, in his extraordinary scheme, Lucy was so intimately interwoven, that it seemed impossible for him at all to cast his future without some way having that heart's love in view. But ignorant of its quantity as yet, or fearful of ascertaining it; like an algebraist, for the real Lucy he, in his scheming thoughts, had substituted but a sign—some empty *x*—and in the ultimate solution of the problem, that empty *x* still figured; not the real Lucy.

But now, when risen from the abasement of his chamber-floor, and risen from the still profounder prostration of his soul, Pierre had thought that all the horizon of his dark fate was commanded by him; all his resolutions clearly defined, and immovably decreed; now finally, to top all, there suddenly slid into his inmost heart the living and breathing form of Lucy. His lungs collapsed; his eyeballs glared; for the sweet imagined form, so long buried alive in him, seemed now as gliding on him from the grave; and her light hair swept far adown her shroud.

Then, for the time, all minor things were whelmed in him; his mother, Isabel, the whole wide world; and one only thing remained to him;—this all-including query—Lucy or God?

But here we draw a vail. Some nameless struggles of the soul can not be painted, and some woes will not be told. Let the ambiguous procession of events reveal their own ambiguousness.

Book XI

He Crosses the Rubicon

SUCKED WITHIN THE MAELSTROM, man must go round. Strike at one end the longest conceivable row of billiard balls in close contact, and the furthermost ball will start forth, while all the rest stand still; and yet that last ball was not struck at all. So, through long previous generations, whether of births or thoughts, Fate strikes the present man. Idly he disowns the blow's effect, because he felt no blow, and indeed, received no blow. But Pierre was not arguing Fixed Fate and Free Will, now; Fixed Fate and Free Will were arguing him, and Fixed Fate got the better in the debate.

The peculiarities of those influences which on the night and early morning following the last interview with Isabel, persuaded Pierre to the adoption of his final resolve, did now irresistibly impel him to a remarkable instantaneousness in his actions, even as before he had proved a lagger.

Without being consciously that way pointed, through the desire of anticipating any objections on the part of Isabel to the assumption of a marriage between himself and her; Pierre was now impetuously hurried into an act, which should have the effective virtue of such an executed intention, without its corresponding motive. Because, as the primitive resolve so deplorably involved Lucy, her image was then prominent in his mind; and hence, because he felt all eagerness to hold her no longer in suspence, but by a certain sort of charity of cruelty, at once to pronounce to her her fate; therefore, it was among his first final thoughts that morning to go to Lucy. And to this, undoubtedly, so trifling a circumstance as her being nearer to him, geographically, than Isabel, must have contributed some added, though unconscious influence, in his present fateful frame of mind.

On the previous undetermined days, Pierre had solicitously sought to disguise his emotions from his mother, by a certain carefulness and choiceness in his dress. But now, since his very soul was forced to wear a mask, he would wear no paltry palliatives and disguisements on his body. He went to the cottage of Lucy as disordered in his person, as haggard in his face.

ii

She was not risen yet. So, the strange imperious instantaneousness in him, impelled him to go straight to her chamber-door, and in a voice of mild invincibleness, demand immediate audience, for the matter pressed.

Already namelessly concerned and alarmed for her lover, now eight-and-forty hours absent on some mysterious and undisclosable affair; Lucy, at this surprising summons was overwhelmed with sudden terror; and in oblivion of all ordinary proprieties, responded to Pierre's call, by an immediate assent.

Opening the door, he advanced slowly and deliberately toward her; and as Lucy caught his pale determined figure, she gave a cry of groping misery, which knew not the pang that caused it, and lifted herself trembling in her bed; but without uttering one word.

Pierre sat down on the bedside; and his set eyes met her terrified and virgin aspect.

"Decked in snow-white, and pale of cheek, thou indeed art fitted for the altar; but not that one of which thy fond heart did'st dream:—so fair a victim!"

"Pierre!"

"'Tis the last cruelty of tyrants to make their enemies slay each other."

"My heart! my heart!"

"Nay;——Lucy, I am married."

The girl was no more pale, but white as any leper; the bed-clothes trembled to the concealed shudderings of all her limbs; one moment she sat looking vacantly into the blank eyes of Pierre, and then fell over toward him in a swoon.

Swift madness mounted into the brain of Pierre; all the past seemed as a dream, and all the present an unintelligible horror. He lifted her, and extended her motionless form upon the bed, and stamped for succor. The maid Martha came running into the room, and beholding those two inexplicable figures, shrieked, and turned in terror. But Pierre's repeated cry rallied Martha from this, and darting out of the chamber, she returned with a sharp restorative, which at length brought Lucy back to life.

"Martha! Martha!" now murmured Lucy, in a scarce audible whispering, and shuddering in the maid's own shuddering arms, "quick, quick; come to me—drive it away! wake me! wake me!"

"Nay, pray God to sleep again," cried Martha, bending over her and embracing her, and half-turning upon Pierre with a glance of loathing indignation. "In God's holy name, sir, what may this be? How came you here; accursed!"

"Accursed?—it is well. Is she herself again, Martha?"

"Thou hast somehow murdered her; how then be herself again? My sweet mistress! oh, my young mistress! Tell me! tell me!" and she bent low over her.

Pierre now advanced toward the bed, making a gesture for the maid to leave them; but soon as Lucy re-caught his haggard form, she whisperingly wailed again, "Martha! Martha! drive it away!—there—there! him—him!" and shut her eyes convulsively, with arms abhorrently outstretched.

"Monster! incomprehensible fiend!" cried the anew terror-smitten maid—"depart! See! she dies away at the sight of thee—begone! Wouldst thou murder her afresh? Begone!"

Starched and frozen by his own emotion, Pierre silently turned and quitted the chamber; and heavily descending the stairs, tramped heavily—as a man slowly bearing a great burden—through a long narrow passage leading to a wing in the rear of the cottage, and knocking at Miss Llanyllyn's door, summoned her to Lucy, who, he briefly said, had fainted. Then, without waiting for any response, left the house, and went directly to the mansion.

iii

"Is my mother up yet?" said he to Dates, whom he met in the hall.

"Not yet, sir;—heavens, sir! are you sick?"

"To death! Let me pass."

Ascending toward his mother's chamber, he heard a coming step, and met her on the great middle landing of the stairs, where in an ample niche, a marble group of the temple-polluting Laocoon and his two innocent children, caught in inextricable snarls of snakes, writhed in eternal torments.

"Mother, go back with me to thy chamber."

She eyed his sudden presence with a dark but repressed foreboding; drew herself up haughtily and repellingly, and with a quivering lip, said, "Pierre, thou thyself hast denied me thy confidence, and thou shalt not force me back to it so easily. Speak! what is that now between thee and me?"

"I am married, mother."

"Great God! To whom?"

"Not to Lucy Tartan, mother."

"That thou merely sayest 'tis not Lucy, without saying who indeed it is, this is good proof she is something vile. Does Lucy know thy marriage?"

"I am but just from Lucy's."

Thus far Mrs. Glendinning's rigidity had been slowly relaxing. Now she clutched the balluster, bent over, and trembled, for a moment. Then erected all her haughtiness again, and stood before Pierre in incurious, unappeasable grief and scorn for him.

"My dark soul prophesied something dark. If already thou hast not found other lodgment, and other table than this house supplies, then seek it straight. Beneath my roof, and at my table, he who was once Pierre Glendinning no more puts himself."

She turned from him, and with a tottering step climbed the winding stairs, and disappeared from him; while in the balluster he held, Pierre seemed to feel the sudden thrill running down to him from his mother's convulsive grasp.

He stared about him with an idiot eye; staggered to the floor below, to dumbly quit the house; but as he crossed its threshold, his foot tripped upon its raised ledge; he pitched forward upon the stone portico, and fell. He seemed as jeeringly hurled from beneath his own ancestral roof.

iv

Passing through the broad court-yard's postern, Pierre closed it after him, and then turned and leaned upon it, his eyes fixed upon the great central chimney of the mansion, from which a light blue smoke was wreathing gently into the morning air.

"The hearth-stone from which thou risest, never more, I inly feel, will these feet press. Oh God, what callest thou that which has thus made Pierre a vagabond?"

He walked slowly away, and passing the windows of Lucy, looked up, and saw the white curtains closely drawn, the white cottage profoundly still, and a white saddle-horse tied before the gate.

"I would enter, but again would her abhorrent wails repel; what more can I now say or do to her? I can not explain. She knows all I purposed to disclose. Ay, but thou didst cruelly burst upon her with it; thy impetuousness, thy instantaneousness hath killed her, Pierre!—Nay, nay, nay!—Cruel tidings who can gently break? If to stab be inevitable; then instant be the dagger! Those curtains are close drawn upon her; so let me upon her sweet image draw the curtains of my soul. Sleep, sleep, sleep, sleep, thou angel! —wake no more to Pierre, nor to thyself, my Lucy!"

Passing on now hurriedly and blindly, he jostled against some oppositely-going wayfarer. The man paused amazed; and looking up, Pierre recognized a domestic of the Mansion. That instantaneousness which now impelled him in all his actions, again seized the ascendency in him. Ignoring the dismayed expression of the man at thus encountering his young master, Pierre commanded him to follow him. Going straight to the "Black Swan," the little village Inn, he entered the first vacant room, and bidding the man be seated, sought the keeper of the house, and ordered pen and paper.

If fit opportunity offer in the hour of unusual affliction, minds of a certain temperament find a strange, hysterical relief, in a wild, perverse humorousness, the more alluring from its entire unsuitableness to the occasion; although they seldom manifest this trait toward those individuals more immediately involved in the cause or the effect of their suffering. The cool censoriousness of the mere philosopher would denominate such conduct as nothing short of temporary madness; and perhaps it is, since, in the inexorable and inhuman eye of mere undiluted reason, all grief, whether on our own account, or that of others, is the sheerest unreason and insanity.

The note now written was the following:

"For that Fine Old Fellow, Dates.

"Dates, my old boy, bestir thyself now. Go to my room, Dates, and bring me down my mahogany strong-box and lockup, the thing covered with blue chintz; strap it very carefully, my sweet Dates, it is rather heavy, and set it just without the postern. Then back and bring me down my writing-desk, and set that, too, just without the postern. Then back yet again, and bring me down the old camp-bed (see that all the parts be there), and bind the case well with a cord. Then go to the left corner little drawer in my wardrobe, and thou wilt find my visiting-cards. Tack one on the chest, and the desk, and the camp-bed case. Then get all my clothes together, and pack them in trunks (not forgetting the two old military cloaks, my boy), and tack cards on them also, my good Dates. Then fly round three times indefinitely, my good Dates, and wipe a little of the perspiration off. And then—let me see—then, my good Dates—why what then? Why, this much. Pick up all papers of all sorts that may be lying round my chamber; and see them burned. And then—have old White Hoof put to the lightest farm-wagon, and send the chest, and the desk, and the camp-bed, and the trunks to the 'Black Swan,' where I shall call for them, when I am ready, and not before, sweet Dates. So God bless thee, my fine, old, imperturbable Dates, and adieu!

"Thy old young master, PIERRE.

"*Nota bene*—Mark well, though, Dates. Should my mother possibly interrupt thee, say that it is my orders, and mention what it is I send for; but on no account show this to thy mistress—D'ye hear? PIERRE again."

Folding this scrawl into a grotesque shape, Pierre ordered the man to take it forthwith to Dates. But the man, all perplexed, hesitated, turning the billet over in his hand; till Pierre loudly and violently bade him begone; but as the man was then rapidly departing in a panic, Pierre called him back and retracted his rude words; but as the servant now lingered again, perhaps thinking to avail himself of this repentant mood in Pierre, to say something in sympathy or remonstrance to him, Pierre ordered him off with augmented violence, and stamped for him to begone.

Apprising the equally perplexed old landlord that certain things would in the course of that forenoon be left for him, (Pierre,) at the Inn; and also desiring him to prepare a chamber for himself and wife that night; some chamber with a commodious connecting room, which might answer for a dressing-room; and likewise still another chamber for a servant; Pierre departed the place, leaving the old landlord staring vacantly at him, and dumbly marveling what horrible thing had happened to turn the brain of his fine young favorite and old shooting comrade, Master Piérre.

Soon the stout old man went out bare-headed upon the low porch of the Inn, descended its one step, and crossed over to the middle of the road, gazing after Pierre. And only as Pierre turned up a distant lane, did his amazement and his solicitude find utterance.

"I taught him—yes, old Casks;—the best shot in all the country round is Master Pierre;—pray God he hits not now the bull's eye in himself.—Married? married? and coming here?—This is pesky strange!"

Book XII

Isabel: Mrs. Glendinning: The Portrait: and Lucy

WHEN ON THE PREVIOUS NIGHT Pierre had left the farm-house where Isabel harbored, it will be remembered that no hour, either of night or day, no special time at all had been assigned for a succeeding interview. It was Isabel, who for some doubtlessly sufficient reason of her own, had, for the first meeting, assigned the early hour of darkness.

As now, when the full sun was well up the heavens, Pierre drew near the farm-house of the Ulvers, he descried Isabel, standing without the little dairy-wing, occupied in vertically arranging numerous glittering shield-like milk-pans on a long shelf, where they might purifyingly meet the sun. Her back was toward him. As Pierre passed through the open wicket and crossed the short soft green sward, he unconsciously muffled his footsteps, and now standing close behind his sister, touched her shoulder and stood still.

She started, trembled, turned upon him swiftly, made a low, strange cry, and then gazed rivetedly and imploringly upon him.

"I look rather queerish, sweet Isabel, do I not?" said Pierre at last with a writhed and painful smile.

"My brother, my blessed brother!—speak—tell me—what has happened—what hast thou done? Oh! Oh! I should have warned thee before, Pierre, Pierre; it is my fault—mine, mine!"

"*What* is thy fault, sweet Isabel?"

"Thou hast revealed Isabel to thy mother, Pierre."

"I have not, Isabel. Mrs. Glendinning knows not thy secret at all."

"Mrs. Glendinning?—that's,—that's thine own mother, Pierre! In heaven's name, my brother, explain thyself. Knows not my secret, and yet thou here so suddenly, and with such a fatal aspect? Come, come with me into the house. Quick, Pierre, why dost thou not stir? Oh, my God! if mad myself sometimes, I am to make mad him who loves me best, and who, I fear, has in some way ruined himself for me;—then, let me no more stand upright on this sod, but fall prone beneath it, that I may be hidden! Tell me!" catching Pierre's arms in both her frantic hands—"tell me, do I blast where I look? is my face Gorgon's?"

"Nay, sweet Isabel; but it hath a more sovereign power; that turned to stone; thine might turn white marble into mother's milk."

"Come with me—come quickly."

They passed into the dairy, and sat down on a bench by the honey-suckled casement.

"Pierre, forever fatal and accursed be the day my longing heart called thee to me, if now, in the very spring-time of our related love, thou art minded to play deceivingly with me, even though thou should'st fancy it for my good. Speak to me; oh speak to me, my brother!"

"Thou hintest of deceiving one for one's good. Now supposing, sweet Isabel, that in no case would I affirmatively deceive thee;—in no case whatever;—would'st thou then be willing for thee and me to piously deceive others, for both their and our united good?—Thou sayest nothing. Now, then, is it *my* turn, sweet Isabel, to bid thee speak to me, oh speak to me!"

"That unknown, approaching thing, seemeth ever ill, my brother, which must have unfrank heralds to go before. Oh, Pierre, dear, dear Pierre; be very careful with me! This strange, mysterious, unexampled love between us, makes me all plastic in thy hand. Be very careful with me. I know little out of me. The world seems all one unknown India to me. Look up, look on me, Pierre; say now, thou wilt be very careful; say so, say so, Pierre!"

"If the most exquisite, and fragile filagree of Genoa be carefully handled by its artisan; if sacred nature carefully folds, and warms, and by inconceivable attentivenesses eggs round and round her minute and marvelous embryoes; then, Isabel, do I most carefully and most tenderly egg thee, gentlest one, and the fate of thee! Short of the great God, Isabel, there lives none who will be more careful with thee, more infinitely considerate and delicate with thee."

"From my deepest heart, do I believe thee, Pierre. Yet thou mayest be very delicate in some point, where delicateness is not all essential, and in some quick impulsive hour, omit thy fullest heedfulness somewhere where heedlessness were most fatal. Nay, nay, my brother; bleach these locks snow-white, thou sun! if I have any thought to reproach thee, Pierre, or betray distrust of thee. But earnestness must sometimes seem suspicious, else it is none. Pierre, Pierre, all thy aspect speaks eloquently of some already executed resolution, born in suddenness. Since I last saw thee, Pierre, some deed irrevocable has been done by thee. My soul is stiff and starched to it; now tell me what it is?"

"Thou, and I, and Delly Ulver, to-morrow morning depart this whole neighborhood, and go to the distant city.—That is it."

"No more?"

"Is it not enough?"

"There is something more, Pierre."

"Thou hast not yet answered a question I put to thee but just now. Bethink thee, Isabel. The deceiving of others by thee and me, in a thing wholly pertaining to ourselves, for their and our united good. Wouldst thou?"

"I would do any thing that does not tend to the marring of thy best lasting fortunes, Pierre. What is it thou wouldst have thee and me to do together? I wait; I wait!"

"Let us go into the room of the double casement, my sister," said Pierre, rising.

"Nay, then; if it can not be said here, then can I not do it anywhere, my brother; for it would harm thee."

"Girl!" cried Pierre, sternly, "if for thee I have lost"—but he checked himself.

"Lost? for me? Now does the very worst blacken on me. Pierre! Pierre!"

"I was foolish, and sought but to frighten thee, my sister. It was very foolish. Do thou now go on with thine innocent work here, and I will come again a few hours hence. Let me go now."

He was turning from her, when Isabel sprang forward to him, caught him with both her arms round him, and held him so convulsively, that her hair sideways swept over him, and half concealed him.

"Pierre, if indeed my soul hath cast on thee the same black shadow that my hair now flings on thee; if thou hast lost aught for me; then eternally is Isabel lost to Isabel, and Isabel will not outlive this night. If I am indeed an accursing thing, I will not act the given part, but cheat the air, and die from it. See; I let thee go, lest some poison I know not of distill upon thee from me."

She slowly drooped, and trembled from him. But Pierre caught her, and supported her.

"Foolish, foolish one! Behold, in the very bodily act of loosing hold of me, thou dost reel and fall;—unanswerable emblem of the indispensable heart-stay, I am to thee, my sweet, sweet Isabel! Prate not then of parting."

"What hast thou lost for me? Tell me!"

"A gainful loss, my sister!"

"'Tis mere rhetoric! What hast thou lost?"

"Nothing that my inmost heart would now recall. I have bought inner love and glory by a price, which, large or small, I would not now have paid me back, so I must return the thing I bought."

"Is love then cold, and glory white? Thy cheek is snowy, Pierre."

"It should be, for I believe to God that I am pure, let the world think how it may."

"What hast thou lost?"

"Not thee, nor the pride and glory of ever loving thee, and being a continual brother to thee, my best sister. Nay, why dost thou now turn thy face from me?"

"With fine words he wheedles me, and coaxes me, not to know some secret thing. Go, go, Pierre, come to me when thou wilt. I am steeled now to the worst, and to the last. Again I tell thee, I will do any thing—yes, any thing that Pierre commands—for, though outer ill do lower upon us, still, deep within, thou wilt be careful, very careful with me, Pierre?"

"Thou art made of that fine, unshared stuff of which God makes his seraphim. But thy divine devotedness to me, is met by mine to thee. Well mayest thou trust me, Isabel; and whatever strangest thing I may yet propose to thee, thy confidence,—will it not bear me out? Surely thou will not hesitate to plunge, when I plunge first;—already have I plunged! now thou canst not stay upon the bank. Hearken, hearken to me.—I seek not now to gain thy prior assent to a thing as yet undone; but I call to thee now, Isabel, from the depth of a foregone act, to ratify it, backward, by thy consent. Look not so hard upon me. Listen. I will tell all. Isabel, though thou art all fearfulness to injure any living thing, least of all, thy brother; still thy true heart foreknoweth not the myriad alliances and criss-crossings among mankind, the infinite entanglements of all social things, which forbid that one thread should fly the general fabric, on some new line of duty, without tearing itself and tearing others. Listen. All that has happened up to this moment, and all that may be yet to happen, some sudden inspiration now assures me, inevitably proceeded from the first hour I saw thee. Not possibly could it, or can it, be otherwise. Therefore feel I, that I have some patience. Listen. Whatever outer things might possibly be mine; whatever seeming brightest blessings; yet now to live uncomforting and unloving to thee, Isabel; now to dwell domestically away from thee; so that only by stealth, and base connivances of the night, I could come to thee as thy related brother; this would be, and is, unutterably impossible. In my bosom a secret adder of self-reproach and self-infamy would never leave off its sting. Listen. But without gratuitous dishonor to a memory which—for right cause or wrong—is ever sacred and inviolate to me, I can not be an open brother to thee, Isabel. But thou wantest not the openness; for thou dost not pine for empty nominalness, but for vital realness; what thou wantest, is not the occasional openness of my brotherly love; but its continual domestic confidence. Do I not speak thine own hidden heart to thee? say, Isabel? Well, then, still listen to me. One only way presents to this; a most strange way, Isabel; to the world, that never throbbed for thee in love, a most deceitful way; but to all a harmless way; so harmless in its essence, Isabel, that, seems to me, Pierre hath consulted heaven itself upon it, and heaven itself did not say Nay. Still, listen to me; mark me. As thou knowest that thou wouldst now droop and die without me; so would I without thee. We are equal there; mark *that*, too, Isabel. I do not stoop to thee, nor thou to me; but we both reach up alike to a glorious ideal! Now the continualness, the secretness, yet the always present domesticness of our love; how may we best compass that, without jeopardizing the ever-sacred memory I hinted of? One way—one way—only one! A strange way, but most pure. Listen. Brace thyself: here, let me hold thee now; and then whisper it to thee, Isabel. Come, I holding thee, thou canst not fall."

He held her tremblingly; she bent over toward him; his mouth wet her ear; he whispered it.

The girl moved not; was done with all her tremblings; leaned closer to him, with an inexpressible strangeness of an intense love, new and inexplicable. Over the face of Pierre there shot a terrible self-revelation; he imprinted repeated burning kisses upon her; pressed hard her hand; would not let go her sweet and awful passiveness.

Then they changed; they coiled together, and entangledly stood mute.

ii

Mrs. Glendinning walked her chamber; her dress loosened.

"That such accursed vileness should proceed from me! Now will the tongued world say—See the vile boy of Mary Glendinning!—Deceitful! thick with guilt, where I thought it was all guilelessness and gentlest docility to me. It has not happened! It is not day! Were this thing so, I should go mad, and be shut up, and not walk here where every door is open to me.—My own only son married to an unknown—thing! My own only son, false to his holiest plighted public vow—and the wide world knowing to it! He bears my name—Glendinning. I will disown it; were it like this dress, I would tear my name off from me, and burn it till it shriveled to a crisp!—Pierre! Pierre! come back, come back, and swear it is not so! It can not be! Wait: I will ring the bell, and see if it be so."

She rung the bell with violence, and soon heard a responsive knock.

"Come in!—Nay, falter not;" (throwing a shawl over her) "come in. Stand there and tell me if thou darest, that my son was in this house this morning and met me on the stairs. Darest thou say that?"

Dates looked confounded at her most unwonted aspect.

"Say it! find thy tongue! Or I will root mine out and fling it at thee! Say it!"

"My dear mistress!"

"I am not thy mistress! but thou my master; for, if thou sayest it, thou commandest me to madness.—Oh, vile boy!—Begone from me!"

She locked the door upon him, and swiftly and distractedly walked her chamber. She paused, and tossing down the curtains, shut out the sun from the two windows.

Another, but an unsummoned knock, was at the door. She opened it.

"My mistress, his Reverence is below. I would not call you, but he insisted."

"Let him come up."

"Here? Immediately?"

"Didst thou hear me? Let Mr. Falsgrave come up."

As if suddenly and admonishingly made aware, by Dates, of the ungovernable mood of Mrs. Glendinning, the clergyman entered the open door of her chamber with a most deprecating but honest reluctance, and apprehensiveness of he knew not what.

"Be seated, sir; stay, shut the door and lock it."

"Madam!"

"*I* will do it. Be seated. Hast thou seen him?"

"Whom, Madam?—Master Pierre?"

"Him!—quick!"

"It was to speak of him I came, Madam. He made a most extraordinary call upon me last night—midnight."

"And thou marriedst him?—Damn thee!"

"Nay, nay, nay, Madam; there is something here I know not of—I came to tell thee news, but thou hast some o'erwhelming tidings to reveal to me."

"I beg no pardons; but I may be sorry. Mr. Falsgrave, my son, standing publicly plighted to Lucy Tartan, has privately wedded some other girl—some slut!"

"Impossible!"

"True as thou art there. Thou knowest nothing of it then?"

"Nothing, nothing—not one grain till now. Who is it he has wedded?"

"Some *slut*, I tell thee!—I am no lady now, but something deeper,—a woman!—an outraged and pride-poisoned woman!"

She turned from him swiftly, and again paced the room, as frantic and entirely regardless of any presence. Waiting for her to pause, but in vain, Mr. Falsgrave advanced toward her cautiously, and with the profoundest deference, which was almost a cringing, spoke:—

"It is the hour of woe to thee; and I confess my cloth hath no consolation for thee yet awhile. Permit me to withdraw from thee, leaving my best prayers for thee, that thou mayst know some peace, ere this now shut-out sun goes down. Send for me whenever thou desirest me.—May I go now?"

"Begone! and let me not hear thy soft, mincing voice, which is an infamy to a man! Begone, thou helpless, and unhelping one!"

She swiftly paced the room again, swiftly muttering to herself. "Now, now, now, now I see it clearer, clearer—clear now as day! My first dim suspicions pointed right!—too right! Ay—the sewing! it was the sewing!—The shriek!—I saw him gazing rooted at her. He would not speak going home with me. I charged him with his silence; he put me off with lies, lies, lies! Ay, ay, he is married to her, to her;—to her!—perhaps was then. And yet,—and yet,—how can it be?—Lucy, Lucy—I saw him, after that, look on her as if he would be glad to die for her, and go to hell for her, whither he deserves to go!—Oh! oh! oh! Thus ruthlessly to cut off, at one gross sensual dash, the fair succession of an honorable race! Mixing the choicest wine with filthy water from the plebeian pool, and so turning all to undistinguishable rankness!—Oh viper! had I thee now in me, I would be a suicide and a murderer with one blow!"

A third knock was at the door. She opened it.

"My mistress, I thought it would disturb you,—it is so just overhead,—so I have not removed them yet."

"Unravel thy gibberish!—what is it?"

"Pardon, my mistress, I somehow thought you knew it, but you can not."

"What is that writing crumpling in thy hand? Give it me."

"I have promised my young master not to, my mistress."

"I will snatch it, then, and so leave thee blameless.—What? what? what?—He's mad sure!—'Fine old fellow Dates'—what? what?—mad and merry!—chest?—clothes?—trunks?—he wants them?—Tumble them out of his window!—and if he stand right beneath, tumble them out! Dismantle that whole room. Tear up the carpet. I swear, he shall leave no smallest vestige in this house.—Here! this very spot—here, here, where I stand, he may have stood upon;—yes, he tied my shoe-string here; it's slippery! Dates!"

"My mistress."

"Do his bidding. By reflection he has made me infamous to the world; and I will make him infamous to it. Listen, and do not delude thyself that I am crazy. Go up to yonder room" (pointing upward), "and remove every article in it, and where he bid thee set down the chest and trunks, there set down all the contents of that room."

"'Twas before the house—this house!"

"And if it had not been there, I would order thee to put them there. Dunce! I would have the world know that I disown and scorn him! Do my bidding!—Stay. Let the room stand; but take him what he asks for."

"I will, my mistress."

As Dates left the chamber, Mrs. Glendinning again paced it swiftly, and again swiftly muttered: "Now, if I were less a strong and haughty woman, the fit would have gone by ere now. But deep volcanoes long burn, ere they burn out.—Oh, that the world were made of such malleable stuff, that we could recklessly do our fieriest heart's-wish before it, and not falter. Accursed be those four syllables of sound which make up that vile word Propriety. It is a chain and ball to drag;—drag? what sound is that? there's dragging—his trunks—the traveler's—dragging out. Oh would I could so drag my heart, as fishers for the drowned do, as that I might drag up my sunken happiness! Boy! boy! worse than brought in dripping drowned to me,—drowned in icy infamy! Oh! oh! oh!"

She threw herself upon the bed, covered her face, and lay motionless. But suddenly rose again, and hurriedly rang the bell.

"Open that desk, and draw the stand to me. Now wait and take this to Miss Lucy."

With a pencil she rapidly traced these lines:—

"My heart bleeds for thee, sweet Lucy. I can not speak—I know it all. Look for me the first hour I regain myself."

Again she threw herself upon the bed, and lay motionless.

iii

Toward sundown that evening, Pierre stood in one of the three bespoken chambers in the Black Swan Inn; the blue chintz-covered chest and the writing-desk before him. His hands were eagerly searching through his pockets.

"The key! the key! Nay, then, I must force it open. It bodes ill, too. Yet lucky is it, some bankers can break into their own vaults, when other means do fail. Not so, ever. Let me see:—yes, the tongs there. Now then for the sweet sight of gold and silver. I never loved it till this day. How long it has been hoarded;—little token pieces, of years ago, from aunts, uncles, cousins innumerable, and from—but I won't mention *them*; dead henceforth to me! Sure there'll be a premium on such ancient gold. There's some broad bits, token pieces to my—I name him not—more than half a century ago. Well, well, I never thought to cast them back into the sordid circulations whence they came. But if they must be spent, now is the time, in this last necessity, and in this sacred cause. 'Tis a most stupid, dunderheaded crowbar. Hoy! so! ah, now for it:—snake's nest!"

Forced suddenly back, the chest-lid had as suddenly revealed to him the chair-portrait lying on top of all the rest, where he had secreted it some days before. Face up, it met him with its noiseless, ever-nameless, and ambiguous, unchanging smile. Now his first repugnance was augmented by an emotion altogether new. That certain lurking lineament in the portrait, whose strange transfer, blended with far other, and sweeter, and nobler characteristics, was visible in the countenance of Isabel; that lineament in the portrait was somehow now detestable; nay, altogether loathsome, ineffably so, to Pierre. He argued not with himself why this was so; he only felt it, and most keenly.

Omitting more subtile inquisition into this deftly-winding theme, it will be enough to hint, perhaps, that possibly one source of this new hatefulness had its primary and unconscious rise in one of those profound ideas, which at times atmospherically, as it were, do insinuate themselves even into very ordinary minds. In the strange relativeness, reciprocalness, and transmittedness, between the long-dead father's portrait, and the living daughter's face, Pierre might have seemed to see reflected to him, by visible and uncontradictable symbols, the tyranny of Time and Fate. Painted before the daughter was conceived or born, like a dumb seer, the portrait still seemed leveling its prophetic finger at that empty air, from which Isabel did finally emerge. There seemed to lurk some mystical intelligence and vitality in the picture; because, since in his own memory of his father, Pierre could not recall any distinct lineament transmitted to Isabel, but vaguely saw such in the portrait; therefore, not Pierre's parent, as any way rememberable by him, but the portrait's painted *self* seemed the real father of Isabel; for, so far as all sense went, Isabel had inherited one peculiar trait nowhither traceable but to it.

And as his father was now sought to be banished from his mind, as a most bitter presence there, but Isabel was become a thing of intense and fearful love for him; therefore, it was loathsome to him, that in the smiling and ambiguous portrait, her sweet mournful image should be so sinisterly becrooked, bemixed, and mutilated to him.

When the first shock, and then the pause were over, he lifted the portrait in his two hands, and held it averted from him.

"It shall not live. Hitherto I have hoarded up mementoes and monuments of the past; been a worshiper of all heir-looms; a fond filer away of letters, locks of hair, bits of ribbon, flowers, and the thousand-and-one minutenesses which love and memory think they sanctify:—but it is forever over now! If to me any memory shall henceforth be dear, I will not mummy it in a visible memorial for every passing beggar's dust to gather on. Love's museum is vain and foolish as the Catacombs, where grinning apes and abject lizards are embalmed, as, forsooth, significant of some imagined charm. It speaks merely of decay and death, and nothing more; decay and death of endless innumerable generations; it makes of earth one mold. How can lifelessness be fit memorial of life?—So far, for mementoes of the sweetest. As for the rest—now I know this, that in commonest memorials, the twilight fact of death first discloses in some secret way, all the ambiguities of that departed thing or person; obliquely it casts hints, and insinuates surmises base, and eternally incapable of being cleared. Decreed by God Omnipotent it is, that Death should be the last scene of the last act of man's play;—a play, which begin how it may, in farce or comedy, ever hath its tragic end; the curtain inevitably falls upon a corpse. Therefore, never more will I play the vile pigmy, and by small memorials after death, attempt to reverse the decree of death, by essaying the poor perpetuating of the image of the original. Let all die, and mix again! As for this—this!—why longer should I preserve it? Why preserve that on which one can not patient look? If I am resolved to hold his public memory inviolate,—destroy this thing; for here is the one great, condemning, and unsuborned proof, whose mysticalness drives me half mad.—Of old Greek times, before man's brain went into doting bondage, and bleached and beaten in Baconian fulling-mills, his four limbs lost their barbaric tan and beauty; when the round world was fresh, and rosy, and spicy, as a new-plucked apple;—all's wilted now!—in those bold times, the great dead were not, turkey-like, dished in trenchers, and set down all garnished in the ground, to glut the damned Cyclops like a cannibal; but nobly envious Life cheated the glutton worm, and gloriously burned the corpse; so that the spirit up-pointed, and visibly forked to heaven!

"So now will I serve thee. Though that solidity of which thou art the unsolid duplicate, hath long gone to its hideous church-yard account;—and though, God knows! but for one part of thee it may have been fit auditing; —yet will I now a second time see thy obsequies performed, and by now burning thee, urn thee in the great vase of air! Come now!"

A small wood-fire had been kindled on the hearth to purify the long-closed room; it was now diminished to a small pointed heap of glowing embers. Detaching and dismembering the gilded but tarnished frame, Pierre laid the four pieces on the coals; as their dryness soon caught the sparks, he rolled the reversed canvas into a scroll, and tied it, and committed it to the now crackling, clamorous flames. Steadfastly Pierre watched the first crispings and blackenings of the painted scroll, but started as suddenly unwinding from the burnt string that had tied it, for one swift instant, seen through the flame and smoke, the upwrithing portrait tormentedly stared at him in beseeching horror, and then, wrapped in one broad sheet of oily fire, disappeared forever.

Yielding to a sudden ungovernable impulse, Pierre darted his hand among the flames, to rescue the imploring face; but as swiftly drew back his scorched and bootless grasp. His hand was burnt and blackened, but he did not heed it.

He ran back to the chest, and seizing repeated packages of family letters, and all sorts of miscellaneous memorials in paper, he threw them one after the other upon the fire.

"Thus, and thus, and thus! on thy manes I fling fresh spoils; pour out all my memory in one libation!—so, so, so—lower, lower, lower; now all is done, and all is ashes! Henceforth, cast-out Pierre hath no paternity, and no past; and since the Future is one blank to all; therefore, twice-disinherited Pierre stands untrammeledly his ever-present self!—free to do his own self-will and present fancy to whatever end!"

iv

That same sunset Lucy lay in her chamber. A knock was heard at its door, and the responding Martha was met by the now self-controlled and resolute face of Mrs. Glendinning.

"How is your young mistress, Martha? May I come in?"

But waiting for no answer, with the same breath she passed the maid, and determinately entered the room.

She sat down by the bed, and met the open eye, but closed and pallid mouth of Lucy. She gazed rivetedly and inquisitively a moment; then turned a quick aghast look toward Martha, as if seeking warrant for some shuddering thought.

"Miss Lucy"—said Martha—"it is your—it is Mrs. Glendinning. Speak to her, Miss Lucy."

As if left in the last helpless attitude of some spent contortion of her grief, Lucy was not lying in the ordinary posture of one in bed, but lay half crosswise upon it, with the pale pillows propping her hueless form, and but a single sheet thrown over her, as though she were so heart overladen, that her white body could not bear one added feather. And as in any snowy, marble statue, the drapery clings to the limbs; so as one found drowned, the thin, defining sheet invested Lucy.

"It is Mrs. Glendinning. Will you speak to her, Miss Lucy?"

The thin lips moved and trembled for a moment, and then were still again, and augmented pallor shrouded her.

Martha brought restoratives; and when all was as before, she made a gesture for the lady to depart, and in a whisper, said, "She will not speak to any; she does not speak to me. The doctor has just left—he has been here five times since morning—and says she must be kept entirely quiet." Then pointing to the stand, added, "You see what he has left—mere restoratives. Quiet is her best medicine now, he says. Quiet, quiet, quiet! Oh, sweet quiet, wilt thou now ever come?"

"Has Mrs. Tartan been written to?" whispered the lady. Martha nodded.

So the lady moved to quit the room, saying that once every two hours she would send to know how Lucy fared.

"But where, where is her aunt, Martha?" she exclaimed, lowly, pausing at the door, and glancing in sudden astonishment about the room; "surely, surely, Mrs. Llanyllyn—"

"Poor, poor old lady," weepingly whispered Martha, "she hath caught infection from sweet Lucy's woe; she hurried hither, caught one glimpse of that bed, and fell like dead upon the floor. The Doctor hath two patients now, lady"—glancing at the bed, and tenderly feeling Lucy's bosom, to mark if yet it heaved; "Alack! Alack! oh, reptile! reptile! that could sting so sweet a breast! fire would be too cold for him—accursed!"

"Thy own tongue blister the roof of thy mouth!" cried Mrs. Glendinning, in a half-stifled, whispering scream. "'Tis not for thee, hired one, to rail at my son, though he were Lucifer, simmering in Hell! Mend thy manners, minx!"

And she left the chamber, dilated with her unconquerable pride, leaving Martha aghast at such venom in such beauty.

Book XIII

They Depart the Meadows

IT WAS JUST DUSK when Pierre approached the Ulver farm-house, in a wagon belonging to the Black Swan Inn. He met his sister shawled and bonneted in the porch.

"Now then, Isabel, is all ready? Where is Delly? I see two most small and inconsiderable portmanteaux. Wee is the chest that holds the goods of the disowned! The wagon waits, Isabel. Now is all ready? and nothing left?"

"Nothing, Pierre; unless in going hence—but I'll not think of that; all's fated."

"Delly! where is she? Let us go in for her," said Pierre, catching the hand of Isabel, and turning rapidly. As he thus half dragged her into the little lighted entry, and then dropping her hand, placed his touch on the catch of the inner door, Isabel stayed his arm, as if to keep him back, till she should forewarn him against something concerning Delly; but suddenly she started herself; and for one instant, eagerly pointing at his right hand, seemed almost to half shrink from Pierre.

"'Tis nothing. I am not hurt; a slight burn—the merest accidental scorch this morning. But what's this?" he added, lifting his hand higher; "smoke! soot! this comes of going in the dark; sunlight, and I had seen it. But I have not touched thee, Isabel?"

Isabel lifted her hand and showed the marks.—"But it came from thee, my brother; and I would catch the plague from thee, so that it should make me share thee. Do thou clean thy hand; let mine alone."

"Delly! Delly!"—cried Pierre—"why may I not go to her, to bring her forth?"

Placing her finger upon her lip, Isabel softly opened the door, and showed the object of his inquiry avertedly seated, muffled, on a chair.

"Do not speak to her, my brother," whispered Isabel, "and do not seek to behold her face, as yet. It will pass over now, ere long, I trust. Come, shall we go now? Take Delly forth, but do not speak to her. I have bidden all good-by; the old people are in yonder room in the rear; I am glad that they chose not to come out, to attend our going forth. Come now, be very quick, Pierre; this is an hour I like not; be it swiftly past."

Soon all three alighted at the inn. Ordering lights, Pierre led the way above-stairs, and ushered his two companions into one of the two outermost rooms of the three adjoining chambers prepared for all.

"See," said he, to the mute and still self-averting figure of Delly;—"see, this is thy room, Miss Ulver; Isabel has told thee all; thou know'st our till now secret marriage; she will stay with thee now, till I return from a little business down the street. To-morrow, thou know'st, very early, we take the stage. I may not see thee again till then, so, be steadfast, and cheer up a very little, Miss Ulver, and good-night. All will be well."

ii

Next morning, by break of day, at four o'clock, the four swift hours were personified in four impatient horses, which shook their trappings beneath the windows of the inn. Three figures emerged into the cool dim air and took their places in the coach.

The old landlord had silently and despondently shaken Pierre by the hand; the vainglorious driver was on his box, threadingly adjusting the four reins among the fingers of his buck-skin gloves; the usual thin company of admiring ostlers and other early on-lookers were gathered about the porch; when—on his companions' account—all eager to cut short any vain delay, at such a painful crisis, Pierre impetuously shouted for the coach to move. In a moment, the four meadow-fed young horses leaped forward their own generous lengths, and the four responsive wheels rolled their complete circles; while making vast rearward flourishes with his whip, the elated driver seemed as a bravado-hero signing his ostentatious farewell signature in the empty air. And so, in the dim of the dawn—and to the defiant crackings of that long and sharp-resounding whip, the three forever fled the sweet fields of Saddle Meadows.

The stout old landlord gazed after the coach awhile, and then re-entering the inn, stroked his gray beard and muttered to himself:—"I have kept this house, now, three-and-thirty years, and have had plenty of bridal-parties come and go; in their long train of wagons, break-downs, buggies, gigs—a gay and giggling train—Ha!—there's a pun! popt out like a cork—ay, and once in ox-carts, all garlanded; ay, and once, the merry bride was bedded on a load of sweet-scented new-cut clover. But such a bridal-party as this morning's—why, it's as sad as funerals. And brave Master Pierre Glendinning is the groom! Well, well, wonders is all the go. I thought I had done with wondering when I passed fifty; but I keep wondering still. Ah, somehow, now, I feel as though I had just come from lowering some old friend beneath the sod, and yet felt the grating cord-marks in my palms.—'Tis early, but I'll drink. Let's see; cider,—a mug of cider;—'tis sharp, and pricks like a game-cock's spur,—cider's the drink for grief. Oh, Lord! that fat men should be so thin-skinned, and suffer in pure sympathy on others' account. A thin-skinned, thin man, he don't suffer so, because there ain't so much stuff in him for his thin skin to cover. Well, well, well, well, well; of all colics, save me from the melloncholics; green melons is the greenest thing!"

Book XIV

The Journey and the Pamphlet

ALL PROFOUND THINGS, and emotions of things are preceded and attended by Silence. What a silence is that with which the pale bride precedes the responsive *I will*, to the priest's solemn question, *Wilt thou have this man for thy husband?* In silence, too, the wedded hands are clasped. Yea, in silence the child Christ was born into the world. Silence is the general consecration of the universe. Silence is the invisible laying on of the Divine Pontiff's hands upon the world. Silence is at once the most harmless and the most awful thing in all nature. It speaks of the Reserved Forces of Fate. Silence is the only Voice of our God.

Nor is this so august Silence confined to things simply touching or grand. Like the air, Silence permeates all things, and produces its magical power, as well during that peculiar mood which prevails at a solitary traveler's first setting forth on a journey, as at the unimaginable time when before the world was, Silence brooded on the face of the waters.

No word was spoken by its inmates, as the coach bearing our young Enthusiast, Pierre, and his mournful party, sped forth through the dim dawn into the deep midnight, which still occupied, unrepulsed, the hearts of the old woods through which the road wound, very shortly after quitting the village.

When, first entering the coach, Pierre had pressed his hand upon the cushioned seat to steady his way, some crumpled leaves of paper had met his fingers. He had instinctively clutched them; and the same strange clutching mood of his soul which had prompted that instinctive act, did also prevail in causing him now to retain the crumpled paper in his hand for an hour or more of that wonderful intense silence, which the rapid coach bore through the heart of the general stirless morning silence of the fields and the woods.

His thoughts were very dark and wild; for a space there was rebellion and horrid anarchy and infidelity in his soul. This temporary mood may best be likened to that, which—according to a singular story once told in the pulpit by a reverend man of God—invaded the heart of an excellent priest. In the midst of a solemn cathedral, upon a cloudy Sunday afternoon, this priest was in the act of publicly administering the bread at the Holy Sacrament of the Supper, when the Evil One suddenly propounded to him the possibility of the mere moonshine of the Christian Religion. Just such now was the mood of Pierre; to him the Evil One propounded the possibility of the mere moonshine of all his self-renouncing Enthusiasm. The Evil One hooted at him, and called him a fool. But by instant and earnest prayer—closing his two eyes, with his two hands still holding the sacramental bread—the devout priest had vanquished the impious Devil. Not so with Pierre. The imperishable monument of his holy Catholic Church; the imperishable record of his Holy Bible; the imperishable intuition of the innate truth of Christianity;—these were the indestructible anchors which still held the priest to his firm Faith's rock, when the sudden storm raised by the Evil One assailed him. But Pierre—where could *he* find the Church, the monument, the Bible, which unequivocally said to him—"Go on; thou art in the Right; I endorse thee all over; go on."—So the difference between the Priest and Pierre was herein:—with the priest it was a matter, whether certain bodiless thoughts of his were true or not true; but with Pierre it was a question whether certain vital acts of his were right or wrong. In this little nut lie germ-like the possible solution of some puzzling problems; and also the discovery of additional, and still more profound problems ensuing upon the solution of the former. For so true is this last, that some men refuse to solve any present problem, for fear of making still more work for themselves in that way.

Now, Pierre thought of the magical, mournful letter of Isabel, he recalled the divine inspiration of that hour when the heroic words burst from his heart—"Comfort thee, and stand by thee, and fight for thee, will thy leapingly-acknowledging brother!" These remembrances unfurled themselves in proud exultations in his soul; and from before such glorious banners of Virtue, the club-footed Evil One limped away in dismay. But now the dread, fateful parting look of his mother came over him; anew he heard the heart-proscribing words—"Beneath my roof and at my table, he who was once Pierre Glendinning no more puts himself;"—swooning in her snow-white bed, the lifeless Lucy lay before him, wrapt as in the reverberating echoings of her own agonizing shriek: "My heart! my heart!" Then how swift the recurrence to Isabel, and the nameless awfulness of his still imperfectly conscious, incipient, new-mingled emotion toward this mysterious being. "Lo! I leave corpses wherever I go!" groaned Pierre to himself—"Can then my conduct be right? Lo! by my conduct I seem threatened by the possibility of a sin anomalous and accursed, so anomalous, it may well be the one for which Scripture says, there is never forgiveness. Corpses behind me, and the last sin before, how then can my conduct be right?"

In this mood, the silence accompanied him, and the first visible rays of the morning sun in this same mood found him and saluted him. The excitement and the sleepless night just passed, and the strange narcotic of a quiet, steady anguish, and the sweet quiescence of the air, and the monotonous cradle-like motion of the coach over a road made firm and smooth by a refreshing shower over night; these had wrought their wonted effect upon Isabel and Delly; with hidden faces they leaned fast asleep in Pierre's sight. Fast asleep—thus unconscious, oh sweet Isabel, oh forlorn Delly, your swift destinies I bear in my own!

Suddenly, as his sad eye fell lower and lower from scanning their magically quiescent persons, his glance lit upon his own clutched hand, which rested on his knee. Some paper protruded from that clutch. He knew not how it had got there, or whence it had come, though himself had closed his own gripe upon it. He lifted his hand and slowly unfingered and unbolted the paper, and unrolled it, and carefully smoothed it, to see what it might be.

It was a thin, tattered, dried-fish-like thing; printed with blurred ink upon mean, sleazy paper. It seemed the opening pages of some ruinous old pamphlet—a pamphlet containing a chapter or so of some very voluminous disquisition. The conclusion was gone. It must have been accidentally left there by some previous traveler, who perhaps in drawing out his handkerchief, had ignorantly extracted his waste paper.

There is a singular infatuation in most men, which leads them in odd moments, intermitting between their regular occupations, and when they find themselves all alone in some quiet corner or nook, to fasten with unaccountable fondness upon the merest rag of old printed paper—some shred of a long-exploded advertisement perhaps—and read it, and study it, and re-read it, and pore over it, and fairly agonize themselves over this miserable, sleazy paper-rag, which at any other time, or in any other place, they would hardly touch with St. Dunstan's long tongs. So now, in a degree, with Pierre. But notwithstanding that he, with most other human beings, shared in the strange hallucination above mentioned, yet the first glimpse of the title of the dried-fish-like, pamphlet-shaped rag, did almost tempt him to pitch it out of the window. For, be a man's mood what it may, what sensible and ordinary mortal could have patience for any considerable period, to knowingly hold in his conscious hand a printed document (and that too a very blurred one as to ink, and a very sleazy one as to paper), so metaphysically and insufferably entitled as this:—"Chronometricals & Horologicals?"

Doubtless, it was something vastly profound; but it is to be observed, that when a man is in a really profound mood, then all merely verbal or written profundities are unspeakably repulsive, and seem downright childish to him. Nevertheless, the silence still continued; the road ran through an almost unplowed and uninhabited region; the slumberers still slumbered before him; the evil mood was becoming well nigh insupportable to him; so, more to force his mind away from the dark realities of things than from any other motive, Pierre finally tried his best to plunge himself into the pamphlet.

ii

Sooner or later in this life, the earnest, or enthusiastic youth comes to know, and more or less appreciate this startling solecism:—That while, as the grand condition of acceptance to God, Christianity calls upon all men to renounce this world; yet by all odds the most Mammonish part of this world—Europe and America—are owned by none but professed Christian nations, who glory in the owning, and seem to have some reason therefor.

This solecism once vividly and practically apparent; then comes the earnest reperusal of the Gospels: the intense self-absorption into that greatest real miracle of all religions, the Sermon on the Mount. From that divine mount, to all earnest-loving youths, flows an inexhaustible soul-melting stream of tenderness and loving-kindness; and they leap exulting to their feet, to think that the founder of their holy religion gave utterance to sentences so infinitely sweet and soothing as these; sentences which embody all the love of the Past, and all the love which can be imagined in any conceivable Future. Such emotions as that Sermon raises in the enthusiastic heart; such emotions all youthful hearts refuse to ascribe to humanity as their origin. This is of God! cries the heart, and in that cry ceases all inquisition. Now, with this fresh-read sermon in his soul, the youth again gazes abroad upon the world. Instantly, in aggravation of the former solecism, an overpowering sense of the world's downright positive falsity comes over him; the world seems to lie saturated and soaking with lies. The sense of this thing is so overpowering, that at first the youth is apt to refuse the evidence of his own senses; even as he does that same evidence in the matter of the movement of the visible sun in the heavens, which with his own eyes he plainly sees to go round the world, but nevertheless on the authority of other persons,—the Copernican astronomers, whom he never saw—he believes it *not* to go round the world, but the world round it. Just so, too, he hears good and wise people sincerely say: This world only *seems* to be saturated and soaking with lies; but in reality it does not so lie soaking and saturate; along with some lies, there is much truth in this world. But again he refers to his Bible, and there he reads most explicitly, that this world is unconditionally depraved and accursed; and that at all hazards men must come out of it. But why come out of it, if it be a True World and not a Lying World? Assuredly, then, this world is a lie.

Hereupon then in the soul of the enthusiast youth two armies come to the shock; and unless he prove recreant, or unless he prove gullible, or unless he can find the talismanic secret, to reconcile this world with his own soul, then there is no peace for him, no slightest truce for him in this life. Now without doubt this Talismanic Secret has never yet been found; and in the nature of human things it seems as though it never can be. Certain philosophers have time and again pretended to have found it; but if they do not in the end discover their own delusion, other people soon discover it for themselves, and so those philosophers and their vain philosophy are let glide away into practical oblivion. Plato, and Spinoza, and Goethe, and many more belong to this guild of self-impostors, with a preposterous rabble of Muggletonian Scots and Yankees, whose vile brogue still the more bestreaks the stripedness of their Greek or German Neoplatonical originals. That profound Silence, that only Voice of our God, which I before spoke of; from that divine thing without a name, those impostor philosophers pretend somehow to have got an answer; which is as absurd, as though they should say they had got water out of stone; for how can a man get a Voice out of Silence?

Certainly, all must admit, that if for any one this problem of the possible reconcilement of this world with our own souls possessed a peculiar and potential interest, that one was Pierre Glendinning at the period we now write of. For in obedience to the loftiest behest of his soul, he had done certain vital acts, which had already lost him his worldly felicity, and which he felt must in the end indirectly work him some still additional and not-to-be-thought-of woe.

Soon then, as after his first distaste at the mystical title, and after his then reading on, merely to drown himself, Pierre at last began to obtain a glimmering into the profound intent of the writer of the sleazy rag pamphlet, he felt a great interest awakened in him. The more he read and re-read, the more this interest deepened, but still the more likewise did his failure to comprehend the writer increase. He seemed somehow to derive some general vague inkling concerning it, but the central conceit refused to become clear to him. The reason whereof is not so easy to be laid down; seeing that the reason-originating heart and mind of man, these organic things themselves are not so easily to be expounded. Something, however, more or less to the point, may be adventured here.

If a man be in any vague latent doubt about the intrinsic correctness and excellence of his general life-theory and practical course of life; then, if that man chance to light on any other man, or any little treatise, or sermon, which unintendingly, as it were, yet very palpably illustrates to him the intrinsic incorrectness and non-excellence of both the theory and the practice of his life; then that man will—more or less unconsciously—try hard to hold himself back from the self-admitted comprehension of a matter which thus condemns him. For in this case, to comprehend, is himself to condemn himself, which is always highly inconvenient and uncomfortable to a man. Again. If a man be told a thing wholly new, then—during the time of its first announcement to him—it is entirely impossible for him to comprehend it. For—absurd as it may seem—men are only made to comprehend things which they comprehended before (though but in the embryo, as it were). Things new it is impossible to make them comprehend, by merely talking to them about it. True, sometimes they pretend to comprehend; in their own hearts they really believe they do comprehend; outwardly look as though they *did* comprehend; wag their bushy tails comprehendingly; but for all that, they do not comprehend. Possibly, they may afterward come, of themselves, to inhale this new idea from the circumambient air, and so come to comprehend it; but not otherwise at all. It will be observed, that neither points of the above speculations do we, in set terms, attribute to Pierre in connection with the rag pamphlet. Possibly both might be applicable; possibly neither. Certain it is, however, that at the time, in his own heart, he seemed to think that he did not fully comprehend the strange writer's conceit in all its bearings. Yet was this conceit apparently one of the plainest in the world; so natural, a child might almost have originated it. Nevertheless, again so profound, that scarce Jugglarius himself could be the author; and still again so exceedingly trivial, that Jugglarius' smallest child might well have been ashamed of it.

Seeing then that this curious paper rag so puzzled Pierre; foreseeing, too, that Pierre may not in the end be entirely uninfluenced in his conduct by the torn pamphlet, when afterwards perhaps by other means he shall come to understand it; or, peradventure, come to know that he, in the first place, did —seeing too that the author thereof came to be made known to him by reputation, and though Pierre never spoke to him, yet exerted a surprising sorcery upon his spirit by the mere distant glimpse of his countenance;— all these reasons I account sufficient apology for inserting in the following chapter the initial part of what seems to me a very fanciful and mystical, rather than philosophical Lecture, from which, I confess, that I myself can derive no conclusion which permanently satisfies those peculiar motions in my soul, to which that Lecture seems more particularly addressed. For to me it seems more the excellently illustrated re-statement of a problem, than the solution of the problem itself. But as such mere illustrations are almost universally taken for solutions (and perhaps they are the only possible human solutions), therefore it may help to the temporary quiet of some inquiring mind; and so not be wholly without use. At the worst, each person can now skip, or read and rail for himself.

iii

"*EI,*"

BY

PLOTINUS PLINLIMMON,

(*In Three Hundred and Thirty-three Lectures.*)

LECTURE FIRST.

CHRONOMETRICALS AND HOROLOGICALS,

(*Being not so much the Portal, as part of the temporary Scaffold to the Portal of this new Philosophy.*)

"Few of us doubt, gentlemen, that human life on this earth is but a state of probation; which among other things implies, that here below, we mortals have only to do with things provisional. Accordingly, I hold that all our so-called wisdom is likewise but provisional.

"This preamble laid down, I begin.

"It seems to me, in my visions, that there is a certain most rare order of human souls, which if carefully carried in the body will almost always and everywhere give Heaven's own Truth, with some small grains of variance. For peculiarly coming from God, the sole source of that heavenly truth, and the great Greenwich hill and tower from which the universal meridians are far out into infinity reckoned; such souls seem as London sea-chronometers (*Greek*, time-namers) which as the London ship floats past Greenwich down the Thames, are accurately adjusted by Greenwich time, and if heedfully kept, will still give that same time, even though carried to the Azores. True, in nearly all cases of long, remote voyages—to China, say—chronometers of the best make, and the most carefully treated, will gradually more or less vary from Greenwich time, without the possibility of the error being corrected by direct comparison with their great standard; but skillful and devout observations of the stars by the sextant will serve materially to lessen such errors. And besides, there is such a thing as *rating* a chronometer; that is, having ascertained its degree of organic inaccuracy, however small, then in all subsequent chronometrical calculations, that ascertained loss or gain can be readily added or deducted, as the case may be. Then again, on these long voyages, the chronometer may be corrected by comparing it with the chronometer of some other ship at sea, more recently from home.

"Now in an artificial world like ours, the soul of man is further removed from its God and the Heavenly Truth, than the chronometer carried to China, is from Greenwich. And, as that chronometer, if at all accurate, will pronounce it to be 12 o'clock high-noon, when the China local watches say, perhaps, it is 12 o'clock midnight; so the chronometric soul, if in this world true to its great Greenwich in the other, will always, in its so-called intuitions of right and wrong, be contradicting the mere local standards and watch-maker's brains of this earth.

"Bacon's brains were mere watch-maker's brains; but Christ was a chronometer; and the most exquisitely adjusted and exact one, and the least affected by all terrestrial jarrings, of any that have ever come to us. And the reason why his teachings seemed folly to the Jews, was because he carried that Heaven's time in Jerusalem, while the Jews carried Jerusalem time there. Did he not expressly say—My wisdom (time) is not of this world? But whatever is really peculiar in the wisdom of Christ seems precisely the same folly to-day as it did 1850 years ago. Because, in all that interval his bequeathed chronometer has still preserved its original Heaven's time, and the general Jerusalem of this world has likewise carefully preserved its own.

"But though the chronometer carried from Greenwich to China, should truly exhibit in China what the time may be at Greenwich at any moment; yet, though thereby it must necessarily contradict China time, it does by no means thence follow, that with respect to China, the China watches are at all out of the way. Precisely the reverse. For the fact of that variance is a presumption that, with respect to China, the Chinese watches must be all right; and consequently as the China watches are right as to China, so the Greenwich chronometers must be wrong as to China. Besides, of what use to the Chinaman would a Greenwich chronometer, keeping Greenwich time, be? Were he thereby to regulate his daily actions, he would be guilty of all manner of absurdities:—going to bed at noon, say, when his neighbors would be sitting down to dinner. And thus, though the earthly wisdom of man be heavenly folly to God; so also, conversely, is the heavenly wisdom of God an earthly folly to man. Literally speaking, this is so. Nor does the God at the heavenly Greenwich expect common men to keep Greenwich wisdom in this remote Chinese world of ours; because such a thing were unprofitable for them here, and, indeed, a falsification of Himself, inasmuch as in that case, China time would be identical with Greenwich time, which would make Greenwich time wrong.

"But why then does God now and then send a heavenly chronometer (as a meteoric stone) into the world, uselessly as it would seem, to give the lie to all the world's time-keepers? Because he is unwilling to leave man without some occasional testimony to this:—that though man's Chinese notions of things may answer well enough here, they are by no means universally applicable, and that the central Greenwich in which He dwells goes by a somewhat different method from this world. And yet it follows not from this, that God's truth is one thing and man's truth another; but—as above hinted, and as will be further elucidated in subsequent lectures—by their very contradictions they are made to correspond.

"By inference it follows, also, that he who finding in himself a chronometrical soul, seeks practically to force that heavenly time upon the earth; in such an attempt he can never succeed, with an absolute and essential success. And as for himself, if he seek to regulate his own daily conduct by it, he will but array all men's earthly time-keepers against him, and thereby work himself woe and death. Both these things are plainly evinced in the character and fate of Christ, and the past and present condition of the religion he taught. But here one thing is to be especially observed. Though Christ encountered woe in both the precept and the practice of his chronometricals, yet did he remain throughout entirely without folly or sin. Whereas, almost invariably, with inferior beings, the absolute effort to live in this world according to the strict letter of the chronometricals is, somehow, apt to involve those inferior beings eventually in strange, *unique* follies and sins, unimagined before. It is the story of the Ephesian matron, allegorized.

"To any earnest man of insight, a faithful contemplation of these ideas concerning Chronometricals and Horologicals, will serve to render provisionally far less dark some few of the otherwise obscurest things which have hitherto tormented the honest-thinking men of all ages. What man who carries a heavenly soul in him, has not groaned to perceive, that unless he committed a sort of suicide as to the practical things of this world, he never can hope to regulate his earthly conduct by that same heavenly soul? And yet by an infallible instinct he knows, that that monitor can not be wrong in itself.

"And where is the earnest and righteous philosopher, gentlemen, who looking right and left, and up and down, through all the ages of the world, the present included; where is there such an one who has not a thousand times been struck with a sort of infidel idea, that whatever other worlds God may be Lord of, he is not the Lord of this; for else this world would seem to give the lie to Him; so utterly repugnant seem its ways to the instinctively known ways of Heaven. But it is not, and can not be so; nor will he who regards this chronometrical conceit aright, ever more be conscious of that horrible idea. For he will then see, or seem to see, that this world's seeming incompatibility with God, absolutely results from its meridianal correspondence with him.

* * * *

"This chronometrical conceit does by no means involve the justification of all the acts which wicked men may perform. For in their wickedness downright wicked men sin as much against their own horologes, as against the heavenly chronometer. That this is so, their spontaneous liability to remorse does plainly evince. No, this conceit merely goes to show, that for the mass of men, the highest abstract heavenly righteousness is not only impossible, but would be entirely out of place, and positively wrong in a world like this. To turn the left cheek if the right be smitten, is chronometrical; hence, no average son of man ever did such a thing. To give *all* that thou hast to the poor, this too is chronometrical; hence no average son of man ever did such a thing. Nevertheless, if a man gives with a certain self-considerate generosity to the poor; abstains from doing downright ill to any man; does his convenient best in a general way to do good to his whole race; takes watchful loving care of his wife and children, relatives, and friends; is perfectly tolerant to all other men's opinions, whatever they may be; is an honest dealer, an honest citizen, and all that; and more especially if he believe that there is a God for infidels, as well as for believers, and acts upon that belief; then, though such a man falls infinitely short of the chronometrical standard, though all his actions are entirely horologic;—yet such a man need never lastingly despond, because he is sometimes guilty of some minor offense:—hasty words, impulsively returning a blow, fits of domestic petulance, selfish enjoyment of a glass of wine while he knows there are those around him who lack a loaf of bread. I say he need never lastingly despond on account of his perpetual liability to these things; because *not* to do them, and their like, would be to be an angel, a chronometer; whereas, he is a man and a horologe.

"Yet does the horologe itself teach, that all liabilities to these things should be checked as much as possible, though it is certain they can never be utterly eradicated. They are only to be checked, then, because, if entirely unrestrained, they would finally run into utter selfishness and human demonism, which, as before hinted, are not by any means justified by the horologe.

"In short, this Chronometrical and Horological conceit, in sum, seems to teach this:—That in things terrestrial (horological) a man must not be governed by ideas celestial (chronometrical); that certain minor self-renunciations in this life his own mere instinct for his own every-day general well-being will teach him to make, but he must by no means make a complete unconditional sacrifice of himself in behalf of any other being, or any cause, or any conceit. (For, does aught else completely and unconditionally sacrifice itself for him? God's own sun does not abate one tittle of its heat in July, however you swoon with that heat in the sun. And if it *did* abate its heat on your behalf, then the wheat and the rye would not ripen; and so, for the incidental benefit of one, a whole population would suffer.)

"A virtuous expediency, then, seems the highest desirable or attainable earthly excellence for the mass of men, and is the only earthly excellence that their Creator intended for them. When they go to heaven, it will be quite another thing. There, they can freely turn the left cheek, because there the right cheek will never be smitten. There they can freely give all to the poor, for *there* there will be no poor to give to. A due appreciation of this matter will do good to man. For, hitherto, being authoritatively taught by his dogmatical teachers that he must, while on earth, aim at heaven, and attain it, too, in all his earthly acts, on pain of eternal wrath; and finding by experience that this is utterly impossible; in his despair, he is too apt to run clean away into all manner of moral abandonment, self-deceit, and hypocrisy (cloaked, however, mostly under an aspect of the most respectable devotion); or else he openly runs, like a mad dog, into atheism. Whereas, let men be taught those Chronometricals and Horologicals, and while still retaining every common-sense incentive to whatever of virtue be practicable and desirable, and having these incentives strengthened, too, by the consciousness of powers to attain their mark; then there would be an end to that fatal despair of becoming all good, which has too often proved the vice-producing result in many minds of the undiluted chronometrical doctrines hitherto taught to mankind. But if any man say, that such a doctrine as this I lay down is false, is impious; I would charitably refer that man to the history of Christendom for the last 1800 years; and ask him, whether, in spite of all the maxims of Christ, that history is not just as full of blood, violence, wrong, and iniquity of every kind, as any previous portion of the world's story? Therefore, it follows, that so far as practical results are concerned—regarded in a purely earthly light—the only great original moral doctrine of Christianity (*i.e.* the chronometrical gratuitous return of good for evil, as distinguished from the horological forgiveness of injuries taught by some of the Pagan philosophers), has been found (horologically) a false one; because after 1800 years' inculcation from tens of thousands of pulpits, it has proved entirely impracticable.

"I but lay down, then, what the best mortal men do daily practice; and what all really wicked men are very far removed from. I present consolation to the earnest man, who, among all his human frailties, is still agonizingly conscious of the beauty of chronometrical excellence. I hold up a practicable virtue to the vicious; and interfere not with the eternal truth, that, sooner or later, in all cases, downright vice is downright woe.

"Moreover: if——"

But here the pamphlet was torn, and came to a most untidy termination.

Book XV

The Cousins

THOUGH RESOLVED to face all out to the last, at whatever desperate hazard, Pierre had not started for the city without some reasonable plans, both with reference to his more immediate circumstances, and his ulterior condition.

There resided in the city a cousin of his, Glendinning Stanly, better known in the general family as Glen Stanly, and by Pierre, as Cousin Glen. Like Pierre, he was an only son; his parents had died in his early childhood; and within the present year he had returned from a protracted sojourn in Europe, to enter, at the age of twenty-one, into the untrammeled possession of a noble property, which in the hands of faithful guardians, had largely accumulated.

In their boyhood and earlier adolescence, Pierre and Glen had cherished a much more than cousinly attachment. At the age of ten, they had furnished an example of the truth, that the friendship of fine-hearted, generous boys, nurtured amid the romance-engendering comforts and elegancies of life, sometimes transcends the bounds of mere boyishness, and revels for a while in the empyrean of a love which only comes short, by one degree, of the sweetest sentiment entertained between the sexes. Nor is this boy-love without the occasional fillips and spicinesses, which at times, by an apparent abatement, enhance the permanent delights of those more advanced lovers who love beneath the cestus of Venus. Jealousies are felt. The sight of another lad too much consorting with the boy's beloved object, shall fill him with emotions akin to those of Othello's; a fancied slight, or lessening of the every-day indications of warm feelings, shall prompt him to bitter upbraidings and reproaches; or shall plunge him into evil moods, for which grim solitude only is congenial.

Nor are the letters of Aphroditean devotees more charged with headlong vows and protestations, more cross-written and crammed with discursive sentimentalities, more undeviating in their semi-weekliness, or dayliness, as the case may be, than are the love-friendship missives of boys. Among those bundles of papers which Pierre, in an ill hour, so frantically destroyed in the chamber of the inn, were two large packages of letters, densely written, and in many cases inscribed crosswise throughout with red ink upon black; so that the love in those letters was two layers deep, and one pen and one pigment were insufficient to paint it. The first package contained the letters of Glen to Pierre, the other those of Pierre to Glen, which, just prior to Glen's departure for Europe, Pierre had obtained from him, in order to re-read them in his absence, and so fortify himself the more in his affection, by reviving reference to the young, ardent hours of its earliest manifestations.

But as the advancing fruit itself extrudes the beautiful blossom, so in many cases, does the eventual love for the other sex forever dismiss the preliminary love-friendship of boys. The mere outer friendship may in some degree—greater or less—survive; but the singular love in it has perishingly dropped away.

If in the eye of unyielding reality and truth, the earthly heart of man do indeed ever fix upon some one woman, to whom alone, thenceforth eternally to be a devotee, without a single shadow of the misgiving of its faith; and who, to him, does perfectly embody his finest, loftiest dream of feminine loveliness, if this indeed be so—and may Heaven grant that it be—nevertheless, in metropolitan cases, the love of the most single-eyed lover, almost invariably, is nothing more than the ultimate settling of innumerable wandering glances upon some one specific object; as admonished, that the wonderful scope and variety of female loveliness, if too long suffered to sway us without decision, shall finally confound all power of selection. The confirmed bachelor is, in America, at least, quite as often the victim of a too profound appreciation of the infinite charmingness of woman, as made solitary for life by the legitimate empire of a cold and tasteless temperament.

Though the peculiar heart-longings pertaining to his age, had at last found their glowing response in the bosom of Lucy; yet for some period prior to that, Pierre had not been insensible to the miscellaneous promptings of the passion. So that even before he became a declarative lover, Love had yet made him her general votary; and so already there had gradually come a cooling over that ardent sentiment which in earlier years he had cherished for Glen.

All round and round does the world lie as in a sharp-shooter's ambush, to pick off the beautiful illusions of youth, by the pitiless cracking rifles of the realities of age. If the general love for women, had in Pierre sensibly modified his particular sentiment toward Glen; neither had the thousand nameless fascinations of the then brilliant paradises of France and Italy, failed to exert their seductive influence on many of the previous feelings of Glen. For as the very best advantages of life are not without some envious drawback, so it is among the evils of enlarged foreign travel, that in young and unsolid minds, it dislodges some of the finest feelings of the home-born nature; replacing them with a fastidious superciliousness, which like the alledged bigoted Federalism of old times would not—according to a political legend—grind its daily coffee in any mill save of European manufacture, and was satirically said to have thought of importing European air for domestic consumption. The mutually curtailed, lessening, long-postponed, and at last altogether ceasing letters of Pierre and Glen were the melancholy attestations of a fact, which perhaps neither of them took very severely to heart, as certainly, concerning it, neither took the other to task.

In the earlier periods of that strange transition from the generous impulsiveness of youth to the provident circumspectness of age, there generally intervenes a brief pause of unpleasant reconsidering; when finding itself all wide of its former spontaneous self, the soul hesitates to commit itself wholly to selfishness; more than repents its wanderings;—yet all this is but transient; and again hurried on by the swift current of life, the prompt-hearted boy scarce longer is to be recognized in matured man,—very slow to feel, deliberate even in love, and statistical even in piety. During the sway of this peculiar period, the boy shall still make some strenuous efforts to retrieve his departing spontaneities; but so alloyed are all such endeavors with the incipiencies of selfishness, that they were best not made at all; since too often they seem but empty and self-deceptive sallies, or still worse, the merest hypocritical assumptions.

Upon the return of Glen from abroad, the commonest courtesy, not to say the blood-relation between them, prompted Pierre to welcome him home, with a letter, which though not over-long, and little enthusiastic, still breathed a spirit of cousinly consideration and kindness, pervadingly touched by the then naturally frank and all-attractive spirit of Pierre. To this, the less earnest and now Europeanized Glen had replied in a letter all sudden suavity; and in a strain of artistic artlessness, mourned the apparent decline of their friendship; yet fondly trusted that now, notwithstanding their long separation, it would revive with added sincerity. Yet upon accidentally fixing his glànce upon the opening salutation of this delicate missive, Pierre thought he perceived certain, not wholly disguisable chirographic tokens, that the "My very dear Pierre," with which the letter seemed to have been begun, had originally been written "Dear Pierre;" but that when all was concluded, and Glen's signature put to it, then the ardent words "My very" had been prefixed to the reconsidered "Dear Pierre;" a casual supposition, which possibly, however unfounded, materially retarded any answering warmth in Pierre, lest his generous flame should only embrace a flaunted feather. Nor was this idea altogether unreinforced, when on the reception of a second, and now half-business letter (of which mixed sort nearly all the subsequent ones were), from Glen, he found that the "My very dear Pierre" had already retreated into "My dear Pierre;" and on a third occasion, into "Dear Pierre;" and on a fourth, had made a forced and very spirited advanced march up to "My dearest Pierre." All of which fluctuations augured ill for the determinateness of that love, which, however immensely devoted to one cause, could yet hoist and sail under the flags of all nations. Nor could he but now applaud a still subsequent letter from Glen, which abruptly, and almost with apparent indecorousness, under the circumstances, commenced the strain of friendship without any overture of salutation whatever; as if at last, owing to its infinite delicateness, entirely hopeless of precisely defining the nature of their mystical love, Glen chose rather to leave that precise definition to the sympathetical heart and imagination of Pierre; while he himself would go on to celebrate the general relation, by many a sugared sentence of miscellaneous devotion. It was a little curious and rather sardonically diverting, to compare these masterly, yet not wholly successful, and indeterminate tactics of the accomplished Glen, with the unfaltering stream of *Beloved Pierres*, which not only flowed along the top margin of all his earlier letters, but here and there, from their subterranean channel, flashed out in bright intervals, through all the succeeding lines. Nor had the chance recollection of these things at all restrained the reckless hand of Pierre, when he threw the whole package of letters, both new and old, into that most honest and summary of all elements, which is neither a respecter of persons, nor a finical critic of what manner of writings it burns; but like ultimate Truth itself, of which it is the eloquent symbol, consumes all, and only consumes.

When the betrothment of Pierre to Lucy had become an acknowledged thing, the courtly Glen, besides the customary felicitations upon that event, had not omitted so fit an opportunity to re-tender to his cousin all his previous jars of honey and treacle, accompanied by additional boxes of candied citron and plums. Pierre thanked him kindly; but in certain little roguish ambiguities begged leave, on the ground of cloying, to return him inclosed by far the greater portion of his present; whose non-substantialness was allegorically typified in the containing letter itself, prepaid with only the usual postage.

True love, as every one knows, will still withstand many repulses, even though rude. But whether it was the love or the politeness of Glen, which on this occasion proved invincible, is a matter we will not discuss. Certain it was, that quite undaunted, Glen nobly returned to the charge, and in a very prompt and unexpected answer, extended to Pierre all the courtesies of the general city, and all the hospitalities of five sumptuous chambers, which he and his luxurious environments contrived nominally to occupy in the most fashionable private hotel of a very opulent town. Nor did Glen rest here; but like Napoleon, now seemed bent upon gaining the battle by throwing all his regiments upon one point of attack, and gaining that point at all hazards. Hearing of some rumor at the tables of his relatives that the day was being fixed for the positive nuptials of Pierre; Glen culled all his Parisian portfolios for his rosiest sheet, and with scented ink, and a pen of gold, indited a most burnished and redolent letter, which, after invoking all the blessings of Apollo and Venus, and the Nine Muses, and the Cardinal Virtues upon the coming event; concluded at last with a really magnificent testimonial to his love.

According to this letter, among his other real estate in the city, Glen had inherited a very charming, little, old house, completely furnished in the style of the last century, in a quarter of the city which, though now not so garishly fashionable as of yore, still in its quiet secludedness, possessed great attractions for the retired billings and cooings of a honeymoon. Indeed he begged leave now to christen it the Cooery, and if after his wedding jaunt, Pierre would deign to visit the city with his bride for a month or two's sojourn, then the Cooery would be but too happy in affording him a harbor. His sweet cousin need be under no apprehension. Owing to the absence of any fit applicant for it, the house had now long been without a tenant, save an old, confidential, bachelor clerk of his father's, who on a nominal rent, and more by way of safe-keeping to the house than any thing else, was now hanging up his well-furbished hat in its hall. This accommodating old clerk would quickly unpeg his beaver at the first hint of new occupants. Glen would charge himself with supplying the house in advance with a proper retinue of servants; fires would be made in the long-unoccupied chambers; the venerable, grotesque, old mahoganies, and marbles, and mirror-frames, and moldings could be very soon dusted and burnished; the kitchen was amply provided with the necessary utensils for cooking; the strong box of old silver immemorially pertaining to the mansion, could be readily carted round from the vaults of the neighboring Bank; while the hampers of old china, still retained in the house, needed but little trouble to unpack; so that silver and china would soon stand assorted in their appropriate closets; at the turning of a faucet in the cellar, the best of the city's water would not fail to contribute its ingredient to the concocting of a welcoming glass of negus before retiring on the first night of their arrival.

The over-fastidiousness of some unhealthily critical minds, as well as the moral pusillanimity of others, equally bars the acceptance of effectually substantial favors from persons whose motive in proffering them, is not altogether clear and unimpeachable; and toward whom, perhaps, some prior coolness or indifference has been shown. But when the acceptance of such a favor would be really convenient and desirable to the one party, and completely unattended with any serious distress to the other; there would seem to be no sensible objection to an immediate embrace of the offer. And when the acceptor is in rank and fortune the general equal of the profferer, and perhaps his superior, so that any courtesy he receives, can be amply returned in the natural course of future events, then all motives to decline are very materially lessened. And as for the thousand inconceivable finicalnesses of small pros and cons about imaginary fitnesses, and proprieties, and self-consistencies; thank heaven, in the hour of heart-health, none such shilly-shallying sail-trimmers ever balk the onward course of a bluff-minded man. He takes the world as it is; and carelessly accommodates himself to its whimsical humors; nor ever feels any compunction at receiving the greatest possible favors from those who are as able to grant, as free to bestow. He himself bestows upon occasion; so that, at bottom, common charity steps in to dictate a favorable consideration for all possible profferings; seeing that the acceptance shall only the more enrich him, indirectly, for new and larger beneficences of his own.

And as for those who noways pretend with themselves to regulate their deportment by considerations of genuine benevolence, and to whom such courteous profferings hypocritically come from persons whom they suspect for secret enemies; then to such minds not only will their own worldly tactics at once forbid the uncivil blank repulse of such offers; but if they are secretly malicious as well as frigid, or if they are at all capable of being fully gratified by the sense of concealed superiority and mastership (which precious few men are) then how delightful for such persons under the guise of mere acquiescence in his own voluntary civilities, to make genteel use of their foe. For one would like to know, what were foes made for except to be used? In the rude ages men hunted and javelined the tiger, because they hated him for a mischief-minded wild-beast; but in these enlightened times, though we love the tiger as little as ever, still we mostly hunt him for the sake of his skin. A wise man then will wear his tiger; every morning put on his tiger for a robe to keep him warm and adorn him. In this view, foes are far more desirable than friends; for who would hunt and kill his own faithful affectionate dog for the sake of his skin? and is a dog's skin as valuable as a tiger's? Cases there are where it becomes soberly advisable, by direct arts to convert some well-wishers into foes. It is false that in point of policy a man should never make enemies. As well-wishers some men may not only be nugatory but positive obstacles in your peculiar plans; but as foes you may subordinately cement them into your general design.

But into these ulterior refinements of cool Tuscan policy, Pierre as yet had never become initiated; his experiences hitherto not having been varied and ripe enough for that; besides, he had altogether too much generous blood in his heart. Nevertheless, thereafter, in a less immature hour, though still he shall not have the heart to practice upon such maxims as the above, yet shall he have the brain thoroughly to comprehend their practicability; which is not always the case. And generally, in worldly wisdom, men will deny to one the possession of all insight, which one does not by his every-day outward life practically reveal. It is a very common error of some unscrupulously infidel-minded, selfish, unprincipled, or downright knavish men, to suppose that believing men, or benevolent-hearted men, or good men, do not know enough to be unscrupulously selfish, do not know enough to be unscrupulous knaves. And thus—thanks to the world!—are there many spies in the world's camp, who are mistaken for strolling simpletons. And these strolling simpletons seem to act upon the principle, that in certain things, we do not so much learn, by showing that already we know a vast deal, as by negatively seeming rather ignorant. But here we press upon the frontiers of that sort of wisdom, which it is very well to possess, but not sagacious to show that you possess. Still, men there are, who having quite done with the world, all its mere worldly contents are become so far indifferent, that they care little of what mere worldly imprudence they may be guilty.

Now, if it were not conscious considerations like the really benevolent or neutral ones first mentioned above, it was certainly something akin to them, which had induced Pierre to return a straightforward, manly, and entire acceptance to his cousin of the offer of the house; thanking him, over and over, for his most supererogatory kindness concerning the pre-engagement of servants and so forth, and the setting in order of the silver and china; but reminding him, nevertheless, that he had overlooked all special mention of wines, and begged him to store the bins with a few of the very best brands. He would likewise be obliged, if he would personally purchase at a certain celebrated grocer's, a small bag of undoubted Mocha coffee; but Glen need not order it to be roasted or ground, because Pierre preferred that both those highly important and flavor-deciding operations should be performed instantaneously previous to the final boiling and serving. Nor did he say that he would pay for the wines and the Mocha; he contented himself with merely stating the remissness on the part of his cousin, and pointing out the best way of remedying it.

He concluded his letter by intimating that though the rumor of a set day, and a near one, for his nuptials, was unhappily but ill-founded, yet he would not hold Glen's generous offer as merely based upon that presumption, and consequently falling with it; but on the contrary, would consider it entirely good for whatever time it might prove available to Pierre. He was betrothed beyond a peradventure; and hoped to be married ere death. Meanwhile, Glen would further oblige him by giving the confidential clerk a standing notice to quit.

Though at first quite amazed at this letter,—for indeed, his offer might possibly have proceeded as much from ostentation as any thing else, nor had he dreamed of so unhesitating an acceptance,—Pierre's cousin was too much of a precocious young man of the world, disclosedly to take it in any other than a very friendly, and cousinly, and humorous, and yet practical way; which he plainly evinced by a reply far more sincere and every way creditable, apparently, both to his heart and head, than any letter he had written to Pierre since the days of their boyhood. And thus, by the bluffness and, in some sort, uncompunctuousness of Pierre, this very artificial youth was well betrayed into an act of effective kindness; being forced now to drop the empty mask of ostentation, and put on the solid hearty features of a genuine face. And just so, are some people in the world to be joked into occasional effective goodness, when all coyness, and coolness, all resentments, and all solemn preaching, would fail.

ii

But little would we comprehend the peculiar relation between Pierre and Glen—a relation involving in the end the most serious results—were there not here thrown over the whole equivocal, preceding account of it, another and more comprehensive equivocalness, which shall absorb all minor ones in itself; and so make one pervading ambiguity the only possible explanation for all the ambiguous details.

It had long been imagined by Pierre, that prior to his own special devotion to Lucy, the splendid Glen had not been entirely insensible to her surprising charms. Yet this conceit in its incipiency, he knew not how to account for. Assuredly his cousin had never in the slightest conceivable hint betrayed it; and as for Lucy, the same intuitive delicacy which forever forbade Pierre to question her on the subject, did equally close her own voluntary lips. Between Pierre and Lucy, delicateness put her sacred signet on this chest of secrecy; which like the wax of an executor upon a desk, though capable of being melted into nothing by the smallest candle, for all this, still possesses to the reverent the prohibitive virtue of inexorable bars and bolts.

If Pierre superficially considered the deportment of Glen toward him, therein he could find no possible warrant for indulging the suspicious idea. Doth jealousy smile so benignantly and offer its house to the bride? Still, on the other hand, to quit the mere surface of the deportment of Glen, and penetrate beneath its brocaded vesture; there Pierre sometimes seemed to see the long-lurking and yet unhealed wound of all a rejected lover's most rankling detestation of a supplanting rival, only intensified by their former friendship, and the unimpairable blood-relation between them. Now, viewed by the light of this master-solution, all the singular enigmas in Glen; his capriciousness in the matter of the epistolary—"Dear Pierres" and "Dearest Pierres;" the mercurial fall from the fever-heat of cordiality, to below the Zero of indifference; then the contrary rise to fever-heat; and, above all, his emphatic redundancy of devotion so soon as the positive espousals of Pierre seemed on the point of consummation; thus read, all these riddles apparently found their cunning solution. For the deeper that some men feel a secret and poignant feeling, the higher they pile the belying surfaces. The friendly deportment of Glen then was to be considered as in direct proportion to his hoarded hate; and the climax of that hate was evinced in throwing open his house to the bride. Yet if hate was the abstract cause, hate could not be the immediate motive of the conduct of Glen. Is hate so hospitable? The immediate motive of Glen then must be the intense desire to disguise from the wide world, a fact unspeakably humiliating to his gold-laced and haughty soul: the fact that in the profoundest desire of his heart, Pierre had so victoriously supplanted him. Yet was it that very artful deportment in Glen, which Glen profoundly assumed to this grand end; that consummately artful deportment it was, which first obtruded upon Pierre the surmise, which by that identical method his cousin was so absorbedly intent upon rendering impossible to him. Hence we here see that as in the negative way the secrecy of any strong emotion is exceedingly difficult to be kept lastingly private to one's own bosom by any human being; so it is one of the most fruitless undertakings in the world, to attempt by affirmative assumptions to tender to men, the precisely opposite emotion as yours. Therefore the final wisdom decrees, that if you have aught which you desire to keep a secret to yourself, be a Quietist there, and do and say nothing at all about it. For among all the poor chances, this is the least poor. Pretensions and substitutions are only the recourse of under-graduates in the science of the world; in which science, on his own ground, my Lord Chesterfield, is the poorest possible preceptor. The earliest instinct of the child, and the ripest experience of age, unite in affirming simplicity to be the truest and profoundest part for man. Likewise this simplicity is so universal and all-containing as a rule for human life, that the subtlest bad man, and the purest good man, as well as the profoundest wise man, do all alike present it on that side which they socially turn to the inquisitive and unscrupulous world.

iii

Now the matter of the house had remained in precisely the above-stated awaiting predicament, down to the time of Pierre's great life-revolution, the receipt of Isabel's letter. And though, indeed, Pierre could not but naturally hesitate at still accepting the use of the dwelling, under the widely different circumstances in which he now found himself; and though at first the strongest possible spontaneous objections on the ground of personal independence, pride, and general scorn, all clamorously declared in his breast against such a course; yet, finally, the same uncompunctuous, ever-adaptive sort of motive which had induced his original acceptation, prompted him, in the end, still to maintain it unrevoked. It would at once set him at rest from all immediate tribulations of mere bed and board; and by affording him a shelter, for an indefinite term, enable him the better to look about him, and consider what could best be done to further the permanent comfort of those whom Fate had intrusted to his charge.

Irrespective, it would seem, of that wide general awaking of his profounder being, consequent upon the extraordinary trials he had so aggregatively encountered of late; the thought was indignantly suggested to him, that the world must indeed be organically despicable, if it held that an offer, superfluously accepted in the hour of his abundance, should now, be rejected in that of his utmost need. And without at all imputing any singularity of benevolent-mindedness to his cousin, he did not for a moment question, that under the changed aspect of affairs, Glen would at least pretend the more eagerly to welcome him to the house, now that the mere thing of apparent courtesy had become transformed into something like a thing of positive and urgent necessity. When Pierre also considered that not himself only was concerned, but likewise two peculiarly helpless fellow-beings, one of them bound to him from the first by the most sacred ties, and lately inspiring an emotion which passed all human precedent in its mixed and mystical import; these added considerations completely overthrew in Pierre all remaining dictates of his vague pride and false independence, if such indeed had ever been his.

Though the interval elapsing between his decision to depart with his companions for the city, and his actual start in the coach, had not enabled him to receive any replying word from his cousin; and though Pierre knew better than to expect it; yet a preparative letter to him he had sent; and did not doubt that this proceeding would prove well-advised in the end.

In naturally strong-minded men, however young and inexperienced in some things, those great and sudden emergencies, which but confound the timid and the weak, only serve to call forth all their generous latentness, and teach them, as by inspiration, extraordinary maxims of conduct, whose counterpart, in other men, is only the result of a long, variously-tried and pains-taking life. One of those maxims is, that when, through whatever cause, we are suddenly translated from opulence to need, or from a fair fame to a foul; and straightway it becomes necessary not to contradict the thing—so far at least as the mere imputation goes,—to some one previously entertaining high conventional regard for us, and from whom we would now solicit some genuine helping offices; then, all explanation or palliation should be scorned; promptness, boldness, utter gladiatorianism, and a defiant non-humility should mark every syllable we breathe, and every line we trace.

The preparative letter of Pierre to Glen, plunged at once into the very heart of the matter, and was perhaps the briefest letter he had ever written him. Though by no means are such characteristics invariable exponents of the predominant mood or general disposition of a man (since so accidental a thing as a numb finger, or a bad quill, or poor ink, or squalid paper, or a rickety desk may produce all sorts of modifications), yet in the present instance, the handwriting of Pierre happened plainly to attest and corroborate the spirit of his communication. The sheet was large; but the words were placarded upon it in heavy though rapid lines, only six or eight to the page. And as the footman of a haughty visitor—some Count or Duke—announces the chariot of his lord by a thunderous knock on the portal; so to Glen did Pierre, in the broad, sweeping, and prodigious superscription of his letter, forewarn him what manner of man was on the road.

In the moment of strong feeling a wonderful condensativeness points the tongue and pen; so that ideas, then enunciated sharp and quick as minute-guns, in some other hour of unruffledness or unstimulatedness, require considerable time and trouble to verbally recall.

Not here and now can we set down the precise contents of Pierre's letter, without a tautology illy doing justice to the ideas themselves. And though indeed the dread of tautology be the continual torment of some earnest minds, and, as such, is surely a weakness in them; and though no wise man will wonder at conscientious Virgil all eager at death to burn his Æniad for a monstrous heap of inefficient superfluity; yet not to dread tautology at times only belongs to those enviable dunces, whom the partial God hath blessed, over all the earth, with the inexhaustible self-riches of vanity, and folly, and a blind self-complacency.

Some rumor of the discontinuance of his betrothment to Lucy Tartan; of his already consummated marriage with a poor and friendless orphan; of his mother's disowning him consequent upon these events; such rumors, Pierre now wrote to his cousin, would very probably, in the parlors of his city-relatives and acquaintances, precede his arrival in town. But he hinted no word of any possible commentary on these things. He simply went on to say, that now, through the fortune of life— which was but the proverbially unreliable fortune of war—he was, for the present, thrown entirely upon his own resources, both for his own support and that of his wife, as well as for the temporary maintenance of a girl, whom he had lately had excellent reason for taking under his especial protection. He proposed a permanent residence in the city; not without some nearly quite settled plans as to the procuring of a competent income, without any ulterior reference to any member of their wealthy and widely ramified family. The house, whose temporary occupancy Glen had before so handsomely proffered him, would now be doubly and trebly desirable to him. But the pre-engaged servants, and the old china, and the old silver, and the old wines, and the Mocha, were now become altogether unnecessary. Pierre would merely take the place—for a short interval—of the worthy old clerk; and, so far as Glen was concerned, simply stand guardian of the dwelling, till his plans were matured. His cousin had originally made his most bounteous overture, to welcome the coming of the presumed bride of Pierre; and though another lady had now taken her place at the altar, yet Pierre would still regard the offer of Glen as impersonal in that respect, and bearing equal reference to any young lady, who should prove her claim to the possessed hand of Pierre.

Since there was no universal law of opinion in such matters, Glen, on general worldly grounds, might not consider the real Mrs. Glendinning altogether so suitable a match for Pierre, as he possibly might have held numerous other young ladies in his eye: nevertheless, Glen would find her ready to return with sincerity all his cousinly regard and attention. In conclusion, Pierre said, that he and his party meditated an immediate departure, and would very probably arrive in town in eight-and-forty hours after the mailing of the present letter. He therefore begged Glen to see the more indispensable domestic appliances of the house set in some little order against their arrival; to have the rooms aired and lighted; and also forewarn the confidential clerk of what he might soon expect. Then, without any tapering sequel of—"*Yours, very truly and faithfully, my dear Cousin Glen,*" he finished the letter with the abrupt and isolated signature of—"PIERRE."

Book XVI

First Night of Their Arrival in the City

THE STAGE WAS BELATED.

The country road they traveled entered the city by a remarkably wide and winding street, a great thoroughfare for its less opulent inhabitants. There was no moon and few stars. It was that preluding hour of the night when the shops are just closing, and the aspect of almost every wayfarer, as he passes through the unequal light reflected from the windows, speaks of one hurrying not abroad, but homeward. Though the thoroughfare was winding, yet no sweep that it made greatly obstructed its long and imposing vista; so that when the coach gained the top of the long and very gradual slope running toward the obscure heart of the town, and the twinkling perspective of two long and parallel rows of lamps was revealed —lamps which seemed not so much intended to dispel the general gloom, as to show some dim path leading through it, into some gloom still deeper beyond—when the coach gained this critical point, the whole vast triangular town, for a moment, seemed dimly and despondently to capitulate to the eye.

And now, ere descending the gradually-sloping declivity, and just on its summit as it were, the inmates of the coach, by numerous hard, painful joltings, and ponderous, dragging trundlings, are suddenly made sensible of some great change in the character of the road. The coach seems rolling over cannon-balls of all calibers. Grasping Pierre's arm, Isabel eagerly and forebodingly demands what is the cause of this most strange and unpleasant transition.

"The pavements, Isabel; this is the town."

Isabel was silent.

But, the first time for many weeks, Delly voluntarily spoke:

"It feels not so soft as the green sward, Master Pierre."

"No, Miss Ulver," said Pierre, very bitterly, "the buried hearts of some dead citizens have perhaps come to the surface."

"Sir?" said Delly.

"And are they so hard-hearted here?" asked Isabel.

"Ask yonder pavements, Isabel. Milk dropt from the milkman's can in December, freezes not more quickly on those stones, than does snow-white innocence, if in poverty, it chance to fall in these streets."

"Then God help my hard fate, Master Pierre," sobbed Delly. "Why didst thou drag hither a poor outcast like me?"

"Forgive me, Miss Ulver," exclaimed Pierre, with sudden warmth, and yet most marked respect; "forgive me; never yet have I entered the city by night, but, somehow, it made me feel both bitter and sad. Come, be cheerful, we shall soon be comfortably housed, and have our comfort all to ourselves; the old clerk I spoke to you about, is now doubtless ruefully eying his hat on the peg. Come, cheer up, Isabel;—'tis a long ride, but here we are, at last. Come! 'Tis not very far now to our welcome."

"I hear a strange shuffling and clattering," said Delly, with a shudder.

"It does not seem so light as just now," said Isabel.

"Yes," returned Pierre, "it is the shop-shutters being put on; it is the locking, and bolting, and barring of windows and doors; the town's-people are going to their rest."

"Please God they may find it!" sighed Delly.

"They lock and bar out, then, when they rest, do they, Pierre?" said Isabel.

"Yes, and you were thinking that does not bode well for the welcome I spoke of."

"Thou read'st all my soul; yes, I was thinking of that. But whither lead these long, narrow, dismal side-glooms we pass every now and then? What are they? They seem terribly still. I see scarce any body in them;—there's another, now. See how haggardly look its criss-cross, far-separate lamps.—What are these side-glooms, dear Pierre; whither lead they?"

"They are the thin tributaries, sweet Isabel, to the great Oronoco thoroughfare we are in; and like true tributaries, they come from the far-hidden places; from under dark beetling secrecies of mortar and stone; through the long marsh-grasses of villainy, and by many a transplanted bough-beam, where the wretched have hung."

"I know nothing of these things, Pierre. But I like not the town. Think'st thou, Pierre, the time will ever come when all the earth shall be paved?"

"Thank God, that never can be!"

"These silent side-glooms are horrible;—look! Methinks, not for the world would I turn into one."

That moment the nigh fore-wheel sharply grated under the body of the coach.

"Courage!" cried Pierre, "we are in it!—Not so very solitary either; here comes a traveler."

"Hark, what is that?" said Delly, "that keen iron-ringing sound? It passed us just now."

"The keen traveler," said Pierre, "he has steel plates to his boot-heels;—some tender-souled elder son, I suppose."

"Pierre," said Isabel, "this silence is unnatural, is fearful. The forests are never so still."

"Because brick and mortar have deeper secrets than wood or fell, sweet Isabel. But here we turn again; now if I guess right, two more turns will bring us to the door. Courage, all will be well; doubtless he has prepared a famous supper. Courage, Isabel. Come, shall it be tea or coffee? Some bread, or crisp toast? We'll have eggs, too; and some cold chicken, perhaps."—Then muttering to himself—"I hope not that, either; no cold collations! there's too much of that in these paving-stones here, set out for the famishing beggars to eat. No. I won't have the cold chicken." Then aloud—"But here we turn again; yes, just as I thought. Ho, driver!" (thrusting his head out of the window) "to the right! to the right! it should be on the right! the first house with a light on the right!"

"No lights yet but the street's," answered the surly voice of the driver.

"Stupid! he has passed it—yes, yes—he has! Ho! ho! stop; turn back. Have you not passed lighted windows?"

"No lights but the street's," was the rough reply. "What's the number? the number? Don't keep me beating about here all night! The number, I say!"

"I do not know it," returned Pierre; "but I well know the house; you must have passed it, I repeat. You must turn back. Surely you have passed lighted windows?"

"Then them lights must burn black; there's no lighted windows in the street; I knows the city; old maids lives here, and they are all to bed; rest is warehouses."

"Will you stop the coach, or not?" cried Pierre, now incensed at his surliness in continuing to drive on.

"I obeys orders: the first house with a light; and 'cording to my reck'-ning—though to be sure, I don't know nothing of the city where I was born and bred all my life—no, I knows nothing at all about it—'cording to my reck'ning, the first light in this here street will be the watch-house of the ward—yes, there it is—all right! cheap lodgings ye've engaged—nothing to pay, and wictuals in."

To certain temperaments, especially when previously agitated by any deep feeling, there is perhaps nothing more exasperating, and which sooner explodes all self-command, than the coarse, jeering insolence of a porter, cabman, or hack-driver. Fetchers and carriers of the worst city infamy as many of them are; professionally familiar with the most abandoned haunts; in the heart of misery, they drive one of the most mercenary of all the trades of guilt. Day-dozers and sluggards on their lazy boxes in the sunlight, and felinely wakeful and cat-eyed in the dark; most habituated to midnight streets, only trod by sneaking burglars, wantons, and debauchees; often in actual pandering league with the most abhorrent sinks; so that they are equally solicitous and suspectful that every customer they encounter in the dark, will prove a profligate or a knave; this hideous tribe of ogres, and Charon ferry-men to corruption and death, naturally slide into the most practically Calvinistical view of humanity, and hold every man at bottom a fit subject for the coarsest ribaldry and jest; only fine coats and full pockets can whip such mangy hounds into decency. The least impatience, any quickness of temper, a sharp remonstrating word from a customer in a seedy coat, or betraying any other evidence of poverty, however minute and indirect (for in that pecuniary respect they are the most piercing and infallible of all the judgers of men), will be almost sure to provoke, in such cases, their least endurable disdain.

Perhaps it was the unconscious transfer to the stage-driver of some such ideas as these, which now prompted the highly irritated Pierre to an act, which, in a more benignant hour, his better reason would have restrained him from.

He did not see the light to which the driver had referred; and was heedless, in his sudden wrath, that the coach was now going slower in approaching it. Ere Isabel could prevent him, he burst open the door, and leaping to the pavement, sprang ahead of the horses, and violently reined back the leaders by their heads. The driver seized his four-in-hand whip, and with a volley of oaths was about striking out its long, coiling lash at Pierre, when his arm was arrested by a policeman, who suddenly leaping on the stayed coach, commanded him to keep the peace.

"Speak! what is the difficulty here? Be quiet, ladies, nothing serious has happened. Speak you!"

"Pierre! Pierre!" cried the alarmed Isabel. In an instant Pierre was at her side by the window; and now turning to the officer, explained to him that the driver had persisted in passing the house at which he was ordered to stop.

"Then he shall turn to the right about with you, sir;—in double quick time too; do ye hear? I know you rascals well enough. Turn about, you sir, and take the gentleman where he directed."

The cowed driver was beginning a long string of criminating explanations, when turning to Pierre, the policeman calmly desired him to re-enter the coach; he would see him safely at his destination; and then seating himself beside the driver on the box, commanded him to tell the number given him by the gentleman.

"He don't know no numbers—didn't I say he didn't—that's what I got mad about."

"Be still"—said the officer. "Sir"—turning round and addressing Pierre within; "where do you wish to go?"

"I do not know the number, but it is a house in this street; we have passed it; it is, I think, the fourth or fifth house this side of the last corner we turned. It must be lighted up too. It is the small old-fashioned dwelling with stone lion-heads above the windows. But make him turn round, and drive slowly, and I will soon point it out."

"Can't see lions in the dark"—growled the driver—"lions; ha! ha! jackasses more likely!"

"Look you," said the officer, "I shall see you tightly housed this night, my fine fellow, if you don't cease your jabber. Sir," he added, resuming with Pierre, "I am sure there is some mistake here. I perfectly well know now the house you mean. I passed it within the last half-hour; all as quiet there as ever. No one lives there, I think; I never saw a light in it. Are you not mistaken in something, then?"

Pierre paused in perplexity and foreboding. Was it possible that Glen had willfully and utterly neglected his letter? Not possible. But it might not have come to his hand; the mails sometimes delayed. Then again, it was not wholly out of the question, that the house was prepared for them after all, even though it showed no outward sign. But that was not probable. At any rate, as the driver protested, that his four horses and lumbering vehicle could not turn short round in that street; and that if he must go back, it could only be done by driving on, and going round the block, and so retracing his road; and as after such a procedure, on his part, then in case of a confirmed disappointment respecting the house, the driver would seem warranted, at least in some of his unmannerliness; and as Pierre loathed the villain altogether, therefore, in order to run no such risks, he came to a sudden determination on the spot.

"I owe you very much, my good friend," said he to the officer, "for your timely assistance. To be frank, what you have just told me has indeed perplexed me not a little concerning the place where I proposed to stop. Is there no hotel in this neighborhood, where I could leave these ladies while I seek my friend?"

Wonted to all manner of deceitfulness, and engaged in a calling which unavoidably makes one distrustful of mere appearances, however specious, however honest; the really good-hearted officer, now eyed Pierre in the dubious light with a most unpleasant scrutiny; and he abandoned the "Sir," and the tone of his voice sensibly changed, as he replied:—"There is no hotel in this neighborhood; it is too off the thoroughfares."

"Come! come!"—cried the driver, now growing bold again—"though you're an officer, I'm a citizen for all that. You havn't any further right to keep me out of my bed now. He don't know where he wants to go to, cause he haint got no place at all to go to; so I'll just dump him here, and you dar'n't stay me."

"Don't be impertinent now," said the officer, but not so sternly as before.

"I'll have my rights though, I tell you that! Leave go of my arm; damn ye, get off the box; I've the law now. I say mister, come tramp, here goes your luggage," and so saying he dragged toward him a light trunk on the top of the stage.

"Keep a clean tongue in ye now"—said the officer—"and don't be in quite so great a hurry," then addressing Pierre, who had now re-alighted from the coach—"Well, this can't continue; what do you intend to do?"

"Not to ride further with that man, at any rate," said Pierre; "I will stop right here for the present."

"He! he!" laughed the driver; "he! he! 'mazing 'commodating now—

we hitches now, we do—stops right afore the watch-house—he! he!—that's funny!"

"Off with the luggage then, driver," said the policeman—"here hand the small trunk, and now away and unlash there behind."

During all this scene, Delly had remained perfectly silent in her trembling and rustic alarm; while Isabel, by occasional cries to Pierre, had vainly besought some explanation. But though their complete ignorance of city life had caused Pierre's two companions to regard the scene thus far with too much trepidation; yet now, when in the obscurity of night, and in the heart of a strange town, Pierre handed them out of the coach into the naked street, and they saw their luggage piled so near the white light of a watch-house, the same ignorance, in some sort, reversed its effects on them; for they little fancied in what really untoward and wretched circumstances they first touched the flagging of the city.

As the coach lumbered off, and went rolling into the wide murkiness beyond, Pierre spoke to the officer.

"It is a rather strange accident, I confess, my friend, but strange accidents will sometimes happen."

"In the best of families," rejoined the other, a little ironically.

Now, I must not quarrel with this man, thought Pierre to himself, stung at the officer's tone. Then said:—"Is there any one in your—office?"

"No one as yet—not late enough."

"Will you have the kindness then to house these ladies there for the present, while I make haste to provide them with better lodgment? Lead on, if you please."

The man seemed to hesitate a moment, but finally acquiesced; and soon they passed under the white light, and entered a large, plain, and most forbidding-looking room, with hacked wooden benches and bunks ranged along the sides, and a railing before a desk in one corner. The permanent keeper of the place was quietly reading a paper by the long central double bat's-wing gas-light; and three officers off duty were nodding on a bench.

"Not very liberal accommodations"—said the officer, quietly; "nor always the best of company, but we try to be civil. Be seated, ladies," politely drawing a small bench toward them.

"Hallo, my friends," said Pierre, approaching the nodding three beyond, and tapping them on the shoulder—"Hallo, I say! Will you do me a little favor? Will you help bring some trunks in from the street? I will satisfy you for your trouble, and be much obliged into the bargain."

Instantly the three noddies, used to sudden awakenings, opened their eyes, and stared hard; and being further enlightened by the bat's-wings and first officer, promptly brought in the luggage as desired.

Pierre hurriedly sat down by Isabel, and in a few words gave her to understand, that she was now in a perfectly secure place, however unwelcoming; that the officers would take every care of her, while he made all possible speed in running to the house, and indubitably ascertaining how matters stood there. He hoped to be back in less than ten minutes with good tidings. Explaining his intention to the first officer, and begging him not to leave the girls till he should return, he forthwith sallied into the street. He quickly came to the house, and immediately identified it. But all was profoundly silent and dark. He rang the bell, but no answer; and waiting long enough to be certain, that either the house was indeed deserted, or else the old clerk was unawakeable or absent; and at all events, certain that no slightest preparation had been made for their arrival; Pierre, bitterly disappointed, returned to Isabel with this most unpleasant information.

Nevertheless something must be done, and quickly. Turning to one of the officers, he begged him to go and seek a hack, that the whole party might be taken to some respectable lodging. But the man, as well as his comrades, declined the errand on the score, that there was no stand on their beat, and they could not, on any account, leave their beat. So Pierre himself must go. He by no means liked to leave Isabel and Delly again, on an expedition which might occupy some time. But there seemed no resource, and time now imperiously pressed. Communicating his intention therefore to Isabel, and again entreating the officer's particular services as before, and promising not to leave him unrequited; Pierre again sallied out. He looked up and down the street, and listened; but no sound of any approaching vehicle was audible. He ran on, and turning the first corner, bent his rapid steps toward the greatest and most central avenue of the city, assured that there, if anywhere, he would find what he wanted. It was some distance off; and he was not without hope that an empty hack would meet him ere he arrived there. But the few stray ones he encountered had all muffled fares. He continued on, and at last gained the great avenue. Not habitually used to such scenes, Pierre for a moment was surprised, that the instant he turned out of the narrow, and dark, and death-like bye-street, he should find himself suddenly precipitated into the not-yet-repressed noise and contention, and all the garish night-life of a vast thoroughfare, crowded and wedged by day, and even now, at this late hour, brilliant with occasional illuminations, and echoing to very many swift wheels and footfalls.

ii

"I say, my pretty one! Dear! Dear! young man! Oh, love, you are in a vast hurry, aint you? Can't you stop a bit, now, my dear: do—there's a sweet fellow."

Pierre turned; and in the flashing, sinister, evil cross-lights of a druggist's window, his eye caught the person of a wonderfully beautifully-featured girl; scarlet-cheeked, glaringly-arrayed, and of a figure all natural grace but unnatural vivacity. Her whole form, however, was horribly lit by the green and yellow rays from the druggist's.

"My God!" shuddered Pierre, hurrying forward, "the town's first welcome to youth!"

He was just crossing over to where a line of hacks were drawn up against the opposite curb, when his eye was arrested by a short, gilded name, rather reservedly and aristocratically denominating a large and very handsome house, the second story of which was profusely lighted. He looked up, and was very certain that in this house were the apartments of Glen. Yielding to a sudden impulse, he mounted the single step toward the door, and rang the bell, which was quickly responded to by a very civil black.

As the door opened, he heard the distant interior sound of dancing-music and merriment.

"Is Mr. Stanly in?"

"Mr. Stanly? Yes, but he's engaged."

"How?"

"He is somewhere in the drawing rooms. My mistress is giving a party to the lodgers."

"Ay? Tell Mr. Stanly I wish to see him for one moment if you please; only one moment."

"I dare not call him, sir. He said that possibly some one might call for him to-night—they are calling every night for Mr. Stanly—but I must admit no one, on the plea of the party."

A dark and bitter suspicion now darted through the mind of Pierre; and ungovernably yielding to it, and resolved to prove or falsify it without delay, he said to the black:

"My business is pressing. I must see Mr. Stanly."

"I am sorry, sir, but orders are orders: I am his particular servant here—the one that sees his silver every holyday. I can't disobey him. May I shut the door, sir? for as it is, I can not admit you."

"The drawing-rooms are on the second floor, are they not?" said Pierre quietly.

"Yes," said the black pausing in surprise, and holding the door.

"Yonder are the stairs, I think?"

"That way, sir; but this is yours;" and the now suspicious black was just on the point of closing the portal violently upon him, when Pierre thrust him suddenly aside, and springing up the long stairs, found himself facing an open door, from whence proceeded a burst of combined brilliancy and melody, doubly confusing to one just emerged from the street. But bewildered and all demented as he momentarily felt, he instantly stalked in, and confounded the amazed company with his unremoved slouched hat, pale cheek, and whole dusty, travel-stained, and ferocious aspect.

"Mr. Stanly! where is Mr. Stanly?" he cried, advancing straight through a startled quadrille, while all the music suddenly hushed, and every eye was fixed in vague affright upon him.

"Mr. Stanly! Mr. Stanly!" cried several bladish voices, toward the further end of the further drawing-room, into which the first one widely opened, "Here is a most peculiar fellow after you; who the devil is he?"

"I think I see him," replied a singularly cool, deliberate, and rather drawling voice, yet a very silvery one, and at bottom perhaps a very resolute one; "I think I see him; stand aside, my good fellow, will you; ladies, remove, remove from between me and yonder hat."

The polite compliance of the company thus addressed, now revealed to the advancing Pierre, the tall, robust figure of a remarkably splendid-looking, and brown-bearded young man, dressed with surprising plainness, almost demureness, for such an occasion; but this plainness of his dress was not so obvious at first, the material was so fine, and admirably fitted. He was carelessly lounging in a half side-long attitude upon a large sofa, and appeared as if but just interrupted in some very agreeable chat with a diminutive but vivacious brunette, occupying the other end. The dandy and the man; strength and effeminacy; courage and indolence, were so strangely blended in this superb-eyed youth, that at first sight, it seemed impossible to decide whether there was any genuine mettle in him, or not.

Some years had gone by since the cousins had met; years peculiarly productive of the greatest conceivable changes in the general personal aspect of human beings. Nevertheless, the eye seldom alters. The instant their eyes met, they mutually recognized each other. But both did not betray the recognition.

"Glen!" cried Pierre, and paused a few steps from him.

But the superb-eyed only settled himself lower down in his lounging attitude, and slowly withdrawing a small, unpretending, and unribboned glass from his vest pocket, steadily, yet not entirely insultingly, notwithstanding the circumstances, scrutinized Pierre. Then, dropping his glass, turned slowly round upon the gentlemen near him, saying in the same peculiar, mixed, and musical voice as before:

"I do not know him; it is an entire mistake; why don't the servants take him out, and the music go on?——As I was saying, Miss Clara, the statues you saw in the Louvre are not to be mentioned with those in Florence and Rome. Why, there now is that vaunted *chef d'œuvre*, the Fighting Gladiator of the Louvre———"

"Fighting Gladiator it is!" yelled Pierre, leaping toward him like Spartacus. But the savage impulse in him was restrained by the alarmed female shrieks and wild gestures around him. As he paused, several gentlemen made motions to pinion him; but shaking them off fiercely, he stood erect, and isolated for an instant, and fastening his glance upon his still reclining, and apparently unmoved cousin, thus spoke:—

"Glendinning Stanly, thou disown'st Pierre not so abhorrently as Pierre does thee. By Heaven, had I a knife, Glen, I could prick thee on the spot; let out all thy Glendinning blood, and then sew up the vile remainder. Hound, and base blot upon the general humanity!"

"This is very extraordinary:—remarkable case of combined imposture and insanity; but where are the servants? why don't that black advance? Lead him out, my good Doc, lead him out. Carefully, carefully! stay"—putting his hand in his pocket—"there, take that, and have the poor fellow driven off somewhere."

Bolting his rage in him, as impossible to be sated by any conduct, in such a place, Pierre now turned, sprang down the stairs, and fled the house.

iii

"Hack, sir? Hack, sir? Hack, sir?"

"Cab, sir? Cab, sir? Cab, sir?"

"This way, sir! This way, sir! This way, sir!"

"He's a rogue! Not him! he's a rogue!"

Pierre was surrounded by a crowd of contending hackmen, all holding long whips in their hands; while others eagerly beckoned to him from their boxes, where they sat elevated between their two coach-lamps like shabby, discarded saints. The whip-stalks thickened around him, and several reports of the cracking lashes sharply sounded in his ears. Just bursting from a scene so goading as his interview with the scornful Glen in the dazzling drawing-room, to Pierre, this sudden tumultuous surrounding of him by whip-stalks and lashes, seemed like the onset of the chastising fiends upon Orestes. But, breaking away from them, he seized the first plated door-handle near him, and, leaping into the hack, shouted for whoever was the keeper of it, to mount his box forthwith and drive off in a given direction.

The vehicle had proceeded some way down the great avenue when it paused, and the driver demanded whither now; what place?

"The Watch-house of the——Ward," cried Pierre.

"Hi! hi! Goin' to deliver himself up, hey?" grinned the fellow to himself—"Well, that's a sort of honest, any way:—g'lang, you dogs!—whist! whee! wha!—g'lang!"

The sights and sounds which met the eye of Pierre on re-entering the watch-house, filled him with inexpressible horror and fury. The before decent, drowsy place, now fairly reeked with all things unseemly. Hardly possible was it to tell what conceivable cause or occasion had, in the comparatively short absence of Pierre, collected such a base congregation. In indescribable disorder, frantic, diseased-looking men and women of all colors, and in all imaginable flaunting, immodest, grotesque, and shattered dresses, were leaping, yelling, and cursing around him. The torn Madras handkerchiefs of negresses, and the red gowns of yellow girls, hanging in tatters from their naked bosoms, mixed with the rent dresses of deep-rouged white women, and the split coats, checkered vests, and protruding shirts of pale, or whiskered, or haggard, or mustached fellows of all nations, some of whom seemed scared from their beds, and others seemingly arrested in the midst of some crazy and wanton dance. On all sides, were heard drunken male and female voices, in English, French, Spanish, and Portuguese, interlarded now and then, with the foulest of all human lingoes, that dialect of sin and death, known as the Cant language, or the Flash.

Running among this combined babel of persons and voices, several of the police were vainly striving to still the tumult; while others were busy handcuffing the more desperate; and here and there the distracted wretches, both men and women, gave downright battle to the officers; and still others already handcuffed struck out at them with their joined ironed arms. Meanwhile, words and phrases unrepeatable in God's sunlight, and whose very existence was utterly unknown, and undreamed of by tens of thousands of the decent people of the city; syllables obscene and accursed were shouted forth in tones plainly evincing that they were the common household breath of their utterers. The thieves'-quarters, and all the brothels, Lock-and-Sin hospitals for incurables, and infirmaries and infernoes of hell seemed to have made one combined sortie, and poured out upon earth through the vile vomitory of some unmentionable cellar.

Though the hitherto imperfect and casual city experiences of Pierre, illy fitted him entirely to comprehend the specific purport of this terrific spectacle; still he knew enough by hearsay of the more infamous life of the town, to imagine from whence, and who, were the objects before him. But all his consciousness at the time was absorbed by the one horrified thought of Isabel and Delly, forced to witness a sight hardly endurable for Pierre himself; or, possibly, sucked into the tumult, and in close personal contact with its loathsomeness. Rushing into the crowd, regardless of the random blows and curses he encountered, he wildly sought for Isabel, and soon descried her struggling from the delirious reaching arms of a half-clad reeling whiskerando. With an immense blow of his mailed fist, he sent the wretch humming, and seizing Isabel, cried out to two officers near, to clear a path for him to the door. They did so. And in a few minutes the panting Isabel was safe in the open air. He would have stayed by her, but she conjured him to return for Delly, exposed to worse insults than herself. An additional posse of officers now approaching, Pierre committing her to the care of one of them, and summoning two others to join himself, now re-entered the room. In another quarter of it, he saw Delly seized on each hand by two bleared and half-bloody women, who with fiendish grimaces were ironically twitting her upon her close-necked dress, and had already stript her handkerchief from her. She uttered a cry of mixed anguish and joy at the sight of him; and Pierre soon succeeded in returning with her to Isabel.

During the absence of Pierre in quest of the hack, and while Isabel and Delly were quietly awaiting his return, the door had suddenly burst open, and a detachment of the police drove in, and caged, the entire miscellaneous night-occupants of a notorious stew, which they had stormed and carried during the height of some outrageous orgie. The first sight of the interior of the watch-house, and their being so quickly huddled together within its four blank walls, had suddenly lashed the mob into frenzy; so that for the time, oblivious of all other considerations, the entire force of the police was directed to the quelling of the in-door riot; and consequently, abandoned to their own protection, Isabel and Delly had been temporarily left to its mercy.

It was no time for Pierre to manifest his indignation at the officer—even if he could now find him—who had thus falsified his individual pledge concerning the precious charge committed to him. Nor was it any time to distress himself about his luggage, still somewhere within. Quitting all, he thrust the bewildered and half-lifeless girls into the waiting hack, which, by his orders, drove back in the direction of the stand, where Pierre had first taken it up.

When the coach had rolled them well away from the tumult, Pierre stopped it, and said to the man, that he desired to be taken to the nearest respectable hotel or boarding-house of any kind, that he knew of. The fellow —maliciously diverted by what had happened thus far—made some ambiguous and rudely merry rejoinder. But warned by his previous rash quarrel with the stage-driver, Pierre passed this unnoticed, and in a controlled, calm, decided manner repeated his directions.

The issue was, that after a rather roundabout drive they drew up in a very respectable side-street, before a large respectable-looking house, illuminated by two tall white lights flanking its portico. Pierre was glad to notice some little remaining stir within, spite of the comparative lateness of the hour. A bare-headed, tidily-dressed, and very intelligent-looking man, with a broom clothes-brush in his hand, appearing, scrutinized him rather sharply at first; but as Pierre advanced further into the light, and his countenance became visible, the man, assuming a respectful but still slightly perplexed air, invited the whole party into a closely adjoining parlor, whose disordered chairs and general dustiness, evinced that after a day's activity it now awaited the morning offices of the housemaids.

"Baggage, sir?"

"I have left my baggage at another place," said Pierre, "I shall send for it to-morrow."

"Ah!" exclaimed the very intelligent-looking man, rather dubiously, "shall I discharge the hack, then?"

"Stay," said Pierre, bethinking him, that it would be well not to let the man know from whence they had last come, "I will discharge it myself, thank you."

So returning to the sidewalk, without debate, he paid the hackman an exorbitant fare, who, anxious to secure such illegal gains beyond all hope of recovery, quickly mounted his box and drove off at a gallop.

"Will you step into the office, sir, now?" said the man, slightly flourishing with his brush—"this way, sir, if you please."

Pierre followed him, into an almost deserted, dimly lit room with a stand in it. Going behind the stand, the man turned round to him a large ledger-like book, thickly inscribed with names, like any directory, and offered him a pen ready dipped in ink.

Understanding the general hint, though secretly irritated at something in the manner of the man, Pierre drew the book to him, and wrote in a firm hand, at the bottom of the last-named column,—

"Mr. and Mrs. Pierre Glendinning, and Miss Ulver."

The man glanced at the writing inquiringly, and then said—"The other column, sir—where from."

"True," said Pierre, and wrote "Saddle Meadows."

The very intelligent-looking man re-examined the page, and then slowly stroking his shaven chin, with a fork, made of his thumb for one tine, and his united four fingers for the other, said softly and whisperingly—"Anywheres in this country, sir?"

"Yes, in the country," said Pierre, evasively, and bridling his ire. "But now show me to two chambers, will you; the one for myself and wife, I desire to have opening into another, a third one, never mind how small; but I must have a dressing-room."

"Dressing-room," repeated the man, in an ironically deliberative voice—"Dressing-room;—Hem!—You will have your luggage taken into the dressing-room, then, I suppose.—Oh, I forgot—your luggage aint come yet—ah, yes, yes, yes—luggage is coming to-morrow—Oh, yes, yes,—certainly—to-morrow—of course. By the way, sir; I dislike to seem at all uncivil, and I am sure you will not deem me so; but—"

"Well," said Pierre, mustering all his self-command for the coming impertinence.

"When stranger gentlemen come to this house without luggage, we think ourselves bound to ask them to pay their bills in advance, sir; that is all, sir."

"I shall stay here to-night and the whole of to-morrow, at any rate," rejoined Pierre, thankful that this was all; "how much will it be?" and he drew out his purse.

The man's eyes fastened with eagerness on the purse; he looked from it to the face of him who held it; then seemed half hesitating an instant; then brightening up, said, with sudden suavity—"Never mind, sir, never mind, sir; though rogues sometimes be gentlemanly; gentlemen that are gentlemen never go abroad without their diplomas. Their diplomas are their friends; and their only friends are their dollars; you have a purse-full of friends.—We have chambers, sir, that will exactly suit you, I think. Bring your ladies and I will show you up to them immediately." So saying, dropping his brush, the very intelligent-looking man lighted one lamp, and taking two unlighted ones in his other hand, led the way down the dusky lead-sheeted hall, Pierre following him with Isabel and Delly.

Book XVII

Young America in Literature

AMONG THE VARIOUS CONFLICTING MODES of writing history, there would seem to be two grand practical distinctions, under which all the rest must subordinately range. By the one mode, all contemporaneous circumstances, facts, and events must be set down contemporaneously; by the other, they are only to be set down as the general stream of the narrative shall dictate; for matters which are kindred in time, may be very irrelative in themselves. I elect neither of these; I am careless of either; both are well enough in their way; I write precisely as I please.

In the earlier chapters of this volume, it has somewhere been passingly intimated, that Pierre was not only a reader of the poets and other fine writers, but likewise—and what is a very different thing from the other—a thorough allegorical understander of them, a profound emotional sympathizer with them; in other words, Pierre himself possessed the poetic nature; in himself absolutely, though but latently and floatingly, possessed every whit of the imaginative wealth which he so admired, when by vast pains-takings, and all manner of unrecompensed agonies, systematized on the printed page. Not that as yet his young and immature soul had been accosted by the Wonderful Mutes, and through the vast halls of Silent Truth, had been ushered into the full, secret, eternally inviolable Sanhedrim, where the Poetic Magi discuss, in glorious gibberish, the Alpha and Omega of the Universe. But among the beautiful imaginings of the second and third degree of poets, he freely and comprehendingly ranged.

But it still remains to be said, that Pierre himself had written many a fugitive thing, which had brought him, not only vast credit and compliments from his more immediate acquaintances, but the less partial applauses of the always intelligent, and extremely discriminating public. In short, Pierre had frequently done that, which many other boys have done—published. Not in the imposing form of a book, but in the more modest and becoming way of occasional contributions to magazines and other polite periodicals. His magnificent and victorious *debut* had been made in that delightful love-sonnet, entitled "The Tropical Summer." Not only the public had applauded his gemmed little sketches of thought and fancy, whether in poetry or prose; but the high and mighty Campbell clan of editors of all sorts had bestowed upon him those generous commendations, which, with one instantaneous glance, they had immediately perceived was his due. They spoke in high terms of his surprising command of language; they begged to express their wonder at his euphonious construction of sentences; they regarded with reverence the pervading symmetry of his general style. But transcending even this profound insight into the deep merits of Pierre, they looked infinitely beyond, and confessed their complete inability to restrain their unqualified admiration for the highly judicious smoothness and genteelness of the sentiments and fancies expressed. "This writer," said one,—in an ungovernable burst of admiring fury—"is characterized throughout by Perfect Taste." Another, after endorsingly quoting that sapient, suppressed maxim of Dr. Goldsmith's, which asserts that whatever is new is false, went on to apply it to the excellent productions before him; concluding with this: "He has translated the unruffled gentleman from the drawing-room into the general levee of letters; he never permits himself to astonish; is never betrayed into any thing coarse or new; as assured that whatever astonishes is vulgar, and whatever is new must be crude. Yes, it is the glory of this admirable young author, that vulgarity and vigor—two inseparable adjuncts—are equally removed from him."

A third, perorated a long and beautifully written review, by the bold and startling announcement—"This writer is unquestionably a highly respectable youth."

Nor had the editors of various moral and religious periodicals failed to render the tribute of their severer appreciation, and more enviable, because more chary applause. A renowned clerical and philological conductor of a weekly publication of this kind, whose surprising proficiency in the Greek, Hebrew, and Chaldaic, to which he had devoted by far the greater part of his life, peculiarly fitted him to pronounce unerring judgment upon works of taste in the English, had unhesitatingly delivered himself thus:—"He is blameless in morals, and harmless throughout." Another, had unhesitatingly recommended his effusions to the family-circle. A third, had no reserve in saying, that the predominant end and aim of this author was evangelical piety.

A mind less naturally strong than Pierre's might well have been hurried into vast self-complacency, by such eulogy as this, especially as there could be no possible doubt, that the primitive verdict pronounced by the editors was irreversible, except in the highly improbable event of the near approach of the Millennium, which might establish a different dynasty of taste, and possibly eject the editors. It is true, that in view of the general practical vagueness of these panegyrics, and the circumstance that, in essence, they were all somehow of the prudently indecisive sort; and, considering that they were panegyrics, and nothing but panegyrics, without any thing analytical about them; an elderly friend of a literary turn, had made bold to say to our hero—"Pierre, this is very high praise, I grant, and you are a surprisingly young author to receive it; but I do not see any criticisms as yet."

"Criticisms?" cried Pierre, in amazement; "why, sir, they are all criticisms! I am the idol of the critics!"

"Ah!" sighed the elderly friend, as if suddenly reminded that that was true after all—"Ah!" and went on with his inoffensive, non-committal cigar.

Nevertheless, thanks to the editors, such at last became the popular literary enthusiasm in behalf of Pierre, that two young men, recently abandoning the ignoble pursuit of tailoring for the more honorable trade of the publisher (probably with an economical view of working up in books, the linen and cotton shreds of the cutter's counter, after having been subjected to the action of the paper-mill), had on the daintiest scolloped-edged paper, and in the neatest possible, and fine-needle-work hand, addressed him a letter, couched in the following terms; the general style of which letter will sufficiently evince that, though—thanks to the manufacturer—their linen and cotton shreds may have been very completely transmuted into paper, yet the cutters themselves were not yet entirely out of the metamorphosing mill.

"Hon. Pierre Glendinning,

"Revered Sir,

"The fine cut, the judicious fit of your productions fill us with amazement. The fabric is excellent—the finest broadcloth of genius. We have just started in business. Your pantaloons—productions, we mean—have never yet been collected. They should be published in the Library form. The tailors—we mean the librarians, demand it. Your fame is now in its finest nap. Now—before the gloss is off—now is the time for the library form. We have recently received an invoice of Chamois——Russia leather. The library form should be a durable form. We respectfully offer to dress your amazing productions in the library form. If you please, we will transmit you a sample of the cloth——we mean a sample-page, with a pattern of the leather. We are ready to give you one tenth of the profits (less discount) for the privilege of arraying your wonderful productions in the library form:—you cashing the seamstresses'——printer's and binder's bills on the day of publication. An answer at your earliest convenience will greatly oblige,—

"Sir, your most obsequious servants,

"WONDER & WEN."

"P.S.—We respectfully submit the enclosed block——sheet, as some earnest of our intentions to do every thing in your behalf possible to any firm in the trade.

"N.B.—If the list does not comprise all your illustrious wardrobe——works, we mean——, we shall exceedingly regret it. We have hunted through all the drawers——magazines.

"Sample of a coat——title for the works of Glendinning:

THE

COMPLETE WORKS

OF

GLENDINNING

AUTHOR OF

That world-famed production, "The Tropical Summer: a Sonnet." "The Weather: a Thought." "Life: an Impromptu." "The late Reverend Mark Graceman: an Obituary." "Honor: a Stanza." "Beauty: an Acrostic." "Edgar: an Anagram." "The Pippin: a Paragraph."

&c. &c. &c. &c.

&c. &c. &c.

&c. &c.

&c."

From a designer, Pierre had received the following:

"Sir: I approach you with unfeigned trepidation. For though you are young in age, you are old in fame and ability. I can not express to you my ardent admiration of your works; nor can I but deeply regret that the productions of such graphic descriptive power, should be unaccompanied by the humbler illustrative labors of the designer. My services in this line are entirely at your command. I need not say how proud I should be, if this hint, on my part, however presuming, should induce you to reply in terms upon which I could found the hope of honoring myself and my profession by a few designs for the works of the illustrious Glendinning. But the cursory mention of your name here fills me with such swelling emotions, that I can say nothing more. I would only add, however, that not being at all connected with the Trade, my business situation unpleasantly forces me to make cash down on delivery of each design, the basis of all my professional arrangements. Your noble soul, however, would disdain to suppose, that this sordid necessity, in my merely business concerns, could ever impair——

"That profound private veneration and admiration
"With which I unmercenarily am,
"Great and good Glendinning,
"Yours most humbly,
"PETER PENCE."

ii

These were stirring letters. The Library Form! an Illustrated Edition! His whole heart swelled.

But unfortunately it occurred to Pierre, that as all his writings were not only fugitive, but if put together could not possibly fill more than a very small duodecimo; therefore the Library Edition seemed a little premature, perhaps; possibly, in a slight degree, preposterous. Then, as they were chiefly made up of little sonnets, brief meditative poems, and moral essays, the matter for the designer ran some small risk of being but meager. In his inexperience, he did not know that such was the great height of invention to which the designer's art had been carried, that certain gentlemen of that profession had gone to an eminent publishing-house with overtures for an illustrated edition of "Coke upon Lyttleton." Even the City Directory was beautifully illustrated with exquisite engravings of bricks, tongs, and flat-irons.

Concerning the draught for the title-page, it must be confessed, that on seeing the imposing enumeration of his titles—long and magnificent as those preceding the proclamations of some German Prince ("*Hereditary Lord of the back-yard of Crantz Jacobi; Undoubted Proprietor by Seizure of the bedstead of the late Widow Van Lorn; Heir Apparent to the Bankrupt Bakery of Fletz and Flitz; Residuary Legatee of the Confiscated Pin-Money of the Late Dowager Dunker; &c. &c. &c.*") Pierre could not entirely repress a momentary feeling of elation. Yet did he also bow low under the weight of his own ponderosity, as the author of such a vast load of literature. It occasioned him some slight misgivings, however, when he considered, that already in his eighteenth year, his title-page should so immensely surpass in voluminous statisticals the simple page, which in his father's edition prefixed the vast speculations of Plato. Still, he comforted himself with the thought, that as he could not presume to interfere with the bill-stickers of the Gazelle Magazine, who every month covered the walls of the city with gigantic announcements of his name among the other contributors; so neither could he now—in the highly improbable event of closing with the offer of Messrs. Wonder and Wen—presume to interfere with the bill-sticking department of their business concern; for it was plain that they esteemed one's title-page but another unwindowed wall, infinitely more available than most walls, since here was at least one spot in the city where no rival bill-stickers dared to encroach. Nevertheless, resolved as he was to let all such bill-sticking matters take care of themselves, he was sensible of some coy inclination toward that modest method of certain kid-gloved and dainty authors, who scorning the vulgarity of a sounding parade, contented themselves with simply subscribing their name to the title-page; as confident, that that was sufficient guarantee to the notice of all true gentlemen of taste. It was for petty German princes to sound their prolonged titular flourishes. The Czar of Russia contented himself with putting the simple word "NICHOLAS" to his loftiest decrees.

This train of thought terminated at last in various considerations upon the subject of anonymousness in authorship. He regretted that he had not started his literary career under that mask. At present, it might be too late; already the whole universe knew him, and it was in vain at this late day to attempt to hood himself. But when he considered the essential dignity and propriety at all points, of the inviolably anonymous method, he could not but feel the sincerest sympathy for those unfortunate fellows, who, not only naturally averse to any sort of publicity, but progressively ashamed of their own successive productions—written chiefly for the merest cash—were yet cruelly coerced into sounding title-pages by sundry baker's and butcher's bills, and other financial considerations; inasmuch as the placard of the title-page indubitably must assist the publisher in his sales.

But perhaps the ruling, though not altogether conscious motive of Pierre in finally declining—as he did—the services of Messrs. Wonder and Wen, those eager applicants for the privilege of extending and solidifying his fame, arose from the idea that being at this time not very far advanced in years, the probability was, that his future productions might at least equal, if not surpass, in some small degree, those already given to the world. He resolved to wait for his literary canonization until he should at least have outgrown the sophomorean insinuation of the Law; which, with a singular affectation of benignity, pronounced him an "infant." His modesty obscured from him the circumstance, that the greatest lettered celebrities of the time, had, by the divine power of genius, become full graduates in the University of Fame, while yet as legal minors forced to go to their mammas for pennies wherewith to keep them in peanuts.

Not seldom Pierre's social placidity was ruffled by polite entreaties from the young ladies that he would be pleased to grace their Albums with some nice little song. We say that here his social placidity was ruffled; for the true charm of agreeable parlor society is, that there you lose your own sharp individuality and become delightfully merged in that soft social Pantheism, as it were, that rosy melting of all into one, ever prevailing in those drawing-rooms, which pacifically and deliciously belie their own name; inasmuch as there no one draws the sword of his own individuality, but all such ugly weapons are left—as of old—with your hat and cane in the hall. It was very awkward to decline the albums; but somehow it was still worse, and peculiarly distasteful for Pierre to comply. With equal justice apparently, you might either have called this his weakness or his idiosyncrasy. He summoned all his suavity, and refused. And the refusal of Pierre—according to Miss Angelica Amabilia of Ambleside—was sweeter than the compliance of others. But then—prior to the proffer of her album—in a copse at Ambleside, Pierre in a gallant whim had in the lady's own presence voluntarily carved Miss Angelica's initials upon the bark of a beautiful maple. But all young ladies are not Miss Angelicas. Blandly denied in the parlor, they courted repulse in the study. In lovely envelopes they dispatched their albums to Pierre, not omitting to drop a little attar-of-rose in the palm of the domestic who carried them. While now Pierre—pushed to the wall in his gallantry—shilly-shallied as to what he must do, the awaiting albums multiplied upon him; and by-and-by monopolized an entire shelf in his chamber; so that while their combined ornate bindings fairly dazzled his eyes, their excessive redolence all but made him to faint, though indeed, in moderation, he was very partial to perfumes. So that of really chilly afternoons, he was still obliged to drop the upper sashes a few inches.

The simplest of all things it is to write in a lady's album. But Cui Bono? Is there such a dearth of printed reading, that the monkish times must be revived, and ladies books be in manuscript? What could Pierre write of his own on Love or any thing else, that would surpass what divine Hafiz wrote so many long centuries ago? Was there not Anacreon too, and Catullus, and Ovid—all translated, and readily accessible? And then—bless all their souls!—had the dear creatures forgotten Tom Moore? But the handwriting, Pierre,—they want the sight of your hand. Well, thought Pierre, actual feeling is better than transmitted sight, any day. I will give them the actual feeling of my hand, as much as they want. And lips are still better than hands. Let them send their sweet faces to me, and I will kiss *lipographs* upon them forever and a day. This was a felicitous idea. He called Dates, and had the albums carried down by the basket-full into the dining-room. He opened and spread them all out upon the extension-table there; then, modeling himself by the Pope, when His Holiness collectively blesses long crates of rosaries—he waved one devout kiss to the albums; and summoning three servants sent the albums all home, with his best compliments, accompanied with a confectioner's *kiss* for each album, rolled up in the most ethereal tissue.

From various quarters of the land, both town and country, and especially during the preliminary season of autumn, Pierre received various pressing invitations to lecture before Lyceums, Young Men's Associations, and other Literary and Scientific Societies. The letters conveying these invitations possessed quite an imposing and most flattering aspect to the unsophisticated Pierre. One was as follows:—

"Urquhartian Club for the Immediate Extension
of the Limits of all Knowledge,
both Human and Divine.

"ZADOCKPRATTSVILLE,
"June 11th, 18—.

"Author of the 'Tropical Summer,' &c.

"HONORED AND DEAR SIR:—

"Official duty and private inclination in this present case most delightfully blend. What was the ardent desire of my heart, has now by the action of the *Committee on Lectures* become professionally obligatory upon me. As Chairman of our *Committee on Lectures*, I hereby beg the privilege of entreating that you will honor this Society by lecturing before it on any subject you may choose, and at any day most convenient to yourself. The subject of Human Destiny we would respectfully suggest, without however at all wishing to impede you in your own unbiased selection.

"If you honor us by complying with this invitation, be assured, sir, that the Committee on Lectures will take the best care of you throughout your stay, and endeavor to make Zadockprattsville agreeable to you. A carriage will be in attendance at the Stage-house to convey yourself and luggage to the Inn, under full escort of the *Committee on Lectures,* with the Chairman at their head.

"Permit me to join my private homage
To my high official consideration for you,
And to subscribe myself
Very humbly your servant,

"DONALD DUNDONALD."

iii

But it was more especially the Lecture invitations coming from venerable, gray-headed metropolitan Societies, and indited by venerable gray-headed Secretaries, which far from elating filled the youthful Pierre with the sincerest sense of humility. Lecture? lecture? such a stripling as I lecture to fifty benches, with ten gray heads on each? five hundred gray heads in all! Shall my one, poor, inexperienced brain presume to lay down the law in a lecture to five hundred life-ripened understandings? It seemed too absurd for thought. Yet the five hundred, through their spokesman, had voluntarily extended this identical invitation to him. Then how could it be otherwise, than that an incipient Timonism should slide into Pierre, when he considered all the disgraceful inferences to be derived from such a fact. He called to mind, how that once upon a time, during a visit of his to the city, the police were called out to quell a portentous riot, occasioned by the vast press and contention for seats at the first lecture of an illustrious lad of nineteen, the author of "A Week at Coney Island."

It is needless to say that Pierre most conscientiously and respectfully declined all polite overtures of this sort.

Similar disenchantments of his cooler judgment did likewise deprive of their full lusciousness several other equally marked demonstrations of his literary celebrity. Applications for autographs showered in upon him; but in sometimes humorously gratifying the more urgent requests of these singular people Pierre could not but feel a pang of regret, that owing to the very youthful and quite unformed character of his handwriting, his signature did not possess that inflexible uniformity, which—for mere prudential reasons, if nothing more—should always mark the hand of illustrious men. His heart thrilled with sympathetic anguish for posterity, which would be certain to stand hopelessly perplexed before so many contradictory signatures of one supereminent name. Alas! posterity would be sure to conclude that they were forgeries all; that no chirographic relic of the sublime poet Glendinning survived to their miserable times.

From the proprietors of the Magazines whose pages were honored by his effusions, he received very pressing epistolary solicitations for the loan of his portrait in oil, in order to take an engraving therefrom, for a frontispiece to their periodicals. But here again the most melancholy considerations obtruded. It had always been one of the lesser ambitions of Pierre, to sport a flowing beard, which he deemed the most noble corporeal badge of the man, not to speak of the illustrious author. But as yet he was beardless; and no cunning compound of Rowland and Son could force a beard which should arrive at maturity in any reasonable time for the frontispiece. Besides, his boyish features and whole expression were daily changing. Would he lend his authority to this unprincipled imposture upon Posterity? Honor forbade.

These epistolary petitions were generally couched in an elaborately respectful style; thereby intimating with what deep reverence his portrait would be handled, while unavoidably subjected to the discipline indispensable to obtain from it the engraved copy they prayed for. But one or two of the persons who made occasional oral requisitions upon him in this matter of his engraved portrait, seemed less regardful of the inherent respect due to every man's portrait, much more, to that of a genius so celebrated as Pierre. They did not even seem to remember that the portrait of any man generally receives, and indeed is entitled to more reverence than the original man himself; since one may freely clap a celebrated friend on the shoulder, yet would by no means tweak his nose in his portrait. The reason whereof may be this: that the portrait is better entitled to reverence than the man; inasmuch as nothing belittling can be imagined concerning the portrait, whereas many unavoidably belittling things can be fancied as touching the man.

Upon one occasion, happening suddenly to encounter a literary acquaintance—a joint editor of the "Captain Kidd Monthly"—who suddenly popped upon him round a corner, Pierre was startled by a rapid—

"Good-morning, good-morning;—just the man I wanted:—come, step round now with me, and have your Daguerreotype taken;—get it engraved then in no time;—want it for the next issue."

So saying, this chief mate of Captain Kidd seized Pierre's arm, and in the most vigorous manner was walking him off, like an officer a pickpocket, when Pierre civilly said—"Pray, sir, hold, if you please, I shall do no such thing."—"Pooh, pooh—must have it—public property—come along—only a door or two now."—"Public property!" rejoined Pierre, "that may do very well for the 'Captain Kidd Monthly;'—it's very Captain Kiddish to say so. But I beg to repeat that I do not intend to accede."—"Don't? Really?" cried the other, amazedly staring Pierre full in the countenance; —"why bless your soul, *my* portrait is published—long ago published!"—"Can't help that, sir"—said Pierre. "Oh! come along, come along," and the chief mate seized him again with the most uncompunctious familiarity by the arm. Though the sweetest-tempered youth in the world when but decently treated, Pierre had an ugly devil in him sometimes, very apt to be evoked by the personal profaneness of gentlemen of the Captain Kidd school of literature. "Look you, my good fellow," said he, submitting to his impartial inspection a determinately double fist,—"drop my arm now—or I'll drop you. To the devil with you and your Daguerreotype!"

This incident, suggestive as it was at the time, in the sequel had a surprising effect upon Pierre. For he considered with what infinite readiness now, the most faithful portrait of any one could be taken by the Daguerreotype, whereas in former times a faithful portrait was only within the power of the moneyed, or mental aristocrats of the earth. How natural then the inference, that instead of, as in old times, immortalizing a genius, a portrait now only *dayalized* a dunce. Besides, when every body has his portrait published, true distinction lies in not having yours published at all. For if you are published along with Tom, Dick, and Harry, and wear a coat of their cut, how then are you distinct from Tom, Dick, and Harry? Therefore, even so miserable a motive as downright personal vanity helped to operate in this matter with Pierre.

Some zealous lovers of the general literature of the age, as well as declared devotees to his own great genius, frequently petitioned him for the materials wherewith to frame his biography. They assured him, that life of all things was most insecure. He might feel many years in him yet; time might go lightly by him; but in any sudden and fatal sickness, how would his last hours be embittered by the thought, that he was about to depart forever, leaving the world utterly unprovided with the knowledge of what were the precise texture and hue of the first trowsers he wore. These representations did certainly touch him in a very tender spot, not previously unknown to the schoolmaster. But when Pierre considered, that owing to his extreme youth, his own recollections of the past soon merged into all manner of half-memories and a general vagueness, he could not find it in his conscience to present such materials to the impatient biographers, especially as his chief verifying authority in these matters of his past career, was now eternally departed beyond all human appeal. His excellent nurse Clarissa had been dead four years and more. In vain a young literary friend, the well-known author of two Indexes and one Epic, to whom the subject happened to be mentioned, warmly espoused the cause of the distressed biographers; saying that however unpleasant, one must needs pay the penalty of celebrity; it was no use to stand back; and concluded by taking from the crown of his hat the proof-sheets of his own biography, which, with the most thoughtful consideration for the masses, was shortly to be published in the pamphlet form, price only a shilling.

It only the more bewildered and pained him, when still other and less delicate applicants sent him their regularly printed *Biographico-Solicito Circulars*, with his name written in ink; begging him to honor them and the world with a neat draft of his life, including criticisms on his own writings; the printed circular indiscriminately protesting, that undoubtedly he knew more of his own life than any other living man; and that only he who had put together the great works of Glendinning could be fully qualified thoroughly to analyze them, and cast the ultimate judgment upon their remarkable construction.

Now, it was under the influence of the humiliating emotions engendered by things like the above; it was when thus haunted by publishers, engravers, editors, critics, autograph-collectors, portrait-fanciers, biographers, and petitioning and remonstrating literary friends of all sorts; it was then, that there stole into the youthful soul of Pierre melancholy forebodings of the utter unsatisfactoriness of all human fame; since the most ardent profferings of the most martyrizing demonstrations in his behalf,—these he was sorrowfully obliged to turn away.

And it may well be believed, that after the wonderful vital world-revelation so suddenly made to Pierre at the Meadows—a revelation which, at moments, in some certain things, fairly Timonized him—he had not failed to clutch with peculiar nervous detestation and contempt that ample parcel, containing the letters of his Biographico and other silly correspondents, which, in a less ferocious hour, he had filed away as curiosities. It was with an almost infernal grin, that he saw that particular heap of rubbish eternally quenched in the fire, and felt that as it was consumed before his eyes, so in his soul was forever killed the last and minutest undeveloped microscopic germ of that most despicable vanity to which those absurd correspondents thought to appeal.

Book XVIII

Pierre, as a Juvenile Author, Reconsidered

INASMUCH AS BY VARIOUS INDIRECT INTIMATIONS much more than ordinary natural genius has been imputed to Pierre, it may have seemed an inconsistency, that only the merest magazine papers should have been thus far the sole productions of his mind. Nor need it be added, that, in the soberest earnest, those papers contained nothing uncommon; indeed—entirely now to drop all irony, if hitherto any thing like that has been indulged in—those fugitive things of Master Pierre's were the veriest common-place.

It is true, as I long before said, that Nature at Saddle Meadows had very early been as a benediction to Pierre;—had blown her wind-clarion to him from the blue hills, and murmured melodious secrecies to him by her streams and her woods. But while nature thus very early and very abundantly feeds us, she is very late in tutoring us as to the proper methodization of our diet. Or,—to change the metaphor,—there are immense quarries of fine marble; but how to get it out; how to chisel it; how to construct any temple? Youth must wholly quit, then, the quarry, for awhile; and not only go forth, and get tools to use in the quarry, but must go and thoroughly study architecture. Now the quarry-discoverer is long before the stone-cutter; and the stone-cutter is long before the architect; and the architect is long before the temple; for the temple is the crown of the world.

Yes; Pierre was not only very unarchitectural at that time, but Pierre was very young, indeed, at that time. And it is often to be observed, that as in digging for precious metals in the mines, much earthy rubbish has first to be troublesomely handled and thrown out; so, in digging in one's soul for the fine gold of genius, much dullness and common-place is first brought to light. Happy would it be, if the man possessed in himself some receptacle for his own rubbish of this sort: but he is like the occupant of a dwelling, whose refuse can not be clapped into his own cellar, but must be deposited in the street before his own door, for the public functionaries to take care of. No common-place is ever effectually got rid of, except by essentially emptying one's self of it into a book; for once trapped in a book, then the book can be put into the fire, and all will be well. But they are not always put into the fire; and this accounts for the vast majority of miserable books over those of positive merit. Nor will any thoroughly sincere man, who is an author, ever be rash in precisely defining the period, when he has completely ridded himself of his rubbish, and come to the latent gold in his mine. It holds true, in every case, that the wiser a man is, the more misgivings he has on certain points.

It is well enough known, that the best productions of the best human intellects, are generally regarded by those intellects as mere immature freshman exercises, wholly worthless in themselves, except as initiatives for entering the great University of God after death. Certain it is, that if any inferences can be drawn from observations of the familiar lives of men of the greatest mark, their finest things, those which become the foolish glory of the world, are not only very poor and inconsiderable to themselves, but often positively distasteful; they would rather not have the book in the room. In minds comparatively inferior as compared with the above, these surmising considerations so sadden and unfit, that they become careless of what they write; go to their desks with discontent, and only remain there —victims to headache, and pain in the back—by the hard constraint of some social necessity. Equally paltry and despicable to them, are the works thus composed; born of unwillingness and the bill of the baker; the rickety offspring of a parent, careless of life herself, and reckless of the germ-life she contains. Let not the short-sighted world for a moment imagine, that any vanity lurks in such minds; only hired to appear on the stage, not voluntarily claiming the public attention; their utmost life-redness and glow is but rouge, washed off in private with bitterest tears; their laugh only rings because it is hollow; and the answering laugh is no laughter to them.

There is nothing so slipperily alluring as sadness; we become sad in the first place by having nothing stirring to do; we continue in it, because we have found a snug sofa at last. Even so, it may possibly be, that arrived at this quiet retrospective little episode in the career of my hero—this shallowly expansive embayed Tappan Zee of my otherwise deep-heady Hudson—I too begin to loungingly expand, and wax harmlessly sad and sentimental.

Now, what has been hitherto presented in reference to Pierre, concerning rubbish, as in some cases the unavoidable first-fruits of genius, is in no wise contradicted by the fact, that the first published works of many meritorious authors have given mature token of genius; for we do not know how many they previously published to the flames; or privately published in their own brains, and suppressed there as quickly. And in the inferior instances of an immediate literary success, in very young writers, it will be almost invariably observable, that for that instant success they were chiefly indebted to some rich and peculiar experience in life, embodied in a book, which because, for that cause, containing original matter, the author himself, forsooth, is to be considered original; in this way, many very original books, being the product of very unoriginal minds. Indeed, man has only to be but a little circumspect, and away flies the last rag of his vanity. The world is forever babbling of originality; but there never yet was an original man, in the sense intended by the world; the first man himself—who according to the Rabbins was also the first author—not being an original; the only original author being God. Had Milton's been the lot of Caspar Hauser, Milton would have been vacant as he. For though the naked soul of man doth assuredly contain one latent element of intellectual productiveness; yet never was there a child born solely from one parent; the visible world of experience being that procreative thing which impregnates the muses; self-reciprocally efficient hermaphrodites being but a fable.

There is infinite nonsense in the world on all of these matters; hence blame me not if I contribute my mite. It is impossible to talk or to write without apparently throwing oneself helplessly open; the Invulnerable Knight wears his visor down. Still, it is pleasant to chat; for it passes the time ere we go to our beds; and speech is further incited, when like strolling improvisatores of Italy, we are paid for our breath. And we are only too thankful when the gapes of the audience dismiss us with the few ducats we earn.

ii

It may have been already inferred, that the pecuniary plans of Pierre touching his independent means of support in the city were based upon his presumed literary capabilities. For what else could he do? He knew no profession, no trade. Glad now perhaps might he have been, if Fate had made him a blacksmith, and not a gentleman, a Glendinning, and a genius. But here he would have been unpardonably rash, had he not already, in some degree, actually tested the fact, in his own personal experience, that it is not altogether impossible for a magazine contributor to Juvenile American literature to receive a few pence in exchange for his ditties. Such cases stand upon imperishable record, and it were both folly and ingratitude to disown them.

But since the fine social position and noble patrimony of Pierre, had thus far rendered it altogether unnecessary for him to earn the least farthing of his own in the world, whether by hand or by brain; it may seem desirable to explain a little here as we go. We shall do so, but always including, the preamble.

Sometimes every possible maxim or thought seems an old one; yet it is among the elder of the things in that unaugmentable stock, that never mind what one's situation may be, however prosperous and happy, he will still be impatient of it; he will still reach out of himself, and beyond every present condition. So, while many a poor be-inked galley-slave, toiling with the heavy oar of a quill, to gain something wherewithal to stave off the cravings of nature; and in his hours of morbid self-reproach, regarding his paltry wages, at all events, as an unavoidable disgrace to him; while this galley-slave of letters would have leaped with delight—reckless of the feeble seams of his pantaloons—at the most distant prospect of inheriting the broad farms of Saddle Meadows, lord of an all-sufficing income, and forever exempt from wearing on his hands those treacherous plague-spots of indigence—videlicet, blots from the inkstand;—Pierre himself, the undoubted and actual possessor of the things only longingly and hopelessly imagined by the other; the then top of Pierre's worldly ambition, was the being able to boast that he had written such matters as publishers would pay something for in the way of a mere business transaction, which they thought would prove profitable. Yet altogether weak and silly as this may seem in Pierre, let us preambillically examine a little further, and see if it be so indeed.

Pierre was proud; and a proud man—proud with the sort of pride now meant—ever holds but lightly those things, however beneficent, which he did not for himself procure. Were such pride carried out to its legitimate end, the man would eat no bread, the seeds whereof he had not himself put into the soil, not entirely without humiliation, that even that seed must be borrowed from some previous planter. A proud man likes to feel himself in himself, and not by reflection in others. He likes to be not only his own Alpha and Omega, but to be distinctly all the intermediate gradations, and then to slope off on his own spine either way, into the endless impalpable ether. What a glory it was then to Pierre, when first in his two gentlemanly hands he jingled the wages of labor! Talk of drums and the fife; the echo of coin of one's own earning is more inspiring than all the trumpets of Sparta. How disdainfully now he eyed the sumptuousness of his hereditary halls—the hangings, and the pictures, and the bragging historic armorials and the banners of the Glendinning renown; confident, that if need should come, he would not be forced to turn resurrectionist, and dig up his grandfather's Indian-chief grave for the ancestral sword and shield, ignominiously to pawn them for a living! He could live on himself. Oh, twice-blessed now, in the feeling of practical capacity, was Pierre.

The mechanic, the day-laborer, has but one way to live; his body must provide for his body. But not only could Pierre in some sort, do that; he could do the other; and letting his body stay lazily at home, send off his soul to labor, and his soul would come faithfully back and pay his body her wages. So, some unprofessional gentlemen of the aristocratic South, who happen to own slaves, give those slaves liberty to go and seek work, and every night return with their wages, which constitute those idle gentlemen's income. Both ambidexter and quadruple-armed is that man, who in a day-laborer's body, possesses a day-laboring soul. Yet let not such an one be over-confident. Our God is a jealous God; He wills not that any man should permanently possess the least shadow of His own self-sufficient attributes. Yoke the body to the soul, and put both to the plough, and the one or the other must in the end assuredly drop in the furrow. Keep, then, thy body effeminate for labor, and thy soul laboriously robust; or else thy soul effeminate for labor, and thy body laboriously robust. Elect! the two will not lastingly abide in one yoke. Thus over the most vigorous and soaring conceits, doth the cloud of Truth come stealing; thus doth the shot, even of a sixty-two-pounder pointed upward, light at last on the earth; for strive we how we may, we can not overshoot the earth's orbit, to receive the attractions of other planets; Earth's law of gravitation extends far beyond her own atmosphere.

In the operative opinion of this world, he who is already fully provided with what is necessary for him, that man shall have more; while he who is deplorably destitute of the same, he shall have taken away from him even that which he hath. Yet the world vows it is a very plain, downright matter-of-fact, plodding, humane sort of world. It is governed only by the simplest principles, and scorns all ambiguities, all transcendentals, and all manner of juggling. Now some imaginatively heterodoxical men are often surprisingly twitted upon their willful inverting of all common-sense notions, their absurd and all-displacing transcendentals, which say three is four, and two and two make ten. But if the eminent Jugglarius himself ever advocated in mere words a doctrine one thousandth part so ridiculous and subversive of all practical sense, as that doctrine which the world actually and eternally practices, of giving unto him who already hath more than enough, still more of the superfluous article, and taking away from him who hath nothing at all, even that which he hath,—then is the truest book in the world a lie.

Wherefore we see that the so-called Transcendentalists are not the only people who deal in Transcendentals. On the contrary, we seem to see that the Utilitarians,—the every-day world's people themselves, far transcend those inferior Transcendentalists by their own incomprehensible worldly maxims. And—what is vastly more—with the one party, their Transcendentals are but theoretic and inactive, and therefore harmless; whereas with the other, they are actually clothed in living deeds.

The highly graveling doctrine and practice of the world, above cited, had in some small degree been manifested in the case of Pierre. He prospectively possessed the fee of several hundred farms scattered over part of two adjoining counties; and now the proprietor of that popular periodical, the Gazelle Magazine, sent him several additional dollars for his sonnets. That proprietor (though in sooth, he never read the sonnets, but referred them to his professional adviser; and was so ignorant, that, for a long time previous to the periodical's actually being started, he insisted upon spelling the Gazelle with a *g* for the *z*, as thus: *Gagelle;* maintaining, that in the Gazelle connection, the *z* was a mere impostor, and that the *g* was soft; for he was a judge of softness, and could speak from experience); that proprietor was undoubtedly a Transcendentalist; for did he not act upon the Transcendental doctrine previously set forth?

Now, the dollars derived from his ditties, these Pierre had always invested in cigars; so that the puffs which indirectly brought him his dollars were again returned, but as perfumed puffs; perfumed with the sweet leaf of Havanna. So that this highly-celebrated and world-renowned Pierre—the great author—whose likeness the world had never seen (for had he not repeatedly refused the world his likeness?), this famous poet, and philosopher, author of "*The Tropical Summer: a Sonnet;*" against whose very life several desperadoes were darkly plotting (for had not the biographers sworn they would have it?); this towering celebrity—there he would sit smoking, and smoking, mild and self-festooned as a vapory mountain. It was very involuntarily and satisfactorily reciprocal. His cigars were lighted in two ways: lighted by the sale of his sonnets, and lighted by the printed sonnets themselves.

For even at that early time in his authorial life, Pierre, however vain of his fame, was not at all proud of his paper. Not only did he make allumettes of his sonnets when published, but was very careless about his discarded manuscripts; they were to be found lying all round the house; gave a great deal of trouble to the housemaids in sweeping; went for kindlings to the fires; and were forever flitting out of the windows, and under the door-sills, into the faces of people passing the manorial mansion. In this reckless, indifferent way of his, Pierre himself was a sort of publisher. It is true his more familiar admirers often earnestly remonstrated with him, against this irreverence to the primitive vestments of his immortal productions; saying, that whatever had once felt the nib of his mighty pen, was thenceforth sacred as the lips which had but once saluted the great toe of the Pope. But hardened as he was to these friendly censurings, Pierre never forbade that ardent appreciator of "The Tear," who, finding a small fragment of the original manuscript containing a dot (*tear*), over an *i* (*eye*), esteemed the significant event providential; and begged the distinguished favor of being permitted to have it for a brooch; and ousted a cameo-head of Homer, to replace it with the more invaluable gem. He became inconsolable, when being caught in a rain, the dot (*tear*) disappeared from over the *i* (*eye*); so that the strangeness and wonderfulness of the sonnet was still conspicuous; in that though the least fragment of it could weep in a drought, yet did it become all tearless in a shower.

But this indifferent and supercilious amateur—deaf to the admiration of the world; the enigmatically merry and renowned author of "The Tear;" the pride of the Gazelle Magazine, on whose flaunting cover his name figured at the head of all contributors—(no small men either; for their lives had all been fraternally written by each other, and they had clubbed, and had their likenesses all taken by the aggregate job, and published on paper, all bought at one shop) this high-prestiged Pierre—whose future popularity and voluminousness had become so startlingly announced by what he had already written, that certain speculators came to the Meadows to survey its water-power, if any, with a view to start a paper-mill expressly for the great author, and so monopolize his stationery dealings; —this vast being,—spoken of with awe by all merely youthful aspirants for fame; this age-neutralizing Pierre;—before whom an old gentleman of sixty-five, formerly librarian to Congress, on being introduced to him at the Magazine publishers', devoutly took off his hat, and kept it so, and remained standing, though Pierre was socially seated with his hat on;—this wonderful, disdainful genius—but only life-amateur as yet—is now soon to appear in a far different guise. He shall now learn, and very bitterly learn, that though the world worship Mediocrity and Common Place, yet hath it fire and sword for all contemporary Grandeur; that though it swears that it fiercely assails all Hypocrisy, yet hath it not always an ear for Earnestness.

And though this state of things, united with the ever multiplying freshets of new books, seems inevitably to point to a coming time, when the mass of humanity reduced to one level of dotage, authors shall be scarce as alchymists are to-day, and the printing-press be reckoned a small invention: —yet even now, in the foretaste of this let us hug ourselves, oh, my Aurelian! that though the age of authors be passing, the hours of earnestness shall remain!

Book XIX

The Church of the Apostles

IN THE LOWER OLD-FASHIONED PART of the city, in a narrow street—almost a lane—once filled with demure-looking dwellings, but now chiefly with immense lofty warehouses of foreign importers; and not far from the corner where the lane intersected with a very considerable but contracted thoroughfare for merchants and their clerks, and their carmen and porters; stood at this period a rather singular and ancient edifice, a relic of the more primitive time. The material was a grayish stone, rudely cut and masoned into walls of surprising thickness and strength; along two of which walls—the side ones—were distributed as many rows of arched and stately windows. A capacious, square, and wholly unornamented tower rose in front to twice the height of the body of the church; three sides of this tower were pierced with small and narrow apertures. Thus far, in its external aspect, the building—now more than a century old,—sufficiently attested for what purpose it had originally been founded. In its rear, was a large and lofty plain brick structure, with its front to the rearward street, but its back presented to the back of the church, leaving a small, flagged, and quadrangular vacancy between. At the sides of this quadrangle, three stories of homely brick colonnades afforded covered communication between the ancient church, and its less elderly adjunct. A dismantled, rusted, and forlorn old railing of iron fencing in a small courtyard in front of the rearward building, seemed to hint, that the latter had usurped an unoccupied space formerly sacred as the old church's burial inclosure. Such a fancy would have been entirely true. Built when that part of the city was devoted to private residences, and not to warehouses and offices as now, the old Church of the Apostles had had its days of sanctification and grace; but the tide of change and progress had rolled clean through its broad-aisle and side-aisles, and swept by far the greater part of its congregation two or three miles up town. Some stubborn and elderly old merchants and accountants, lingered awhile among its dusty pews, listening to the exhortations of a faithful old pastor, who, sticking to his post in this flight of his congregation, still propped his half-palsied form in the worm-eaten pulpit, and occasionally pounded—though now with less vigorous hand—the moth-eaten covering of its desk. But it came to pass, that this good old clergyman died; and when the gray-headed and bald-headed remaining merchants and accountants followed his coffin out of the broad-aisle to see it reverently interred; then that was the last time that ever the old edifice witnessed the departure of a regular worshiping assembly from its walls. The venerable merchants and accountants held a meeting, at which it was finally decided, that, hard and unwelcome as the necessity might be, yet it was now no use to disguise the fact, that the building could no longer be efficiently devoted to its primitive purpose. It must be divided into stores; cut into offices; and given for a roost to the gregarious lawyers. This intention was executed, even to the making offices high up in the tower; and so well did the thing succeed, that ultimately the church-yard was invaded for a supplemental edifice, likewise to be promiscuously rented to the legal crowd. But this new building very much exceeded the body of the church in height. It was some seven stories; a fearful pile of Titanic bricks, lifting its tiled roof almost to a level with the top of the sacred tower.

In this ambitious erection the proprietors went a few steps, or rather a few stories, too far. For as people would seldom willingly fall into legal altercations unless the lawyers were always very handy to help them; so it is ever an object with lawyers to have their offices as convenient as feasible to the street; on the ground-floor, if possible, without a single acclivity of a step; but at any rate not in the seventh story of any house, where their clients might be deterred from employing them at all, if they were compelled to mount seven long flights of stairs, one over the other, with very brief landings, in order even to pay their preliminary retaining fees. So, from some time after its throwing open, the upper stories of the less ancient attached edifice remained almost wholly without occupants; and by the forlorn echoes of their vacuities, right over the head of the business-thriving legal gentlemen below, must—to some few of them at least—have suggested unwelcome similitudes, having reference to the crowded state of their basement-pockets, as compared with the melancholy condition of their attics;—alas! full purses and empty heads! This dreary posture of affairs, however, was at last much altered for the better, by the gradual filling up of the vacant chambers on high, by scores of those miscellaneous, bread-and-cheese adventurers, and ambiguously professional nondescripts in very genteel but shabby black, and unaccountable foreign-looking fellows in blue spectacles; who, previously issuing from unknown parts of the world, like storks in Holland, light on the eaves, and in the attics of lofty old buildings in most large sea-port towns. Here they sit and talk like magpies; or descending in quest of improbable dinners, are to be seen drawn up along the curb in front of the eating-houses, like lean rows of broken-hearted pelicans on a beach; their pockets loose, hanging down and flabby, like the pelican's pouches when fish are hard to be caught. But these poor, penniless devils still strive to make ample amends for their physical forlornness, by resolutely reveling in the region of blissful ideals.

They are mostly artists of various sorts; painters, or sculptors, or indigent students, or teachers of languages, or poets, or fugitive French politicians, or German philosophers. Their mental tendencies, however heterodox at times, are still very fine and spiritual upon the whole; since the vacuity of their exchequers leads them to reject the coarse materialism of Hobbes, and incline to the airy exaltations of the Berkelyan philosophy. Often groping in vain in their pockets, they can not but give in to the Descartian vortices; while the abundance of leisure in their attics (physical and figurative), unites with the leisure in their stomachs, to fit them in an eminent degree for that undivided attention indispensable to the proper digesting of the sublimated Categories of Kant; especially as Kant (can't) is the one great palpable fact in their pervadingly impalpable lives. These are the glorious paupers, from whom I learn the profoundest mysteries of things; since their very existence in the midst of such a terrible precariousness of the commonest means of support, affords a problem on which many speculative nut-crackers have been vainly employed. Yet let me here offer up three locks of my hair, to the memory of all such glorious paupers who have lived and died in this world. Surely, and truly I honor them—noble men often at bottom—and for that very reason I make bold to be gamesome about them; for where fundamental nobleness is, and fundamental honor is due, merriment is never accounted irreverent. The fools and pretenders of humanity, and the impostors and baboons among the gods, these only are offended with raillery; since both those gods and men whose titles to eminence are secure, seldom worry themselves about the seditious gossip of old apple-women, and the skylarkings of funny little boys in the street.

When the substance is gone, men cling to the shadow. Places once set apart to lofty purposes, still retain the name of that loftiness, even when converted to the meanest uses. It would seem, as if forced by imperative Fate to renounce the reality of the romantic and lofty, the people of the present would fain make a compromise by retaining some purely imaginative remainder. The curious effects of this tendency are oftenest evinced in those venerable countries of the old transatlantic world; where still over the Thames one bridge yet retains the monastic title of Blackfriars; though not a single Black Friar, but many a pickpocket, has stood on that bank since a good ways beyond the days of Queen Bess; where still innumerable other historic anomalies sweetly and sadly remind the present man of the wonderful procession that preceded him in his new generation. Nor—though the comparative recentness of our own foundation upon these Columbian shores, excludes any considerable participation in these attractive anomalies, —yet are we not altogether, in our more elderly towns, wholly without some touch of them, here and there. It was thus with the ancient Church of the Apostles—better known, even in its primitive day, under the abbreviative of The Apostles—which, though now converted from its original purpose to one so widely contrasting, yet still retained its majestical name. The lawyer or artist tenanting its chambers, whether in the new building or the old, when asked where he was to be found, invariably replied,—*At the Apostles*'. But because now, at last, in the course of the inevitable transplantations of the more notable localities of the various professions in a thriving and amplifying town, the venerable spot offered not such inducements as before to the legal gentlemen; and as the strange nondescript adventurers and artists, and indigent philosophers of all sorts, crowded in as fast as the others left; therefore, in reference to the metaphysical strangeness of these curious inhabitants, and owing in some sort to the circumstance, that several of them were well-known Teleological Theorists, and Social Reformers, and political propagandists of all manner of heterodoxical tenets; therefore, I say, and partly, peradventure, from some slight waggishness in the public; the immemorial popular name of the ancient church itself was participatingly transferred to the dwellers therein. So it came to pass, that in the general fashion of the day, he who had chambers in the old church was familiarly styled an *Apostle*.

But as every effect is but the cause of another and a subsequent one, so it now happened that finding themselves thus clannishly, and not altogether infelicitously entitled, the occupants of the venerable church began to come together out of their various dens, in more social communion; attracted toward each other by a title common to all. By-and-by, from this, they went further; and insensibly, at last became organized in a peculiar society, which, though exceedingly inconspicuous, and hardly perceptible in its public demonstrations, was still secretly suspected to have some mysterious ulterior object, vaguely connected with the absolute overturning of Church and State, and the hasty and premature advance of some unknown great political and religious Millennium. Still, though some zealous conservatives and devotees of morals, several times left warning at the police-office, to keep a wary eye on the old church; and though, indeed, sometimes an officer would look up inquiringly at the suspicious narrow window-slits in the lofty tower; yet, to say the truth, was the place, to all appearance, a very quiet and decorous one, and its occupants a company of harmless people, whose greatest reproach was efflorescent coats and crack-crowned hats all podding in the sun.

Though in the middle of the day many bales and boxes would be trundled along the stores in front of the Apostles'; and along its critically narrow sidewalk, the merchants would now and then hurry to meet their checks ere the banks should close: yet the street, being mostly devoted to mere warehousing purposes, and not used as a general thoroughfare, it was at all times a rather secluded and silent place. But from an hour or two before sundown to ten or eleven o'clock the next morning, it was remarkably silent and depopulated, except by the Apostles themselves; while every Sunday it presented an aspect of surprising and startling quiescence; showing nothing but one long vista of six or seven stories of inexorable iron shutters on both sides of the way. It was pretty much the same with the other street, which, as before said, intersected with the warehousing lane, not very far from the Apostles'. For though that street was indeed a different one from the latter, being full of cheap refectories for clerks, foreign restaurants, and other places of commercial resort; yet the only hum in it was restricted to business hours; by night it was deserted of every occupant but the lamp-posts; and on Sunday, to walk through it, was like walking through an avenue of sphinxes.

Such, then, was the present condition of the ancient Church of the Apostles; buzzing with a few lingering, equivocal lawyers in the basement, and populous with all sorts of poets, painters, paupers and philosophers above. A mysterious professor of the flute was perched in one of the upper stories of the tower; and often, of silent, moonlight nights, his lofty, melodious notes would be warbled forth over the roofs of the ten thousand warehouses around him—as of yore, the bell had pealed over the domestic gables of a long-departed generation.

ii

On the third night following the arrival of the party in the city, Pierre sat at twilight by a lofty window in the rear building of the Apostles'. The chamber was meager even to meanness. No carpet on the floor, no picture on the wall; nothing but a low, long, and very curious-looking single bedstead, that might possibly serve for an indigent bachelor's pallet, a large, blue, chintz-covered chest, a rickety, rheumatic, and most ancient mahogany chair, and a wide board of the toughest live-oak, about six feet long, laid upon two upright empty flour-barrels, and loaded with a large bottle of ink, an unfastened bundle of quills, a pen-knife, a folder, and a still unbound ream of foolscap paper, significantly stamped, "Ruled; Blue."

There, on the third night, at twilight, sat Pierre by that lofty window of a beggarly room in the rear-building of the Apostles'. He was entirely idle, apparently; there was nothing in his hands; but there might have been something on his heart. Now and then he fixedly gazes at the curious-looking, rusty old bedstead. It seemed powerfully symbolical to him; and most symbolical it was. For it was the ancient dismemberable and portable camp-bedstead of his grandfather, the defiant defender of the Fort, the valiant captain in many an unsuccumbing campaign. On that very camp-bedstead, there, beneath his tent on the field, the glorious old mild-eyed and warrior-hearted general had slept, and but waked to buckle his knight-making sword by his side; for it was noble knighthood to be slain by grand Pierre; in the other world his foes' ghosts bragged of the hand that had given them their passports.

But has that hard bed of War, descended for an inheritance to the soft body of Peace? In the peaceful time of full barns, and when the noise of the peaceful flail is abroad, and the hum of peaceful commerce resounds, is the grandson of two Generals a warrior too? Oh, not for naught, in the time of this seeming peace, are warrior grandsires given to Pierre! For Pierre is a warrior too; Life his campaign, and three fierce allies, Woe and Scorn and Want, his foes. The wide world is banded against him; for lo you! he holds up the standard of Right, and swears by the Eternal and True! But ah, Pierre,

Pierre, when thou goest to that bed, how humbling the thought, that thy most extended length measures not the proud six feet four of thy grand John of Gaunt sire! The stature of the warrior is cut down to the dwindled glory of the fight. For more glorious in real tented field to strike down your valiant foe, than in the conflicts of a noble soul with a dastardly world to chase a vile enemy who ne'er will show front.

There, then, on the third night, at twilight, by the lofty window of that beggarly room, sat Pierre in the rear building of the Apostles'. He is gazing out from the window now. But except the donjon form of the old gray tower, seemingly there is nothing to see but a wilderness of tiles, slate, shingles, and tin;—the desolate hanging wildernesses of tiles, slate, shingles and tin, wherewith we modern Babylonians replace the fair hanging-gardens of the fine old Asiatic times when the excellent Nebuchadnezzar was king.

There he sits, a strange exotic, transplanted from the delectable alcoves of the old manorial mansion, to take root in this niggard soil. No more do the sweet purple airs of the hills round about the green fields of Saddle Meadows come revivingly wafted to his cheek. Like a flower he feels the change; his bloom is gone from his cheek; his cheek is wilted and pale.

From the lofty window of that beggarly room, what is it that Pierre is so intently eying? There is no street at his feet; like a profound black gulf the open area of the quadrangle gapes beneath him. But across it, and at the further end of the steep roof of the ancient church, there looms the gray and grand old tower; emblem to Pierre of an unshakable fortitude, which, deep-rooted in the heart of the earth, defied all the howls of the air.

There is a door in Pierre's room opposite the window of Pierre: and now a soft knock is heard in that direction, accompanied by gentle words, asking whether the speaker might enter.

"Yes, always, sweet Isabel"—answered Pierre, rising and approaching the door;—"here: let us drag out the old camp-bed for a sofa; come, sit down now, my sister, and let us fancy ourselves anywhere thou wilt."

"Then, my brother, let us fancy ourselves in realms of everlasting twilight and peace, where no bright sun shall rise, because the black night is always its follower. Twilight and peace, my brother, twilight and peace!"

"It is twilight now, my sister; and surely, this part of the city at least seems still."

"Twilight now, but night soon; then a brief sun, and then another long night. Peace now, but sleep and nothingness soon, and then hard work for thee, my brother, till the sweet twilight come again."

"Let us light a candle, my sister; the evening is deepening."

"For what light a candle, dear Pierre?—Sit close to me, my brother."

He moved nearer to her, and stole one arm around her; her sweet head leaned against his breast; each felt the other's throbbing.

"Oh, my dear Pierre, why should we always be longing for peace, and then be impatient of peace when it comes? Tell me, my brother! Not two hours ago, thou wert wishing for twilight, and now thou wantest a candle to hurry the twilight's last lingering away."

But Pierre did not seem to hear her; his arm embraced her tighter; his whole frame was invisibly trembling. Then suddenly in a low tone of wonderful intensity he breathed:

"Isabel! Isabel!"

She caught one arm around him, as his was around herself; the tremor ran from him to her; both sat dumb.

He rose, and paced the room.

"Well, Pierre; thou camest in here to arrange thy matters, thou saidst. Now what hast thou done? Come, we will light a candle now."

The candle was lighted, and their talk went on.

"How about the papers, my brother? Dost thou find every thing right? Hast thou decided upon what to publish first, while thou art writing the new thing thou didst hint of?"

"Look at that chest, my sister. Seest thou not that the cords are yet untied?"

"Then thou hast not been into it at all as yet?"

"Not at all, Isabel. In ten days I have lived ten thousand years. Forewarned now of the rubbish in that chest, I can not summon the heart to open it. Trash! Dross! Dirt!"

"Pierre! Pierre! what change is this? Didst thou not tell me, ere we came hither, that thy chest not only contained some silver and gold, but likewise far more precious things, readily convertible into silver and gold? Ah, Pierre, thou didst swear we had naught to fear!"

"If I have ever willfully deceived thee, Isabel, may the high gods prove Benedict Arnolds to me, and go over to the devils to reinforce them against me! But to have ignorantly deceived myself and thee together, Isabel; that is a very different thing. Oh, what a vile juggler and cheat is man! Isabel, in that chest are things which in the hour of composition, I thought the very heavens looked in from the windows in astonishment at their beauty and power. Then, afterward, when days cooled me down, and again I took them up and scanned them, some underlying suspicions intruded; but when in the open air, I recalled the fresh, unwritten images of the bunglingly written things; then I felt buoyant and triumphant again; as if by that act of ideal recalling, I had, forsooth, transferred the perfect ideal to the miserable written attempt at embodying it. This mood remained. So that afterward how I talked to thee about the wonderful things I had done; the gold and the silver mine I had long before sprung for thee and for me, who never were to come to want in body or mind. Yet all this time, there was the latent suspicion of folly; but I would not admit it; I shut my soul's door in its face. Yet now, the ten thousand universal revealings brand me on the forehead with fool! and like protested notes at the Bankers, all those written things of mine, are jaggingly cut through and through with the protesting hammer of Truth!—Oh, I am sick, sick, sick!"

"Let the arms that never were filled but by thee, lure thee back again, Pierre, to the peace of the twilight, even though it be of the dimmest!"

She blew out the light, and made Pierre sit down by her; and their hands were placed in each other's.

"Say, are not thy torments now gone, my brother?"

"But replaced by—by—by—Oh God, Isabel, unhand me!" cried Pierre, starting up. "Ye heavens, that have hidden yourselves in the black hood of the night, I call to ye! If to follow Virtue to her uttermost vista, where common souls never go; if by that I take hold on hell, and the uttermost virtue, after all, prove but a betraying pander to the monstrousest vice,—then close in and crush me, ye stony walls, and into one gulf let all things tumble together!"

"My brother! this is some incomprehensible raving," pealed Isabel, throwing both arms around him;—"my brother, my brother!"

"Hark thee to thy furthest inland soul"—thrilled Pierre in a steeled and quivering voice. "Call me brother no more! How knowest thou I am thy brother? Did thy mother tell thee? Did my father say so to me?—I am Pierre, and thou Isabel, wide brother and sister in the common humanity,—no more. For the rest, let the gods look after their own combustibles. If they have put powder-casks in me—let them look to it! let them look to it! Ah! now I catch glimpses, and seem to half-see, somehow, that the uttermost ideal of moral perfection in man is wide of the mark. The demigods trample on trash, and Virtue and Vice are trash! Isabel, I will write such things—I will gospelize the world anew, and show them deeper secrets than the Apocalypse!—I will write it, I will write it!"

"Pierre, I am a poor girl, born in the midst of a mystery, bred in mystery, and still surviving to mystery. So mysterious myself, the air and the earth are unutterable to me; no word have I to express them. But these are the circumambient mysteries; thy words, thy thoughts, open other wonder-worlds to me, whither by myself I might fear to go. But trust to me, Pierre. With thee, with thee, I would boldly swim a starless sea, and be buoy to thee, there, when thou the strong swimmer shouldst faint. Thou, Pierre, speakest of Virtue and Vice; life-secluded Isabel knows neither the one nor the other, but by hearsay. What are they, in their real selves, Pierre? Tell me first what is Virtue:—begin!"

"If on that point the gods are dumb, shall a pigmy speak? Ask the air!"

"Then Virtue is nothing."

"Not that!"

"Then Vice?"

"Look: a nothing is the substance, it casts one shadow one way, and another the other way; and these two shadows cast from one nothing; these, seems to me, are Virtue and Vice."

"Then why torment thyself so, dearest Pierre?"

"It is the law."

"What?"

"That a nothing should torment a nothing; for I am a nothing. It is all a dream—we dream that we dreamed we dream."

"Pierre, when thou just hovered on the verge, thou wert a riddle to me; but now, that thou art deep down in the gulf of the soul,—now, when thou wouldst be lunatic to wise men, perhaps—now doth poor ignorant Isabel begin to comprehend thee. Thy feeling hath long been mine, Pierre. Long loneliness and anguish have opened miracles to me. Yes, it is all a dream!"

Swiftly he caught her in his arms:—"From nothing proceeds nothing, Isabel! How can one sin in a dream?"

"First what is sin, Pierre?"

"Another name for the other name, Isabel."

"For Virtue, Pierre?"

"No, for Vice."

"Let us sit down again, my brother."

"I am Pierre."

"Let us sit down again, Pierre; sit close; thy arm!"

And so, on the third night, when the twilight was gone, and no lamp was lit, within the lofty window of that beggarly room, sat Pierre and Isabel hushed.

Book XX

Charlie Millthorpe

PIERRE HAD BEEN INDUCED to take chambers at the Apostles', by one of the Apostles themselves, an old acquaintance of his, and a native of Saddle Meadows.

Millthorpe was the son of a very respectable farmer—now dead—of more than common intelligence, and whose bowed shoulders and homely garb had still been surmounted by a head fit for a Greek philosopher, and features so fine and regular that they would have well graced an opulent gentleman. The political and social levelings and confoundings of all manner of human elements in America, produce many striking individual anomalies unknown in other lands. Pierre well remembered old farmer Millthorpe:—the handsome, melancholy, calm-tempered, mute, old man; in whose countenance—refinedly ennobled by nature, and yet coarsely tanned and attenuated by many a prolonged day's work in the harvest—rusticity and classicalness were strangely united. The delicate profile of his face, bespoke the loftiest aristocracy; his knobbed and bony hands resembled a beggar's.

Though for several generations the Millthorpes had lived on the Glendinning lands, they loosely and unostentatiously traced their origin to an emigrating English Knight, who had crossed the sea in the time of the elder Charles. But that indigence which had prompted the knight to forsake his courtly country for the howling wilderness, was the only remaining hereditament left to his bedwindled descendants in the fourth and fifth remove. At the time that Pierre first recollected this interesting man, he had, a year or two previous, abandoned an ample farm on account of absolute inability to meet the manorial rent, and was become the occupant of a very poor and contracted little place, on which was a small and half-ruinous house. There, he then harbored with his wife,—a very gentle and retiring person,—his three little daughters, and his only son, a lad of Pierre's own age. The hereditary beauty and youthful bloom of this boy; his sweetness of temper, and something of natural refinement as contrasted with the unrelieved rudeness, and oftentimes sordidness, of his neighbors; these things had early attracted the sympathetic, spontaneous friendliness of Pierre. They were often wont to take their boyish rambles together; and even the severely critical Mrs. Glendinning, always fastidiously cautious as to the companions of Pierre, had never objected to his intimacy with so prepossessing and handsome a rustic as Charles.

Boys are often very swiftly acute in forming a judgment on character. The lads had not long companioned, ere Pierre concluded, that however fine his face, and sweet his temper, young Millthorpe was but little vigorous in mind; besides possessing a certain constitutional, sophomorean presumption and egotism; which, however, having nothing to feed on but his father's meal and potatoes, and his own essentially timid and humane disposition, merely presented an amusing and harmless, though incurable, anomalous feature in his character, not at all impairing the good-will and companionableness of Pierre; for even in his boyhood, Pierre possessed a sterling charity, which could cheerfully overlook all minor blemishes in his inferiors, whether in fortune or mind; content and glad to embrace the good whenever presented, or with whatever conjoined. So, in youth, do we unconsciously act upon those peculiar principles, which in conscious and verbalized maxims shall systematically regulate our maturer lives;—a fact, which forcibly illustrates the necessitarian dependence of our lives, and their subordination, not to ourselves, but to Fate.

If the grown man of taste, possess not only some eye to detect the picturesque in the natural landscape, so also, has he as keen a perception of what may not unfitly be here styled, the *povertiresque* in the social landscape. To such an one, not more picturesquely conspicuous is the dismantled thatch in a painted cottage of Gainsborough, than the time-tangled and want-thinned locks of a beggar, *povertiresquely* diversifying those snug little cabinet-pictures of the world, which, exquisitely varnished and framed, are hung up in the drawing-room minds of humane men of taste, and amiable philosophers of either the "Compensation," or "Optimist" school. They deny that any misery is in the world, except for the purpose of throwing the fine *povertiresque* element into its general picture. Go to! God hath deposited cash in the Bank subject to our gentlemanly order; he hath bounteously blessed the world with a summer carpet of green. Begone, Heraclitus! The lamentations of the rain are but to make us our rainbows!

Not that in equivocal reference to the *povertiresque* old farmer Millthorpe, Pierre is here intended to be hinted at. Still, man can not wholly escape his surroundings. Unconsciously Mrs. Glendinning had always been one of these curious Optimists; and in his boyish life Pierre had not wholly escaped the maternal contagion. Yet often, in calling at the old farmer's for Charles of some early winter mornings, and meeting the painfully embarrassed, thin, feeble features of Mrs. Millthorpe, and the sadly inquisitive and hopelessly half-envious glances of the three little girls; and standing on the threshold, Pierre would catch low, aged, life-weary groans from a recess out of sight from the door; then would Pierre have some boyish inklings of something else than the pure *povertiresque* in poverty: some inklings of what it might be, to be old, and poor, and worn, and rheumatic, with shivering death drawing nigh, and present life itself but a dull and a chill! some inklings of what it might be, for him who in youth had vivaciously leaped from his bed, impatient to meet the earliest sun, and lose no sweet drop of his life, now hating the beams he once so dearly loved; turning round in his bed to the wall to avoid them; and still postponing the foot which should bring him back to the dismal day; when the sun is not gold, but copper; and the sky is not blue, but gray; and the blood, like Rhenish wine, too long unquaffed by Death, grows thin and sour in the veins.

Pierre had not forgotten that the augmented penury of the Millthorpes' was, at the time we now retrospectively treat of, gravely imputed by the gossiping frequenters of the Black Swan Inn, to certain insinuated moral derelictions of the farmer. "The old man tipped his elbow too often," once said in Pierre's hearing an old bottle-necked fellow, performing the identical same act with a half-emptied glass in his hand. But though the form of old Millthorpe was broken, his countenance, however sad and thin, betrayed no slightest sign of the sot, either past or present. He never was publicly known to frequent the inn, and seldom quitted the few acres he cultivated with his son. And though, alas, indigent enough, yet was he most punctually honest in paying his little debts of shillings and pence for his groceries. And though, heaven knows, he had plenty of occasion for all the money he could possibly earn, yet Pierre remembered, that when, one autumn, a hog was bought of him for the servants' hall at the Mansion, the old man never called for his money till the midwinter following; and then, as with trembling fingers he eagerly clutched the silver, he unsteadily said, "I have no use for it now; it might just as well have stood over." It was then, that chancing to overhear this, Mrs. Glendinning had looked at the old man, with a kindly and benignantly interested eye to the *povertiresque;* and murmured, "Ah! the old English Knight is not yet out of his blood. Bravo, old man!"

One day, in Pierre's sight, nine silent figures emerged from the door of old Millthorpe; a coffin was put into a neighbor's farm-wagon; and a procession, some thirty feet long, including the elongated pole and box of the wagon, wound along Saddle Meadows to a hill, where, at last, old Millthorpe was laid down in a bed, where the rising sun should affront him no more. Oh, softest and daintiest of Holland linen is the motherly earth! There, beneath the sublime tester of the infinite sky, like emperors and kings, sleep, in grand state, the beggars and paupers of earth! I joy that Death is this Democrat; and hopeless of all other real and permanent democracies, still hug the thought, that though in life some heads are crowned with gold, and some bound round with thorns, yet chisel them how they will, headstones are all alike.

This somewhat particular account of the father of young Millthorpe, will better set forth the less immature condition and character of the son, on whom had now descended the maintenance of his mother and sisters. But, though the son of a farmer, Charles was peculiarly averse to hard labor. It was not impossible that by resolute hard labor he might eventually have succeeded in placing his family in a far more comfortable situation than he had ever remembered them. But it was not so fated; the benevolent State had in its great wisdom decreed otherwise.

In the village of Saddle Meadows there was an institution, half common-school and half academy, but mainly supported by a general ordinance and financial provision of the government. Here, not only were the rudiments of an English education taught, but likewise some touch of belles lettres, and composition, and that great American bulwark and bore—elocution. On the high-raised, stage platform of the Saddle Meadows Academy, the sons of the most indigent day-laborers were wont to drawl out the fiery revolutionary rhetoric of Patrick Henry, or gesticulate impetuously through the soft cadences of Drake's "Culprit Fay." What wonder, then, that of Saturdays, when there was no elocution and poesy, these boys should grow melancholy and disdainful over the heavy, plodding handles of dung-forks and hoes?

At the age of fifteen, the ambition of Charles Millthorpe was to be either an orator, or a poet; at any rate, a great genius of one sort or other. He recalled the ancestral Knight, and indignantly spurned the plow. Detecting in him the first germ of this inclination, old Millthorpe had very seriously reasoned with his son; warning him against the evils of his vagrant ambition. Ambition of that sort was either for undoubted genius, rich boys, or poor boys, standing entirely alone in the world, with no one relying upon them. Charles had better consider the case; his father was old and infirm; he could not last very long; he had nothing to leave behind him but his plow and his hoe; his mother was sickly; his sisters pale and delicate; and finally, life was a fact, and the winters in that part of the country exceedingly bitter and long. Seven months out of the twelve the pastures bore nothing, and all cattle must be fed in the barns. But Charles was a boy; advice often seems the most wantonly wasted of all human breath; man will not take wisdom on trust; may be, it is well; for such wisdom is worthless; we must find the true gem for ourselves; and so we go groping and groping for many and many a day.

Yet was Charles Millthorpe as affectionate and dutiful a boy as ever boasted of his brain, and knew not that he possessed a far more excellent and angelical thing in the possession of a generous heart. His father died; to his family he resolved to be a second father, and a careful provider now. But not by hard toil of his hand; but by gentler practices of his mind. Already he had read many books—history, poetry, romance, essays, and all. The manorial book-shelves had often been honored by his visits, and Pierre had kindly been his librarian. Not to lengthen the tale, at the age of seventeen, Charles sold the horse, the cow, the pig, the plow, the hoe, and almost every movable thing on the premises; and, converting all into cash, departed with his mother and sisters for the city; chiefly basing his expectations of success on some vague representations of an apothecary relative there resident. How he and his mother and sisters battled it out; how they pined and half-starved for a while; how they took in sewing; and Charles took in copying; and all but scantily sufficed for a livelihood; all this may be easily imagined. But some mysterious latent good-will of Fate toward him, had not only thus far kept Charles from the Poor-House, but had really advanced his fortunes in a degree. At any rate, that certain harmless presumption and innocent egotism which have been previously adverted to as sharing in his general character, these had by no means retarded him;

for it is often to be observed of the shallower men, that they are the very last to despond. It is the glory of the bladder that nothing can sink it; it is the reproach of a box of treasure, that once overboard it must down.

ii

When arrived in the city, and discovering the heartless neglect of Glen, Pierre,—looking about him for whom to apply to in this strait,—bethought him of his old boy-companion Charlie, and went out to seek him, and found him at last; he saw before him, a tall, well-grown, but rather thin and pale yet strikingly handsome young man of two-and-twenty; occupying a small dusty law-office on the third floor of the older building of the Apostles; assuming to be doing a very large, and hourly increasing business among empty pigeon-holes, and directly under the eye of an unopened bottle of ink; his mother and sisters dwelling in a chamber overhead; and himself, not only following the law for a corporeal living, but likewise interlinked with the peculiar secret, theologico-politico-social schemes of the masonic order of the seedy-coated Apostles; and pursuing some crude, transcendental Philosophy, for both a contributory means of support, as well as for his complete intellectual aliment.

Pierre was at first somewhat startled by his exceedingly frank and familiar manner; all old manorial deference for Pierre was clean gone and departed; though at the first shock of their encounter, Charlie could not possibly have known that Pierre was cast off.

"Ha, Pierre! glad to see you, my boy! Hark ye, next month I am to deliver an address before the Omega order of the Apostles. The Grand Master, Plinlimmon, will be there. I have heard on the best authority that he once said of me—'That youth has the Primitive Categories in him; he is destined to astonish the world.' Why, lad, I have received propositions from the Editors of the Spinozaist to contribute a weekly column to their paper, and you know how very few can understand the Spinozaist; nothing is admitted there but the Ultimate Transcendentals. Hark now, in your ear; I think of throwing off the Apostolic disguise and coming boldly out; Pierre! I think of stumping the State, and preaching our philosophy to the masses.—When did you arrive in town?"

Spite of all his tribulations, Pierre could not restrain a smile at this highly diverting reception; but well knowing the youth, he did not conclude from this audacious burst of enthusiastic egotism that his heart had at all corroded; for egotism is one thing, and selfishness another. No sooner did Pierre intimate his condition to him, than immediately, Charlie was all earnest and practical kindness; recommended the Apostles as the best possible lodgment for him,—cheap, snug, and convenient to most public places; he offered to procure a cart and see himself to the transport of Pierre's luggage; but finally thought it best to mount the stairs and show him the vacant rooms. But when these at last were decided upon; and Charlie, all cheerfulness and alacrity, started with Pierre for the hotel, to assist him in the removal; grasping his arm the moment they emerged from the great arched door under the tower of the Apostles; he instantly launched into his amusing heroics, and continued the strain till the trunks were fairly in sight.

"Lord! my law-business overwhelms me! I must drive away some of my clients; I must have my exercise, and this ever-growing business denies it to me. Besides, I owe something to the sublime cause of the general humanity; I must displace some of my briefs for my metaphysical treatises. I can not waste all my oil over bonds and mortgages.—You said you were married, I think?"

But without stopping for any reply, he rattled on. "Well, I suppose it is wise after all. It settles, centralizes, and confirms a man, I have heard.—No, I didn't; it is a random thought of my own, that!—Yes, it makes the world definite to him; it removes his morbid *sub*jectiveness, and makes all things *ob*jective; nine small children, for instance, may be considered *ob*jective. Marriage, hey!—A fine thing, no doubt, no doubt:—domestic—pretty—nice, all round. But I owe something to the world, my boy! By marriage, I might contribute to the population of men, but not to the census of mind. The great men are all bachelors, you know. Their family is the universe: I should say the planet Saturn was their elder son; and Plato their uncle.—So you are married?"

But again, reckless of answers, Charlie went on. "Pierre, a thought, my boy;—a thought for you! You do not say it, but you hint of a low purse. Now I shall help you to fill it—Stump the State on the Kantian Philosophy! A dollar a head, my boy! Pass round your beaver, and you'll get it. I have every confidence in the penetration and magnanimousness of the people! Pierre, hark in your ear;—it's my opinion the world is all wrong. Hist, I say—an entire mistake. Society demands an Avatar,—a Curtius, my boy! to leap into the fiery gulf, and by perishing himself, save the whole empire of men! Pierre, I have long renounced the allurements of life and fashion. Look at my coat, and see how I spurn them! Pierre! but, stop, have you ever a shilling? let's take a cold cut here—it's a cheap place; I go here sometimes. Come, let's in."

Book XXI

Pierre Immaturely Attempts a Mature Work • Tidings from the Meadows • Plinlimmon

WE ARE NOW TO BEHOLD Pierre permanently lodged in three lofty adjoining chambers of the Apostles. And passing on a little further in time, and overlooking the hundred and one domestic details, of how their internal arrangements were finally put into steady working order; how poor Delly, now giving over the sharper pangs of her grief, found in the lighter occupations of a handmaid and familiar companion to Isabel, the only practical relief from the memories of her miserable past; how Isabel herself in the otherwise occupied hours of Pierre, passed some of her time in mastering the chirographical incoherencies of his manuscripts, with a view to eventually copying them out in a legible hand for the printer; or went below stairs to the rooms of the Millthorpes, and in the modest and amiable society of the three young ladies and their excellent mother, found some little solace for the absence of Pierre; or, when his day's work was done, sat by him in the twilight, and played her mystic guitar till Pierre felt chapter after chapter born of its wondrous suggestiveness; but alas! eternally incapable of being translated into words; for where the deepest words end, there music begins with its supersensuous and all-confounding intimations.

Disowning now all previous exertions of his mind, and burning in scorn even those fine fruits of a care-free fancy, which, written at Saddle

Meadows in the sweet legendary time of Lucy and her love, he had jealously kept from the publishers, as too true and good to be published; renouncing all his foregone self, Pierre was now engaged in a comprehensive compacted work, to whose speedy completion two tremendous motives unitedly impelled;—the burning desire to deliver what he thought to be new, or at least miserably neglected Truth to the world; and the prospective menace of being absolutely penniless, unless by the sale of his book, he could realize money. Swayed to universality of thought by the widely-explosive mental tendencies of the profound events which had lately befallen him, and the unprecedented situation in which he now found himself; and perceiving, by presentiment, that most grand productions of the best human intellects ever are built round a circle, as atolls (*i.e.* the primitive coral islets which, raising themselves in the depths of profoundest seas, rise funnel-like to the surface, and present there a hoop of white rock, which though on the outside everywhere lashed by the ocean, yet excludes all tempests from the quiet lagoon within), digestively including the whole range of all that can be known or dreamed; Pierre was resolved to give the world a book, which the world should hail with surprise and delight. A varied scope of reading, little suspected by his friends, and randomly acquired by a random but lynx-eyed mind, in the course of the multifarious, incidental, bibliographic encounterings of almost any civilized young inquirer after Truth; this poured one considerable contributary stream into that bottomless spring of original thought which the occasion and time had caused to burst out in himself. Now he congratulated himself upon all his cursory acquisitions of this sort; ignorant that in reality to a mind bent on producing some thoughtful thing of absolute Truth, all mere reading is apt to prove but an obstacle hard to overcome; and not an accelerator helpingly pushing him along.

While Pierre was thinking that he was entirely transplanted into a new and wonderful element of Beauty and Power, he was, in fact, but in one of the stages of the transition. That ultimate element once fairly gained, then books no more are needed for buoys to our souls; our own strong limbs support us, and we float over all bottomlessnesses with a jeering impunity. He did not see,—or if he did, he could not yet name the true cause for it,—that already, in the incipiency of his work, the heavy unmalleable element of mere book-knowledge would not congenially weld with the wide fluidness and ethereal airiness of spontaneous creative thought. He would climb Parnassus with a pile of folios on his back. He did not see, that it was nothing at all to him, what other men had written; that though

Plato was indeed a transcendently great man in himself, yet Plato must not be transcendently great to him (Pierre), so long as he (Pierre himself) would also do something transcendently great. He did not see that there is no such thing as a standard for the creative spirit; that no one great book must ever be separately regarded, and permitted to domineer with its own uniqueness upon the creative mind; but that all existing great works must be federated in the fancy; and so regarded as a miscellaneous and Pantheistic whole; and then,—without at all dictating to his own mind, or unduly biasing it any way,—thus combined, they would prove simply an exhilarative and provocative to him. He did not see, that even when thus combined, all was but one small mite, compared to the latent infiniteness and inexhaustibility in himself; that all the great books in the world are but the mutilated shadowings-forth of invisible and eternally unembodied images in the soul; so that they are but the mirrors, distortedly reflecting to us our own things; and never mind what the mirror may be, if we would see the object, we must look at the object itself, and not at its reflection.

But, as to the resolute traveler in Switzerland, the Alps do never in one wide and comprehensive sweep, instantaneously reveal their full awfulness of amplitude—their overawing extent of peak crowded on peak, and spur sloping on spur, and chain jammed behind chain, and all their wonderful battalionings of might; so hath heaven wisely ordained, that on first entering into the Switzerland of his soul, man shall not at once perceive its tremendous immensity; lest illy prepared for such an encounter, his spirit should sink and perish in the lowermost snows. Only by judicious degrees, appointed of God, does man come at last to gain his Mont Blanc and take an overtopping view of these Alps; and even then, the tithe is not shown; and far over the invisible Atlantic, the Rocky Mountains and the Andes are yet unbeheld. Appalling is the soul of a man! Better might one be pushed off into the material spaces beyond the uttermost orbit of our sun, than once feel himself fairly afloat in himself!

But not now to consider these ulterior things, Pierre, though strangely and very newly alive to many before unregarded wonders in the general world; still, had he not as yet procured for himself that enchanter's wand of the soul, which but touching the humblest experiences in one's life, straightway it starts up all eyes, in every one of which are endless significancies. Not yet had he dropped his angle into the well of his childhood, to find what fish might be there; for who dreams to find fish in a well? the running stream of the outer world, there doubtless swim the golden perch and the pickerel! Ten million things were as yet uncovered to Pierre. The old mummy lies buried in cloth on cloth; it takes time to unwrap this Egyptian king. Yet now, forsooth, because Pierre began to see through the first superficiality of the world, he fondly weens he has come to the unlayered substance. But, far as any geologist has yet gone down into the world, it is found to consist of nothing but surface stratified on surface. To its axis, the world being nothing but superinduced superficies. By vast pains we mine into the pyramid; by horrible gropings we come to the central room; with joy we espy the sarcophagus; but we lift the lid—and no body is there!—appallingly vacant as vast is the soul of a man!

ii

He had been engaged some weeks upon his book—in pursuance of his settled plan avoiding all contact with any of his city-connections or friends, even as in his social downfall they sedulously avoided seeking him out—nor ever once going or sending to the post-office, though it was but a little round the corner from where he was, since having dispatched no letters himself, he expected none; thus isolated from the world, and intent upon his literary enterprise, Pierre had passed some weeks, when verbal tidings came to him, of three most momentous events.

First: his mother was dead.

Second: all Saddle Meadows was become Glen Stanly's.

Third: Glen Stanly was believed to be the suitor of Lucy; who, convalescent from an almost mortal illness, was now dwelling at her mother's house in town.

It was chiefly the first-mentioned of these events which darted a sharp natural anguish into Pierre. No letter had come to him; no smallest ring or memorial been sent him; no slightest mention made of him in the will; and yet it was reported that an inconsolable grief had induced his mother's mortal malady, and driven her at length into insanity, which suddenly terminated in death; and when he first heard of that event, she had been cold in the ground for twenty-five days.

How plainly did all this speak of the equally immense pride and grief of his once magnificent mother; and how agonizedly now did it hint of her mortally-wounded love for her only and best-beloved Pierre! In vain he reasoned with himself; in vain remonstrated with himself; in vain sought to parade all his stoic arguments to drive off the onslaught of natural passion. Nature prevailed; and with tears that like acid burned and scorched as they flowed, he wept, he raved, at the bitter loss of his parent; whose eyes had been closed by unrelated hands that were hired; but whose heart had been broken, and whose very reason been ruined, by the related hands of her son.

For some interval it almost seemed as if his own heart would snap; his own reason go down. Unendurable grief of a man, when Death itself gives the stab, and then snatches all availments to solacement away. For in the grave is no help, no prayer thither may go, no forgiveness thence come; so that the penitent whose sad victim lies in the ground, for that useless penitent his doom is eternal, and though it be Christmas-day with all Christendom, with him it is Hell-day and an eaten liver forever.

With what marvelous precision and exactitude he now went over in his mind all the minutest details of his old joyous life with his mother at Saddle Meadows. He began with his own toilet in the morning; then his mild stroll into the fields; then his cheerful return to call his mother in her chamber; then the gay breakfast—and so on, and on, all through the sweet day, till mother and son kissed, and with light, loving hearts separated to their beds, to prepare themselves for still another day of affectionate delight. This recalling of innocence and joy in the hour of remorsefulness and woe; this is as heating red-hot the pincers that tear us. But in this delirium of his soul, Pierre could not define where that line was, which separated the natural grief for the loss of a parent from that other one which was born of compunction. He strove hard to define it, but could not. He tried to cozen himself into believing that all his grief was but natural, or if there existed any other, that must spring—not from the consciousness of having done any possible wrong—but from the pang at what terrible cost the more exalted virtues are gained. Nor did he wholly fail in this endeavor. At last he dismissed his mother's memory into that same profound vault where hitherto had reposed the swooned form of his Lucy. But, as sometimes men are coffined in a trance, being thereby mistaken for dead; so it is possible to bury a tranced grief in the soul, erroneously supposing that it hath no more vitality of suffering. Now, immortal things only can beget immortality. It would almost seem one presumptive argument for the endless duration of the human soul, that it is impossible in time and space to kill any compunction arising from having cruelly injured a departed fellow-being.

Ere he finally committed his mother to the profoundest vault of his soul, fain would he have drawn one poor alleviation from a circumstance, which nevertheless, impartially viewed, seemed equally capable either of soothing or intensifying his grief. His mother's will, which without the least mention of his own name, bequeathed several legacies to her friends, and concluded by leaving all Saddle Meadows and its rent-rolls to Glendinning Stanly; this will bore the date of the day immediately succeeding his fatal announcement on the landing of the stairs, of his assumed nuptials with Isabel. It plausibly pressed upon him, that as all the evidences of his mother's dying unrelentingness toward him were negative; and the only positive evidence—so to speak—of even that negativeness, was the will which omitted all mention of Pierre; therefore, as that will bore so significant a date, it must needs be most reasonable to conclude, that it was dictated in the not yet subsided transports of his mother's first indignation. But small consolation was this, when he considered the final insanity of his mother; for whence that insanity but from a hate-grief unrelenting, even as his father must have become insane from a sin-grief irreparable? Nor did this remarkable double-doom of his parents wholly fail to impress his mind with presentiments concerning his own fate—his own hereditary liability to madness. Presentiment, I say; but what is a presentiment? how shall you coherently define a presentiment, or how make any thing out of it which is at all lucid, unless you say that a presentiment is but a judgment in disguise? And if a judgment in disguise, and yet possessing this preternaturalness of prophecy, how then shall you escape the fateful conclusion, that you are helplessly held in the six hands of the Sisters? For while still dreading your doom, you foreknow it. Yet how foreknow and dread in one breath, unless with this divine seeming power of prescience, you blend the actual slimy powerlessness of defense?

That his cousin, Glen Stanly, had been chosen by his mother to inherit the domain of the Meadows, was not entirely surprising to Pierre. Not only had Glen always been a favorite with his mother by reason of his superb person and his congeniality of worldly views with herself, but excepting only Pierre, he was her nearest surviving blood relation; and moreover, in his christian name, bore the hereditary syllables, Glendinning. So that if to any one but Pierre the Meadows must descend, Glen, on these general grounds, seemed the appropriate heir.

But it is not natural for a man, never mind who he may be, to see a noble patrimony, rightfully his, go over to a soul-alien, and that alien once his rival in love, and now his heartless, sneering foe; for so Pierre could not but now argue of Glen; it is not natural for a man to see this without singular emotions of discomfort and hate. Nor in Pierre were these feelings at all soothed by the report of Glen's renewed attentions to Lucy. For there is something in the breast of almost every man, which at bottom takes offense at the attentions of any other man offered to a woman, the hope of whose nuptial love he himself may have discarded. Fain would a man selfishly appropriate all the hearts which have ever in any way confessed themselves his. Besides, in Pierre's case, this resentment was heightened by Glen's previous hypocritical demeanor. For now all his suspicions seemed abundantly verified; and comparing all dates, he inferred that Glen's visit to Europe had only been undertaken to wear off the pang of his rejection by Lucy, a rejection tacitly consequent upon her not denying her affianced relation to Pierre.

But now, under the mask of profound sympathy—in time, ripening into love—for a most beautiful girl, ruffianly deserted by her betrothed, Glen could afford to be entirely open in his new suit, without at all exposing his old scar to the world. So at least it now seemed to Pierre. Moreover, Glen could now approach Lucy under the most favorable possible auspices. He could approach her as a deeply sympathizing friend, all wishful to assuage her sorrow, but hinting nothing, at present, of any selfish matrimonial intent; by enacting this prudent and unclamorous part, the mere sight of such tranquil, disinterested, but indestructible devotedness, could not but suggest in Lucy's mind, very natural comparisons between Glen and Pierre, most deplorably abasing to the latter. Then, no woman—as it would sometimes seem—no woman is utterly free from the influence of a princely social position in her suitor, especially if he be handsome and young. And Glen would come to her now the master of two immense fortunes, and the heir, by voluntary election, no less than by blood propinquity, to the ancestral bannered hall, and the broad manorial meadows of the Glendinnings. And thus, too, the spirit of Pierre's own mother would seem to press Glen's suit. Indeed, situated now as he was Glen would seem all the finest part of Pierre, without any of Pierre's shame; would almost seem Pierre himself—what Pierre had once been to Lucy. And as in the case of a man who has lost a sweet wife, and who long refuses the least consolation; as this man at last finds a singular solace in the companionship of his wife's sister, who happens to bear a peculiar family resemblance to the dead; and as he, in the end, proposes marriage to this sister, merely from the force of such magical associative influences; so it did not seem wholly out of reason to suppose, that the great manly beauty of Glen, possessing a strong related similitude to Pierre's, might raise in Lucy's heart associations, which would lead her at least to seek—if she could not find—solace for one now regarded as dead and gone to her forever, in the devotedness of another, who would notwithstanding almost seem as that dead one brought back to life.

Deep, deep, and still deep and deeper must we go, if we would find out the heart of a man; descending into which is as descending a spiral stair in a shaft, without any end, and where that endlessness is only concealed by the spiralness of the stair, and the blackness of the shaft.

As Pierre conjured up this phantom of Glen transformed into the seeming semblance of himself; as he figured it advancing toward Lucy and raising her hand in devotion; an infinite quenchless rage and malice possessed him. Many commingled emotions combined to provoke this storm. But chief of all was something strangely akin to that indefinable detestation which one feels for any imposter who has dared to assume one's own name and aspect in any equivocal or dishonorable affair; an emotion greatly intensified if this impostor be known for a mean villain at bottom, and also, by the freak of nature to be almost the personal duplicate of the man whose identity he assumes. All these and a host of other distressful and resentful fancies now ran through the breast of Pierre. All his Faith-born, enthusiastic, high-wrought, stoic, and philosophic defenses, were now beaten down by this sudden storm of nature in his soul. For there is no faith, and no stoicism, and no philosophy, that a mortal man can possibly evoke, which will stand the final test of a real impassioned onset of Life and Passion upon him. Then all the fair philosophic or Faith-phantoms that he raised from the mist, slide away and disappear as ghosts at cock-crow. For Faith and philosophy are air, but events are brass. Amidst his gray philosophizings, Life breaks upon a man like a morning.

While this mood was on him, Pierre cursed himself for a heartless villain and an idiot fool;—heartless villain, as the murderer of his mother—idiot fool, because he had thrown away all his felicity; because he had himself, as it were, resigned his noble birthright to a cunning kinsman for a mess of pottage, which now proved all but ashes in his mouth.

Resolved to hide these new, and—as it latently seemed to him—unworthy pangs, from Isabel, as also their cause, he quitted his chamber, intending a long vagabond stroll in the suburbs of the town, to wear off his sharper grief, ere he should again return into her sight.

iii

As Pierre, now hurrying from his chamber, was rapidly passing through one of the higher brick colonnades connecting the ancient building with the modern, there advanced toward him from the direction of the latter, a very plain, composed, manly figure, with a countenance rather pale if any thing, but quite clear and without wrinkle. Though the brow and the beard, and the steadiness of the head and settledness of the step indicated mature age, yet the blue, bright, but still quiescent eye offered a very striking contrast. In that eye, the gay immortal youth Apollo, seemed enshrined; while on that ivory-throned brow, old Saturn cross-legged sat. The whole countenance of this man, the whole air and look of this man, expressed a cheerful content. Cheerful is the adjective, for it was the contrary of gloom; content—perhaps acquiescence—is the substantive, for it was not Happiness or Delight. But while the personal look and air of this man were thus winning, there was still something latently visible in him which repelled. That something may best be characterized as non-Benevolence. Non-Benevolence seems the best word, for it was neither Malice nor Ill-will; but something passive. To crown all, a certain floating atmosphere seemed to invest and go along with this man. That atmosphere seems only renderable in words by the term Inscrutableness. Though the clothes worn by this man were strictly in accordance with the general style of any unobtrusive gentleman's dress, yet his clothes seemed to disguise this man. One would almost have said, his very face, the apparently natural glance of his very eye disguised this man.

Now, as this person deliberately passed by Pierre, he lifted his hat, gracefully bowed, smiled gently, and passed on. But Pierre was all confusion; he flushed, looked askance, stammered with his hand at his hat to return the courtesy of the other; he seemed thoroughly upset by the mere sight of this hat-lifting, gracefully bowing, gently-smiling, and most miraculously self-possessed, non-benevolent man.

Now who was this man? This man was Plotinus Plinlimmon. Pierre had read a treatise of his in a stage-coach coming to the city, and had heard him often spoken of by Millthorpe and others as the Grand Master of a certain mystic Society among the Apostles. Whence he came, no one could tell. His surname was Welsh, but he was a Tennesseean by birth. He seemed to have no family or blood ties of any sort. He never was known to work with his hands; never to write with his hands (he would not even write a letter); he never was known to open a book. There were no books in his chamber. Nevertheless, some day or other he must have read books, but that time seemed gone now; as for the sleazy works that went under his name, they were nothing more than his verbal things, taken down at random, and bunglingly methodized by his young disciples.

Finding Plinlimmon thus unfurnished either with books or pen and paper, and imputing it to something like indigence, a foreign scholar, a rich nobleman, who chanced to meet him once, sent him a fine supply of stationery, with a very fine set of volumes,—Cardan, Epictetus, the Book of Mormon, Abraham Tucker, Condorcet and the Zend-Avesta. But this noble foreign scholar calling next day—perhaps in expectation of some compliment for his great kindness—started aghast at his own package deposited just without the door of Plinlimmon, and with all fastenings untouched.

"Missent," said Plotinus Plinlimmon placidly: "if any thing, I looked for some choice Curaçoa from a nobleman like you. I should be very happy, my dear Count, to accept a few jugs of choice Curaçoa."

"I thought that the society of which you are the head, excluded all things of that sort"—replied the Count.

"Dear Count, so they do; but Mohammed hath his own dispensation."

"Ah! I see," said the noble scholar archly.

"I am afraid you do not see, dear Count"—said Plinlimmon; and instantly before the eyes of the Count, the inscrutable atmosphere eddied and eddied roundabout this Plotinus Plinlimmon.

His chance brushing encounter in the corridor was the first time that ever Pierre had without medium beheld the form or the face of Plinlimmon. Very early after taking chambers at the Apostles', he had been struck by a steady observant blue-eyed countenance at one of the loftiest windows of the old gray tower, which on the opposite side of the quadrangular space, rose prominently before his own chamber. Only through two panes of glass—his own and the stranger's—had Pierre hitherto beheld that remarkable face of repose,—repose neither divine nor human, nor any thing made up of either or both—but a repose separate and apart—a repose of a face by itself. One adequate look at that face conveyed to most philosophical observers a notion of something not before included in their scheme of the Universe.

Now as to the mild sun, glass is no hindrance at all, but he transmits his light and life through the glass; even so through Pierre's panes did the tower face transmit its strange mystery.

Becoming more and more interested in this face, he had questioned Millthorpe concerning it. "Bless your soul"—replied Millthorpe—"that is Plotinus Plinlimmon! our Grand Master, Plotinus Plinlimmon! By gad, you must know Plotinus thoroughly, as I have long done. Come away with me, now, and let me introduce you instanter to Plotinus Plinlimmon."

But Pierre declined; and could not help thinking, that though in all human probability Plotinus well understood Millthorpe, yet Millthorpe could hardly yet have wound himself into Plotinus;—though indeed

Plotinus—who at times was capable of assuming a very off-hand, confidential, and simple, sophomorean air—might, for reasons best known to himself, have tacitly pretended to Millthorpe, that he (Millthorpe) had thoroughly wriggled himself into his (Plotinus') innermost soul.

A man will be given a book, and when the donor's back is turned, will carelessly drop it in the first corner; he is not over-anxious to be bothered with the book. But now personally point out to him the author, and ten to one he goes back to the corner, picks up the book, dusts the cover, and very carefully reads that invaluable work. One does not vitally believe in a man till one's own two eyes have beheld him. If then, by the force of peculiar circumstances, Pierre while in the stage, had formerly been drawn into an attentive perusal of the work on "Chronometricals and Horologicals;" how then was his original interest heightened by catching a subsequent glimpse of the author. But at the first reading, not being able—as he thought—to master the pivot-idea of the pamphlet; and as every incomprehended idea is not only a perplexity but a taunting reproach to one's mind, Pierre had at last ceased studying it altogether; nor consciously troubled himself further about it during the remainder of the journey. But still thinking now it might possibly have been mechanically retained by him, he searched all the pockets of his clothes, but without success. He begged Millthorpe to do his best toward procuring him another copy; but it proved impossible to find one. Plotinus himself could not furnish it.

Among other efforts, Pierre in person had accosted a limping half-deaf old book-stall man, not very far from the Apostles'. "Have you the '*Chronometrics*,' my friend?" forgetting the exact title.

"Very bad, very bad!" said the old man, rubbing his back;—"has had the *chronic-rheumatics* ever so long; what's good for 'em?"

Perceiving his mistake, Pierre replied that he did not know what was the infallible remedy.

"Whist! let me tell ye, then, young 'un," said the old cripple, limping close up to him, and putting his mouth in Pierre's ear—"Never catch 'em! —now's the time, while you're young:—never catch 'em!"

By-and-by the blue-eyed, mystic-mild face in the upper window of the old gray tower began to domineer in a very remarkable manner upon Pierre. When in his moods of peculiar depression and despair; when dark thoughts of his miserable condition would steal over him; and black doubts as to the integrity of his unprecedented course in life would most malignantly suggest themselves; when a thought of the vanity of his deep book would glidingly intrude; if glancing at his closet-window that mystic-mild face met Pierre's; under any of these influences the effect was surprising, and not to be adequately detailed in any possible words.

Vain! vain! vain! said the face to him. Fool! fool! fool! said the face to him. Quit! quit! quit! said the face to him. But when he mentally interrogated the face as to why it thrice said Vain! Fool! Quit! to him; here there was no response. For that face did not respond to any thing. Did I not say before that that face was something separate, and apart; a face by itself? Now, any thing which is thus a thing by itself never responds to any other thing. If to affirm, be to expand one's isolated self; and if to deny, be to contract one's isolated self; then to respond is a suspension of all isolation. Though this face in the tower was so clear and so mild; though the gay youth Apollo was enshrined in that eye, and paternal old Saturn sat cross-legged on that ivory brow; yet somehow to Pierre the face at last wore a sort of malicious leer to him. But the Kantists might say, that this was a *subjective* sort of leer in Pierre. Any way, the face seemed to leer upon Pierre. And now it said to him—*Ass! ass! ass!* This expression was insufferable. He procured some muslin for his closet-window; and the face became curtained like any portrait. But this did not mend the leer. Pierre knew that still the face leered behind the muslin. What was most terrible was the idea that by some magical means or other the face had got hold of his secret. "Ay," shuddered Pierre, "the face knows that Isabel is not my wife! And that seems the reason it leers."

Then would all manner of wild fancyings float through his soul, and detached sentences of the "Chronometrics" would vividly recur to him—sentences before but imperfectly comprehended, but now shedding a strange, baleful light upon his peculiar condition, and emphatically denouncing it. Again he tried his best to procure the pamphlet, to read it now by the commentary of the mystic-mild face; again he searched through the pockets of his clothes for the stage-coach copy, but in vain.

And when—at the critical moment of quitting his chambers that morning of the receipt of the fatal tidings—the face itself—the man himself—this inscrutable Plotinus Plinlimmon himself—did visibly brush by him in the brick corridor, and all the trepidation he had ever before felt at the mild-mystic aspect in the tower window, now redoubled upon him, so that, as before said, he flushed, looked askance, and stammered with his saluting hand to his hat;—then anew did there burn in him the desire of procuring the pamphlet. "Cursed fate that I should have lost it"—he cried;—"more cursed, that when I did have it, and did read it, I was such a ninny as not to comprehend; and now it is all too late!"

Yet—to anticipate here—when years after, an old Jew Clothesman rummaged over a surtout of Pierre's—which by some means had come into his hands—his lynx-like fingers happened to feel something foreign between the cloth and the heavy quilted bombazine lining. He ripped open the skirt, and found several old pamphlet pages, soft and worn almost to tissue, but still legible enough to reveal the title—"Chronometricals and Horologicals." Pierre must have ignorantly thrust it into his pocket, in the stage, and it had worked through a rent there, and worked its way clean down into the skirt, and there helped pad the padding. So that all the time he was hunting for this pamphlet, he himself was wearing the pamphlet. When he brushed past Plinlimmon in the brick corridor, and felt that renewed intense longing for the pamphlet, then his right hand was not two inches from the pamphlet.

Possibly this curious circumstance may in some sort illustrate his self-supposed non-understanding of the pamphlet, as first read by him in the stage. Could he likewise have carried about with him in his mind the thorough understanding of the book, and yet not be aware that he so understood it? I think that—regarded in one light—the final career of Pierre will seem to show, that he *did* understand it. And here it may be randomly suggested, by way of bagatelle, whether some things that men think they do not know, are not for all that thoroughly comprehended by them; and yet, so to speak, though contained in themselves, are kept a secret from themselves? The idea of Death seems such a thing.

Book XXII

The Flower-Curtain Lifted from before a Tropical Author, with Some Remarks on the Transcendental Flesh-Brush Philosophy

SOME DAYS PASSED after the fatal tidings from the Meadows, and at length, somewhat mastering his emotions, Pierre again sits down in his chamber; for grieve how he will, yet work he must. And now day succeeds day, and week follows week, and Pierre still sits in his chamber. The long rows of cooled brick-kilns around him scarce know of the change; but from the fair fields of his great-great-great-grandfather's manor, Summer hath flown like a swallow-guest; the perfidious wight, Autumn, hath peeped in at the groves of the maple, and under pretense of clothing them in rich russet and gold, hath stript them at last of the slightest rag, and then ran away laughing; prophetic icicles depend from the arbors round about the old manorial mansion—now locked up and abandoned; and the little, round, marble table in the viny summer-house where, of July mornings, he had sat chatting and drinking negus with his gay mother, is now spread with a shivering napkin of frost; sleety varnish hath encrusted that once gay mother's grave, preparing it for its final cerements of wrapping snow upon snow; wild howl the winds in the woods: it is Winter. Sweet Summer is done; and Autumn is done; but the book, like the bitter winter, is yet to be finished.

That season's wheat is long garnered, Pierre; that season's ripe apples and grapes are in; no crop, no plant, no fruit is out; the whole harvest is done. Oh, woe to that belated winter-overtaken plant, which the summer could not bring to maturity! The drifting winter snows shall whelm it. Think, Pierre, doth not thy plant belong to some other and tropical clime? Though transplanted to northern Maine, the orange-tree of the Floridas will put forth leaves in that parsimonious summer, and show some few tokens of fruitage; yet November will find no golden globes thereon; and the passionate old lumber-man, December, shall peel the whole tree, wrench it off at the ground, and toss it for a fagot to some lime-kiln. Ah, Pierre, Pierre, make haste! make haste! force thy fruitage, lest the winter force thee.

Watch yon little toddler, how long it is learning to stand by itself! First it shrieks and implores, and will not try to stand at all, unless both father and mother uphold it; then a little more bold, it must, at least, feel one parental hand, else again the cry and the tremble; long time is it ere by degrees this child comes to stand without any support. But, by-and-by, grown up to man's estate, it shall leave the very mother that bore it, and the father that begot it, and cross the seas, perhaps, or settle in far Oregon lands. There now, do you see the soul. In its germ on all sides it is closely folded by the world, as the husk folds the tenderest fruit; then it is born from the world-husk, but still now outwardly clings to it;—still clamors for the support of its mother the world, and its father the Deity. But it shall yet learn to stand independent, though not without many a bitter wail, and many a miserable fall.

That hour of the life of a man when first the help of humanity fails him, and he learns that in his obscurity and indigence humanity holds him a dog and no man: that hour is a hard one, but not the hardest. There is still another hour which follows, when he learns that in his infinite comparative minuteness and abjectness, the gods do likewise despise him, and own him not of their clan. Divinity and humanity then are equally willing that he should starve in the street for all that either will do for him. Now cruel father and mother have both let go his hand, and the little soul-toddler, now you shall hear his shriek and his wail, and often his fall.

When at Saddle Meadows, Pierre had wavered and trembled in those first wretched hours ensuing upon the receipt of Isabel's letter; then humanity had let go the hand of Pierre, and therefore his cry; but when at last inured to this, Pierre was seated at his book, willing that humanity should desert him, so long as he thought he felt a far higher support; then, ere long, he began to feel the utter loss of that other support, too; ay, even the paternal gods themselves did now desert Pierre; the toddler was toddling entirely alone, and not without shrieks.

If man must wrestle, perhaps it is well that it should be on the nakedest possible plain.

The three chambers of Pierre at the Apostles' were connecting ones. The first—having a little retreat where Delly slept—was used for the more exacting domestic purposes: here also their meals were taken; the second was the chamber of Isabel; the third was the closet of Pierre. In the first—the dining room, as they called it—there was a stove which boiled the water for their coffee and tea, and where Delly concocted their light repasts. This was their only fire; for, warned again and again to economize to the uttermost, Pierre did not dare to purchase any additional warmth. But by prudent management, a very little warmth may go a great way. In the present case, it went some forty feet or more. A horizontal pipe, after elbowing away from above the stove in the dining-room, pierced the partition wall, and passing straight through Isabel's chamber, entered the closet of Pierre at one corner, and then abruptly disappeared into the wall, where all further caloric—if any—went up through the chimney into the air, to help warm the December sun. Now, the great distance of Pierre's calorical stream from its fountain, sadly impaired it, and weakened it. It hardly had the flavor of heat. It would have had but very inconsiderable influence in raising the depressed spirits of the most mercurial thermometer; certainly it was not very elevating to the spirits of Pierre. Besides, this calorical stream, small as it was, did not flow through the room, but only entered it, to elbow right out of it, as some coquettish maidens enter the heart; moreover, it was in the furthest corner from the only place where, with a judicious view to the light, Pierre's desk-barrels and board could advantageously stand. Often, Isabel insisted upon his having a separate stove to himself; but Pierre would not listen to such a thing. Then Isabel would offer her own room to him; saying it was of no indispensable use to her by day; she could easily spend her time in the dining-room; but Pierre would not listen to such a thing: he would not deprive her of the comfort of a continually accessible privacy; besides, he was now used to his own room, and must sit by that particular window there, and no other. Then Isabel would insist upon keeping her connecting door open while Pierre was employed at his desk, that so the heat of her room might bodily go into his; but Pierre would not listen to such a thing: because he must be religiously locked up while at work; outer love and hate must alike be excluded then. In vain Isabel said she would make not the slightest noise, and muffle the point of the very needle she used. All in vain. Pierre was inflexible here.

Yes, he was resolved to battle it out in his own solitary closet; though a strange, transcendental conceit of one of the more erratic and non-conforming Apostles,—who was also at this time engaged upon a profound work above stairs, and who denied himself his full sufficiency of food, in order to insure an abundant fire;—the strange conceit of this Apostle, I say,—accidentally communicated to Pierre,—that, through all the kingdoms of Nature, caloric was the great universal producer and vivifyer, and could not be prudently excluded from the spot where great books were in the act of creation; and therefore, he (the Apostle) for one, was resolved to plant his head in a hot-bed of stove-warmed air, and so force his brain to germinate and blossom, and bud, and put forth the eventual, crowning, victorious flower;—though indeed this conceit rather staggered Pierre—for in truth, there was no small smack of plausible analogy in it—yet one thought of his purse would wholly expel the unwelcome intrusion, and reinforce his own previous resolve.

However lofty and magnificent the movements of the stars; whatever celestial melodies they may thereby beget; yet the astronomers assure us that they are the most rigidly methodical of all the things that exist. No old housewife goes her daily domestic round with one millionth part the precision of the great planet Jupiter in his stated and unalterable revolutions. He has found his orbit, and stays in it; he has timed himself, and adheres to his periods. So, in some degree with Pierre, now revolving in the troubled orbit of his book.

Pierre rose moderately early; and the better to inure himself to the permanent chill of his room, and to defy and beard to its face, the cruelest cold of the outer air; he would—behind the curtain—throw down the upper sash of his window; and on a square of old painted canvas, formerly wrapping some bale of goods in the neighborhood, treat his limbs, of those early December mornings, to a copious ablution, in water thickened with incipient ice. Nor, in this stoic performance, was he at all without company,—not present, but adjoiningly sympathetic; for scarce an Apostle in all those scores and scores of chambers, but undeviatingly took his daily December bath. Pierre had only to peep out of his pane and glance round the multi-windowed, inclosing walls of the quadrangle, to catch plentiful half-glimpses, all round him, of many a lean, philosophical nudity, refreshing his meager bones with crash-towel and cold water. "Quick be the play," was their motto: "Lively our elbows, and nimble all our tenuities." Oh, the dismal echoings of the raspings of flesh-brushes, perverted to the filing and polishing of the merest ribs! Oh, the shuddersome splashings of pails of ice-water over feverish heads, not unfamiliar with aches! Oh, the rheumatical cracklings of rusted joints, in that defied air of December! for every thick-frosted sash was down, and every lean nudity courted the zephyr!

Among all the innate, hyena-like repellants to the reception of any set form of a spiritually-minded and pure archetypical faith, there is nothing so potent in its skeptical tendencies, as that inevitable perverse ridiculousness, which so often bestreaks some of the essentially finest and noblest aspirations of those men, who disgusted with the common conventional quackeries, strive, in their clogged terrestrial humanities, after some imperfectly discerned, but heavenly ideals: ideals, not only imperfectly discerned in themselves, but the path to them so little traceable, that no two minds will entirely agree upon it.

Hardly a new-light Apostle, but who, in superaddition to his revolutionary scheme for the minds and philosophies of men, entertains some insane, heterodoxical notions about the economy of his body. His soul, introduced by the gentlemanly gods, into the supernal society,—practically rejects that most sensible maxim of men of the world, who chancing to gain the friendship of any great character, never make that the ground of boring him with the supplemental acquaintance of their next friend, who perhaps, is some miserable ninny. Love me, love my dog, is only an adage for the old country-women who affectionately kiss their cows. The gods love the soul of a man; often, they will frankly accost it; but they abominate his body; and will forever cut it dead, both here and hereafter. So, if thou wouldst go to the gods, leave thy dog of a body behind thee. And most impotently thou strivest with thy purifying cold baths, and thy diligent scrubbings with flesh-brushes, to prepare it as a meet offering for their altar. Nor shall all thy Pythagorean and Shellian dietings on apple-parings, dried prunes, and crumbs of oat-meal cracker, ever fit thy body for heaven. Feed all things with food convenient for them,—that is, if the food be procurable. The food of thy soul is light and space; feed it then on light and space. But the food of thy body is champagne and oysters; feed it then on champagne and oysters; and so shall it merit a joyful resurrection, if there is any to be. Say, wouldst thou rise with a lantern jaw and a spavined knee? Rise with brawn on thee, and a most royal corporation before thee; so shalt thou in that day claim respectful attention. Know this: that while many a consumptive dietarian has but produced the merest literary flatulencies to the world; convivial authors have alike given utterance to the sublimest wisdom, and created the least gross and most ethereal forms. And for men of demonstrative muscle and action, consider that right royal epitaph which Cyrus the Great caused to be engraved on his tomb—"I could drink a great deal of wine, and it did me a great deal of good." Ah, foolish! to think that by starving thy body, thou shalt fatten thy soul! Is yonder ox fatted because yonder lean fox starves in the winter wood? And prate not of despising thy body, while still thou flourishest thy flesh-brush! The finest houses are most cared for within; the outer walls are freely left to the dust and the soot. Put venison in thee, and so wit shall come out of thee. It is one thing in the mill, but another in the sack.

Now it was the continual, quadrangular example of those forlorn fellows, the Apostles, who, in this period of his half-developments and transitions, had deluded Pierre into the Flesh-Brush Philosophy, and had almost tempted him into the Apple-Parings Dialectics. For all the long wards, corridors, and multitudinous chambers of the Apostles' were scattered with the stems of apples, the stones of prunes, and the shells of pea-nuts. They went about huskily muttering the Kantian Categories through teeth and lips dry and dusty as any miller's, with the crumbs of Graham crackers. A tumbler of cold water was the utmost welcome to their reception rooms; at the grand supposed Sanhedrim presided over by one of the deputies of Plotinus Plinlimmon, a huge jug of Adam's Ale, and a bushel-basket of Graham crackers were the only convivials. Continually bits of cheese were dropping from their pockets, and old shiny apple parchments were ignorantly exhibited every time they drew out a manuscript to read you. Some were curious in the vintages of waters; and in three glass decanters set before you, Fairmount, Croton, and Cochituate; they held that Croton was the most potent, Fairmount a gentle tonic, and Cochituate the mildest and least inebriating of all. Take some more of the Croton, my dear sir! Be brisk with the Fairmount! Why stops that Cochituate? So on their philosophical tables went round their Port, their Sherry, and their Claret.

Some, further advanced, rejected mere water in the bath, as altogether too coarse an element; and so, took to the Vapor-baths, and steamed their lean ribs every morning. The smoke which issued from their heads, and overspread their pages, was prefigured in the mists that issued from under their door-sills and out of their windows. Some could not sit down of a morning until after first applying the Vapor-bath outside, and then thoroughly rinsing out their interiors with five cups of cold Croton. They were as faithfully replenished fire-buckets; and could they, standing in one cordon, have consecutively pumped themselves into each other, then the great fire of 1835 had been far less wide-spread and disastrous.

Ah! ye poor lean ones! ye wretched Soakites and Vaporites! have not your niggardly fortunes enough rinsed ye out, and wizened ye, but ye must still be dragging the hose-pipe, and throwing still more cold Croton on yourselves and the world? Ah! attach the screw of your hose-pipe to some fine old butt of Madeira! pump us some sparkling wine into the world! see, see, already, from all eternity, two-thirds of it have lain helplessly soaking!

ii

With cheek rather pale, then, and lips rather blue, Pierre sits down to his plank.

But is Pierre packed in the mail for St. Petersburg this morning? Over his boots are his moccasins; over his ordinary coat is his surtout; and over that, a cloak of Isabel's. Now he is squared to his plank; and at his hint, the affectionate Isabel gently pushes his chair closer to it, for he is so muffled, he can hardly move of himself. Now Delly comes in with bricks hot from the stove; and now Isabel and she with devoted solicitude pack away these comforting stones in the folds of an old blue cloak, a military garment of the grandfather of Pierre, and tenderly arrange it both over and under his feet; but putting the warm flagging beneath. Then Delly brings still another hot brick to put under his inkstand, to prevent the ink from thickening. Then Isabel drags the camp-bedstead nearer to him, on which are the two or three books he may possibly have occasion to refer to that day, with a biscuit or two, and some water, and a clean towel, and a basin. Then she leans against the plank by the elbow of Pierre, a crook-ended stick. Is Pierre a shepherd, or a bishop, or a cripple? No, but he has in effect, reduced himself to the miserable condition of the last. With the crook-ended cane, Pierre—unable to rise without sadly impairing his manifold intrenchments, and admitting the cold air into their innermost nooks,—Pierre, if in his solitude, he should chance to need any thing beyond the reach of his arm, then the crook-ended cane drags it to his immediate vicinity.

Pierre glances slowly all round him; every thing seems to be right; he looks up with a grateful, melancholy satisfaction at Isabel; a tear gathers in her eye; but she conceals it from him by coming very close to him, stooping over, and kissing his brow. 'Tis her lips that leave the warm moisture there; not her tears, she says.

"I suppose I must go now, Pierre. Now don't, don't be so long to-day. I will call thee at half-past four. Thou shalt not strain thine eyes in the twilight."

"We will *see* about that," says Pierre, with an unobserved attempt at a very sad pun. "Come, thou must go. Leave me."

And there he is left.

Pierre is young; heaven gave him the divinest, freshest form of a man; put light into his eye, and fire into his blood, and brawn into his arm, and a joyous, jubilant, overflowing, upbubbling, universal life in him everywhere. Now look around in that most miserable room, and at that most miserable of all the pursuits of a man, and say if here be the place, and this be the trade, that God intended him for. A rickety chair, two hollow barrels, a plank, paper, pens, and infernally black ink, four leprously dingy white walls, no carpet, a cup of water, and a dry biscuit or two. Oh, I hear the leap of the Texan Camanche, as at this moment he goes crashing like a wild deer through the green underbrush; I hear his glorious whoop of savage and untamable health; and then I look in at Pierre. If physical, practical unreason make the savage, which is he? Civilization, Philosophy, Ideal Virtue! behold your victim!

iii

Some hours pass. Let us peep over the shoulder of Pierre, and see what it is he is writing there, in that most melancholy closet. Here, topping the reeking pile by his side, is the last sheet from his hand, the frenzied ink not yet entirely dry. It is much to our purpose; for in this sheet, he seems to have directly plagiarized from his own experiences, to fill out the mood of his apparent author-hero, Vivia, who thus soliloquizes: "A deep-down, unutterable mournfulness is in me. Now I drop all humorous or indifferent disguises, and all philosophical pretensions. I own myself a brother of the clod, a child of the Primeval Gloom. Hopelessness and despair are over me, as pall on pall. Away, ye chattering apes of a sophomorean Spinoza and Plato, who once didst all but delude me that the night was day, and pain only a tickle. Explain this darkness, exorcise this devil, ye can not. Tell me not, thou inconceivable coxcomb of a Goethe, that the universe can not spare thee and thy immortality, so long as—like a hired waiter—thou makest thyself 'generally useful.' Already the universe gets on without thee, and could still spare a million more of the same identical kidney. Corporations have no souls, and thy Pantheism, what was that? Thou wert but the pretensious, heartless part of a man. Lo! I hold thee in this hand, and thou art crushed in it like an egg from which the meat hath been sucked."

Here is a slip from the floor.

"Whence flow the panegyrical melodies that precede the march of these heroes? From what but from a sounding brass and a tinkling cymbal!"

And here is a second.

"Cast thy eye in there on Vivia; tell me why those four limbs should be clapt in a dismal jail—day out, day in—week out, week in—month out, month in—and himself the voluntary jailer! Is this the end of philosophy? This the larger, and spiritual life? This your boasted empyrean? Is it for this that a man should grow wise, and leave off his most excellent and calumniated folly?"

And here is a third.

"Cast thy eye in there on Vivia; he, who in the pursuit of the highest health of virtue and truth, shows but a pallid cheek! Weigh his heart in thy hand, oh, thou gold-laced, virtuoso Goethe! and tell me whether it does not exceed thy standard weight!"

And here is a fourth.

"Oh God, that man should spoil and rust on the stalk, and be wilted and threshed ere the harvest hath come! And oh God, that men that call themselves men should still insist on a laugh! I hate the world, and could trample all lungs of mankind as grapes, and heel them out of their breath, to think of the woe and the cant,—to think of the Truth and the Lie! Oh! blessed be the twenty-first day of December, and cursed be the twenty-first day of June!"

From these random slips, it would seem, that Pierre is quite conscious of much that is so anomalously hard and bitter in his lot, of much that is so black and terrific in his soul. Yet that knowing his fatal condition does not one whit enable him to change or better his condition. Conclusive proof that he has no power over his condition. For in tremendous extremities human souls are like drowning men; well enough they know they are in peril; well enough they know the causes of that peril;—nevertheless, the sea is the sea, and these drowning men do drown.

iv

From eight o'clock in the morning till half-past four in the evening, Pierre sits there in his room;—eight hours and a half!

From throbbing neck-bands, and swinging belly-bands of gay-hearted horses, the sleigh-bells chimingly jingle;—but Pierre sits there in his room; Thanksgiving comes, with its glad thanks, and crisp turkeys;—but Pierre sits there in his room; soft through the snows, on tinted Indian moccasin, Merry Christmas comes stealing;—but Pierre sits there in his room; it is New-Year's, and like a great flagon, the vast city overbrims at all curbstones, wharves, and piers, with bubbling jubilations;—but Pierre sits there in his room:—Nor jingling sleigh-bells at throbbing neck-band, or swinging belly-band; nor glad thanks, and crisp turkeys of Thanksgiving; nor tinted Indian moccasin of Merry Christmas softly stealing through the snows; nor New-Year's curb-stones, wharves, and piers, over-brimming with bubbling jubilations:—Nor jingling sleigh-bells, nor glad Thanksgiving, nor Merry Christmas, nor jubilating New Year's:—Nor Bell, Thank, Christ, Year;—none of these are for Pierre. In the midst of the merriments of the mutations of Time, Pierre hath ringed himself in with the grief of Eternity. Pierre is a peak inflexible in the heart of Time, as the isle-peak, Piko, stands unassaultable in the midst of waves.

He will not be called to; he will not be stirred. Sometimes the intent ear of Isabel in the next room, overhears the alternate silence, and then the long lonely scratch of his pen. It is, as if she heard the busy claw of some midnight mole in the ground. Sometimes, she hears a low cough, and sometimes the scrape of his crook-handled cane.

Here surely is a wonderful stillness of eight hours and a half, repeated day after day. In the heart of such silence, surely something is at work. Is it creation, or destruction? Builds Pierre the noble world of a new book? or does the Pale Haggardness unbuild the lungs and the life in him?—Unutterable, that a man should be thus!

When in the meridian flush of the day, we recall the black apex of night; then night seems impossible; this sun can never go down. Oh that the memory of the uttermost gloom as an already tasted thing to the dregs, should be no security against its return. One may be passably well one day, but the next, he may sup at black broth with Pluto.

Is there then all this work to one book, which shall be read in a very few hours; and, far more frequently, utterly skipped in one second; and which, in the end, whatever it be, must undoubtedly go to the worms?

Not so; that which now absorbs the time and the life of Pierre, is not the book, but the primitive elementalizing of the strange stuff, which in the act of attempting that book, has upheaved and upgushed in his soul. Two books are being writ; of which the world shall only see one, and that the bungled one. The larger book, and the infinitely better, is for Pierre's own private shelf. That it is, whose unfathomable cravings drink his blood; the other only demands his ink. But circumstances have so decreed, that the one can not be composed on the paper, but only as the other is writ down in his soul. And the one of the soul is elephantinely sluggish, and will not budge at a breath. Thus Pierre is fastened on by two leeches;—how then can the life of Pierre last? Lo! he is fitting himself for the highest life, by thinning his blood and collapsing his heart. He is learning how to live, by rehearsing the part of death.

Who shall tell all the thoughts and feelings of Pierre in that desolate and shivering room, when at last the idea obtruded, that the wiser and the profounder he should grow, the more and the more he lessened the chances for bread; that could he now hurl his deep book out of the window, and fall to on some shallow nothing of a novel, composable in a month at the longest, then could he reasonably hope for both appreciation and cash. But the devouring profundities, now opened up in him, consume all his vigor; would he, he could not now be entertainingly and profitably shallow in some pellucid and merry romance. Now he sees, that with every accession of the personal divine to him, some great land-slide of the general surrounding divineness slips from him, and falls crashing away. Said I not that the gods, as well as mankind, had unhanded themselves from this Pierre? So now in him you behold the baby toddler I spoke of; forced now to stand and toddle alone.

Now and then he turns to the camp-bed, and wetting his towel in the basin, presses it against his brow. Now he leans back in his chair, as if to give up; but again bends over and plods.

Twilight draws on, the summons of Isabel is heard from the door; the poor, frozen, blue-lipped, soul-shivering traveler for St. Petersburg is unpacked; and for a moment stands toddling on the floor. Then his hat, and his cane, and out he sallies for fresh air. A most comfortless staggering of a stroll! People gaze at him passing, as at some imprudent sick man, willfully burst from his bed. If an acquaintance is met, and would say a pleasant newsmonger's word in his ear, that acquaintance turns from him, affronted at his hard aspect of icy discourtesy. "Bad-hearted," mutters the man, and goes on.

He comes back to his chambers, and sits down at the neat table of Delly; and Isabel soothingly eyes him, and presses him to eat and be strong. But his is the famishing which loathes all food. He can not eat but by force. He has assassinated the natural day; how then can he eat with an appetite? If he lays him down, he can not sleep; he has waked the infinite wakefulness in him; then how can he slumber? Still his book, like a vast lumbering planet, revolves in his aching head. He can not command the thing out of its orbit; fain would he behead himself, to gain one night's repose. At last the heavy hours move on; and sheer exhaustion overtakes him, and he lies still—not asleep as children and day-laborers sleep—but he lies still from his throbbings, and for that interval holdingly sheaths the beak of the vulture in his hand, and lets it not enter his heart.

Morning comes; again the dropt sash, the icy water, the flesh-brush, the breakfast, the hot bricks, the ink, the pen, the from-eight-o'clock-to-half-past-four, and the whole general inclusive hell of the same departed day.

Ah! shivering thus day after day in his wrappers and cloaks, is this the warm lad that once sung to the world of the Tropical Summer?

Book XXIII

A Letter for Pierre • Isabel • Arrival of Lucy's Easel and Trunks at the Apostles'

IF A FRONTIER MAN be seized by wild Indians, and carried far and deep into the wilderness, and there held a captive, with no slightest probability of eventual deliverance; then the wisest thing for that man is to exclude from his memory by every possible method, the least images of those beloved objects now forever reft from him. For the more delicious they were to him in the now departed possession, so much the more agonizing shall they be in the present recalling. And though a strong man may sometimes succeed in strangling such tormenting memories; yet, if in the beginning permitted to encroach upon him unchecked, the same man shall, in the end, become as an idiot. With a continent and an ocean between him and his wife—thus sundered from her, by whatever imperative cause, for a term of long years;—the husband, if passionately devoted to her, and by nature broodingly sensitive of soul, is wise to forget her till he embrace her again;—is wise never to remember her if he hear of her death. And though such complete suicidal forgettings prove practically impossible, yet is it the shallow and ostentatious affections alone which are bustling in the offices of obituarian memories. *The love deep as death*—what mean those five words, but that such love can not live, and be continually remembering that the loved one is no more? If it be thus then in cases where entire unremorsefulness as regards the beloved absent objects is presumed, how much more intolerable, when the knowledge of their hopeless wretchedness occurs, attended by the visitations of before latent upbraidings in the rememberer as having been any way—even unwillingly—the producers of their sufferings. There seems no other sane recourse for some moody organizations on whom such things, under such circumstances intrude, but right and left to flee them, whatever betide.

If little or nothing hitherto has been said of Lucy Tartan in reference to the condition of Pierre after his departure from the Meadows, it has only been because her image did not willingly occupy his soul. He had striven his utmost to banish it thence; and only once—on receiving the tidings of Glen's renewed attentions—did he remit the intensity of those strivings, or rather feel them, as impotent in him in that hour of his manifold and overwhelming prostration.

Not that the pale form of Lucy, swooning on her snow-white bed; not that the inexpressible anguish of the shriek—"My heart! my heart!" would not now at times force themselves upon him, and cause his whole being to thrill with a nameless horror and terror. But the very thrillingness of the phantom made him to shun it, with all remaining might of his spirit.

Nor were there wanting still other, and far more wonderful, though but dimly conscious influences in the breast of Pierre, to meet as repellants the imploring form. Not to speak of his being devoured by the all-exacting theme of his book, there were sinister preoccupations in him of a still subtler and more fearful sort, of which some inklings have already been given.

It was while seated solitary in his room one morning; his flagging faculties seeking a momentary respite; his head sideways turned toward the naked floor, following the seams in it, which, as wires, led straight from where he sat to the connecting door, and disappeared beneath it into the chamber of Isabel; that he started at a tap at that very door, followed by the wonted, low, sweet voice,—

"Pierre! a letter for thee—dost thou hear? a letter,—may I come in?"

At once he felt a dart of surprise and apprehension; for he was precisely in that general condition with respect to the outer world, that he could not reasonably look for any tidings but disastrous, or at least, unwelcome ones. He assented; and Isabel entered, holding out the billet in her hand.

"'Tis from some lady, Pierre; who can it be?—not thy mother though, of that I am certain;—the expression of her face, as seen by me, not at all answering to the expression of this handwriting here."

"My mother? from my mother?" muttered Pierre, in wild vacancy—

"no! no! it can scarce be from her.—Oh, she writes no more, even in her own private tablets now! Death hath stolen the last leaf, and rubbed all out, to scribble his own ineffaceable *hic jacet* there!"

"Pierre!" cried Isabel, in affright.

"Give it me!" he shouted, vehemently, extending his hand. "Forgive me, sweet, sweet Isabel, I have wandered in my mind; this book makes me mad. There; I have it now"—in a tone of indifference—"now, leave me again. It is from some pretty aunt, or cousin, I suppose," carelessly balancing the letter in his hand.

Isabel quitted the room; the moment the door closed upon her, Pierre eagerly split open the letter, and read:—

ii

"This morning I vowed it, my own dearest, dearest Pierre. I feel stronger to-day; for to-day I have still more thought of thine own superhuman, angelical strength; which so, has a very little been transferred to me. Oh, Pierre, Pierre, with what words shall I write thee now;—now, when still knowing nothing, yet something of thy secret I, as a seer, suspect. Grief,—deep, unspeakable grief, hath made me this seer. I could murder myself, Pierre, when I think of my previous blindness; but that only came from my swoon. It was horrible and most murdersome; but now I see thou wert right in being so instantaneous with me, and in never afterward writing to me, Pierre; yes, now I see it, and adore thee the more.

"Ah! thou too noble and angelical Pierre, now I feel that a being like thee, can possibly have no love as other men love; but thou lovest as angels do; not for thyself, but wholly for others. But still are we one, Pierre; thou art sacrificing thyself, and I hasten to re-tie myself to thee, that so I may catch thy fire, and all the ardent multitudinous arms of our common flames may embrace. I will ask of thee nothing, Pierre; thou shalt tell me no secret. Very right wert thou, Pierre, when, in that ride to the hills, thou wouldst not swear the fond, foolish oath I demanded. Very right, very right; now I see it.

"If then I solemnly vow, never to seek from thee any slightest thing which thou wouldst not willingly have me know; if ever I, in all outward actions, shall recognize, just as thou dost, the peculiar position of that mysterious, and ever-sacred being;—then, may I not come and live with thee? I will be no encumbrance to thee. I know just where thou art, and how thou art living; and only just there, Pierre, and only just so, is any further life endurable, or possible for me. She will never know—for thus far I am sure thou thyself hast never disclosed it to her what I once was to thee. Let it seem, as though I were some nun-like cousin immovably vowed to dwell with thee in thy strange exile. Show not to me,—never show more any visible conscious token of love. I will never to thee. Our mortal lives, oh, my heavenly Pierre, shall henceforth be one mute wooing of each other; with no declaration; no bridal; till we meet in the pure realms of God's final blessedness for us;—till we meet where the ever-interrupting and ever-marring world can not and shall not come; where all thy hidden, glorious unselfishness shall be gloriously revealed in the full splendor of that heavenly light; where, no more forced to these cruelest disguises, she, *she* too shall assume her own glorious place, nor take it hard, but rather feel the more blessed, when, there, thy sweet heart, shall be openly and unreservedly mine. Pierre, Pierre, my Pierre!—only this thought, this hope, this sublime faith now supports me. Well was it, that the swoon, in which thou didst leave me, that long eternity ago—well was it, dear Pierre, that though I came out of it to stare and grope, yet it was only to stare and grope, and then I swooned again, and then groped again, and then again swooned. But all this was vacancy; little I clutched; nothing I knew; 'twas less than a dream, my Pierre, I had no conscious thought of thee, love; but felt an utter blank, a vacancy;—for wert thou not then utterly gone from me? and what could there then be left of poor Lucy?—But now, this long, long swoon is past; I come out again into life and light; but how could I come out, how could I any way *be*, my Pierre, if not in thee? So the moment I came out of the long, long swoon, straightway came to me the immortal faith in thee, which though it could offer no one slightest possible argument of mere sense in thy behalf, yet was it only the more mysteriously imperative for that, my Pierre. Know then, dearest Pierre, that with every most glaring earthly reason to disbelieve in thy love; I do yet wholly give myself up to the unshakable belief in it. For I feel, that always is love love, and can not know change, Pierre; I feel that heaven hath called me to a wonderful office toward thee. By throwing me into that long, long swoon,—during which, Martha tells me, I hardly ate altogether, three ordinary meals,—by that, heaven, I feel now, was preparing me for the superhuman office I speak of; was wholly estranging me from this earth, even while I yet lingered in it; was fitting me for a celestial mission in terrestrial elements. Oh, give to me of thine own dear strength! I am but a poor weak girl, dear Pierre; one that didst once love thee but too fondly, and with earthly frailty. But now I shall be wafted far upward from that; shall soar up to thee, where thou sittest in thine own calm, sublime heaven of heroism.

"Oh seek not to dissuade me, Pierre. Wouldst thou slay me, and slay me a million times more? and never have done with murdering me? I must come! I must come! God himself can not stay me, for it is He that commands me.—I know all that will follow my flight to thee;—my amazed mother, my enraged brothers, the whole taunting and despising world.—But thou art my mother and my brothers, and all the world, and all heaven, and all the universe to me—thou *art* my Pierre. One only being does this soul in me serve—and that is thee, Pierre.—So I am coming to thee, Pierre, and quickly;—to-morrow it shall be, and never more will I quit thee, Pierre. Speak thou immediately to her about me; thou shalt know best what to say. Is there not some connection between our families, Pierre? I have heard my mother sometimes trace such a thing out,—some indirect cousinship. If thou approvest, then, thou shalt say to her, I am thy cousin, Pierre;—thy resolved and immovable nun-like cousin; vowed to dwell with thee forever; to serve thee and her, to guard thee and her without end. Prepare some little corner for me somewhere; but let it be very near. Ere I come, I shall send a few little things,—the tools I shall work by, Pierre, and so contribute to the welfare of all. Look for me then. I am coming! I am coming, my Pierre; for a deep, deep voice assures me, that all noble as thou art, Pierre, some terrible jeopardy involves thee, which my continual presence only can drive away. I am coming! I am coming!"

LUCY.

iii

When surrounded by the base and mercenary crew, man, too long wonted to eye his race with a suspicious disdain, suddenly is brushed by some angelical plume of humanity, and the human accents of superhuman love, and the human eyes of superhuman beauty and glory, suddenly burst on his being; then how wonderful and fearful the shock! It is as if the sky-cope were rent, and from the black valley of Jehoshaphat, he caught upper glimpses of the seraphim in the visible act of adoring.

He held the artless, angelical letter in his unrealizing hand; he started, and gazed round his room, and out at the window, commanding the bare, desolate, all-forbidding quadrangle, and then asked himself whether this was the place that an angel should choose for its visit to earth. Then he felt a vast, out-swelling triumphantness, that the girl whose rare merits his intuitive soul had once so clearly and passionately discerned, should indeed, in this most tremendous of all trials, have acquitted herself with such infinite majesty. Then again, he sunk utterly down from her, as in a bottomless gulf, and ran shuddering through hideous galleries of despair, in pursuit of some vague, white shape, and lo! two unfathomable dark eyes met his, and Isabel stood mutely and mournfully, yet all-ravishingly before him.

He started up from his plank; cast off his manifold wrappings, and crossed the floor to remove himself from the spot, where such sweet, such sublime, such terrific revelations had been made him.

Then a timid little rap was heard at the door.

"Pierre, Pierre; now that thou art risen, may I not come in—just for a moment, Pierre."

"Come in, Isabel."

She was approaching him in her wonted most strange and sweetly mournful manner, when he retreated a step from her, and held out his arm, not seemingly to invite, but rather as if to warn.

She looked fixedly in his face, and stood rooted.

"Isabel, another is coming to me. Thou dost not speak, Isabel. She is coming to dwell with us so long as we live, Isabel. Wilt thou not speak?"

The girl still stood rooted; the eyes, which she had first fixed on him, still remained wide-openly riveted.

"Wilt thou not speak, Isabel?" said Pierre, terrified at her frozen, immovable aspect, yet too terrified to manifest his own terror to her; and still coming slowly near her. She slightly raised one arm, as if to grasp some support; then turned her head slowly sideways toward the door by which she had entered; then her dry lips slowly parted—"My bed; lay me; lay me!"

The verbal effort broke her stiffening enchantment of frost; her thawed form sloped sidelong into the air; but Pierre caught her, and bore her into her own chamber, and laid her there on the bed.

"Fan me; fan me!"

He fanned the fainting flame of her life; by-and-by she turned slowly toward him.

"Oh! that feminine word from thy mouth, dear Pierre:—that *she*, that *she!*"

Pierre sat silent, fanning her.

"Oh, I want none in the world but thee, my brother—but thee, but thee! and, oh God! am *I* not enough for thee? Bare earth with my brother were all heaven for me; but all my life, all my full soul, contents not my brother."

Pierre spoke not; he but listened; a terrible, burning curiosity was in him, that made him as heartless. But still all that she had said thus far was ambiguous.

"Had I known—had I but known it before! Oh bitterly cruel to reveal it now. That *she!* That *she!*"

She raised herself suddenly, and almost fiercely confronted him.

"Either thou hast told thy secret, or she is not worthy the commonest love of man! Speak Pierre,—which?"

"The secret is still a secret, Isabel."

"Then is she worthless, Pierre, whoever she be—foolishly, madly fond! —Doth not the world know me for thy wife?—She shall not come! 'Twere a foul blot on thee and me. She shall not come! One look from me shall murder her, Pierre!"

"This is madness, Isabel. Look: now reason with me. Did I not before opening the letter, say to thee, that doubtless it was from some pretty young aunt or cousin?"

"Speak quick!—a cousin?"

"A cousin, Isabel."

"Yet, yet, that is not wholly out of the degree, I have heard. Tell me more, and quicker! more! more!"

"A very strange cousin, Isabel; almost a nun in her notions. Hearing of our mysterious exile, she, without knowing the cause, hath yet as mysteriously vowed herself ours—not so much mine, Isabel, as ours, *ours*—to serve *us;* and by some sweet heavenly fancying, to guide us and guard us here."

"Then, possibly, it may be all very well, Pierre, my brother—my *brother*—I can say that now?"

"Any,—all words are thine, Isabel; words and worlds with all their containings, shall be slaves to thee, Isabel."

She looked eagerly and inquiringly at him; then dropped her eyes, and touched his hand; then gazed again. "Speak so more to me, Pierre! Thou art my brother; art thou not my brother?—But tell me now more of—her; it is all newness, and utter strangeness to me, Pierre."

"I have said, my sweetest sister, that she has this wild, nun-like notion in her. She is willful in it; in this letter she vows she must and will come, and nothing on earth shall stay her. Do not have any sisterly jealousy, then, my sister. Thou wilt find her a most gentle, unobtrusive, ministering girl, Isabel. She will never name the not-to-be-named things to thee; nor hint of them; because she knows them not. Still, without knowing the secret, she yet hath the vague, unspecializing sensation of the secret—the mystical presentiment, somehow, of the secret. And her divineness hath drowned all womanly curiosity in her; so that she desires not, in any way, to verify the presentiment; content with the vague presentiment only; for in that, she thinks, the heavenly summons to come to us, lies;—even there, in that, Isabel. Dost thou now comprehend me?"

"I comprehend nothing, Pierre; there is nothing these eyes have ever looked upon, Pierre, that this soul comprehended. Ever, as now, do I go all a-grope amid the wide mysteriousness of things. Yes, she shall come; it is only one mystery the more. Doth she talk in her sleep, Pierre? Would it be well, if I slept with her, my brother?"

"On thy account; wishful for thy sake; to leave thee incommoded; and —and—not knowing precisely how things really are;—she probably anticipates and desires otherwise, my sister."

She gazed steadfastly at his outwardly firm, but not interiorly unfaltering aspect; and then dropped her glance in silence.

"Yes, she shall come, my brother; she shall come. But it weaves its thread into the general riddle, my brother.—Hath she that which they call the memory, Pierre; the memory? Hath she that?"

"We all have the memory, my sister."

"Not all! not all!—poor Bell hath but very little. Pierre! I have seen her in some dream. She is fair-haired—blue eyes—she is not quite so tall as I, yet a very little slighter."

Pierre started. "Thou hast seen Lucy Tartan, at Saddle Meadows?"

"Is Lucy Tartan the name?—Perhaps, perhaps;—but also, in the dream, Pierre; she came, with her blue eyes turned beseechingly on me; she seemed as if persuading me from thee;—methought she was then more than thy cousin;—methought she was that good angel, which some say, hovers over every human soul; and methought—oh, methought that I was thy other, —thy other angel, Pierre. Look: see these eyes,—this hair—nay, this cheek; —all dark, dark, dark,—and she—the blue-eyed—the fair-haired—oh, once the red-cheeked!"

She tossed her ebon tresses over her; she fixed her ebon eyes on him.

"Say, Pierre; doth not a funerealness invest me? Was ever hearse so plumed?—Oh, God! that I had been born with blue eyes, and fair hair! Those make the livery of heaven! Heard ye ever yet of a good angel with dark eyes, Pierre?—no, no, no—all blue, blue, blue—heaven's own blue— the clear, vivid, unspeakable blue, which we see in June skies, when all clouds are swept by.—But the good angel shall come to thee, Pierre. Then both will be close by thee, my brother; and thou mayest perhaps elect,— elect!—She shall come; she shall come.—When is it to be, dear Pierre?"

"To-morrow, Isabel. So it is here written."

She fixed her eye on the crumpled billet in his hand. "It were vile to ask, but not wrong to suppose the asking.—Pierre,—no, I need not say it,—wouldst thou?"

"No; I would not let thee read it, my sister; I would not; because I have no right to—no right—no right;—that is it; no: I have no right. I will burn it this instant, Isabel."

He stepped from her into the adjoining room; threw the billet into the stove, and watching its last ashes, returned to Isabel.

She looked with endless intimations upon him.

"It is burnt, but not consumed; it is gone, but not lost. Through stove, pipe, and flue, it hath mounted in flame, and gone as a scroll to heaven! It shall appear again, my brother.—Woe is me—woe, woe!—woe is me, oh, woe! Do not speak to me, Pierre; leave me now. She shall come. The Bad angel shall tend the Good; she shall dwell with us, Pierre. Mistrust me not; her considerateness to me, shall be outdone by mine to her.—Let me be alone now, my brother."

iv

Though by the unexpected petition to enter his privacy—a petition he could scarce ever deny to Isabel, since she so religiously abstained from preferring it, unless for some very reasonable cause, Pierre, in the midst of those conflicting, secondary emotions, immediately following the first wonderful effect of Lucy's strange letter, had been forced to put on, toward Isabel, some air of assurance and understanding concerning its contents; yet at bottom, he was still a prey to all manner of devouring mysteries.

Soon, now, as he left the chamber of Isabel, these mysteriousnesses re-mastered him completely; and as he mechanically sat down in the dining-room chair, gently offered him by Delly—for the silent girl saw that some strangeness that sought stillness was in him;—Pierre's mind was revolving how it was possible, or any way conceivable, that Lucy should have been inspired with such seemingly wonderful presentiments of something assumed, or disguising, or non-substantial, somewhere and somehow, in his present most singular apparent position in the eye of the world. The wild words of Isabel yet rang in his ears. It were an outrage upon all womanhood to imagine that Lucy, however yet devoted to him in her hidden heart, should be willing to come to him, so long as she supposed, with the rest of the world, that Pierre was an ordinarily married man. But how—

what possible reason—what possible intimation could she have had to suspect the contrary, or to suspect any thing unsound? For neither at this present time, nor at any subsequent period, did Pierre, or could Pierre, possibly imagine that in her marvelous presentiments of Love she had any definite conceit of the precise nature of the secret which so unrevealingly and enchantedly wrapt him. But a peculiar thought passingly recurred to him here.

Within his social recollections there was a very remarkable case of a youth, who, while all but affianced to a beautiful girl—one returning his own throbbings with incipient passion—became somehow casually and momentarily betrayed into an imprudent manifested tenderness toward a second lady; or else, that second lady's deeply-concerned friends caused it to be made known to the poor youth, that such committal tenderness toward her he had displayed, nor had it failed to exert its natural effect upon her; certain it is, this second lady drooped and drooped, and came nigh to dying, all the while raving of the cruel infidelity of her supposed lover; so that those agonizing appeals, from so really lovely a girl, that seemed dying of grief for him, at last so moved the youth, that—morbidly disregardful of the fact, that inasmuch as two ladies claimed him, the prior lady had the best title to his hand—his conscience insanely upbraided him concerning the second lady; he thought that eternal woe would surely overtake him both here and hereafter if he did not renounce his first love—terrible as the effort would be both to him and her—and wed with the second lady; which he accordingly did; while, through his whole subsequent life, delicacy and honor toward his thus wedded wife, forbade that by explaining to his first love how it was with him in this matter, he should tranquilize her heart; and, therefore, in her complete ignorance, she believed that he was willfully and heartlessly false to her; and so came to a lunatic's death on his account.

This strange story of real life, Pierre knew to be also familiar to Lucy; for they had several times conversed upon it; and the first love of the demented youth had been a school-mate of Lucy's, and Lucy had counted upon standing up with her as bridemaid. Now, the passing idea was self-suggested to Pierre, whether into Lucy's mind some such conceit as this, concerning himself and Isabel, might not possibly have stolen. But then again such a supposition proved wholly untenable in the end; for it did by no means suffice for a satisfactory solution of the absolute motive of the extraordinary proposed step of Lucy; nor indeed by any ordinary law of propriety, did it at all seem to justify that step. Therefore, he knew not what to think; hardly what to dream. Wonders, nay, downright miracles and no less were sung about Love; but here was the absolute miracle itself—the out-acted miracle. For infallibly certain he inwardly felt, that whatever her strange conceit; whatever her enigmatical delusion; whatever her most secret and inexplicable motive; still Lucy in her own virgin heart remained transparently immaculate, without shadow of flaw or vein. Nevertheless, what inconceivable conduct this was in her, which she in her letter so passionately proposed! Altogether, it amazed him; it confounded him.

Now, that vague, fearful feeling stole into him, that, rail as all atheists will, there is a mysterious, inscrutable divineness in the world—a God—a Being positively present everywhere;—nay, He is now in this room; the air did part when I here sat down. I displaced the Spirit then—condensed it a little off from this spot. He looked apprehensively around him; he felt overjoyed at the sight of the humanness of Delly.

While he was thus plunged into this mysteriousness, a knock was heard at the door.

Delly hesitatingly rose—"Shall I let any one in, sir?—I think it is Mr. Millthorpe's knock."

"Go and see—go and see"—said Pierre, vacantly.

The moment the door was opened, Millthorpe—for it was he—catching a glimpse of Pierre's seated form, brushed past Delly, and loudly entered the room.

"Ha, ha! well, my boy, how comes on the Inferno? That is it you are writing; one is apt to look black while writing Infernoes; you always loved Dante. My lad! I have finished ten metaphysical treatises; argued five cases before the court; attended all our society's meetings; accompanied our great Professor, Monsieur Volvoon, the lecturer, through his circuit in the philosophical saloons, sharing all the honors of his illustrious triumph; and by the way, let me tell you, Volvoon secretly gives me even more credit than is my due; for 'pon my soul, I did not help write more than one half, at most, of his Lectures; edited—anonymously, though—a learned, scientific work on 'The Precise Cause of the Modifications in the Undulatory Motion in Waves,' a posthumous work of a poor fellow—fine lad he was, too—a friend of mine. Yes, here I have been doing all this, while you still are hammering away at that one poor plaguy Inferno! Oh, there's a secret in dispatching these things; patience! patience! you will yet learn the secret. Time! time! I can't teach it to you, my boy, but Time can: I wish I could, but I can't."

There was another knock at the door.

"Oh!" cried Millthorpe, suddenly turning round to it, "I forgot, my boy. I came to tell you that there is a porter, with some queer things, inquiring for you. I happened to meet him down stairs in the corridors, and I told him to follow me up—I would show him the road; here he is; let him in, let him in, good Delly, my girl."

Thus far, the rattlings of Millthorpe, if producing any effect at all, had but stunned the averted Pierre. But now he started to his feet. A man with his hat on, stood in the door, holding an easel before him.

"Is this Mr. Glendinning's room, gentlemen?"

"Oh, come in, come in," cried Millthorpe, "all right.".

"Oh! is that *you*, sir? well, well, then;" and the man set down the easel.

"Well, my boy," exclaimed Millthorpe to Pierre; "you are in the Inferno dream yet. Look; that's what people call an *easel*, my boy. An *easel*, an *easel*—not a *weasel;* you look at it as though you thought it a weasel. Come; wake up, wake up! You ordered it, I suppose, and here it is. Going to paint and illustrate the Inferno, as you go along, I suppose. Well, my friends tell me it is a great pity my own things aint illustrated. But I can't afford it. There now is that Hymn to the Niger, which I threw into a pigeon-hole, a year or two ago—that would be fine for illustrations."

"Is it for Mr. Glendinning you inquire?" said Pierre now, in a slow, icy tone, to the porter.

"Mr. Glendinning, sir; all right, aint it?"

"Perfectly," said Pierre mechanically, and casting another strange, rapt, bewildered glance at the easel. "But something seems strangely wanting here. Ay, now I see, I see it:—Villain!—the vines! Thou hast torn the green heart-strings! Thou hast but left the cold skeleton of the sweet arbor wherein she once nestled! Thou besotted, heartless hind and fiend, dost thou so much as dream in thy shriveled liver of the eternal mischief thou hast done? Restore thou the green vines! untrample them, thou accursed!—Oh my God, my God, trampled vines pounded and crushed in all fibers, how can they live over again, even though they be replanted! Curse thee, thou!—Nay, nay," he added moodily—"I was but wandering to myself." Then rapidly and mockingly—"Pardon, pardon!—porter; I most humbly crave thy most haughty pardon." Then imperiously—"Come, stir thyself, man; thou hast more below: bring all up."

As the astounded porter turned, he whispered to Millthorpe—"Is he safe?—shall I bring 'em?"

"Oh certainly," smiled Millthorpe: "I'll look out for him; he's never really dangerous when I'm present; there, go!"

Two trunks now followed, with "L. T." blurredly marked upon the ends.

"Is that all, my man?" said Pierre, as the trunks were being put down before him; "well, how much?"—that moment his eyes first caught the blurred letters.

"Prepaid, sir; but no objection to more."

Pierre stood mute and unmindful, still fixedly eying the blurred letters; his body contorted, and one side drooping, as though that moment half-way down-stricken with a paralysis, and yet unconscious of the stroke.

His two companions momentarily stood motionless in those respective attitudes, in which they had first caught sight of the remarkable change that had come over him. But, as if ashamed of having been thus affected, Millthorpe summoning a loud, merry voice, advanced toward Pierre, and, tapping his shoulder, cried, "Wake up, wake up, my boy!—He says he is prepaid, but no objection to more."

"Prepaid;—what's that? Go, go, and jabber to apes!"

"A curious young gentleman, is he not?" said Millthorpe lightly to the porter;—"Look you, my boy, I'll repeat:—He says he's prepaid, but no objection to more."

"Ah?—take that then," said Pierre, vacantly putting something into the porter's hand.

"And what shall I do with this, sir?" said the porter, staring.

"Drink a health; but not mine; that were mockery!"

"With a key, sir? This is a key you gave me."

"Ah!—well, you at least shall not have the thing that unlocks me. Give me the key, and take this."

"Ay, ay!—here's the chink! Thank 'ee sir, thank 'ee. This'll drink. I aint called a porter for nothing; Stout's the word; 2151 is my number; any jobs, call on me."

"Do you ever cart a coffin, my man?" said Pierre.

"'Pon my soul!" cried Millthorpe, gayly laughing, "if you aint writing an Inferno, then—but never mind. Porter! this gentleman is under medical treatment at present. You had better—ab'—you understand—'squatulate, porter! There, my boy, he is gone; I understand how to manage these fellows; there's a trick in it, my boy—an off-handed sort of what d'ye call it?—you understand—the trick! the trick!—the whole world's a trick. Know the trick of it, all's right; don't know, all's wrong. Ha! ha!"

"The porter is gone then?" said Pierre, calmly. "Well, Mr. Millthorpe, you will have the goodness to follow him."

"Rare joke! admirable!—Good morning, sir. Ha, ha!"

And with his unruffleable hilariousness, Millthorpe quitted the room. But hardly had the door closed upon him, nor had he yet removed his hand from its outer knob, when suddenly it swung half open again, and thrusting his fair curly head within, Millthorpe cried: "By the way, my boy, I have a word for you. You know that greasy fellow who has been dunning you so of late. Well, be at rest there; he's paid. I was suddenly made flush yesterday:—regular flood-tide. You can return it any day, you know—no hurry; that's all.—But, by the way,—as you look as though you were going to have company here—just send for me in case you want to use me—any bedstead to put up, or heavy things to be lifted about. Don't you and the women do it, now, mind! That's all again. Addios, my boy. Take care of yourself!"

"Stay!" cried Pierre, reaching forth one hand, but moving neither foot—"Stay!"—in the midst of all his prior emotions struck by these singular traits in Millthorpe. But the door was abruptly closed; and singing Fa, la, la: Millthorpe in his seedy coat went tripping down the corridor.

"Plus heart, minus head," muttered Pierre, his eyes fixed on the door. "Now, by heaven! the god that made Millthorpe was both a better and a greater than the god that made Napoleon or Byron.—Plus head, minus heart—Pah! the brains grow maggoty without a heart; but the heart's the preserving salt itself, and can keep sweet without the head.—Delly!"

"Sir?"

"My cousin Miss Tartan is coming here to live with us, Delly. That easel,—those trunks are hers."

"Good heavens!—coming here?—your cousin?—Miss Tartan?"

"Yes, I thought you must have heard of her and me;—but it was broken off, Delly."

"Sir? Sir?"

"I have no explanation, Delly; and from you, I must have no amazement. My cousin,—mind, my *cousin*, Miss Tartan, is coming to live with us. The next room to this, on the other side there, is unoccupied. That room shall be hers. You must wait upon her, too, Delly."

"Certainly sir, certainly; I will do any thing;" said Delly trembling; "but,—but—does Mrs. Glendin-din—does my mistress know this?"

"My wife knows all"—said Pierre sternly. "I will go down and get the key of the room; and you must sweep it out."

"What is to be put into it, sir?" said Delly. "Miss Tartan—why, she is used to all sorts of fine things,—rich carpets—wardrobes—mirrors—curtains;—why, why, why!"

"Look," said Pierre, touching an old rug with his foot;—"here is a bit of carpet; drag that into her room; here is a chair, put that in; and for a bed, —ay, ay," he muttered to himself; "I have made it for her, and she ignorantly lies on it now!—as made—so lie. Oh God!"

"Hark! my mistress is calling"—cried Delly, moving toward the opposite room.

"Stay!"—cried Pierre, grasping her shoulder; "if both called at one time from these opposite chambers, and both were swooning, which door would you first fly to?"

The girl gazed at him uncomprehendingly and affrighted a moment; and then said,—"This one, sir"—out of mere confusion perhaps, putting her hand on Isabel's latch.

"It is well. Now go."

He stood in an intent unchanged attitude till Delly returned.

"How is my wife, now?"

Again startled by the peculiar emphasis placed on the magical word *wife,* Delly, who had long before this, been occasionally struck with the infrequency of his using that term; she looked at him perplexedly, and said half-unconsciously—

"Your wife, sir?"

"Ay, is she not?"

"God grant that she be—Oh, 'tis most cruel to ask that of poor, poor Delly, sir!"

"Tut for thy tears! Never deny it again then!—I swear to heaven, she is!"

With these wild words, Pierre seized his hat, and departed the room, muttering something about bringing the key of the additional chamber.

As the door closed on him, Delly dropped on her knees. She lifted her head toward the ceiling, but dropped it again, as if tyrannically awed downward, and bent it low over, till her whole form tremulously cringed to the floor.

"God that made me, and that wast not so hard to me as wicked Delly deserved,—God that made me, I pray to thee! ward it off from me, if it be coming to me. Be not deaf to me; these stony walls—Thou canst hear through them. Pity! pity!—mercy, my God!—If they are not married; if I, penitentially seeking to be pure, am now but the servant to a greater sin, than I myself committed: then, pity! pity! pity! pity! pity! Oh God that made me,—See me, see me here—what can Delly do? If I go hence, none will take me in but villains. If I stay, then—for stay I must—and they be not married,—then pity, pity, pity, pity, pity!"

Book XXIV

Lucy at the Apostles

NEXT MORNING, the recently appropriated room adjoining on the other side of the dining-room, presented a different aspect from that which met the eye of Delly upon first unlocking it with Pierre on the previous evening. Two squares of faded carpeting of different patterns, covered the middle of the floor, leaving, toward the surbase, a wide, blank margin around them. A small glass hung in the pier; beneath that, a little stand, with a foot or two of carpet before it. In one corner was a cot, neatly equipped with bedding. At the outer side of the cot, another strip of carpeting was placed. Lucy's delicate feet should not shiver on the naked floor.

Pierre, Isabel, and Delly were standing in the room; Isabel's eyes were fixed on the cot.

"I think it will be pretty cosy now," said Delly, palely glancing all round, and then adjusting the pillow anew.

"There is no warmth, though," said Isabel. "Pierre, there is no stove in the room. She will be very cold. The pipe—can we not send it this way?" And she looked more intently at him, than the question seemed to warrant.

"Let the pipe stay where it is, Isabel," said Pierre, answering her own pointed gaze. "The dining-room door can stand open. She never liked sleeping in a heated room. Let all be; it is well. Eh! but there is a grate here, I see. I will buy coals. Yes, yes—that can be easily done; a little fire of a morning—the expense will be nothing. Stay, we will have a little fire here now for a welcome. She shall always have fire."

"Better change the pipe, Pierre," said Isabel, "that will be permanent, and save the coals."

"It shall not be done, Isabel. Doth not that pipe and that warmth go into thy room? Shall I rob my wife, good Delly, even to benefit my most devoted and true-hearted cousin?"

"Oh! I should say not, sir; not at all," said Delly hysterically.

A triumphant fire flashed in Isabel's eye; her full bosom arched out; but she was silent.

"She may be here, now, at any moment, Isabel," said Pierre; "come, we will meet her in the dining-room; that is our reception-place, thou knowest."

So the three went into the dining-room.

ii

They had not been there long, when Pierre, who had been pacing up and down, suddenly paused, as if struck by some laggard thought, which had just occurred to him at the eleventh hour. First he looked toward Delly, as if about to bid her quit the apartment, while he should say something private to Isabel; but as if, on a second thought, holding the contrary of this procedure most advisable, he, without preface, at once addressed Isabel, in his ordinary conversational tone, so that Delly could not but plainly hear him, whether she would or no.

"My dear Isabel, though, as I said to thee before, my cousin, Miss Tartan, that strange, and willful, nun-like girl, is at all hazards, mystically resolved to come and live with us, yet it must be quite impossible that her friends can approve in her such a singular step; a step even more singular, Isabel, than thou, in thy unsophisticatedness, can'st at all imagine. I shall be immensely deceived if they do not, to their very utmost, strive against it. Now what I am going to add may be quite unnecessary, but I can not avoid speaking it, for all that."

Isabel with empty hands sat silent, but intently and expectantly eying him; while behind her chair, Delly was bending her face low over her knitting—which she had seized so soon as Pierre had begun speaking—and with trembling fingers was nervously twitching the points of her long needles. It was plain that she awaited Pierre's accents with hardly much less eagerness than Isabel. Marking well this expression in Delly, and apparently not unpleased with it, Pierre continued; but by no slightest outward tone or look seemed addressing his remarks to any one but Isabel.

"Now what I mean, dear Isabel, is this: if that very probable hostility on the part of Miss Tartan's friends to her fulfilling her strange resolution—if any of that hostility should chance to be manifested under thine eye, then thou certainly wilt know how to account for it; and as certainly wilt draw no inference from it in the minutest conceivable degree involving any thing sinister in me. No, I am sure thou wilt not, my dearest Isabel. For, understand me, regarding this strange mood in my cousin as a thing wholly above my comprehension, and indeed regarding my poor cousin herself as a rapt enthusiast in some wild mystery utterly unknown to me; and unwilling ignorantly to interfere in what almost seems some supernatural thing, I shall not repulse her coming, however violently her friends may seek to stay it. I shall not repulse, as certainly as I have not invited. But a neutral attitude sometimes seems a suspicious one. Now what I mean is this: let all such vague suspicions of me, if any, be confined to Lucy's friends; but let not such absurd misgivings come near my dearest Isabel, to give the least uneasiness. Isabel! tell me; have I not now said enough to make plain what I mean? Or, indeed, is not all I have said wholly unnecessary; seeing that when one feels deeply conscientious, one is often apt to seem superfluously, and indeed unpleasantly and unbeseemingly scrupulous? Speak, my own Isabel,"—and he stept nearer to her, reaching forth his arm.

"Thy hand is the caster's ladle, Pierre, which holds me entirely fluid. Into thy forms and slightest moods of thought, thou pourest me; and I there solidify to that form, and take it on, and thenceforth wear it, till once more thou moldest me anew. If what thou tellest me be thy thought, then how can I help its being mine, my Pierre?"

"The gods made thee of a holyday, when all the common world was done, and shaped thee leisurely in elaborate hours, thou paragon!"

So saying, in a burst of admiring love and wonder, Pierre paced the room; while Isabel sat silent, leaning on her hand, and half-vailed with her hair. Delly's nervous stitches became less convulsive. She seemed soothed; some dark and vague conceit seemed driven out of her by something either directly expressed by Pierre, or inferred from his expressions.

iii

"Pierre! Pierre!—Quick! Quick!—They are dragging me back!—oh, quick, dear Pierre!"

"What is that?" swiftly cried Isabel, rising to her feet, and amazedly glancing toward the door leading into the corridor.

But Pierre darted from the room, prohibiting any one from following him.

Half-way down the stairs, a slight, airy, almost unearthly figure was clinging to the balluster; and two young men, one in naval uniform, were vainly seeking to remove the two thin white hands without hurting them. They were Glen Stanly, and Frederic, the elder brother of Lucy.

In a moment, Pierre's hands were among the rest.

"Villain!—Damn thee!" cried Frederic; and letting go the hand of his sister, he struck fiercely at Pierre.

But the blow was intercepted by Pierre.

"Thou hast bewitched, thou damned juggler, the sweetest angel! Defend thyself!"

"Nay, nay," cried Glen, catching the drawn rapier of the frantic brother, and holding him in his powerful grasp; "he is unarmed; this is no time or place to settle our feud with him. Thy sister,—sweet Lucy—let us save her first, and then what thou wilt. Pierre Glendinning—if thou art but the little finger of a man—begone with thee from hence! Thy depravity, thy pollutedness, is that of a fiend!—Thou canst not desire this thing:—the sweet girl is mad!"

Pierre stepped back a little, and looked palely and haggardly at all three.

"I render no accounts: I am what I am. This sweet girl—this angel whom ye two defile by your touches—she is of age by the law:—she is her own mistress by the law. And now, I swear she shall have her will! Unhand the girl! Let her stand alone. See; she will faint; let her go, I say!" And again his hands were among them.

Suddenly, as they all, for the one instant vaguely struggled, the pale girl drooped, and fell sideways toward Pierre; and, unprepared for this, the two opposite champions, unconsciously relinquished their hold, tripped, and stumbled against each other, and both fell on the stairs. Snatching Lucy in his arms, Pierre darted from them; gained the door; drove before him Isabel and Delly,—who, affrighted, had been lingering there;—and bursting into the prepared chamber, laid Lucy on her cot; then swiftly turned out of the room, and locked them all three in: and so swiftly—like lightning—was this whole thing done, that not till the lock clicked, did he find Glen and Frederic fiercely fronting him.

"Gentlemen, it is all over. This door is locked. She is in women's hands. —Stand back!"

As the two infuriated young men now caught at him to hurl him aside, several of the Apostles rapidly entered, having been attracted by the noise.

"Drag them off from me!" cried Pierre. "They are trespassers! drag them off!"

Immediately Glen and Frederic were pinioned by twenty hands; and, in obedience to a sign from Pierre, were dragged out of the room, and dragged down stairs; and given into the custody of a passing officer, as two disorderly youths invading the sanctuary of a private retreat.

In vain they fiercely expostulated; but at last, as if now aware that nothing further could be done without some previous legal action, they most reluctantly and chafingly declared themselves ready to depart. Accordingly they were let go; but not without a terrible menace of swift retribution directed to Pierre.

iv

Happy is the dumb man in the hour of passion. He makes no impulsive threats, and therefore seldom falsifies himself in the transition from choler to calm.

Proceeding into the thoroughfare, after leaving the Apostles', it was not very long ere Glen and Frederic concluded between themselves, that Lucy could not so easily be rescued by threat or force. The pale, inscrutable determinateness, and flinchless intrepidity of Pierre, now began to domineer upon them; for any social unusualness or greatness is sometimes most impressive in the retrospect. What Pierre had said concerning Lucy's being her own mistress in the eye of the law; this now recurred to them. After much tribulation of thought, the more collected Glen proposed, that Frederic's mother should visit the rooms of Pierre; he imagined, that though insensible to their own united intimidations, Lucy might not prove deaf to the maternal prayers. Had Mrs. Tartan been a different woman than she was; had she indeed any disinterested agonies of a generous heart, and not mere match-making mortifications, however poignant; then the hope of Frederic and Glen might have had more likelihood in it. Nevertheless, the experiment was tried, but signally failed.

In the combined presence of her mother, Pierre, Isabel, and Delly; and addressing Pierre and Isabel as Mr. and Mrs. Glendinning; Lucy took the most solemn vows upon herself, to reside with her present host and hostess until they should cast her off. In vain her by turns suppliant, and exasperated mother went down on her knees to her, or seemed almost on the point of smiting her; in vain she painted all the scorn and the loathing; sideways hinted of the handsome and gallant Glen; threatened her that in case she persisted, her entire family would renounce her; and though she should be starving, would not bestow one morsel upon such a recreant, and infinitely worse than dishonorable girl.

To all this, Lucy—now entirely unmenaced in person—replied in the gentlest and most heavenly manner; yet with a collectedness, and steadfastness, from which there was nothing to hope. What she was doing was not of herself; she had been moved to it by all-encompassing influences above, around, and beneath. She felt no pain for her own condition; her only suffering was sympathetic. She looked for no reward; the essence of well-doing was the consciousness of having done well without the least hope of reward. Concerning the loss of worldly wealth and sumptuousness, and all the brocaded applauses of drawing-rooms; these were no loss to her, for they had always been valueless. Nothing was she now renouncing; but in acting upon her present inspiration she was inheriting every thing. Indifferent to scorn, she craved no pity. As to the question of her sanity, that matter she referred to the verdict of angels, and not to the sordid opinions of man. If any one protested that she was defying the sacred counsels of her mother, she had nothing to answer but this: that her mother possessed all her daughterly deference, but her unconditional obedience was elsewhere due. Let all hope of moving her be immediately, and once for all, abandoned. One only thing could move her; and that would only move her, to make her forever immovable;—that thing was death.

Such wonderful strength in such wonderful sweetness; such inflexibility in one so fragile, would have been matter for marvel to any observer. But to her mother it was very much more; for, like many other superficial observers, forming her previous opinion of Lucy upon the slightness of her person, and the dulcetness of her temper, Mrs. Tartan had always imagined that her daughter was quite incapable of any such daring act. As if sterling heavenliness were incompatible with heroicness. These two are never found apart. Nor, though Pierre knew more of Lucy than any one else, did this most singular behavior in her fail to amaze him. Seldom even had the mystery of Isabel fascinated him more, with a fascination partaking of the terrible. The mere bodily aspect of Lucy, as changed by her more recent life, filled him with the most powerful and novel emotions. That unsullied complexion of bloom was now entirely gone, without being any way replaced by sallowness, as is usual in similar instances. And as if her body indeed were the temple of God, and marble indeed were the only fit material for so holy a shrine, a brilliant, supernatural whiteness now gleamed in her cheek. Her head sat on her shoulders as a chiseled statue's head; and the soft, firm light in her eye seemed as much a prodigy, as though a chiseled statue should give token of vision and intelligence.

Isabel also was most strangely moved by this sweet unearthliness in the aspect of Lucy. But it did not so much persuade her by any common appeals to her heart, as irrespectively commend her by the very signet of heaven. In the deference with which she ministered to Lucy's little occasional wants, there was more of blank spontaneousness than compassionate voluntariness. And when it so chanced, that—owing perhaps to some momentary jarring of the distant and lonely guitar—as Lucy was so mildly speaking in the presence of her mother, a sudden, just audible, submissively answering musical, stringed tone, came through the open door from the adjoining chamber; then Isabel, as if seized by some spiritual awe, fell on her knees before Lucy, and made a rapid gesture of homage; yet still, somehow, as it were, without evidence of voluntary will.

Finding all her most ardent efforts ineffectual, Mrs. Tartan now distressedly motioned to Pierre and Isabel to quit the chamber, that she might urge her entreaties and menaces in private. But Lucy gently waved them to stay; and then turned to her mother. Henceforth she had no secrets but those which would also be secrets in heaven. Whatever was publicly known in heaven, should be publicly known on earth. There was no slightest secret between her and her mother.

Wholly confounded by this inscrutableness of her so alienated and infatuated daughter, Mrs. Tartan turned inflamedly upon Pierre, and bade him follow her forth. But again Lucy said nay, there were no secrets between her mother and Pierre. She would anticipate every thing there. Calling for pen and paper, and a book to hold on her knee and write, she traced the following lines, and reached them to her mother:

"I am Lucy Tartan. I have come to dwell during their pleasure with Mr. and Mrs. Pierre Glendinning, of my own unsolicited free-will. If they desire it, I shall go; but no other power shall remove me, except by violence; and against any violence I have the ordinary appeal to the law."

"Read this, madam," said Mrs. Tartan, tremblingly handing it to Isabel, and eying her with a passionate and disdainful significance.

"I have read it," said Isabel, quietly, after a glance, and handing it to Pierre, as if by that act to show, that she had no separate decision in the matter.

"And do you, sir, too, indirectly connive?" said Mrs. Tartan to Pierre, when he had read it.

"I render no accounts, madam. This seems to be the written and final calm will of your daughter. As such, you had best respect it, and depart."

Mrs. Tartan glanced despairingly and incensedly about her; then fixing her eyes on her daughter, spoke.

"Girl! here where I stand, I forever cast thee off. Never more shalt thou be vexed by my maternal entreaties. I shall instruct thy brothers to disown thee; I shall instruct Glen Stanly to banish thy worthless image from his heart, if banished thence it be not already by thine own incredible folly and depravity. For thee, Mr. Monster! the judgment of God will overtake thee for this. And for thee, madam, I have no words for the woman who will connivingly permit her own husband's paramour to dwell beneath her roof. For thee, frail one," (to Delly), "thou needest no amplification.—A nest of vileness! And now, surely, whom God himself hath abandoned forever, a mother may quit, never more to revisit."

This parting maternal malediction seemed to work no visibly corresponding effect upon Lucy; already she was so marble-white, that fear could no more blanch her, if indeed fear was then at all within her heart. For as the highest, and purest, and thinnest ether remains unvexed by all the tumults of the inferior air; so that transparent ether of her cheek, that clear mild azure of her eye, showed no sign of passion, as her terrestrial mother stormed below. Helpings she had from unstirring arms; glimpses she caught of aid invisible; sustained she was by those high powers of immortal Love, that once siding with the weakest reed which the utmost tempest tosses; then that utmost tempest shall be broken down before the irresistible resistings of that weakest reed.

Book XXV

Lucy, Isabel, and Pierre • Pierre at His Book • Enceladus

A DAY OR TWO after the arrival of Lucy, when she had quite recovered from any possible ill-effects of recent events,—events conveying such a shock to both Pierre and Isabel,—though to each in a quite different way,—but not, apparently, at least, moving Lucy so intensely—as they were all three sitting at coffee, Lucy expressed her intention to practice her crayon art professionally. It would be so pleasant an employment for her, besides contributing to their common fund. Pierre well knew her expertness in catching likenesses, and judiciously and truthfully beautifying them; not by altering the features so much, as by steeping them in a beautifying atmosphere. For even so, said Lucy, thrown into the Lagoon, and there beheld—as I have heard—the roughest stones, without transformation, put on the softest aspects. If Pierre would only take a little trouble to bring sitters to her room, she doubted not a fine harvest of heads might easily be secured. Certainly, among the numerous inmates of the old Church, Pierre must know many who would have no objections to being sketched. Moreover, though as yet she had had small opportunity to see them; yet among such a remarkable company of poets, philosophers, and mystics of all sorts, there must be some striking heads. In conclusion, she expressed her satisfaction at the chamber prepared for her, inasmuch as having been formerly the studio of an artist, one window had been considerably elevated, while by a singular arrangement of the interior shutters, the light could in any direction be thrown about at will.

Already Pierre had anticipated something of this sort; the first sight of the easel having suggested it to him. His reply was therefore not wholly unconsidered. He said, that so far as she herself was concerned, the systematic practice of her art at present would certainly be a great advantage in supplying her with a very delightful occupation. But since she could hardly hope for any patronage from her mother's fashionable and wealthy associates; indeed, as such a thing must be very far from her own desires; and as it was only from the Apostles she could—for some time to come, at least—reasonably anticipate sitters; and as those Apostles were almost universally a very forlorn and penniless set—though in truth there were some wonderfully rich-looking heads among them—therefore, Lucy must not look for much immediate pecuniary emolument. Ere long she might indeed do something very handsome; but at the outset, it was well to be moderate in her expectations. This admonishment came, modifiedly, from that certain stoic, dogged mood of Pierre, born of his recent life, which taught him never to expect any good from any thing; but always to anticipate ill; however not in unreadiness to meet the contrary; and then, if good came, so much the better. He added that he would that very morning go among the rooms and corridors of the Apostles, familiarly announcing that his cousin, a lady-artist in crayons, occupied a room adjoining his, where she would be very happy to receive any sitters.

"And now, Lucy, what shall be the terms? That is a very important point, thou knowest."

"I suppose, Pierre, they must be very low," said Lucy, looking at him meditatively.

"Very low, Lucy; very low, indeed."

"Well, ten dollars, then."

"Ten Banks of England, Lucy!" exclaimed Pierre. "Why, Lucy, that were almost a quarter's income for some of the Apostles!"

"Four dollars, Pierre."

"I will tell thee now, Lucy—but first, how long does it take to complete one portrait?"

"Two sittings; and two mornings' work by myself, Pierre."

"And let me see; what are thy materials? They are not very costly, I believe. 'Tis not like cutting glass,—thy tools must not be pointed with diamonds, Lucy?"

"See, Pierre!" said Lucy, holding out her little palm, "see; this handful of charcoal, a bit of bread, a crayon or two, and a square of paper:—that is all."

"Well, then, thou shalt charge one-seventy-five for a portrait."

"Only one-seventy-five, Pierre?"

"I am half afraid now we have set it far too high, Lucy. Thou must not be extravagant. Look: if thy terms were ten dollars, and thou didst crayon on trust; then thou wouldst have plenty of sitters, but small returns. But if thou puttest thy terms right-down, and also sayest thou must have thy cash right-down too—don't start so at that *cash*—then not so many sitters to be sure, but more returns. Thou understandest."

"It shall be just as thou say'st, Pierre."

"Well, then, I will write a card for thee, stating thy terms; and put it up conspicuously in thy room, so that every Apostle may know what he has to expect."

"Thank thee, thank thee, cousin Pierre," said Lucy, rising. "I rejoice at thy pleasant and not entirely unhopeful view of my poor little plan. But I must be doing something; I must be earning money. See, I have eaten ever so much bread this morning, but have not earned one penny."

With a humorous sadness Pierre measured the large remainder of the one only piece she had touched, and then would have spoken banteringly to her; but she had slid away into her own room.

He was presently roused from the strange revery into which the conclusion of this scene had thrown him, by the touch of Isabel's hand upon his knee, and her large expressive glance upon his face. During all the foregoing colloquy, she had remained entirely silent; but an unoccupied observer would perhaps have noticed, that some new and very strong emotions were restrainedly stirring within her.

"Pierre!" she said, intently bending over toward him.

"Well, well, Isabel," stammeringly replied Pierre; while a mysterious color suffused itself over his whole face, neck, and brow; and involuntarily he started a little back from her self-proffering form.

Arrested by this movement Isabel eyed him fixedly; then slowly rose, and with immense mournful stateliness, drew herself up, and said: "If thy sister can ever come too nigh to thee, Pierre, tell thy sister so, beforehand; for the September sun draws not up the valley-vapor more jealously from the disdainful earth, than my secret god shall draw me up from thee, if ever I can come too nigh to thee."

Thus speaking, one hand was on her bosom, as if resolutely feeling of something deadly there concealed; but, riveted by her general manner more than by her particular gesture, Pierre, at the instant, did not so particularly note the all-significant movement of the hand upon her bosom, though afterward he recalled it, and darkly and thoroughly comprehended its meaning.

"Too nigh to me, Isabel? Sun or dew, thou fertilizest me! Can sunbeams or drops of dew come too nigh the thing they warm and water? Then sit down by me, Isabel, and sit close; wind in within my ribs,—if so thou canst,—that my one frame may be the continent of two."

"Fine feathers make fine birds, so I have heard," said Isabel, most bitterly—"but do fine sayings always make fine deeds? Pierre, thou didst but just now draw away from me!"

"When we would most dearly embrace, we first throw back our arms, Isabel; I but drew away, to draw so much the closer to thee."

"Well; all words are arrant skirmishers; deeds are the army's self! be it as thou sayest. I yet trust to thee.—Pierre."

"My breath waits thine; what is it, Isabel?"

"I have been more blockish than a block; I am mad to think of it! More mad, that her great sweetness should first remind me of mine own stupidity. But she shall not get the start of me! Pierre, some way I must work for thee! See, I will sell this hair; have these teeth pulled out; but some way I will earn money for thee!"

Pierre now eyed her startledly. Touches of a determinate meaning shone in her; some hidden thing was deeply wounded in her. An affectionate soothing syllable was on his tongue; his arm was out; when shifting his expression, he whisperingly and alarmedly exclaimed—"Hark! she is coming.—Be still."

But rising boldly, Isabel threw open the connecting door, exclaiming half-hysterically—"Look, Lucy; here is the strangest husband; fearful of being caught speaking to his wife!"

With an artist's little box before her—whose rattling, perhaps, had startled Pierre—Lucy was sitting mid-way in her room, opposite the opened door; so that at that moment, both Pierre and Isabel were plainly visible to her. The singular tone of Isabel's voice instantly caused her to look up intently. At once, a sudden irradiation of some subtile intelligence—but whether welcome to her, or otherwise, could not be determined—shot over her whole aspect. She murmured some vague random reply; and then bent low over her box, saying she was very busy.

Isabel closed the door, and sat down again by Pierre. Her countenance wore a mixed and writhing, impatient look. She seemed as one in whom the most powerful emotion of life is caught in inextricable toils of circumstances, and while longing to disengage itself, still knows that all struggles will prove worse than vain; and so, for the moment, grows madly reckless and defiant of all obstacles. Pierre trembled as he gazed upon her. But soon the mood passed from her; her old, sweet mournfulness returned; again the clear unfathomableness was in her mystic eye.

"Pierre, ere now,—ere I ever knew thee—I have done mad things, which I have never been conscious of, but in the dim recalling. I hold such things no things of mine. What I now remember, as just now done, was one of them."

"Thou hast done nothing but shown thy strength, while I have shown my weakness, Isabel;—yes, to the whole world thou art my wife—to her, too, thou art my wife. Have I not told her so, myself? I was weaker than a kitten, Isabel; and thou, strong as those high things angelical, from which utmost beauty takes not strength."

"Pierre, once such syllables from thee, were all refreshing, and bedewing to me; now, though they drop as warmly and as fluidly from thee, yet falling through another and an intercepting zone, they freeze on the way, and clatter on my heart like hail, Pierre.——Thou didst not speak thus to her!"

"She is not Isabel."

The girl gazed at him with a quick and piercing scrutiny; then looked quite calm, and spoke. "My guitar, Pierre: thou know'st how complete a mistress I am of it; now, before thou gettest sitters for the portrait-sketcher, thou shalt get pupils for the music-teacher. Wilt thou?" and she looked at him with a persuasiveness and touchingness, which to Pierre, seemed more than mortal.

"My poor poor, Isabel!" cried Pierre; "thou art the mistress of the natural sweetness of the guitar, not of its invented regulated artifices; and these are all that the silly pupil will pay for learning. And what thou hast can not be taught. Ah, thy sweet ignorance is all transporting to me! my sweet, my sweet!—dear, divine girl!" And impulsively he caught her in his arms.

While the first fire of his feeling plainly glowed upon him, but ere he had yet caught her to him, Isabel had backward glided close to the connecting door; which, at the instant of his embrace, suddenly opened, as by its own volition.

Before the eyes of seated Lucy, Pierre and Isabel stood locked; Pierre's lips upon her cheek.

ii

Notwithstanding the maternal visit of Mrs. Tartan, and the peremptoriness with which it had been closed by her declared departure never to return, and her vow to teach all Lucy's relatives and friends, and Lucy's own brothers, and her suitor, to disown her, and forget her; yet Pierre fancied that he knew too much in general of the human heart, and too much in particular of the character of both Glen and Frederic, to remain entirely untouched by disquietude, concerning what those two fiery youths might now be plotting against him, as the imagined monster, by whose infernal tricks Lucy Tartan was supposed to have been seduced from every earthly seemliness. Not happily, but only so much the more gloomily, did he augur from the fact, that Mrs. Tartan had come to Lucy unattended; and that Glen and Frederic had let eight-and-forty hours and more go by, without giving the slightest hostile or neutral sign. At first he thought, that bridling their impulsive fierceness, they were resolved to take the slower, but perhaps the surer method, to wrest Lucy back to them, by instituting some legal process. But this idea was repulsed by more than one consideration.

Not only was Frederic of that sort of temper, peculiar to military men, which would prompt him, in so closely personal and intensely private and family a matter, to scorn the hireling publicity of the law's lingering arm; and impel him, as by the furiousness of fire, to be his own righter and avenger; for, in him, it was perhaps quite as much the feeling of an outrageous family affront to himself, through Lucy, as her own presumed separate wrong, however black, which stung him to the quick: not only were these things so respecting Frederic; but concerning Glen, Pierre well knew, that be Glen heartless as he might, to do a deed of love, Glen was not heartless to do a deed of hate; that though, on that memorable night of his arrival in the city, Glen had heartlessly closed his door upon him, yet now Glen might heartfully burst Pierre's open, if by that he at all believed, that permanent success would crown the fray.

Besides, Pierre knew this;—that so invincible is the natural, untamable, latent spirit of a courageous manliness in man, that though now socially educated for thousands of years in an arbitrary homage to the Law, as the one only appointed redress for every injured person; yet immemorially and universally, among all gentlemen of spirit, once to have uttered independent personal threats of personal vengeance against your foe, and then, after that, to fall back slinking into a court, and hire with sops a pack of yelping pettifoggers to fight the battle so valiantly proclaimed; this, on the surface, is ever deemed very decorous, and very prudent—a most wise second thought; but, at bottom, a miserably ignoble thing. Frederic was not the watery man for that,—Glen had more grapey blood in him.

Moreover, it seemed quite clear to Pierre, that only by making out Lucy absolutely mad, and striving to prove it by a thousand despicable little particulars, could the law succeed in tearing her from the refuge she had voluntarily sought; a course equally abhorrent to all the parties possibly to be concerned on either side.

What then would those two boiling bloods do? Perhaps they would patrol the streets; and at the first glimpse of lonely Lucy, kidnap her home. Or, if Pierre were with her, then, smite him down by hook or crook, fair play or foul; and then, away with Lucy! Or if Lucy systematically kept her room, then fall on Pierre in the most public way, fell him, and cover him from all decent recognition beneath heaps on heaps of hate and insult; so that broken on the wheel of such dishonor, Pierre might feel himself unstrung, and basely yield the prize.

Not the gibbering of ghosts in any old haunted house; no sulphurous and portentous sign at night beheld in heaven, will so make the hair to stand, as when a proud and honorable man is revolving in his soul the possibilities of some gross public and corporeal disgrace. It is not fear; it is a pride-horror, which is more terrible than any fear. Then, by tremendous imagery, the murderer's mark of Cain is felt burning on the brow, and the already acquitted knife blood-rusts in the clutch of the anticipating hand.

Certain that those two youths must be plotting something furious against him; with the echoes of their scorning curses on the stairs still ringing in his ears—curses, whose swift responses from himself, he, at the time, had had much ado to check;—thoroughly alive to the supernaturalism of that mad frothing hate which a spirited brother forks forth at the insulter of a sister's honor—beyond doubt the most uncompromising of all the social passions known to man—and not blind to the anomalous fact, that if such a brother stab his foe at his own mother's table, all people and all juries would bear him out, accounting every thing allowable to a noble soul made mad by a sweet sister's shame caused by a damned seducer;—imagining to himself his own feelings, if he were actually in the position which Frederic so vividly fancied to be his; remembering that in love matters jealousy is as an adder, and that the jealousy of Glen was double-addered by the extraordinary malice of the apparent circumstances under which Lucy had spurned Glen's arms, and fled to his always successful and now married rival, as if wantonly and shamelessly to nestle there;—remembering all these intense incitements of both those foes of his, Pierre could not but look forward to wild work very soon to come. Nor was the storm of passion in his soul unratified by the decision of his coolest possible hour. Storm and calm both said to him,—Look to thyself, oh Pierre!

Murders are done by maniacs; but the earnest thoughts of murder, these are the collected desperadoes. Pierre was such; fate, or what you will, had made him such. But such he was. And when these things now swam before him; when he thought of all the ambiguities which hemmed him in; the stony walls all round that he could not overleap; the million aggravations of his most malicious lot; the last lingering hope of happiness licked up from him as by flames of fire, and his one only prospect a black, bottomless gulf of guilt, upon whose verge he imminently teetered every hour;—then the utmost hate of Glen and Frederic were jubilantly welcome to him; and murder, done in the act of warding off their ignominious public blow, seemed the one only congenial sequel to such a desperate career.

iii

As a statue, planted on a revolving pedestal, shows now this limb, now that; now front, now back, now side; continually changing, too, its general profile; so does the pivoted, statued soul of man, when turned by the hand of Truth. Lies only never vary; look for no invariableness in Pierre. Nor does any canting showman here stand by to announce his phases as he revolves. Catch his phases as your insight may.

Another day passed on; Glen and Frederic still absenting themselves, and Pierre and Isabel and Lucy all dwelling together. The domestic presence of Lucy had begun to produce a remarkable effect upon Pierre. Sometimes, to the covertly watchful eye of Isabel, he would seem to look upon Lucy with an expression illy befitting their singular and so-supposed merely cousinly relation; and yet again, with another expression still more unaccountable to her,—one of fear and awe, not unmixed with impatience. But his general detailed manner toward Lucy was that of the most delicate and affectionate considerateness—nothing more. He was never alone with her; though, as before, at times alone with Isabel.

Lucy seemed entirely undesirous of usurping any place about him; manifested no slightest unwelcome curiosity as to Pierre, and no painful embarrassment as to Isabel. Nevertheless, more and more did she seem, hour by hour, to be somehow inexplicably sliding between them, without touching them. Pierre felt that some strange heavenly influence was near him, to keep him from some uttermost harm; Isabel was alive to some untraceable displacing agency. Though when all three were together, the marvelous serenity, and sweetness, and utter unsuspectingness of Lucy obviated any thing like a common embarrassment: yet if there was any embarrassment at all beneath that roof, it was sometimes when Pierre was alone with Isabel, after Lucy would innocently quit them.

Meantime Pierre was still going on with his book; every moment becoming still the more sensible of the intensely inauspicious circumstances of all sorts under which that labor was proceeding. And as the now advancing and concentring enterprise demanded more and more compacted vigor from him, he felt that he was having less and less to bring to it. For not only was it the signal misery of Pierre, to be invisibly—though but accidentally—goaded, in the hour of mental immaturity, to the attempt at a mature work,—a circumstance sufficiently lamentable in itself; but also, in the hour of his clamorous pennilessness, he was additionally goaded into an enterprise long and protracted in the execution, and of all things least calculated for pecuniary profit in the end. How these things were so, whence they originated, might be thoroughly and very beneficially explained; but space and time here forbid.

At length, domestic matters—rent and bread—had come to such a pass with him, that whether or no, the first pages must go to the printer; and thus was added still another tribulation; because the printed pages now dictated to the following manuscript, and said to all subsequent thoughts and inventions of Pierre—*Thus and thus; so and so; else an ill match.* Therefore, was his book already limited, bound over, and committed to imperfection, even before it had come to any confirmed form or conclusion at all. Oh, who shall reveal the horrors of poverty in authorship that is high? While the silly Millthorpe was railing against his delay of a few weeks and months; how bitterly did unreplying Pierre feel in his heart, that to most of the great works of humanity, their authors had given, not weeks and months, not years and years, but their wholly surrendered and dedicated lives. On either hand clung to by a girl who would have laid down her life for him; Pierre, nevertheless, in his deepest, highest part, was utterly without sympathy from any thing divine, human, brute, or vegetable. One in a city of hundreds of thousands of human beings, Pierre was solitary as at the Pole.

And the great woe of all was this: that all these things were unsuspected without, and undivulgible from within; the very daggers that stabbed him were joked at by Imbecility, Ignorance, Blockheadedness, Self-Complacency, and the universal Blearedness and Besottedness around him. Now he began to feel that in him, the thews of a Titan were forestallingly cut by the scissors of Fate. He felt as a moose, hamstrung. All things that think, or move, or lie still, seemed as created to mock and torment him. He seemed gifted with loftiness, merely that it might be dragged down to the mud. Still, the profound willfulness in him would not give up. Against the breaking heart, and the bursting head; against all the dismal lassitude, and deathful faintness and sleeplessness, and whirlingness, and craziness, still he like a demigod bore up. His soul's ship foresaw the inevitable rocks, but resolved to sail on, and make a courageous wreck. Now he gave jeer for jeer, and taunted the apes that jibed him. With the soul of an Atheist, he wrote down the godliest things; with the feeling of misery and death in him, he created forms of gladness and life. For the pangs in his heart, he put down hoots on the paper. And every thing else he disguised under the so conveniently adjustable drapery of all-stretchable Philosophy. For the more and the more that he wrote, and the deeper and the deeper that he dived, Pierre saw the everlasting elusiveness of Truth; the universal lurking insincerity of even the greatest and purest written thoughts. Like knavish cards, the leaves of all great books were covertly packed. He was but packing one set the more; and that a very poor jaded set and pack indeed. So that there was nothing he more spurned, than his own aspirations; nothing he more abhorred than the loftiest part of himself. The brightest success, now seemed intolerable to him, since he so plainly saw, that the brightest success could not be the sole offspring of Merit; but of Merit for the one thousandth part, and nine hundred and ninety-nine combining and dovetailing accidents for the rest. So beforehand he despised those laurels which in the very nature of things, can never be impartially bestowed. But while thus all the earth was depopulated of ambition for him; still circumstances had put him in the attitude of an eager contender for renown. So beforehand he felt the unrevealable sting of receiving either plaudits or censures, equally unsought for, and equally loathed ere given. So, beforehand he felt the pyramidical scorn of the genuine loftiness for the whole infinite company of infinitesimal critics. His was the scorn which thinks it not worth the while to be scornful. Those he most scorned, never knew it. In that lonely little closet of his, Pierre foretasted all that this world hath either of praise or dispraise; and thus foretasting both goblets, anticipatingly hurled them both in its teeth. All panegyric, all denunciation, all criticism of any sort, would come too late for Pierre.

But man does never give himself up thus, a doorless and shutterless house for the four loosened winds of heaven to howl through, without still additional dilapidations. Much oftener than before, Pierre laid back in his chair with the deadly feeling of faintness. Much oftener than before, came staggering home from his evening walk, and from sheer bodily exhaustion economized the breath that answered the anxious inquiries as to what might be done for him. And as if all the leagued spiritual inveteracies and malices, combined with his general bodily exhaustion, were not enough, a special corporeal affliction now descended like a sky-hawk upon him. His incessant application told upon his eyes. They became so affected, that some days he wrote with the lids nearly closed, fearful of opening them wide to the light. Through the lashes he peered upon the paper, which so seemed fretted with wires. Sometimes he blindly wrote with his eyes turned away from the paper;—thus unconsciously symbolizing the hostile necessity and distaste, the former whereof made of him this most unwilling states-prisoner of letters.

As every evening, after his day's writing was done, the proofs of the beginning of his work came home for correction, Isabel would read them to him. They were replete with errors; but preoccupied by the thronging, and undiluted, pure imaginings of things, he became impatient of such minute, gnat-like torments; he randomly corrected the worst, and let the rest go; jeering with himself at the rich harvest thus furnished to the entomological critics.

But at last he received a tremendous interior intimation, to hold off—to be still from his unnatural struggle.

In the earlier progress of his book, he had found some relief in making his regular evening walk through the greatest thoroughfare of the city; that so, the utter isolation of his soul, might feel itself the more intensely from the incessant jogglings of his body against the bodies of the hurrying thousands. Then he began to be sensible of more fancying stormy nights, than pleasant ones; for then, the great thoroughfares were less thronged, and the innumerable shop-awnings flapped and beat like schooners' broad sails in a gale, and the shutters banged like lashed bulwarks; and the slates fell hurtling like displaced ship's blocks from aloft. Stemming such tempests through the deserted streets, Pierre felt a dark, triumphant joy; that while others had crawled in fear to their kennels, he alone defied the storm-admiral, whose most vindictive peltings of hail-stones,—striking his iron-framed fiery furnace of a body,—melted into soft dew, and so, harmlessly trickled from off him.

By-and-by, of such howling, pelting nights, he began to bend his steps down the dark, narrow side-streets, in quest of the more secluded and mysterious tap-rooms. There he would feel a singular satisfaction, in sitting down all dripping in a chair, ordering his half-pint of ale before him, and drawing over his cap to protect his eyes from the light, eye the varied faces of the social castaways, who here had their haunts from the bitterest midnights.

But at last he began to feel a distaste for even these; and now nothing but the utter night-desolation of the obscurest warehousing lanes would content him, or be at all sufferable to him. Among these he had now been accustomed to wind in and out every evening; till one night as he paused a moment previous to turning about for home, a sudden, unwonted, and all-pervading sensation seized him. He knew not where he was; he did not have any ordinary life-feeling at all. He could not see; though instinctively putting his hand to his eyes, he seemed to feel that the lids were open. Then he was sensible of a combined blindness, and vertigo, and staggering; before his eyes a million green meteors danced; he felt his foot tottering upon the curb, he put out his hands, and knew no more for the time. When he came to himself he found that he was lying crosswise in the gutter, dabbled with mud and slime. He raised himself to try if he could stand; but the fit was entirely gone. Immediately he quickened his steps homeward, forbearing to rest or pause at all on the way, lest that rush of blood to his head, consequent upon his sudden cessation from walking, should again smite him down. This circumstance warned him away from those desolate streets, lest the repetition of the fit should leave him there to perish by night in unknown and unsuspected loneliness. But if that terrible vertigo had been also intended for another and deeper warning, he regarded such added warning not at all; but again plied heart and brain as before.

But now at last since the very blood in his body had in vain rebelled against his Titanic soul; now the only visible outward symbols of that soul—his eyes—did also turn downright traitors to him, and with more success than the rebellious blood. He had abused them so recklessly, that now they absolutely refused to look on paper. He turned them on paper, and they blinked and shut. The pupils of his eyes rolled away from him in their own orbits. He put his hand up to them, and sat back in his seat. Then, without saying one word, he continued there for his usual term, suspended, motionless, blank.

But next morning—it was some few days after the arrival of Lucy—still feeling that a certain downright infatuation, and no less, is both unavoidable and indispensable in the composition of any great, deep book, or even any wholly unsuccessful attempt at any great, deep book; next morning he returned to the charge. But again the pupils of his eyes rolled away from him in their orbits: and now a general and nameless torpor—some horrible foretaste of death itself—seemed stealing upon him.

iv

During this state of semi-unconsciousness, or rather trance, a remarkable dream or vision came to him. The actual artificial objects around him slid from him, and were replaced by a baseless yet most imposing spectacle of natural scenery. But though a baseless vision in itself, this airy spectacle assumed very familiar features to Pierre. It was the phantasmagoria of the Mount of the Titans, a singular height standing quite detached in a wide solitude not far from the grand range of dark blue hills encircling his ancestral manor.

Say what some poets will, Nature is not so much her own ever-sweet interpreter, as the mere supplier of that cunning alphabet, whereby selecting and combining as he pleases, each man reads his own peculiar lesson according to his own peculiar mind and mood. Thus a high-aspiring, but most moody, disappointed bard, chancing once to visit the Meadows and beholding that fine eminence, christened it by the name it ever after bore; completely extinguishing its former title—The Delectable Mountain—one long ago bestowed by an old Baptist farmer, an hereditary admirer of Bunyan and his most marvelous book. From the spell of that name the mountain never afterward escaped; for now, gazing upon it by the light of those suggestive syllables, no poetical observer could resist the apparent felicity of the title. For as if indeed the immemorial mount would fain adapt itself to its so recent name, some people said that it had insensibly changed its pervading aspect within a score or two of winters. Nor was this strange conceit entirely without foundation, seeing that the annual displacements of huge rocks and gigantic trees were continually modifying its whole front and general contour.

On the north side, where it fronted the old Manor-house, some fifteen miles distant, the height, viewed from the piazza of a soft haze-canopied summer's noon, presented a long and beautiful, but not entirely inaccessible-looking purple precipice, some two thousand feet in air, and on each hand sideways sloping down to lofty terraces of pastures.

Those hill-side pastures, be it said, were thickly sown with a small white amaranthine flower, which, being irreconcilably distasteful to the cattle, and wholly rejected by them, and yet, continually multiplying on every hand, did by no means contribute to the agricultural value of those elevated lands. Insomuch, that for this cause, the disheartened dairy tenants of that part of the Manor, had petitioned their lady-landlord for some abatement in their annual tribute of upland grasses, in the Juny-load; rolls of butter in the October crock; and steers and heifers on the October hoof; with turkeys in the Christmas sleigh.

"The small white flower, it is our bane!" the imploring tenants cried. "The aspiring amaranth, every year it climbs and adds new terraces to its sway! The immortal amaranth, it will not die, but last year's flowers survive to this! The terraced pastures grow glittering white, and in warm June still show like banks of snow:—fit token of the sterileness the amaranth begets! Then free us from the amaranth, good lady, or be pleased to abate our rent!"

Now, on a somewhat nearer approach, the precipice did not belie its purple promise from the manorial piazza;—that sweet imposing purple promise, which seemed fully to vindicate the Bunyanish old title originally bestowed;—but showed the profuse aërial foliage of a hanging forest. Nevertheless, coming still more nigh, long and frequent rents among the mass of leaves revealed horrible glimpses of dark-dripping rocks, and mysterious mouths of wolfish caves. Struck by this most unanticipated view, the tourist now quickened his impulsive steps to verify the change by coming into direct contact with so chameleon a height. As he would now speed on, the lower ground, which from the manor-house piazza seemed all a grassy level, suddenly merged into a very long and weary acclivity, slowly rising close up to the precipice's base; so that the efflorescent grasses rippled against it, as the efflorescent waves of some great swell or long rolling billow ripple against the water-line of a steep gigantic war-ship on the sea. And, as among the rolling sea-like sands of Egypt, disordered rows of broken Sphinxes lead to the Cheopian pyramid itself; so this long acclivity was thickly strewn with enormous rocky masses, grotesque in shape, and with wonderful features on them, which seemed to express that slumbering intelligence visible in some recumbent beasts—beasts whose intelligence seems struck dumb in them by some sorrowful and inexplicable spell. Nevertheless, round and round those still enchanted rocks, hard by their utmost rims, and in among their cunning crevices, the misanthropic hill-scaling goat nibbled his sweetest food; for the rocks, so barren in themselves, distilled a subtile moisture, which fed with greenness all things that grew about their igneous marge.

Quitting those recumbent rocks, you still ascended toward the hanging forest, and piercing within its lowermost fringe, then suddenly you stood transfixed, as a marching soldier confounded at the sight of an impregnable redoubt, where he had fancied it a practicable vault to his courageous thews. Cunningly masked hitherto, by the green tapestry of the interlacing leaves, a terrific towering palisade of dark mossy massiveness confronted you; and, trickling with unevaporable moisture, distilled upon you from its beetling brow slow thunder-showers of water-drops, chill as the last dews of death. Now you stood and shivered in that twilight, though it were high noon and burning August down the meads. All round and round, the grim scarred rocks rallied and re-rallied themselves; shot up, protruded, stretched, swelled, and eagerly reached forth; on every side bristlingly radiating with a hideous repellingness. Tossed, and piled, and indiscriminate among these, like bridging rifts of logs up-jammed in alluvial-rushing streams of far Arkansas: or, like great masts and yards of overwhelmed fleets hurled high and dashed amain, all splintering together, on hovering ridges of the Atlantic sea,—you saw the melancholy trophies which the North Wind, championing the unquenchable quarrel of the Winter, had wrested from the forests, and dismembered them on their own chosen battle-ground, in barbarous disdain. 'Mid this spectacle of wide and wanton spoil, insular noises of falling rocks would boomingly explode upon the silence and fright all the echoes, which ran shrieking in and out among the caves, as wailing women and children in some assaulted town.

Stark desolation; ruin, merciless and ceaseless; chills and gloom,—all here lived a hidden life, curtained by that cunning purpleness, which, from the piazza of the manor house, so beautifully invested the mountain once called Delectable, but now styled Titanic.

Beaten off by such undreamed-of glooms and steeps, you now sadly retraced your steps, and, mayhap, went skirting the inferior sideway terraces of pastures; where the multiple and most sterile inodorous immortalness of the small, white flower furnished no aliment for the mild cow's meditative cud. But here and there you still might smell from far the sweet aromaticness of clumps of catnip, that dear farm-house herb. Soon you would see the modest verdure of the plant itself; and wheresoever you saw that sight, old foundation stones and rotting timbers of log-houses long extinct would also meet your eye; their desolation illy hid by the green solicitudes of the unemigrating herb. Most fitly named the catnip; since, like the unrunagate cat, though all that's human forsake the place, that plant will long abide, long bask and bloom on the abandoned hearth. Illy hid; for every spring the amaranthine and celestial flower gained on the mortal household herb; for every autumn the catnip died, but never an autumn made the amaranth to wane. The catnip and the amaranth!—man's earthly household peace, and the ever-encroaching appetite for God.

No more now you sideways followed the sad pasture's skirt, but took your way adown the long declivity, fronting the mystic height. In mid field again you paused among the recumbent sphinx-like shapes thrown off from the rocky steep. You paused; fixed by a form defiant, a form of awfulness. You saw Enceladus the Titan, the most potent of all the giants, writhing from out the imprisoning earth;—turbaned with upborne moss he writhed; still, though armless, resisting with his whole striving trunk, the Pelion and the Ossa hurled back at him;—turbaned with upborne moss he writhed; still turning his unconquerable front toward that majestic mount eternally in vain assailed by him, and which, when it had stormed him off, had heaved his undoffable incubus upon him, and deridingly left him there to bay out his ineffectual howl.

To Pierre this wondrous shape had always been a thing of interest, though hitherto all its latent significance had never fully and intelligibly smitten him. In his earlier boyhood a strolling company of young collegian pedestrians had chanced to light upon the rock; and, struck with its remarkableness, had brought a score of picks and spades, and dug round it to unearth it, and find whether indeed it were a demoniac freak of nature, or some stern thing of antediluvian art. Accompanying this eager party, Pierre first beheld that deathless son of Terra. At that time, in its untouched natural state, the statue presented nothing but the turbaned head of igneous rock rising from out the soil, with its unabasable face turned upward toward the mountain, and the bull-like neck clearly defined. With distorted features, scarred and broken, and a black brow mocked by the upborne moss, Enceladus there subterraneously stood, fast frozen into the earth at the junction of the neck. Spades and picks soon heaved part of his Ossa from him, till at last a circular well was opened round him to the depth of some thirteen feet. At that point the wearied young collegians gave over their enterprise in despair. With all their toil, they had not yet come to the girdle of Enceladus. But they had bared good part of his mighty chest, and exposed his mutilated shoulders, and the stumps of his once audacious arms. Thus far uncovering his shame, in that cruel plight they had abandoned him, leaving stark naked his in vain indignant chest to the defilements of the birds, which for untold ages had cast their foulness on his vanquished crest.

Not unworthy to be compared with that leaden Titan, wherewith the art of Marsy and the broad-flung pride of Bourbon enriched the enchanted gardens of Versailles;—and from whose still twisted mouth for sixty feet the waters yet upgush, in elemental rivalry with those Etna flames, of old asserted to be the malicious breath of the borne-down giant;—not unworthy to be compared with that leaden demi-god—piled with costly rocks, and with one bent wrenching knee protruding from the broken bronze;—not unworthy to be compared with that bold trophy of high art, this American Enceladus, wrought by the vigorous hand of Nature's self, it did go further than compare;—it did far surpass that fine figure molded by the inferior skill of man. Marsy gave arms to the eternally defenseless; but Nature, more truthful, performed an amputation, and left the impotent Titan without one serviceable ball-and-socket above the thigh.

Such was the wild scenery—the Mount of Titans, and the repulsed group of heaven-assaulters, with Enceladus in their midst shamefully recumbent at its base;—such was the wild scenery, which now to Pierre, in his strange vision, displaced the four blank walls, the desk, and camp-bed, and domineered upon his trance. But no longer petrified in all their ignominious attitudes, the herded Titans now sprung to their feet; flung themselves up the slope; and anew battered at the precipice's unresounding wall. Foremost among them all, he saw a moss-turbaned, armless giant, who despairing of any other mode of wreaking his immitigable hate, turned his vast trunk into a battering-ram, and hurled his own arched-out ribs again and yet again against the invulnerable steep.

"Enceladus! it is Enceladus!"—Pierre cried out in his sleep. That moment the phantom faced him; and Pierre saw Enceladus no more; but on the Titan's armless trunk, his own duplicate face and features magnifiedly gleamed upon him with prophetic discomfiture and woe. With trembling frame he started from his chair, and woke from that ideal horror to all his actual grief.

V

Nor did Pierre's random knowledge of the ancient fables fail still further to elucidate the vision which so strangely had supplied a tongue to muteness. But that elucidation was most repulsively fateful and foreboding; possibly because Pierre did not leap the final barrier of gloom; possibly because Pierre did not willfully wrest some final comfort from the fable; did not flog this stubborn rock as Moses his, and force even aridity itself to quench his painful thirst.

Thus smitten, the Mount of Titans seems to yield this following stream:—

Old Titan's self was the son of incestuous Cœlus and Terra, the son of incestuous Heaven and Earth. And Titan married his mother Terra, another and accumulatively incestuous match. And thereof Enceladus was one issue. So Enceladus was both the son and grandson of an incest; and even thus, there had been born from the organic blended heavenliness and earthliness of Pierre, another mixed, uncertain, heaven-aspiring, but still not wholly earth-emancipated mood; which again, by its terrestrial taint held down to its terrestrial mother, generated there the present doubly incestuous Enceladus within him; so that the present mood of Pierre—that reckless sky-assaulting mood of his, was nevertheless on one side the grandson of the sky. For it is according to eternal fitness, that the precipitated Titan should still seek to regain his paternal birthright even by fierce escalade. Wherefore whoso storms the sky gives best proof he came from thither! But whatso crawls contented in the moat before that crystal fort, shows it was born within that slime, and there forever will abide.

Recovered somewhat from the after-spell of this wild vision folded in his trance, Pierre composed his front as best he might, and straightway left his fatal closet. Concentrating all the remaining stuff in him, he resolved by an entire and violent change, and by a willful act against his own most habitual inclinations, to wrestle with the strange malady of his eyes, this new death-fiend of the trance, and this Inferno of his Titanic vision.

And now, just as he crossed the threshold of the closet, he writhingly strove to assume an expression intended to be not uncheerful—though how indeed his countenance at all looked, he could not tell; for dreading some insupportably dark revealments in his glass, he had of late wholly abstained from appealing to it—and in his mind he rapidly conned over, what indifferent, disguising, or light-hearted gamesome things he should say, when proposing to his companions the little design he cherished.

And even so, to grim Enceladus, the world the gods had chained for a ball to drag at his o'erfreighted feet;—even so that globe put forth a thousand flowers, whose fragile smiles disguised his ponderous load.

Book XXVI

A Walk: a Foreign Portrait: a Sail: and the End

COME, ISABEL, COME, LUCY; we have not had a single walk together yet. It is cold, but clear; and once out of the city, we shall find it sunny. Come: get ready now, and away for a stroll down to the wharf, and then for some of the steamers on the bay. No doubt, Lucy, you will find in the bay scenery some hints for that secret sketch you are so busily occupied with—ere real living sitters do come—and which you so devotedly work at, all alone and behind closed doors."

Upon this, Lucy's original look of pale-rippling pleasantness and surprise—evoked by Pierre's unforeseen proposition to give himself some relaxation—changed into one of infinite, mute, but unrenderable meaning, while her swimming eyes gently, yet all-bewildered, fell to the floor.

"It is finished, then," cried Isabel,—not unmindful of this by-scene, and passionately stepping forward so as to intercept Pierre's momentary rapt glance at the agitated Lucy,—"That vile book, it is finished!—Thank Heaven!"

"Not so," said Pierre; and, displacing all disguisements, a hectic unsummoned expression suddenly came to his face;—"but ere that vile book be finished, I must get on some other element than earth. I have sat on earth's saddle till I am weary; I must now vault over to the other saddle awhile. Oh, seems to me, there should be two ceaseless steeds for a bold man to ride,—the Land and the Sea; and like circus-men we should never dismount, but only be steadied and rested by leaping from one to the other, while still, side by side, they both race round the sun. I have been on the Land steed so long, oh I am dizzy!"

"Thou wilt never listen to me, Pierre," said Lucy lowly; "there is no need of this incessant straining. See, Isabel and I have both offered to be thy amanuenses;—not in mere copying, but in the original writing; I am sure that would greatly assist thee."

"Impossible! I fight a duel in which all seconds are forbid."

"Ah Pierre! Pierre!" cried Lucy, dropping the shawl in her hand, and gazing at him with unspeakable longings of some unfathomable emotion.

Namelessly glancing at Lucy, Isabel slid near to him, seized his hand and spoke.

"I would go blind for thee, Pierre; here, take out these eyes, and use them for glasses." So saying, she looked with a strange momentary haughtiness and defiance at Lucy.

A general half involuntary movement was now made, as if they were about to depart.

"Ye are ready; go ye before"—said Lucy meekly; "I will follow."

"Nay, one on each arm"—said Pierre—"come!"

As they passed through the low arched vestibule into the street, a cheek-burnt, gamesome sailor passing, exclaimed—"Steer small, my lad; 'tis a narrow strait thou art in!"

"What says he?"—said Lucy gently. "Yes, it is a narrow strait of a street indeed."

But Pierre felt a sudden tremble transferred to him from Isabel, who whispered something inarticulate in his ear.

Gaining one of the thoroughfares, they drew near to a conspicuous placard over a door, announcing that above stairs was a gallery of paintings, recently imported from Europe, and now on free exhibition preparatory to their sale by auction. Though this encounter had been entirely unforeseen by Pierre, yet yielding to the sudden impulse, he at once proposed their visiting the pictures. The girls assented, and they ascended the stairs.

In the anteroom, a catalogue was put into his hand. He paused to give one hurried, comprehensive glance at it. Among long columns of such names as Rubens, Raphael, Angelo, Domenichino, Da Vinci, all shamelessly prefaced with the words "undoubted," or "testified," Pierre met the following brief line:—"*No. 99. A stranger's head, by an unknown hand.*"

It seemed plain that the whole must be a collection of those wretched imported daubs, which with the incredible effrontery peculiar to some of the foreign picture-dealers in America, were christened by the loftiest names known to Art. But as the most mutilated torsoes of the perfections of antiquity are not unworthy the student's attention, neither are the most bungling modern incompletenesses: for both are torsoes; one of perished perfections in the past; the other, by anticipation, of yet unfulfilled perfections in the future. Still, as Pierre walked along by the thickly hung walls, and seemed to detect the infatuated vanity which must have prompted many of these utterly unknown artists in the attempted execution by feeble hand of vigorous themes; he could not repress the most melancholy foreboding concerning himself. All the walls of the world seemed thickly hung with the empty and impotent scope of pictures, grandly outlined, but miserably filled. The smaller and humbler pictures, representing little familiar things, were by far the best executed; but these, though touching him not unpleasingly, in one restricted sense, awoke no dormant majesties in his soul, and therefore, upon the whole, were contemptibly inadequate and unsatisfactory.

At last Pierre and Isabel came to that painting of which Pierre was capriciously in search—No. 99.

"My God! see! see!" cried Isabel, under strong excitement, "only my mirror has ever shown me that look before! See! see!"

By some mere hocus-pocus of chance, or subtly designing knavery, a real Italian gem of art had found its way into this most hybrid collection of impostures.

No one who has passed through the great galleries of Europe, unbewildered by their wonderful multitudinousness of surpassing excellence —a redundancy which neutralizes all discrimination or individualizing capacity in most ordinary minds—no calm, penetrative person can have victoriously run that painted gauntlet of the gods, without certain very special emotions, called forth by some one or more individual paintings, to which, however, both the catalogues and the criticisms of the greatest connoisseurs deny any all-transcending merit, at all answering to the effect thus casually produced. There is no time now to show fully how this is; suffice it, that in such instances, it is not the abstract excellence always, but often the accidental congeniality, which occasions this wonderful emotion. Still, the individual himself is apt to impute it to a different cause; hence, the headlong enthusiastic admiration of some one or two men for things not at all praised by—or at most, which are indifferent to—the rest of the world;—a matter so often considered inexplicable.

But in this Stranger's Head by the Unknown Hand, the abstract general excellence united with the all-surprising, accidental congeniality in producing an accumulated impression of power upon both Pierre and Isabel. Nor was the strangeness of this at all impaired by the apparent uninterestedness of Lucy concerning that very picture. Indeed, Lucy—who, owing to the occasional jolting of the crowd, had loosened her arm from Pierre's, and so, gradually, had gone on along the pictured hall in advance—Lucy had thus passed the strange painting, without the least special pause, and had now wandered round to the precisely opposite side of the hall; where, at this present time, she was standing motionless before a very tolerable copy (the only other good thing in the collection) of that sweetest, most touching, but most awful of all feminine heads—The Cenci of Guido. The wonderfulness of which head consists chiefly, perhaps, in a striking, suggested contrast, half-identical with, and half-analogous to, that almost supernatural one—sometimes visible in the maidens of tropical nations—namely, soft and light blue eyes, with an extremely fair complexion, vailed by funereally jetty hair. But with blue eyes and fair complexion, the Cenci's hair is golden—physically, therefore, all is in strict, natural keeping; which, nevertheless, still the more intensifies the suggested fanciful anomaly of so sweetly and seraphically *blonde* a being, being double-hooded, as it were, by the black crape of the two most horrible crimes (of one of which she is the object, and of the other the agent) possible to civilized humanity—incest and parricide.

Now, this Cenci and "the Stranger" were hung at a good elevation in one of the upper tiers; and, from the opposite walls, exactly faced each other; so that in secret they seemed pantomimically talking over and across the heads of the living spectators below.

With the aspect of the Cenci every one is familiar. "The Stranger" was a dark, comely, youthful man's head, portentously looking out of a dark, shaded ground, and ambiguously smiling. There was no discoverable drapery; the dark head, with its crisp, curly, jetty hair, seemed just disentangling itself from out of curtains and clouds. But to Isabel, in the eye and on the brow, were certain shadowy traces of her own unmistakable likeness; while to Pierre, this face was in part as the resurrection of the one he had burnt at the Inn. Not that the separate features were the same; but the pervading look of it, the subtler interior keeping of the entirety, was almost identical; still, for all this, there was an unequivocal aspect of foreignness, of Europeanism, about both the face itself and the general painting.

"Is it? Is it? Can it be?" whispered Isabel, intensely.

Now, Isabel knew nothing of the painting which Pierre had destroyed. But she solely referred to the living being who—under the designation of her father—had visited her at the cheerful house to which she had been removed during childhood from the large and unnamable one by the pleasant woman in the coach. Without doubt—though indeed she might not have been at all conscious of it in her own mystic mind—she must have somehow vaguely fancied, that this being had always through life worn the same aspect to every body else which he had to her, for so very brief an interval of his possible existence. Solely knowing him—or dreaming of him, it may have been—under that one aspect, she could not conceive of him under any other. Whether or not these considerations touching Isabel's ideas occurred to Pierre at this moment is very improbable. At any rate, he said nothing to her, either to deceive or undeceive, either to enlighten or obscure. For, indeed, he was too much riveted by his own far-interior emotions to analyze now the cotemporary ones of Isabel. So that there here came to pass a not unremarkable thing: for though both were intensely excited by one object, yet their two minds and memories were thereby directed to entirely different contemplations; while still each, for the time—however unreasonably—might have vaguely supposed the other occupied by one and the same contemplation. Pierre was thinking of the chair-portrait: Isabel, of the living face. Yet Isabel's fervid exclamations having reference to the living face, were now, as it were, mechanically responded to by Pierre, in syllables having reference to the chair-portrait. Nevertheless, so subtile and spontaneous was it all, that neither perhaps ever afterward discovered this contradiction; for, events whirled them so rapidly and peremptorily after this, that they had no time for those calm retrospective reveries indispensable perhaps to such a discovery.

"Is it? is it? can it be?" was the intense whisper of Isabel.

"No, it can not be, it is not," replied Pierre; "one of the wonderful coincidences, nothing more."

"Oh, by that word, Pierre, we but vainly seek to explain the inexplicable. Tell me: it is! it must be! it is wonderful!"

"Let us begone; and let us keep eternal silence," said Pierre, quickly; and, seeking Lucy, they abruptly left the place; as before, Pierre, seemingly unwilling to be accosted by any one he knew, or who knew his companions, unconsciously accelerating their steps while forced for a space to tread the thoroughfares.

ii

As they hurried on, Pierre was silent; but wild thoughts were hurrying and shouting in his heart. The most tremendous displacing and revolutionizing thoughts were upheaving in him, with reference to Isabel; nor—though at the time he was hardly conscious of such a thing—were these thoughts wholly unwelcome to him.

How did he know that Isabel was his sister? Setting aside Aunt Dorothea's nebulous legend, to which, in some shadowy points, here and there Isabel's still more nebulous story seemed to fit on,—though but uncertainly enough—and both of which thus blurredly conjoining narrations, regarded in the unscrupulous light of real naked reason, were any thing but legitimately conclusive; and setting aside his own dim reminiscences of his wandering father's death-bed; (for though, in one point of view, those reminiscences might have afforded some degree of presumption as to his father's having been the parent of an unacknowledged daughter, yet were they entirely inconclusive as to that presumed daughter's identity; and the grand point now with Pierre was, not the general question whether his father had had a daughter, but whether, assuming that he had had, *Isabel*, rather than any other living being, *was that daughter*;)—and setting aside all his own manifold and inter-enfolding mystic and transcendental persuasions,—originally born, as he now seemed to feel, purely of an intense procreative enthusiasm:—an enthusiasm no longer so all-potential with him as of yore; setting all these aside, and coming to the plain, palpable facts,—how did he *know* that Isabel was his sister? Nothing that he saw in her face could he remember as having seen in his father's. The chair-portrait, *that* was the entire sum and substance of all possible, rakable, downright presumptive evidence, which peculiarly appealed to his own separate self. Yet here was another portrait of a complete stranger—a European; a portrait imported from across the seas, and to be sold at public auction, which was just as strong an evidence as the other. Then, the original of this second portrait was as much the father of Isabel as the original of the chair-portrait. But perhaps there was no original at all to this second portrait; it might have been a pure fancy piece; to which conceit, indeed, the uncharacterizing style of the filling-up seemed to furnish no small testimony.

With such bewildering meditations as these in him, running up like clasping waves upon the strand of the most latent secrecies of his soul, and with both Isabel and Lucy bodily touching his sides as he walked; the feelings of Pierre were entirely untranslatable into any words that can be used.

Of late to Pierre, much more vividly than ever before, the whole story of Isabel had seemed an enigma, a mystery, an imaginative delirium; especially since he had got so deep into the inventional mysteries of his book. For he who is most practically and deeply conversant with mysticisms and mysteries; he who professionally deals in mysticisms and mysteries himself; often that man, more than any body else, is disposed to regard such things in others as very deceptively bejuggling; and likewise is apt to be rather materialistic in all his own merely personal notions (as in their practical lives, with priests of Eleusinian religions), and more than any other man, is often inclined, at the bottom of his soul, to be uncompromisingly skeptical on all novel visionary hypotheses of any kind. It is only the no-mystics, or the half-mystics, who, properly speaking, are credulous. So that in Pierre, was presented the apparent anomaly of a mind, which by becoming really profound in itself, grew skeptical of all tendered profundities; whereas, the contrary is generally supposed.

By some strange arts Isabel's wonderful story might have been, someway, and for some cause, forged for her, in her childhood, and craftily impressed upon her youthful mind; which so—like a slight mark in a young tree—had now enlargingly grown with her growth, till it had become this immense staring marvel. Tested by any thing real, practical, and reasonable, what less probable, for instance, than that fancied crossing of the sea in her childhood, when upon Pierre's subsequent questioning of her, she did not even know that the sea was salt.

iii

In the midst of all these mental confusions they arrived at the wharf; and selecting the most inviting of the various boats which lay about them in three or four adjacent ferry-slips, and one which was bound for a half-hour's sail across the wide beauty of that glorious bay; they soon found themselves afloat and in swift gliding motion.

They stood leaning on the rail of the guard, as the sharp craft darted out from among the lofty pine-forests of ships'-masts, and the tangled under-brush and cane-brakes of the dwarfed sticks of sloops and scows. Soon, the spires of stone on the land, blent with the masts of wood on the water; the crotch of the twin-rivers pressed the great wedged city almost out of sight. They swept by two little islets distant from the shore; they wholly curved away from the domes of free-stone and marble, and gained the great sublime dome of the bay's wide-open waters.

Small breeze had been felt in the pent city that day, but the fair breeze of naked nature now blew in their faces. The waves began to gather and roll; and just as they gained a point, where—still beyond—between high promontories of fortresses, the wide bay visibly sluiced into the Atlantic, Isabel convulsively grasped the arm of Pierre and convulsively spoke.

"I feel it! I feel it! It is! It is!"

"What feelest thou?—what is it?"

"The motion! the motion!"

"Dost thou not understand, Pierre?" said Lucy, eying with concern and wonder his pale, staring aspect—"The waves: it is the motion of the waves that Isabel speaks of. Look, they are rolling, direct from the sea now."

Again Pierre lapsed into a still stranger silence and revery.

It was impossible altogether to resist the force of this striking corroboration of by far the most surprising and improbable thing in the whole surprising and improbable story of Isabel. Well did he remember her vague reminiscence of the teetering sea, that did not slope exactly as the floors of the unknown, abandoned, old house among the French-like mountains.

While plunged in these mutually neutralizing thoughts of the strange picture and the last exclamations of Isabel, the boat arrived at its destination—a little hamlet on the beach, not very far from the great blue sluice-way into the ocean, which was now yet more distinctly visible than before.

"Don't let us stop here"—cried Isabel. "Look, let us go through there! Bell must go through there! See! see! out there upon the blue! yonder, yonder! far away—out, out!—far, far away, and away, and away, out there! where the two blues meet, and are nothing—Bell must go!"

"Why, Isabel," murmured Lucy, "that would be to go to far England or France; thou wouldst find but few friends in far France, Isabel."

"Friends in far France? And what friends have I here?—Art thou my friend? In thy secret heart dost *thou* wish me well? And for thee, Pierre, what am I but a vile clog to thee; dragging thee back from all thy felicity? Yes, I will go yonder—yonder; out there! I will, I will! Unhand me! Let me plunge!"

For an instant, Lucy looked incoherently from one to the other. But both she and Pierre now mechanically again seized Isabel's frantic arms, as they were thrown again over the outer rail of the boat. They dragged her back; they spoke to her; they soothed her; but though less vehement, Isabel still looked deeply distrustfully at Lucy, and deeply reproachfully at Pierre.

They did not leave the boat as intended; too glad were they all, when it unloosed from its fastenings, and turned about upon the backward trip.

Stepping to shore, Pierre once more hurried his companions through the unavoidable publicity of the thoroughfares; but less rapidly proceeded, soon as they gained the more secluded streets.

IV

Gaining the Apostles', and leaving his two companions to the privacy of their chambers, Pierre sat silent and intent by the stove in the dining-room for a time, and then was on the point of entering his closet from the corridor, when Delly, suddenly following him, said to him, that she had forgotten to mention it before, but he would find two letters in his room, which had been separately left at the door during the absence of the party.

He passed into the closet, and slowly shooting the bolt—which, for want of something better, happened to be an old blunted dagger—walked, with his cap yet unmoved, slowly up to the table, and beheld the letters. They were lying with their sealed sides up; one in either hand, he lifted them; and held them straight out sideways from him.

"I see not the writing; know not yet, by mine own eye, that they are meant for me; yet, in these hands I feel that I now hold the final poniards that shall stab me; and by stabbing me, make *me* too a most swift stabber in the recoil. Which point first?—this!"

He tore open the left-hand letter:—

"SIR:—You are a swindler. Upon the pretense of writing a popular novel for us, you have been receiving cash advances from us, while passing through our press the sheets of a blasphemous rhapsody, filched from the vile Atheists, Lucian and Voltaire. Our great press of publication has hitherto prevented our slightest inspection of our reader's proofs of your book. Send not another sheet to us. Our bill for printing thus far, and also for our cash advances, swindled out of us by you, is now in the hands of our lawyer, who is instructed to proceed with instant rigor.

(*Signed*) STEEL, FLINT & ASBESTOS."

He folded the left-hand letter, and put it beneath his left heel, and stood upon it so; and then opened the right-hand letter.

"Thou, Pierre Glendinning, art a villainous and perjured liar. It is the sole object of this letter imprintedly to convey the point blank lie to thee; that taken in at thy heart, it may be thence pulsed with thy blood, throughout thy system. We have let some interval pass inactive, to confirm and solidify our hate. Separately, and together, we brand thee, in thy every lung-cell, a liar;—liar, because that is the scornfullest and loathsomest title for a man; which in itself is the compend of all infamous things.

(*Signed*) GLENDINNING STANLY,
FREDERIC TARTAN."

He folded the right-hand letter, and put it beneath his right heel; then folding his two arms, stood upon both the letters.

"These are most small circumstances; but happening just now to me, become indices to all immensities. For now am I hate-shod! On these I will skate to my acquittal! No longer do I hold terms with aught. World's bread of life, and world's breath of honor, both are snatched from me; but I defy all world's bread and breath. Here I step out before the drawn-up worlds in widest space, and challenge one and all of them to battle! Oh, Glen! oh, Fred! most fraternally do I leap to your rib-crushing hugs! Oh, how I love ye two, that yet can make me lively hate, in a world which elsewise only merits stagnant scorn!—Now, then, where is this swindler's, this coiner's book? Here, on this vile counter, over which the coiner thought to pass it to the world, here will I nail it fast, for a detected cheat! And thus nailed fast now, do I spit upon it, and so get the start of the wise world's worst abuse of it! Now I go out to meet my fate, walking toward me in the street."

As with hat on, and Glen and Frederic's letter invisibly crumpled in his hand, he—as it were somnambulously—passed into the room of Isabel, she gave loose to a thin, long shriek, at his wondrous white and haggard plight; and then, without the power to stir toward him, sat petrified in her chair, as one embalmed and glazed with icy varnish.

He heeded her not, but passed straight on through both intervening rooms, and without a knock unpremeditatedly entered Lucy's chamber. He would have passed out of that, also, into the corridor, without one word; but something stayed him.

The marble girl sat before her easel; a small box of pointed charcoal, and some pencils by her side; her painter's wand held out against the frame; the charcoal-pencil suspended in two fingers, while with the same hand, holding a crust of bread, she was lightly brushing the portrait-paper, to efface some ill-considered stroke. The floor was scattered with the bread-crumbs and charcoal-dust; he looked behind the easel, and saw his own portrait, in the skeleton.

At the first glimpse of him, Lucy started not, nor stirred; but as if her own wand had there enchanted her, sat tranced.

"Dead embers of departed fires lie by thee, thou pale girl; with dead embers thou seekest to relume the flame of all extinguished love! Waste not so that bread; eat it—in bitterness!"

He turned, and entered the corridor, and then, with outstretched arms, paused between the two outer doors of Isabel and Lucy.

"For ye two, my most undiluted prayer is now, that from your here unseen and frozen chairs ye may never stir alive;—the fool of Truth, the fool of Virtue, the fool of Fate, now quits ye forever!"

As he now sped down the long winding passage, some one eagerly hailed him from a stair.

"What, what, my boy? where now in such a squally hurry? Hallo, I say!"

But without heeding him at all, Pierre drove on. Millthorpe looked anxiously and alarmedly after him a moment, then made a movement in pursuit, but paused again.

"There was ever a black vein in this Glendinning; and now that vein is swelled, as if it were just one peg above a tournequet drawn over-tight. I scarce durst dog him now; yet my heart misgives me that I should.—Shall I go to his rooms and ask what black thing this is that hath befallen him?—No; not yet;—might be thought officious—they say I'm given to that. I'll wait; something may turn up soon. I'll into the front street, and saunter some; and then—we'll see."

V

Pierre passed on to a remote quarter of the building, and abruptly entered the room of one of the Apostles whom he knew. There was no one in it. He hesitated an instant; then walked up to a book-case, with a chest of drawers in the lower part.

"Here I saw him put them:—this,—no—here—ay—we'll try this."

Wrenching open the locked drawer, a brace of pistols, a powder flask, a bullet-bag, and a round green box of percussion-caps lay before him.

"Ha! what wondrous tools Prometheus used, who knows? but more wondrous these, that in an instant, can unmake the topmost three-score-years-and-ten of all Prometheus' makings. Come: here's two tubes that'll outroar the thousand pipes of Harlem.—Is the music in 'em?—No?—Well then, here's powder for the shrill treble; and wadding for the tenor; and a lead bullet for the concluding bass! And,—and,—and,—ay; for the top-wadding, I'll send 'em back their lie, and plant it scorching in their brains!"

He tore off that part of Glen and Fred's letter, which more particularly gave the lie; and halving it, rammed it home upon the bullets.

He thrust a pistol into either breast of his coat; and taking the rearward passages, went down into the back street; directing his rapid steps toward the grand central thoroughfare of the city.

It was a cold, but clear, quiet, and slantingly sunny day; it was between four and five of the afternoon; that hour, when the great glaring avenue was most thronged with haughty-rolling carriages, and proud-rustling promenaders, both men and women. But these last were mostly confined to the one wide pavement to the West; the other pavement was well nigh deserted, save by porters, waiters, and parcel-carriers of the shops. On the west pave, up and down, for three long miles, two streams of glossy, shawled, or broadcloth life unceasingly brushed by each other, as long, resplendent, drooping trains of rival peacocks brush.

Mixing with neither of these, Pierre stalked midway between. From his wild and fatal aspect, one way the people took the wall, the other way they took the curb. Unentangledly Pierre threaded all their host, though in its inmost heart. Bent he was, on a straightforward, mathematical intent. His eyes were all about him as he went; especially he glanced over to the deserted pavement opposite; for that emptiness did not deceive him; he himself had often walked that side, the better to scan the pouring throng upon the other.

Just as he gained a large, open, triangular space, built round with the stateliest public erections;—the very proscenium of the town;—he saw Glen and Fred advancing, in the distance, on the other side. He continued on; and soon he saw them crossing over to him obliquely, so as to take him face-and-face. He continued on; when suddenly running ahead of Fred, who now chafingly stood still (because Fred would not make two, in the direct personal assault upon one) and shouting "Liar! Villain!" Glen leaped toward Pierre from front, and with such lightning-like ferocity, that the simultaneous blow of his cow-hide smote Pierre across the cheek, and left a half-livid and half-bloody brand.

For that one moment, the people fell back on all sides from them; and left them—momentarily recoiled from each other—in a ring of panics.

But clapping both hands to his two breasts, Pierre, on both sides shaking off the sudden white grasp of two rushing girls, tore out both pistols, and rushed headlong upon Glen.

"For thy one blow, take here two deaths! 'Tis speechless sweet to murder thee!"

Spatterings of his own kindred blood were upon the pavement; his own hand had extinguished his house in slaughtering the only unoutlawed human being by the name of Glendinning;—and Pierre was seized by a hundred contending hands.

vi

That sundown, Pierre stood solitary in a low dungeon of the city prison. The cumbersome stone ceiling almost rested on his brow; so that the long tiers of massive cell-galleries above seemed partly piled on him. His immortal, immovable, bleached cheek was dry; but the stone cheeks of the walls were trickling. The pent twilight of the contracted yard, coming through the barred arrow-slit, fell in dim bars upon the granite floor.

"Here, then, is the untimely, timely end;—Life's last chapter well stitched into the middle! Nor book, nor author of the book, hath any sequel, though each hath its last lettering!—It is ambiguous still. Had I been heartless now, disowned, and spurningly portioned off the girl at Saddle Meadows, then had I been happy through a long life on earth, and perchance through a long eternity in heaven! Now, 'tis merely hell in both worlds. Well, be it hell. I will mold a trumpet of the flames, and, with my breath of flame, breathe back my defiance! But give me first another body! I long and long to die, to be rid of this dishonored cheek. *Hung by the neck till thou be dead.*—Not if I forestall you, though!—Oh now to live is death, and now to die is life; now, to my soul, were a sword my midwife!—Hark! —the hangman?—who comes?"

"Thy wife and cousin—so they say;—hope they may be; they may stay till twelve;" wheezingly answered a turnkey, pushing the tottering girls into the cell, and locking the door upon them.

"Ye two pale ghosts, were this the other world, ye were not welcome. Away!—Good Angel and Bad Angel both!—For Pierre is neuter now!"

"Oh, ye stony roofs, and seven-fold stony skies!—not thou art the murderer, but thy sister hath murdered thee, my brother, oh my brother!"

At these wailed words from Isabel, Lucy shrunk up like a scroll, and noiselessly fell at the feet of Pierre.

He touched her heart.—"Dead!—Girl! wife or sister, saint or fiend!"—seizing Isabel in his grasp—"in thy breasts, life for infants lodgeth not, but death-milk for thee and me!—The drug!" and tearing her bosom loose, he seized the secret vial nesting there.

vii

At night the squat-framed, asthmatic turnkey tramped the dim-lit iron gallery before one of the long honey-combed rows of cells.

"Mighty still there, in that hole, them two mice I let in;—humph!"

Suddenly, at the further end of the gallery, he discerned a shadowy figure emerging from the archway there, and running on before an officer, and impetuously approaching where the turnkey stood.

"More relations coming. These wind-broken chaps are always in before the second death, seeing they always miss the first.—Humph! What a froth the fellow's in!—Wheezes worse than me!"

"Where is she?" cried Fred Tartan, fiercely, to him; "she's not at the murderer's rooms! I sought the sweet girl there, instant upon the blow; but the lone dumb thing I found there only wrung her speechless hands and pointed to the door;—both birds were flown! Where is she, turnkey? I've searched all lengths and breadths but this. Hath any angel swept adown and lighted in your granite hell?"

"Broken his wind, and broken loose, too, aint he?" wheezed the turnkey to the officer who now came up.

"This gentleman seeks a young lady, his sister, someway innocently connected with the prisoner last brought in. Have any females been here to see him?"

"Oh, ay,—two of 'em in there now;" jerking his stumped thumb behind him.

Fred darted toward the designated cell.

"Oh, easy, easy, young gentleman"—jingling at his huge bunch of keys—"easy, easy, till I get the picks—I'm housewife here.—Hallo, here comes another."

Hurrying through the same archway toward them, there now rapidly advanced a second impetuous figure, running on in advance of a second officer.

"Where is the cell?" demanded Millthorpe.

"He seeks an interview with the last prisoner," explained the second officer.

"Kill 'em both with one stone, then," wheezed the turnkey, gratingly throwing open the door of the cell. "There's his pretty parlor, gentlemen; step in. Reg'lar mouse-hole, arn't it?—Might hear a rabbit burrow on the world's t'other side;—are they all 'sleep?"

"I stumble!" cried Fred, from within; "Lucy! A light! a light!—Lucy!"

Lucy!" And he wildly groped about the cell, and blindly caught Millthorpe, who was also wildly groping.

"Blister me not! take off thy bloody touch!—Ho, ho, the light!—Lucy! Lucy!—she's fainted!"

Then both stumbled again, and fell from each other in the cell: and for a moment all seemed still, as though all breaths were held.

As the light was now thrust in, Fred was seen on the floor holding his sister in his arms; and Millthorpe kneeling by the side of Pierre, the unresponsive hand in his; while Isabel, feebly moving, reclined between, against the wall.

"Yes! Yes!—Dead! Dead! Dead!—without one visible wound—her sweet plumage hides it.—Thou hellish carrion, this is thy hellish work! Thy juggler's rifle brought down this heavenly bird! Oh, my God, my God! Thou scalpest me with this sight!"

"The dark vein's burst, and here's the deluge-wreck—all stranded here! Ah, Pierre! my old companion, Pierre;—school-mate—play-mate—friend! —Our sweet boy's walks within the woods!—Oh, I would have rallied thee, and banteringly warned thee from thy too moody ways, but thou wouldst never heed! What scornful innocence rests on thy lips, my friend! —Hand scorched with murderer's powder, yet how woman-soft!—By heaven, these fingers move!—one speechless clasp!—all's o'er!"

"All's o'er, and ye know him not!" came gasping from the wall; and from the fingers of Isabel dropped an empty vial—as it had been a run-out sand-glass—and shivered upon the floor; and her whole form sloped sideways, and she fell upon Pierre's heart, and her long hair ran over him, and arbored him in ebon vines.

FINIS

Editorial Appendix

HISTORICAL NOTE

By Leon Howard
and Hershel Parker

TEXTUAL RECORD

By the Editors

THE FIRST *of the two parts of this* APPENDIX *is a note on the composition, publication, reception, and later critical history of* Pierre, *contributed by Leon Howard (Section I) and Hershel Parker (Sections II–IV). The second, which records textual information, has been prepared by the editors, Harrison Hayford, Hershel Parker, and G. Thomas Tanselle. It consists of a note on the textual history of* Pierre *and on the editorial principles of this edition, followed by discussions of certain problematical readings, a list of emendations, and a report of line-end hyphenation. In verifying the information in the* APPENDIX, *the editors have been aided by the bibliographical associate, Richard Colles Johnson, and the editorial associate, Joel Myerson. Two contributing scholars for other volumes in the Edition, Watson G. Branch and Amy Puett, also worked closely with the editors and assisted in many ways. To insure uniform policy, the same three editors bear full responsibility for establishing the texts in all volumes of the Edition, except when other editors are specifically named (as in the case of certain writings edited from manuscript). Although most of the historical notes have been written by other contributing scholars, the task of writing textual commentary and of preparing the textual lists has been the joint responsibility of the three editors. Hershel Parker is the editor who coordinated the preparation of this volume.*

At appropriate points in the APPENDIX *acknowledgment is made for generous assistance received from scholars not directly connected with the Edition. The editors also wish to recognize the indispensable services of these members of their staff: Eugene Perchak, R. E. Steinhauer, and Justine Smith. The authors of the* HISTORICAL NOTE *are grateful to Mrs. David Bennett for securing information from the British Museum.*

Proofreading expenses for this volume have been in part supported by a grant from the National Endowment for the Humanities administered through the Center for Editions of American Authors of the Modern Language Association.

Historical Note

MELVILLE'S *Pierre; or, The Ambiguities* was written at Arrowhead, the author's new home near Pittsfield, Massachusetts, during the winter of 1851–52.[1] The seventh of the nine book-length prose works to be published during his lifetime, it was written under pressure by a man who had just invested an extra year in raising *Moby-Dick* from the level of a whaling narrative to that of an intensely dramatic and philosophical book, who had come to doubt his wisdom in doing so, and who knew that he had overdrawn his account with his publishers and needed a new book which would sell well enough to carry him over the next winter. Melville's circumstances were similar to those which followed the completion of *Mardi* and impelled him to write *Redburn* and *White-Jacket* as commercial jobs that would compensate him for a year's indulgence in writing the sort of book he wanted to write. But by now he had fairly well exhausted his best source of literary material—his experience as a merchant sailor, a whaleman, and a seaman in the U.S. Navy—and he

1. See the section on "Sources" at the end of this NOTE, where the documentation is explained. Quotations from Melville's letters follow the Davis-Gilman transcription (1960), retaining Melville's erratic spelling. All other documents are likewise quoted *literatim*.

needed to do something new. His mind was turning toward the feminine audience which formed the largest novel-reading public in his time, but he was to find himself unable to escape the conflict between a calculated desire to please the public and an inner compulsion to write as he pleased. The result was to be a book which was possibly the most carefully planned of all his novels but which exceeded its planned length and remains a puzzle to critics who attempt to fathom its intent and significance.

Melville apparently began planning some sort of new book as soon as *Moby-Dick* was off his hands and its proof sheets were on their way to England, for in September he wrote his neighbor, Sarah Morewood, that he would have to postpone reading two romances, Harriet Martineau's *The Hour and the Man* and Edward Bulwer-Lytton's *Zanoni*, which she had recently sent him. He would surmount the difficult fine print of the latter, he explained, but: "At present, however, the Fates have plunged me into certain silly thoughts and wayward speculations, which will prevent me, for a time, from falling into the reveries of these books—for a fine book is a sort of revery to us—is it not?—So I shall regard them as my Paradise in store. . . ." If these thoughts and speculations were about his own new book, it is hardly likely that they would have been about one in any way resembling *Moby-Dick*. Of it he warned Mrs. Morewood, in the same letter: "Dont you buy it—dont you read it, when it does come out, because it is by no means the sort of book for you. It is not a peice of fine feminine Spitalfields silk—but is of the horrible texture of a fabric that should be woven of ships' cables & hausers."

Work on his farm and the normal distractions accompanying the birth of his second son would have prevented serious composition until he finished getting in his winter's supply of wood in November. His thoughts, however, were in two directions. Hawthorne's understanding and appreciation of *Moby-Dick* had led him to think of doing something more in the same line: "So, now," he wrote his friend in November, "let us add Moby Dick to our blessing, and step from that. Leviathan is not the biggest fish;—I have heard of Krakens." But in his extant correspondence the first clear reference to *Pierre*, as a book rather than as a wayward speculation, occurs in a letter of January 8, 1852, when he wrote Sophia Hawthorne to express his amazement that she, a woman, should find any satisfaction in *Moby-Dick*. "My Dear Lady," he promised, "I shall not again send you a bowl of salt water. The next chalice I shall commend, will be a rural bowl of milk." He clearly had made a distinction in his own mind between the tastes of masculine and feminine readers and was planning, when he wrote

Mrs. Hawthorne (whatever he may have contemplated earlier), to address his seventh book to the latter.

By February he was sufficiently far along to offer his new work to his English publisher, Richard Bentley, with an estimate of its length. Melville's letter is lost, but Bentley's reply, on March 4, was discouraging. Because of the state of the copyright at the time and the poor sales of Melville's three earlier works he had published, Bentley offered publication only on the basis of half profits (rather than a lump sum in advance) and added a gratuitous observation that Melville's books were "produced in too rapid succession." Bentley's letter is important because it stirred Melville to make his only comments on record concerning the finished *Pierre*.

Melville deferred his response to Bentley's proposal until April 16, when he had proofs of the American edition to send with his letter, and then rejected it with a counteroffer of the book for £100 "to be drawn for by me at thirty days' sight, immediately upon my being apprised of your acquiescence" and with the added inducement that the finished work was 150 pages longer than he had expected it to be when he first wrote about it. He admitted a disadvantage in the rapid succession in which his books had been "published" (but not in the rapidity with which he had "produced" or written them) and said that this was one of "several accounts" which made him consider dissociating *Pierre* from his sea stories and think that "it might not prove unadvisable to publish this present book anonymously, or under an assumed name:—'*By a Vermonter*' say," or, he added in a footnote, "'*By Guy Winthrop*.'" But the crucial passage in his letter was a long and incoherent sentence in which he set forth the qualities he expected his publisher to find in *Pierre*:

> And more especially am I impelled to decline those overtures [Bentley's offer to publish at half profits] upon the ground that my new book possessing unquestionable novelty, as regards my former ones,—treating of utterly new scenes & characters;—and, as I beleive, very much more calculated for popularity than anything you have yet published of mine—being a regular romance, with a mysterious plot to it, & stirring passions at work, and withall, representing a new & elevated aspect of American life—all these considerations warrant me strongly in not closing with terms greatly inferior to those upon which our previous negotiations have proceeded.

The seriousness of this description of a book which neither Bentley nor any contemporary reviewer found "calculated for popularity" has taxed the credulity of many modern scholars.

Yet it is difficult to believe that Melville was either being facetious or trying to fool a shrewd and friendly publisher in a letter which has every appearance of being a rather desperate effort to sell a book that would be in Bentley's hands when he read the description. Some misunderstanding is involved in the considerable difference between the book itself and Melville's comments upon it. The misunderstanding could be either on the part of readers who find more in *Pierre* than Melville thought he had put there, or on the part of the author who was blinded to his actual performance by the limited nature of his first intentions. Such an alternative makes it unusually desirable to examine the book itself, its literary milieu, and its author's state of mind and habits of composition in an effort to infer from such textual and circumstantial evidence as much as possible about the way it came into being.

First it should be observed that there is no incompatibility between Melville's representation of the finished volume to Bentley and his allusion to it in the letter to Mrs. Hawthorne or to his possible plans for it in the letter to Mrs. Morewood. Nor are these references incompatible with the first eight "Books" of the published work. The opening sections might well have been inspired by the desire to do something quite different from *Moby-Dick*, to appeal to the taste of someone like Sarah Morewood, and to astonish such English readers as the *Blackwood's* reviewer of *Omoo* who found the name "Herman Melville" too romantic to be real and was "wholly incredulous" of "the existence of Uncle Gansevoort, of Gansevoort, Saratoga County." In these sections Melville presented "a new & elevated aspect of American life" based upon such verifiable material as his own family background and the existence of an old landed aristocracy.

The Glendinning estate of Saddle Meadows was a combination of his Uncle Herman's home in Gansevoort and his own Arrowhead, with perhaps some features of the neighboring Broadhall which had once belonged to relatives and was now owned by the Morewoods. The Mount of the Titans was Mt. Greylock, to whose "Most Excellent Majesty" the book was dedicated, and the Memnon Stone was a local curiosity. His descriptions of upstate New York landholdings were accurate, and his account of the person and deeds of Pierre's paternal grandfather was in large part a meticulous representation of the family traditions surrounding his own maternal grandfather, General Peter Gansevoort, a hero of the Revolution. The two oil portraits of Pierre's father closely resembled those of Melville's own father who, like Mr. Glendinning, had lived abroad and died when his son was entering his teens. There was a considerable amount of reality in the "new & elevated aspect of American life" he presented in the opening sections of his book.

Its style, however, was far removed from the language of real life. Melville had tried his hand at romantic fiction before, first in *Mardi* and again in the Harry Bolton sections of *Redburn,* and in each instance he lost the plausibility he achieved when using a persona and spinning a yarn. In *Pierre,* writing as an omniscient narrator, he was artificial to the point of absurdity in his handling of dialogue. But he was trying to represent the relationship of Pierre and Lucy as idyllic and was deliberately creating an artificial relationship between Pierre and Mrs. Glendinning. When he allowed Isabel to tell her story, in Books VI and VIII, he shifted to the high but less precious style of the "regular romance."

These eight Books would have constituted two-thirds of the volume he had in mind when he accepted an advance of $500 from the Harpers on February 20 and wrote Bentley the lost letter, before he added the unanticipated pages. They foreshadow a plot which would have some resemblance to that of *Romeo and Juliet* in its representation of fate-stricken lovers and the deplorable end of a too ardent and impetuous hero, and they develop fully a tragically romantic motivation in Pierre's longing for a sister he could "love, and protect, and fight for" (p. 7) and his obsession with the mysterious face of a girl who might have been such a sister. They also provide valuable hints concerning the literary milieu in which *Pierre* was conceived and begun, but little if any anticipation of the anti-romantic skepticism and questioning with which it was completed.

There can be little doubt, from what Melville said of his new book, that he conceived of it in terms of a novel or romance of the type currently popular; and Henry A. Murray, in his edition of *Pierre*, has noted numerous verbal echoes or incidental parallels between it and various English novels by Borrow, Carlyle, Dickens, Disraeli, Godwin, Scott, Mary Shelley, and Thackeray, and American works of fiction by Cooper, Hawthorne, Longfellow, and Poe. Other scholars have mentioned the possible influence of Mme de Staël's *Corinne* (which had been published by Bentley and obtained from him by Melville) and Sylvester Judd's *Margaret* (which Melville had borrowed from Evert A. Duyckinck in 1850), and contemporary reviewers related *Pierre* to the morbidity of Hawthorne's works, the excesses of Transcendentalism, the extravagances of Eugène Sue, the "indiscretions" of the younger Goethe, and to the stylistic qualities of Carlyle, Richter in a translation, Lamartine, and Martin Farquhar Tupper. This is too mixed a group to provide the clue to Melville's literary intention—especially when one adds to the writers of fiction the pervasive influence of such Romantics as Byron, Shelley, and De Quincey, of Shakespeare, and (especially in the later sections) of Dante. Yet they can be sorted out.

There are, for example, unmistakable Dickensian touches (and perhaps some from Thackeray) in the book, especially in the various letters addressed to Pierre, but not enough to suggest that Melville was consciously undertaking a novel in the manner of either of these writers. It was their humor rather than their realism which appealed to him. There is a great deal of Carlyle's *Bildungsroman* in the latter part of *Pierre,* as there had been in *Moby-Dick,* but none in the early part when Melville was firmly in control of his intentions. These appear to have been directed entirely toward the creation of what his friend Hawthorne had called a romance, which must conform to "the truth of the human heart" but not to "the probable and ordinary course of man's experience." His frequent insistence in the book itself that *Pierre* was not a "novel" is supported by his practice and by the nature of the books that seem most likely to have provided him with his literary models.

Melville's interest in the romance, like Hawthorne's, included an interest in the marvelous and mysterious, and he was attracted to the Gothic tale. But, despite the elements of mystery and madness in *Pierre,* he was not trying to write in the Gothic genre. His ambiguities were designed to do something more than thrill the reader. There are possible resemblances between his book and Judd's *Margaret* (which was subtitled "A Tale of the Real and the Ideal, Blight and Bloom") but nothing to suggest the unlikely hypothesis that he took it as a model. *Corinne,* on the other hand, was a book with a mysterious heroine like Isabel and a good angel named Lucy which had been a highly successful publishing venture by Bentley and might have attracted a calculating interest. The book that did most to transform his "silly thoughts and wayward speculations" into a definite plan for *Pierre,* however, may have been the one he postponed reading while first indulging in them—Edward Bulwer-Lytton's *Zanoni.*

On the surface the two books are quite dissimilar, for *Zanoni* is a romance of the eighteenth century with a Rosicrucian hero whose character and actions are far removed from the world of reality. But it has, as another major character, a young man who resembles Pierre in everything but determination. Glyndon in Bulwer's novel fears "the world's opinion," fears his "own impulses when most generous," fears his "own powers" when his "genius is most bold," and fears "that virtue is not eternal."

Glyndon almost misses his opportunity for initiation into Rosicrucian mysteries because he is unable to realize that "There are times in life when, from the imagination, and not reason, should wisdom come"; and after he fails his initiation he is refused a second chance because he cannot say, consistently, "Come what may, to Virtue I will cling." Pierre has none of these shortcomings. He passes all the tests that Glyndon fails, and the tragic consequences of his "success" may have reflected Melville's ironic reaction to Bulwer's belief in the superiority of the "Ideal" to the "Actual."

This possibility is supported by the existence of another character in Bulwer's novel who bears a close resemblance to *Pierre*'s Plotinus Plinlimmon and whose cold and distant wisdom is like that implied in the pamphlet on "Chronometricals and Horologicals" and is equally incomprehensible to a young man of ardent disposition. There are other parallels between the two works which reinforce the possibility that Bulwer had a strong suggestive effect upon Melville's imagination. Glyndon had the same kind of dreams that Pierre did and was comparably obsessed by a girl who played the guitar and died in a dungeon, and Bulwer used the device (although he was by no means unique in doing so) which Melville adopted of dividing his narrative into numerous "books" and subdividing it within them. But the most important of these parallels may be found in Bulwer's method of treating the conflict between the Ideal and the Actual. As contemporary reviewers realized and as Bulwer was to explain in a later edition, *Zanoni* was a book of "mysteries." It was not an allegory which personified "distinct and definite things" but a story in which "typical meanings" were concealed, and, as the author was to say, "the essence of type is mystery" which "none of us can elucidate" (not even the creating artist) although each "mystery" or "enigma" might lend itself to a variety of interpretations by different individuals. *Pierre* was announced on its title page as a book of "ambiguities," and like Bulwer, whether consciously or not, Melville took no responsibility for elucidating them.

It is impossible to prove that Melville's first thoughts and speculations were brought to a focus by Bulwer's novel. But the hypothesis that they were provides an explanation of the "Krakens" allusion in his November letter to Hawthorne and reconciles the inconsistency of that with his other early references to *Pierre*. For the moral values in Bulwer's book were consciously Christian. Zanoni lost the whole world but gained his own soul, and Glyndon, who could not remain steadfast in his pursuit of the Ideal, failed. Pierre, who was steadfast, lost everything. If Melville was consciously denying Bulwer's values, as he appears to have been, he would have been planning, from the beginning, a book more "wicked" than *Moby-Dick*.

Such a plan could have been concealed from all but the most perceptive of readers by a multitude of ambiguities and by the manner and style of a "regular romance" which was otherwise "calculated for popularity." What Melville could not anticipate—or, apparently, recognize afterward—was his own compulsion to "write precisely as I please" (p. 244) and the effect this would have on the tone of his book. This change in tone marked the opening of Book IX when he began to scold his hero in the manner of Carlyle. From this point on he was more openly satiric in the treatment of Pierre, more skeptical about his motives, and more inclined to dramatize him as a Romeo-turned-Hamlet. It must have been after adopting this new attitude that he wrote the extra 150 pages he mentioned to Bentley in April without indicating what may have inspired them. But the introduction of new and unforeseen material into an almost completed book was characteristic of Melville. There is positive evidence that he had done so in *Typee, Mardi,* and *Redburn;* he may have done so in *White-Jacket;* and he had recast *Moby-Dick* after one version of it was nearly finished. In *Pierre,* however, he seems to have been firmly determined to follow his original plot. The "unprecedented final resolution" of Pierre to give Isabel the Glendinning name by a pretense of marriage was what Melville might have considered an "original stroke" of invention in a romance after the fashion of Bulwer, for both the resolution and Mrs. Glendinning's reaction were prepared for in the opening sections of the book. The removal to the city, the appearance of Plinlimmon and his pamphlet, the arrival of Lucy, and the events leading up to a final catastrophe were also quite compatible with such a plan. The change was not in the plot of his romance but in his attitude toward it.

Most of the last half—and slightly more—of *Pierre* is clearly written by the author of *Moby-Dick,* rather than by a potential "Guy Winthrop," and it reflects Melville's intellectual and compositional experiences of the preceding year. Many of its discursive passages are in the style of Carlyle, just as Ishmael fell into Carlylese in the cetological chapters of the whaling novel. But Melville, as an omniscient narrator, is a more sardonic, less whimsical Carlyle than the narrator Ishmael had been. He dissociates himself from the thoughts he attributes to Pierre and becomes recurrently scornful of his hero's youthful naïveté, his pretensions, and his errors in judgment. Isabel becomes less the mysterious heroine of romance and more the simple-minded girl with a selfish need for emotional security. The proportion of discursive to narrative passages increases.

The influence of Shakespeare, which had been so strong in *Moby-Dick*, became increasingly dominant in the latter part of *Pierre*. It had existed from the beginning, of course, for Pierre was obviously imagined as a Romeo and there are a number of Shakespearean allusions in the first eight Books. But in the second portion the characters became almost parodies of Shakespearean counterparts. Pierre became a Hamlet, with a melancholy awareness of the lesson to be learned from his prototype but with an inability to act effectively. Lucy was an Ophelia until she recovered from her long swoon and her brother Fred took over the role of Laertes. Mrs. Glendinning became a vengeful Lady Macbeth or Volumnia who went insane and died. Glen Stanly played Tybalt to what was left of Pierre's Romeo, and Charlie Millthorpe was a Shakespearean clown until he disavowed his artificial pose and became Horatio at the end. Pierre's Lear-like wanderings in the storm and Melville's references to his Timonism and to a jealousy like Othello's all bear witness to the conscious Shakespearean quality in the author's later imagination.

Yet the Shakespearean quality of *Pierre* is different from that of *Moby-Dick*. It is more artificial and is at times cynical. It reflects the state of mind which led Melville to adopt the more sardonic attitudes of Carlyle for his direct commentary. And it was in this state of mind that Melville began his most serious inquiry into the genuineness of Pierre's perception of the Ideal and his motives for pursuing it.

There had been a vein of philosophical seriousness in *Pierre* from the beginning, for Melville could not entirely dismiss or submerge some of the intellectual problems with which he had been so intensely preoccupied in *Moby-Dick*. Though Pierre was handicapped as a hero by his unwillingness to "ruffle any domestic brow" (p. 20) and his tendency to shrink from "the infernal catacombs of thought" (p. 51), he was capable of sounding like Ahab when, challenged by Isabel's first claim to be his sister, he pictured the Truth as a "Black Knight" with his visor down and exclaimed: "I strike through thy helm, and will see thy face, be it Gorgon!" (p. 66). Pierre can easily be seen, whether or not Melville intended it so at the beginning, as an immature Ahab. He was trying to do the same thing—to see the Truth behind the mask of the actual—and Melville was still preoccupied with the problem of deciding whether a true vision would be of good or of evil.

When Melville became sardonic about his romance and serious about his preoccupation, however, he did not treat evil as abstract and absolute or the perception of it as a question of madness or sanity. Instead, it became an individual problem to be explored psychologically through a person's unconscious motives. In the first eight Books Pierre's emotions were explicitly pure: having longed for a sister and found one, he was mystified by her reluctance to permit a "brotherly embrace" but "the thought of any other caress, which took hold of any domesticness, was entirely vacant from his uncontaminated soul" (p. 142). As with many Romantic writers of the early nineteenth century (including Bulwer), Melville was willing to play with the idea of a potentially incestuous situation but not, in the early part of his book, with the possibility of incestuous passion. He had made Isabel attractive, beautiful rather than ugly, but was careful to explain that he gave her a "mere contingent" quality in order to represent Pierre as being made of human "clay" and not as completely "immaculate" (pp. 107–8).

The underlying nature of Isabel's attractiveness, however, is one of the major ambiguities of the book. Melville may have originally conceived it as that mysterious something identified in his day by the chemical term (adopted by Goethe for human relationships) "elective affinity," and he may have been trying to reassert this conception, near the end, when he had Isabel exclaim that after Lucy joined their menage "thou mayest perhaps elect,—elect!" But in the meantime he had certainly contrived two scenes to suggest a sexual relationship. The first described Isabel's reaction to Pierre's whispered proposal of a pretended marriage (p. 192):

> The girl moved not; was done with all her tremblings; leaned closer to him, with an inexpressible strangeness of an intense love, new and inexplicable. Over the face of Pierre there shot a terrible self-revelation; he imprinted repeated burning kisses upon her; pressed hard her hand; would not let go her sweet and awful passiveness.
>
> Then they changed; they coiled together, and entangledly stood mute.

The second described the evening of their third night in the city, when they had just settled into their new apartment and were holding hands in the twilight. "Say, are not thy torments now gone, my brother?" asks Isabel (p. 273).

> "But replaced by—by—by—Oh God, Isabel, unhand me!" cried Pierre, starting up. "Ye heavens, that have hidden yourselves in the black hood of the night, I call to ye! If to follow Virtue to her uttermost vista, where common souls never go; if by that I take hold on hell, and the uttermost virtue, after all, prove but a betraying pander to the monstrousest

> vice,—then close in and crush me, ye stony walls, and into one gulf let all things tumble together!"

Isabel finds this "incomprehensible raving" and throws her arms around him while he continues "in a steeled and quivering voice":

> "Call me brother no more! How knowest thou I am thy brother? Did thy mother tell thee? Did my father say so to me?—I am Pierre, and thou Isabel, wide brother and sister in the common humanity,—no more. For the rest, let the gods look after their own combustibles. If they have put powder-casks in me—let them look to it! let them look to it! Ah! now I catch glimpses, and seem to half-see, somehow, that the uttermost ideal of moral perfection in man is wide of the mark. The demigods trample on trash, and Virtue and Vice are trash! Isabel, I will write such things—I will gospelize the world anew, and show them deeper secrets than the Apocalypse!—I will write it, I will write it!"

Melville attributed to Isabel an instinctive understanding of Pierre's apparent lunacy and—after another embrace following Pierre's question "How can one sin in a dream?" (p. 274) and another denial of brotherhood—closed the scene with them sitting hushed in the darkness.

The emotional implication of these scenes is clear. But Melville was extremely careful to provide no evidence that these "stirring passions" were ever consummated. They may have been sublimated into the "blasphemous rhapsody, filched from the vile Atheists, Lucian and Voltaire," which Pierre's publishers found in his book (p. 356). On the other hand, by giving Pierre and Isabel a privacy which he explicitly denied Pierre and Lucy, he was equally careful to avoid a denial of their physical intimacy. Whether Pierre remained pure in body is ambiguous to the end. That he was not pure in heart, in the last half of the work, is abundantly clear. In his letter to Bentley, Melville was trying to be persuasive about one—but only one—of the possible interpretations of his ambiguous romance.

The relevance of Melville's changed attitude toward his romance may be found in his treatment of Pierre as an author. This is the section most probably responsible for the greatest number of his unforeseen pages. It was always difficult if not impossible for him to write a book unrelated to his own experiences, either in the past or at the time of writing, and his representation of Pierre's effort to support his menage by authorship is related both to his earlier literary activities and to what he was doing or rebelling against doing at the time.

Melville's first treatment of the subject (in Books XVII and XVIII) was an interpolation into the narrative and was introduced as such. It seems to have begun with a delayed petulant reaction against parts of his friend Evert A. Duyckinck's review of *Moby-Dick* in the *Literary World* and may have been composed at about the time (Valentine's Day, 1852) he abruptly canceled his subscription to that journal. For the title of Book XVII, "Young America in Literature," has an unmistakable reference to the "Young America" movement in which Duyckinck was an active participant and was a superficial satire upon the willingness of a literary clique to admire anything providing it was trivial. Whether the satire has the serious political implications which have been attributed to it may be doubtful, but Melville was certainly irritated with his old friend and characterized him as the "chief mate" of the "Captain Kidd Monthly" when he parodied his refusal of Duyckinck's request of the year before to have his daguerreotype taken for *Holden's Dollar Magazine*. His reconsideration of Pierre as a juvenile author, in Book XVIII, was in the same tone but more serious because it related Pierre to the young Melville, who, having "no profession, no trade," turned to writing as a means of support. "For what else could he do?" (p. 260) but become "a poor be-inked galley-slave, toiling with the heavy oar of a quill."

In the section on authorship (which was continued in Books XXI, XXII, and XXV) thoughts such as had appeared the year before in his letters to Hawthorne provided him with material. The Melville who dreaded going down to posterity as a "man who lived among the cannibals" reappeared in his reflections upon very young writers who were "chiefly indebted to some rich and peculiar experience in life" (p. 259) for their reputed originality. The sacrifice of a robust body to a soul robust for writing (p. 261) was Melville's sacrifice. "Swayed to universality of thought by the widely-explosive mental tendencies of the profound events which had lately befallen him" (p. 283), Pierre was not unlike the author of the revised version of *Moby-Dick*, who realized, as Pierre did not (p. 284), that great works should not be imitated but "be federated in the fancy" before they could prove "an exhilarative and provocative to him." Pierre had "not as yet procured for himself that enchanter's wand of the soul" which could touch "the humblest experiences in one's life" and produce "endless significancies" (p. 284), but he was to unfold and learn that the secret of the pyramid was an empty sarcophagus, realize the futility of trying to earn a living by telling the Truth, and present the world with only a "bungled" version of the "infinitely better" book on his "own private shelf" (p. 304).

In a more sardonic tone, Melville presented Pierre at work in a grotesque parody of his own working habits as he had described them in a letter to Duyckinck in December, 1850. Shut in the strict privacy of his own room, for long uninterrupted hours, Pierre forces himself to severe self-discipline despite the eyestrain he shared with his creator. "Who shall tell all the thoughts and feelings of Pierre in that desolate and shivering room, when at last the idea obtruded, that the wiser and the profounder he should grow, the more and the more he lessened the chances for bread" (p. 305). Melville had revealed his own thoughts in a letter to Hawthorne the previous June, while writing *Moby-Dick* under similar circumstances, and he was pushing himself to even greater extremes of effort with *Pierre*. Sarah Morewood had written George Duyckinck on December 28 that he was so engaged on his new work "as frequently not to leave his room till quite dark in the evening—when he for the first time during the whole day partakes of solid food." This was the routine he attributed to Pierre, and he also attributed to his hero the sort of morbid excitement which Mrs. Morewood feared might injure his health as well as the recluse life which she told him made his city friends "think that he was slightly insane." He had told Mrs. Morewood that he had long ago come to the same conclusion himself and amplified it in his book when he said of Pierre, in Carlylese (p. 302): "Oh, I hear the leap of the Texan Camanche, as at this moment he goes crashing like a wild deer through the green underbrush; I hear his glorious whoop of savage and untamable health; and then I look in at Pierre. If physical, practical unreason make the savage, which is he? Civilization, Philosophy, Ideal Virtue! behold your victim!"

Melville's serious comments upon Pierre as an author, in fact, are so relevant to his own situation that one is tempted to look in them for some oblique indication of unknown facts related to *Pierre*'s composition. Surely the alternative he suggested for the lessened "chances for bread" implies that he had second thoughts about the wisdom of the new tack he had taken in Book IX: "could he now hurl his deep book out of the window, and fall to on some shallow nothing of a novel, composable in a month at the longest, then could he reasonably hope for both appreciation and cash" (p. 305). But, as he had said to Hawthorne of *Moby-Dick,* what he was most moved to write was banned in the marketplace, and altogether to write "the *other* way" he could not. He faced this fact again in *Pierre*: "But the devouring profundities, now opened up in him, consume all his vigor; would he, he could not now be entertainingly and profitably shallow in some pellucid and merry romance" (p. 305).

There is no evidence that Melville himself had planned to be pellucid or merry in his own romance. Ambiguities and tragic implications were in *Pierre* from the beginning. But the most "devouring" profundities which opened up to him while writing appear to have been psychological. He was certainly exploring his own impulses—his compulsions and his doubts—as a writer, and his efforts to descend into "the cavern of man" and discover the secret of Pierre's impulses toward Isabel may also have been introspective. However this may be and whatever he may have planned, he managed to make of *Pierre* a book which, in its understanding of human nature, was more profound than any he had yet written.

The likelihood that Melville made a number of allusions, within *Pierre*, to his problems in writing the book suggests a possibility that he might also have alluded, in its concluding pages, to his problems with regard to publishing it. He had allowed Pierre to start sending his masterpiece—as he himself had sent *Moby-Dick*—through the press before the book was finished, and he attributed to Pierre's publishers a letter of denunciation when they got around to reading it. Could he have followed the same procedure with *Pierre* and received an unhappy communication from his own publishers? The evidence is against such a speculation. His brother Allan had signed, on Herman's behalf, a contract with the Harpers on February 20, 1852, providing for the publication of a book of "about 360 pages" entitled "Pierre or the Ambiguities," which would be sold for $1.00 a copy and pay the author 20 cents per copy royalty after the proceeds of the first 1,190 copies were used "to liquidate the cost of the stereotype plates and of the copies usually given to editors." The published book actually contained 495 pages of text, sold for $1.25 in muslin and $1.00 in paper, and provided Melville with a royalty of 25 cents per copy. Although the contract provided for an increase or decrease in the number of copies required to pay the cost of stereotyping if the book was not of the estimated length, and although a large number of copies (150) were given away, the publishers only claimed the first 1,190 for costs. It was probably a just claim in view of the increased retail price, but, within the terms of the contract, they could have claimed the proceeds from 400 more and probably would have done so if they had been unhappy about the manuscript or antagonistic toward its author.

The book was finished and in type by the middle of April, and the Harpers provided Melville with the proof sheets which he sent to Bentley on April 16 before it was stereotyped. Bentley's response, despite Melville's awkward attempt at salesmanship in the accompanying letter, was a polite version of the reaction Melville had already attributed to Pierre's publishers. Although Bentley was still willing to honor his original offer to publish the book on the basis of half profits and no advance, as he indicated in a letter of May 5, he would do so only on condition that he be allowed to "make or have made by a judicious literary friend such alterations as are absolutely necessary to 'Pierre' being properly appreciated" in England. Bentley's objection was apparently to Melville's unrestrained imagination and to a style incomprehensible to "the great mass of readers" as well as to the fact that he had already "offended the feelings of many sensitive readers." Melville presumably did not accede to the conditions, and was probably offended by Bentley's blunt criticisms. There was apparently no further correspondence between them.

Although Bentley had suggested that perhaps "somebody ignorant of the absolute failure of your former works might be tempted to make a trifling advance on the chance" of the success of *Pierre*, it is not known whether Melville approached any other publisher in England. The only reason for supposing he might have done so is that the Harpers, who had contracted to defer publication until an English edition appeared or for a maximum period of three months after the delivery of proof, actually waited two extra weeks before bringing the book out around the end of July. The only English issue was in the form of American sheets, bound and published in November under the imprint of the Harpers' London agent, Sampson, Low, Son, and Co.

II

Harper's advertised *Pierre* in some New York City papers and gave away 150 review copies, twenty-five more than usual, but only two dozen notices have been found, some of them fiercely hostile. Judging only by financial standards, *Pierre* was a disaster for Melville. Of the 2,310 copies printed, the Harper distribution system and Melville's name carried off 1,423 by March 21, 1853—a figure which includes whatever sets of the American sheets Sampson Low bought for sale in England. Since by terms of the cautious Harper contract Melville was not to receive payment for the first 1,190 copies, his royalty (25 cents each on the 233 copies sold above that number) amounted only to $58.25. Because of the $500 advanced him on February 20, 1852, his account, even with credit from his other works, showed him owing his publishers $298.71. Sales continued to be so slow that a new printing would not have been required for many years if the

Harper fire in December, 1853, had not destroyed 494 copies; as a result, a second printing (of 260 copies, as can be inferred from the records) was made in 1855. Thirty-two years later Melville's last Harper account recorded 79 copies still on hand; judging from these records, *Pierre* was probably his only book, apart from *Battle-Pieces* (and perhaps *Mardi*), to remain in print throughout his lifetime.

Melville's refusal to allow Bentley to publish an expurgated edition had lost *Pierre* at one stroke the chance to be widely reviewed in England and the chance to be sold to the English circulating libraries in the customary three-decker form. Sampson Low sent out a few review copies and listed the book in at least one advertisement, but the only English review known is the contemptuous one in the *Athenæum* (November 20, 1852). The lack of British reviews makes the reception of *Pierre* fragmentary, for the most intelligent reviews of Melville's earlier books had usually been British.

Pierre had no chance to be thoughtfully and impartially reviewed in the United States, for lurid rumors about it swept through the New York publishing clique, probably even before review copies were distributed. The writer for the New York *Herald* on July 29, 1852, had evidently not seen the book:

> In fiction, Herman Melville has a new book, "Pierre or the Ambiguities," in which it is understood that he has dressed up and exhibited in Berkshire, where he is living, some of the ancient and most repulsive inventions of the George Walker and Anne Radcliffe sort—desperate passion at first sight, for a young woman who turns out to be the hero's sister, &c., &c., &c. It is conceded that Mr. Melville has written himself out. The book is advertised by the Harpers.

Prepublication gossip must have influenced some of the metropolitan reviews, even while the reviews stimulated some aghast news items. On the first page, where it never reviewed books, the Philadelphia *Public Ledger* (August 11) offered "THE PLOT OF A NEW AMERICAN WORK," as drawn from the outraged review in the Boston *Post* (August 4). The *Ledger* reprinted the *Post*'s judgment that anyone who bought the book would be "cheating himself of his money." Under the stark heading "HERMAN MELVILLE CRAZY" the New York *Day Book* (September 7) used a quotation about *Pierre* from a hard-to-please friend ("it appeared to be composed of the ravings and reveries of a madman") as the lead-in to the report of a newsworthy rumor:[2]

2. It is uncertain just how many and widespread were such journalistic items as these previously unnoticed *Herald* and *Day Book* squibs.

> We were somewhat startled at the remark; but still more at learning, a few days after, that Melville was really supposed to be deranged, and that his friends were taking measures to place him under treatment. We hope one of the earliest precautions will be to keep him stringently secluded from pen and ink.

Less slanderous but perhaps as damning was the straight-faced account of a "FATAL OCCURRENCE" in a comic weekly, the New York *Lantern* (October 2), about "an intelligent young man" who was seen entering the store of Stringer and Townsend to deliberately purchase a copy of Melville's latest work: "He has, of course, not since been heard of." Such news items and reviews that made *Pierre* something between a literary laughing-stock and an outrage to public morality were often explicitly worded so as to discourage it from becoming a *succès de scandale*.

The six longest American reviews denounced *Pierre* in terms excessive even in the journalism of that day. They were evidently written mainly out of genuine disgust with the book, not on the basis of metropolitan gossip, though personal animosity toward Melville himself or his earlier works tinged all but one of them.[3] The Boston *Post* declared that the "amount of utter trash" in *Pierre* was "almost infinite—trash of conception, execution, dialogue and sentiment." The New York *Albion* (August 21) pronounced it "a dead failure, seeing that neither in design or execution does it merit praise," and a "crazy rigmarole" by which Melville had periled his literary standing. In the *Literary World* (August 21) the Duyckincks branded it "a literary mare's nest," "a mystic romance, in

3. Charles Gordon Greene, the editor of the Boston *Post*, knew members of Melville's family, and if he did not write the reviews himself he at least had lent his columns to direct scoldings for Melville's abuse of his talent in fictions like *Mardi* and *Moby-Dick*. The exasperation in the *Post*'s review of *Pierre* was cumulative. The same is true of the *Albion*, in a much more temperate way, and of the *Southern Literary Messenger*. Whatever else it was, the review in the Duyckinck brothers' *Literary World* was a private act of self-justification and a personal reproof to Melville. (Since Evert A. and George L. Duyckinck were co-editors, the review is here attributed to both. Evert is the more likely writer, but they must have shared responsibility for publishing an essay so certain to grieve their estranged friend.) Hugh W. Hetherington, who made tentative identifications of several reviewers of *Pierre*, has suggested that the author of the essay in the *American Whig Review* was G. W. Peck, who wrote that magazine's prurient attack on *Omoo*. Peck or not, the reviewer carried forward an *ad hominem* attack on Melville's vanity that had been launched in the reviews of *Mardi* in the *Southern Literary Messenger* (May, 1849) and the *Whig Review* itself (September, 1849). Two uninfluential reviews were laudatory precisely because of the writers' personal knowledge of the Melvilles and pride in Melville as a local talent: one in the Lansingburgh *Gazette* (August 3) and one in the Albany *Argus* (August 10).

which are conjured up unreal nightmare-conceptions, a confused phantasmagoria of distorted fancies and conceits, ghostly abstractions, and fitful shadows." The Richmond *Southern Literary Messenger* (September) advised that "if one does not desire to look at virtue and religion with the eye of Mephistopheles, or, at least, through a haze of *ambiguous* meaning, in which they may readily be taken for their opposites, he had better leave 'Pierre or the Ambiguities' unbought on the shelves of the bookseller." "Ambiguities, indeed!" said the New York *Herald* (September 18):

> One long brain-muddling, soul-bewildering ambiguity (to borrow Mr. Melville's style), like Melchisedeck, without beginning or end—a labyrinth without a clue—an Irish bog without so much as a Jack o' th'-lantern to guide the wanderer's footsteps—the dream of a distempered stomach, disordered by a hasty supper on half-cooked pork chops.

The New York *American Whig Review* (November) began by calling it "A bad book! Affected in dialect, unnatural in conception, repulsive in plot, and inartistic in construction." The motivations of the reviewers in the *Albion*, the *Southern Literary Messenger*, and the *Whig Review* are somewhat clouded by the perceptible influence of the *Post* (either directly or through the September 4 reprinting in the Boston *Littell's Living Age)* or the *Literary World*. Of the long reviews only the one in the *Herald* seems to contain no *ad hominem* elements in its attack, yet the writers of all six could honestly have agreed with the purpose of novel-reading later defined by the *Athenæum:*

> We take up novels to be amused—not bewildered,—in search of pleasure for the mind—not in pursuit of cloudy metaphysics; and it is no refreshment after the daily toils and troubles of life, for a reader to be soused into a torrent rhapsody uttered in defiance of taste and sense.

Such literary predilections, along with varied personal biases, kept all the authors of the longer reviews from examining *Pierre* seriously as a psychological novel.

By October two Philadelphia magazines, *Godey's* and *Graham's*, were saying that *Pierre* was, as the latter put it, "generally considered a failure," but in fact some of the shorter reviews were not uniformly hostile. Half a dozen were perfunctory notices a sentence or two long, but the eight or ten paragraph-length reviews were more thoughtful and judicious than their brevity would suggest. The ambivalent analysis in *Graham's*, especially, shows more awareness of what Melville was attempting than anything in the longer and more conspicuous reviews:

> None of Melville's novels equals the present in force and subtlety of thinking and unity of purpose. Many of the scenes are wrought out with great splendor and vigor, and a capacity is evinced of holding with a firm grasp, and describing with a masterly distinctness, some of the most evanescent phenomena of morbid emotions. But the spirit pervading the whole book is intolerably unhealthy, and the most friendly reader is obliged at the end to protest against such a provoking perversion of talent and waste of power.

The few such attempts to comprehend *Pierre* were submerged in the foul wash of publishing gossip, old literary feuds, new personal attacks, and morally and aesthetically outraged diatribes.

In all the reviews, long or short, the most common complaint was that, as the Washington *National Era* (August 19) said, the momentary reminders of "Typee, Omoo, &c." were "speedily swallowed up in the slough of metaphysical speculation, which constitutes the largest portion of the work." The reviewer in the *Albion* mentioned his favorable notice of "that bold, original work 'Moby-Dick,'" and called for "a fresh romance of the Ocean." He would have settled for something rather less ambitious than *Moby-Dick*: "Peter Simple is worth a ship-load of your Peter the Ambiguous." In their letters and diaries the Duyckincks had always regarded Melville more as a sailor-author than a genuine literary man, and in the *Literary World* they complained that "the substantial author of 'Omoo' and 'Typee,' the jovial and hearty narrator of the traveller's tale of incident and adventure," had been transformed to a specter of himself in *Pierre*. "Is Polynesia used up?" asked the *Herald*: "Is there not a solitary whale left, whose cetaceous biography might have added another stone to the monumental fame of the author of Moby-Dick?" *Godey's* hoped "the severity of the critical notices" would persuade Melville of his error in leaving "his native element, the ocean, and his original business of harpooning whales, for the mysteries and 'ambiguities' of metaphysics, love and romance." In a virulent personal attack, the Charleston *Southern Quarterly Review* (October) decided that Melville had probably "gone 'clean daft'" to follow clever books "by such a farrago as this of 'Pierre.'" The *Whig Review* speculated that *Pierre* was the sad result of Melville's having come to fancy himself a genius and offered this concluding advice:

> Let him continue, then, if he must write, his pleasant sea and island tales. We will be always happy to hear Mr. Melville discourse about savages, but we must protest against any more Absurdities, misnamed "Ambiguities."

Only the loyal Lansingburgh *Gazette* was rash enough to speculate as to whether Melville might possibly "find more admirers ashore than afloat."

To forsake the sea was bad enough, but it struck reviewers as far worse to imitate non-nautical fiction which was inartistic, unwholesome, foreign, or all three. The *Albion* felt that Melville had thrown away a great dramatic opportunity by relying on a Gallic model in Pierre's pretended marriage:

> A clash and a catastrophe are foreseen at the moment. Would that Mr. Melville had hit upon a less Frenchified mode of carrying us through the one, and bringing about the other! What fatality could have tempted him to call upon the spirit of Eugène Sue, to help him in such extreme emergency!

The rest of the book reminded the reviewer of "a Porte St. Martin tragedy," overlaid with the additional horror of incest. The *Herald* deplored that Melville had become a "copyist" of the worst features of Carlyle:

> No book was ever such a compendium of Carlyle's faults, with so few of his redeeming qualities, as this Pierre. We have the same German English—the same transcendental flights of fancy—the same abrupt starts—the same incoherent ravings, and unearthly visions. . . . Herds of pretenders to literary fame have ranged themselves under the banner of the Edinburgh reviewer, and, fancying they were establishing a Carlyle-ist school, have borrowed their master's hump, without stealing a single ray from the flashing of his eye, or a single tone from the harmony of his tongue. Sorry, indeed, are we to class Mr. Melville among these. Could he but sound the depths of his own soul, he would discover pearls of matchless price, that 'twere a sin and a shame to set in pinchbeck finery. Let him but study the classic writers of his own language—dissect their system—brood over their plain, honest, Saxon style—not more French than German—the search would soon convince him that he might still be attractive, though clad in his homely mother tongue. *Soyons de notre pays,* says the poet-philosopher of Passy, it will satisfy our wants, without borrowing tinsel imagery of a Lamartine, or the obscure mysticism of a Goethe or a Kant.

Quoting Isabel's speech to Pierre when he "entreats her not to demur to Lucy's living with them" (p. 324.25–29), the *Herald* laid its particular faults not "to the deleterious influence of deep, untempered draughts of Carlyle" but to the influence of "a man who has done no good to our literature—Martin Farquhar Tupper." *Graham's* decided that Melville had seemingly attempted to combine in *Pierre* "the peculiarities of Poe and Hawthorne," and had succeeded in producing "nothing but a powerfully unpleasant caricature of morbid thought and passion." The *Whig Review* thought the style was "disfigured by every paltry affectation of the worst German school," and suspected the malign influence of Jean Paul Richter. The Toronto *Anglo-American* (September) and the London *Athenæum* also discerned German influences, the latter seeing "nothing either American or original in its pages" and calling it "one of the most diffuse doses of transcendentalism offered for a long time to the public." After the reviews had stopped, a Methodist paper, the New York *National Magazine* (January, 1853), moved from a discussion of Hawthorne's "morbid propensity for morbid characters" to generalize that a "strong predilection for this sort of writing seems to be developing itself in our national literature." A prime example was "the late miserable abortion of Melville."

Concerned as the reviewers were to define *Pierre* as an anomaly in Melville's career and to associate it with undesirable models, they also judged it more particularly as a work of fiction. Their comments, which dealt most often with the plot, the characterizations, and the style, reveal something about *Pierre* and a great deal about the standards of naturalness by which it was weighed.

Rather long and more or less sarcastic plot summaries were offered by the *Post*, the *Albion*, the *Literary World* (from which the New York *Evening Mirror* took its "outline" of the book on August 27), the *Southern Literary Messenger*, the *Herald*, and the *Whig Review*. Many of the comments were moralistic, like the *Post*'s declaration that the plot itself ("this string of nonsense") was bad enough without "the nonsense that is strung upon it, in the way of crazy sentiment and exaggerated passion" or the *Whig Review*'s claim that the plot was "repulsive, unnatural and indecent." Still, a few strictures were based only on literary criteria. The *Albion* remarked briefly on Melville's over-obvious manipulation of plot for the sake of advancing his hero's quandary:

> The author (and here is our first serious quarrel with him) drags in a bit of episodical and gratuitous seduction, in order that any such vague idea in Pierre's mind [i.e., any idea that Mrs. Glendinning "would acknowledge poor Isabel"] may be quietly knocked on the head. Delly Ulver, a daughter of the farmer with whom Isabel has been serving, is abominably made to have a little convenient mishap.

Less specifically, the *Literary World* allowed that Melville "may have constructed his story upon some new theory of art to a knowledge of which we have not yet transcended," but pronounced that he had not constructed it according to the "established principles," since true art grows out of truth and nature. In an apparent echo, the *Southern Literary Messenger* also condemned "the absurdity of the principle" upon which the plot was constructed:

> The truth is, Mr. Melville's theory is wrong. It should be the object of fiction to delineate life and character either as it is around us, or as it ought to be. Now, Pierre never did exist, and it is very certain that he never ought to exist. Consequently, in the production of Pierre, Mr. Melville has deviated from the legitimate line of the novelist.

The *Whig Review* speculated about Melville's failure to plan the book fully before writing it:

> Just in this part of the book it comes out suddenly that Pierre is an author, a fact not even once hinted at in the preceding pages. . . . All this is told in a manner that proves it very clearly to be nothing more than an afterthought of Mr. Melville's, and not contemplated in the original plan of the book, that is, if it ever had a plan.

The *Athenæum* also supposed that when Melville "sat down to compose it" he "evidently had not determined what he was going to write about"; in consequence, the plot was "amongst the inexplicable 'ambiguities' of the book."

The characterizations in *Pierre* were regularly condemned, though some of the comments showed that Melville had partly succeeded in copying at least one novelistic stereotype. The characters were called "false to nature" (the *Post*), "exceedingly unnatural and bearing but little resemblance to living realities" (the Boston *Daily Traveller*, August 17), and "absurdly paradoxical and greatly overdrawn" (the *National Era*). The *Albion* saw Lucy Tartan as a typical romantic heroine "not differing much from some scores of Lucies in your book acquaintance, if it be extensive," and the *Literary World* and the *Southern Literary Messenger* said almost the same thing. Distressed as he was by the unreality of the characters, the writer in the *Herald* was sympathetic to them:

> We own to a sneaking partiality for Pierre, rough and unnatural as he is, and share his fiery rebellion against the yoke of conventional proprieties, and the world's cold rules of esteem. Weep we, too, with gentle Isabel; poor bud, blighted by a hereditary canker. And, need we blush to avow that our pulse beat faster than our physician in ordinary would have

> sanctioned, when the heartless Stanly disclaimed his poverty stricken cousin, and strove to wrest his reluctant bride from the arms of her chosen lover?

But once Pierre had committed murder that partiality was cast off: "Let him hang like a dog!" *Graham's* was alone in seeing a "unity of purpose," even in the characterization of the hero:

> Pierre, we take it, is crazy, and the merit of the book is in clearly presenting the psychology of his madness; but the details of such a mental malady as that which afflicts Pierre are almost as disgusting as those of physical disease itself.

This remark was altogether unironic, but with cruel wit the *Southern Quarterly Review* said the "*dramatis personae* are all mad as March hares, every mother's son of them, and every father's daughter of them." The *Whig Review* sarcastically analyzed the peculiar behavior of the characters, while the *Athenæum* dismissed them as "a marrowless tribe of phantoms, flitting through dense clouds of transcendental mysticism."

The style offended almost every reviewer, though some of the early discussions were mild enough. The Hartford *Daily Courant* (August 4) called it a strange style, "not at all natural and too much in the mystic, transcendental vein of affectation that characterizes some of our best writers," but decided that it belonged "to the new era of progress" and must be submitted to. The Springfield *Republican* (August 16) focused almost entirely on the style, taking its metaphorical description from Melville's dedication of the book "to the mystical Greylock":

> Of mist-caps, and ravines, and sky piercing peaks, and tangled underwoods, and barren rocks of language and incident, the book is made. Genteel hifalutin, painful, though ingenious involutions of language, and high-flown incidental detail, characterize the work, to the uprooting of our affection for the graceful and simple writer of Omoo and Typee. Melville has changed his style entirely, and is to be judged of as a new author.

The reviewer in the *Albion* announced that in *Pierre* as in *Moby-Dick* Melville could not "make his characters talk." He saw the stylization of the language but made no attempt to perceive its function, merely complaining that almost "every spoken word reminds you of the chorus of the old Greek Tragedies." Among his strictures he generously mentioned one example of believable speech:

> With the exception of some few sentences very naturally suited to the mouth of the Revd. Mr. Falsgrave, a sleek, smooth-tongued clergyman,

> there is scarcely a page of dialogue that is not absurd to the last degree. It would really pain us to give extracts, and we decline doing so; but the truth is as we state it. We allow the greatest stretch to the imagination of an author, so far as situations and persons are concerned; but if they can't speak as such men and women would be likely to speak, under such and such circumstances, the reader cannot sympathise with them.

The *Literary World* complained elaborately about the language:

> Such infelicities of expression, such unknown words as these, to wit: "human*ness*," "heroic*ness*," "patriarchal*ness*," "descended*ness*," "flushful-*ness*," "amaranthi*ness*," "instantaneous*ness*," "leapingly acknowledging," "fateful frame of mind," "protecting*ness*," "young*ness*," "infantile*ness*," "visible*ness*," *ed id genus omne*!

On the charitable theory that Melville had "merely assumed his present transcendental metamorphosis" in order to satirize "the ridiculous pretensions of some of our modern literati," *Godey's* offered its "very best off-hand effort" in parody of the style:

> Melodiously breathing an inane mysteriousness, into the impalpable airiness of our unsearchable sanctum, this wonderful creation of its ineffable author's sublime-winging imagination has been fluttering its snow-like-invested pinions upon our multitudinous table.

The reviewer claimed to have found in *Pierre* "an infinite, unbounded, inexpressible mysteriousness of nothingness."

The *Whig Review* was harshest of all, objecting "particularly" to "the painful habit" Pierre and Lucy "have contracted of *tutoyer*-ing each other through whole pages of insane rhapsody." Later the writer devoted two and a half two-column pages to an exposition of the stylistic faults, beginning with this:

> Mr. Melville's style of writing in this book is probably the most extraordinary thing that an American press ever beheld. It is precisely what a raving lunatic who had read Jean Paul Richter *in a translation* might be supposed to spout under the influence of a particularly moonlight night. Word piled upon word, and syllable heaped upon syllable, until the tongue grows as bewildered as the mind, and both refuse to perform their offices from sheer inability to grasp the magnitude of the absurdities.

With extravagant sarcasm he quoted objectionable passages and denounced Melville's "scheme for accomplishing" the improvement of the English language: "The essence of this great eureka, this philological reform, consists in 'est' and 'ness,' added to every word to which they have no earthly right to belong." Appending a list of twenty-one words like "Magnifiedly" and "Undoffable," along with page citations, he exclaimed: "After such a list, what shall we say? Shall we leave Mr. Melville to the tender mercies of the Purists, or shall we execute vengeance upon him ourselves?" He complimented Melville ironically upon "the boldness of the metaphors with which it is so thickly studded,"[4] then relapsed for nearly a full column to what seems intended as a grimly hilarious indictment of Melville's invention of "a new substantive," namely "instantaneousness." By contrast with such sustained vindictiveness, the *Athenæum* was tolerant enough in merely observing that the style was "a prolonged succession of spasms."[5]

Far from contenting themselves with analyzing the "execution" of the book, the reviewers offered judgments on what they called the "conception" or the "design"; indeed, they were more often distressed by *Pierre* as an outrage against morality than as an artistic failure. As the *Southern Literary Messenger* said, no matter how bad it was as a work of fiction, it was "infinitely worse" in "its moral tendency." The *Albion* was the first to mention the treatment of incest:

> We wish we could close here, but we regret to add that in several places the ambiguities are still further thickened by hints at that fearfullest of all

4. The reviewer suggested that Isabel's head must have undergone some operation like trephining "in order to warrant her forehead being likened to a 'vivid buckler.'" His greatest contempt was for this sentence: "An infixing stillness now thrust a long rivet through the night, and fast nailed it to that side of the world!" Offering it on his "critical pin" for "the admiration of scientific etymologists," he declared: "This is a grand and simple metaphor. To realize it thoroughly, all we have to do is to imagine some Titantic upholsterer armed with a gigantic nail, and hammer to match, hanging one hemisphere with black crape."

5. Normally reviews contained lengthy "extracts" but most quotations from *Pierre* were short examples of bad writing. Perhaps quoting from *Pierre* would have pained others as much as the *Albion*. In any case, only two reviewers included extracts. The *Literary World* prefaced a long passage from Isabel's story with this comment: "There is a spectral, ghost-like air about the description, that conveys powerfully to the imagination the intended effect of gloom and remote indistinctness." After an elaborate defense against being thought "envious or malicious" the writer in the *Whig Review* saw fit to "subjoin" the description of Pierre's grandfather, qualified by these remarks: "It is not by any means with a view of proving our magnanimity that we quote the following passage from Pierre as a specimen of Mr. Melville's better genius. Even this very passage is disfigured by affectations and faults, which, in any other book, would condemn it to exclusion; but in a work like Pierre, where all else is so intensely bad, and this is probably the only passage in it that could be extracted with advantage, we feel that we would be doing our author an injustice if, after setting forth all his sins so systematically, we did not present to our readers some favorable specimen of his powers."

human crimes, which one shrinks from naming, but to which the narrative alludes when it brings some of its personages face to face with a copy of the Cenci portrait.

The Duyckincks began their essay with a statement of the theme:

> The purpose of Mr. Melville's story, though vaguely hinted, rather than directly stated, seems to be to illustrate the possible antagonism of a sense of duty, conceived in the heat and impetuosity of youth, to all the recognised laws of social morality; and to exhibit a conflict between the virtues.

After summarizing the plot, they attempted a sharper definition:

> The most immoral *moral* of the story, if it has any moral at all, seems to be the impracticability of virtue; a leering demoniacal spectre of an idea seems to be speering at us through the dim obscure of this dark book, and mocking us with this dismal falsehood.

They were the only reviewers to mention the chapter on "Chronometricals and Horologicals," and they did so with horror, saying that "if it has any meaning at all" it "simply means that virtue and religion are only for gods and not to be attempted by man." They were glad that "ordinary novel readers" would "never unkennel this loathsome suggestion." Almost as loathsome to them, apparently, was "the supersensuousness with which the holy relations of the family are described." The theme of incest wrought the critic in the *Whig Review* to this extraordinary pitch:

> Now, in this matter Mr. Melville has done a very serious thing, a thing which not even unsoundness of intellect could excuse. He might have been mad to the very pinnacle of insanity; he might have torn our poor language into tatters, and made from the shreds a harlequin suit in which to play his tricks; he might have piled up word upon word, and adjective upon adjective, until he had built a pyramid of nonsense, which should last to the admiration of all men; he might have done all this and a great deal more, and we should not have complained. But when he dares to outrage every principle of virtue; when he strikes with an impious, though, happily, weak hand, at the very foundations of society, we feel it our duty to tear off the veil with which he has thought to soften the hideous features of the idea, and warn the public against the reception of such atrocious doctrines.

Even reviewers who wrote vaguely of the "metaphysics" sensed enough foulness to condemn the whole book.

The reception of *Pierre* leaves some tantalizing questions, for all the near-unanimity of opinion. Was there something like a journalistic conspiracy of silence, or did the book simply bore or baffle most of the men who received review copies? Exactly how far into it did reviewers get before deciding it was abominable? Why did only *Godey's* allude to the literary satire, when others must have understood it and been stung by it? Did the *Whig Review*, which had ignored the well-publicized *Moby-Dick*, review *Pierre* only because it offered an opportunity for attacking Melville? After the review in the *Athenæum* appeared, why did some of the enthusiastic reviewers of *The Whale* not rout out a copy of *Pierre* and review it? Most speculatively, how would *Pierre* have fared if it had been published pseudonymously in England (or the United States) as by "Guy Winthrop"?

Also puzzling is how Melville's family responded to *Pierre* itself and to its reception. No comment survives from Melville's sister Helen, who had copied it, or from anyone else who may have seen it in manuscript or during the proofreading. No comment survives concerning Melville's failure to obtain an English publisher. Reverberations of family distress would seem to inform this account by Melville's granddaughter, Eleanor Melville Metcalf:

> Here is a sick man writing of some matters known to be true, some entirely untrue, combined in such a way that the family feared its members and their friends might assume all to be true—that is, factual. Well they knew the description of the soul-searching trials of a young author to be autobiographical. That the young author's story was not autobiographical they also knew: but would others be able to separate fact from invention?

Yet Mrs. Metcalf's account was apparently based not on her memory of family traditions but on evidence now generally available, none of which indicates that Melville was sick in 1852 or that the family was alarmed about *Pierre* before its publication. Melville spent a pleasant vacation in Nantucket with his father-in-law, Judge Lemuel Shaw, in July, 1852, apparently without discussing his forthcoming book. However, the Judge's letter on August 17 to his son Lemuel, then in Europe, may be more conspicuous for diplomacy than veracity, given the currency of the review of *Pierre* in the Boston *Post*:

> Herman has just published his new work. . . . I have not read it, & do not know, how it is received; it does not I believe relate to incidents, or characters, connected with the sea. I hope it will have a run & succeed well, & realize his hopes & expectations.

The next surviving family allusion is John Oakes Shaw's on August 31, also in a letter to the younger Lemuel, his and Lizzie Melville's half-brother:

"Herman has published another book some *high faluting* romance which is spoken of with any thing but praise at least so far as I have heard." Judge Shaw and his wife visited the Melvilles for four days in the third week of September, and while all of them must have seen reviews by then, they had "a very agreeable visit." In October, a maternal uncle, Peter Gansevoort, drafted an indignant reproach for Melville's unaccountable rudeness to one of his Albany neighbors who had visited Pittsfield: "Oh Herman, Herman, Herman truly thou art an 'Ambiguity.'" Yet Gansevoort made no complaint about Herman's less than reverential literary appropriation of events and paraphernalia associated with the family. One particularly tantalizing possibility is that the immediate family reacted less to any new oddness in Melville's behavior or to their own readings of *Pierre* than to the reviews and defamatory news items. For as the responses to *Pierre* accumulated, even before any surviving documents show that Melville was in bad health or that he wanted to stop writing, the family evidently held nervous councils, in which they talked "the matter over again & again," concluding that his literary career was finished and that the best prospect for him was "some foreign Consulship."

Melville's own response to the reception of *Pierre* must be sought in his later behavior, such as his failure to complete his next literary projects and his beginning to write short magazine tales instead of book-length fictions, as well as in oblique comments, such as this one which Evert A. Duyckinck tellingly marked in his copy of *The Confidence-Man* (Chapter 33):

> Though every one knows how bootless it is to be in all cases vindicating one's self, never mind how convinced one may be that he is never in the wrong; yet, so precious to man is the approbation of his kind, that to rest, though but under an imaginary censure applied to but a work of imagination, is no easy thing.

The censures applied to *Pierre* were anything but imaginary, and during the fall of 1852 Melville could have taken only cold comfort in remembering the lesson Pierre bitterly learns—"that though the world worship Mediocrity and Common Place, yet hath it fire and sword for all contemporary Grandeur."

III

After the 1,423 copies of *Pierre* sold during the initial promotion, sales dwindled quickly. By October 6, 1854, 133 more copies had been sold, but it took twelve years to sell another 139. Thereafter during Melville's lifetime *Pierre* sold at a miniscule but erratic rate: 35 sales were reported in 1865, while no copies at all were sold between 1872 and 1875. In the thirty-three years between 1854 and 1887, exactly 300 copies were sold. The last Harper's report, on March 4, 1887, showed 79 copies on hand; the plates were melted five days later.[6]

With the important exception of Fitz-James O'Brien's essay on Melville in the second issue of the influential New York magazine, *Putnam's Monthly* (February, 1853), commentary on *Pierre* died away with the last of the reviews. Though what O'Brien had to say about *Pierre* as a piece of fiction amounted to hardly more than a judicious and eloquent version of what many reviewers had said, he did give the only nineteenth-century expression of the notion that *Pierre* might almost be read as parody:

> When first we read Pierre, we felt a strong inclination to believe the whole thing to be a well-got-up hoax. We remembered having read a novel in six volumes once of the same order, called "The Abbess," in which the stilted style of writing is exposed very funnily; and, as a specimen of unparalleled bombast, we believed it to be unequalled until we met with Pierre.

What distinguished O'Brien's comments on *Pierre* was his awareness of its significance in relation to the whole of Melville's early literary career. He was the first to treat *Pierre* not as an isolated aberration from the simplicities of *Typee* and *Omoo* but as the culmination of the tendency toward stylistic and philosophic extravagances which Melville had manifested all along, especially in *Mardi* and *Moby-Dick*. He took *Pierre* as evidence that Melville was in a "state of ferment" like that which Keats described in the preface to *Endymion*, or, in O'Brien's paraphrase, an "interregnum of nonsense." He concluded with a blunt warning:

> Let Mr. Melville stay his step in time. He totters on the edge of a precipice, over which all his hard-earned fame may tumble with such

6. From an entry in the Harper ledgers: "The plates of Pierre & Mardi were melted Mar 9, 1887, 'at the author's request.'" See *Secretary's News Sheet* [Bibliographical Society of the University of Virginia], No. 37 (September, 1957), p. 6, where the secretary reports having copied the entry in 1952.

> another weight as Pierre attached to it. He has peculiar talents, which may be turned to rare advantage. Let him diet himself for a year or two on Addison, and avoid Sir Thomas Browne, and there is little doubt but that he will make a notch on the American Pine.

Unlike the reviewers, O'Brien made no simplistic demand that Melville write more books like *Typee* and *Omoo*. He saw Melville's career as still developing and implicitly, at least, allowed for the chance that it would take a new direction. The honor of being accorded such an essay, for all its strictures, may have encouraged Melville to accept an invitation to contribute to the magazine. In any case, *Putnam's Monthly* published "Bartleby, the Scrivener" in November and December, 1853, and became for the next two years the main outlet for Melville's writings.

Isolated comments on *Pierre* during these years merely echoed the initial reviews, and between 1857 and Melville's death in 1891 the book was almost ignored except for routine listing in literary histories and encyclopedias.[7] The major exception was the English critic H. S. Salt's comments in his essay on Melville in the *Scottish Art Review* in November, 1889, at a time when many English literary men were rediscovering Melville. As the first to do research on the course of Melville's literary career rather than witnessing it, Salt had read the "contemporary critics" and had been influenced by them. His reading of *Pierre* obviously derived from O'Brien. He pronounced it "perhaps the *ne plus ultra* in the way of metaphysical absurdity," and raised but did not pursue the question of whether "the transcendental obscurities in which he [Melville] latterly ran riot were the cause or the consequence of the failure of his artistic powers." Salt's friend J. W. Barrs sent Melville the article along with his detailed

7. The Melville entry in the biographical dictionary *Men of the Time, or Sketches of Living Notables* (London, 1853) was derived from the *Literary World*: "His latest production is 'Pierre, or the Ambiguities,' an unhealthy mystic romance, in which are conjured up 'unreal night-mare conceptions, a confused phantasmagoria of distorted fancies and conceits, ghostly abstractions, and fitful shadows,' altogether different from the hale and sturdy sailors and fresh sea-breezes of his earlier productions. It met with a decided non-success, and has not been reprinted in this country." In their *Cyclopædia of American Literature* (1855) the Duyckincks commented briefly: "Its conception and execution were both literary mistakes. The author was off the track of his true genius. The passion which he sought to evolve was morbid or unreal, in the worst school of the mixed French and German melodramatic." A few reviewers of *Israel Potter* (1855) and *The Piazza Tales* (1856) praised these later books in explicit contrast to *Pierre*. In 1870 Dante Gabriel Rossetti tried to obtain a copy, but whether he succeeded is not known (*Log*, II, 716). In *Confessions and Criticisms* (1887) Julian Hawthorne cited *Pierre* as "really a terrible example of the enormities which a man of genius may perpetrate when working in a direction unsuited to him"; by contrast Bret Harte had "done something both new and good."

exceptions to it, specifying that he did not think Salt did *Pierre* "anything like justice." Though Salt quickly came to think even better of *Moby-Dick*, in a second essay (1892) he still dismissed *Pierre* as transcendental in thought and bombastic in language.

A few weeks after Melville's death J. E. A. Smith, his old Berkshire acquaintance, gave a disproportionate amount of attention to *Pierre* in a series of memorial articles in the Pittsfield *Evening Journal*, partly in refuting the assertion of some obituary writers that the reception of *Pierre* was the immediate cause for Melville's ceasing to write, partly in acknowledging that "keen and just thoughts" are "scattered here and there through the book," but mostly in quoting from the "score of pages of local interest" which Berkshire inhabitants "could ill afford to lose." He offered the "true story of the Memnon naming"— an apparently reliable account in which the heroine may be Sarah Morewood[8]—and he asserted, as a matter of his own knowledge, that certain characters and household objects in *Pierre* had counterparts in Melville's own life. Specifically, he saw in Pierre's Aunt Dorothea "a shadowy vision of the author's maiden aunt" (presumably Priscilla Melvill, whose home in Boston he had visited), and he caught in the two paintings of Pierre's father "glimpses of the family portraits." He took Pierre as being in some degree Melville's idealization of himself:

> Even in books where he was not avowedly his own hero, he often idealized himself in portions of the story of some of his characters; or it may be more correct to say that he often, and sometimes very closely, modelled incidents in his stories upon real ones in his own experience; very often in cases where he had been magna pars. Of course he did not incorporate these incidents literally and bodily into the story; and still less was his idealization of himself a portrait of what he was in his own eyes. Like other novelists, he adapted both to the exigencies of the plot.

8. "One charming summer day, Mr. Melville, passing with his accustomed party of merry ladies and gentlemen, over smooth roads, came to the rock, and there had their usual picnic. While the party were enjoying their woodland meal one of the ladies crept into that fearful recess under the rock into which no man dare venture. And soon there issued from its depths sweet and mysterious music. This cunning priestess had hidden there a magnificent music box whose delicious strains must still be remembered, by some in Pittsfield and New York. This mysterious music completed in Mr. Melville's mind the resemblance to the Egyptian Memnon suggested by the size and form of the rock. And voila—Pierre's Memnon!" In the 1852 edition of his *Taghconic* Smith had told of having "heard the story of the merry hour when 'Memnon' was inscribed" on the stone "by a hand which has written many a witty and clever volume." Since he was mentioning no names he was free to say archly: "I wonder if ever there was anything in that broken champagne bottle which lay at the foot of the rock."

When Mrs. Melville had Smith's articles printed as a pamphlet in 1897 to preserve them from "oblivion,"[9] she retained his description of *Pierre* as a "strange vagary" and his insistence that those who attributed Melville's withdrawal from literary work "to the unlimited censure of Pierre, show a strange forgetfulness of dates," but she deleted the whole of the passage on Melville's idealization of himself, along with Smith's comment on his own censoring of one of Melville's "irrelevant rhapsodies" from "the pen picture of our pet local monster and geological mystery," the Balanced Rock. During the next two decades almost nothing was written of *Pierre*. Even Carl Van Doren, one of the initiators of the Melville revival, dismissed it in the *Cambridge History of American Literature* (1917) as "hopelessly frantic."

IV

From Melville's centennial in 1919 through the 1930's the general literary reputation of *Pierre* was created by critics struck by the extraordinary modernity of its psychological probings and by its anticipations of modern fictional techniques.[10] The later academic reputation of *Pierre* developed primarily from the two major biographers of the revival, both of whom found in the book revelations about Melville's own psychology and life. Raymond Weaver in 1921 presented an autobiographical interpretation which has flourished intermittently ever since:

> Melville's disillusionment began at home. The romantic idealisation of his mother gave place to a recoil into a realisation of the cold, "scaly,

9. Mrs. Melville's letter to Melville's cousin, Catherine Gansevoort Lansing, from Pittsfield, September 5, 1897, in V. H. Paltsits, ed., *Family Correspondence of Herman Melville, 1830–1904* (New York: New York Public Library, 1929), p. 67. A discussion of the differences between the newspaper articles and the pamphlet is in Harrison Hayford's dissertation, "Melville and Hawthorne" (Yale University, 1945), pp. 312–23.

10. In three centennial articles, Raymond Weaver called *Pierre* "worthily comparable to Meredith's 'Egoist' in elaborate subtlety and mercilessness of psychological analysis" and "a prophetic parody of Hardy's most poisonous pessimism"; Frank Jewett Mather, Jr., compared its "leading motive" to that of Meredith's *The Ordeal of Richard Feverel;* and Arthur Johnson declared that D. H. Lawrence "hasn't exceeded it for morbid unhealthy pathology." By 1938 Willard Thorp could say that the methods of Melville which were "utterly confusing" to an earlier generation are now not so to readers who easily read Meredith, James, and Woolf and think themselves able to fathom "the expressionism" of Joyce's *Ulysses* and Lawrence's *The Rainbow*. In his literary column for the *Saturday Review* (May 1, 1926), Christopher Morley quoted this ecstatic praise from a correspondent in England: "Melville, it is supposed, has been re-discovered recently. Actually, folk here rave hysterically about 'Moby Dick,' principally, and apparently lack the wit to know that 'Pierre' is one of the most important books in the world, profound beyond description in its metaphysic."

> glittering folds of pride" that rebuffed his tormented love; and he studied the portrait of his father, and found it a defaming image.

Disillusioned with his parents, with Western civilization, with American Protestantism, with the "criminal stupidity of war," and with romantic marital love, "Melville coiled down into the night of his soul, to write an anatomy of despair"—that is, to write *Pierre*. The book was "an apologia of Melville's own defeat" and after it any more writing "was both an impertinence and an irrelevancy." In 1929 Lewis Mumford argued bluntly that the failure of *Pierre* "as a work of art gives us a certain licence to deal with it as biography." Mumford took the book as a self-betrayal of Melville's sexual "regression" and sought to discover "what event, or series of occurrences, caused a hiatus in Melville's emotional and sexual development."[11] Seeing in the "sexual symbols" of *Pierre* "the unconscious revelation of his dilemmas as a writer," Mumford decided that Lucy might "signify the naïve writings of his youth" (*Typee* and *Omoo*), while Isabel might "stand for that darker consciousness in himself that goads him to all his most heroic efforts." In this view, *Pierre* "was a blow, aimed at his family with their cold pride, and at the critics, with their low standards, their failure to see where Melville's true vocation lay." In their autobiographical interpretations both Weaver and Mumford, having access to relatively little of the factual information that has since been made available, regularly deduced Melville's attitudes toward his own family from Pierre's attitudes toward his.

A variation on Weaver's and Mumford's psychoanalytic readings was offered by E. L. Grant Watson in 1930. Watson was interested in Melville's "psychic history" more than whatever details of his life could be discovered by research or deduced from his fictions. He took *Pierre* as "a record (for a certain period) of Melville's mystical experience," a darker and more profound version of the fall of man. His reading was explicitly "symbolical": Pierre at the outset "shows the white, glittering side of the bright coin of Puritan America"—"developed only on one side, on that white shining side which is called goodness and is what society would have us believe that we wish ourselves to be." Mrs. Glendinning "represents the complex of the social instinct." Lucy symbolizes "those *conscious* elements of his [Pierre's] soul that appear as yet all purity and goodness." Isabel is

11. Mumford decided that Melville had longed "for the pre-nuptial state" after his marriage: "Sex meant marriage; marriage meant a household and a tired wife and children and debts. No wonder he retreated: no wonder his fantasy attached him to a mother who could not surrender, to a half-sister who could not bear children!"

"the hitherto unapprehended" manifestation "of the dark half of his soul," the half that "has, in the purity of his upbringing, been left unregarded."[12] Pierre's father "is in the image of God, and as God he [Pierre] had known him as the original source." Watson defined minor characters as "representing tendencies or complexes within the *psyche*": Delly Ulver is the "earthly double" of Isabel, her "primitive, quite innocent, but sensual, and unconscious counterpart"; Glen Stanly is "the respectable counterpart and worldly double of Pierre."

Watson also related events in *Pierre* to crises in the psyche, in one instance defining the symbolic meaning of Isabel's memories of the asylum:

> Thus it is that the awakening consciousness of the soul, is closely and dangerously beset, in its lonely infancy, by the undifferentiated and demented-seeming forms of the collective unconscious. She tells of the death of these undifferentiated forces, of the consciousness of death, which came to her, and of the increasingly tragic consciousness which is her being.

In a similar manner he explained Pierre's behavior after his rejection by Glen Stanly:

> For the first time in unguarded contact with the brutalities of the world, Pierre not only tastes the bitterness of his new experience, but is assailed by tumult from within, the upspewings of anger and disgust, and other half-recognised tendencies, which, symbolised in the rabble from a brothel, fight and claw one other.

He read the book, finally, as "the story of a conscious soul attempting to draw itself free from the psychic world-material in which most of mankind is unconsciously always wrapped and enfolded, as a foetus in the womb." For Watson, *Pierre* was Melville's masterpiece:

> In *Pierre* a luxuriant imagination meets with an adequate controlling power and an artistic appreciation of reticence. The book is a far better artistic whole than *Moby Dick*; there is less matter irrelevant to the main theme, and the elaborate fabric in which Melville's thought and intuition meet and

12. "She is no earthly or physical representation, but is a soul-image, an image, too, of an awakening universe. She is a symbol of the consciousness of the tragic aspect of life; she is his angel of experience as contrasted with Lucy, who is his angel of innocence. As a symbol of the Tragic Muse, blood-related to himself, born of the same life-spring, Pierre must accept from her the wider vision that in her complete purity she brings; he must descend into the depths of the underworld; she is the gate and the way; and at the first uncomprehending sight of her, his fate, though he knows it not, is already sealed."

> are interwoven, is a quality quite unmatched by any other work of his time.

No other critic has so elaborately justified such a tribute to *Pierre*.

The first challenge to the Weaver-Mumford view of *Pierre* as autobiographical was offered by Robert S. Forsythe in his edition of the book in the Americana Deserta series (1930). Forsythe declared that there was "no evidence whatsoever for connecting the story of Isabel's mother with any actual happening" in the life of Melville's father, and he reproached the "Freudian enthusiasts" who had identified Isabel with Melville's "vigorous and highly pious sister" (Augusta Melville).[13] He treated Melville's own experiences merely as source materials for the highly conscious "satirical narrative of his hero's early adventures in authorship and his encounters with magazine editors," and he made a crucial distinction about Melville's use of fact in *Pierre*:

> It is true that there is much in *Pierre* that is factual in origin. A large part of this, is autobiographical or relating to Melville's family history. Yet it must be observed that these are almost always mere details used in heightening character or rendering settings more vivid: hardly ever do they enter into the plot. And they are employed with Melville's usual disregard for painstaking accuracy, being twisted and distorted to suit his purpose as a novelist.

Forsythe's picture of Melville as a conscious literary artist precipitated a controversy that swirled about in scholarly journals without much clarification until 1938, when Willard Thorp made a sensible contribution by surveying Melville's life separately then taking up each major work for a literary evaluation.[14] Like Forsythe, he stressed that biographers had

13. Forsythe's point is clarified by Mumford's review of the Dutton edition of *Pierre* in the *Saturday Review* (June 29, 1929): "Much of the materials of 'Pierre' are plainly autobiographical: the hero's patrician background, his relation to his father and mother, the effect of his father's image, his attachment to his cousin, his career as a writer: the novel, in fact, is full of identifiable landscapes and people, and, according to Dr. Henry Murray, Jr., whose researches into the actualities of Melville's life have gone farther than either Mr. Weaver's or my own, there is even a certain amount of evidence which might link the dark, mysterious Isabel, half-sister to Pierre, with the real sister who during the early part of his literary career had so patiently made fair copies of his manuscripts." Reviewing Mumford's book in *New England Quarterly* the next month, Murray himself said that Mumford had not gone far enough in his exploration of Melville's unconscious.

14. The quarrel quickly became personal. See in "Sources": Starke; the anonymous item in the *New York Times Book Review* section (July 20, 1930); MacLean; Forsythe (November, 1930); Eby; and Murray (April, 1931). The most understated comment was Dr. Murray's observation that Forsythe's "accurate, thorough and most gentlemanly introduction does not mention the word incest."

followed "a dangerous course" in identifying Melville and his parents with Pierre and *his* parents.

The publication of Henry A. Murray's Hendricks House edition of *Pierre* in 1949 and of Leon Howard's biography of Melville in 1951 in effect continued the Weaver-Mumford *vs.* Forsythe-Thorp controversy.[15] Dr. Murray declared that "today scarcely anyone denies that *Pierre* is, in some sense and in some degree, autobiographical," and placed himself among those who believed that the autobiographical elements were numerous and "were influential in the shaping of the novel." He listed what he called highly probable "originals" for "all the natural objects and scenes" in the book and devoted a long paragraph to the identifications of the principal characters with real people whom Melville knew. He was at pains to insist that the book was not "a transcription of fact" and that Melville had thrown "a disguise over each of his originals," but he believed that Melville "*intended* his future biographers to recognize that he was writing the hushed story of his life"—that Melville was not "experimenting with the novel and incidentally making use of some personal experiences" but was deliberately writing "his spiritual autobiography in the form of a novel." Somewhat in the spirit of Forsythe and Thorp, but with a closer scrutiny of the composition of *Pierre*, Leon Howard treated the book as Melville's flawed attempt "to turn out a genuinely popular story" and minimized the autobiographical aspects: "For once, he would not have to borrow or buy a book from which to get material: he could draw upon his own family background and his boyhood impressions of fact and legend."

15. Dr. Murray's edition is a special case in Melville scholarship—a major interpretation that was formed in large part more than twenty years before it was published. Murray, whose assistance was acknowledged by Mumford, seemed to echo him in arraying "natural objects and scenes" and "all the principal characters" in *Pierre* against their "originals" and seemed to echo Watson in seeing Isabel as "the personification of Pierre's unconscious" who leads him to acquire "the tragic sense of life." Nor did his edition resolve many important critical issues such as the problem of the style. Even though he had declared in 1931 that for him the value of *Pierre* was in "the consummate sorcery of Melville's language," his focus in 1949 was such that reviewers complained of his ignoring "many of the esthetic questions" and forgetting "to look at the work of art." He actually created some new controversies by making debatable identifications between characters in the book and real people, particularly between Plinlimmon and Hawthorne. One of Murray's major contributions was as literary scholar rather than eminent psychiatrist: his knowledgeable examination of predecessors of *Pierre* among British novels. Besides his introductory essay of ninety pages, Murray contributed seventy-six pages of scholarly notes. As the best-edited and the only annotated edition available (and as one of the earliest volumes in the Hendricks House edition), Murray's edition became the starting point for almost all new criticism on *Pierre* for more than two decades.

The degree to which *Pierre* can be read as autobiography (or "spiritual autobiography") has been the dominant theme of interpretation since the revival, but its style was analyzed frequently, beginning with Arthur Johnson's centennial essay. Johnson compared Henry James and Melville as "mannered" writers, illustrating his points by quotations from *Pierre* and concluding with this thoughtful comment:

> The technique and texture of it are, of course, essentially different to the master's [James's]. In relation to his, it is as crude and stark as warp without any woof. Melville ramified along the way to elementary goals, punctilious to leave no stone unturned that should add to the complexity of what he fancied was to him alone obvious; whereas James, exploring and groping ahead, coped with inspiration upon inspiration, and concentric inspirations, so to speak, the very poignancy and multiplicity of which, and his zeal not to miss an impression, absorbed the least dread of obscurity. Yet their thoroughness, thus dissimilarly acquired perhaps, involved devices and idiosyncracies grotesquely alike—all quite aside, I mean, from whatever in their methods of presentation I've hinted may appear rather to tally. Melville, it is told, had a proclivity to metaphysics, and James's inheritance possibly included an aptitude for the elaborations which such a field seems inevitably to engender. At any rate, one queries if there isn't a something about the convolutions of both that savors of philosophers' painstakingness.

Carl Van Vechten in 1922 replied to critics who had "protested against the author's use of 'Gothic dialogue'" in *Moby-Dick* and *Pierre*, arguing that it "was a perfectly conscious device" which served to remove Ahab and Pierre "from any particular environment or period."[16] In his biography Lewis Mumford pointed to the oddity in *Pierre* of both "passages that are the finest utterances" of Melville's spirit and "passages that would scarcely honour Laura Jean Libbey." He contrasted its style with that of *Moby-Dick*, calling the language in *Pierre* disproportionate to the events. In language, he said, *Pierre* was "perfervid and poetical in a mawkish way," with opening dialogue in which "the style becomes a perfumed silk, taken from an Elizabethan chamber romance." Melville had "suddenly lost both taste

16. One of the most extreme attacks on the style was in John Freeman's 1926 critical biography in the English Men of Letters Series. Freeman thought Melville "had thrown aside the enchanter's wand when he finished *Redburn*, and now bore a serpent"; the "passages of lovely prose in *Pierre*, leisured, deep-breathed prose," were "all wasted." Freeman was repelled by more than the style: "The psychology is intolerably followed, with the sly and thirsty fury of a stoat; nothing outside the Russians could be more subtle or less scrupulous."

and discretion" and the style had become "tedious, intolerable, ridiculous." The next year, 1930, E. L. Grant Watson took a quite different view, describing the "trance-like quality" of the opening scene as Melville's device for leading the reader into a conventional—a stylized—realm "far from actuality." Tacitly refuting Mumford for taking the "artificial coloring" at face value, Watson argued that it was admirably functional:

> There is a viscous and somewhat cloying quality about the style, which like the substance of the subconscious world, with which it deals, is at first repellent. Like some alien particle, unable to fuse or to accommodate itself to this deliberate artifice, the mind, which can not at once shake off the values of normal existence, rebels against the exaggerated virtuousness of the Glendinning family.

Furthermore, Watson defended the alternation of styles that had disturbed Mumford, both the early "deliberate artificiality" and such a later style as the "vivid imaginative realism" of Isabel's story.

In 1936 William Braswell combined the two major approaches to *Pierre* by accounting for the style in terms of Melville's life, thereby precipitating a fresh critical debate. Assuming on the basis of information and opinion in Weaver's biography that Melville "was in profound grief" when he wrote *Pierre* (partly from the "comparatively poor reception" of *Moby-Dick*), Braswell declared that Melville "expected *Pierre* to be his final publication":

> In this novel he was having his last fling. He was satirizing his own too idealistic self, and he was giving a parting blow to a world that had struck him many a blow.

Braswell saw "a two-edged purpose" in the mannered dialogue: Melville was secretly satirizing "certain elements in his own spiritual world" and giving "critics more to carp about." The style was meant to offend readers and to bring down upon Melville the condemnation of the reviewers. In 1946 Harrison Hayford argued that the Weaver-Braswell theory of Melville's intentions in writing *Pierre* was "substantially refuted" by the evidence in the letter to Bentley on April 16, 1852, and in the later "Agatha letters" to Hawthorne. Hayford rejected the possibility that Melville's whole letter to Bentley was "an utterly insincere sales-promotion designed to dupe and mulct his publisher." He acknowledged that Melville completely misjudged either *Pierre* or "the literary taste of the public" (or perhaps both) in thinking his readers "would gag not at all over the lumps of satire and the strong flavoring of unorthodox morality," but he suggested that Melville honestly believed he had written a book that would be both popular and profound:

> Melville's letter is of course not to be interpreted as denying the existence of deeper meanings. From at least the time of "Hawthorne and His Mosses" he had held the theory that literary works can please the mob of superficial readers on a surface level of noise and show and at the same time speak to a few profounder readers on a level of deep truth. Probably Melville saw well enough that the superficial public taste would be pleased by "a regular romance with a mysterious plot to it, and stirring emotions at work," but deceived himself in thinking he had submerged the profounder elements of his book far enough below the surface to allow the ordinary reader clear sailing through the romance.

In an apparent modification of his theory (1950), Braswell did not repeat his claim that *Pierre* was Melville's farewell to writing but argued instead that passages which Mumford and F. O. Matthiessen had "unfortunately read as a serious attempt at beautiful prose" were parody of the sentimental style of certain popular fiction of the day. Rather than being "insipidly sentimental," such passages were "mock-romantic." Again Braswell relied on the language of *Pierre* to be self-evident parody rather than demonstrating its similarities to contemporary sentimental fiction. The next year, however, Braswell in effect restated his position of fifteen years before. During the 1950's and 1960's scholars accepted Hayford's evidence that Melville never intended *Pierre* to be his last work, but they were slow to explore the other issues that Braswell and Hayford had raised.

Since 1951 no study has been as broadly interpretative as Lewis Mumford's, E. L. Grant Watson's, and Henry A. Murray's, and no biographical studies have appreciably supplemented Willard Thorp's, Harrison Hayford's, and Leon Howard's. Scholarly criticism of *Pierre* during the 1950's and 1960's is unified not so much by its focus on common problems of interpretation as by its use of the same methods of literary analysis. Most readings have stressed the significance of literary allusions, of mythic patterns, of imagery, and of metaphors. One critic said that about half of *Pierre* "pivots on references to the *Inferno*"; another that the *Divine Comedy*, particularly the *Inferno*, was Melville's "primary frame of reference, both structurally and symbolically"; another that "Melville's use of the imagery of the Fall of Man defines the structure, action, and theme of the novel"; another that the "language, imagery, and symbolism of rocks, stones, bricks, and marble" permeate the pages of the book and that the brick tower of the Apostles' is "symbol of the central structural principle" (the same writer held that the "petrification image is central"); and another that "the narrator's metaphors define the writer's relationship to both the fictional and the material world."[17] In 1955, well before this method of analysis had become the most popular approach to *Pierre*, James Kissane used one such reading as a way of exploring "some inherent limitations" of the "tendency to approach fiction through imagery and myth."

Certain topics have recurred in all recent criticism of *Pierre*, regardless of the differences in approaches: the possible sources in British, Continental, and American literature; the relationships to themes and characters in Melville's other works; and the meanings of particular symbols or passages in *Pierre*.

The motley lot of suggested sources in British literature includes Shakespeare (*Romeo and Juliet* and *Hamlet*, in particular); Bacon; "the old novel of sensibility, the Gothic romance, the novel of romantic sophistication"; and such nineteenth-century writers as Byron (especially *Manfred*), De Quincey, Carlyle, Disraeli, Bulwer-Lytton, Dickens, and Thackeray. Several critics have examined Melville's debt to Dante. Others, including S. Foster Damon, E. H. Eby, and F. O. Matthiessen, have unconvincingly proposed Sylvester Judd's *Margaret* as a source, and Braswell (1936) apparently thought Melville might have used "Susan Warner's *The Wide, Wide World* (1850), Donald Grant Mitchell's *Reveries of a Bachelor* (1850), *Godey's Lady's Book, Graham's Magazine*, and the gift-books."[18]

Critics have often linked *Pierre* with *Moby-Dick*. One standard formulation sees it as Melville's attempt to arrive at a "sort of psychological truth" comparable to the metaphysical truth he had achieved in *Moby-Dick*—a story of "not the universe, but the ego." Another analysis takes *Moby-Dick* as "a close examination of universal society in terms of religion" and *Pierre* as "an equally close examination of the individual in terms of morality." Especially in the 1920's and 1930's, *Pierre* was often linked with *Mardi* and *Moby-Dick* as the third in a "trilogy." In 1926 Carl Van Vechten added this passage to a reprinting of his essay on Melville's later works:

> Of the three major later novels it may, roughly speaking, be said that they form a kind of tragic triptych: Mardi is a tragedy of the intellect, Moby Dick a tragedy of the spirit, and Pierre, a tragedy of the flesh; Mardi is a tragedy of heaven, Moby Dick, a tragedy of hell, and Pierre, a tragedy of the world we live in.

17. These quotations are, in this order, from Giovannini, Schless, Moorman (1953), Franklin, and Dryden. For full citations, see "Sources," at the end of this NOTE.

18. The quotation in the first sentence is from Arvin. The fullest treatment of literary influences on *Pierre* is in Dr. Murray's introduction; other discussions, with self-explanatory titles, are listed in "Sources."

Other critics, beginning with Merton M. Sealts, Jr., have found in *Pierre* foreshadowings of images and themes that became dominant in the tales Melville began to write in late 1852 or early 1853. One has seen *The Confidence-Man* as "a more sardonic, more mordant version of the contrast between chronometrical and horological ethics in *Pierre*," while another has associated the pamphlet in *Pierre* with the Indian-hater episode of *The Confidence-Man*, which he sees as a tragic study of "the impracticability of Christianity" and a satiric study of "the nominal practice of Christianity." Still another has seen the action of *Pierre* as a "fumbled" version of that of *Billy Budd*.[19]

Several critics have compared characters in *Pierre* and Melville's other works. Pierre and Ahab are often seen as Promethean heroes, although an opposing view holds that Pierre can never feel the "topmost greatness" which Ahab feels before he dies. One critic sees Isabel as being "of the same world-substance (mother-substance) as Moby Dick," the main difference being "the aspect from which they are viewed"; another links her by a set of word-plays to "Jezebel ('devotee of Bel'), the wife of Ahab." Another has related Pierre implicitly to the "wilful boy" in *Mardi* (Chapter 112) and explicitly to Colonel Moredock in *The Confidence-Man*, all of whom aim "at the absolute imitation of Christ." Yet another argues that in crucial ways Plotinus Plinlimmon is like two other characters in *The Confidence-Man*, Mark Winsome and Egbert, and that a knowledge of the pamphlet clarifies "the nature of Winsome's and Egbert's offences."[20]

Critics focusing on particular symbols in *Pierre* have taken Isabel's guitar as "the Teh, namely the immanent manifestation within the individual soul of the transcendental reality of Life" (Watson) and, more simply, as "a womb symbol" (Murray). Melville's own explication of two symbols has often been cited: "The catnip and the amaranth!—man's earthly household peace, and the ever-encroaching appetite for God." This sentence occurs in the Enceladus passage, which is widely quoted from but rarely analyzed, although George C. Homans in 1932 made an elaborate "chart" by superimposing the "symbolic genealogy" of Pierre's mood on its "spiritual genealogy."

A section of *Pierre* mentioned in only one contemporary review is seen by recent critics as central to the meaning of the whole book: the pamphlet

19. Unattributed quotations in this paragraph are from Mumford, Mason, Foster, Parker, and Lewis. For other discussions of the "trilogy," see Homans and Thorp.

20. Geist and Sedgwick respectively argue for and against taking Pierre and Ahab as Promethean heroes. Unattributed quotations in this paragraph are from Watson, Murray (1949), Parker, and Higgins.

on "Chronometricals and Horologicals" which Melville offers in Book XIV, Chapter III, as a somewhat bungled transcription of a lecture by the philosopher Plotinus Plinlimmon. Agreed as they are on the importance of the pamphlet, critics are at odds on its precise meaning, most obviously in their notions of Melville's attitude toward what is said in the pamphlet. Thorp was sure that if Melville had "sided with Plinlimmon" the book "would contain insoluble contradictions." Dr. Murray held that "Plinlimmon's egocentric, non-benevolent, prudential morality is patently inadequate" and called the pamphlet "an indictment by Melville of Plinlimmon in particular and of society in general." Thinking the pamphlet which embodies Plinlimmon's "mature sagacity" should at least on the rational level "be taken at its face value," Newton Arvin (1950) repudiated such readings as Thorp's and Murray's:

> Many readers of *Pierre* have imagined that Melville's simple purpose in this whole passage was to deride the preachers of a low, expedient, comfortable morality of compromise and adjustment; but surely this was not at all his conscious intention.

Lawrance Thompson (1952) in a variation of Murray's interpretation held that Plinlimmon's major conclusion about a virtuous expediency was, on Plinlimmon's part but not Melville's, "unintentionally stupid and ridiculous." Melville's "ulterior joke," Thompson thought, lay "in the fun of permitting Plinlimmon to make an ass not merely of himself but also of exactly those readers who are able to take Plinlimmon seriously." After a survey of opinion on the pamphlet, Floyd C. Watkins (1964) identified Melville's point of view with Plinlimmon's:

> If Plinlimmon states Melville's theme in *Pierre,* if Melville seems to be merely a compromiser, if he seems too expedient in his virtue, the reader must see that some expediency and reconciliation are necessary for sanity and existence.

Although criticism is so disparate, several of the major commentators, including Dr. Murray, Arvin, and Thompson, have partially indicated a way of resolving the difficulties: by accepting that on an intellectual level Melville might often if not always agree with the ideas attributed to Plinlimmon while altogether dissociating himself from the blandly rational and self-satisfied tone in which Plinlimmon is reported to express them.

After four decades of analysis, *Pierre* remains to a remarkable degree a challenge to its readers. Critics are still confused by the extent and the function of autobiographical elements, by Melville's intentions and actual accomplishments in plot and style, by the book's precise relationships to its literary ancestors, and—most conspicuously—by the meaning of the set-piece which constitutes the philosophical crux of the novel. Naturally enough, there is no consensus as to either the value or the success of *Pierre*. Largely on the basis of this book Dr. Murray could hail Melville "as the literary discoverer" of "the Darkest Africa of the mind, the mythological unconscious," yet he declared that "here and there" in *Pierre* "Melville errs miserably, for the first time, in his use of language." Arvin saw the doubloon in *Moby-Dick* and the pamphlet in *Pierre* as representing Melville's "most serious and mature wisdom, a wisdom that he doubtless bought at a painful cost," yet he thought that the "great theme" of *Pierre* was "not embodied in a great action," that the "gap between the conception and the performance" was never bridged. In his view the result was "fiasco," a book "four-fifths claptrap, and sickly claptrap to boot." Other critics have been more casually contemptuous of the book in part or in whole. For all the cogency of E. L. Grant Watson's early psychological analysis, no critic of comparable stature has followed him in calling *Pierre* "the greatest of Melville's books." Yet none of Melville's other "secondary" works has so regularly evoked from its most thorough critics the sense that they are in the presence of grandeur, however flawed.

SOURCES

REFERENCES TO DATES AND EVENTS in Melville's life, unless otherwise ascribed in footnotes, are based upon the following printed sources: *The Letters of Herman Melville*, ed. Merrell R. Davis and William H. Gilman (New Haven: Yale University Press, 1960); Bernard R. Jerman, "'With Real Admiration': More Correspondence between Melville and Bentley," *American Literature*, XXV (November, 1953), 307–13; Jay Leyda, *The Melville Log* (New York: Harcourt, Brace, 1951); and Eleanor Melville Metcalf, *Herman Melville: Cycle and Epicycle* (Cambridge: Harvard University Press, 1953). Most references can be checked in the *Log*, which is arranged chronologically. The most detailed documentation of Melville's and his family's attitude toward his career just after the publication of *Pierre* is in Harrison Hayford and Merrell Davis, "Herman Melville as Office-Seeker," *Modern Language Quarterly*, X (June, 1949), 168–83, and (September, 1949), 377–88. Information concerning nineteenth-century American and English contracts, printings, sales, and profits was derived from the Harper records; many details from those records are available in G. Thomas Tanselle, "The Sales of Melville's Books," *Harvard Library Bulletin*, XVIII (April, 1969), 195–215. The prices for *Pierre* in muslin and paper are taken from the William Demarest ledger in the Morgan Library. Excerpts from reviews of *Pierre* are assembled, with some differences in transcription, in Leyda's *Log* and in Hugh W. Hetherington, *Melville's Reviewers: British and American, 1846–1891* (Chapel Hill: University of North Carolina Press, 1961). The reviews in the *Post*, the *Literary World*, the *Southern Literary Messenger*, and the *Athenæum* are reprinted in Hershel Parker, *The Recognition of Herman Melville* (Ann Arbor: University of Michigan Press, 1967), pp. 48–62. For reasons explained in Hershel Parker, "A Reexamination of *Melville's Reviewers*," *American Literature*, XLII (May, 1970), 226–32, all quotations from the reviews are drawn from the original magazine and newspaper printings.

These articles and books are quoted from or referred to in the NOTE without full bibliographical information: Anonymous, Review of the Knopf edition of *Pierre*, *New York Times Book Review* (July 20, 1930); Newton Arvin, *Herman Melville* (New York: William Sloane Associates, 1950); William Braswell, "The Satirical Temper of Melville's *Pierre*," *American Literature*, VII (January, 1936), 424–38; William Braswell, "The Early Love Scenes in Melville's *Pierre*," *American Literature*, XXII (November, 1950), 283–89; William Braswell, "Melville's Opinion of *Pierre*," *American Literature*, XXIII (May, 1951), 246–50; Harvey Breit, Review of the Hendricks House edition of *Pierre*, *New York Times Book Review* (March 20, 1949)—the words "many of the esthetic questions" in footnote 15; Richard Chase, Review of the Hendricks House edition of *Pierre*, *Modern Language Notes*, LXV (May, 1950), 358–59—the words "to look at the work of art" in footnote 15; S. Foster Damon, "Pierre the Ambiguous," *Hound & Horn*, II (January–March, 1929), 107–18; Edgar A. Dryden, *Melville's Thematics of Form* (Baltimore: Johns Hopkins Press, 1968); E. H. Eby, Review of the Knopf edition of *Pierre*, *American Literature*, II (November, 1930), 319–21; Robert S. Forsythe, "Mr. Lewis Mumford and Melville's *Pierre*," *American Literature*, II (November, 1930), 286–89; Robert S. Forsythe, Introduction to *Pierre* (New York: Alfred A. Knopf, 1930), xix–xxxviii; Elizabeth S. Foster, Introduction to *The Confidence-Man* (New York: Hendricks House, 1954), xiii–xcv; H. Bruce Franklin, *The Wake of the Gods: Melville's Mythology* (Stanford: Stanford University Press, 1963); John Freeman, *Herman Melville* (New York: Macmillan, 1926); Stanley Geist, *Herman Melville: The Tragic Vision and the Heroic Ideal* (Cambridge: Harvard University Press, 1939); G. Giovannini, "Melville's *Pierre* and Dante's *Inferno*," *PMLA*, LXIV (March, 1949), 70–78; Rita Gollin, "*Pierre's* Metamorphosis of Dante's *Inferno*," *American Literature*, XXXIX (January, 1968), 542–45; Harrison Hayford, "The Significance of Melville's 'Agatha' Letters," *ELH, A Journal of English Literary History*, XIII (December, 1946), 299–310 (at 403.9 Melville's letter is quoted from an inaccurate transcription—see 367.32); Brian Higgins, "Mark Winsome and Egbert," in *The Confidence-Man*, ed. Hershel Parker (New York: W. W. Norton, 1971), pp. 339–43; George C. Homans, "The Dark Angel: The Tragedy of Herman Melville," *New England Quarterly*, V (October, 1932), 699–730; Leon Howard, *Herman Melville: A Biography* (Berkeley and Los Angeles: University of California Press, 1951); Arthur Johnson, "A Comparison of Manners," *New Republic*, XX (August 27, 1919), 113–15; James Kissane, "Imagery, Myth, and Melville's *Pierre*," *American Literature*, XXVI (January, 1955), 564–72; R. W. B. Lewis, *The American Adam* (Chicago: University of Chicago Press, 1955); Edward G. Lueders, "The Melville-Hawthorne Relationship in *Pierre* and *The Blithedale Romance*," *Western Humanities Review*, IV (Autumn, 1950), 323–34; Malcolm S. MacLean, "A Restoration," [University of North Dakota] *Quarterly Journal*, XXI (Fall, 1930), 76–78; Ronald Mason, *The Spirit Above the Dust* (London: John Lehmann, 1951); Frank Jewett Mather, Jr., "Herman Melville," *Review*, I (August 16, 1919), 298–301; F. O. Matthiessen, *American Renaissance* (New York: Oxford University Press, 1941); Joseph J. Mogan, Jr., "*Pierre* and *Manfred*: Melville's Study of the Byronic Hero," *Papers on English Language and Literature*, I (Summer, 1965), 230–40; John Brooks Moore, Introduction to *Pierre* (New York: E. P. Dutton, 1929), xxi–xxvii; Charles Moorman, "Melville's *Pierre* and the Fortunate Fall," *American Literature*, XXV (March, 1953), 13–30; Charles Moorman, "Melville's Pierre in the City," *American Literature*, XXVII (January, 1956), 571–77; Lewis Mumford, *Herman Melville* (New York: Harcourt, Brace, 1929); Henry A. Murray, Review of Mumford's *Herman Melville, New England Quarterly*, II (July, 1929), 523–26; Henry A. Murray, Review of the Knopf edition of *Pierre, New England Quarterly*, IV (April, 1931), 333–37; Henry A. Murray, Introduction and Explanatory Notes to *Pierre* (New York: Hendricks House, 1949), xiii–ciii and 429–504; Hershel Parker, "The Metaphysics of Indian-hating," *Nineteenth-Century Fiction*, XVIII (September, 1963), 165–73; Ben Ray Redman, "Old Wine in New Bottles," *New York Herald Tribune Books* (October 20, 1929); Howard H. Schless, "Flaxman, Dante, and Melville's *Pierre*," *Bulletin of the New York Public Library*, LXIV (February, 1960), 65–82; Merton M.

Sealts, Jr., "Herman Melville's 'I and My Chimney,'" *American Literature*, XIII (May, 1941), 142–54; Merton M. Sealts, Jr., "Melville's Chimney, Revisited," in *Themes and Directions in American Literature*, ed. Ray B. Browne and Donald Pizer (Lafayette: Purdue University Studies, 1969), pp. 80–102; William Ellery Sedgwick, *Herman Melville: The Tragedy of Mind* (Cambridge: Harvard University Press, 1944); A. H. Starke, "A Note on Lewis Mumford's Life of Herman Melville," *American Literature*, I (November, 1929), 304–5; Lawrance Thompson, *Melville's Quarrel with God* (Princeton: Princeton University Press, 1952); Willard Thorp, *Herman Melville: Representative Selections* (New York: American Book Company, 1938); Carl Van Vechten, "The Later Work of Herman Melville," *Double Dealer*, III (January, 1922), 9–20; Carl Van Vechten, *Excavations: A Book of Advocacies* (New York: Alfred A. Knopf, 1926); Floyd C. Watkins, "Melville's Plotinus Plinlimmon and Pierre," in *Reality and Myth*, ed. William E. Walker and Robert L. Welker (Nashville: Vanderbilt University Press, 1964), pp. 39–51; E. L. Grant Watson, "Melville's *Pierre*,' *New England Quarterly*, III (April, 1930), 195–234; Raymond Weaver, "The Centennial of Herman Melville," *Nation* [New York], CIX (August 2, 1919), 145–46; Raymond Weaver, *Herman Melville: Mariner and Mystic* (New York: George H. Doran, 1921); Nathalia Wright, "*Pierre:* Herman Melville's *Inferno*," *American Literature*, XXXII (May, 1960), 167–81; and Elinor Yaggy, "Shakespeare and Melville's *Pierre*," *Boston Public Library Quarterly*, VI (January, 1954), 43–51.

Note on the Text

THIS EDITION of *Pierre* presents an unmodernized critical text, reconstructed according to the theory of copy-text formulated by Sir Walter Greg.[1] Central to that theory is the distinction between substantive variants (those which affect meaning, such as verbal changes) and accidental variants (those which affect form, such as changes in punctuation and spelling).[2] When an author makes substantive revisions in printed forms of his work, he is not always equally concerned with accidentals. The fact that he does not alter certain accidentals which were not his own but were changes made by the copyist, publisher, or compositor does not amount to an endorsement of those accidentals. Since the aim of a critical edition is to establish a text which represents as nearly as possible the author's intentions, it follows that the formal texture of his work will

1. "The Rationale of Copy-Text," *Studies in Bibliography*, III (1950–51), 19–36. For an application of this method to the period of Melville, see Fredson Bowers, "Some Principles for Scholarly Editions of Nineteenth-Century American Authors," *Studies in Bibliography*, XVII (1964), 223–28; and his "A Preface to the Text," in the Centenary Edition of Hawthorne's *The Scarlet Letter* (Columbus: Ohio State University Press, 1962), pp. xxix–xlvii (reprinted in the later volumes of the Centenary Edition).

2. The line between the two is not rigid, for some changes of punctuation and spelling do affect meaning and accordingly could be classed as substantives.

be most accurately reproduced by adopting as copy-text[3] either the fair-copy manuscript or the first printing based on it. The printed form is chosen if the manuscript does not exist or if the author worked in such a way that corrected proof became in effect the final form of the manuscript. This basic text may then be emended with any later authorial alterations (whether substantive or accidental) and with other obvious corrections. Following this procedure maximizes the probability of keeping authorial readings when evidence is inconclusive as to the source of an alteration in a later authorized edition. The resulting text is *critical* in that it does not correspond exactly to any single authorized edition, but it is closer to the author's intentions—insofar as they are recoverable—than any such edition.

As the preceding HISTORICAL NOTE has shown, the Harper edition of *Pierre* was the only authorized edition during Melville's lifetime; in the absence of the manuscript Melville furnished the publisher, the first impression of the Harper edition becomes the copy-text for the present edition.[4] Any later impressions of this edition published before Melville's death in 1891 are a potential source for emendations in that copy-text, since theoretically it would have been possible for Melville to make corrections or changes in them. The only such impression (Harper, 1855) has therefore been collated with the American issue of the first impression, and in addition the 1852 Sampson Low issue has been collated with that first issue to make certain that the sheets are from the same impression:

1. Issues of the First Impression
   One machine collation[5] of the American issue (1852) against the English issue (1852) of the first impression
2. Impressions of the American Edition
   Two machine collations of the first impression of this edition (1852) against the last (1855)[6]

3. "Copy-text" is the text accepted as the basis for an edition.

4. The particular copy of the first impression which served (in the form of a marked Xerox reproduction) as printer's copy is M66–2471–53 (see footnote 6).

5. Collations between *impressions* of the same edition (or copies of an impression) are "machine collations"—so called because the Hinman Collator, by superimposing page images, enables the human collator's eye to see differences, including minute changes not otherwise easily detected, such as resettings and type or plate damage. The terms *edition, impression (printing), issue*, and *state*, as used here, follow the definitions of Fredson Bowers in *Principles of Bibliographical Description* (Princeton: Princeton University Press, 1949), pp. 379–426.

6. The copies used for these collations are here recorded by identification number (for books in the Melville Collection, now in The Newberry Library) or by library name and call number (for books not in the Melville Collection): (1) M68–1396–3 *vs.* Newberry

The text was thus collated for record three times.[7] In addition, routine procedures in the process of compiling, checking, and preparing the information for publication have resulted in a larger total number of collations.[8]

Analysis of the variants (in both substantives and accidentals) disclosed by these collations has not resulted in the adoption of any emendations in the copy-text; but 104 emendations to correct errors found in both Harper impressions have been made by the present editors. In order to make clear the evidence and rationale on which these decisions rest, an account of the textual history of the work is given below, followed by a discussion of the treatment in this text of substantives and accidentals, and an explanation of the editorial apparatus through which the evidence is presented.

THE TEXTS

NO MANUSCRIPT of *Pierre* survives. Therefore the only authoritative text is that of the first edition, published by Harper & Brothers in the late summer of 1852—on August 6, according to the contemporary record of William Demarest of Harpers, but perhaps available a week or so earlier, when the first reviews appeared. Copies of this Harper edition dated 1852 on the title page exist in several states, distinguishable by the setting of A128 and by the presence or absence of plate damage at a number of other points. A128 occurs in two settings—in one, there is no punctuation after the divisional numeral at 94.30,[9] the word "seated" (94.33) is spelled

Case Y255M5154; (2) M67-1601-3 *vs.* Gift M71-1 (James Albert FitzSimmons copy); Newberry Case Y255M5153 *vs.* New York City College YR.M46p.

7. The number of collations which must be performed in order to detect all significant variations in a given text can never be prescribed with certainty, since chance determines, at least to some extent, the particular copies available for collation. Whether or not variant states of a first impression are detected, for example, depends largely upon whether or not at least one copy of an earlier state is present in the collection of copies assembled for collation; regardless of the size of this collection, there is always the chance that an unknown earlier state is missing. To reduce the element of chance somewhat, the present editors have checked many points in every copy of *Pierre* in the Melville Collection at The Newberry Library and have examined numerous copies in other collections. For making copies of *Pierre* available, the editors are indebted to William Braswell, James Albert FitzSimmons, William M. Gibson, Jay Leyda, and Willard Thorp.

8. Proofreading provided the chief opportunity for making these additional collations. Separate sets of page proofs were read for a total of five complete readings. In addition there were repeated readings of corrected passages and a complete matching of final films against initial page proofs.

9. Reference numbers with a prefixed A refer to page and line of the original American edition; when this letter does not appear, reference is to the Northwestern-Newberry Edition.

correctly, and the dash at the end of 95.6 is outside the quotation marks; in the other, there is a period after the numeral, "seated" appears as "steated", and the dash falls within the quotation marks. The order of these two settings can be determined by noting that the one with the "steated" reading reappears in the 1855 impression of the book and that damage along the right margin of A137 occurs only in copies with the "steated" reading on A128. This edge of A137 would have been adjacent to A128 in the forme on the press (the outer forme of sheet F); the damage could have resulted from an accident which also damaged A128 seriously enough to require resetting, or it could have occurred at the time when the reset plate of A128 was placed in the forme. In any case, one may conclude that the resetting (with only three accidental variants) was not made for the purpose of incorporating textual revision and that the setting of A128 with the word "seated" spelled correctly is the earlier of the two.

The other points of variation among 1852 copies do not involve resetting but are simply instances of plate damage. Two of them, however, create textual differences: on page 201 of the Harper edition, the comma after "guitar" (148.14) is completely absent in some copies; and the damage along the right edge of A204 in some copies causes the semicolon after "loose" (150.20) to look like a comma. In addition, there is damage in some copies in "throughout" at 23.34, "prisoner" at 91.14, "join" at 143.19, and the left margin of A409. (What appears to be damage to the first two letters of "chronometer" (A286.28) in some copies of the 1852 printing is actually failure to print and the letters print properly in the 1855 impression.) Since all these instances of damage recur in the 1855 impression, there is no doubt that the damaged states are later. The copy-text for *Pierre* may therefore be defined as the Harper printing with 1852 on the title page, with the original setting of page 128, and without these instances of plate damage. Since, however, the instances of damage do not always occur together in the same copies, for practical purposes those instances which do not involve textual differences may be ignored in selecting the copy which is to provide the copy-text. For this reason the copy-text for the present edition can more simply be defined as the 1852 Harper printing with "seated" at A128.5, with a comma after "guitar" at A201.5, and with a semicolon after "loose" at A204.3.[10]

10. Historical facts about the dates, sizes, and background of the issues and impressions are given in the HISTORICAL NOTE; precise physical descriptions will appear in the full-scale bibliography to be published in conjunction with the Northwestern-Newberry Edition. The present discussion is not concerned with bibliographical details discovered in the

The 1852 Sampson Low issue consists of 1852 Harper sheets with a cancel title leaf; it need not be discussed separately here, since no other instances of cancel leaves or sheets have been discovered in it. The Harper edition was printed once more from the 1852 plates, in 1855, with no deliberate changes; because all of the slight variations resulted from plate damage none has any textual authority.[11]

No other editions appeared in the nineteenth century. Since the Melville revival, *Pierre* has been set in type four times.[12] The Constable edition of *Pierre*—in the collected *Works* (London, 1923; reissued by Russell & Russell, New York, 1963)—is significant because it was the first edition of the book after Melville's death and because it is part of the only complete set of his work that has been available in the past (and is therefore often cited as standard). Its text, however, departs from that of the original Harper edition occasionally in substantive readings and frequently in capitalization, punctuation, and spelling (especially through the substitution of British forms), and it offers no explanation of its editorial policy.[13]

---

process of collation, unless they bear on textual questions. Type or plate damage, for example, which may distinguish the states within an impression, is not reported here if it does not create a textual variant (as defined in the following footnote) and if the states involved are not otherwise of textual significance.

11. Of the many variations produced in the 1855 impression by plate damage, only the following nine might create textual ambiguity: the loss of commas after "pauper" at 10.4, "folly" at 227.28, and "gently" at 348.13; the loss of line-end hyphens after "bright" at 23.30, "crayon" at 39.4, and "her" (in "herself") at 194.26; the loss of a semicolon after "are" at 88.28; and the failure to print of the first "l" in "lowly" at 200.1 and the "r" in the first "her" at 317.4. In this NOTE, when changes are listed within the American edition (that is, within either impression or between the two), the many instances of battered type or plates and missing letters are not included when it is clear what letter is intended, nor is missing end-punctuation mentioned when the absent mark is a period; and missing hyphens at the ends of lines are not reported when the divided word is not a possible compound. Missing commas, however, which might pass unnoticed, are listed. In other words, type or plate wear is noted only when it could pass unnoticed or be mistaken for intentional revision.

12. Details of these editions will be included in the forthcoming descriptive bibliography. The Melville Collection being formed at The Newberry Library in connection with the preparation of the Northwestern-Newberry Edition contains these later editions. Charles Roberts Anderson, in *Melville in the South Seas* (New York: Columbia University Press, 1939), states that four "new editions" of *Pierre* had been published by 1938 (p. 439); but he is not using "edition" in the sense employed here, as a technical bibliographical term which encompasses all the impressions from a given setting of type.

13. This generalization is based on a partial collation of a copy of the 1852 edition (M67–1601–3) with a copy of the Constable edition (M67–1601–4). For some background relating to the Constable texts, see Philip Durham, "Prelude to the Constable Edition of Melville," *Huntington Library Quarterly*, XXI (1957–58), 285–89.

This Constable edition was reprinted in 1929 by Dutton and in 1957 by Grove Press. In contrast to the Constable edition, the next two editions of the book included explicit statements about editorial procedure. The 1930 Knopf edition, carefully edited by Robert S. Forsythe for the "Americana Deserta" series and reprinted as an "Alblabook Edition" in 1941 (not 1940 as mistakenly given on the verso of the title page), incorporates 338 emendations (listed on pp. 405–16), which fall into two categories, according to the preface: "the correction of obvious typographical and grammatical errors" and "the systematizing, according to Melville's own usage, of spelling, capitalization, hyphenation, and punctuation" (p. ix). Two decades later (in 1949), Henry A. Murray edited *Pierre* as a volume in the Hendricks House edition of Melville and adopted a total of 342 emendations (listed on pp. 505–14); as he says in the preface (pp. v–vi), his text is similar to Forsythe's, since he made changes which "rectified indubitable errors" in spelling and punctuation and sought to achieve consistency. The Signet Classic paperback edition of *Pierre* (1964) is identified as "reprinted" (i.e., reset) from the Hendricks House edition but contains some inadvertent departures from Murray's text. Thus although only four twentieth-century editions of *Pierre* have been published, one well-edited text was available in hard cover in the 1930's and 1940's and another has been steadily available in hard cover since 1949 and in a paperback reprint since 1964.

TREATMENT OF SUBSTANTIVES

THE TEXTUAL HISTORY of *Pierre* is simple: there was only one authorized edition of the book and Melville made no revisions in the second (and final) impression of that edition. An editor's only task is to locate and correct any errors in this copy-text—readings, that is, which cannot be the ones Melville intended, either obvious mistakes such as typographical errors or less obvious mistakes which are recognized when the sense of a passage is carefully considered.[14]

14. While the famous passage on proofreading (p. 340) cannot be literally true of Melville's proofreading of *Pierre*, it probably suggests some of the reasons for the many errors in the Harper text (such as those listed in footnotes 17 and 19): "As every evening, after his day's writing was done, the proofs of the beginning of his work came home for correction, Isabel would read them to him. They were replete with errors; but preoccupied by the thronging, and undiluted, pure imaginings of things, he became impatient of such minute, gnat-like torments; he randomly corrected the worst, and let the rest go; jeering with himself at the rich harvest thus furnished to the entomological critics."

Of the errors discovered in editing the Northwestern-Newberry *Pierre*, fewer than three dozen involve substantives. Among the obvious errors several are incorrect verb forms—either the wrong number (as "seem" for "seems" at 11.4) or the wrong person (as "standest" for "standeth" at 59.36 or "flourisheth" for "flourishest" at 300.4). A few obvious errors result from possible confusion regarding syntax—errors such as the use of "whom" for "who" (164.3). Several are instances in which the presence of one incorrect letter creates a different word—"where" for "were" (107.35), "fells" for "falls" (154.27), and "bell" for "ball" (195.33). In one case a necessary "the" is omitted (before "world" at 315.33) and in another a superfluous "the" is included (before "age" at 218.9). Among the less obvious errors there are similar slips and corruptions—the presence of "into" before "which" (175.26), the excrescent letter in "countries" (for "counties" at 11.2), the presence of "at" before "all good" (215.12), and such possible vestiges of manuscript confusion as the duplicative words in "wee little bit scrap" (14.12). None of these readings, whether compositor's errors or slips of the author's (or copyist's) pen, can represent Melville's intention and are accordingly corrected here.

Simple as the textual history of *Pierre* is, the text does present some problems with substantives beyond emending these relatively few errors. Still other words in the Harper text may not be the ones Melville intended, for the copyist who had to deal with his sometimes difficult handwriting was his sister Helen rather than his usual copyist, his wife, and he may have had less opportunity than usual to exercise immediate control over the proofreading. In any event, some copy-text readings seem slightly askew, even though they make adequate sense: an example is "quite legibly but still fadedly gilded" at 148.1–2. Since one cannot be sure in such instances that editorial emendations would in fact restore what Melville intended, rather than "improve" upon the text in a nonauthorial way, several minor cruxes are considered in the DISCUSSIONS OF ADOPTED READINGS but not emended.

TREATMENT OF ACCIDENTALS

IN THE ABSENCE of a final manuscript, the degree to which the author was responsible for the accidentals—the punctuation and spelling—of a printed text is a matter impossible to settle conclusively. Even though changes in the spelling and punctuation of *Pierre* were undoubtedly made at Harper & Brothers, the Harper edition is nevertheless the only source of the text, and its accidentals, when they are not Melville's own, at least represent contemporary practice. Accordingly, the accidentals of the first American impression of *Pierre* have been retained in the present edition except in a few unusual instances, even when the spelling and punctuation may appear incorrect or inconsistent by mid-twentieth-century standards. Some of the inconsistencies in the spelling and punctuation may have been in the manuscript, and, although Melville presumably did not intend them, they constitute a suggestive part of his total expression, since patterns of accidentals do affect the texture of a literary work. On the other hand, some of the inconsistencies in accidentals may have resulted either from an imperfectly realized attempt to make the manuscript conform to a house style or from compositorial alterations. To regularize the punctuation and spelling would be to risk choosing nonauthorial forms.[15] Therefore no attempt has been made to impose general consistency on either spelling or punctuation,[16] and any changes have been made sparingly, according to the following guidelines:

SPELLING. The general rule adopted here is to correct spellings which were unacceptable by the standards of 1852, but to retain any acceptable variants. One available guide for decisions about spelling is the 1847 revision of Webster's *American Dictionary of the English Language* (Springfield, Mass., 1848). Webster's was the dictionary used by Harper & Brothers at the time, for Melville remarked, in his letter to Murray on January 28, 1849, that "my printers here 'go for' Webster." The Harper accounts show that Melville ordered at least three copies of Webster's (on April 10 and November 15, 1847, and on November 16, 1848), the third of which could have been the 1848 edition. In any case, the 1848 Webster's can be taken as a generally accepted standard in use when Melville was writing *Pierre*. Recourse to it and to other contemporary dictionaries (and to editions of American novels and other works published in the 1840's and 1850's by Harpers and other American publishers), as well as to such sources for the historical study of spelling as the *Oxford English Dictionary*, has resulted in the retention of some anomalous-appearing copy-text

15. Melville's habits in the extant manuscripts and letters are not definite enough to offer grounds to emend for consistency (and in any case the letters, not intended for publication, do not provide a parallel situation). Neither is the Harper house styling consistent enough to be helpful in determining precisely what elements of the punctuation of *Pierre* resulted from it.

16. For example, no emendations are made to secure consistency in the use (or nonuse) of apostrophes in contractions, or of italics or of quotation marks (or both at once) for such items as foreign words and titles of poems and books.

forms, such as "Berkelyan", "Buccleugh", "Camanche", "Carrisbrook", "Descartian", "Josh" (for "Joss"), "minister" (for "minster"), "Shellian", "suspence", "tournequet", and "uncompunctuousness". A few other forms, not found in reliable parallels in such contemporary sources, have been corrected: "direlictions", "Hobbs", "*lapsus-lingua*", "perlieus", "sylables", and "Zenda-Vesta". Any changes to bring spelling into conformity with an 1852 standard have been made cautiously so as to preserve the wide latitude allowed in contemporary usage, especially for proper names.

PUNCTUATION. Emendations in punctuation are made to correct obvious typographical errors and to eliminate serious ambiguity; but no alterations are made in punctuation simply in an effort to bring it into conformity with some presumed standard. Most of the obvious errors, which have been emended, fall into two categories: (1) the absence of periods at the ends of sentences or the presence of periods within sentences;[17] and (2) the absence of quotation marks where they are required or the presence of them where they are not needed.[18] In a number of instances a mark of punctuation has slipped out of position before plating; these marks are placed properly in the present text. Such alterations merely correct the typography of the copy-text but do not emend the text itself, and are not recorded in the LIST OF EMENDATIONS.[19] Since it is not the aim

17. For example, the periods now present in the following lines are absent in the copy-text: 8.35, 79.14, 125.17, 213.12, 291.33, 309.13. The commas now present after "head" (93.12) and "askance" (293.35) are periods in the copy-text.

18. Thus superfluous double quotation marks are present in the copy-text after "briefer" (121.30), while necessary double quotation marks are absent after "eye" (159.15), "strange" (187.38), and "him" (245.34); and single, rather than double, quotation marks are required for the two quotations in 120.35–36. In none of these instances does the emendation involve a decision affecting the meaning, since in none does the misuse or omission of quotation marks seriously call into question who is speaking or what is said.

19. Commas in the copy-text which printed either above or below the proper position occur after the following words: "soul" (142.25), "snowy" (199.22), the second "man" (225.25), "lives" (276.31), "romance" (279.25), "doom" (287.19), and "so" (330.12). Similarly placed periods occur after "knees" (321.27) and "taught" (334.29). A related category of defects in the copy-text not reported in the LIST OF EMENDATIONS consists of plate damage which creates no textual problems. Thus seriously damaged letters occur in the copy-text in these words: "their" (91.15), "her" (179.39), "here" (231.37), "the" (231.39), "better" (232.37), "Yet" (273.7), "yet" (280.9), "important" (331.24), "looking" (331.26), "despicable" (336.5), "her" (336.6), "or" (339.30), and "made" (358.14). Seriously damaged marks of punctuation occur in the copy-text after these words: "mystery" (41.26), "happy" (119.4), the second "Mystery" (126.26), "heart" (135.19), and "him" (141.19). None of these damaged letters or marks of punctuation prevents one from knowing what is intended. Finally, line-end hyphens which fail to print in the copy-text (though there is space for them) are not reported here when the words involved are

of the present edition to modernize and since contemporary practice did not demand accuracy in the use of accents on foreign words (indeed, contemporary dictionaries sometimes listed them without accents), such words as "*recherche*" (52.31) and "*debut*" (245.11) are allowed to stand, without accents, as they appear in the copy-text. The only instances in which punctuation not obviously wrong has been emended occur at four points where the copy-text punctuation (or absence of it) creates an ambiguity serious enough to interfere with the meaning of a sentence (100.5, 148.2–3, 196.29, and 204.22).

EDITORIAL APPARATUS

THE BASIC EVIDENCE for textual decisions in the present edition is given in the preceding parts of this NOTE and in the three sections which follow it and complete the TEXTUAL RECORD:

DISCUSSIONS OF ADOPTED READINGS. These discussions take up any reading (whether a copy-text reading or an emendation) adopted in the Northwestern–Newberry text which seems to require discussion or explanation beyond the general guidelines already stated. Certain instances of decisions not to emend, as well as some actual emendations, are commented upon.

LIST OF EMENDATIONS. This list records every change made in the copy-text for the present edition, accidentals as well as substantives. The left column gives the Northwestern–Newberry readings,[20] the right column the rejected copy-text readings. Items marked with an asterisk are commented on in the DISCUSSIONS OF ADOPTED READINGS. Seventy emendations have been made in accidentals, and thirty-four in substantives. No emendations of any sort have been made silently; using the LIST OF EMENDATIONS and the REPORT OF LINE-END HYPHENATION, one can reconstruct the copy-text in every detail.[21]

not possible compounds and therefore appear as single unhyphenated words in the present edition (a dozen such instances occur in the copy-text).

20. Calling these emendations "Northwestern–Newberry readings" signifies only that the readings do not occur in the original edition; it does not imply that no one has ever thought of them before.

21. That is, every *textual* detail: features of the styling or design of the copy-text print—such as length of lines; the form and content of the title page and running titles; the typography, punctuation, and capitalization of the "Book" and "chapter" numbers and titles; and the display capitalization of chapter openings—are of course not recoverable from these lists. In the copy-text all letters of Book titles were capitalized both in the table of contents and at the heads of the Books in the text; in the Northwestern–Newberry Edition these titles have been styled in capitals and small capitals.

REPORT OF LINE-END HYPHENATION. Since some possible compound words are hyphenated at the ends of lines in the copy-text, the intended forms of these words become a matter for editorial decision. When such a word appears elsewhere in the copy-text in only one form, that form is followed; when its treatment is not consistent (and the inconsistency is an acceptable one, to be retained in the present text), the form which occurs more times in analogous situations is followed. If the word does not occur elsewhere in the copy-text, the form is determined by a survey of similar words, by the usage in the 1848 Webster's, and by any relevant evidence in a Melville manuscript. The first list in the REPORT OF LINE-END HYPHENATION records these decisions, by listing the adopted Northwestern–Newberry forms of possible compounds which are hyphenated at the ends of lines in the copy-text. The second list is a guide to the established copy-text forms of compounds which are hyphenated at the ends of lines in the Northwestern–Newberry Edition. No editorial decisions are involved in this second list,[22] but the information recorded is essential for reconstructing the copy-text and making exact quotations from the present edition.

In these three lists the reader has before him all the copy-text readings which have been emended here. With the lists he can examine and reconsider for himself the textual decisions for the present edition and in the process see more clearly the relationship between the text of *Pierre* available during Melville's lifetime and the one which is offered here as a more faithful representation of the author's intentions.

22. Except in the cases of words hyphenated at the ends of lines in the copy-text as well. These words, which appear in both lists and are marked with daggers, are given in the forms which the present editors adopted but which are obscured by hyphenation at the ends of lines in this edition.

Discussions of Adopted Readings

IN THESE COMMENTS on emendations and on decisions not to emend, the following symbols are employed:

A American Edition (1852–1855)
NN Northwestern–Newberry Edition

10.28 Cæsar] The singular form indicates that the word is used collectively here, but it is possible that Melville meant a plural and that the copyist did not see the "s", since his final "s" was frequently indeterminate.

14.12 wee scrap] The Harper reading "wee little bit scrap" is so unidiomatic (despite the Scottish use of "bit" to mean "bit of") that it can hardly be the intended reading in this context. Some emendation is called for; the simplest would be the deletion of one of the nouns, "bit" or "scrap". NN deletes "little bit" on the grounds that it may be considered a phrase unit, as in the preceding line, and that Melville may first have merely repeated the phrase then decided to substitute a synonymous one ("wee scrap") without adequately marking the first for deletion. Various plausible conjectures about what may have been intended and what went wrong (including the one suggested here) offer no certain grounds for recovering exactly what Melville wrote or meant to write. See the entry at 108.5.

34.12 Love is busy] Here and in the next line the copy-text reading "love" is emended to "Love". Since the word occurs capitalized nearly two dozen times in the passage, these two uncapitalized occurrences might be mistaken as implying a shift in meaning when none is intended.

61.30 faintly, starting] It may be that the comma is superfluous and that Pierre was "faintly starting at the strangeness of the encounter" as he made his exclamation.

68.1 temples] Possibly "temples" should read "temple", since two sentences later and repeatedly to the end of the section the metaphor of a "shrine" or "temple" in Pierre's soul is used; but "temples" makes sense here if it is taken separately, not as the introductory instance of the metaphor.

75.33 Among] The copy-text "among" is emended to make entirely clear that a new sentence begins at this point.

100.5 Pierre—now,"] A has double quotation marks after "Pierre" and none after "now". That reading is obviously wrong, since it leaves "now" dangling. Of the different ways of correcting this unsatisfactory reading, the simplest is to delete the comma after "now" so that it will modify "said", but a more likely supposition is that Mrs. Glendinning uses the "now" rhetorically, as she turns to her son with an earnest proposition.

108.5 as immaculate] The copy-text reading "as perfect as immaculate", though barely possible syntactically (assuming that the first "as" stands for "as being as"), yields so little plausible meaning that some corruption of Melville's intention must be assumed. One possibility is that both phrases belong but that a necessary mark of punctuation between them is missing in the copy-text. Another is that either "as perfect" or "as immaculate" is an uncanceled manuscript reading. While none of the possible conjectural emendations can demonstrably restore what Melville intended, NN assumes that only one phrase was intended and deletes "as perfect", considering the first phrase the more likely one for Melville to have meant to cancel. See a possibly analogous error at 14.12.

141.24 tribes] The plural here and the singular at 141.26 are both retained from A, although one would have expected Melville to use the same form in both occurrences. There seems no satisfactory way of determining which form he would have preferred, though the probabilities favor the plural, since his final "s" was often hard to discern. See the entry on "eye" at 168.12.

148.1–2 quite legibly but still fadedly gilded] The emphasis in this construction seems awry, since the degree of fadedness should be stressed more than the degree of legibility. However, if one takes "still" to mean "nevertheless" the copy-text reading is reasonably adequate. One might speculate that what Melville meant was rather "fadedly but still quite legibly gilded" or "quite fadedly but still legibly gilded".

161.3 pivoted] The A reading makes sense but it may be a misreading for the word "riveted" since "rivet" occurs in a parallel passage below, at 161.35. In Melville's hand a peaked initial "r" could be mistaken for other letters, including "h" and "p".

168.12 eye] Melville may have intended the plural rather than the singular form but failed to make his final "s" clear enough; in either case, he probably intended to use the same form in this sentence and at 168.24, where the reading is "eyes". Because the whole passage employs exact repetition, the variation between singular and plural suggests a change of signification apparently not intended. See the note at 141.24.

175.26 which] In the copy-text the sentence is rendered incoherent by the word "into" before "which". To clarify the sense, NN omits "into" as an excrescence, presumably a relic of an incomplete revision which involved a shift of construction.

210.4 Jugglarius] The copy-text form "Juggularius" (repeated with an apostrophe at 210.5) is emended to the variant copy-text form "Jugglarius" as at 262.8, where the context makes clear that Melville associated the word with "juggle."

215.12 all] The A reading "at all" is here emended by the omission of the intrusive "at". Plinlimmon's point in this passage (215.1–14) is not that man, under the old teaching, despairs of becoming good in any degree ("at all good") but rather that he despairs of becoming entirely good ("all good").

245.17 was] The singular verb is retained here because the antecedent of "which" ("commendations") can be taken in a singular sense.

260.36 preambillically] The peculiar form of this nonce word is insufficient reason for emending it. Idiosyncratic adverbs are characteristic of Melville's style in *Pierre* and in any case no regular form seems available for the word.

282.2 *Pierre*] The copy-text misspelling "PIERE" is here corrected; the change from capital letters to italics is made in conformity with the styling of NN.

304.2 Thanksgiving] The A reading is "thanksgiving" but the context shows that the name of the holiday, not the common noun, is intended.

343.4 Juny-load] The somewhat unusual word "Juny" might be taken as an error for "July" since the form "Juny" is not exactly parallel with "October" and since July would perhaps be the more common month for haying. However, the phrase "Juny morning" occurs in Melville's poem "Ball's Bluff" (*Battle-Pieces*) and the month intended here is evidently established as June in the next paragraph.

343.15 piazza;] In all examined copies of A the punctuation mark after "piazza" registered only as a single dot which could be taken as the top member of either a colon or a semicolon. The use of a semicolon with a dash later in the sentence to mark the end of the interrupting appositive phrase indicates that a semicolon and a dash are also required at this point to mark the beginning of it.

362.17 boy's] The copy-text placing of the apostrophe is retained, although the context involves two boys. Melville's practice in general with such apostrophes cannot be determined; in any case idiom does not require literal construction of the sense.

List of Emendations

In this list of changes made in the copy-text by the present editors, the following abbreviations are used to designate the sources of readings:

A American Edition (1852–1855)
NN Northwestern–Newberry Edition

For further comment on this list, see p. 420 above; for discussions of the emendations marked with an asterisk (*), see the Discussions of Adopted Readings, pp. 423–26. The wavy dash (~) stands for the word cited in the left column and signals that only a punctuation mark is emended. The caret (‸) indicates the absence of a punctuation mark.

	NN Reading	Copy-Text (A) Reading
5.24–25	amaranthineness	amaranthiness
8.35	condition.	~‸
11.2	counties	countries
11.4	seems	seem
11.5	patroons	patrons
*14.12	scrap	little bit scrap

	NN Reading	Copy-Text (A) Reading
24.31	Empire	Fmpire
26.16	Llanyllyn	Lanyllyn
26.20	Llanyllyn's	Lanyllyn's
*34.12	Love is	love is
34.13	Love	love
36.18	earth's!	~?
37.19	agitateth	agitatest
38.3	purlieus	perlieus
42.23	Paolo	Palola
56.30	*lapsus-linguae*	*lapsus-lingua*
59.36	standeth	standest
66.5	life!	~?
71.34	Tadmor	Tadmore
*75.33	Among	among
77.14	something	somethings
79.14	subject.	~^
81.1	and	aud
87.30	desolation	deso-/ation
89.28	syllables	sylables
91.27	hopelessness	hopelessnes
93.12	head,	~.
97.34	Glendinning	Gendinning
*100.5	Pierre^	~"
*100.5	now,"	~,^
104.33	prevailing	pervailing
107.35	were	where
*108.5	as	as perfect as
120.35	'Feel	"~
120.36	break.'	~."
120.36	'Broken	"~
120.36	broken'	~"
121.30	briefer.^	~."
125.17	guitar.	~^

	NN Reading	Copy-Text (A) Reading
129.14	society of	societyof
134.32	Virtue	virtue
150.16	casement	casemeut
153.4	christian name	surname
153.4	Glendinning	Glendining
154.27	falls	fells
157.28	hast	hath
159.15	eye."	~.‸
164.3	who	whom
166.27	Mr.	~‸
*175.26	which	into which
176.8	purpose	purpese
184.6	length	lenght
184.28	Llanyllyn's	Lanyllyn's
186.1	white‸cottage	~-~
187.38	strange!"	~!‸
191.23	and	aud
191.37	forbid	forbids
195.22	order	not order
195.33	ball	bell
196.29	transfer,	~‸
198.12	Cyclops	Cyclop
200.3	Llanyllyn	Lanyllyn
204.22	When,	~‸
*210.4	Jugglarius	Juggularius
210.5	Jugglarius'	Juggularius'
210.14	chapter	chapters
213.12	ages.	~‸
*215.12	all	at all
218.9	age	the age
218.33	spontaneities	spontanieties
221.16	unhealthily	uuhealthily
224.30	Pierres"	~'"

	NN Reading	Copy-Text (A) Reading
226.38	palliation	palation
243.20	but—"	~—‸
245.34	him."	~.‸
254.26	instead of	instead
263.22	appreciator	appreciation
267.24	Hobbes	Hobbs
267.27	unites	unite
268.10	are	is
272.1	deepening	deepning
276.23	anomalous	anomolous
276.34	picturesque	pieturesque
277.28	Millthorpes'	Millthorpe's
277.31	derelictions	direlictions
*282.2	*Pierre*	PIERE
291.2	Zend-Avesta	Zenda-Vesta
291.33	it.	~‸
293.35	askance,	~.
300.4	flourishest	flourisheth
*304.2	Thanksgiving	thanksgiving
304.24	passably	passibly
304.31	has	have
309.13	Pierre.	~‸
315.33	the world	world
316.39	knew	know
325.2	"Pierre	‸Pierre
333.24	and	aud
333.24	exclaimed	exclaimcd
*343.15	piazza;	~.
345.9	upborne	upborn
345.11	upborne	upborn
345.27	upborne	upborn
361.10	in!	~?

Report of Line-End Hyphenation

THE FIRST LIST below records the forms adopted in the present edition (NN) for possible compound words which were hyphenated at line-ends in the copy-text (A) and which the editors had to decide whether to print as single-word compounds without hyphens or as hyphenated compounds. The second list enables one to determine the established reading (present in A or established by the editors) of compounds which happen to be hyphenated at the ends of lines in NN; any possible compound hyphenated at the end of a line in NN should be transcribed as one unhyphenated word unless it appears in this list. Those words coincidentally hyphenated between the same elements at line-ends in both A and NN are marked with daggers (†); in the first list they are given in the forms which would have been adopted if they had fallen within a line in NN. A slash (/) indicates the line-end break in A in a word which might possibly be hyphenated in more than one place. For further comment on these lists, see p. 421 above.

I. NN *forms of possible compounds which were hyphenated at copy-text line-ends*

vii.17	Greylock
5.13	clear-cut
9.9	all-fertile
9.18	ever-shifting
10.26	tea-canister
13.12	thorough-going
13.33	twenty-four
18.7	low-spirited
23.30	bright-cheeked
24.14	†after-birth
25.21	†love-pauses
28.16	all-persuasive
29.13	playfellow
29.36	quarter-cask
30.2	blue-eyed
30.6	after-dinner
30.8	blue-eyed
31.1	saddle-beast
31.8	mid-summer
31.27	kettle-drum
32.8	horse-ghosts
34.3	†rose-leaves
35.34	uplands
36.5	foretastes
36.12	over-charged
38.14	ice-floes
39.4	crayon-sketching
39.30	snow-white
49.3	sad-eyed
50.6	by-gone
50.12	regained
51.29	interlocks
52.31	chit-chat
58.7	good-bye
59.37	double-arches
60.7	forecastingly
60.35	sunlight
64.29	farm-house
66.20	bare-headed
69.19	overlaid
71.18	henbane
72.2	gay-hearted
74.17	handkerchief
78.32	chair-portrait
79.28	huge-figured
79.31	white-figured
79.32	neckcloth
80.20	neckcloth
84.34	half-suggestions
86.21	dragon-footed
87.28	rebuilded
90.21	heart-vacancies
90.21	ice-gilded
92.25	over-tasked
100.14	episcopal-looking
102.33	half-openly
105.11	cloud-rent
105.38	master-event
110.6	rain-shakings
110.17	dairy-shed
110.23	ridge-pole
115.7	fire-places
115.10	hearth-stone
117.15	pine-trees
117.26	tree-like
118.30	farm-houses
120.20	soul-composed
129.15	new-found
131.37	beech-trees
132.26	spring-tide
132.39	long-settled
133.24	†white-haired
134.20	predetermination
134.31	foreordained
135.11	head-stone
137.21	chateau-like
138.35	every-days
138.36	two-score
139.32	ever-shifting
141.32	dark-lantern

144.23	household
146.18	handkerchief
147.24	half-smile
152.4	deep-seated
157.22	bright-budding
158.20	sideways
160.24	ground-lightnings
161.25	true-hearted
169.1	counterpart
173.18	world-wide
175.10	true-hearted
179.38	forepainted
181.5	hamlet-home
181.19	chamber-floor
183.13	chamber-door
183.33	bed-clothes
184.22	terror-smitten
186.31	lockup
187.28	dressing-room
192.9	self-reproach
197.22	heir-looms
198.10	turkey-like
201.3	farm-house
203.2	sharp-resounding
206.35	handkerchief
207.3	re-read
207.33	earnest-loving
221.30	shilly-shallying
221.30	†bluff-minded
222.31	benevolent-hearted
223.8	pre-engagement
225.24	all-containing
230.1	cannon-balls
230.12	milkman's
234.20	good-hearted
234.23	thoroughfares
243.14	dressing-room
246.33	scolloped-edged
249.4	*bedstead*
249.21	bill-sticking
249.23	kid-gloved
254.15	sweetest-tempered
261.26	over-confident
266.6	side-aisles
267.34	nut-crackers
270.13	live-oak
270.14	flour-barrels
270.26	warrior-hearted
270.26	†knight-making
271.25	deep-rooted
271.30	camp-bed
271.32	everlasting
277.1	drawing-room
277.7	rainbows
279.35	good-will
280.15	interlinked
286.33	fellow-being
289.19	Faith-phantoms
290.4	ivory-throned
291.20	blue-eyed
292.6	over-anxious
292.39	closet-window
295.9	brick-kilns
296.4	orange-tree
297.25	desk-barrels
298.35	crash-towel
299.2	thick-frosted
299.25	flesh-brushes
299.26	apple-parings
300.9	half-developments
300.19	bushel-basket
300.29	Vapor-baths
308.26	sideways
311.9	to-morrow
311.28	†sky-cope
311.35	out-swelling
313.32	nun-like
329.21	marble-white
331.22	lady-artist
332.30	self-proffering
339.25	dovetailing
340.13	states-prisoner
344.7	water-drops
357.12	drawn-up

358.4 outstretched
358.30 percussion-caps
359.8 haughty-rolling
359.31 cow-hide
361.26 housewife
362.20 woman-soft

II. *Compounds containing line-end hyphens in* NN *which should be retained in transcription*

3.22 snow-white
5.27 side-ways
7.10 great-grand-/father's
11.31 great-uncle's
12.22 hearth-stone
20.18 pictured-bannered
24.14 †after-birth
24.20 death-drops
25.21 †love-pauses
29.10 shirt-collar
29.35 fair-sized
31.21 sword-points
34.3 †rose-leaves
35.34 long-stretching
36.7 shepherd-king
44.32 good-evening
45.7 long-drawn
45.34 powder-horn
46.2 well-snuffed
49.27 bed-clothes
55.14 wine-bibber
56.15 well-bred
58.28 flower-bud
71.32 twin-brother
72.24 drawing-room
76.17 good-hearted
77.10 sitting-chair
80.35 half-unconscious
82.36 drawing-room
84.26 thick-fallen
88.16 gay-hearted
89.5 lady-counsellor
96.21 well-considered
102.8 self-possession
103.15 surplice-like
106.1 life-chart
110.7 forest-ghosts
110.15 chimney-bricks
110.20 snow-white
112.25 death-like
113.26 death-like
122.24 pleasant-looking
125.34 bird-twitterings
126.3 abundant-haired
129.24 re-entered
129.32 good-morning
131.9 shame-faced
131.30 half-way
132.2 wedge-shaped
132.4 lengthwise-sharpened
132.16 winter-evenings
133.4 half-obliterate
133.24 †white-haired
133.38 head-stone
135.14 after-times
137.6 well-doings
139.26 all-controlling
149.36 double-casement
151.2 half-anticipated
153.37 new-born
155.19 seldom-pausing
173.5 self-renouncing
177.7 above-named
183.15 eight-and-forty
186.11 oppositely-going
187.7 farm-wagon

188.3	farm-house
188.11	shield-like
189.16	honey-suckled
198.7	fulling-mills
198.20	long-closed
209.3	not-to-be-thought-of
211.32	watch-maker's
214.25	self-renunciations
215.12	vice-producing
218.29	prompt-hearted
221.30	†bluff-minded
225.5	gold-laced
225.36	ever-adaptive
226.17	fellow-beings
231.2	far-hidden
235.11	watch-house
237.19	dancing-music
238.22	splendid-looking
239.37	drawing-room
240.1	whip-stalks
240.21	deep-rouged
240.38	Lock-and-Sin
252.18	gray-headed
257.20	stone-cutter
260.25	galley-slave
261.24	day-laborer's
262.2	matter-of-fact
267.7	bread-and-cheese
270.20	curious-looking
270.24	camp-bedstead
270.26	†knight-making
271.12	hanging-gardens
274.2	wonder-worlds
278.20	head-stones
278.30	common-school
283.8	widely-explosive
290.11	Ill-will
293.12	cross-legged
293.33	mild-mystic
294.14	self-supposed
298.33	half-glimpses
298.38	ice-water
301.26	crook-ended
303.36	curb-stones
304.9	isle-peak
306.2	from-eight-o'clock-to-half-past-four
311.28	†sky-cope
315.26	re-mastered
315.27	dining-room
316.33	self-suggested
319.8	half-way
327.15	well-doing
340.34	storm-admiral
340.35	iron-framed
342.32	inaccessible-looking
343.35	hill-scaling
349.21	cheek-burnt
352.21	chair-portrait
353.31	chair-portrait
354.26	half-hour's
356.5	dining-room
357.34	bread-crumbs
358.32	three-score-years-and-ten
358.36	top-wadding